I enjoy sharing my books as I do my friends, asking only that you treat them well and see them safely home

LONDON

SHORT STORIES
OF
IRWIN SHAW

SHORT STORIES

OF

IRWIN
SHAW

RANDOM HOUSE • NEW YORK

CONTENTS

SAILOR OFF THE BREMEN

THEY SAT in the small white kitchen, Ernest and Charley and Preminger and Dr. Stryker, all bunched around the porcelain-topped table, so that the kitchen seemed to be overflowing with men. Sally stood at the stove turning griddle-cakes over thoughtfully, listening intently to what Preminger was saying.

"So," Preminger said, carefully working his knife and fork, "everything was excellent. The comrades arrived, dressed like ladies and gentlemen at the opera, in evening gowns and what do you call them?"

"Tuxedoes," Charley said. "Black ties."

"Tuxedoes," Preminger nodded, speaking with his precise educated German accent. "Very handsome people, mixing with all the other handsome people who came to say good-bye to their friends on the boat; everybody very gay, everybody with a little whisky on the breath; nobody would suspect they were Party members, they were so clean and upper class." He laughed lightly at his own joke. He looked like a young boy from a nice Middle Western college, with crew-cut hair and a straight nose and blue eyes and an easy laugh. His laugh was a little high and short, and he talked fast, as though he wanted to get a great many words out to beat a certain deadline, but otherwise, being a Communist in Germany and a deck officer on the *Bremen* hadn't made any obvious changes in him. "It is a wonderful thing," he said, "how many pretty girls there are in the Party in the United States. Wonderful!"

They all laughed, even Ernest, who put his hand up to cover the empty spaces in the front row of his teeth every time he smiled. His hand covered his mouth and the fingers cupped around the neat black patch over his eye, and he smiled secretly and swiftly behind that concealment, getting his merriment over with swiftly, so he could take his hand down and compose his face into its usual unmoved, distant expression, cultivated from the time he got out of the hospital. Sally watched him from the stove, knowing each step: the grudging smile, the hand, the consciousness and memory of deformity, the wrench to composure, the lie of peace when he took his hand down.

She shook her head, dumped three brown cakes onto a plate.

"Here," she said, putting them before Preminger. "Better than Childs restaurant."

"Wonderful," Preminger said, dousing them with syrup. "Each time I come to America I feast on these. There is nothing like it in the whole continent of Europe."

"All right," Charley said, leaning out across the kitchen table, practically covering it, because he was so big, "finish the story."

"So I gave the signal," Preminger said, waving his fork. "When everything was nice and ready, everybody having a good time, stewards running this way, that way, with champagne, a nice little signal and we had a very nice little demonstration. Nice signs, good loud yelling, the Nazi flag cut down, one, two, three, from the pole. The girls standing together singing like angels, everybody running there from all parts of the ship, everybody getting the idea very, very clear—a very nice little demonstration." He smeared butter methodically on the top cake. "So then, the rough business. Expected. Naturally. After all, we all know it is no cocktail party for Lady Astor." He pursed his lips and squinted at his plate, looking like a small boy making believe he's the head of a family. "A little pushing, expected, maybe a little crack over the head here and there, expected. Justice comes with a headache these days, we all know that. But my people, the Germans. You must always expect the worst from them. They organize like lightning. Method. How to treat a riot on a ship. Every steward, every oiler, every sailor, was there in a minute and a half. Two men would hold a comrade, the other would beat him. Nothing left to accident."

"The hell with it," Ernest said. "What's the sense in going through the whole thing again? It's all over."

"Shut up," Charley said.

"Two stewards got hold of Ernest," Preminger said softly. "And another one did the beating. Stewards are worse than sailors. All day long they take orders, they hate the world. Ernest was unlucky. All the others did their jobs, but they were human beings. The steward is a member of the Nazi party. He is an Austrian; he is not a normal man."

"Sally," Ernest said, "give Mr. Preminger some more milk."

"He kept hitting Ernest," Preminger tapped absently on the porcelain top with his fork, "and he kept laughing and laughing."

"You know who he is?" Charley asked. "You're sure you know who he is?"

"I know who he is. He is twenty-five years old, very dark and good-looking, and he sleeps with at least two ladies a voyage." Preminger slopped his milk around in the bottom of his glass. "His name is Lueger. He spies on the crew for the Nazis. He has sent two men already to concentration camps. He is a very serious character. He knew what he was doing," Preminger said clearly, "when he kept hitting Ernest in the eye. I tried to get to him, but I was in the middle of a thousand people, screaming and running. If something happens to that Lueger that will be a very good thing."

"Have a cigar," Ernest said, pulling two out of his pocket.

"Something will happen to him," Charley said, taking a deep breath, and leaning back from the table. "Something will damn sure happen to him."

"You're a dumb kid," Ernest said, in the weary tone he used now in all serious discussions. "What do you prove if you beat up one stupid sailor?"

"I don't prove anything," Charley said. "I don't prove a goddamn thing. I am just going to have a good time with the boy that knocked my brother's eye out. That's all."

"It is not a personal thing," Ernest said, in the tired voice. "It is the movement of Fascism. You don't stop Fascism with a personal crusade against one German. If I thought it would do some good, I'd say, sure, go ahead . . ."

"My brother, the Communist," Charley said bitterly. "He goes out and he gets ruined and still he talks dialectics. The Red Saint with the long view. The long view gives me a pain in the ass. I am taking a very short view of Mr. Lueger. I am going to kick the living guts out of his belly. Preminger, what do you say?"

"Speaking as a Party member," Preminger said, "I approve of your brother's attitude, Charley."

"Nuts," Charley said.

"Speaking as a man, Charley," Preminger went on, "please put Lueger on his back for at least six months. Where is that cigar, Ernest?"

Dr. Stryker spoke up in his dry, polite, dentist's voice. "As you know," he said, "I am not the type for violence." Dr. Stryker weighed a hundred and thirty-three pounds and it was almost possible to see through his wrists, he was so frail. "But as Ernest's friends, I think there would be a definite satisfaction for all of us, including Ernest, if this Lueger was taken care of. You may count on me for anything within my powers." He was very scared, Dr. Stryker, and his voice was even drier than usual, but he spoke up after reasoning the whole thing out slowly and carefully, disregarding the fear, the worry, the possible great damage. "That is my opinion," he said.

"Sally," Ernest said, "talk to these damn fools."

"I think," Sally said slowly, looking steadily at her husband's face, always stiffly composed now, like a corpse's face, "I think they know what they're talking about."

Ernest shrugged. "Emotionalism. A large useless gesture. You're all tainted by Charley's philosophy. He's a football player. He has a football player's philosophy. Somebody knocks you down, you knock him down, everything is fine."

"I want a glass of milk, too," Charley said. "Please, Sally."

"Whom're you playing this week?" Ernest said.

"Georgetown."

"Won't that be enough violence for one week?" Ernest asked.

"Nope," Charley said. "I'll take care of Georgetown first, then Lueger."

"Anything I can do," Dr. Stryker said. "Remember, anything I can do. I am at your service."

"The coach'll be sore," Ernest said, "if you get banged up, Charley."

"The hell with the coach. Please shut up, Ernest. I have got my stomachful of Communist tactics. No more. Get this in your head, Ernest." Charley stood up and banged the table. "I am disregarding the class struggle, I am disregarding the education of the proletariat, I am disregarding the fact that you are a good Communist. I am acting strictly in the capacity of your brother. If you'd had any brains you would have stayed away from that lousy boat. You're a painter, an artist, you make water colors, what the hell is it your business if lunatics're running Germany? But all right. You've got no brains. You go and get your eye beat out. O.K. Now I step in. Purely personal. None of your business. Shut your trap. I will fix everything to my own satisfaction. Please go and lie down in the bedroom. We have arrangements to make here."

Ernest stood up, hiding his mouth, which was twitching, and walked into the bedroom and closed the door and lay down on the bed, in the dark, with his eye open.

The next day, an hour before sailing time, Charley and Dr. Stryker and Sally went down to the *Bremen*, and boarded the ship on different gangplanks. They stood separately on the A Deck, up forward, waiting for Preminger. Preminger came, very boyish and crisp in his blue uniform, looked coldly past them, touched a steward on the arm, a dark, good-looking young steward, said something to him, and went aft. Charley and Dr. Stryker examined the steward closely, so that two weeks later, on a dark street, there would be no mistake, and left, leaving Sally there, smiling at Lueger.

"Yes," Sally said two weeks later, "it is very clear. I'll have dinner with him, and I'll go to a movie with him, and I'll get him to take at least two drinks, and I'll tell him I live on West Twelfth Street, near West Street. There is a whole block of apartment houses there, and I'll get him down to West Twelfth Street between a quarter to one and one in the morning, and you'll be waiting there, you and Stryker, under the Ninth Avenue L, and you'll say, 'Pardon me, can you direct me to Sheridan Square?' and I'll start running."

"That's right," Charley said, "that's fine." He blew reflectively on his huge hands, knotted and cleat-marked from last Saturday's game. "That is the whole story for Mr. Lueger. You'll go through with it now?" he asked. "You're sure you can manage it?"

"I'll go through with it," Sally said. "I had a long talk with him today when the boat came in. He is very . . . anxious. He likes small girls like me, he says, with black hair. I told him I lived alone, downtown. He looked at me very significantly. I know why he manages to sleep with two ladies a voyage, like Preminger says. I'll manage it."

"What is Ernest going to do tonight?" Dr. Stryker asked. In the two weeks of waiting his voice had become so dry he had to swallow desperately every five words. "Somebody ought to take care of Ernest tonight."

"He's going to Carnegie Hall tonight," Sally said. "They're playing Brahms and Debussy."

"That's a good way to spend an evening," Charley said. He opened his collar absently, and pulled down his tie. "The only place I can go with Ernest these days is the movies. It's dark, so I don't have to look at him."

"He'll pull through," Dr. Stryker said professionally. "I'm making him new teeth; he won't be so self-conscious, he'll adjust himself."

"He hardly paints any more," Sally said. "He just sits around the house and looks at his old pictures."

"Mr. Lueger," Charley said. "Our pal, Mr. Lueger."

"He carries a picture of Hitler," Sally said. "In his watch. He showed me. He says he's lonely."

"How big is he?" Stryker asked nervously.

"He's a large, strong man," Sally said.

"I think you ought to have an instrument of some kind, Charley," Stryker said dryly. "Really, I do."

Charley laughed. He extended his two hands, palms up, the broken fingers curled a little, broad and muscular. "I want to do this with my own hands," he said. "I want to take care of Mr. Lueger with my bare fists. I want it to be a very personal affair."

"There is no telling what . . ." Stryker said.

"Don't worry, Stryker," Charley said. "Don't worry one bit."

At twelve that night Sally and Lueger walked down Eighth Avenue from the Fourteenth Street subway station. Lueger held Sally's arm as they walked, his fingers moving gently up and down, occasionally grasping tightly the loose cloth of her coat and the firm flesh of her arm just above the elbow.

"Oh," Sally said. "Don't. That hurts."

Lueger laughed. "It does not hurt much," he said. He pinched her playfully. "You don't mind if it hurt, nevertheless," he said. His English was very complicated, with a thick accent.

"I mind," Sally said. "Honest, I mind."

"I like you," he said, walking very close to her. "You are a good girl. You are made excellent. I am happy to accompany you home. You are sure you live alone?"

"I'm sure," Sally said. "Don't worry. I would like a drink."

"Aaah," Lueger said. "Waste time."

"I'll pay for it," Sally said. She had learned a lot about him in one evening. "My own money. Drinks for you and me."

"If you say so," Lueger said, steering her into a bar. "One drink, because we have something to do tonight." He pinched her hard and laughed, looking obliquely into her eyes with a kind of technical suggestiveness he used on the two ladies a voyage on the *Bremen*.

Under the Ninth Avenue L on Twelfth Street, Charley and Dr. Stryker leaned against an elevated post, in deep shadow.

"I . . . I . . ." Stryker said. Then he had to swallow to wet his throat so that the words would come out. "I wonder if they're coming," he said finally in a flat, high whisper.

"They'll come," Charley said, keeping his eyes on the little triangular park up Twelfth Street where it joins Eighth Avenue. "That Sally has guts. That Sally loves my dumb brother like he was the President of the United States. As if he was a combination of Lenin and Michelangelo. And he had to go and get his eye batted out."

"He's a very fine man," Stryker said. "Your brother Ernest. A man with true ideals. I am very sorry to see what has happened to his character since . . . Is that them?"

"No," Charley said. "It's two girls from the YWCA on the corner."

"He used to be a very merry man," Stryker said, swallowing rapidly. "Always laughing. Always sure of what he was saying. Before he was married we used to go out together all the time and all the time the girls, my girl and his girl, no matter who they were, would give all their attention to him. All the time. I didn't mind. I love your brother Ernest as if he was my young brother. I could cry when I see him sitting now, covering his eye and his teeth, not saying anything, just listening to what other people have to say."

"Yeah," Charley said. "Yeah. Why don't you keep quiet, Stryker?"

"Excuse me," Stryker said, talking fast and dry. "I don't like to bother you. But I must talk. Otherwise, if I just stand here keeping still, I will suddenly start running and I'll run right up to Forty-second Street. I can't keep quiet at the moment, excuse me."

"Go ahead and talk, Stryker," Charley said gently, patting him on the shoulder. "Shoot your mouth right off, all you want."

"I am only doing this because I think it will help Ernest," Stryker said, leaning hard against the post, in the shadow, to keep his knees straight. "I have a theory. My theory is that when Ernest finds out what happens to this Lueger, he will pick up. It will be a kind of springboard to him. It is my private notion of the psychology of the situation. We should have brought an instrument with us, though. A club, a knife, brass knuckles." Stryker put his hands in his pockets, holding them tight against the cloth to keep them from trembling. "It will be very bad if we mess this up. Won't it be very bad, Charley? Say, Charley . . ."

"Sssh," said Charley.

Stryker looked up the street. "That's them. That's Sally, that's her coat. That's the bastard. The lousy German bastard."

"Sssh, Stryker. Sssh."

"I feel very cold, Charley. Do you feel cold? It's a warm night but I . . ."

"For Christ's sake, shut up!"

"We'll fix him," Stryker whispered. "Yes, Charley, I'll shut up, sure, I'll shut up, depend on me, Charley . . ."

Sally and Lueger walked slowly down Twelfth Street. Lueger had his arm around Sally's waist and their hips rubbed as they walked.

"That was a very fine film tonight," Lueger was saying. "I enjoy Deanna Durbin. Very young, fresh, sweet. Like you." He grinned at Sally in the dark and held tighter to her waist. "A small young maid. You are just the kind I like." He tried to kiss her. Sally turned her head away.

"Listen, Mr. Lueger," she said, not because she liked him, but because he was a human being and thoughtless and unsuspecting and because her heart was softer than she had thought. "Listen, I think you'd better leave me here."

"I do not understand English," Lueger said, enjoying this last coyness.

"Thank you very much for a pleasant evening," Sally said desperately, stopping in her tracks. "Thank you for taking me home. You can't come up. I was lying to you. I don't live alone . . ."

Lueger laughed. "Little frightened girl. That's nice. I love you for it."

"My brother," Sally said. "I swear to God I live with my brother."

Lueger grabbed her and kissed her, hard, bruising her lips against her teeth, his hands pressing harshly into the flesh of her back. She sobbed into his mouth with the pain, helpless. He released her. He was laughing.

"Come," he said, holding her close, "I am anxious to meet your brother. Little liar."

"All right," she said, watching Charley and Stryker move out from the L shadow. "All right. Let's not wait. Let's walk fast. Very fast. Let's not waste time."

Lueger laughed happily. "That's it. That's the way a girl should talk."

They walked swiftly toward the elevated ramp, Lueger laughing, his hand on her hip in certainty and possession.

"Pardon me," Stryker said. "Could you direct me to Sheridan Square?"

"Well," said Sally, stopping, "it's . . ."

Charley swung and Sally started running as soon as she heard the wooden little noise a fist makes on a man's face. Charley held Lueger up with one hand and chopped the lolling head with the other. He carried Lueger back into the shadows against a high iron railing. He hung Lueger by his overcoat against one of the iron points, so he could use both hands on him. Stryker watched for a moment, then turned and looked toward Eighth Avenue.

Charley worked very methodically, getting his two hundred pounds behind short, accurate, smashing blows that made Lueger's head jump and loll and roll against the iron pikes. Charley hit him in the nose three times, squarely, using his fist the way a carpenter uses a hammer. Each time Charley heard the sound of bone breaking, cartilage tearing. When he got through with the nose, Charley went after the mouth, hooking along the side of the jaws with both hands, until teeth fell out and the jaw hung open, smashed, loose with the queer looseness of flesh that is no longer moored to solid bone. Charley started crying, the tears running down into his mouth, the sobs shaking him as he swung his fists. Even then Stryker didn't turn around. He just put his hands to his ears and looked steadfastly at Eighth Avenue.

When he started on Lueger's eye, Charley talked. "You bastard. Oh, you lousy goddamn bastard," came out with the sobs and the tears as he hit at the eye with his right hand, cutting it, smashing it, tearing it again and again, his hand coming away splattered with blood each time. "Oh, you dumb, mean, skirtchasing, sonofabitch, bastard." And he kept hitting with fury and deliberation at the shattered eye . . .

A car came up Twelfth Street from the waterfront and slowed down at the corner. Stryker jumped on the running board. "Keep moving," he said, very tough, "if you know what's good for you."

He jumped off the running board and watched the car speed away.

Charley, still sobbing, pounded Lueger in the chest and belly. With each blow Lueger slammed against the iron fence with a noise like a carpet being beaten, until his coat ripped off the pike and he slid to the sidewalk.

Charley stood back, his fists swaying, the tears still coming, the sweat running down his face inside his collar, his clothes stained with blood.

"O.K.," he said, "O.K., you bastard."

He walked swiftly up under the L in the shadows, and Stryker hurried after him.

Much later, in the hospital, Preminger stood over the bed in which Lueger lay, unconscious, in splints and bandages.

"Yes," he said to the detective and the doctor. "That's our man. Lueger. A steward. The papers on him are correct."

"Who do you think done it?" the detective asked in a routine voice. "Did he have any enemies?"

"Not that I know of," Preminger said. "He was a very popular boy. Especially with the ladies."

The detective started out of the ward. "Well," he said, "he won't be a very popular boy when he gets out of here."

Preminger shook his head. "You must be very careful in a strange city," he said to the interne, and went back to the ship.

I STAND BY DEMPSEY

THE CROWD came out of Madison Square Garden with the sorrowful, meditative air that hangs over it when the fights have been bad. Flanagan pushed Gurske and Flora quickly through the frustrated fans and into a cab. Gurske sat on the folding seat, Flanagan with Flora in the back.

"I want a drink," he said to her as the cab started. "I want to forget what I saw tonight."

"They were not so bad," Gurske said. "They were scientific."

"Not a bloody nose," Flanagan said. "Not a single drop of blood. Heavyweights! Heavyweight pansies!"

"As an exhibition of skill," Gurske said, "I found it interesting."

"Joe Louis could've wiped them all up in the short space of two minutes," Flanagan said.

"Joe Louis is overrated," Gurske said, leaning across from the little folding seat and tapping Flanagan on the knee. "He is highly overrated."

"Yeah," Flanagan said. "He is overrated like the S. S. *Texas* is overrated. I saw the Schmeling fight."

"That German is a old man," Gurske said.

"When Louis hit him in the belly," Flora said, "he cried. Like a baby. Louis' hand went in up to the wrist. I saw with my own eyes."

"He left his legs in Hamburg," Gurske said. "A slight wind woulda knocked him over."

"That is some slight wind," said Flanagan, "that Louis."

"He's built like a brick privy," Flora remarked.

"I woulda liked to see Dempsey in there with him." Gurske rolled his eyes at the thought. "Dempsey. In his prime. The blood would flow."

"Louis would make chopmeat outa Dempsey. Who did Dempsey ever beat?" Flanagan wanted to know.

"Listen to that!" Gurske pushed Flora's knee in amazement. "Dempsey! The Manassa Mauler!"

"Louis is a master boxer," Flanagan said. "Also, he punches like he had a baseball bat in his both hands. Dempsey! Eugene, you are a goddamn fool."

"Boys!" Flora said.

"Dempsey was a panther in action. Bobbing and weaving." Gurske bobbed and weaved and knocked his derby off his small, neat head. "He carried destruction in either fist." Gurske bent over for his hat. "He had the heart of a wounded lion."

"He certainly would be wounded if he stepped into the ring with Joe Louis." Flanagan thought this was funny and roared with laughter. He slapped Gurske's face playfully with his huge hand and Gurske's hat fell off.

"You're very funny," Gurske said, bending over for his hat again. "You're a very funny man."

"The trouble with you, Eugene," Flanagan said, "is you don't have no sense of humor."

"I laugh when something's funny." Gurske brushed his hat off.

"Am I right?" Flanagan asked Flora. "Has Eugene got a sense of humor?"

"He is a very serious character, Eugene," Flora said.

"Go to hell," Gurske said.

"Hey, you." Flanagan tapped him on the shoulder. "Don't you talk like that."

"Aaah," Gurske said. "Aaah—"

"You don't know how to argue like a gentleman," Flanagan said. "That's what's the matter with you. All little guys're like that."

"Aaah!"

"A guy is under five foot six, every time he gets in a argument he gets excited. Ain't that so, Flora?"

"Who's excited?" Gurske yelled. "I am merely stating a fact. Dempsey would lay Louis out like a carpet. That is all I'm saying."

"You are making too much noise," Flanagan said. "Lower your voice."

"I seen 'em both. With my own eyes!"

"What the hell do you know about fighting, anyway?" Flanagan asked.

"Fighting!" Gurske trembled on his seat. "The only kind of fighting *you* know about is waiting at the end of a alley with a gun for drunks."

Flanagan put his hand over Gurske's mouth. With his other hand he held the back of Gurske's neck. "Shut up, Eugene," he said. "I am asking you to shut up."

Gurske's eyes rolled for a moment behind the huge hand. Then he relaxed.

Flanagan sighed and released him. "You are my best friend, Eugene," he said, "but sometimes you gotta shut up."

"A party," Flora said. "We go out on a party. Two gorillas. A little gorilla and a big gorilla."

They rolled downtown in silence. They brightened, however, when they got to Savage's Café and had two Old-Fashioneds each. The five-piece college-boy band played fast numbers and the Old-Fashioneds warmed the blood and friends gathered around the table. Flanagan stretched out his hand and patted Gurske amiably on the head.

"All right," he said. "All right, Eugene. We're friends. You and me, we are lifelong comrades."

"All right," Gurske said reluctantly. "This is a party."

Everybody drank because it was a party, and Flora said, "Now, boys, you see how foolish it was—over two guys you never even met to talk to?"

"It was a question of attitude," Gurske said. "Just because he's a big slob with meat axes for hands he takes a superior attitude."

"All I said was Louis was a master boxer." Flanagan opened his collar. "That's all he said!"

"Dempsey was a slugger. That's all—a slugger. Look what that big ox from South America did to him. That Firpo. Dempsey had to be put on his feet by newspapermen. No newspaperman has to stand Joe Louis on his feet."

"That's all he said," Gurske repeated. "That's all he said. My God!"

"Boys," Flora pleaded, "it's history. Have a good time."

Flanagan toyed with his glass. "That Eugene," he said. "You say one thing, he says another. Automatic. The whole world agrees there never was nothing like Joe Louis, he brings up Dempsey."

"The whole world!" Gurske said. "Flanagan, the whole world!"

"I want to dance," Flora said.

"Sit down," Flanagan said. "I want to talk with my friend, Eugene Gurske."

"Stick to the facts," Gurske said. "That's all I ask, stick to the facts."

"A small man can't get along in human society," Flanagan said to the company at the table. "He can't agree with no one. He should live in a cage."

"That's right," Gurske said. "Make it personal. You can't win by reason, use insults. Typical."

"I would give Dempsey two rounds. Two," Flanagan said. "There! As far as I am concerned the argument is over. I want a drink."

"Let me tell you something," Gurske said loudly. "Louis wouldn't—"

"The discussion is closed."

"Who says it's closed? In Shelby, Montana, when Dempsey—"

"I ain't interested."

"He met 'em all and he beat 'em all—"

"Listen, Eugene," Flanagan said seriously. "I don't want to hear no more. I want to listen to the music."

Gurske jumped up from his chair in a rage. "I'm goin' to talk, see, and you're not going to stop me, see, and—"

"Eugene," Flanagan said. Slowly he lifted his hand, palm open.

"I—" Gurske watched the big red hand, with the heavy gold rings on the fingers, waggle back and forth. His lips quivered. He stooped suddenly and picked up his derby and rushed out of the room, the laughter of the guests at the table ringing in his ears.

"He'll be back," Flanagan said. "He's excitable, Eugene. Like a little rooster. He has got to be toned down now and then. Now, Flora. Let's dance."

They danced pleasantly for a half-hour, taking time out for another Old-Fashioned between numbers. They were on the dance floor when Gurske appeared in the doorway with a large soda bottle in each hand.

"Flanagan!" Gurske shouted from the doorway. "I'm looking for Vincent Flanagan!"

"My God!" Flora shrieked. "He'll kill somebody!"

"Flanagan," Gurske repeated. "Come on out of that crowd. Step out here."

Flora pulled at Flanagan as the dancers melted to both sides. "Vinnie," she cried, "there's a back door."

"Give me a ginger-ale bottle," Flanagan said, taking a step toward Gurske. "Somebody put a ginger-ale bottle in my hand."

"Don't come no nearer, Flanagan! This is one argument you won't win with yer lousy big hands."

"Where is that ginger-ale bottle?" Flanagan asked, advancing on Gurske step by step, keeping Gurske's eyes fixed with his.

"I warn you, Flanagan!"

Gurske threw one of the bottles. Flanagan ducked and it smashed against the back wall.

"You are going to regret this," Flanagan said.

Gurske lifted the other bottle nervously. Flanagan took another step, and then another.

"Oh, my God!" Gurske cried, and threw the bottle at Flanagan's head and turned tail and ran.

Flanagan caught the bottle in mid-flight, took careful aim with it, and let it go across the dance floor. It hit Gurske at the ankle and he went sailing over a table like a duckpin caught all alone on a bowling alley. Flanagan was on him and had him by the collar immediately. He lifted Gurske into the air with one hand and held him there.

"Gurske," he said. "You cockeyed Gurske. The hundred-and-thirty-pound Napoleon."

"Don't kill him!" Flora came running over to them distractedly. "For God's sake, don't kill him, Vinnie!"

For a moment Flanagan looked at Gurske hanging limply from his hand. Then he turned to the other guests. "Ladies and gentlemen," he said, "no damage has occurred."

"I missed," Gurske said bitterly. "I ought to wear glasses."

"Let everybody dance," Flanagan announced. "I apologize for my friend. I guarantee he won't cause no more trouble."

The orchestra struck up "The Dipsy Doodle" and the guests swung back with animation into their dancing.

Flanagan carried Gurske to their table and set him down. "All right," he said. "We will finish our discussion. Once and for all."

"Aaah!" Gurske said, but without spirit.

"Eugene," Flanagan said, "come here."

Gurske sidled up toward Flanagan, who was sitting with his feet out from the table, his legs spread comfortably apart.

"What about those prizefighters we mentioned some time ago?"

"Dempsey," Gurske said hoarsely. "I stand by Dempsey."

Flanagan laid his hand on Gurske's arm and pulled. Gurske fell face downward, seat up, over Flanagan's knees.

"The old woodshed," Flanagan said. He began to spank Gurske with wide, deliberate strokes. The orchestra stopped playing after a moment and the smacks resounded in the silent room.

"Oh!" Gurske said at the seventh stroke.

"Oh!" the roomful of people answered in a single hushed tone.

At the ninth stroke the drummer of the band took up the beat and from then on the bass drum sounded simultaneously with the hard, unrelenting hand.

"Well," Flanagan said on the twenty-fifth stroke. "Well, Mr. Gurske?"

"I stand by Dempsey!"

"O.K.," Flanagan said, and continued with the spanking.

After stroke thirty-two Gurske called tearfully, "All right. That's all, Flanagan."

Flanagan lifted Eugene to his feet. "I am glad that matter is settled. Now sit down and have a drink."

The guests applauded and the orchestra struck up and the dancing began again. Flanagan and Flora and Gurske sat at their table drinking Old-Fashioneds.

"The drinks are on me," Flanagan said. "Drink hearty. Who do you stand by, Eugene?"

"I stand by Louis," Gurske said.

"What round would he win in?"

"In the second round," Gurske said. The tears streamed down his face, and he sipped his Old-Fashioned. "He would win in the second round."

"My friend Eugene," Flanagan said.

THE GIRLS
IN THEIR SUMMER DRESSES

Fɪғᴛʜ Aᴠᴇɴᴜᴇ ᴡᴀs shining in the sun when they left the Brevoort and started walking toward Washington Square. The sun was warm, even though it was November and everything looked like Sunday morning— the buses, and the well-dressed people walking slowly in couples and the quiet buildings with the windows closed.

Michael held Frances' arm tightly as they walked downtown in the sunlight. They walked lightly, almost smiling, because they had slept late and had a good breakfast and it was Sunday. Michael unbuttoned his coat and let it flap around him in the mild wind. They walked, without saying anything, among the young and pleasant-looking people who somehow seem to make up most of the population of that section of New York City.

"Look out," Frances said, as they crossed Eighth Street. "You'll break your neck."

Michael laughed and Frances laughed with him.

"She's not so pretty, anyway," Frances said. "Anyway, not pretty enough to take a chance breaking your neck looking at her."

Michael laughed again. He laughed louder this time, but not as solidly. "She wasn't a bad-looking girl. She had a nice complexion. Country-girl complexion. How did you know I was looking at her?"

Frances cocked her head to one side and smiled at her husband under the tip-tilted brim of her hat. "Mike, darling . . ." she said.

Michael laughed, just a little laugh this time. "O.K.," he said. "The evidence is in. Excuse me. It was the complexion. It's not the sort of complexion you see much in New York. Excuse me."

Frances patted his arm lightly and pulled him along a little faster toward Washington Square.

"This is a nice morning," she said. "This is a wonderful morning. When I have breakfast with you it makes me feel good all day."

"Tonic," Michael said. "Morning pick-up. Rolls and coffee with Mike and you're on the alkali side, guaranteed."

"That's the story. Also, I slept all night, wound around you like a rope."

"Saturday night," he said. "I permit such liberties only when the week's work is done."

"You're getting fat," she said.

"Isn't it the truth? The lean man from Ohio."

"I love it," she said, "an extra five pounds of husband."

"I love it, too," Michael said gravely.

"I have an idea," Frances said.

"My wife has an idea. That pretty girl."

"Let's not see anybody all day," Frances said. "Let's just hang around with each other. You and me. We're always up to our neck in people, drinking their Scotch, or drinking our Scotch, we only see each other in bed . . ."

"The Great Meeting Place," Michael said. "Stay in bed long enough and everybody you ever knew will show up there."

"Wise guy," Frances said. "I'm talking serious."

"O.K., I'm listening serious."

"I want to go out with my husband all day long. I want him to talk only to me and listen only to me."

"What's to stop us?" Michael asked. "What party intends to prevent me from seeing my wife alone on Sunday? What party?"

"The Stevensons. They want us to drop by around one o'clock and they'll drive us into the country."

"The lousy Stevensons," Mike said. "Transparent. They can whistle. They can go driving in the country by themselves. My wife and I have to stay in New York and bore each other tête-à-tête."

"Is it a date?"

"It's a date."

Frances leaned over and kissed him on the tip of the ear.

"Darling," Michael said. "This is Fifth Avenue."

"Let me arrange a program," Frances said. "A planned Sunday in New York for a young couple with money to throw away."

"Go easy."

"First let's go see a football game. A professional football game,"

Frances said, because she knew Michael loved to watch them. "The Giants are playing. And it'll be nice to be outside all day today and get hungry and later we'll go down to Cavanagh's and get a steak as big as a blacksmith's apron, with a bottle of wine, and after that, there's a new French picture at the Filmarte that everybody says . . . Say, are you listening to me?"

"Sure," he said. He took his eyes off the hatless girl with the dark hair, cut dancer-style, like a helmet, who was walking past him with the self-conscious strength and grace dancers have. She was walking without a coat and she looked very solid and strong and her belly was flat, like a boy's, under her skirt, and her hips swung boldly because she was a dancer and also because she knew Michael was looking at her. She smiled a little to herself as she went past and Michael noticed all these things before he looked back at his wife. "Sure," he said, "we're going to watch the Giants and we're going to eat steak and we're going to see a French picture. How do you like that?"

"That's it," Frances said flatly. "That's the program for the day. Or maybe you'd just rather walk up and down Fifth Avenue."

"No," Michael said carefully. "Not at all."

"You always look at other women," Frances said. "At every damn woman in the City of New York."

"Oh, come now," Michael said, pretending to joke. "Only pretty ones. And, after all, how many pretty women *are* there in New York? Seventeen?"

"More. At least you seem to think so. Wherever you go."

"Not the truth. Occasionally, maybe, I look at a woman as she passes. In the street. I admit, perhaps in the street I look at a woman once in a while . . ."

"Everywhere," Frances said. "Every damned place we go. Restaurants, subways, theaters, lectures, concerts."

"Now, darling," Michael said, "I look at everything. God gave me eyes and I look at women and men and subway excavations and moving pictures and the little flowers of the field. I casually inspect the universe."

"You ought to see the look in your eye," Frances said, "as you casually inspect the universe on Fifth Avenue."

"I'm a happily married man." Michael pressed her elbow tenderly, knowing what he was doing. "Example for the whole twentieth century, Mr. and Mrs. Mike Loomis."

"You mean it?"

"Frances, baby . . ."

"Are you *really* happily married?"

"Sure," Michael said, feeling the whole Sunday morning sinking like lead inside him. "Now what the hell is the sense in talking like that?"

"I would like to know." Frances walked faster now, looking straight ahead, her face showing nothing, which was the way she always managed it when she was arguing or feeling bad.

"I'm wonderfully happily married," Michael said patiently. "I am the envy of all men between the ages of fifteen and sixty in the State of New York."

"Stop kidding," Frances said.

"I have a fine home," Michael said. "I got nice books and a phonograph and nice friends. I live in a town I like the way I like and I do the work I like and I live with the woman I like. Whenever something good happens, don't I run to you? When something bad happens, don't I cry on your shoulder?"

"Yes," Frances said. "You look at every woman that passes."

"That's an exaggeration."

"Every woman." Frances took her hand off Michael's arm. "If she's not pretty you turn away fairly quickly. If she's halfway pretty you watch her for about seven steps . . ."

"My lord, Frances!"

"If she's pretty you practically break your neck . . ."

"Hey, let's have a drink," Michael said, stopping.

"We just had breakfast."

"Now, listen, darling," Mike said, choosing his words with care, "it's a nice day and we both feel good and there's no reason why we have to break it up. Let's have a nice Sunday."

"I could have a fine Sunday if you didn't look as though you were dying to run after every skirt on Fifth Avenue."

"Let's have a drink," Michael said.

"I don't want a drink."

"What do you want, a fight?"

"No," Frances said so unhappily that Michael felt terribly sorry for her. "I don't want a fight. I don't know why I started this. All right, let's drop it. Let's have a good time."

They joined hands consciously and walked without talking among the baby carriages and the old Italian men in their Sunday clothes and the young women with Scotties in Washington Square Park.

"I hope it's a good game today," Frances said after a while, her tone a good imitation of the tone she had used at breakfast and at the beginning of their walk. "I like professional football games. They hit each other as though they're made out of concrete. When they tackle each other," she said, trying to make Michael laugh, "they make divots. It's very exciting."

"I want to tell you something," Michael said very seriously. "I have not touched another woman. Not once. In all the five years."

"All right," Frances said.

"You believe that, don't you?"

"All right."

They walked between the crowded benches, under the scrubby city park trees.

"I try not to notice it," Frances said, as though she were talking to herself. "I try to make believe it doesn't mean anything. Some men're like that, I tell myself, they have to see what they're missing."

"Some women're like that, too," Michael said. "In my time I've seen a couple of ladies."

"I haven't even looked at another man," Frances said, walking straight ahead, "since the second time I went out with you."

"There's no law," Michael said.

"I feel rotten inside, in my stomach, when we pass a woman and you look at her and I see that look in your eye and that's the way you looked at me the first time, in Alice Maxwell's house. Standing there in the living room, next to the radio, with a green hat on and all those people."

"I remember the hat," Michael said.

"The same look," Frances said. "And it makes me feel bad. It makes me feel terrible."

"Sssh, please, darling, sssh . . ."

"I think I would like a drink now," Frances said.

They walked over to a bar on Eighth Street, not saying anything, Michael automatically helping her over curbstones, and guiding her past automobiles. He walked, buttoning his coat, looking thoughtfully at his neatly shined heavy brown shoes as they made the steps toward the bar. They sat near a window in the bar and the sun streamed in, and there was a small cheerful fire in the fireplace. A little Japanese waiter came over and put down some pretzels and smiled happily at them.

"What do you order after breakfast?" Michael asked.

"Brandy, I suppose," Frances said.

"Courvoisier," Michael told the waiter. "Two Courvoisier."

The waiter came with the glasses and they sat drinking the brandy, in the sunlight. Michael finished half his and drank a little water.

"I look at women," he said. "Correct. I don't say it's wrong or right, I look at them. If I pass them on the street and I don't look at them, I'm fooling you, I'm fooling myself."

"You look at them as though you want them," Frances said, playing with her brandy glass. "Every one of them."

"In a way," Michael said, speaking softly and not to his wife, "in a way that's true. I don't do anything about it, but it's true."

"I know it. That's why I feel bad."

"Another brandy," Michael called. "Waiter, two more brandies."

"Why do you hurt me?" Frances asked. "What're you doing?"

Michael sighed and closed his eyes and rubbed them gently with his fingertips. "I love the way women look. One of the things I like best about New York is the battalions of women. When I first came to New York from Ohio that was the first thing I noticed, the million wonderful women, all over the city. I walked around with my heart in my throat."

"A kid," Frances said. "That's a kid's feeling."

"Guess again," Michael said. "Guess again. I'm older now, I'm a man getting near middle age, putting on a little fat and I still love to walk along Fifth Avenue at three o'clock on the east side of the street between Fiftieth and Fifty-seventh Streets, they're all out then, making believe they're shopping, in their furs and their crazy hats, everything all concentrated from all over the world into eight blocks, the best furs, the best clothes, the handsomest women, out to spend money and feeling good about it, looking coldly at you, making believe they're not looking at you as you go past."

The Japanese waiter put the two drinks down, smiling with great happiness.

"Everything is all right?" he asked.

"Everything is wonderful," Michael said.

"If it's just a couple of fur coats," Frances said, "and forty-five-dollar hats . . ."

"It's not the fur coats. Or the hats. That's just the scenery for that particular kind of woman. Understand," he said, "you don't have to listen to this."

"I want to listen."

"I like the girls in the offices. Neat, with their eye-glasses, smart, chipper, knowing what everything is about, taking care of themselves all the time." He kept his eye on the people going slowly past outside the window. "I like the girls on Forty-fourth Street at lunch time, the actresses, all dressed up on nothing a week, talking to the good-looking boys, wearing themselves out being young and vivacious outside Sardi's, waiting for producers to look at them. I like the salesgirls in Macy's, paying attention to you first because you're a man, leaving lady customers waiting, flirting with you over socks and books and phonograph needles. I got all this stuff accumulated in me because I've been thinking about it for ten years and now you've asked for it and here it is."

"Go ahead," Frances said.

"When I think of New York City, I think of all the girls, the Jewish girls, the Italian girls, the Irish, Polack, Chinese, German, Negro, Spanish, Russian girls, all on parade in the city. I don't know whether it's something special with me or whether every man in the city walks around with the same feeling inside him, but I feel as though I'm at a picnic in this city. I like to sit near the women in the theaters, the famous beauties who've taken six hours to get ready and look it. And the young girls at the football games, with the red cheeks, and when the warm weather comes, the girls in their summer dresses . . ." He finished his drink. "That's the story. You asked for it, remember. I can't help but look at them. I can't help but want them."

"You want them," Frances repeated without expression. "You said that."

"Right," Michael said, being cruel now and not caring, because she had made him expose himself. "You brought this subject up for discussion, we will discuss it fully."

Frances finished her drink and swallowed two or three times extra. "You say you love me?"

"I love you, but I also want them. O.K."

"I'm pretty, too," Frances said. "As pretty as any of them."

"You're beautiful," Michael said, meaning it.

"I'm good for you," Frances said, pleading. "I've made a good wife, a good housekeeper, a good friend. I'd do any damn thing for you."

"I know," Michael said. He put his hand out and grasped hers.

"You'd like to be free to . . ." Frances said.

"Sssh."

"Tell the truth." She took her hand away from under his.

Michael flicked the edge of his glass with his finger. "O.K.," he said gently. "Sometimes I feel I would like to be free."

"Well," Frances said defiantly, drumming on the table, "anytime you say . . ."

"Don't be foolish," Michael swung his chair around to her side of the table and patted her thigh.

She began to cry, silently, into her handkerchief, bent over just enough so that nobody else in the bar would notice. "Some day," she said, crying, "you're going to make a move . . ."

Michael didn't say anything. He sat watching the bartender slowly peel a lemon.

"Aren't you?" Frances asked harshly. "Come on, tell me. Talk. Aren't you?"

"Maybe," Michael said. He moved his chair back again. "How the hell do I know?"

"You know," Frances persisted. "Don't you know?"

"Yes," Michael said after a while, "I know."

Frances stopped crying then. Two or three snuffles into the handkerchief and she put it away and her face didn't tell anything to anybody. "At least do me one favor," she said.

"Sure."

"Stop talking about how pretty this woman is, or that one. Nice eyes, nice breasts, a pretty figure, good voice," she mimicked his voice. "Keep it to yourself. I'm not interested."

"Excuse me." Michael waved to the waiter. "I'll keep it to myself."

Frances flicked the corner of her eyes. "Another brandy," she told the waiter.

"Two," Michael said.

"Yes, ma'am, yes, sir," said the waiter, backing away.

Frances regarded him coolly across the table. "Do you want me to call the Stevensons?" she asked. "It'll be nice in the country."

"Sure," Michael said. "Call them up."

She got up from the table and walked across the room toward the telephone. Michael watched her walk, thinking, what a pretty girl, what nice legs.

RETURN TO KANSAS CITY

ARLINE OPENED the bedroom door and softly went over between the twin beds, the silk of her dress making a slight rustle in the quiet room. The dark shades were down and the late afternoon sun came in only in one or two places along the sides of the window frames, in sharp, thin rays.

Arline looked down at her husband, sleeping under the blankets. His fighter's face with the mashed nose was very peaceful on the pillow and his hair was curled like a baby's and he snored gently because he breathed through his mouth. A light sweat stood out on his face. Eddie always sweated, any season, any place. But now, when she saw Eddie begin to sweat, it made Arline a little angry.

She stood there, watching the serene, glove-marked face. She sat down on the other bed, still watching her husband. She took a lace-bordered handkerchief out of a pocket and dabbed at her eyes. They were dry. She sniffed a little and the tears started. For a moment she cried silently, then she sobbed aloud. In a minute the tears and the sobs were regular, loud in the still room.

Eddie stirred in his bed. He closed his mouth, turned over on his side.

"Oh, my," Arline sobbed, "oh, my God."

She saw, despite the fact that Eddie's back was toward her, that he had awakened.

"Oh," Arline wept, "sweet Mother of God."

She knew that Eddie was wide awake listening to her and he knew that she knew it, but he hopefully pretended he hadn't been roused. He even snored experimentally once or twice. Arline's sobs shook her and the mascara ran down her cheeks in straight black lines.

Eddie sighed and turned around and sat up, rubbing his hair with his hands.

"What's the matter?" he asked. "What's bothering you, Arline?"

"Nothing," Arline sobbed.

"If nothing's the matter," Eddie said mildly, "what're you crying for?"

Arline didn't say anything. She stopped sobbing aloud and turned the grief inward upon herself and wept all the more bitterly, in silence. Eddie wiped his eye with the heel of his hand, looked wearily at the dark shades that shut out the slanting rays of the sun.

"There are six rooms in this house, Arline darling," he said. "If you have to cry why is it necessary to pick the exact room where I am sleeping?"

Arline's head sank low on her breast, her beautiful beauty-shop straw-colored hair falling tragically over her face. "You don't care," she murmured, "you don't care one dime's worth if I break my heart."

She squeezed the handkerchief and the tears ran down her wrist.

"I care," Eddie said, throwing back the covers neatly and putting his stockinged feet onto the floor. He had been sleeping in his pants and shirt, which were very wrinkled now. He shook his head two or three times as he sat on the edge of the bed and hit himself smartly on the cheek with the back of his hand to awaken himself. He looked unhappily across at his wife, sitting on the other bed, her hands wrung in her lap, her face covered by her careless hair, sorrow and despair in every line of her. "Honest, Arline, I care." He went over and sat next to her on the bed and put his arm around her. "Baby," he said. "Now, baby."

She just sat there crying silently, her round, soft shoulders shaking now and then under his arm. Eddie began to feel more and more uncomfortable. He squeezed her shoulder two or three times, exhausting his methods of consolation. "Well," he said finally, "I think maybe I'll put the kid in the carriage and take him for a walk. A little air. Maybe when I come back you'll feel better."

"I won't feel better," Arline promised him, without moving. "I won't feel one ounce better."

"Arline," Eddie said.

"The kid." She sat up erect now and looked at him. "If you paid as much attention to me as to the kid."

"I pay equal attention. My wife and my kid." Eddie stood up and padded around the room uneasily in his socks.

Arline watched him intently, the creased flannel trousers and the wrinkled shirt not concealing the bulky muscles.

"The male sleeping beauty," she said. "The long-distance sleeping champion. My husband."

"I don't sleep so awful much," Eddie protested.

"Fifteen hours a day," Arline said. "Is it natural?"

"I had a hard workout this morning," Eddie said, standing at the window. "I went six fast rounds. I got to get rest. I got to store up my energy. I am not so young as some people any more. I got to take care of myself. Don't I have to store up energy?"

"Store up your energy!" Arline said loudly. "All day long you store up energy. What is your wife supposed to do when you are storing up energy?"

Eddie let the window shade fly up. The light shot into the room, making it harder for Arline to cry.

"You ought to have friends," Eddie suggested without hope.

"I have friends."

"Why don't you go out with them?"

"They're in Kansas City," Arline said.

There was silence in the room. Eddie sat down and began putting on his shoes.

"My mother's in Kansas City," Arline said. "My two sisters are in Kansas City. My two brothers. I went to high school in Kansas City. Here I am, in Brooklyn, New York."

"You were in Kansas City two and a half months ago," Eddie said, buttoning his collar and knotting his tie. "A mere two and a half months ago."

"Two and a half months are a long time," Arline said, clearing away the mascara lines from her cheeks, but still weeping. "A person can die in two and a half months."

"What person?" Eddie asked.

Arline ignored him. "Mama writes she wants to see the baby again. After all, that is not unnatural, a grandmother wants to see her grandchild. Tell me, is it unnatural?"

"No," said Eddie, "it is not unnatural." He combed his hair swiftly. "If Mama wants to see the baby," he said, "explain to me why she can't come here. Kindly explain to me."

"My husband is of the opinion that they are handing out gold pieces with movie tickets in Kansas City," Arline said with cold sarcasm.

"Huh?" Eddie asked, honestly puzzled. "What did you say?"

"How can Mama afford to come here?" Arline asked. "After all, you know, there are no great prizefighters in *our* family. I had to *marry* to bring one into the family. Oh, my God!" Once more she wept.

"Lissen, Arline," Eddie ran over to her and spoke pleadingly, his tough, battered face very gentle and sad, "I can't afford to have you go to Kansas City every time I take a nap in the afternoon. We have been married a year and a half and you have gone to Kansas City five times. I feel like I am fighting for the New York Central Railroad, Arline!"

Arline shook her head obstinately. "There is nothing to do in New York," she said.

"There is nothing to do in New York!" Eddie's mouth opened in surprise. "My God! There's something to do in Kansas City?" he cried. "What the hell is there to do in Kansas City? Remember, I have been in that town myself. I married you in that town."

"I didn't know how it was going to be," Arline said flatly. "It was nice in Kansas City. I was an innocent young girl."

"Please," said Eddie. "Let us not rake up the past."

"I was surrounded by my family," Arline went on shakily. "I went to high school there."

She bent over and grief took possession once more. Eddie licked his lips uncomfortably. They were dry from the morning's workout and the lower lip was split a little and smarted when he ran his tongue over it. He searched his brain for a helpful phrase.

"The kid," he ventured timidly, "why don't you play more with the kid?"

"The kid!" Arline cried defiantly. "I take very good care of the kid. I have to stay in every night minding the kid while you are busy storing up your energy." The phrase enraged her and she stood up, waving her arms. "What a business! You fight thirty minutes a month, you got to sleep three hundred and fifty hours. Why, it's laughable. It is very laughable! You are some fighter!" She shook her fist at him in derision. "With all the energy you store up you ought to be able to beat the German army!"

"That is the business I am in," Eddie tried to explain gently. "That is the nature of my profession."

"Don't tell me that!" Arline said. "I have gone out with other fighters. They don't sleep all the time."

"I am not interested," Eddie said. "I do not want to hear anything about your life before our marriage."

"They go to night clubs," Arline went on irresistibly, "and they dance and they take a drink once in a while and they take a girl to see a musical show!"

Eddie nodded. "They are after something," he said. "That is the whole story."

"I wish to God you were after something!"

"I meet the type of fighter you mention, too," Eddie said. "The night-club boys. They knock my head off for three rounds and then they start breathing through the mouth. By the time they reach the eighth round they wish they never saw a naked lady on a dance floor. And by the time I get through with them they are storing up energy, flat on their backs. With five thousand people watching them. You want me to be that kind of a fighter?"

"You're wonderful," Arline said, wrinkling her nose, sneering. "My Joe Louis. Big-Purse Eddie Megaffin. I don't notice you bringing back the million-dollar gate."

"I am progressing slowly," Eddie said, looking at the picture of Mary and Jesus over his bed. "I am planning for the future."

"I am linked for life to a goddamn health-enthusiast," Arline said despairingly.

"Why do you talk like that, Arline?"

"Because I want to be in Kansas City," she wailed.

"Explain to me," Eddie said, "why in the name of God you are so crazy for Kansas City?"

"I'm lonesome," Arline wept with true bitterness. "I'm awful lonesome. I'm only twenty-one years old, Eddie."

Eddie patted her gently on the shoulder. "Look, Arline." He tried to make his voice very warm and at the same time logical. "If you would only go easy. If you would go by coach and not buy presents for everybody, maybe I can borrow a coupla bucks and swing it."

"I would rather die," Arline said. "I would rather never see Kansas City again for the rest of my life than let them know my husband has to watch pennies like a street-car conductor. A man with his name in the papers every week. It would be shameful!"

"But, Arline, darling," Eddie's face was tortured, "you go four times a year, you spread presents like the WPA and you always buy new clothes . . ."

"I can't appear in Kansas City in rags!" Arline pulled at a stocking, righting it on her well-curved leg. "I would rather . . ."

"Some day, darling," Eddie interrupted. "We're working up. Right now I can't."

"You can!" Arline said. "You're lying to me, Eddie Megaffin. Jake Blucher called up this morning and he told me he offered you a thousand dollars to fight Joe Principe."

Eddie sat down in a chair. He looked down at the floor, understanding why Arline had picked this particular afternoon.

"You would come out of that fight with seven hundred and fifty dollars," Arline's voice was soft and inviting. "I could go to Kansas . . ."

"Joe Principe will knock my ears off."

Arline sighed. "I am so anxious to see my mother. She is an old woman and soon she will die."

"At this stage," Eddie said slowly, "I am not ready for Joe Principe. He is too strong and too smart for me."

"Jake Blucher told me he thought you had a wonderful chance."

"I have a wonderful chance to land in the hospital," Eddie said. "That Joe Principe is made out of springs and cement. If you gave him a pair of horns it would be legal to kill him with a sword."

"He is only a man with two fists just like you," Arline said.

"Yeah."

"You're always telling me how good you are."

"In two years," Eddie said, "taking it very easy and careful, making sure I don't get knocked apart . . ."

"You could make the money easy!" Arline pointed her finger dramatically at him. "You just don't want to. You don't want me to be happy. I see through you, Eddie Megaffin!"

"I just don't want to get beaten up," Eddie said, shaking his head.

"A fine fighter!" Arline laughed. "What kind of fighter are you, anyhow? A fighter is supposed to get beaten up, isn't he? That's his business, isn't it? You don't care for me. All you wanted was somebody to give you a kid and cook your goddamn steaks and lamb chops. In Brooklyn! I got to stay in a lousy little house day in and . . ."

"I'll take you to the movies tonight," Eddie promised.

"I don't want to go to the movies. I want to go to Kansas City." Arline threw herself face down on the bed and sobbed. "I'm caught. I'm caught! You don't love me! You won't let me go to people who love me! Mama! Mama!"

Eddie closed his eyes in pain. "I love you," he said, meaning it. "I swear to God."

"You say it." Her voice was smothered in the pillow. "But you don't prove it! Prove it! I never knew a young man could be so stingy. Prove it . . ." The words trailed off in sorrow.

Eddie went over and bent down to kiss her. She shook her shoulders to send him away and cried like a heartbroken child. From the next room, where the baby had been sleeping, came the sound of his wailing.

Eddie walked over to the window and looked out at the peaceful Brooklyn street, at the trees and the little boys and girls skating.

"O.K.," he said, "I'll call Blucher."

Arline stopped crying. The baby still wailed in the next room.

"I'll try to raise him to twelve hundred," Eddie said. "You can go to Kansas City. You happy?"

Arline sat up and nodded. "I'll write Mama right away," she said.

"Take the kid out for a walk, will you?" Eddie said, as Arline started repairing her face before the mirror. "I want to take a little nap."

"Sure," Arline said, "sure, Eddie."

Eddie took off his shoes and lay down on the bed to start storing up his energy.

THE DEPUTY SHERIFF

MACOMBER SAT in the sheriff's swivel chair, his feet in the waste-basket because he was too fat to lift them to the desk. He sat there looking across at the poster on the opposite wall that said, "Wanted, for Murder, Walter Cooper, Reward Four Hundred Dollars." He sometimes sat for seven days on end looking at the spot that said "Four Hundred Dollars," going out only for meals and ten hours' sleep a night.

Macomber was the third deputy sheriff and he took care of the office because he didn't like to go home to his wife. In the afternoon the second deputy sheriff came in, too, and sat tilted against the wall, also looking at the spot that said, "Four Hundred Dollars."

"I read in the newspapers," Macomber said, feeling the sweat roll deliberately down his neck into his shirt, "that New Mexico has the healthiest climate in the world. Look at me sweat. Do you call that healthy?"

"You're too goddamn fat," the second deputy sheriff said, never taking his eyes off the "Four Hundred Dollars." "What do you expect?"

"You could fry eggs," Macomber said, looking for an instant at the street blazing outside his window. "I need a vacation. You need a vacation. Everybody needs a vacation." He shifted his gun wearily, where it dug into the fat. "Why can't Walter Cooper walk in here this minute? Why can't he?" he asked.

The telephone rang. Macomber picked it up. He listened, said, "Yes, no, the sheriff's taking a nap. I'll tell him, good-bye."

He put the telephone down slowly, thought in his eyes. "That was Los Angeles," he said. "They caught Brisbane. They got him in the jail there."

"He'll get fifteen years," the second deputy said. "His accomplice got fifteen years. They can sing to each other."

"That's my case," Macomber said, slowly, putting on his hat. "I was the first one to look at the boxcar after they bust into it." He turned at the door. "Somebody's got to go bring Brisbane back from Los Angeles. I'm the man, wouldn't you say?"

"You're the man," the second deputy said. "That's a nice trip. Hollywood. There is nothing wrong with the girls in Hollywood." He nodded his head dreamily. "I wouldn't mind shaking a hip in that city."

Macomber walked slowly toward the sheriff's house, smiling a little to himself, despite the heat, as he thought of Hollywood. He walked briskly, his two hundred and forty pounds purposeful and alert.

"Oh, for Christ's sake," the sheriff said when he told him about Brisbane, "what the hell turns up in Los Angeles." The sheriff was sleepy and annoyed, sitting on the edge of the sofa on which he'd been lying without shoes, his pants open for the first three buttons, after lunch. "We got a conviction out of that, already."

"Brisbane is a known criminal," Macomber said. "He committed entry."

"So he committed entry," the sheriff said. "Into a boxcar. He took two overcoats and a pair of socks and I have to send a man to Los Angeles for him! If you asked them for a murderer you'd never get him out of Los Angeles in twenty years! Why did you have to wake me up?" he asked Macomber testily.

"Los Angeles asked me to have you call back as soon as possible," Macomber said smoothly. "They want to know what to do with him. They want to get rid of him. He cries all day, they told me, at the top of his voice. He's got a whole cell-block yelling their heads off in Los Angeles, they told me."

"I need a man like that here," the sheriff said. "I need him very bad."

But he put his shoes on and buttoned his pants and started back to the office with Macomber.

"Do you mind going to Los Angeles?" the sheriff asked Macomber.

Macomber shrugged. "Somebody's got to do it."

"Good old Macomber," the sheriff said sarcastically. "The backbone of the force. Ever loyal."

"I know the case," Macomber said. "Inside out."

The sheriff looked at him over his shoulder. "There are so many girls there, I read, that even a fat man ought to be able to do business. Taking your wife, Macomber?" He jabbed with his thumb into the fat over the ribs, and laughed.

"Somebody's got to go. I admit," Macomber said earnestly, "it would be nice to see Hollywood. I've read about it."

When they got into the office the second deputy got up out of the swivel chair, and the sheriff dropped into it, unbuttoning the top three buttons of his pants. The sheriff opened a drawer and took out a ledger, panting from the heat. "Why is it," the sheriff wanted to know, "that anybody lives in a place like this?" He looked with annoyance at the opened ledger. "We have not got a penny," the sheriff said, "not a stinking penny. That trip to Needles after Bucher cleaned out the fund. We don't get another appropriation for two months. This is a beautiful county. Catch one crook and you got to go out of business for the season. So what are you looking at me like that for, Macomber?"

"It wouldn't cost more than ninety dollars to send a man to Los Angeles." Macomber sat down gently on a small chair.

"You got ninety dollars?" the sheriff asked.

"This got nothing to do with me," Macomber said. "Only it's a known criminal."

"Maybe," the second deputy said, "you could get Los Angeles to hold onto him for two months."

"I got brain workers in this office," the sheriff said. "Regular brain workers." But he turned to the phone and said, "Get me the police headquarters at Los Angeles."

"Swanson is the name of the man who is handling the matter," Macomber said. "He's waiting for your call."

"Ask them to catch a murderer in Los Angeles," the sheriff said bitterly, "and see what you get . . . They're wonderful on people who break into boxcars."

While the sheriff was waiting for the call to be put through, Macomber turned ponderously, the seat of his pants sticking to the yellow varnish of the chair, and looked out at the deserted street, white with sunlight, the tar boiling up in little black bubbles out in the road from the heat. For a moment, deep under the fat, he couldn't bear Gatlin, New Mexico. A suburb of the desert, a fine place for people with tuberculosis. For twelve years he'd been there, going to the movies twice a week, listening to his wife talk. The fat man. Before you died in Gatlin, New Mexico, you got fat. Twelve years, he thought, looking out on a street that was empty except on Saturday night. He could see himself stepping out of a barber shop in Hollywood, walking lightly to a bar with a blonde girl, thin in the waist, drinking a beer or two, talking and laughing in the middle of a million other people talking and laughing. Greta Garbo walked the streets there, and Carole Lombard, and Alice Faye. "Sarah," he would say to his wife, "I have got to go to Los Angeles. On State business. I will not be back for a week."

"Well . . . ?" the sheriff was calling into the phone. "*Well?* Where is Los Angeles?"

Ninety dollars, ninety lousy dollars . . . He turned away from looking at the street. He put his hands on his knees and was surprised to see them shake as he heard the sheriff say, "Hello, is this Swanson?"

He couldn't sit still and listen to the sheriff talk over the phone, so he got up and walked slowly through the back room to the lavatory. He went in, closed the door, and looked carefully at his face in the mirror. That's what his face looked like, that's what the twelve years, listening to his wife talk, had done. Without expression he went back to the office.

"All right," the sheriff was saying, "you don't have to keep him for two months. I know you're crowded. I know it's against the constitution. I know, I said, for Christ's sake. It was just a suggestion. I'm sorry he's crying. Is it my fault he's crying? Maybe you'd cry, too, if you were going to jail for fifteen years. Stop yelling, for Christ's sake, this call is costing the county of Gatlin a million dollars. I'll call you back. All right, by six o'clock. All right, I said. All right."

The sheriff put the telephone down. For a moment he sat wearily, looking at the open top of his pants. He sighed, buttoned his pants. "That is some city," he said, "Los Angeles." He shook his head. "I got a good mind to say the hell with it. Why should I run myself into an early grave for a man who broke into a boxcar? Who can tell me?"

"He's a known criminal," Macomber said. "We got a whole case." His voice was smooth but he felt the eager tremor deep under it. "Justice is justice."

The sheriff looked at him bitterly. "The voice of conscience. The sheriff's white light, Macomber."

Macomber shrugged. "What's it to me? I just like to see a case closed."

The sheriff turned back to the telephone. "Get me the county treasurer's office," he said. He sat there, waiting, looking at Macomber, with the receiver against his ear. Macomber walked over to the door and looked out across the street. He saw his wife sitting at the window of their house up the street, her fat elbows crossed, with the sweat dripping off them. He looked the other way.

He heard the sheriff's voice, as though distant and indistinct, talking to the county treasurer. He heard the county treasurer's voice rise in anger through the phone, mechanical and shrill. "Everybody spends money," the county treasurer screamed. "Nobody brings in money, but everybody spends money. I'll be lucky to have my own salary left over at the end of the month and you want ninety dollars to go joy-riding to Los Angeles to get a man who stole nine dollars' worth of second-hand goods. The hell with you! I said the hell with you!"

Macomber put his hands in his pockets so that nobody could see how tense they were as he heard the receiver slam on the other end of the wire. Coldly he watched the sheriff put the phone gently down.

"Macomber," the sheriff said, feeling his deputy's eyes on him, hard and accusing, "I'm afraid Joan Crawford will have to get along without you, this year."

"They will hang crepe on the studios when they hear about this," the second deputy said.

"I don't care for myself," Macomber said evenly, "but it will sound awfully funny to people if they find out that the sheriff's office let a known criminal go free after he was caught."

The sheriff stood up abruptly. "What do you want me to do?" he asked with violence. "Tell me what the hell more you want me to do? Can I create the ninety dollars? Talk to the State of New Mexico!"

Macomber shrugged. "It's not my business," he said. "Only I think we can't let criminals laugh at New Mexican justice."

"All right," the sheriff shouted. "Do something. Go do something! I don't have to call back until six o'clock! You got three hours to see justice done. My hands are washed." He sat down and opened the top three buttons of his pants and put his feet on the desk. "If it means so much to you," he said, as Macomber started through the door, "arrange it yourself."

Macomber passed his house on the way to the district attorney's office. His wife was still sitting at the window with the sweat dripping off her. She looked at her husband out of her dry eyes, and he looked at her as he walked thoughtfully past. No smile lit her face or his, no word was passed. For a moment they looked at each other with the arid recognition of twelve years. Then Macomber walked deliberately on, feeling the heat rising through his shoes, tiring his legs right up to his hips.

In Hollywood he would walk firmly and briskly, not like a fat man, over the clean pavements, ringing to the sharp attractive clicks of high heels all around him. For ten steps he closed his eyes as he turned into the main street of Gatlin, New Mexico.

He went into the huge Greek building that the WPA had built for the County of Gatlin. As he passed down the quiet halls, rich with marble, cool, even in the mid-afternoon, he said, looking harshly around him, "Ninety dollars—ninety lousy dollars."

In front of the door that said "Office of the District Attorney" he stopped. He stood there for a moment, feeling nervousness rise and fall in him like a wave. His hand sweated on the doorknob when he opened the door. He went in casually, carefully appearing like a man carrying out impersonal government business.

The door to the private office was open a little and he could see the district attorney's wife standing there and could hear the district attorney yelling, "For God's sake, Carol, have a heart! Do I look like a man who is made of money? Answer me, do I?"

"All I want," the district attorney's wife said stubbornly, "is a little vacation. Three weeks, that's all. I can't stand the heat here. I'll lie down and die if I have to stay here another week. Do you want me to lie down and die? You make me live in this oasis, do I have to die here, too?" She started to cry, shaking her careful blonde hair.

"All right," the district attorney said. "All right, Carol. Go ahead. Go home and pack. Stop crying. For the love of God, stop crying!"

She went over and kissed the district attorney and came out, past Macomber, drying the tip of her nose. The district attorney took her through the office and opened the door for her. She kissed him again and went down the hall. The district attorney closed the door and leaned against it wearily. "She's got to go to Wisconsin," he said to Macomber. "She knows people in Wisconsin. There are lakes there. What do you want?"

Macomber explained about Brisbane and Los Angeles and the sheriff's fund and what the county treasurer had said. The district attorney sat down on the bench against the wall and listened with his head down.

"What do you want me to do?" he asked when Macomber finished.

"That Brisbane is a man who should be behind bars for fifteen years. There wouldn't be any doubt about it, once we got him here. He's a known criminal. After all, it would only cost ninety dollars . . . If you said something, if you made a protest . . ."

The district attorney sat on the bench with his head down, his hands loose between his knees. "Everybody wants to spend money to go some place that isn't Gatlin, New Mexico. You know how much it's going to cost to send my wife to Wisconsin for three weeks? Three hundred dollars. Oh, my God!"

"This is another matter," Macomber said very softly and reasonably. "This is a matter of your record. A sure conviction."

"There's nothing wrong with my record." The district attorney stood up. "My record's fine. I got a conviction on that case already. What do you want me to do—spend my life getting convictions on a nine-dollar robbery?"

"If you only said one word to the county treasurer . . ." Macomber tagged after the district attorney as he started for his inner office.

"If the county treasurer wants to save money, I say, 'That's the sort of man we need.' Somebody has to save money. Somebody has got to do something else besides supporting the railroads."

"It's a bad precedent, a guilty man . . ." Macomber said a little louder than he wanted.

"Leave me alone," the district attorney said. "I'm tired." He went into the inner office and closed the door firmly.

Macomber said, "Son of a bitch, you bastard!" softly to the imitation oak door, and went out into the marble hall. He bent over and drank from the shining porcelain fountain that the WPA had put there. His mouth felt dry and sandy, with an old taste in it.

Outside he walked down the burning sidewalk, his feet dragging. His belly stretched against the top of his trousers uncomfortably, and he belched, remembering his wife's cooking. In Hollywood he would sit down in a restaurant where the stars ate, no matter what it cost, and have light French dishes, served with silver covers, and wine out of iced bottles. Ninety lousy dollars. He walked in the shade of store-awnings, sweating, wrenching his mind to thought. "Goddamn it, god-damn it!" he said to himself because he could think of nothing further to do. For the rest of his life, in Gatlin, New Mexico, with never another chance to get even a short breath of joy . . . The back of his eyes ached from thinking. Suddenly he strode out from under the awning, walked up the steps that led to the office of the Gatlin *Herald*.

The city editor was sitting at a big desk covered with dust and tangled copy. He was wearily blue-penciling a long white sheet. He listened abstractedly as Macomber talked, using his pencil from time to time.

"You could show the voters of Gatlin," Macomber was leaning close over the desk, talking fast, "what sort of men they got serving them. You could show the property owners of this county what sort of protection they can expect to get from the sheriff, the district attorney, and the county treasurer they put into office. That would make interesting reading-matter, that would, letting men who committed crimes in this county go off thumbing their noses at law enforcement here. If I was you I would write one hell of an editorial, I would. For ninety lousy dollars. One expression of opinion like that in the paper and the sheriff's office would have a man in Los Angeles tomorrow. Are you listening to me?"

"Yeah," the city editor said, judiciously running his pencil in straight blue lines three times across the page. "Why don't you go back to being the third deputy sheriff, Macomber?"

"You're a party paper," Macomber said bitterly, "that's what's the matter with you. You're Democrats and you wouldn't say anything if a Democratic politician walked off with Main Street in a truck. You're a very corrupt organization."

"Yes," the city editor said. "You hit the nail on the head." He used the pencil again.

"Aaah!" Macomber said, turning away. "For Christ's sake."

"The trouble with you," the city editor said, "is you don't get enough nourishment. You need nourishment." He poised the pencil thoughtfully over a sentence as Macomber went out, slamming the door.

Macomber walked dully down the street, regardless of the heat beating solidly against him.

He passed his house on the way back to the office. His wife was still sitting there, looking out at the street that was always empty except on Saturday night. Macomber regarded her with his aching eyes, from the other side of the street. "Is that all you have to do," he called, "sit there?"

She didn't say anything, but looked at him for a moment, then calmly glanced up the street.

Macomber entered the sheriff's office and sat down heavily. The sheriff was still there, his feet on the desk.

"Well?" the sheriff said.

"The hell with it." Macomber dried the sweat off his face with a colored handkerchief. "It's no skin off my back." He loosened the laces of his shoes and sat back as the sheriff got Los Angeles on the phone. "Swanson?" the sheriff said into the phone. "This is Sheriff Hadley of Gatlin, New Mexico. You can go tell Brisbane he can stop crying. Turn him loose. We're not coming for him. We can't be bothered. Thanks." He hung up, sighed as a man sighs at the end of a day's work. "I'm going home to dinner," he said, and went out.

"I'll stay here while you go home to eat," the second deputy said to Macomber.

"Never mind," Macomber said. "I'm not hungry."

"O.K.," the second deputy stood up and went to the door. "So long, Barrymore." He departed, whistling.

Macomber hobbled over to the sheriff's swivel chair in his open shoes. He leaned back in the chair, looked up at the poster, "Wanted for Murder . . . Four Hundred Dollars" lit now by the lengthening rays of the sun. He put his feet into the waste-basket, "Goddamn Walter Cooper," he said.

SECOND MORTGAGE

THE BELL RANG and I went to the window to see who it was.

"Don't answer it," my father called. "It may be a summons."

"They can't serve summonses on Sunday," I said, parting the curtains cautiously.

"Don't answer it, anyway." My father came into the living room. He didn't know how to handle bill-collectors. They bullied him and he made wild promises, very seriously, to pay, and never did and they'd come and hound him terribly. When he was home alone he never answered the doorbell. He never even went to see who it was. He just sat in the kitchen reading the paper while the bell clanged over his head. Even the postman couldn't get the front door opened when my father was home alone.

The bell rang again. "What the hell," I said, "it's only a little old lady. She's probably selling something. We can open the door."

"What for?" my father asked. "We can't buy anything."

I opened the door anyway. The little old lady jumped when the door swung back. Her hands fluttered. They were plump little hands, swollen, without gloves. "I'm Mrs. Shapiro," she said, waiting.

I waited. She tried a smile. I waited sternly. Strangers are never friends at the doors of the poor. I was only seventeen but I had learned that anyone who rang our doorbell might turn out to be the Edison Electric Company or the Brooklyn Borough Gas Company, intent on shutting off the electricity or the gas.

Mrs. Shapiro hunched inside her shapeless little coat. "I own the second mortgage," she said.

Still I waited, sternly. Another enemy.

Her hand came out, cold, plump, and pleading. "I want to speak to your father, maybe," she said.

My father had retreated to the kitchen and the Sunday *Times*, hoping that nothing would happen at the front door that would require his tearing himself out of that peaceful welter of journalism.

"Pop!" I called. I heard him sigh and the rustle of the Sunday *Times* as he put down the editorial page. Mrs. Shapiro came in and I closed the door. My father came in, wiping his glasses, longing for the kitchen.

"This is Mrs. Shapiro, Pop," I said. "She owns the second mortgage . . ."

"Yes," Mrs. Shapiro was eager and bright and apologetic for a moment. She moved into the middle of the room. There were runs in her fat little stockings and her shoes were shapeless. "I came because . . ."

"Yes," my father said, with his imitation of a businesslike attitude, that he always tried on bill-collectors and which he lost as soon as they started to bully him. "Yes. Of course. Just wait a moment . . . My wife . . . my wife knows more about this than . . . Oh . . . Helen! Helen!"

My mother came down from upstairs, fixing her hair.

"Mrs. Shapiro," my father said. "The second mortgage . . ."

"It's this way," Mrs. Shapiro said, moving toward my mother. "In 1929, I . . ."

"Won't you sit down?" My mother pointed to a chair. She glanced at my father, tightening her mouth. My mother was always contemptuous of my father at those times when my father proved unequal to the task of beating off the representatives of our poverty.

Mrs. Shapiro sat on the very edge of the chair, leaning forward, her knees together. "The second mortgage is eight hundred dollars," Mrs. Shapiro said. We all sat silent. Mrs. Shapiro was disheartened by the silence, but she went on, her fat gray cheeks moving anxiously over her words. "Eight hundred dollars is a lot of money," she said.

We didn't contradict her.

"In 1929," Mrs. Shapiro said, "I had eight thousand dollars." She looked to our faces for pity, envy, anything. We sat there expressionless, with the faces of people who have become used to owing money. "Eight thousand dollars. I worked all my life for it. I had a vegetable store. It's hard to make money in vegetables nowadays. Vegetables are expensive and they spoil and there is always somebody else who sells them cheaper than you can . . ."

"Yes," my mother said, "vegetables are very expensive. I paid twenty cents for a head of cauliflower yesterday . . ."

"It wasn't any good, either," my father said. "I don't like cauliflower. It reminds me of cabbage, somehow."

"When Mr. Shapiro died of cancer, it took him two years to die," Mrs. Shapiro went on, trying to please us. "I had eight thousand dollars. I had rheumatism and high-blood pressure and I couldn't take care of the store any more." Once more she begged our faces for that crumb of pity. "I took the eight thousand dollars out of the bank and I went to Mr. Mayer and I said, 'Mr. Mayer, you're a big man, you have a fine reputation, I am giving you a widow's life's savings, invest it for me so that I have enough to live on. I don't need much, Mr. Mayer,' I told him, 'just a few dollars a week until I die, that's all,' I said, 'just a few dollars.'"

"I know Mayer," my father said. "He's not doing so well now. The Trust Company's in receivership now."

"Mr. Mayer," Mrs. Shapiro said with passion, her fists quivering on her little thighs, "is a crook! He took my money and he put it out in second mortgages. Eight thousand dollars' worth of second mortgages!"

She stopped. For the moment she could not say another word.

"Today," my father said, "even first mortgages are no good. Nothing's any good any more."

"In the last two years," Mrs. Shapiro said, her eyes filling with tears, "I haven't got a penny out of them . . . out of eight thousand dollars' worth of second mortgages, not a penny . . ." A little rag of a handkerchief came out and wiped at her eyes. "I used to go to Mr. Mayer and he'd tell me I'd have to wait. How long can I wait? I don't have with what to eat now, as it is! Can I wait longer than that?" Triumphantly she wept. "Now Mr. Mayer won't see me any more. They tell me he's out when I go there. It doesn't do any good to go there." She stopped, wiping her eyes. We sat, uncomfortable and still.

"I'm going to the houses where I have the second mortgages," Mrs. Shapiro said. "Nice houses, they are . . . like this. With rugs and curtains and steam heat and something cooking on the stove that you can smell inside. I have the second mortgage on houses like that, and I don't have enough to eat . . ." Her tears soaked through the rag of a handkerchief. "Please," she cried, "please . . . give me something. I don't want the eight hundred dollars, but something. It's my money . . . I have nobody. I have rheumatism and there's no heat in my room and there're holes in my shoes. I walk on my bare feet . . . Please . . . please . . ."

We tried to stop her but she kept on, crying, "Please . . . please . . . just a little bit. A hundred dollars. Fifty. My money . . ."

"All right, Mrs. Shapiro," my father said. "Come back next Sunday. I'll have it for you then . . ."

The tears stopped. "Oh, God bless you," Mrs. Shapiro said. Before we knew what she was about she flung herself across the room and was on her hands and knees in front of my father and was kissing his hand wildly. "God bless you, God bless you," she cried over and over again. My father sat through it nervously, trying to pick her up with his free hand, looking pleadingly at my mother.

Finally my mother could bear it no longer. "Mrs. Shapiro," she said, breaking in over the "God bless you's", "listen to me! Stop that! Please stop it! We can't give you anything! Next Sunday or any Sunday! We haven't got a cent."

Mrs. Shapiro dropped my father's hand. She stayed on her knees in front of him, though, looking strange there in the middle of our living room. "But Mr. Ross said . . ."

"Mr. Ross is talking nonsense!" my mother said. "We have no money and we're not going to have any! We expect to be thrown out of this house any day now! We can't give you a penny, Mrs. Shapiro."

"But next Sunday . . ." Mrs. Shapiro tried to make my mother understand that she didn't expect it now, not for another week . . .

"We won't have any more next Sunday than we have today. And we have eighty-five cents in the house right now, Mrs. Shapiro!" My mother stood up, went over to Mrs. Shapiro, where she was kneeling on the floor. Before my mother could touch her, Mrs. Shapiro keeled over onto the floor, hitting it heavily, like a packed handbag that's been dropped.

It took us ten minutes to pull her out of her faint. My mother gave her tea, which she drank silently. She didn't seem to recognize us as she drank her tea and made ready to go off. She told us that this was the fifth time in two months that she had fainted like that. She seemed ashamed of herself, somehow. My mother gave her the address of a doctor who would wait for his money and Mrs. Shapiro went out, her fat, shabby stockings shaking as she went down the steps. My mother and I watched her as she shambled down the street and disappeared around the corner, but my father went into the kitchen and the New York *Times.*

She was back the next Sunday and two Sundays after that, ringing the bell, but we didn't open the door. She rang for almost a half-hour each time, but we all sat quietly in the kitchen, waiting for her to go away.

"MARCH, MARCH ON
DOWN THE FIELD"

"For one dollar," Peppe said, "you could buy enough coal to keep this lousy locker room warm all week." He laced up his shoulder pads with numb fingers. "For one stinking dollar. We'll be stiff like concrete by the time we got to kick off. Somebody ought to tell that Scheepers something. For one dollar that Scheepers would freeze his grandmother. In sections. Yeah." He ducked his head into his jersey.

"We ought to get together," Ullman said. "We all ought to stick together and go to Scheepers and say, 'Scheepers,' we ought to say, 'you pay us to play football for you, *but—*'"

"Ullman," Peppe called from inside his jersey, "the City College Boy, Mr. Stalin's right-hand man. Fullbacks of the world, unite."

"Hey, shake your tails," Holstein said. "We want to go out and loosen up before the game starts."

"Loosen up!" Peppe finally got his head through the jersey. "They will have to broil me. On both sides. My God, I wish I was in the south of France. Along the Riviera. With the French girls."

"Put your pants on," Holstein said.

"Look!" Peppe pointed sadly to his naked legs. "I am turning blue. A dark shade of blue. From the ankle up. It's past my knees already. Look, boys. Another foot and that is the end of Peppe."

Klonsky, the right tackle, a tall, thick man, pushed Peppe to one side. "Excuse me," he said. "I want to look in the mirror."

"If I had a face like that—" Peppe began. Klonsky turned and looked at him.

"What did I say?" Peppe asked. "Did I say anything?"

Klonsky looked at himself in the mirror again, pulling down his lower lip. "It's my teeth," he explained without turning from the mirror. "I got three new teeth from the dentist this week."

"They'll sign you for the movies," Holstein said.

"Fifty bucks," Klonsky said. "The lousy dentist charged me fifty bucks. In advance. He wouldn't put the teeth in until I put the money down. My wife, she insisted I got to have teeth in the front of my face. She said it was bad, a college graduate with teeth missing."

"Sure," Holstein said. "Listen to women in a case like that. They know what they're talking about."

"I lost them two years ago in the Manhattan game." Klonsky shook his head and turned from the mirror. "They are very rough—Manhattan. All they were interested in was hitting me in the teeth—they didn't give a damn who won the game."

"Watch out for Krakow," Peppe said. "He runs like a locomotive, that guy. You could chop off his leg, he would still run. He's got no sense. He played for Upsala for three years and he had to make every tackle in every game. It upset his brains. He plays like he don't get paid for it. He will break your back for three yards. Oh, my God, it's cold! That bastard Scheepers!"

The door opened and Scheepers came in, the collar of his pale camel's-hair coat up around his ears. "I heard somebody call me bastard," he said. "I don't like that, boys." He looked at them, his face set under the brim of his soft green hat.

"It's cold in here," Holstein said.

"There's ice in the East River," Ullman said.

"I am responsible," Scheepers said ironically, "I am responsible for the weather all of a sudden?"

"One dollar's worth of coal." Peppe blew on his hands. "That's all you need to keep this locker room warm. One lousy dollar's worth."

"Watch your language," Scheepers said. He turned to the rest of the team. "I ordered coal. I swear to God." He put his collar down and took off his pigskin gloves. "Anyway, it's not so cold. I don't know what you boys are complaining about."

"Some day," Peppe said, "you should get dressed here, Scheepers. That's all I ask. They would use you to freeze ice cubes."

"Lissen, boys!" Scheepers stood up on a bench and addressed the whole room. "I got a matter to discuss, a slight matter of money."

The locker room was silent.

"Call the pickpocket squad," Peppe said after a moment. "Scheepers is discussing money."

"I know you boys are joking." Scheepers smiled. "So I don't get sore."

"Get sore, Scheepers," Peppe said. "Get good and sore."

Scheepers hesitated and then spoke in a confidential voice. "Boys," he said, "it is not a warm day. This is not a pleasant Sunday afternoon, to be perfectly frank with you."

"Secrets," Holstein said. "Keep it to yourself, boys."

"It's cold. It's near the end of the season. It snowed this morning. The Dodgers are playing Pittsburgh at Ebbets Field. You fellers ain't put on such a good show for the last two weeks. In a word, there is not a large crowd today." He looked around him significantly. "I have made a deal with Krakow's All-Stars. I have reduced their guarantee fifty per cent because there is hardly anybody in the stands."

"That's nice," Holstein said. "That's a nice piece of business. You ought to be proud of yourself."

"What I am driving at—" Scheepers said.

"Don't tell us," Peppe said. "Let us guess. Ullman, you guess first."

"What I am driving at," Scheepers continued, "is that I expect you boys to take a small fifty-per-cent reduction for yourself."

"You know what you can do," Holstein said. "With my compliments."

"Scheepers!" Peppe said. "The Season's Leading Louse."

"It ain't hardly worth the risk," Klonsky said, feeling his teeth. "I borrowed that fifty bucks to pay the dentist. I gave a lien on my radio. If they take that radio, my wife is going to raise hell. Go ask somebody else, Scheepers."

"I am being fair," Scheepers said. "Absolutely fair. It is an impartial proposition. Everybody takes a small fifty-per—"

" 'The butcher, the baker, the candlestick-maker,' " sang Peppe, " 'were all in love with Marie.' "

"I am talking serious," Scheepers said. "And I want a serious answer."

"He wants a serious answer," Peppe said.

"I am trying to conduct business!" Scheepers screamed. "I got bills to pay, dammit!"

"Nuts," Peppe said mildly. "Nuts, Mr. Scheepers. That serious enough?"

"I am hereby telling you that I will go outside and pay back every admission ticket unless you boys do business," Scheepers said. "The game will be off. I got to protect myself."

The men looked at each other. Holstein scraped his cleats on the plank floor.

"I was thinking of buying a pair of shoes tomorrow," Ullman said. "I'm walking around in my bare feet."

"It's up to you, boys." Scheepers put his gloves on again.

"I got a date tonight," Peppe said bitterly. "A very fine girl. A girl from Greenwich Village. It will cost me six bucks sure. Scheepers, you're taking advantage."

"Profit and loss," Scheepers insisted. "I am merely trying to balance the books. Take it or leave it, boys."

"O.K.," Holstein said.

"It is strictly not a personal thing," Scheepers said. "I am in the red all season."

"Kindly leave the room, Scheepers," Peppe said, "while we feel sorry for you. The tears are blinding us."

"Wise guys," Scheepers said, sneering. "A collection of very wise guys. Remember, next season there will be games played too." He glanced at Peppe. "Football players are a drug on the market, remember. Every year five thousand boys come out of college who can block and tackle. I don't have to take insults from nobody."

"You stink," Peppe said. "That is my honest opinion. Oh, my God, it's cold!" He went to the first-aid kit and poured liniment over his hands to warm them.

"I got one or two more things to say." Scheepers spoke loudly to hold their attention. "I want you boys to open up today. A little zip. Some fancy stuff. Passes."

"Nobody can hold onto passes today," Holstein said. "It's cold. Your hands get stiff. Also, there's snow all over the field. The ball'll be sliding as though it had butter on it."

"What do you care?" Scheepers said. "They like passes—give them passes. And please, boys, play like you meant it. After all, we're in business, you know."

"On a day like this I got to play games." Peppe shivered. "I could be in Greenwich Village now, drinking beer in my girl's house. I hope Krakow falls and breaks his neck."

"I got a premonition," Klonsky said. "Something is definitely going to happen to my teeth."

"Also," Scheepers said, "there has been some slipup in the helmets. The amateur team that was supposed to play here this morning and leave the helmets didn't play on account of the snow, so you will have to play without helmets."

"Good old Scheepers," Holstein said. "He thinks of everything."

"It was an error," Scheepers said. "An unavoidable error. Lots of guys play without helmets."

"Lots of guys jump off bridges, too," Holstein said.

"What the hell good is a helmet anyway?" Scheepers demanded. "Every time you need it, it falls off."

"Any other little thing on your mind?" Holstein asked. "You're sure you didn't want us to play with only eight men because it's a small crowd?"

The men laughed, and then, one by one, they filed out onto the field, swinging their arms to keep warm in the freezing wind that swept down on them from the north. Scheepers watched them a moment and then he went into the field house and switched on the public-address system. " 'March, march on down the field,'" sang the public-address system as Scheepers' Red Devils lined up to receive the kick, without helmets.

WALK ALONG THE CHARLES RIVER

"Shelley," Hortense said. "Percy Bysshe Shelley. 1792 to 1822. What're the dates?"

"1792 to 1822," Roger said, across the breakfast table. "Romantic poet. Wordsworth, Coleridge, Keats, Byron, Shelley, romantic movement."

"That's right," Hortense said. But she saw his eyelids start down into that half-droop that was like sleep these days for him. "Roger!" she called sharply. "Roger!"

"I'm awake," he said, throwing back his head with the full white hair and the ruddy professor's skin with the latecome wrinkles. "Perfectly awake this morning. The subject is Shelley, poet and dramatist. Perfectly awake, my dear."

"Have some more coffee."

"I hate coffee."

Hortense poured another cup. She had bought cups as large as porridge bowls for morning coffee. He picked up one of his old lecture notebooks and read slowly, rubbing his eyes, then handed it back to Hortense.

"Drink the coffee," Hortense said.

Roger lifted the cup in his soft old-man's hands and drank in the neat, delicate, indoor way that was peculiarly his and still remained with him, even now.

"He was a son of a very good and rich family . . ." Hortense began.

"A paradox. Still, maybe in 1792 good and rich could go together." Roger chuckled. "See," he said, "I'm all right. I'm making professors' jokes. Right on my toes."

Hortense smiled and touched her husband's hand. "That's fine. He was expelled from Cambridge when he wrote *The Necessity of Atheism* and his father refused to talk to him . . ."

"I remember perfectly," Roger said. "Sophomore English. Survey of English literature. I've given that course thirty years, I ought to remember that, don't you think?"

"Yes, dear," said Hortense.

"Everything is clear this morning," Roger said. "Clear as glass. Maybe I'm getting better. What do you think?"

"That's very possible," said Hortense. "Now, darling, Shelley . . ."

"You don't have to bother this morning. Nothing to worry about this morning. I'll hold the class in the palm of my hand. The glories of poetry, gentlemen, music of the centuries. Rhetoric for the young from the old professor . . ." With a sudden sigh he closed his eyes and fell asleep.

Hortense shook her head, played nervously with the bun of straight gray hair at the back of her neck. She went over and shook her husband gently. "All right, now, Roger, you can't go to sleep now. Come on, now. You've got a fifty-minute class at nine o'clock." She shook him more violently. His head lolled on his chest. "Roger!" she shouted. "Roger, you must get up!"

"Let me sleep," he muttered, without opening his eyes. "Please let me sleep. Just five minutes. That's all I ask, five minutes."

"You must open your eyes this minute!" Hortense shouted. "You must keep awake until two this afternoon! Roger, darling, please, please . . ."

"I'm a tired old man," Roger said softly, his eyes still closed. "Go away."

Hortense took his head between her hands and shook hard. Finally he opened his eyes. "Why don't you leave me alone?" he shouted, six inches from her face. "Why don't you get out of here? I can't teach any more! I want to die! Get out of here!"

She pushed the coffee cup to his lips. "Come on," she said. "Drink."

He drank automatically.

"I hate you," he said between gulps. "You're making the last years of my life plain hell. Hell. Let them throw me out! Let them! I don't care any more . . ."

"Remember the influences that are most apparent in Shelley's poetry," Hortense said. "Remember Godwin and Plato."

"All I want is sleep. The hell with the pension, the hell with . . ."

"What are the two leading influences on Shelley's poetry, Roger?"

"Godwin and Plato," said Roger with a weary wave of his hand. "I know. I'm all right. Excuse me. Did I say I hate you?"

"Never mind," said Hortense.

"I don't hate you," Roger said, his voice flat and old. "I love you very much."

"I know. That's all right."

"I have dreams sometimes when I close my eyes," Roger said. "I don't know whether I'm asleep or awake but I have dreams. I walk along the Charles River, looking across toward Harvard, and you're walking with me again. That's when I close my eyes."

"Don't talk about it, darling."

"It won't do any harm. I feel fine again." Roger sipped his coffee. "We should never've left the East. We've been in exile in this town. I never liked it. I would have liked to live my whole life in Boston. What're we doing here?"

"When you get your pension we'll move back to Boston," Hortense said. "We'll walk along the Charles River in the summertime. Now, darling, let's not neglect Mr. Shelley . . ."

"I'd rather talk," said Roger. "That'll keep me up and I really remember all that stuff anyway. It's only that a mist sometimes comes down and I get tired. I feel like talking so seldom, you oughtn't to complain."

"I'm not complaining," Hortense said.

"Little Hortense Sloan." Roger laughed a little. "I had to do practically everything but wash your face for you when we were first married."

"You took good care of me," Hortense said. "All the time."

"And now . . ." Roger rubbed his eyes. "You've turned into a general, lecturer, housekeeper, banker, all in one."

"It wasn't a bad thing," Hortense said softly, "to find out I could do something like that before I died."

"It's too hard for you. Too much of a strain. You look more tired than I do."

"Sssh, Roger."

"Why don't you just go up to the Board and apply for the pension? Right now."

"Sssh, Roger." She had thought of it, but the Board of this small, impoverished school had never given a premature pension yet. And Roger was not popular; they had never liked him.

"After all," Roger said, "there's only two and a half more months to the term and I'll be sixty-five in September, that's the age, that's before another term starts . . ."

"I think we'd better just try to stick in out while we can," Hortense said. "The doctor says you can do it."

"The doctor! A fool! He doesn't know what the hell is happening to me."

The doctor knew and had told Hortense exactly what was happening to her husband, but she nodded, "He's confused, dear," she said. "Now don't get excited."

Roger slapped himself, a common gesture with him now. He drank some more coffee. "If they liked me better here," he said, "if I was . . . well . . . a success . . . we could go and talk to the Board."

"You're a success," Hortense said. "You've made a great success here."

Roger laughed slightly. "You're just a little bit wrong, darling." He leaned back reflectively in his chair. "I talked too much. I always was speaking my little piece. How many schools have I taught in, darling?"

"Fourteen."

"I have enemies in fourteen schools. My monument." He laughed again. "I never could keep my mouth shut. That's been a little hard on you, hasn't it?"

"I didn't mind," Hortense said. "Not one bit."

"Excuse me. I should've shut up for your sake."

"No," Hortense said. "That's the way you were and that's the way I liked you. You going to know all about Shelley?"

"Every breath of his life will be carefully examined." He chuckled. "1792 to 1822. See? If Winter comes can Spring be . . . I weep for Adonais, he is dead . . . My name is Ozymandias, King of Kings, look on my works, ye mighty, and despair . . . See? That doctor's a fool. My brain's as clear as a bell most of the time, there's no reason he can't just keep it that way, no reason . . ."

"We'll talk to him."

"I should've shut up." Roger leaned over the table, his head in his hands. "When I was young I made believe I was going to be Professor of English at Harvard, head of the department. I was going to have twenty brilliant works of research behind me. I talked too much."

"Please, Roger . . ." Hortense tried to hush him.

"This little jerkwater school. I have to be sixty-five." And he fell asleep again.

Hortense shook him and he woke up weeping, shaking his head.

"Stop crying like a little baby!" Hortense snapped at him, though she was crying, too, inside, without tears. "You've got a class to teach." She couldn't be gentle with him, because he would take advantage of her and not go to the lecture room. "Get up now! Get up!"

"Why don't you let me alone?" Roger allowed himself to be dragged up, still weeping. "Why don't you let an old man sleep?"

Hortense put his hat on him and by the time they were outside the door in the fresh spring morning his tears had stopped. They walked slowly together toward the class room.

"I wish I was sixty-five," Roger said as they passed the chapel.

"Yes, darling," said Hortense, nodding at an economics professor.

"I'd just lie down and sleep and sleep and only get up on Saturday afternoons. We'd go walking along the Charles River on Saturday afternoon, you and I, Hortense."

"Yes."

"I have worked for thirty-three years and I have five hundred dollars in the bank," Roger said. "So I must get a pension or the government has to feed us. Thirty-three years. Poor Hortense."

"Sssh, Roger. Here's your class room." She guided him into the well-filled room. The boys were very sympathetic and understanding about Roger and kept what they knew very quiet.

"Shelley, remember Shelley," Hortense whispered, standing Roger at his desk. "Godwin, Plato, the romantic movement . . ."

He just stood there, but with his eyes wide open, staring out over the class. She sighed and went and sat in the back of the room.

The bell rang and the class grew quiet and Roger shuffled some papers on his desk. He read so slowly these days notes were of little help to him. There was a puzzled, absent look on his face and Hortense swallowed nervously, afraid that this was the day . . .

Roger cleared his throat, slapped his face gently. "Shelley," he said. "Gentlemen, today we take up Shelley, romantic poet. Born 1792 of a rich and good family. It sounds like a paradox, gentlemen, but those were different times and perhaps in 1792 good and rich could go together . . ." The class laughed and Roger laughed and his eyes brightened and Hortense sat back with relief in her seat, knowing that another day would pass.

NO JURY WOULD CONVICT

"I COME from Jersey City," the man in the green sweater was saying, "all the way from Jersey City, and I might of just as well stood home. You look at Brooklyn and you look at Jersey City and if you didn't look at the uniforms you'd never tell the difference."

Just then the Giants scored four runs and two men a few rows below stood up with grins on their faces and called to a friend behind us, "Johnny, Johnny! Did you see that, Johnny? You still here, Johnny? We thought you mighta left. What a team, Brooklyn!" They shook their heads in sardonic admiration, "What a team! You still here, Johnny?"

Johnny, wherever he was, didn't say anything. His two friends sat down, laughing.

The man in the green sweater took off his yellow straw hat and carefully wiped the sweatband with his handkerchief. "I been watching the Dodgers for twenty-three years," he said, "and I never seen anything like this." He put his hat on again, over his dark Greek face, the eyes deep and sad, never leaving the field where the Dodgers moved wearily in their green-trimmed uniforms. "Jersey City, Albany and Brooklyn, that would make a good league. One helluva league. I would give Brooklyn twenty-five games headstart and let them fight it out. They would have a hard fight stayin' in the New York-Penn League. They would have to get three new pitchers. They're worse than Jersey City, I swear, worse . . ."

"Ah, now, listen," the man beside him said, "if that's the case why isn't Brooklyn in Jersey City and Jersey City in Brooklyn?"

"I don't know," the man in the green sweater said. "I honestly couldn't tell ye."

"They haven't got such a bad team."

"They ought to move them into the New York-Penn League. A major league team . . ." He laughed sadly. "Look at that!" A man named Wilson was striking out for Brooklyn. "Look at Wilson. Why, he's pitiful. They walk two men to get at him in the International League. I bet Newark could spot them five runs and beat them every day. I'd give odds."

"You can't make a supposition like that," the man beside him protested. "They never play each other. It's not a fair supposition."

"Five runs, every day. If they didn't have those green caps they could play in a twilight league in Connecticut and nobody'd ever tell the difference, not in ten years. Look at that!" The Brooklyn shortstop fell down leaping at a grounder to his right. "No guts," the man from Jersey City said, "a major league shortstop woulda had it and threw the man out. He fell to make a alibi."

"It was a hard-hit ball," his neighbor protested.

"Bartell woulda had it. He ain't no Bartell."

"He's got nine yards of tape on him," the man next to him said. "I saw with my own eyes in the dugout. He's a mass of cuts and bruises."

"That's Brooklyn. Always got tape all over them. They spend more money for tape than for players. Look at that."

One of the Giants hit a home run and three runs scored. The two men in front of us stood up with grins on their faces and called to their friend in back of us, "Still there, Johnny?" and sat down.

"For twenty-three years," the man in the green sweater said, "I been rootin' for this team. I'm gettin' tired of rootin' for a minor league team in a major league. I would hate to see what would happen to those guys in Jersey City."

"I come to see them every day," his neighbor said stubbornly, "and they're a major league team."

"Look at them," the man in the green sweater pointed his scorecard in accusation at the nine weary figures. "Take 'em one by one. Look at Wilson. Why, he's the worst ballplayer in the world. He's even worse than Smead Jolley."

He sat back triumphantly, having silenced his adversary for the moment.

He watched the play quietly for a few seconds, his Greek eyes bitter but resigned. "Why," he continued, "in Jersey City they put a catcher in to play center field instead of him. A catcher. I know Wilson."

"Wilson isn't the only one on the team," his neighbor said.

"All right. Cooney. What can Cooney do?"

"Cooney can field."

"All right, Cooney can field. But he has an air rifle for an arm. He can't reach second base in under seven bounces. Don't talk to me about Cooney."

"His arm's not so bad," the neighbor insisted.

"Not so bad? Why, Mac, if Cooney had an arm he'd be a pitcher."

"I never noticed anything wrong with his arm."

"Mac," the man in the green sweater said, "then you're the one man in the United States that don't know Cooney got a glass arm. The one man."

"How about Winsett?" his neighbor wanted to know.

Winsett was up at the plate by this time and the man in the green sweater watched him critically. "A cigar store Indian," he said finally. "Watch him swing."

"He hit sixty home runs the year before they brought him up," the Brooklyn fan said. "Cigar store Indians don't hit sixty home runs."

"I saw him," the man in the green sweater said, "when he was playin' in the International League. Do you know what he hit in the International League . . . .250 . . . You know why? It's an outcurve league. The National League is also an outcurve league. He ought to be out somewhere playin' night baseball." At the top of his voice he called, "Come on, you cigar store Indian!"

Winsett hit a home run.

"This is a fine time to hit it," the man from Jersey City said, "they're behind seven runs and there's nobody on base and he hits a home run."

In the next inning a pitcher named Cantwell took up the bitter burden of pitching for Brooklyn. The face of the man in the green sweater lightened. "There's a pitcher," he said. "One of the best. Out in Jersey City they were goin' to give him a new automobile but he went to the Giants. Watch him!" he said as Cantwell disposed of the first two batters. "A prince of a fellow. A prince. Everybody likes him."

"He's been pitching lousy," his neighbor said, as Cantwell suddenly filled the bases.

"What do you expect?" the man from Jersey City said, anxiously watching the misery below. "He don't look like the Cantwell of Jersey City. Terry double-crossed him, he wanted to stay in Jersey City, he woulda got an automobile, but Terry took him and double-crossed him and shipped him to Brooklyn. How do you expect him to pitch? He broke his heart."

Cantwell struck out the third batter. The man in the green sweater stood up and applauded as the pitcher trudged into the dugout. "You bet your life he can pitch, the poor son of a gun, he's disgusted, the poor fella. That's it, Ben!" He sat down. "Wonderful pitcher, Ben, he's got a head."

"I never saw him strike out a man before," the Brooklyn fan said.

"There's very few of them makes a living out of strikeouts. Now if they only give Ben something to work on . . ."

Brooklyn scored three runs. Two men died on base when Wilson popped out.

"That Wilson," the man in the green sweater said, "they ought to trade him to the Salvation Army. He's the worst player in the world. Why, he's worse than Smead Jolley."

But he cheered lustily when Cantwell came through another inning unscored upon. "There's a pitcher," he said, "if I had a team, I'd buy him."

"You could buy him for the fare to Jersey City," a man in back said, "eleven cents."

"The only major leaguer on that ball club!" the man in the green sweater said with finality. "If only those cheap bastards would buy a couple more like him, they'd have something. I'm not saying Brooklyn's bad as a town, because it's not, but they got office boys running the ball club, office boys with snot in their ears. That cheap Grimes. I heard he used the groundkeeper's truck to move his furniture in."

The Dodgers scored three more runs and the man in the green sweater was shouting triumphantly, the ancient Greek sorrow gone from his eyes for the first time in the entire afternoon. There was only one out and there was a man on third base and the Dodgers needed only one run to tie the score. Wilson was coming up to bat and the man in the green sweater groaned. "That's what happens when you have some-body like that on a team. He comes up at a time like this. That's always the way it happens. He's pitiful. In the International League they walk two batters to get at him."

But at the last moment somebody else batted for Wilson and struck out. "On low ones," the man in the green sweater said in pain, "a pinch hitter swinging at low ones."

Cantwell was to bat next.

"Let him stay up there!" the man from Jersey City shouted. "Let him win his own game." He turned to his public. "I would like to see old Ben smack one out and win the ball game," he said, "and go right over to Terry and spit in his face."

But old Ben didn't get a chance. Grimes put a man called Spence in to bat for him and Spence popped out.

In the next inning the Brooklyn second baseman juggled a ball and another run scored. All hope fled from the dark Greek face. "Why is it," he asked, "that other teams don't do it?" He got up, preparing to leave. "A man on third and one out," he said, "and no score. They ought to shoot Grimes for that. No jury would convict. Ah," he said, moving down toward the exit gate, "I'm going to root for a winning team from now on. I've been rooting for a losing team long enough. I'm going to root for the Giants. You don't know," he said to the Brooklyn fan moving along with him, "you don't know the pleasure you get out of rooting for a winning team."

And he went back to Jersey City, leaving his heart in Brooklyn.

SANTA CLAUS

SAM KOVEN let himself into his apartment, walked slowly into the living room, and sat down heavily in the old easy chair, without taking off his hat and overcoat, and waited there for his wife. There was no expression on his soft fat face, under the gray bristles of his beard, and his body, slumped in the chair, had the look of a small chunky child's worn to utter weariness by lack of sleep. He sat there, with his eyes open, in his still buttoned overcoat, looking incuriously out across the court to where a neighbor was swiftly preparing a Saturday night supper out of cans and waxed paper. When he heard his wife's key turn in the lock he sighed a little and took off his hat.

"Hello, Sam," she said as she came into the room and saw him there. "Why don't you turn on the light?"

He reached up and switched on the lamp over the chair.

"I was just sitting," he said.

"What's the matter," his wife asked, looking at him sharply, over the bundles in her arms, "you got a headache?"

"Yeah, I got a headache."

"Why don't you go take an aspirin?"

"I just want to sit, Annie. Let me sit."

"All right," Annie said. "It's your headache." She went into the bedroom to put her clothes away.

Sam sat without moving, his small fat legs straight down to reach the floor. He saw, across the court, that his neighbor was going to get tuna fish and sliced onions for dinner.

The doorbell rang and Annie came out, tying on an apron, to answer it. From the door, she called, "Sam!"

"Yeah?" he called back.

"Sam," Annie said, "it's the order from the vegetable store. Let me have some money. Two dollars."

Sam sat quietly. He opened his overcoat slowly and kept watching the woman with the tuna fish across the court.

"Sam!" Annie called. Then, after a little silence, "*Sam!*"

Annie came into the room. "What's the matter, you deaf? I need two dollars for the vegetable man."

Sam sighed. "I haven't got two dollars," he said slowly.

"What do you mean you haven't got two dollars?"

"I mean I haven't got two dollars."

Annie came over and leaned over his chair. "This is Saturday, isn't it?"

Sam nodded, still looking across the court.

"You're supposed to get paid on Saturday, aren't you?"

"Yes, Annie. Yes."

"Then why haven't . . ."

"Mrs. Koven!" the vegetable man shouted from the hall, "I ain't got all day. I can't deliver vegetables all night."

"Sam . . ." Annie began.

"Tell him to go away," Sam said. "We'll pay him some other time."

Annie looked at him thoughtfully, then walked quietly out of the room down the hall, pulling her apron down absently over her neatly corseted figure. Sam got up and took off his coat, letting it drop to the floor next to the chair. He went over and pulled down the shade on the window that gave on the court. He felt through his pockets for a cigarette, but couldn't find one. He was back in his chair when his wife returned.

"All right," Annie said, in the voice she might have used to a confused child. "Now tell me." She sat down across from him, on the couch. "Where's your salary?"

"Now, listen, Annie, don't get angry. Everything will turn out all right. It's just that . . ."

"Don't tell me fairy stories, Sam. The truth for once, Sam, the honest-to-God truth. What happened to your salary?"

Sam's hands kept searching for a cigarette. "I didn't get it today."

"Why not, Sam?"

"Brodsky . . . Brodsky fired me," Sam said uncertainly. "Imagine that, that son-of-a-bitch, I used to buy him drinks in the afternoon when drinks were a dollar and a quarter a piece . . . Imagine . . ."

Annie closed her eyes and sat back.

"You told me for the last four weeks Brodsky liked you, Sam. You're not telling me the whole story, Sam."

"Sure, I'm telling you the whole story," Sam said without conviction. "What've I got to lie about?"

"I want the whole story, Sam."

Sam sighed, then began in a flat, old voice. "I never had the job, Annie."

Annie shook her head, eyes closed, against the back of the chair. "My God," she said without passion, "what happens in this house? Oh, my God."

"Now you know, Annie."

"But every Saturday for the last four Saturdays you brought home a twenty-dollar bill, Sam. How is that?"

"What's the difference. I brought home eighty dollars. That's enough."

"Tell me, Sam. For twenty-five years I've lived with you and I never got the whole story on anything. Tell me this."

"I don't like to worry you."

"Worry me, Sam," Annie said, laughing a little. "Worry me now."

"I borrowed the money. I went down that Monday morning to go to work. I wasn't lying to you, Annie. Brodsky told me to report to work that Monday morning."

"What happened?"

"Brodsky's wife's nephew came down from Buffalo the day before without a penny. That louse, Brodsky. In 1926 I made twenty thousand dollars for him . . ."

"I baked a cake that Monday night to celebrate. Remember?"

"Is it my fault Brodsky's wife's nephew came down from Buffalo?"

"No," Annie said, opening her eyes and leaning forward to look at her husband, sitting in his chair, like a bad little fat boy with gray hair, explaining how he took the quarter from his mother's purse. "No, it wasn't your fault. Why didn't you tell me then?"

"I didn't want to hurt you. Honest, Annie," Sam said painfully, "enough other things hurt you, I don't like to if I can help it. Believe me."

"Remember that Monday night, you told Susan she could go marry Eddie, you would take care of us from now on, she didn't have to throw her salary into the house every week any more. Remember?"

"Yeah," Sam said irritably. "Yeah. Why do you have to keep reminding me?"

"Why did you do it, Sam?"

"Susan's a grown girl, she should have a house of her own."

"We all know that, Sam. Don't worry, we know it."

"It isn't right for her to support us. Every time she looks at me I can see in her eyes she wants to get out of this house. I've heard her crying at night after she's come home from being out with Eddie." Sam looked at his hat, noticing the sweatstains. "So I think she ought to be married, we shouldn't stand in the way."

"But now you haven't got a job, Sam," Annie said patiently, "she'll have to support us, won't she?"

"Let's not talk about it," Sam said, standing up. "I'm going in to lie down."

"Won't she, Sam? Answer me!"

"I suppose so."

Annie shook her head wonderingly. "Yet you could tell her you had a job, go ahead, get married, when you knew you didn't have a job, you would have to fall back on her. Sam, Sam . . ."

"I figured I would find a job in four weeks." Sam walked back and forth now, on his short babyish legs. "A lot of people're still working. Times're supposed to be getting better. Roosevelt's working hard . . ."

"Roosevelt!" Annie laughed bitterly. "For God's sake, Sam!"

"So what should I do?" Sam turned on her defiantly. "Tell me! Should I lay down and die?"

"Who loaned you eighty dollars, Sam? Tell me who was so foolish?"

"What's the difference?" Sam turned from her, went to the street window, looked out at the gathering evening, at the lights going up in warm little spots throughout the city.

"Where did you get the eighty dollars?"

Wearily, Sam gave up his last defense. "All right," he said, talking at the window. "I wrote to Detroit. To Albert."

"My poor brother!" Annie said. "He's got to support you, too. You must owe him a thousand dollars already!"

"Who else could I go to?" Sam asked flatly. "Where else? Where else? Somebody's got to help me."

"Aren't you ashamed to ask Albert for any more money? You never paid him back a cent."

"I'll pay him back. Things'll get better."

Annie laughed.

"Laugh," Sam said stubbornly, "go ahead and laugh. Once I had sixty thousand dollars in the bank. In cash."

"Once the Indians owned the United States. For God's sake, Sam, Santa Claus has stopped visiting the Bronx!" She sat in silence for a moment, looking at the familiar fat round shoulders of her husband. "Well," she asked quietly, "how're you going to tell Susan? Last Saturday they decided they were going to get married on the first of May and go to Vermont for two weeks. That's going to be nice, telling her."

"That's it," Sam said, "I didn't want to tell her that Monday, I didn't want to hurt her."

"It hurts more now, Sam. Can't you get that through your head?"

"I thought I'd get a job," Sam said patiently. "When Albert sent that check I thought that was a good sign. It gave me hope."

"How did you get a letter from Albert without me seeing it?" Annie talked with a kind of impersonal curiosity, like a woman who wants to find out how many eggs you put in a sponge cake.

Sam sighed, remembering the long complicated details. "I told him to send the check to the Dixie Hotel. I know a clerk there. I kept the money in that old valise in the hall closet."

"And every Saturday, like the head of a family, you brought me twenty dollars . . ."

"I didn't want for you to worry, Annie. I didn't want for Susan to worry. I was sure I was going to get a job, Annie, believe me. It would be *too* bad if I couldn't get a job. Bad things've happened to me," Sam said in an even reflective voice, "but anything *this* bad couldn't happen."

"So it happened," Annie said, with a little final gesture of her hands.

"So it happened." Sam sat down and covered his eyes with his little pudgy hands. "I wouldn't believe people could live and have everything go so bad for them. You can only go so far down, Annie."

"Santa Claus," Annie said, but without mockery. "Santa Claus." Then, with the same dull curiosity, "Every day at eight o'clock you left here, like a working man, Sam, and you came back every day at six-thirty. What did you do all day?"

Sam did not lift his eyes as he remembered the days. "In the morning I went from office to office. There are so many offices, Annie, so many people working. Once I used to go into those offices and hand out cigars and they'd bring out drinks. In the afternoon I used to go to the Public Library and sit and read."

"The scholar. The student. Sitting there all day." Annie shook her head slowly, tears for the first time in her eyes. "Poor Sam. What did you read?"

"I read all the old newspapers, the *Times,* the *World,* the old *American,* from 1920 to 1929. It made me feel good, reading about those days, about Lindbergh and Coolidge and John McGraw. Those were good days. I saw my picture in the papers, too—May 17, 1926, there was a Garment Manufacturers' Ball in the Hotel Astor, and you and me, we were sitting right up in front of the picture and I had on a tuxedo and a paper hat. You could tell just from the picture my hair was still black then. Remember?"

"I remember."

"I should've died in 1929," Sam said, taking his hand down from his eyes.

The bell rang, two short, sharp rings.

"That's Susan," Annie said. "She never remembers her keys."

Sam got up. "I'm going in to lie down," he said, starting for the bedroom.

"Take an aspirin, Sam," Annie said.

"Yeah, I'll take an aspirin." Sam went into the bedroom and Annie walked slowly, like an old lady, down the hall, to let Susan in.

THE MONUMENT

"I DO NOT want any of his private stock," McMahon said firmly. He blew on a glass and wiped it carefully. "I have my own opinion of his private stock."

Mr. Grimmet looked sad, sitting across the bar on a high stool, and Thesing shrugged like a salesman, not giving up the fight, but moving to a new position to continue the attack. McMahon picked up another glass in his clean, soft bartender's hands. He wiped it, his face serious and determined and flushed right up to the bald spot that his plastered-down hair couldn't cover. There was nobody else in the bar at the front part of the restaurant.

It was three o'clock in the afternoon. In the rear three waiters stood arguing. Every day at three o'clock the three waiters gathered in the back and argued.

"Fascism," one waiter said, "is a rehearsal for the cemetery."

"You read that some place," another waiter said.

"All right," said the first waiter, "I read it some place."

"An Italian," the third waiter said to the first waiter. "You are one lousy Italian."

Mr. Grimmet turned around and called to the waiters, "Please reserve discussions of that character for when you go home. This is a restaurant, not Madison Square Garden."

He turned back to watching McMahon wiping the glasses. The three waiters looked at him with equal hate.

"Many of the best bars in the city," Thesing said in his musical salesman's voice, "use our private stock."

"Many of the best bars in the city," McMahon said, using the towel very hard, "ought to be turned into riding academies."

"That's funny," Thesing said, laughing almost naturally. "He's very funny, isn't he, Mr. Grimmet?"

"Listen, Billy," Mr. Grimmet said, leaning forward, disregarding Thesing, "listen to reason. In a mixed drink nobody can tell how much you paid for the rye that goes into it. That is the supreme beauty of cocktails."

McMahon didn't say anything. The red got a little deeper on his cheeks and on his bald spot and he put the clean glasses down with a sharp tinkle and the tinkle went through the shining lines of the other glasses on the shelves and sounded thinly through the empty restaurant. He was a little fat man, very compact. He moved with great precision and style behind a bar and you could tell by watching him whether he was merry or sad or perturbed, just from the way he mixed a drink or put down a glass. Just now he was angry and Mr. Grimmet knew it. Mr. Grimmet didn't want a fight, but there was money to be saved. He put out his hand appealingly to Thesing.

"Tell me the truth, Thesing," he said. "Is your private stock bad?"

"Well," Thesing said slowly, "a lot of people like it. It is very superior for a blended product."

"Blended varnish," McMahon said, facing the shelves. "Carefully matched developing fluid."

Thesing laughed, the laugh he used from nine to six. "Witty," he said, "the sparkling bartender." McMahon wheeled and looked at him, head down a little on his chest. "I meant it," Thesing protested. "I sincerely meant it."

"I want to tell you," Mr. Grimmet said to McMahon, fixing him with his eye, "that we can save seven dollars a case on the private stock."

McMahon started whistling the tenor aria from *Pagliacci*. He looked up at the ceiling and wiped a glass and whistled. Mr. Grimmet felt like firing him and remembered that at least twice a month he felt like firing McMahon.

"Please stop whistling," he said politely. "We have a matter to discuss."

McMahon stopped whistling and Mr. Grimmet still felt like firing him.

"Times're not so good," Mr. Grimmet said in a cajoling tone of voice, hating himself for descending to such tactics before an employee of his. "Remember, McMahon, Coolidge is no longer in the White House. I am the last one in the world to compromise with quality, but we must remember, we are in business and it is 1938."

"Thesing's private stock," McMahon said, "would destroy the stomach of a healthy horse."

"Mussolini!" the first waiter's voice came out from the back of the restaurant. "Every day on Broadway I pass forty-five actors who could do his act better."

"I am going to tell you one thing," Mr. Grimmet said with obvious calmness to McMahon. "I am the owner of this restaurant."

McMahon whistled some more from *Pagliacci*. Thesing moved wisely down the bar a bit.

"I am interested in making money," Mr. Grimmet said. "What would you say, Mr. McMahon, if I ordered you to use the private stock?"

"I would say, 'I am through, Mr. Grimmet.' Once and for all."

Mr. Grimmet rubbed his face unhappily and stared coldly at the waiters in the back of the restaurant. The waiters remained silent and stared coldly back at him. "What's it to you?" Mr. Grimmet asked McMahon angrily. "What do you care if we use another whisky. Do you have to drink it?"

"In my bar, Mr. Grimmet," McMahon said, putting down his towel and the glasses and facing his employer squarely, "in my bar, good drinks are served."

"Nobody will know the difference!" Mr. Grimmet got off his stool and jumped up and down gently. "What do Americans know about liquor? Nothing! Read any book on the subject!"

"True," Thesing said judiciously. "The general consensus of opinion is that Americans do not know the difference between red wine and a chocolate malted milk."

"In my bar," McMahon repeated, his face very red, his wide hands spread on the bar, "I serve the best drinks I know how to serve."

"Stubborn!" Mr. Grimmet yelled. "You are a stubborn Irishman! You do this out of malice! You are anxious to see me lose seven dollars on every case of liquor because you dislike me. Let us get down to the bedrock of truth!"

"Keep your voice down," McMahon said, speaking with great control. "I want to remind you of one or two things. I have worked for you since Repeal, Mr. Grimmet. In that time, how many times did we have to enlarge the bar?"

"I am not in the mood for history, McMahon!" Mr. Grimmet shouted. "What good is a bar as long as the *Normandie* if it is not run on a businesslike basis?"

"Answer my question," McMahon said. "How many times?"

"Three," Mr. Grimmet said, "all right, three."

"We are three times as big now as we were six years ago," McMahon said in a professor's tone, explaining proposition one, going on to proposition two. "Why do you think that is?"

"Accident!" Mr. Grimmet looked ironically up to the ceiling. "Fate! Roosevelt! The hand of God! How do I know?"

"I will tell you," McMahon said, continuing in the professorial vein. "People who come in to this bar get the best Manhattans, the best Martinis, the best Daiquiris that are made on the face of the earth. They are made out of the finest ingredients, with great care, Mr. Grimmet."

"One cocktail tastes like another," Mr. Grimmet said. "People make a big fuss and they don't know anything."

"Mr. Grimmet," McMahon said with open contempt, "it is easy to see that you are not a drinking man."

Mr. Grimmet's face reflected his desperate search for a new line of defense. His eyebrows went up with pleasure as he found it. He sat down and spoke softly across the bar to McMahon. "Did it ever occur to you," he asked, "that people come into this place because of the food that is served here?"

"I will give you my final opinion of Greta Garbo," the first waiter's voice sounded out defiantly. "There is nobody like her."

For a moment McMahon looked straight into Mr. Grimmet's eyes. A slight bitter smile played at one corner of his mouth. He breathed deeply, like a man who has just decided to bet on a horse that has not won in fourteen races. "Shall I tell you what I think of the food that is served in your restaurant, Mr. Grimmet?" McMahon asked flatly.

"The best chefs," Mr. Grimmet said quickly, "the best chefs in the City of New York."

McMahon nodded slowly. "The best chefs," he said, "and the worst food."

"Consider," Mr. Grimmet called. "Consider what you're saying."

"Anything a cook can disguise," McMahon said, talking now to Thesing, disregarding Mr. Grimmet, "is wonderful here. Anything with a sauce. Once I ate a sirloin steak in this restaurant . . ."

"Careful, McMahon." Mr. Grimmet jumped off his stool and ran around to face McMahon.

"What can be done to disguise a sirloin steak?" McMahon asked reasonably. "Nothing. You broil it. Simply that. If it was good when it was cut off the steer, it's good on your plate. If it was bad . . ."

"I pay good prices!" Mr. Grimmet yelled. "I'll have no allusions . . ."

"I would not bring a dog into this restaurant to eat sirloin steak," McMahon said. "Not a young dog with the teeth of a lion."

"You're fired!" Mr. Grimmet pounded on the bar. "This restaurant will now do without your services."

McMahon bowed. "That is satisfactory to me," he said. "Perfectly satisfactory."

"Well, now, everybody. Boys!" Thesing said pacifically. "Over a little thing like private stock rye . . ."

McMahon began taking off his apron. "This bar has a reputation. It is my reputation. I am proud of it. I am not interested in remaining at a place in which my reputation will be damaged."

McMahon threw his apron, neatly folded, over a towel rack and picked up the little wooden wedge on which was printed, in gold letters, "William McMahon, *In Charge*." Mr. Grimmet watched him with trouble in his eyes as McMahon lifted the hinged piece of the bar that permitted the bartenders to get out into the restaurant proper.

"What is the sense," Mr. Grimmet asked as the hinges creaked, "of taking a rash step, Billy?" Once more Mr. Grimmet hated himself for his dulcet tone of voice, but William McMahon was one of the five finest bartenders in the City of New York.

McMahon stood there, pushing the hinged piece of the bar a little, back and forth. "Once and for all," he said. He let the hinged piece fall behind him.

"I'll tell you what I'll do, Billy," Mr. Grimmet went on swiftly, hating himself more and more, "I'll make a compromise. I will give you five dollars more per week." He sighed to himself and then looked brightly at McMahon.

McMahon knocked his shingle thoughtfully against the bar. "I will try to make you understand something, Mr. Grimmet," he said, gently. "I am not as fundamentally interested in money as I am fundamentally interested in other things."

"You are not so different from the rest of the world," Mr. Grimmet said with dignity.

"I have been working for twenty-five years," McMahon said, knocking the shingle that said, "William McMahon, *In Charge*," "and I have constantly been able to make a living. I do not work only to make a living. I am more interested in making something else. For the last six years I have worked here night and day. A lot of nice people come in here and drink like ladies and gentlemen. They all like this place. They all like me."

"Nobody is saying anything about anybody not liking you," Mr. Grimmet said impatiently. "I am discussing a matter of business principle."

"I like this place." McMahon looked down at the shingle in his hand. "I think this is a very nice bar. I planned it. Right?" He looked up at Mr. Grimmet.

"You planned it. I will sign an affidavit to the effect that you planned it," Mr. Grimmet said ironically. "What has that got to do with Thesing's private stock?"

"If something is right here," McMahon went on, without raising his voice, "people can say it's William McMahon's doing. If something is wrong here they can say it's William McMahon's fault. I like that, Mr. Grimmet. When I die people can say, 'William McMahon left a monument, the bar at Grimmet's Restaurant. He never served a bad drink in his whole life.' " McMahon took his coat out of the closet next to the bar and put it on. "A monument. I will not have a monument made out of Thesing's private stock. Mr. Grimmet, I think you are a dumb bastard."

McMahon bowed a little to the two men and started out. Mr. Grimmet gulped, then called, his words hard and dry in the empty restaurant. "McMahon!" The bartender turned around. "All right," Mr. Grimmet said. "Come back."

McMahon gestured toward Thesing.

"Any liquor you say," Mr. Grimmet said in a choked voice. "Any goddamn whisky you want!"

McMahon smiled and went back to the closet and took his coat off and took the shingle out of his pocket. He went back of the bar and slipped on his apron, as Thesing and Grimmet watched.

"One thing," Mr. Grimmet said, his eyes twitching from the strain, "one thing I want you to know."

"Yes, sir," said McMahon.

"I don't want you to talk to me," Mr. Grimmet said, "and I don't want to talk to you. Ever."

Thesing quietly picked up his hat and stole out the door.

"Yes, sir," said McMahon.

Mr. Grimmet walked swiftly into the kitchen.

"I will tell you something about debutantes," the first waiter was saying in the rear of the restaurant, "they are overrated."

McMahon tied the bow in his apron strings and, neatly, in the center of the whisky shelves above the bar, placed the shingle, "William McMahon, *In Charge*."

THE GREEK GENERAL

"I DID IT," Alex kept saying. "I swear I did it."

"Tell me more stories," Flanagan said, standing right over him, "I love to hear stories."

"I swear to God," Alex said, beginning to feel scared.

"Come on!" Flanagan jerked Alex to his feet. "We are going to visit New Jersey. We are going to revisit the scene of the crime, except there was no crime."

"I don't understand," Alex said hurriedly, putting on his coat and going down the stairs between Flanagan and Sam, leaving his door unlocked. "I don't understand at all."

Sam drove the car through the empty night streets, and Alex and Flanagan sat in the back seat.

"I did everything very careful," Alex said in a troubled voice. "I soaked the whole goddamn house with naphtha. I didn't forget a single thing. You know me, Flanagan, I know how to do a job . . ."

"Yeah," Flanagan said. "The efficiency expert. Alexander. The Greek general. Only the house didn't burn. That's all."

"I honestly don't understand it." Alex shook his head in puzzlement. "I put a fuse into a pile of rags that had enough naphtha on it to wash a elephant. I swear to God."

"Only the house didn't burn," Flanagan said stubbornly. "Everything was dandy, only the house didn't burn. I would like to kick you in the belly."

"Now, lissen, Flanagan," Alex protested, "what would you want to do that for? Lissen, I meant well. Sam," he appealed to the driver, "you know me, ain't I got a reputation . . . ?"

"Yeah," Sam said, flatly, not taking his eyes off the traffic ahead of him.

"Jesus, Flanagan, why would I want to run out? Answer me that, what's there in it for me if I run out? I ask you that simple question."

"You give me a pain in the belly," Flanagan said. "A terrible pain. Alexander." He took out a cigarette and lit it, without offering one to Alex, and looked moodily out at the policeman who was taking their toll money at the Holland Tunnel entrance.

They rode in silence through the tunnel until Sam said, "This is some tunnel. It's an achievement of engineering. Look, they got a cop every hundred yards."

"You give me a pain in the belly, too," Flanagan said to Sam. So they rode in silence until they came to the skyway. The open starlit sky seemed to loosen Flanagan up a little. He took off his derby and ran his fingers through his sandy hair with a nervous unhappy motion.

"I had to get mixed up with you," he said to Alex. "A simple little thing like burning down a house and you gum it up like flypaper. Twenty-five thousand dollars hanging by a thread. Christ!" he said bitterly. "Maybe I ought to shoot you."

"I don't understand it," Alex said miserably. "That fuse shoulda reached the naphtha in two hours. It shoulda burned like a gas stove."

"You Greek general."

"Lissen, Flanagan," Alex said, tough and businesslike. "I don't like the way you talk. You talk like I threw the job away on purpose. Lissen, do you think I'd throw five thousand bucks out the window like that?"

"I don't know what you'd do," Flanagan said, lighting another cigarette. "I don't think you got enough brains to come in outa the rain. That's my honest opinion."

"Five thousand bucks is five thousand bucks," Alex insisted. "With money like that I could open a poolroom and be a gentleman for the rest of my life." He looked up at the ceiling of the car and spoke softly. "I always wanted to operate a poolroom." Then, harshly, to Flanagan, "You think I'd give up a chance like that? What do you think—I'm crazy?"

"I don't think nothing," Flanagan said stubbornly. "All I know is the house didn't burn. That's all I know."

He looked stonily out his window and there was quiet in the car as it raced across the Jersey meadows through the stockyard, fertilizer, glue-factory smells, and turned off on the fork to Orangeburg. Two miles out of the town they stopped at an intersection and McCracken came out from behind a tree and got into the car. Sam started the car again even before McCracken was seated. McCracken was not in uniform and there was a harried frown on his face. "This is the nuts," McCracken said even before he got the car door closed. "This is wonderful. This is a beautiful kettle of fish."

"If you just come to cry," Flanagan said bluntly, "you can get right out now."

"I have been sitting around in the police station," McCracken wailed, "and I have been going crazy."

"All right. All right!" Flanagan said.

"Everything worked just like we planned," McCracken went right on, pounding his hand on his knee. "Ten minutes before eleven o'clock an alarm was turned in from the other end of town and the whole damned fire department went charging out to put out a brush fire in a vacant lot. I waited and waited and for two hours there was no sign of a fire from the Littleworth house. Twenty-five thousand bucks!" He rocked back and forth in misery. "Then I called you. What're you doing, playing a game?"

Flanagan gestured toward Alex with his thumb. "Look at him. There's the boy. Our efficiency expert. I would like to kick him in the belly."

"Lissen," Alex said coolly and reasonably. "Something went wrong. A mistake. All right."

"What's all right about it?" McCracken shouted. "You tell me! Lissen, Alex, I get four thousand bucks a year for bein' Chief of Police of this town, I can't afford to get mixed up in mistakes."

"I will do the job over," Alex said soothingly. "I will do it good this time."

"You better," Flanagan said grimly. "You'll be served up as pie if you make another mistake."

"That's no way to talk," Alex said, hurt.

"That's the way I talk," Flanagan said. "Sam, go to the Littleworth house."

The car barely stopped for Alex to jump out in front of the Littleworth house. "We'll be back in ten minutes," Flanagan said as he closed the door. "Find out what went wrong. *Alex!*" he said with loathing.

Alex shrugged and looked up at the huge pile of the Littleworth house, black against the sky. By all rights it should've been just a heap of ashes by now with insurance experts probing in the remains to estimate how much damage was done. Why couldn't it've burned? Alex wept inwardly, why couldn't it? Five thousand dollars, he thought as he went swiftly and quietly across the dark lawn. A nice comfortable pool-room, with the balls clicking like music and the boys buying Coca-Cola at ten cents a bottle between shots and the cash register ringing again and again. A gentleman's life. No wondering every time you saw a cop was he looking for you. Why couldn't it've burned?

He slipped silently through the window that he had left open and padded along the thick carpet to the library, his flashlight winking on and off cautiously in the dark hall. He went directly to the pile of rags in the corner, over which still hung the faint odor of naphtha. He played the flashlight on the fuse that he had carefully lighted before slipping out the window. Only ashes remained. The fuse had burned all right. Uncertainly he touched the rags. They were dry as sand. "Nuts," he said softly in the silent library. "Nuts. Smart guy!" He hit his head with both his hands in irritation. "What a smart guy!" He kicked the pile of rags bitterly and went back along the hall and jumped out the window and walked out across the lawn and waited for Flanagan and Sam behind a tree, smoking a cigarette.

Alex breathed deeply, looking around him. This was the way to live, he thought, peering at the big houses set behind trees and lawns off in the darkness, fresh air and birds and quiet, going off to Palm Beach when you wanted your house burned down and you didn't want to know anything about it. He sighed, blotting out his cigarette against the tree. A well-run poolroom ought to be good for six, seven thousand dollars a year. You could live very respectable in Flatbush on six, seven thousand dollars a year, there were trees there, all over the place, and squirrels, live squirrels, in the gardens. Like a park, like a real park, that's how people ought to live . . .

The car drew up to him and Flanagan opened the door and leaned out.

"Well, general?" Flanagan asked without humor.

"Look, Flanagan," Alex said seriously, talking in whispers, "something went wrong."

"No!" Flanagan said with bitter irony. "No! Don't tell me!"

"Do you want to make jokes?" Alex asked. "Or do you want to hear what happened?"

"For God's sake," McCracken whispered, his voice tense and high, "don't be a comedian, Flanagan. Say what you got to say and let's get outa here!" He looked anxiously up and down the street. "For all I know a cop's liable to come walkin' up this street any minute!"

"Our Chief of Police. Old Iron Nerves," Flanagan said.

"I'm sorry I ever got into this," McCracken said hoarsely. "Well, Alex, what the hell happened?"

"It's very simple," Alex said. "I set a two-hour fuse and the naphtha evaporated."

"Evaporated?" Sam said slowly. "What's that, evaporated?"

"He's a student, our boy, Alex," Flanagan said. "He knows big words. Evaporated. You dumb Greek! You efficiency expert! You stupid sonofa-bitch! Trust you to burn down a house! Evaporated! You ought to be washing dishes! *Alexander!*" Deliberately Flanagan spit at Alex.

"You oughtn't to say that," Alex said, wiping his face. "I did my best."

"What're we going to do now?" McCracken wailed. "Somebody tell me what we're going to do now."

Flanagan leaned way over and grabbed Alex fiercely by the collar. "Lissen, Alexander," he said right into Alex's face, "you're goin' back in that house and you're settin' fire to that house, and you're settin' fire to it good! Hear me?"

"Yeah," Alex said, his voice trembling. "Sure I hear you, Flanagan. You don't have to tear my collar off. Say, lissen, Flanagan, this shirt cost me eight bucks . . ."

"You are setting fire to this house personally now," Flanagan's grip tightened on the collar. "You are giving this fire the benefit of your personal attention, see? No fuse, no evaporated, nothing, understand?"

"Yeah," Alex said. "Sure, Flanagan."

"You will be served up as pie, anything goes wrong," Flanagan said slowly, his pale mean eyes glaring straight into Alex's.

"Why don't you leave go my collar?" Alex said, choking a little. "Lissen, Flanagan, this shirt cost me . . ."

Flanagan spat into his face again. "I would like to kick you in the belly," he said. He let go Alex's collar and pushed Alex's face with the heel of his hand.

"Say, Flanagan . . ." Alex protested as he stumbled back.

The car door slammed. "Move, Sam," Flanagan said, sitting back.

The car spurted down the street. Alex wiped his face with a shaking hand. "Oh, Jesus," he said to himself as he walked back across the completely dark lawn to the house. He heard a sparrow cheep in the three o'clock morning hush and he nearly cried under the peaceful trees.

Once in the house, though, he became very businesslike. He went upstairs to where he had set out buckets of naphtha and brought them down in pairs. He tore down all the drapes from the ground-floor windows and piled them at the farther end of the long hall that ran along one side of the house. Then he took all the linen covers off the furniture and piled them on top of the drapes. He went down to the cellar and brought up three egg boxes full of excelsior and put the excelsior on top of the piled cloth. It made a heap about seven feet high at the end of the hall. He worked grimly, swiftly, ripping cloth when it wouldn't give way easily, running up and down steps, sweating in his overcoat, feeling the sweat roll down his neck onto his tight collar. He soaked every piece of furniture with naphtha, then came out and poured ten gallons of naphtha over the pile at the end of the hall. He stepped back, the acrid smell sharp in his nostrils, and surveyed his work with satisfaction. If that didn't work you couldn't burn this house down in a blast-oven. When he got through with it, the home of the Littleworths would be hot. No mistake this time. He got a broom and broke off the handle and wrapped it heavily with rags. He soaked the rags with naphtha until the liquid ran out of the saturated cloth to the floor. He whistled comfortably under his breath "There'll be a hot time in the old town tonight" as he opened the window wide behind him at the end of the hall that was opposite the huge pile of cloth and excelsior. It was a narrow hall, but long. A distance of thirty-five feet separated him from the pyre at the other end.

"There'll be a hot time in the old town tonight," he sang under his breath as he took out a match from the dozen he had lying loose in his pocket. He stood next to the open window, prepared to jump swiftly out as he struck the match, put it to his heavy torch. The torch flared up wildly in his hand and he hurled it with all his strength straight down the hall to the pile of naphtha-soaked cloth and excelsior at the other end. It landed squarely on the pile. For a moment nothing happened. Alex stood, ready at the window, his eyes shining in the fierce light of the flaring torch. Alex smiled and kissed his fingers at the other end of the hall.

Then the whole hall exploded. The pile of cloth became a single huge ball of flame and hurtled down the hall like a flaming shell to the open window behind Alex. With a scream sick in his throat, lost in the immense roar of the exploding house, Alex dove to the floor just as the ball of flame shot over him and through the window to the pull of the open air beyond, carrying his hat and his hair, like smoke going up a chimney to the pull of the sky.

When he came to there was a dusty burned smell in his nostrils. Without surprise he saw that the carpet under his face was quietly afire, burning gently, like coal in a grate. He hit the side of his head three times to put out the fire in what remained of his hair, and sat up dully. Coughing and crying, he dove down to the floor again, escaping the smoke. He crawled along the burning carpet foot by foot, his hands getting black and crisp under him as he slowly made his way to the nearest door. He opened the door and crawled out onto a side porch. Just behind him the hall beams collapsed and a column of flame shot up through the roof, as solid as cement. He sighed and crawled to the edge of the porch and fell off five feet to the loam of a flower bed. The loam was hot and smelled from manure, but he lay there gratefully for a moment, until he realized that something was wrong with his hip. Stiffly he sat up and looked at his hip. Flames were coming out through his overcoat from inside and he could smell his skin broiling. Neatly he unbuttoned his coat and hit at the flames, curling up from the pocket where he had the dozen matches. When he put out the fire on his hip he crawled out to the lawn, shaking his head again and again to clear it, and sat behind a tree. He slid over and went out again, his head on a root.

Far off, far, far off a bell clanged again and again. Alex opened his eyes, singed of their lashes, and listened. He heard the fire trucks turn into the street. He sighed again and crawled, clinging to the cold ground, around the back of the house and through a bare hedge that cut his swelling hands, and away from the house. He stood up and walked off behind a high hedge just as the first fireman came running down toward the back of the house.

Directly, but slowly, like a man walking in a dream, he went to Mc-Cracken's house. It took forty minutes to walk there, walking deliberately down alleys and back streets in the dark, feeling the burned skin crack on his knees with every step.

He rang the bell and waited. The door opened slowly and Mc-Cracken cautiously put his face out.

"My God!" McCracken said and started to slam the door, but Alex had his foot in the way.

"Lemme in," Alex said in a hoarse broken voice.

"You're burned," McCracken said, trying to kick Alex's foot out of the doorway. "I can't have nothing to do with you. Get outa here."

Alex took out his gun and shoved it into McCracken's ribs. "Lemme in," he said.

McCracken slowly opened the door. Alex could feel his ribs shaking against the muzzle of the gun. "Take it easy," McCracken said, his voice high and girlish with fright. "Lissen, Alex, take it easy."

They stepped inside the hall and McCracken closed the door. Mc-

Cracken kept holding on to the doorknob to keep from sliding to the floor from terror. "What do you want from me, Alex?" His necktie jumped up and down with the strain of talking. "What can I do for you?"

"I want a hat," Alex said, "and I want a coat."

"Sure, sure, Alex. Anything I can do to help . . ."

"Also I want for you to drive me to New York."

McCracken swallowed hard. "Now, look, Alex," he wiped his mouth with the back of his hand to dry the lips, "let's be reasonable. It's impossible for me to drive you to New York. I got a four-thousand-dollar job. I'm Chief of Police. I can't take chances like . . ."

Alex started to cry. "I'll give it to you right in the guts. So help me."

"All right, Alex, all right," McCracken said hurriedly. "What're you crying about?"

"It hurts. I can't stand it, it hurts so much." Alex weaved back and forth in the hallway in pain. "I got to get to a doctor before I croak. Come on, you bastard," he wept, "drive me to the city!"

All the way to Jersey City Alex cried as he sat there, jolting in the front seat, wrapped in a big coat of McCracken's, an old hat slipping back and forth on his burnt head as the car sped east into the dawn. McCracken gripped the wheel with tight, sweating hands, his face drawn and pale. From time to time he glanced sidewise fearfully at Alex.

"Yeah," Alex said once when he caught McCracken looking at him. "I'm still here. I ain't dead yet. Watch where you're goin', Chief of Police."

A block from the Jersey entrance of the Holland Tunnel, McCracken stopped the car.

"Please, Alex," he pleaded, "don't make me take you across to New York. I can't take the chance."

"I gotta get to a doctor," Alex said, licking his cracked lips. "I gotta get to a doctor. Nobody's gonna stop me from getting to a doctor. You're goin' to take me through the tunnel and then I'm goin' to let you have it because you're a bastard. You're an Irish bastard. Start this car." He rocked back and forth in the front seat to help him with the pain. "Start this car!" he shouted.

Shaking so that it was hard for him to control the car, McCracken drove Alex all the way to the St. George Hotel in Brooklyn where Flanagan lived. He stopped the car and sat still, slumped exhausted over the wheel.

"O.K., Alex," he said. "Here we are. You're gonna be a good guy, aren't you, Alex, you're not goin' to do anythin' you're goin' to be sorry for, are you? Remember, Alex, I'm a family man, I'm a man with three children. Come on, Alex, why don't you talk? Why would you want to hurt me?"

"Because you're a bastard," Alex said painfully because his jaws were stiffening. "I got a good mind to. You didn't want to help me. I had to make you help me."

"I got a kid aged two years old," McCracken cried. "Do you want to make a orphan of a two-year-old kid? Please, Alex. I'll do anything you say."

Alex sighed. "Go get Flanagan."

McCracken jumped out quickly and came right back with Flanagan and Sam. Alex smiled stiffly when Flanagan opened the door of the car and saw Alex and whistled. "Nice," Flanagan said. "Very nice."

"Look at him," Sam said, shaking his head. "He looks like he been in a war."

"You ought to a' seen what I done to the house," Alex said. "A first-class job."

"Are you goin' to pass out, Alex?" Sam asked anxiously.

Alex waved his gun pointlessly two or three times and then pitched forward, his head hitting the dashboard with a smart crack, like the sound of a baseball bat on a thrown ball.

When he opened his eyes he was in a dark, meagerly furnished room and Flanagan's voice was saying, "Lissen, Doc, this man can't die. He's gotta come through, understand? It is too hard to explain away a dead body. It can't be done. I don't care if he loses both legs and both arms and if it takes five years, but he's got to pull through."

"I should never've gotten mixed up in this," McCracken's voice wailed. "I was a damn fool. Risking a four-thousand-dollar-a-year job. I ought to have my head examined."

"Maybe he will and maybe he won't," a strange professional voice said. "That is a well done young man."

"It looks to me," Sam's voice said, "as if he's marked special delivery to Calvary Cemetery."

"Shut up!" Flanagan said. "And from now on nobody says a word. This is a private case. Alexander. The lousy Greek."

Alex heard them all go out before he dropped off again.

For the next five days, the doctor kept him full of dope, and Flanagan kept Sam at his bedside with a towel for a gag, to keep him quiet when the pain became too much to bear. He would start to yell and Sam would shove the towel into his mouth and say soothingly, "This is a respectable boarding house, Alex. They don't like noise." And he could scream all he wanted to into the towel and bother no one.

Ten days later the doctor told Flanagan, "All right. He'll live."

Flanagan sighed. "The dumb Greek," he said, patting Alex on his bandaged head. "I would like to kick him in the belly. I am going out to get drunk." And he put on his derby hat, square on his head, and went out.

Alex lay in one position for three months in the furnished room. Sam played nursemaid, feeding him, playing rummy with him, reading the sporting news to him.

At times when Sam wasn't there Alex lay straight on his bed, his eyes half-closed, thinking of his poolroom. He would have a neon sign, "Alex's Billiard Parlor" going on and off and new tables and leather chairs just like a club. Ladies could play in "Alex's Billiard Parlor" it would be so refined. He would cater to the better element. Maybe even a refined free lunch, cold meats and Swiss cheese. For the rest of his life he would be a gentleman, sitting behind a cash register with his jacket on. He smiled to himself. When Flanagan gave him his money he would go straight to the pool parlor on Clinton Street and throw his money down on the counter. Cold cash. This was hard-earned money, he nearly died and there were days he'd wished he could die, and his hair was going to grow in patches, like scrub grass on a highway, for the rest of his life, but what the hell. You didn't get nothing for nothing. Five thousand dollars, five thousand dollars, five thousand dollars . . .

On June first he put on his clothes for the first time in three months and twelve days. He had to sit down after he pulled his pants on because the strain hit him at the knees. He got completely dressed, dressing very slowly, and being very careful with his necktie, and then sat down to wait for Flanagan and Sam. He was going to walk out of that lousy little room with five thousand dollars flat in his wallet. Well, he thought, I earned it, I certainly did earn it.

Flanagan and Sam came in without knocking.

"We're in a hurry," Flanagan said. "We're going to the Adirondacks. The Adirondacks in June are supposed to be something. We came to settle up."

"That's right," Alex said. He couldn't help but smile, thinking about the money. "Five thousand dollars. Baby!"

"I think you are making a mistake," Flanagan said slowly.

"Did you say five thousand dollars?" Sam asked politely.

"Yeah," Alex said. "Yeah. Five thousand bucks, that's what we agreed, isn't it?"

"That was in February, Alex," Flanagan explained calmly. "A lot of things've happened since February."

"Great changes have taken place," Sam said. "Read the papers."

"Stop the kiddin'," Alex said, weeping inside his chest. "Come on, stop the bull."

"It is true, general," Flanagan said, looking disinterestedly out the window, "that you was supposed to get five thousand dollars. But doctor bills ate it all up. Ain't it too bad? It's terrible, how expensive doctors are, these days."

"We got a specialist for you, Alex," Sam said. "Nothing but the best. He's very good on gunwounds too. But it costs."

"You lousy Flanagan," Alex shouted. "I'll get you. Don't think I won't get you!"

"You shouldn't yell in your condition," Flanagan said smoothly.

"Yeah," Sam said. "The specialist says you should relax."

"Get out of here," Alex said through tears. "Get the hell out of here."

Flanagan went over to the dresser drawer and took out Alex's gun. Expertly, he broke it and took out the shells and slipped them into his pocket. "This is just in case your hot Greek blood gets the better of you for a minute, Alex," he said. "That would be too bad."

"Lissen, Flanagan," Alex cried, "ain't I going to get anything? Not anything?"

Flanagan looked at Sam, then took out his wallet, threw a fifty-dollar bill at Alex. "Outa my own pocket," he said. "My Irish generosity."

"Some day," Alex said, "I'm going to give it to you. Wait and see. Remember."

Flanagan laughed. "The efficiency expert. Look, Alexander, you ought to get out of this business. Take the advice of an older man. You ain't got the temperament for it."

"I'm going to give it to you," Alex said stubbornly. "Remember what I said."

"The general," Flanagan laughed. "The terrible Greek." He came over and hit Alex's head back with the heel of his hand. "So long, Alexander."

He left the room.

Sam came over and put his hand on Alex's shoulder. "Take care of yourself, Alex," he said. "You've been under a big strain." And he followed Flanagan.

Alex sat for ten minutes, dry-eyed, in his chair. His nose was bleeding a little from Flanagan's push. He sighed and got up and put his coat on. He bent and picked up the fifty-dollar bill and put it in his wallet.

He slipped the empty pistol into his topcoat pocket and went out slowly into the warm June sunshine. He walked slowly the two blocks to Fort Greene Park and sat down panting on the first bench. He sat there reflectively for a few minutes, shaking his head sadly from time to time. Finally he took the gun out of his pocket, looked secretly around him, and dropped it into the waste can next to the bench. It fell with a soft dry plop on the papers in the can. He reached into the can and got out a discarded newspaper and turned to the Help Wanted section. He blinked his eyes in the glare of the sun off the newsprint and traced down the page with his finger to "Help Wanted, Boys." He sat there in the warm June sunshine, with his topcoat on, making neat little checks with a pencil on the margin of the page.

MY GREEN FLOWER

MOLLOY OPENED the door of his home and went quietly into the living room. Gently he put his package down on the yellow oak library table, next to a neat pile of old *Catholic Sentinels*. He looked fondly at the package for a moment, his face cracked with a smile through the signs of weather and age. He took off his hat like a proper man and bawled out, "Bessie! *Bessie!*" his voice clanging like a street car bell throughout the five-room flat.

Bessie came running out of the bedroom, her gray hair flying behind her, her uncorseted flesh shaking in a housedress as she hurried into the living room. "What's wrong?" she called even before she saw Molloy. "Are ye all right, Vincent?"

"My darlin' Bessie," Molloy said. He went over and put his arms tightly around her. "My green flower." He kissed her right eye because she pulled away from him.

"That's a breath," Bessie said coldly, knocking his arms off her. "That's a fine breath."

"Do ye know what day this is?" Molloy grabbed her again.

"Saturday," Bessie said, pushing him into a chair. "You smell exactly like Saturday."

"Today," Molloy said, declaiming from his deep chair, "today is the day on which we married, March 14, a happy day. Gi' me a kiss, Bessie. My green flower. Just twenty-six years ago today, March 14. My virgin bride. Don't ye remember, Bessie?"

"I remember," Bessie said sternly. Then she relented. "Ye remembered, Vincent," she said softly, kissing him on his bald spot, smoothing down the stray gray hairs. "That was a day." She kissed his bald spot again.

Vincent held her hand gently. "Look on the table, Bessie. See what's starin' ye in the eye." With his free hand he gestured widely at the library table. "For the twenty-six years. Go ahead and open it up."

Bessie kissed him once more and went over and tore the paper off the package. "Four Roses!" she cried, holding up the bottle. "You're a thoughtful man, Vincent."

Vincent beamed. "A whole quart," he said. "The best that money can buy. A blend of straight whiskies."

Bessie was swiftly opening the bottle. "I was lyin' on my back in the bedroom, melancholy at the thought of the passin' of the years," she said, wrenching the tin cap off vigorously. "This'll take the pain away." She smelled the bottle luxuriously, closing her eyes. "Isn't it strange how sweet it'll smell at the neck of a bottle and how foul on a man's breath? Vincent, it was real kind of ye to remember me this way. A true husband."

Molloy came over and put his arm around her lovingly, his fingers in the slack flesh of her loose-hanging hip. "Tonight, old lady," he said, "we'll be the happiest couple in the whole of Brooklyn." He took the bottle.

"Ah, Vincent," Bessie whispered, "it's not been so bad, has it? Not out of the bottle, Vincent. It ain't decent out of the bottle. Let's sit in the kitchen, the light's good there."

Arm in arm, with Molloy holding the whisky devotedly, they went into the kitchen. Bessie got out two water tumblers and sat down at the kitchen table, opposite Molloy. She smiled at her husband as he carefully measured the whisky out into the two glasses.

They picked up the drinks. "To undyin' love," Molloy said quietly, through teary eyes.

"To my love an' your love," Bessie answered, blinking.

They drained the glasses and smiled at each other as Molloy poured two more.

"That," he said, "is whisky. Anniversary whisky. On the day of our weddin' Old Overholt flowed like water in a stream. At six in the mornin' the festivities were still at feverish pitch." He shook his head, remembering, and filled his glass.

"That," Bessie said reflectively, "was a lively crowd. There were five men there who'd asked for my hand, all singin' and dancin' and despairin' . . ."

"At that time," Molloy said, "you were the prettiest number in Brooklyn. There is no denyin' it. My green flower." He tilted his head back, emptying the glass. "I got somethin'. I really got somethin'." He laughed aloud as he poured himself and Bessie another drink. "My God, what a thing it is to be twenty years old. Jesus Christ God, what a thing!"

"I remember you," Bessie said, holding his hand across the porcelain top of the kitchen table, "with a red mustache like a cavalryman's on yer young face, drinkin' with any man that would drink with ye, with a slap and a laugh for the girls, handsome as a king, with yer head full of ideas for tearin' the world down piece by piece. Ah, ah, that was a day!" She sighed, drinking.

"Well, the world's still standing," Molloy said soberly. "Vincent Molloy's not done it much damage in these twenty-six years." He filled his glass. "Do ye remember when I told ye I was goin' to be Mayor of the City of New York?"

"I do," Bessie said quietly, sipping. "I believed ye, every word."

"I became a family man," Molloy looked gloomily into his whisky, slopping it around inside the glass. "A postal clerk. A man who was a young man like me," he said bitterly.

"The truth of the matter, Molloy," Bessie said, "is that family man or no family man ye'd be a postal clerk."

"That's a harsh thing," Molloy said with dignity. "A very harsh thing. My own wife. Who was it said, stay at home at nights, entertain me and the babies, when I should've been in the bars and Democratic clubs cultivatin' profitable acquaintances? Who was it?" He drank in a gulp.

"Ye'd have cultivated the scum of God's earth," Bessie said, sitting up straight. "Your natural friends."

"That is no way to talk," Molloy said, "on an anniversary. We should be full of joy and celebration."

"Let me have the bottle," Bessie said. Molloy pushed it over to her and she poured for both of them. "You were the kind of man that could not be allowed around the corner."

"That is hardly the way to talk, Bessie."

"The Mayor of the City of New York. Elected on the women's vote."

"You're unfair, Bessie," Molloy complained, wiping whisky off his chin. "You're an unfair woman. Vincent Molloy has been as true as a brass saint for the whole of the twenty-six years of his married life, so help me."

"Shall I tell ye what I know?" Bessie challenged him.

"Tell me," Molloy said, hitting the kitchen table bravely. "Tell me all ye know. Call names. Announce facts. I am a man who has given up great ambition for his wife. This is the reward. On an anniversary. For Christ's sweet sake."

"Well, tell me about Rose Bowen," Bessie said, "and Mrs. Sloan, and John Gallagher's wife in the year 1922."

Molloy blushed to his scalp, reddening under the sparse hair. "Lies," he shouted. "I throw it in your face. The miserable stories of church-goin' women. Lies!"

"Mrs. Pilowski. Deny Mrs. Pilowski, the summer I spent in New Jersey." Bessie's hand shook as she lifted her glass to her lips and dashed the whisky off. "Deny her!"

"Here I sit," Molloy said, his eyes full of tears, "my heart flowin' with love after twenty-six years, sittin' here drinkin' with ye the best bottle of whisky money can buy, and ye tell me stories like that. Ye should be ashamed. Ye truly should be ashamed." He drank silently for a moment, then spoke with keen logic, leaning forward over the table, pounding his points home. "Why didn't ye talk in 1922? Why did ye keep quiet when ye came home from New Jersey if there was anythin' afoot? Answer me that!" he thundered.

"For the kids' sake," Bessie said quietly. "For the poor innocent darlings with you for a father." She wept and wiped her nose with an apron that was hanging over one end of the table.

"Shut up," Molloy said. "Keep yer mouth shut. Yer husband's talkin'."

"The sweet children." Bessie put her head down on the table and cried as she thought of them. "The pure-white angels livin' in an air of lust and corruption."

"Are ye talkin' about me?" Molloy stood up, shouting, the cords of his throat standing out red against his collar. "I ask ye, are ye talkin' about me?"

"Their father a man who hasn't seen the insides of a church since the World War. A God-hatin', disbelievin', sinnin' man."

Molloy finished the last of the whisky and sat down uncertainly. "You're an old woman with a bitter tongue. Ye've ruined my life, let me live my last few years in peace."

"A bad example to the little ones. From beginning to end," Bessie wailed, rocking back and forth. "Laughin' at the rules of God an' man, instillin' wild an' sinful thoughts in the minds of the young."

"Name a wild thought," Molloy shouted. "Point out a sinful thought I instilled in the minds of my children. Name them!"

"Bringin' the shame of God on our youngest and dearest . . ."

"Blame that on me?" Molloy screamed. "Do ye lay that at my doorstep? Answer me, do ye?" He stood up, weaving.

"Our little one, Katherine, deceived into lovin' her father . . ."

"Deceived! I warn ye, woman, anniversary or no anniversary . . ."

"Darlin' Katherine, the prettiest and lovingest of them all. Child of my old age. Married to a Protestant." Bessie shook back and forth bitterly, uncontrollably.

Molloy stood speechless, gathering fury, his mouth working back and forth seeking words. He spoke with forced calm, finally. "Do ye say it was my doin', her marryin' that Lutheran? Speak straight, ye drunken grandmother, do ye say it was I put her in the arms of the Protestant?"

"Yes," Bessie shouted. "I say it. Jeerin' and laughin' at the true faith, never settin' foot on the inside of a church, takin' yer shoes off in the parlor when a priest came to visit . . ."

"Do ye mean it?" Molloy asked quietly. "Do ye speak what ye think?"

"Katherine, my daughter, can thank her father today," Bessie said, lifting her head, "that she is married for life to a Protestant."

Molloy shook the bottle to make sure it was empty and broke it over Bessie's head. Blood and a little whisky ran down her face as she rocked gently back and forth twice and slid dumbly to the floor.

"There," Molloy said with satisfaction, sitting down with the remnants of the bottle in his hand, looking soberly at his wife curled up comfortably on the linoleum floor, blood slowly sliding out from under her head like fingers from a hand.

After a while Molloy got up and went to the telephone. "Send me an ambulance," he told the operator and hung up and went back to the kitchen table and put his head on it and went to sleep.

When the ambulance surgeon came in Molloy woke up and watched with interest while the surgeon bandaged his wife's head. Bessie was conscious, but heavy-lidded, and sat on the floor saying nothing.

From time to time as the surgeon worked, Molloy said to the neighbors clustered curiously at the door, "A bottle fell on her. A fine woman. But a bottle fell on her."

When the young doctor got through with her, he looked at her, then doubtfully at Molloy. "I think we better take her to the hospital," he said to the driver. "Come on, let's put her on the stretcher."

The driver started to unroll the stretcher but Molloy stopped him with a grand gesture. "Nothing like that, my lad," he said. "Nothing at all like that. No wife of mine needs be carried out of my house."

"Now look here," the doctor said.

"None of that, my lad," Molloy said. "This is a fine woman here. She'll not be carried out to make a show for all the neighbors. Bessie.

Bessie!" he called, "stand up on yer two legs." He pulled at her under the shoulders and she stood up dazedly. "That's the old lady," Molloy said. "This is a family with stamina. A fine specimen of a woman. Take her away, Doctor."

The ambulance surgeon shook his head and walked Bessie out, supporting her, down the three flights of steps.

Molloy stood at the head of the stairs, watching. When they had disappeared he turned to his neighbors. "A fine woman. A noble specimen. A grandmother. Married twenty-six years today, believe it or not. A proud woman. The prettiest girl in the whole of Brooklyn twenty-six years ago today. Anniversary. I would invite ye all in for a drop to celebrate, but I'm afraid the bottle's gone. A quart's a short measure."

Gravely he went through the door and closed it to the neighbors and sat down at the kitchen table and put his head on it and fell asleep.

STRAWBERRY ICE CREAM SODA

Eddie Barnes looked at the huge Adirondack hills, browning in the strong summer afternoon sun. He listened to his brother Lawrence practice finger-exercises on the piano inside the house, onetwothree-four*five*, onetwothreefour*five*, and longed for New York. He lay on his stomach in the long grass of the front lawn and delicately peeled his sunburned nose. Morosely he regarded a grasshopper, stupid with sun, wavering on a bleached blade of grass in front of his nose. Without interest he put out his hand and captured it.

"Give honey," he said, listlessly. "Give honey or I'll kill yuh . . ."

But the grasshopper crouched unmoving, unresponsive, oblivious to Life or Death.

Disgusted, Eddie tossed the grasshopper away. It flew uncertainly, wheeled, darted back to its blade of grass, alighted and hung there dreamily, shaking a little in the breeze in front of Eddie's nose. Eddie turned over on his back and looked at the high blue sky.

The country! Why anybody ever went to the country . . . What things must be doing in New York now, what rash, beautiful deeds on the steaming, rich streets, what expeditions, what joy, what daring sweaty adventure among the trucks, the trolley cars, the baby-carriages! What cries, hoarse and humorous, what light laughter outside the red-painted shop where lemon ice was sold at three cents the double scoop, true nourishment for a man at fifteen.

Eddie looked around him, at the silent, eternal, granite-streaked hills. Trees and birds, that's all. He sighed, torn with thoughts of distant pleasure, stood up, went over to the window behind which Lawrence seriously hammered at the piano, onetwothreefour*five*.

"Lawrrrence," Eddie called, the rrr's rolling with horrible gentility in his nose, "Lawrrrence, you stink."

Lawrence didn't even look up. His thirteen-year-old fingers, still pudgy and babyish, went onetwothreefour*five*, with unswerving precision. He was talented and he was dedicated to his talent and some day they would wheel a huge piano out onto the stage of Carnegie Hall and he would come out and bow politely to the thunder of applause and sit down, flipping his coat-tails back, and play, and men and women would laugh and cry and remember their first loves as they listened to him. So now his fingers went up and down, up and down, taking strength against the great day.

Eddie looked through the window a moment more, watching his brother, sighed and walked around to the side of the house, where a crow was sleepily eating the radish seeds that Eddie had planted three days ago in a fit of boredom. Eddie threw a stone at the crow and the crow silently flew up to the branch of an oak and waited for Eddie to go away. Eddie threw another stone at the crow. The crow moved to another branch. Eddie wound up and threw a curve, but the crow disdained it. Eddie picked his foot up the way he'd seen Carl Hubbell do and sizzled one across not more than three feet from the crow. Without nervousness the crow walked six inches up the branch. In the style now of Dizzy Dean, with terrifying speed, Eddie delivered his fast one. It was wild and the crow didn't even cock his head. You had to expect to be a little wild with such speed. Eddie found a good round stone and rubbed it professionally on his back pocket. He looked over his shoulder to hold the runner close to the bag, watched for the signal. Eddie Hubbell Dean Mungo Feller Ferrell Warnecke Gomez Barnes picked up his foot and let go his high hard one. The crow slowly got off his branch and regretfully sailed away.

Eddie went over, kicked away the loose dirt, and looked at his radish seeds. Nothing was happening to them. They just lay there, baked and inactive, just as he had placed them. No green, no roots, no radishes, no anything. He was sorry he'd ever gone in for farming. The package of seeds had cost him a dime, and the only thing that happened to them was that they were eaten by crows. And now he could use that dime. Tonight he had a date.

"I got a date," he said aloud, savoring the words. He went to the shade of the grape arbor to think about it. He sat down on the bench under the cool flat leaves, and thought about it. He'd never had a date before in his life. He had thirty-five cents. Thirty-five cents ought to be enough for any girl, but if he hadn't bought the radish seeds, he'd have had forty-five cents, really prepared for any eventuality. "Damn crow," he said, thinking of the evil black head feeding on his dime.

Many times he'd wondered how you managed to get a date. Now he knew. It happened all of a sudden. You went up to a girl where she was lying on the raft in a lake and you looked at her, chubby in a blue bathing suit, and she looked seriously at you out of serious blue eyes where you stood dripping with lake water, with no hair on your chest, and suddenly you said, "I don't s'pose yuh're not doing anything t'morra night, are yuh?" You didn't know quite what you meant, but she did, and she said, "Why, no, Eddie. Say about eight o'clock?" And you nodded and dived back into the lake and there you were.

Still, those radish seeds, that crow-food, that extra dime . . .

Lawrence came out, flexing his fingers, very neat in clean khaki shorts and a white blouse. He sat down next to Eddie in the grape arbor.

"I would like a strawberry ice cream soda," he said.

"Got any money?" Eddie asked, hopefully.

Lawrence shook his head.

"No strawberry ice cream soda," Eddie said.

Lawrence nodded seriously. "You got any money?" he asked.

"Some," Eddie said carefully. He pulled down a grape leaf and cracked it between his hands, held up the two parts and looked at them critically.

Lawrence didn't say anything, but Eddie sensed a feeling developing in the grape arbor, like a growth. "I gotta save my money," Eddie said harshly. "I got a date. I got thirty-five cents. How do I know she won't want a banana-split tonight?"

Lawrence nodded again, indicating that he understood, but sorrow washed up in his face like a high tide.

They sat in silence, uncomfortably, listening to the rustle of the grape leaves.

"All the time I was practicing," Lawrence said, finally, "I kept thinking, 'I would like a strawberry ice cream soda, I would like a strawberry ice cream soda . . .'"

Eddie stood up abruptly. "Aaah, let's get outa here. Let's go down to the lake. Maybe something's doing down the lake."

They walked together through the fields to the lake, not saying anything, Lawrence flexing his fingers mechanically.

"Why don't yuh stop that fer once?" Eddie asked, with distaste. "Just fer once?"

"This is good for my fingers. It keeps them loose."

"Yuh give me a pain."

"All right," Lawrence said, "I won't do it now."

They walked on again, Lawrence barely up to Eddie's chin, frailer, cleaner, his hair mahogany dark and smooth on his high, pink, baby brow. Lawrence whistled. Eddie listened with disguised respect.

"That's not so bad," Eddie said. "You don't whistle half bad."

"That's from the Brahms second piano concerto." Lawrence stopped whistling for a moment. "It's easy to whistle."

"Yuh give me a pain," Eddie said, mechanically, "a real pain."

When they got to the lake, there was nobody there. Flat and unruffled it stretched across, like a filled blue cup, to the woods on the other side.

"Nobody here," Eddie said, staring at the raft, unmoving and dry in the still water. "That's good. Too many people here all the time." His eyes roamed the lake, to the farthest corner, to the deepest cove.

"How would yuh like to go rowing in a boat out in that old lake?" Eddie asked.

"We haven't got a boat," Lawrence answered reasonably.

"I didn't ask yuh that. I asked, 'How'd yuh like to go rowing?'"

"I'd like to go rowing if we had a . . ."

"Shut up!" Eddie took Lawrence's arm, led him through tall grass to the water's edge, where a flat-bottomed old boat was drawn up, the water just lapping at the stern, high, an old red color, faded by sun and storm. A pair of heavy oars lay along the bottom of the boat.

"Jump in," Eddie said, "when I tell yuh to."

"But it doesn't belong to us."

"Yuh want to go rowing, don't yuh?"

"Yes, but . . ."

"Then jump in when I give yuh the word."

Lawrence neatly took off his shoes and socks while Eddie hauled the boat into the water.

"Jump in!" Eddie called.

Lawrence jumped. The boat glided out across the still lake. Eddie rowed industriously once they got out of the marsh grass.

"This isn't half bad, is it?" He leaned back on his oars for a moment.

"It's nice," Lawrence said. "It's very peaceful."

"Aaah," said Eddie, "yuh even talk like a pianist." And he rowed. After a while he got tired and let the boat go with the wind. He lay back and thought of the night to come, dabbling his fingers in the water, happy. "They oughta see me now, back on a Hunnerd and Seventy-third Street," he said. "They oughta see me handle this old boat."

"Everything would be perfect," Lawrence agreed, picking his feet up out of the puddle that was collecting on the bottom of the boat, "if we only knew that when we got out of this boat, we were going to get a strawberry ice cream soda."

"Why don't yuh think of somethin' else? Always thinkin' of one thing! Don't yuh get tired?"

"No," Lawrence said, after thinking it over.

"Here!" Eddie pushed the oars toward his brother. "Row! That'll give yuh somethin' else t' think about."

Lawrence took the oars gingerly. "This is bad for my hands," he explained as he pulled dutifully on the oars. "It stiffens the fingers."

"Look where yuh're goin'!" Eddie cried impatiently. "In circles! What the hell's the sense in goin' in circles?"

"That's the way the boat goes," Lawrence said, pulling hard. "I can't help it if that's the way the boat goes."

"A pianist. A regular pianist. That's all yuh are. Gimme those oars."

Gratefully Lawrence yielded the oars up.

"It's not my fault if the boat goes in circles. That's the way it's made," he persisted quietly.

"Aaah, shut up!" Eddie pulled savagely on the oars. The boat surged forward, foam at the prow.

"Hey, out there in the boat! Hey!" A man's voice called over the water.

"Eddie," Lawrence said, "there's a man yelling at us."

"Come on in here, before I beat your pants off!" the man called. "Get out of my boat!"

"He wants us to get out of his boat," Lawrence interpreted. "This must be his boat."

"You don't mean it," Eddie snorted with deep sarcasm. He turned around to shout at the man on the shore, who was waving his arms now. "All right," Eddie called. "All right. We'll give yuh yer old boat. Keep your shirt on."

The man jumped up and down. "I'll beat yer heads off," he shouted.

Lawrence wiped his nose nervously. "Eddie," he said, "why don't we row over to the other side and walk home from there?"

Eddie looked at his brother contemptuously. "What're yuh—afraid?"

"No," Lawrence said, after a pause. "But why should we get into an argument?"

For answer Eddie pulled all the harder on the oars. The boat flew through the water. Lawrence squinted to look at the rapidly nearing figure of the man on the bank.

"He's a great big man, Eddie," Lawrence reported. "You never saw such a big man. And he looks awfully sore. Maybe we shouldn't've gone out in this boat. Maybe he doesn't like people to go out in his boat. Eddie, are you listening to me?"

With a final heroic pull, Eddie drove the boat into the shore. It grated with a horrible noise on the pebbles of the lake bottom.

"Oh, my God," the man said, "that's the end of that boat."

"That doesn't really hurt it, mister," Lawrence said. "It makes a lot of noise, but it doesn't do any damage."

The man reached over and grabbed Lawrence by the back of his neck with one hand and placed him on solid ground. He was a very big man, with tough bristles that grew all over his double chin and farmer's muscles in his arms that were quivering with passion now under a mat of hair. There was a boy of about thirteen with him, obviously, from his look, his son, and the son was angry, too.

"Hit 'im, Pop," the son kept calling. "Wallop 'im!"

The man shook Lawrence again and again. He was almost too overcome with anger to speak. "No damage, eh? Only noise, eh!" he shouted into Lawrence's paling face. "I'll show you damage. I'll show you noise."

Eddie spoke up. Eddie was out of the boat now, an oar gripped in his hand, ready for the worst. "That's not fair," he said. "Look how much bigger yuh are than him. Why'n't yuh pick on somebody yuh size?"

The farmer's boy jumped up and down in passion, exactly as his father had done. "I'll fight him, Pop! I'll fight 'im! I'm his size! Come on, kid, put yer hands up!"

The farmer looked at his son, looked at Lawrence. Slowly he released Lawrence. "O.K." he said. "Show him, Nathan."

Nathan pushed Lawrence. "Come into the woods, kid," he said belligerently. "We cin settle it there."

"One in the eye," Eddie whispered out of the corner of his mouth. "Give 'im one in the eye, Larry!"

But Lawrence stood with eyes lowered, regarding his hands.

"Well?" the farmer asked.

Lawrence still looked at his hands, opening and closing them slowly.

"He don't wanna fight," Nathan taunted Eddie. "He just wants t' row in our boat, he don't wanna fight."

"He wants to fight, all right," Eddie said staunchly, and under his breath, "Come on, Larry, in the kisser, a fast one in the puss . . ."

But Larry stood still, calmly, seeming to be thinking of Brahms and Beethoven, of distant concert halls.

"He's yella, that's what's the matter with him," Nathan roared. "He's a coward, all city kids're cowards!"

"He's no coward," Eddie insisted, knowing in his deepest heart that his brother was a coward. With his knees he nudged Lawrence. "Bring up yuh left! Please, Larry, bring up yuh left!"

Deaf to all pleas, Lawrence kept his hands at his sides.

"Yella! Yella! Yella!" Nathan screamed loudly.

"Well," the farmer wanted to know, "is he goin' to fight or not?"

"Larry!" Fifteen years of desperation was in Eddie's voice, but it made no mark on Lawrence. Eddie turned slowly toward home. "He's not goin' to fight," he said flatly. And then, as one throws a bone to a neighbor's noisy dog, "Come on, you . . ."

Slowly Lawrence bent over, picked up his shoes and socks, took a step after his brother.

"Wait a minute, you!" the farmer called. He went after Eddie, turned him around. "I want to talk to ye."

"Yeah?" Eddie said sadly, with little defiance. "What do yuh wanna say?"

"See that house over there?" the farmer asked, pointing.

"Yeah," Eddie said. "What about it?"

"That's my house," the farmer said. "You stay away from it. See?"

"O.K. O.K.," Eddie said wearily, all pride gone.

"See that boat there?" the farmer asked, pointing at the source of all the trouble.

"I see it," Eddie said.

"That's my boat. Stay away from it or I'll beat hell outa ye. See?"

"Yeah, yeah, I see," Eddie said. "I won't touch yer lousy boat." And once more, to Lawrence, "Come on, *you*. . . ."

"Yella! Yella! Yella!" Nathan kept roaring, jumping up and down, until they passed out of earshot, across the pleasant fields, ripe with the soft sweet smell of clover in the late summer afternoon. Eddie walked before Lawrence, his face grimly contracted, his mouth curled in shame and bitterness. He stepped on the clover blossoms fiercely, as though he hated them, wanted to destroy them, the roots under them, the very ground they grew in.

Holding his shoes in his hands, his head bent on his chest, his hair still mahogany smooth and mahogany dark, Lawrence followed ten feet back in the footsteps, plainly marked in the clover, of his brother.

"Yella," Eddie was muttering, loud enough for the villain behind him to hear clearly. "Yella! Yella as a flower. My own brother," he marveled. "If it was me I'da been glad to get killed before I let anybody call me that. I would let 'em cut my heart out first. My own brother. Yella as a flower. Just one in the eye! Just *one!* Just to show 'im . . . But he stands there, takin' guff from a kid with holes in his pants. A pianist. Lawrrrrence! They knew what they were doin' when they called yuh Lawrrrrence! Don't talk to me! I don't want yuh ever to talk to me again as long as yuh live! Lawrrrrence!"

In sorrow too deep for tears, the two brothers reached home, ten feet, ten million miles apart.

Without looking around, Eddie went to the grape arbor, stretched out on the bench. Lawrence looked after him, his face pale and still, then went into the house.

Face downward on the bench, close to the rich black earth of the arbor, Eddie bit his fingers to keep the tears back. But he could not bite hard enough, and the tears came, a bitter tide, running down his face, dropping on the black soft earth in which the grapes were rooted.

"Eddie!"

Eddie scrambled around, pushing the tears away with iron hands. Lawrence was standing there, carefully pulling on doeskin gloves over his small hands. "Eddie," Lawrence was saying, stonily disregarding the tears. "I want you to come with me."

Silently, but with singing in his heart so deep it called new tears to his wet eyes, Eddie got up, blew his nose, and followed after his brother, caught up with him, walked side by side with him across the field of clover, so lightly that the red and purple blossoms barely bent in their path.

Eddie knocked sternly at the door of the farm house, three knocks, solid, vigorous, the song of trumpets caught in them.

Nathan opened the door. "What do ye want?" he asked suspiciously.

"A little while ago," Eddie said formally, "yuh offered to fight my brother. He's ready now."

Nathan looked at Lawrence, standing there, straight, his head up, his baby lips compressed into a thin tight line, his gloved hands creased in solid fists. He started to close the door. "He had his chance," Nathan said.

Eddie kept the door open firmly. "Yuh offered, remember that," he reminded Nathan politely.

"He shoulda fought then," Nathan said stubbornly. "He had his chance."

"Come on," Eddie almost begged. "Yuh wanted to fight before."

"That was before. Lemme close the door."

"Yuh can't do this!" Eddie was shouting desperately. "Yuh offered!"

Nathan's father, the farmer, appeared in the doorway. He looked bleakly out. "What's goin' on here?" he asked.

"A little while ago," Eddie spoke very fast, "this man here offered to fight this man here." His eloquent hand indicated first Nathan, then Lawrence. "Now we've come to take the offer."

The farmer looked at his son. "Well?"

"He had his chance," Nathan grumbled sullenly.

"Nathan don't want t' fight," the farmer said to Eddie. "Get outa here."

Lawrence stepped up, over to Nathan. He looked Nathan squarely in the eye. "Yella," he said to Nathan.

The farmer pushed his son outside the door. "Go fight him," he ordered.

"We can settle it in the woods," Lawrence said.

"Wipe him up, Larry!" Eddie called as Lawrence and Nathan set out for the woods, abreast, but a polite five yards apart. Eddie watched them disappear behind trees, in silence.

The farmer sat down heavily on the porch, took out a package of cigarettes, offered them to Eddie. "Want one?"

Eddie looked at the cigarettes, suddenly took one. "Thanks," he said.

The farmer struck a match for the cigarettes, leaned back against a pillar, stretched comfortably, in silence. Eddie licked the tobacco of his first cigarette nervously off his lips.

"Sit down," the farmer said, "ye cin never tell how long kids'll fight."

"Thanks," Eddie said, sitting, pulling daringly at the cigarette, exhaling slowly, with natural talent.

In silence they both looked across the field to the woods that shielded the battlefield. The tops of the trees waved a little in the wind and the afternoon was collecting in deep blue shadows among the thick brown tree-trunks where they gripped the ground. A chicken hawk floated lazily over the field, banking and slipping with the wind. The farmer regarded the chicken hawk without malice.

"Some day," the farmer said, "I'm going to get that son of a gun."

"What is it?" Eddie asked, carefully holding the cigarette out so he could talk.

"Chicken hawk. You're from the city, ain't ye?"

"Yeah."

"Like it in the city?"

"Nothing like it."

The farmer puffed reflectively. "Some day I'm goin' to live in the city. No sense in livin' in the country these days."

"Oh, I don't know," Eddie said. "The country's very nice. There's a lot to be said for the country."

The farmer nodded, weighing the matter in his own mind. He put out his cigarette. "Another cigarette?" he asked Eddie.

"No, thanks," Eddie said, "I'm still working on this."

"Say," said the farmer, "do you think your brother'll damage my kid?"

"It's possible," Eddie said. "He's very tough, my brother. He has dozens a' fights, every month. Every kid back home's scared stiff a' him. Why," said Eddie, sailing full into fancy, "I remember one day, Larry fought three kids all in a row. In a half a hour. He busted all their noses. In a half a hour! He's got a terrific left jab—one, two, bang! like this—and it gets 'em in the nose."

"Well, he can't do Nathan's nose any harm." The farmer laughed. "No matter what you did to a nose like that it'd be a improvement."

"He's got a lot of talent, my brother," Eddie said, proud of the warrior in the woods. "He plays the piano. He's a very good piano-player. You ought to hear him."

"A little kid like that," the farmer marveled. "Nathan can't do nothing."

Off in the distance, in the gloom under the trees, two figures appeared, close together, walked slowly out into the sunlight of the field. Eddie and the farmer stood up. Wearily the two fighters approached, together, their arms dangling at their sides.

Eddie looked first at Nathan. Nathan's mouth had been bleeding and there was a lump on his forehead and his ear was red. Eddie smiled with satisfaction. Nathan had been in a fight. Eddie walked slowly toward Lawrence. Lawrence approached with head high. But it was a sadly battered head. The hair was tangled, an eye was closed, the nose was bruised and still bled. Lawrence sucked in the blood from his nose from time to time with his tongue. His collar was torn, his pants covered with forest loam, with his bare knees skinned and raw. But in the one eye that still could be seen shone a clear light, honorable, indomitable.

"Ready to go home now, Eddie?" Lawrence asked.

"Sure." Eddie started to pat Lawrence on the back, pulled his hand back. He turned and waved at the farmer. "So long."

"So long," the farmer called. "Any time you want to use the boat, just step into it."

"Thanks." Eddie waited while Lawrence shook hands gravely with Nathan.

"Good night," Lawrence said. "It was a good fight."

"Yeah," Nathan said.

The two brothers walked away, close together, across the field of clover, fragrant in the long shadows. Half the way they walked in silence, the silence of equals, strong men communicating in a language more eloquent than words, the only sound the thin jingle of the thirty-five cents in Eddie's pocket.

Suddenly Eddie stopped Lawrence. "Let's go this way," he said, pointing off to the right.

"But home's this way, Eddie."

"I know. Let's go into town. Let's get ice cream sodas," Eddie said; "let's get strawberry ice cream sodas."

THE BOSS

THE GOLDSTEINS had a tailor-shop in the basement of our house. The windows of the shop were half above street-level and in all weathers the steam from Mr. Goldstein's press poured out in a thin, hissing vapor.

The Goldsteins were our landlords. Mrs. Goldstein made desperate arrangements with innumerable mortgages and loans and kept at least a nominal title to the house, although she hadn't a cent of her own invested in it. Mrs. Goldstein collected the rents with the conscious pride of a landowner. She was a short, dark woman with black, greedy eyes and an erect figure and her rents were the most punctually collected on all that block of ten-family, cold-flat buildings. Her voice was sharp and shrewd—and woe to that family that did not have its rent ready by the third of the month. Its infamy was proclaimed in piercing oratory throughout the house and its shame kept eloquently alive until Mrs. Goldstein's just dues had been paid.

Mrs. Goldstein also ran the tailor-shop. She called for and delivered the clothes. She made the estimates, paid the bills and collected the money. When a customer asked Mr. Goldstein about the price of a piece of work, he would shrug his fat shoulders, turn back to his machine, and say, "Speak to my wife."

My father used to say that Mr. Goldstein reminded him of the donkeys they had going round and round turning the flour mill in the old country, except that Mr. Goldstein was fatter and wasn't treated as well.

Mr. Goldstein was a tremendous man. He had an enormous bloated belly that he carried the way a man carries a heavy basket held in front of him. He leaned back and balanced his belly on stubby little legs that sometimes seemed to tremble under the load. He had no neck—and when he worked over his steaming press the sweat rolled right down the round, smooth sides of his face into his shirt and stained it greasily. There was something blank and inhuman about Mr. Goldstein's face— as though all thought and emotion were hidden deep under the fat and found it impossible to struggle to the surface where they might be seen. His face moved with slow, deliberate shakings, like a drunkard's legs, and was almost always set in the same apathetic expression of nothing at all. His emotional exercise seemed to be confined to scream- ing heavily at us brats when we scrambled in the yard back of his flat in our games.

One night he chased me ponderously and I climbed up the tall clothes-pole that rose three stories from his yard. He stood at the bottom, calling me names in guttural Yiddish, and shaking the pole. I clung to it like a treed cat while it waved crazily in the dark yard. I remember that I was surprised to see Mr. Goldstein actually getting angry and thereby proclaiming his kinship with the rest of humanity.

He used to work over his press until late at night, drinking incredible quantities of soda-water, belching from the gas in the soda, his face steaming, his hands damp with sweat. He drank out of the bottles them- selves, tall thick bottles that he put in a line on his window sill, from where we would try to steal them and collect the nickel deposit from the drugstore on the corner.

When Mrs. Goldstein was in evidence, we conducted no raids on the row of bottles. Money was the one thing sacred in Mrs. Goldstein's religion of materialism—and a nickel was money. A penny was money. If ever she discovered the identity of the young hoodlum who had snatched one of the bottles, she would make a belligerent excursion to the parents of the thief and cast darkling curses upon the seed of the house that bore one so unmistakably destined for a dishonorable end.

We were all more than a little afraid of Mrs. Goldstein. And not only the children. Customers were afraid of bargaining with her about prices—this in a civilization in which bargaining was second nature and a characteristic as carefully bred as speed in thoroughbreds. Tenants went without food for themselves and charcoal for their stove fires to forestall Mrs. Goldstein's dread malediction on ghetto-scum that did not pay its rent on time. She dressed her table for less than any other woman on the block because the market people fought only half- heartedly against her savage haggling.

The light of a Cause burnt intensely in Mrs. Goldstein's eyes—and like other persons with a Cause that is bigger than they, she had her way with people. Money was Mrs. Goldstein's Cause—but it meant as much to her as France did to Joan of Arc and God did to Saint Francis of Assisi.

The tailor-shop did not supply enough money to please Mrs. Goldstein. My father used to say that Mrs. Goldstein wouldn't be satisfied if the Czar turned over the Crown Jewels to her and old man Rockefeller made her his sole heir. Seeking for new fields to conquer, she undertook to run a poultry stand in the market three blocks away. She didn't tell Mr. Goldstein about her new business until the day before she was to move in. She hardly ever talked to him, anyway, and her opinion of her husband was expressed in the description of him she gave her neighbors, "Mendel is a good tailor—but he is a shlemiel."

Joe Goldstein was one of my partners in vice and much of my information about the Goldstein family came from his ready and slightly moronic lips. He told me about Mrs. Goldstein's announcement of her venture.

"Mendel," she said while he was sitting at his sewing machine, "I'm going into business."

Mr. Goldstein didn't say anything. But the sewing machine stopped —evidence of great emotional stress deep within Mr. Goldstein.

"When?" Mr. Goldstein didn't turn around—so that his wife talked to his back. He probably would have turned around if he had thought of it.

"Tomorrow," Mrs. Goldstein answered, the wild light of her Cause flaring in her eyes. "I signed a lease with Schwartz today. Ten dollars I paid him and I pay him twenty-five dollars at the end of the month. I get the poultry without paying until the end of the week. A good place I got in the market."

Mr. Goldstein nodded slowly. An idea oozed up to his tongue and he asked, "Why did you do it?"

Mrs. Goldstein shook her head impatiently. "To make money, fool."

Mr. Goldstein puzzled over this for a while. "Why?" he finally wanted to know. "Don't we make enough money?"

Mrs. Goldstein tapped her foot intolerantly. "You can never make enough money."

Mr. Goldstein shrugged and started to work his machine again. Suddenly another thought jumped into his mind to worry him. He even turned around to talk to Mrs. Goldstein now. "You won't be able to take care of the tailor-shop," he explained to her. "You'll be busy at the market."

"Yes, I'll be busy at the market."

"Then I'll be alone in the shop?" Mr. Goldstein's fat brow was creased in worriment.

"So? Are you a grown man or aren't you? Do I have to be afraid to leave you to run a tailor-shop? Ah—you are a fool, Mendel." And Mrs. Goldstein went back into the house.

Mr. Goldstein sat where he was for a few moments, shook his head heavily, and very slowly turned back to his sewing machine.

Mrs. Goldstein took up her stand in the H. and W. market and prospered exceedingly. Money was her natural element and profit her inevitable due. She worked long and hard, bullied her customers, insulted her competitors, ruthlessly cut the bills she owed her creditors, and in all ways conducted her business in the manner approved alike by Pennsylvania Avenue and Wall Street. In two weeks she was making more with her poultry than the tailor-shop had ever made.

Not a feather was wasted, not a penny lost at Mrs. Goldstein's stand. The quick-fingered women who walked the market collecting in their voluminous shawls the unwilling largesse of the merchants, avoided Mrs. Goldstein's stand. The other merchants, noticing the stealthy swells under the shawls, would shrug and say, half with irritation, half with pity, "Ah! There is Mrs. Cohen again. She is a thief and that is without doubt one of my best cabbages under her arm—but her poor Samuel has not brought home ten pennies this month and her stringy children look like walking Death and the loss of a cabbage will not ruin me, anyway. The world is a hard place for the poor."

But in Mrs. Goldstein's cult of wealth there was no place for charity to thieves. Her quick eyes noted everything and she would sally out from behind her counter with shrill imprecations and wrest the hidden fowl from the loudly protesting Mrs. Cohen.

"Thief!" Mrs. Goldstein would scream. "Daughter of a bitch! Scavenger! Garbage louse! Stealing the wares of honest women! You should sit in shame for a week on the floor of your house for your sinfulness. You should be denied the light of day and the smiles of your children. You should be forbidden the market and the greetings of your friends— for robbery is the most foul of abominations." And she would toss the disputed rooster into the bin with a triumphant flourish.

Mrs. Goldstein made money—but the tailor-shop suffered. She no longer scoured the neighborhood for suits to be cleaned and pressed and mended. She no longer was able to fix generous prices and maintain them by the ferocity of her arguments. Business fell off.

Mr. Goldstein was now a rudderless hulk on the stern seas of Hebraic commerce. When a customer came in and threw a suit down on the counter and asked, "Well, Mr. Goldstein, it will cost how much?" Mr. Goldstein would look steadily at the suit for almost five minutes, move his shoulders in jelly-like quakings of helplessness, out of habit look into the back room for the efficient shrewdness of his wife, and finally shrug and say, "I don't know. Maybe you should come back later when Mrs. Goldstein will be here."

But usually the customer scented victory and pressed his advantage. "I'm in a hurry," he would say. "My brother's daughter is getting married tomorrow night and it is a matter of life and death I should have this suit. I'll give you—say"—craftily—"seventy-five cents." The customer would know that it should be at least twice as much—but there's no harm in trying, as he would after explain triumphantly to his family. Jews are a merciful and charitable folk and would spare their worst enemies if they found them lying helpless on a battlefield—but business is business and the devil takes the hindmost when coins clink on the counter.

Vaguely in Mr. Goldstein a latent heritage would warn him that seventy-five cents was not enough—but he was glad to be left alone and he would nod his head and turn back to his press, feeling that if Mrs. Goldstein were there things would be different. Late at night, when Mrs. Goldstein came home from the market, she would berate him for his ineptitude. "Lunatic," she would scream at him, while her tenants called down at her to keep quiet and let them sleep, "the rats have done away with your brains! You will be pressing suits for charity, next! Seventy-five cents! I would die first before I gave him a new lining and pressed the suit for seventy-five cents! You are an old woman, Mendel, and I should get someone to take care of you!"

Mr. Goldstein became more and more hesitant in making estimates. One day when I went in to the shop with a suit of my father's that needed mending, he stared at it for a while and said, "Bring it in tonight. Maybe my wife will be here."

"My father needs it by six o'clock," I said, according to instructions from my mother.

Suddenly, Mr. Goldstein rose, a large pair of shears grasped in his hand. "Go away!" he shouted at me. "Go away! Keep out of my store! I don't want you here!" And he waved the shears in his immense pudgy hand and I was glad to be able to run out of the store with my head still on my skinny neck. From then on we had our tailoring done on the next block.

It was not long before Mr. Goldstein's trade had fallen off very con-

siderably. At night when we came in from our games we would see a
strange sight—Mr. Goldstein at the window of his shop reading the
Bible by a single lamp, the inevitable soda-bottles ranged before him,
the press unbelievably at rest and sending no steam into the street. Mr.
Goldstein seemed to be brooding on something.

One day he appeared at his wife's poultry stand. Before Mrs. Goldstein was aware of his arrival, he took out a chair, carried it to the
rear of the counter and firmly sat himself down. Mrs. Goldstein
marched over to him.

"Well, Mendel?" she demanded.

"I have come here," he told her.

"Yes?"

"I am no more going to stay in the tailor-shop," he said. "I cannot
stay there without you. People come in and ask me questions."

Mrs. Goldstein pulled at his shirt. "Go home, Mendel! You are an
idiot! You should have a skirt to wear and a bottle to suck at! Go home
to your business and don't let me see your face here any more!"

Mr. Goldstein went home weeping bitterly. "Ida, Ida," he repeated
over and over. "I cannot go home without you. Ida!"

But the next week he went to the poultry stand and remained there.
He wouldn't move—and Mrs. Goldstein wasn't strong enough to pull
him home. Anyway, as she told her customers, her Sophie was getting
old enough now to think of getting married and it didn't look nice to
have a tailor-shop in the parlor. She sold the press and the sewing
machine and bought new furniture for Sophie's young men to loll on.

Mr. Goldstein swept the floor around the stand every morning and
sat the day through in the rear, plucking chickens in the circle of old
women who, knee-deep in feathers, plucked chickens for Mrs. Goldstein's customers at a nickel a piece. It was the clearing-house for the
neighborhood's gossip—but whether or not any of it made an impression
on Mr. Goldstein was hard to discern. Absolutely wordless, he sat on
his rickety, backless chair, methodically yanking feathers, the old
women hunched in their ragged shawls like feathery witches around
him.

When they got used to his presence they began to chide him. "Bubbe
Mendel" they called him—Grandmama Mendel—and asked him if he
wanted a lace cap for his head. They wanted to know if Mrs. Goldstein
gave him her skirt and wore his pants at home. They took to calling
Mrs. Goldstein "Boss" and found cruel delight in saying to Mr. Goldstein that "his boss" wanted him to go home and stir the soup. Mr.

Goldstein sat stolidly through it all and plucked chickens. And brooded.

Finally they taunted him with reports of Mrs. Goldstein's amours. Mrs. Goldstein was a lusty woman—not yet forty, full-bosomed, fruity-hipped, roving-eyed. My father once said that all the Czar's Cossacks in one bed wouldn't be enough to keep Mrs. Goldstein happy for one night—and he laughed when my mother told him not to say things like that before the children.

"Mendel," one of the witches said to Mr. Goldstein one morning, "have you seen the young man Mrs. Goldstein was out *walking* with last night?"

All the hags tittered. Mr. Goldstein went on with his work.

"Isaac Stern, his name is," the old woman offered slyly. "A fine young man he is—nicer even than the other young men Mrs. Goldstein goes walking with at night."

The hags cackled again.

"He's a box-fighter," she went on. "A big, tall, fine man. Curled hair he's got—and blue eyes—and his ears lay close to his head. His lips are red like cherries in summer and soft and wet. And his arms are tough like a whip-handle and he picks Ida up with one hand and carries her around. His back is broad and his legs are long and straight and his belly is flat—not round and fat like yours so you can't get near a woman. *He* can get near a woman all right!"

All the old women stopped their plucking to laugh and laugh.

Mrs. Goldstein called sharply from the counter, "Mendel!"

"Your boss wants you, Mrs. Mendel." The old hag chuckled in toothless merriment and prodded him with her crooked, scaly finger.

Mr. Goldstein methodically put down the half-plucked fowl he was working on and shuffled over to his wife with the witches' chorus ringing in his ears.

That night I saw Mr. Goldstein at his window as I dove out of the house. It was Friday night—the appointed time for the rat-hunting excursions the youth of the block conducted in the fastnesses of the ice-warehouse across the street. I was in a hurry—but I saw that although the Bible was as usual open before him, Mr. Goldstein was not reading. He seemed to be staring down the street. There were no more bottles of soda, either—ever since he had moved into his wife's stand, Mr. Goldstein had drunk water. The rows of empty bottles, last symbol of his domination in his family, were gone.

The rat hunt was a successful one. It was nearly eleven when we parted with the same rugged masculine joy that lightens the hearts of hunters who have bagged the limit for the day.

I straggled across the street and saw Mr. Goldstein sitting on the steps in front of our house. Sitting down, he looked as though his knees came directly out of his ballooning stomach, without the usual human go-between of thighs. At the end of the street I saw Mrs. Goldstein taking leave of some man or other. It was nothing unusual. I had not yet reached the age of intelligent scandal and I didn't bother to find out who it was this time. Mr. Goldstein obviously saw them, too. He stood up (a tremendous process—hoisting all that belly up into a position in which it could be carried from place to place). He stared at the corner and turned and went into the house.

I sat down on the steps to cool off before I went upstairs and nodded to Mrs. Goldstein when she passed me on her way into the house. I could hardly help looking in to the Goldsteins' flat—and I didn't bother to avert my eyes. Such niceties are not bred in the ghetto.

Mr. Goldstein was sitting facing the door. Sophie and her young man were plumped stiffly on the sofa, earnestly wishing Mr. Goldstein out of the room. When the door opened and Mrs. Goldstein came in, Sophie's young man rose and greeted her. Mr. Goldstein just sat and stared at her. His face, as usual, expressed nothing. Pain, fear, love, hope, anger, washed over Mr. Goldstein's face invisibly for the most part. There was too much flesh there to be moved by mere impulses of the mind.

Mrs. Goldstein was laughing with Sophie and her young man, ignoring her husband. Everybody in the Goldstein family ignored Mr. Goldstein when there was somebody else present. Mr. Goldstein rose slowly and enormously from his chair.

"Whore," he said deliberately.

The other three stood frozen between their phrases.

"Bitch," Mr. Goldstein went on in measured Yiddish with the same deliberation. "You come in here stinking from your lust, foul with your whoring. There is filth in your blood and you make a stench in the nostrils of Heaven. I sweep the floors of your business and take the nickels of your customers—I live on your money and eat of your food— I cannot feed the riot of your lust—but I am your husband and the master of your household. The master of your household, whore! Always must the man be the head of the house—and so shall it be here! You deceive me with tramps from the street because you think that you're the boss, because you think no more I wear the pants in your house! Witch! I wear the pants in this house!" Mr. Goldstein lapsed into English from his rehearsed Yiddish—and shouted, "I'm de boss! *I*'m de boss! Do you hear, you dirty whore, *I'm de boss!*"

Then he started throwing things at her. He threw a lamp, his Bible, a cigarette box, anything he could lay his hands on. She ran around the room screaming and wailing. Sophie's young man, after dodging the cigarette box, picked up his hat and scuttled out into the street. Sophie followed her father imploring him to stop. There were shouts, wails, curses, the sound of shattering glassware and overturned furniture shaking the floor. The noise was terrible.

Grimly Mr. Goldstein pursued his vengeance. He tore the legs out of the table and threw them at Mrs. Goldstein. He was clumsy and he threw things the way a woman does—from his elbow—but there was nothing comical about him. He moved with deadly intensity. He ripped the sofa apart and the stuffing flew all over the floor. He broke a bridge lamp in two. He went inside and pulled down the china closet and kicked the shattered plates around. He pulled out the electrical fixtures from the wall and dashed the bulbs to the floor with reports like gunshots. He took a knife and slashed the wallpaper into shreds. He took eggs and milk out of the icebox and spattered them against the walls. He tore books in half and strewed them on the floor. He ripped Joey's violin from its case and splintered it against the wall and stabbed at Mrs. Goldstein with the torn fret. Whenever he could he fetched Mrs. Goldstein a blow with whatever he had in his hand. Then she'd bawl horribly and Sophie would whine, "Papa, Papa!" and he would grunt, "Bitch!" He threw bottles at her and she shrieked in terror while the broken glass clattered about her. And all the time he kept up a constant stream of dreadful curses in Yiddish and shouted again and again, "I'm de boss! *I'm de boss!*"

Finally Sophie dragged Mrs. Goldstein out of the house. They ran down the street past me. Mr. Goldstein stopped his work of destruction. He was ankle-deep in upholstery and torn wallpaper. Egg yolk had dried in his hair and there were pieces of eggshell tangled in his hair. Blood was dripping from his hand onto a piece of paper at his feet. Bits of china were strewn throughout the room. There was no expression on Mr. Goldstein's face. There was only one electric bulb, high up, that was still working, and it cast a dull and squalid light on the destroyed room.

"Whore," he kept saying to himself. "Whore. I'm de boss."

Two hours later when they came and took him to the Kings County asylum, he went docilely, saying, "I'm de boss."

LITTLE HENRY IRVING

THE DICE ROLLED like cavalry across the concrete floor of the academy basement.

"Eight's the point," Eddie said, pulling at the high collar of his cadet's uniform. "Eight, baby, come eight, oh, you eight." He stood up with a grin, dusting the knife-creases at his knees. "Read them," he said.

The Custodian shook his head and sat down backward. "I might just as well lay down and die. On Christmas. How can a man be as unlucky as me on Christmas?"

"Roll for the pot," Eddie offered seductively.

"My better nature says no," the Custodian said.

"Roll you for the pot."

"If I lose I'm cleaned. I won't even be able to buy a pint of beer for my throat on Christmas."

"O.K.," Eddie said offhandedly, starting to rake in the silver, "if you want to quit, losing . . ."

"Roll for the pot," the Custodian said grimly. He put out his last dollar-twenty with the desperate calm of a man signing his will. "Go ahead, Diamond Jim."

Eddie cooed to the dice, held warm and cozy in his hands, and rocked soothingly back and forth on his skinny knees. "The moment has come," he cried softly into his hands. "Little sweethearts . . ."

"Roll!" the Custodian cried irritably. "No poetry!"

"Four and three, five and two, six and one," Eddie coaxed into his hands. "That's all I ask."

"Roll!" the Custodian yelled.

Delicately Eddie spun the dice along the cold hard floor. They stopped like lovers, nestling together against Fate. "Do we read seven?" Eddie asked gently.

"On Christmas!" the Custodian said despairingly.

Eddie carefully counted and sorted his money. "You put up a good fight," he said comfortingly to the Custodian.

"Yeah," the Custodian muttered. "Oh, yeah. A kid like you. Say, how old *are* you, anyway, a million?"

"I am thirteen years old," Eddie said, pocketing the last coins. "But I come from New York."

"You ought to be home with your family. On Christmas. A kid like you. I wish to hell you was home with yer family!"

"In Connecticut," Eddie said, pulling his skimpy uniform jacket down, "nobody knows anything about crap. I'm telling you for your own good."

"You ought to be home with yer family," the Custodian insisted.

A veil of tears came suddenly over Eddie's large dark eyes. "My Pop told me he don't want to see me for a year."

"What'd ye do?" the Custodian asked. "Win his pants from him last Christmas?"

Eddie blew his nose and the tears left his eyes. "I hit my sister with a lamp. A bridge lamp." His mouth tightened in retrospect. "I would do it again. Her name's Diana. She's fifteen years old."

"That's nice," the Custodian said. "You're a fine little boy, all around."

"It took four stitches. She cried for five hours. *Diana!* She said I mighta ruined her beauty."

"Well, it wouldn't do her beauty no good, hitting her with a bridge lamp," the Custodian said reasonably.

"She's going to be an actress. A stage actress."

"That's nice for a girl," the Custodian said.

"Aaah," Eddie snorted. "What's nice about it? She takes lessons from dancing teachers and French teachers and English teachers and horse-back teachers and music teachers and Pop is always kissin' her and callin' her his little Bernhardt. She stinks."

"That's no way to talk about yer sister," the Custodian said sternly. "I won't listen to a little boy talkin' like that about his sister."

"Aaah, shut up!" Eddie said bitterly. "Little Bernhardt. Pop's an actor, too. The whole damn family's actors. Except me," he said with somber satisfaction.

"You're a crap player," the Custodian said. "You got nothing to worry about."

"Little Bernhardt. Pop takes her with him all over the country. Detroit, Dallas, St. Louis, Hollywood."

"Hollywood!"

"Me they send to Military Academy."

"Military Academy is good for young minds," the Custodian said loyally.

"Aaah," Eddie said. "Little Bernhardt. I would like to step on her face."

"That's no way to talk."

"She goes in three times a week to see my Pop act. My Pop can act better than anybody since Sir Henry Irving."

"Who says so?" the Custodian wanted to know.

"My Pop," Eddie said. "He's a Polack, my Pop. He's got feeling. Real feeling. Everybody says my Pop's got feeling. You oughta see him act."

"I only go to the movies," the Custodian said.

"He's actin' in *The Merchant of Venice*. With a long white beard, you'd never know it was my Pop. When he talks people laugh and cry in the audience. You can hear my Pop's voice for five blocks, I bet."

"That's the kind of actin' I like," the Custodian said.

Eddie threw out his arm in a tragic, pleading gesture. "Hath not a Jew eyes?" he demanded in tones of thunder. "Hath not a Jew hands, organs, dimensions, senses, affections, passions? Like that, that's the way my Pop does it." He sat down slowly on an upturned box. "It's the most beautiful thing in the world, the way my Pop does it," he said softly.

"You shouldn't've hit yer sister with a bridge lamp," the Custodian said morally. "Then you could've been seein' him act tonight."

"He smacked me for fifteen minutes, my Pop. He weighs two hundred and fifteen pounds an' he's built like Lou Gehrig, my Pop, like a truckhorse, an' he was swingin' from his heels, but I didn't cry an' I didn't tell him why I hit her with a bridge lamp. I didn't cry one tear. I showed him. His little Bernhardt." Eddie got up with determination. "What the hell, I might just as well spend Christmas in a Military Academy as any place else." He started out into the bleak December afternoon.

"Lissen, Eddie," the Custodian said hurriedly, before Eddie could get through the door, "I wanna ask you a question."

"What?" Eddie asked coldly, sensing what was coming.

"It's Christmas Eve," the Custodian said, preparation in his voice.

"All right," Eddie said, "it's Christmas Eve."

"I'm an old man." The Custodian brushed his white mustache pitifully. "I'm an old man without kith or kin."

"All right," Eddie said.

"Usually on Christmas, Eddie, I buy myself a little pint of something,
applejack usually, and I warm my old heart in a corner to forget that
I'm deserted by the world. When you get older you'll know what I
mean."

"Yeah," Eddie said.

"This year," the Custodian shifted uneasily, "this year you happen
to've won all my money. Now, I was wonderin', if you would . . ."

"No," Eddie said, starting out.

"On Christmas Eve, for an old man, Eddie."

"You lost," Eddie said without heat. "I won. O.K."

He left and the Custodian settled down in his carpet-seated rocker
next the furnace. The Custodian rocked mournfully back and forth
and shook his head as he watched Eddie go up the cellar steps out into
the gray afternoon.

Eddie shambled aimlessly around the winter-bare school grounds.
"Military School! Aaah!" he said to himself. He should be home in
New York City, blazing with lights, green and red and white lights,
filled with people hurrying happily through the streets with packages
done up in colored ribbon, and Santa Clauses ringing their little bells
on the street corner for the Salvation Army and the thousand movie
houses gaping invitingly along the sidewalks. He should go watch Pop
act tonight and go to dinner with him afterwards on Second Avenue,
and eat duck and potato pancakes and drink spiced wine and go home
and listen to Pop sing German songs at the top of his voice, accompanying himself on the piano loudly, until the neighbors complained to the
police.

He sighed. Here he was, stuck at a Military Academy in Connecticut,
because he was a bad boy. Ever since his sixth birthday he'd been
known as a bad boy. He'd had a party on his sixth birthday and he'd
had a fine time, with cake, candy, ice cream and bicycles, until his
sister Diana had come into the middle of the room and done a scene
from *As You Like It* that her English teacher had coached her in. "All
the world's a stage," she'd piped in her imitation Boston accent that
the English teacher gave her, "and all the men and women in't merely
playahs . . ." At the end of it everybody shouted "Bravo!" and Pop
grabbed her and swung her up and cried on her blonde hair and said
over and over again, "Little Bernhardt, my little Bernhardt!"

Eddie had thrown a plate of ice cream at her and it had spattered all over Pop and Diana had cried for two hours and he'd been spanked and sent to bed.

"I hate Connecticut," he said to a leafless elm, leaning coldly over the dirty snow on the side of the walk.

Since then he had thrown Diana off a porch, tearing ligaments in her arm; he had run away in a rowboat off the coast of New Jersey and had had to be rescued by the Coast Guard at ten o'clock at night; he had played truant from seven different private and public schools, he had been caught coming out of burlesque houses with older friends; he had disobeyed his father on every possible occasion, and had been beaten three times to the month, standing there proud and stubborn, conscious in those moments at last, as Pop stood over him angry and terrible, that, actor or no actor, he was getting some attention, some evidence of paternal love.

He leaned against a tree and closed his eyes. He was in his Pop's dressing room at the theatre and Pop was in his silk bathrobe with pieces of beard stuck here and there over his face and his hair gray with powder. Beautiful women with furs came in, talking and laughing in their womanly musical voices and Pop said, "This is my son, Eddie. He is a little Henry Irving," and the women cried with delight and took him in their arms, among the scented furs and kissed him, their lips cool from the winter outside on his warm red face. And Pop beamed and patted his behind kindly and said, "Eddie, you do not have to go to Military School any longer and you don't have to spend Christmas with your aunt in Duluth, either. You are going to spend Christmas in New York alone with me. Go to the box office and get a ticket for tonight's performance, Row A, center. 'Hath not a Jew eyes? Hath not a Jew hands, organs . . .' Yes, Pop, yes, Pop, yes . . ."

Eddie blinked his eyes and looked around him at the mean wood walls of the Academy. Prison, prison. "I wish you burn," he said with utter hate to the peeling paint and the dead ivy and the ramshackle bell tower. "Burn! *Burn!*"

Abruptly he became quiet. His eyes narrowed and the cast of thought came over his face beneath the stiff short visor of his military cap. He regarded the dreary buildings intently, his lips moving silently over deep unmentionable thoughts, the expression on his face a hunter's expression, marking down prey for the kill far off in the tangled jungle.

If the school burned down he couldn't sleep in the December woods, could he, they would have to send him home, wouldn't they, and if he was rescued from the burning building Pop would be so grateful that his son was not dead that . . . The school would have to burn down completely and they would never send him back and fire burns from the bottom up and the bottom was the cellar and the only person there was the Custodian, sitting lonely there, longing for his Christmas bottle . . .

With a sharp involuntary sigh, Eddie wheeled swiftly and walked toward the cellar entrance, to seize the moment.

"Lissen," he said to the Custodian, rocking mournfully back and forth next to the furnace. "Lissen, I feel sorry for yuh."

"Yeah," the Custodian said hopelessly. "I can see it."

"I swear. An old man like you. All alone on Christmas Eve. Nothin' to comfort yuh. That's terrible."

"Yeah," the Custodian agreed. "Yeah."

"Not even a single drink to warm yuh up."

"Not a drink. On Christmas!" The Custodian rocked bitterly back and forth. "I might as well lay down and die."

"I got a change of heart," Eddie said deliberately. "How much does a bottle of applejack cost?"

"Well," the Custodian said craftily, "there's applejack and applejack."

"The cheapest applejack," Eddie said sternly. "Who do you think I am?"

"You can get a first-rate bottle of applejack for ninety-five cents, Eddie," the Custodian said in haste. "I would take that kindly. That's a thoughtful deed for an old man in the holiday season."

Eddie slowly assorted ninety-five cents out in his pocket. "Understand," he said, "this ain't a usual thing."

"Of course not, Eddie," the Custodian said quickly. "I wouldn't expect . . ."

"I won it honest," Eddie insisted.

"Sure, Eddie."

"But on Christmas . . ."

"Sure, just on Christmas . . ." The Custodian was on the edge of his rocker now, leaning forward, his mouth open, his tongue licking at the corners of his lips.

Eddie put out his hand with the coins in it. "Ninety-five cents," he said. "Take it or leave it."

The Custodian's hand trembled as he took the money. "You got a good heart, Eddie," he said simply. "You don't look it, but you got a good heart."

"I would go get it for you myself," Eddie said, "only I got to write my father a letter."

"That's all right, Eddie, my boy, perfectly all right. I'll take a little walk into town myself." The Custodian laughed nervously. "The clear air. Pick me up. Thank you, Eddie, you're one of the best."

"Well," Eddie said, starting out. "Merry Christmas."

"Merry Christmas," the Custodian said heartily. "Merry Christmas, my boy, *and* a happy New Year."

And he sang "I saw three ships go sailing by, go sailing by," as Eddie went up the cellar steps.

Five hours later Eddie walked down Forty-fifth Street, in New York City, without an overcoat, shivering in the cold, but happy. He marched across from the Grand Central Station through the good-natured holiday crowds, reciting gayly to the lights, the neon signs, the bluecoated policemen, "If you prick us, do we not bleed? if you tickle us, do we not laugh? if you poison us, do we not die?" He crossed Sixth Avenue, turned into the stage-entrance alley of the theater over which the huge sign read in electric bulbs, *The Merchant of Venice* by William Shakespeare. "And if you wrong us, shall we not revenge?" he shouted thickly at the alley walls, as he opened the stage door and ran upstairs to his father's dressing room.

The door was open and his father was sitting at his make-up table, applying grease and false hair carefully, close to the mirror. Eddie sidled in softly.

"Pop," he said, standing at the door. Then again, "Pop."

"Uh." His father touched up an eyebrow with a comb, making it bush out.

"Pop," Eddie said. "It's me."

His father soberly put down the grease-stick, the small comb, the false hair, and turned around.

"Eddie," he said.

"Merry Christmas, Pop," Eddie said, smiling nervously.

"What're you doing here, Eddie?" His father looked him straight and seriously in the eye.

"I'm home, Pop," Eddie said quickly. "I'm home for Christmas."

"I am paying that money-grabbing military academy forty-five dollars extra to keep you there and you tell me you are home for Christmas!" The great voice boomed out with the passion and depth that made audiences of fifteen hundred souls shiver in their seats. "A telephone! I want a telephone! Frederick!" he called for his dresser. "Frederick, by God Almighty, a telephone!"

"But, Pop . . ." Eddie said.

"I will talk to those miserable toy soldiers, those uniformed school-ma'ams! Frederick, in the name of God!"

"Pop, Pop," Eddie wailed. "You can't call them."

His father stood up to his six-foot-three magnificence in his red-silk dressing-gown and looked down on Eddie, one eyebrow high with mockery on the huge domed forehead. "I can't call them, my son says. Little snot-nose tells me what to do and what not to do."

"You can't call, Pop," Eddie yelled, "because there's nothing to talk to. See?"

"Oh," his father said, with searing irony, "the school has disappeared. Poof! and off it goes. The Arabian Nights. In Connecticut."

"That's why I'm here, Pop," Eddie pleaded rapidly. "There ain't no more school. It burned. It burned right down to the ground. This afternoon. Look, even my overcoat. Look, I don't have an overcoat."

His father stood silent, regarding him soberly through the deep-set cold gray eyes under the famous gray brows. One of the famous long thick fingers beat slowly, like the pendulum of doom, on the dressing table, as he listened to his son, standing there, chapped by exposure, in his tight uniform, talking fast, shifting from one foot to another.

"See, Pop, it burned down, I swear to God, you can ask anyone, I was lying in my bed writing a letter and the firemen got me, you can ask them, and there wasn't no place for them to put me and they gave me money for the train and . . . I'll stay here with you, Pop, eh, Pop, for Christmas, what do you say, Pop?" Pleading, pleading . . . His voice broke off under his father's steady unrelenting stare. He stood silent, pleading with his face, his eyes, the twist of his mouth, with his cold, chapped hands. His father moved majestically over to him, raised his hand, and slapped him across the face.

Eddie stood there, his face quivering, but no tears. "Pop," he said, controlling his voice as best he could. "Pop, what're you hitting me for? It ain't my fault. The school burned down, Pop."

"If the school burned down," his father said in measured tones, "and you were there, it was your fault. Frederick," he said to his dresser, who was standing in the doorway, "put Eddie on the next train to his aunt in Duluth." And he turned, immutable as Fate, back to his dressing table and once more carefully started applying false hair to the famous face.

In the train to Duluth an hour later, Eddie sat watching the Hudson River fly past, crying at last.

STOP PUSHING, ROCKY

Mr. Gensel carefully wrapped six feet of adhesive tape around Joey Garr's famous right hand. Joey sat on the edge of the rubbing table, swinging his legs, watching his manager moodily.

"Delicate," Mr. Gensel said, working thoughtfully. "Remember, delicate is the keyword."

"Yeah," Joey said. He belched.

Mr. Gensel frowned and stopped winding the tape. "Joey," he said, "how many times I got to tell you, please, for my sake, don't eat in diners."

"Yeah," Joey said.

"There is a limit to everything, Joey," Mr. Gensel said. "Thrift can be carried too far, Joey. You're not a poor man. You got as much money in the bank as a Hollywood actress, why do you have to eat thirty-five-cent blueplates?"

"Please do not talk so much." Joey stuck out his left hand.

Mr. Gensel turned his attention to the famous left hand. "Ulcers," he complained. "I will have a fighter with ulcers. A wonderful prospect. He has to eat garbage. Garbage and ketchup. The coming welterweight champion. Dynamite in either fist. But he belches forty times a day. My God, Joey."

Joey spat impassively on the floor and squinted at his neatly slicked hair in the mirror. Mr. Gensel sighed and moved his bridge restlessly around in his mouth and finished his job.

"Allow me, some day," he said, "to buy you a meal. A dollar-fifty meal. To give you the taste."

"Save yer money, Mr. Gensel," Joey said, "for your old age."

The door opened and McAlmon came in, flanked on either side by two tall, broad men with flat faces and scarred lips curled in amiable grins.

"I am glad to see you boys," McAlmon said, coming up and patting Joey on the back. "How is my little boy Joey tonight?"

"Yeah," Joey said, lying down on the rubbing table and closing his eyes.

"He belches," Mr. Gensel said. "I never saw a fighter belched so much as Joey in my whole life. Not in thirty-five years in the game. How is your boy?"

"Rocky is fine," McAlmon said. "He wanted to come in here with me. He wanted to make sure that Joey understood."

"I understand," Joey said irritably. "I understand fine. That Rocky. The one thing he is afraid of maybe some day somebody will hit him. A prize-fighter."

"You can't blame him," McAlmon said reasonably. "After all, he knows, if Joey wants he can put him down until the day after Thanksgiving."

"With one hand," Joey said grimly. "That is some fighter, that Rocky."

"He got nothing to worry about," Mr. Gensel said smoothly. "Everything is absolutely clear in everybody's mind. Clear like crystal. We carry him the whole ten rounds."

"Lissen, Joey," McAlmon leaned on the rubbing table right over Joey's upturned face, "let him look good. He has a following in Philadelphia."

"I will make him look wonderful," Joey said wearily. "I will make him look like the British navy. The one thing that worries me all the time is maybe Rocky will lose his following in Philadelphia."

McAlmon spoke very coldly. "I don't like your tone of voice, Joey," he said.

"Yeah." Joey turned over on his belly.

"Just in case," McAlmon said in crisp tones, "just in case any party forgets their agreement, let me introduce you to Mr. Pike and Mr. Petroskas."

The two tall broad men smiled very widely.

Joey sat up slowly and looked at them.

"They will be sitting in the audience," McAlmon said. "Watching proceedings with interest."

The two men smiled from ear to ear, the flat noses flattening even deeper into their faces.

"They got guns, Mr. Gensel," Joey said. "Under their lousy armpits."

"It is just a precaution," McAlmon said. "I know everything will go along smooth. But we got money invested."

"Lissen, you dumb Philadelphia hick," Joey began.

"That isn't the way to talk, Joey," Mr. Gensel said nervously.

"I got money invested, too," Joey yelled. "I got one thousand dollars down even money that that lousy Rocky stays ten rounds with me. You don't need your gorillas. I am only hoping Rocky don't collapse from fright before the tenth round."

"Is that the truth?" McAlmon asked Mr. Gensel.

"I put the bet down through my own brother-in-law," Mr. Gensel said. "I swear to God."

"What do you think, McAlmon?" Joey shouted, "I throw away thousand-dollar bills? I'm a business man."

"Take my word for it," Mr. Gensel said. "Joey is a business man."

"All right, all right." McAlmon put out both his hands placatingly. "There is no harm done in straightening matters out complete beforehand, is there? Now nobody is in the dark about anything. That is the way I like to operate." He turned to Pike and Petroskas. "O.K., boys, just sit in your seats and have a good time."

"Why do those two bums have to be there?" Joey demanded.

"Do you mind if they enjoy themselves?" McAlmon asked with cold sarcasm. "It's going to damage you if they have a good time?"

"That's all right," Mr. Gensel said soothingly. "We don't object. Let the boys have a good time."

"Only get them out of here," Joey said loudly. "I don't like people with guns under their armpits in my room."

"Come on, boys," McAlmon said, opening the door. Both men smiled pleasantly and started out. Petroskas stopped and turned around. "May the best man win," he said, and nodded soberly twice and left, closing the door behind him.

Joey looked at Mr. Gensel and shook his head. "McAlmon's friends," he said. "Philadelphia boys."

The door swung open and an usher chanted "Joey Garr. Joey Garr is on next." Joey spat into his bandaged hands and started up the steps with Mr. Gensel.

When the fight started, Rocky dove immediately into a clinch. Under the thick bush of hair all over his chest and shoulders he was sweating profusely.

"Lissen, Joey," he whispered nervously into Joey's ear, hanging on tightly to his elbows, "you remember the agreement? You remember, don't yuh, Joey?"

"Yeah," Joey said. "Let go of my arm. What're you trying to do, pull it off?"

"Excuse me, Joey," Rocky said, breaking and giving Joey two to the ribs.

As the fight progressed, with the customers yelling loud approval of the footwork, the deft exchanges, the murderous finishers that missed by a hair, Rocky gained in confidence. By the fourth round he was standing up bravely, exposing his chin, moving in and out with his fists brisk and showy. His friends in the crowd screamed with pleasure and a loud voice called out, "Kill the big bum, Rocky! Oh, you Rocky!" Rocky breathed deeply and let a fast one go to Joey's ear. Joey's head shook a little and a look of mild surprise came over his face. "Wipe him out!" the voice thundered from among Rocky's following. Rocky set himself flat on his feet and whistled another across to Joey's ear as the bell rang. He strutted back to his corner smiling confidently at his friends in the arena.

Mr. Gensel bent and worked over Joey. "Lissen, Joey," he whispered, "he is pushing you. Tell him to stop pushing you. They will give him the fight if he don't stop pushing you."

"Aaah," Joey said, "it's nothing. For the crowd. His pals. A little excitement. Makes it look good. Don't worry, Mr. Gensel."

"Please tell him to stop pushing you," Mr. Gensel pleaded. "For my sake, Joey. He is supposed to go ten rounds with us but we are supposed to win. We can't afford to lose to Rocky Pidgeon, Joey."

In the fifth round Rocky kept up his charging attack, keeping both hands going, weaving, aggressive, shoving Joey back and forth across the ring, while the home-town crowd stood in its seats and shouted hoarse support. Joey kept him nicely bottled up, back-pedaling, catching punches on his gloves, sliding with the blows, occasionally jabbing sharply to Rocky's chest. In a corner, with Joey against the ropes, Rocky swung from behind his back with a right hand, grunting deeply as it landed on Joey's side.

Joey clinched, feeling the sting. "Say, Rocky," he whispered politely, "stop pushing."

"Oh," Rocky grunted, as though he'd just remembered, and backed off. They sparred delicately for thirty seconds, Joey still on the ropes.

"Come on, Rocky," the voice shouted. "Finish him. You got the bum going! Oh, you Rocky!"

A light came into Rocky's eyes and he wound up and let one go. It caught Joey on the side of the head as the bell rang. Joey leaned a little wearily against the ropes, scowling thoughtfully at Rocky as Rocky strode lightly across to his corner amid wild applause. Joey went and sat down.

"How's it going?" he asked Mr. Gensel.

"You lost that round," Mr. Gensel said swiftly and nervously. "For God's sake, Joey, tell him to stop pushing. You'll lose the fight. If you lose to Rocky Pidgeon you will have to go fight on the team with the boys from the Hebrew Orphan Asylum. Why don't you tell him to stop pushing?"

"I did," Joey snapped. "He's all hopped up. His friends keep yelling what a great guy he is, so he believes it. He hits me in the ear once more I will take him out in the alley after the fight and I will beat the pants off him."

"Just tell him to take it easy," Mr. Gensel said, worriedly. "Remind him we are carrying him. Just remind him."

"That dumb Rocky," Joey said. "You got to reason with him, you got a job on your hands."

The gong rang and the two men sprang out at each other. The light of battle was still in Rocky's eye and he came out swinging violently. Joey tied him up tight and talked earnestly to him. "Lissen, Rocky, enough is enough. Stop being a hero, please. Everybody thinks you're wonderful. All right. Let it go at that. Stop pushing, Rocky. There is money invested here. What are you, crazy? Say, Rocky, do you know what I'm talking about?"

"Sure," Rocky grunted. "I'm just putting on a good show. You got to put on a good show, don't you?"

"Yeah," Joey said, as the referee finally pulled them apart.

They danced for two minutes after that, but right before the end of the round, from in close, Rocky unleashed a murderous uppercut that sent the blood squirting in all directions from Joey's nose. Rocky wheeled jauntily as the bell rang and shook his hands gaily at his screaming friends. Joey looked after him and spat a long stream of blood at his retreating, swaggering back.

Mr. Gensel rushed anxiously out and led Joey back to his corner. "Why didn't you tell him to stop pushing, Joey?" he asked. "Why don't you do like I say?"

"I told him," Joey said, bitterly. "Look, I got a bloody nose. I got to come to Philadelphia to get a bloody nose. That bastid, Rocky."

"Make sure to tell him to stop pushing," Mr. Gensel said, working swiftly over the nose. "You got to win from here on, Joey. No mistake now."

"I got to come to Starlight Park, in the city of Philadelphia," Joey marveled, "to get a bloody nose from Rocky Pidgeon. Holy Jesus God!"

"Joey," Mr. Gensel implored, "will you remember what I told you? Tell him to stop . . ."

The bell rang and the two men leapt at each other as the crowd took up its roaring from where it had left off. The loud voice had settled into a constant, inspiriting chant of "Oh, Rocky, oh, you Rocky!" over and over again.

Joey grabbed Rocky grimly. "Lissen, you bum," he whispered harshly, "I ask you to stop pushing. I will take you out later and knock all your teeth out. I warn you."

And he rapped Rocky smartly twice across the ear to impress him.

For the next minute Rocky kept a respectful distance and Joey piled up points rapidly. Suddenly half the arena took up the chant, "Oh, Rocky, oh, you Rocky!" On fire with this admiration, Rocky took a deep breath and let sail a roundhouse right. It caught Joey squarely on the injured nose. Once more the blood spurted. Joey shook his head to clear it and took a step toward Rocky, who was charging in wildly. Coldly Joey hooked with his left, like a spring uncoiling, and crossed with his right as Rocky sagged with glass in his eyes. Rocky went fourteen feet across the ring and landed face down. For a split second a smile of satisfaction crossed Joey's face. Then he remembered. He swallowed drily as the roar of the crowd exploded in his ears. He looked at his corner. Mr. Gensel was just turning around to sit with his back to the ring and his head in his hands. He looked at Rocky's corner. McAlmon was jumping up and down, beating his hat with both fists in agony, screaming, "Rocky! Get up, Rocky! Get up or I'll fill you full of lead! Rocky, do you hear me?"

Behind McAlmon, Joey saw Pike and Petroskas, standing in their seats, amiable smiles on their faces, watching him interestedly, their hands under their armpits.

"Rocky!" Joey whispered hoarsely as the referee counted five, "Good old Rocky. Get up, Rocky! For God's sake. Please get up! Please . . . please." He remembered the thousand dollars and tears filled his eyes. "Rocky," he sobbed, half-bending to his knees, in the corner of the ring, as the referee reached seven, "for the love of God . . ."

Rocky turned over, got to one knee.

Joey closed his eyes to spare himself. When he opened them again, there was Rocky, standing, weaving unsteadily, before him. A breath, a prayer, escaped Joey's lips as he jumped across the ring, swinging dramatically. He curled his arm viciously around the back of Rocky's neck. Even at that Rocky started to go again. Joey grabbed him under the armpits and made violent movements with his arms as though he were trying desperately to release them.

"Hold on, Rocky!" he whispered hoarsely, supporting the stricken fighter. "Just keep your knees stiff. You all right? Hey, Rocky, you all right? Hey, Rocky, answer me! Please, Rocky, say something!"

But Rocky said nothing. He just leaned against Joey with the glaze in his eyes, his arms hanging limply at his side, while Joey conducted the fight by himself.

When the bell rang, Joey held Rocky up until McAlmon could come out and drag him back to his corner. The referee eyed Joey narrowly as Joey went over to his own corner.

"A nice, interesting bout," the referee said. "Yes, siree."

"Yeah," Joey said, sinking onto his stool. "Hey, Mr. Gensel," he called. Mr. Gensel turned his face back to the ring for the first time since the middle of the round. Like an old man, he climbed the steps and haphazardly worked on his fighter.

"Explain to me," he said in a flat voice, "what you were thinking of."

"That Rocky," Joey said wearily. "He got the brains of a iceman's horse. He keeps pushing and pushing. I musta lost a quart of blood through the nose. I hit him to teach him a little respect."

"Yes," Mr. Gensel said. "That was fine. We were nearly buried in Philadelphia."

"I didn't hit him hard," Joey protested. "It was strictly a medium punch. He got a chin like a movie star. Like Myrna Loy. He shouldn't oughta be in this business. He should wait on customers in a store. In a dairy. Butter and eggs."

"Please do me a favor," Mr. Gensel said. "Kindly hold him up for the next three rounds. Treat him with care. I am going down to sit in the dressing room."

And Mr. Gensel left as Joey charged out and pounded Rocky's fluttering elbows severely.

Fifteen minutes later, Joey came down to him in the dressing room and lay wearily down on the rubbing table.

"So?" Mr. Gensel asked, not lifting his head.

"So we won," Joey said hoarsely. "I had to carry him like a baby for nine whole minutes. Like a eight-month-old baby girl. That Rocky. Hit him once, he is no good for three years. I never worked so hard in my whole life, not even when I poured rubber in Akron, Ohio."

"Did anybody catch on?" Mr. Gensel asked.

"Thank God we're in Philadelphia," Joey said. "They ain't caught on the war's over yet. They are still standing up there yelling, 'Rocky! Oh, you Rocky!' because he was so goddamn brave and stood in there fighting. My God! Every ten seconds I had to kick him in the knee to straighten it out so he'd keep standing!"

Mr. Gensel sighed. "Well, we made a lot of money."

"Yeah," Joey said without joy.

"I'll treat you to a dollar-fifty dinner, Joey."

"Naah," Joey said, flattening out on the rubbing table. "I just want to stay here and rest. I want to lay here and rest for a long time."

RESIDENTS OF OTHER CITIES

WHEN THE BOLSHEVIKS *came, the men of the city, the peasants and clerks and small merchants, hurriedly put on red badges and ran to greet them, singing the half-learned words of the Internationale. While they remained in possession of the town there were police on the streets at night and an air of purpose and everyone was called "Comrade," even Jews. Then when the Whites recovered the city the men who had not gone with the Bolsheviks ran to greet them and the women hung white sheets out the windows and the houses of the Jews were sacked in pogroms and Jews were killed and the young girls were raped by the city's hoodlums. This was in Kiev, in 1918. The city changed hands many times as the war rocked around it, and the full record of those changes could be read in the eyes of the Jewish residents.*

The riots started at five o'clock in the evening. All afternoon the men had been gathering silently in the square and in the small inns near by. The peasants came in from the fields, armed with axes, and soldiers of the broken army of the Czar sat at the inn-tables with the rifles with which they had fought the Germans.

We knew they were coming and we hid the silver, the good blankets, the money, and my mother's paisley silk scarf. The whole family gathered at my father's house, all eight children—the four boys and four girls, and my uncle and his wife.

We put out all the lights and locked the door and pulled the blinds and sat all together in the living room, in the twilight, and even the small children sat still and hushed on the floor. My uncle's wife suckled her four-weeks-old child in the room because it was less fearsome there, with the family assembled. I watched her carefully. She was a handsome woman, my uncle's wife Sara. She was very young, nineteen, and her breast was full but upright. She sang very softly to the child as it fed and that was the only sound in the whole room.

My father sat alone in the center of the room, on his face that same abstract expression as when he led the prayers in the synagogue and looked as though he were engaged directly with God's angels in elevated but intimate discussion. He had a lean scholar's face, my father. He ate very little and was much concerned with spiritual matters and disliked me to a degree because I looked like a peasant, big and broad for my age, and went to the Academy and painted naked women. He caught me looking at my aunt's bare breast and his nostrils widened for a moment and his lip lifted. I watched for another thirty seconds, resisting.

We heard a yell far away, in the still city. The yell died down. The child sighed in my aunt's arms and fell asleep. My aunt covered her breast, sat without moving, watching her husband, my uncle Samuel, pacing slowly up and down between her and the door. A muscle kept tightening and relaxing in Samuel's jaw, making a little white ball and disappearing, again and again. My mother swiftly pulled books down off the shelves, slipped bank-notes between their leaves, put them back on the shelves. There were two thousand books on the shelves, in Hebrew, Russian, German, and French. I looked at my watch. It was a quarter to five. The watch was new, a wrist watch, such as army officers wore. I was very proud of it. I wished something would happen. I was sixteen years old.

This is what a pogrom is like. First you hear a yell or two far off. Then the sound of a man running, the steps coming nearer swiftly, the sudden opening and slamming of a door near by. Then a moment later more running and more and more, all silent but for the desperate sound of speed on the street, like leaves swift before a wind. Then silence for a moment and then the mob, approaching, with its single noise.

The mob came up to our house and passed. We didn't look out the window. We didn't say anything. My uncle paced up and down and my aunt looked at him. My father closed his eyes as the mob paused at our house, opened them when the mob passed. My seven-year-old sister, Hester, picked her nose. My mother sat with her hands in her lap.

After a little while we heard a woman weeping outside. The woman walked past our windows and around the corner, weeping.

It was a half hour before they came. And then they broke the windows with clubs and knocked the door down with axes and in a moment the house was full of men and the street in front of our house was full of men. There was the smell of sweat and the peasant smell of the farm and a little smell of alcohol and there they were, a blur and confusion of faces and coats and guns and knives and axes and bayonets and clubs in the small neat house my mother dusted three times a day. They lighted the lamps and a big man with a mustache, in the uniform of a sergeant of the Czar's army kept yelling, "Shut up! For Christ's sake, keep your mouths shut!"

We stood huddled in one corner of the room as the big sergeant walked up and down in front of us. My uncle Samuel stood in front of his wife and child and my mother stood in front of my father. Hester cried, the first tears.

The sergeant had a bayonet in his hand and he tapped it on the palm of his other hand. "The oldest son!" he said. "Where's the oldest son?"

Hester wept. None of us said anything.

"Well!" the sergeant yelled. He smacked the bayonet down on a table and splinters flew off. "Goddamnit, where's the stinking oldest son?"

I stepped out. I was sixteen and my brother Eli was older than I and my brother David, but I stepped out.

"What?" I said. "What?"

The sergeant leaned over. "Little one," he pinched my cheek and the men behind him laughed, "little one, you are now going to make yourself useful."

I looked at my father. He was watching me thoughtfully, his face abstracted, his eyes narrowed, conversing with the angels.

"What do you want?" I asked. I was facing the whole roomful of men. I could feel the blood passing through my elbows and knees.

The sergeant grabbed me, not very roughly, by the collar. "Little Jew," he said, "we want everything there is in the house. You will take us from room to room and deliver everything." He shook me. He weighed two hundred and twenty-five pounds.

My mother pushed her way to me. "Give them as little as you can, Daniel," she whispered in Yiddish.

The sergeant pushed my mother back. "Talk Russian," he said. "Everybody talk Russian."

"She doesn't talk Russian," I said, lying, trying to plan swiftly what I could give them and what I could hold back.

I went from room to room with five of the crowd, growing old, cunning, adept, thoughtful at each step, giving them the things they would have found most easily, some of the silver, some of the blankets, a few small trinkets of my mother's. There were other mobs coming and they, too, would have to be satisfied.

When I passed through the living room again my uncle Samuel was lying on the floor bleeding from the head and a big peasant was holding the four-weeks-old child in one hand and Sara was in a corner, crying, with men all around her, pulling playfully at her clothes, lifting her skirt. Hester sat on the floor, with her fist in her mouth. My mother sat stolidly, a little fat figure, in front of the glass doors of the bookcase. My father, thin and tall, stood looking dreamily at the ceiling, pulling from time to time at his little beard. The men were laughing and it was hard to hear what anyone was saying and there was broken glass on the carpet already.

In my mother's bedroom I stopped. The men had made a big pile of goods outside in the hall. "That's all," I said. "You got everything."

The sergeant grinned and pulled my ear. "You're a nice little boy," he said. He was enjoying everything. "You wouldn't lie to me, would you?"

"No."

"You know what happens to little boys who lie to me, don't you?"

"Yes. You're hurting my ear."

"Oh." The sergeant turned to the men behind him with broad concern. "I'm hurting his ear. I'm damaging the poor little Jewboy's ear. Isn't that too bad?"

The men laughed. There was laughter throughout the house. All the mobs that came to our house made the house ring with their laughter.

"Maybe if I cut it off," the sergeant said, "maybe it wouldn't hurt so much. What do you say, boys?"

The boys agreed. "A nice kosher ear," one of them said. "For stew."

"You're absolutely sure, now," the sergeant said, twisting my ear, "that there's nothing left?"

"Yes," I said.

"I hope you're right, little boy. For your sake."

We marched down through the living room and to the small music room right next to it. There were sliding doors between the living room and the music room. "We are now going to search the house, little boy," the sergeant said very loudly. He had a voice you could hear over all the noise. "And if we find anything you haven't shown us, if we find one little silver baby spoon . . ." He touched my throat with the bayonet. I felt the blood come to the skin, drip in a little trickle to my collar. "The end. Poor little Jewboy." The sergeant looked significantly at my mother. She looked back at him firmly. My two older brothers David and Eli, pale and spiritual-looking, like my father, stood together, holding each other's hands. David's eyes were open very wide and there were white lines, like ridges, across his cheeks. They watched me intently, never taking their eyes off me.

The sergeant marched me into the music room after ordering the men to search the house. The sergeant closed the doors firmly. "Sit down, little boy," he said. I sat down and he sat down opposite me, the bayonet across his knee. "One little silver baby spoon," he said. "Sssst!"

I didn't feel that he could kill me. He was a foolish, lumpy man, with spit sliding down his chin. I had read books on French art, I knew what Impressionism was, I had seen reproductions of the paintings of Cézanne and Renoir. It was impossible that a big fool with a torn and muddy uniform could kill me.

"You're still sure there's nothing else?"

"You got the last piece."

"All Jews should be killed," he said. I looked at the bayonet and thought of the searchers passing the bookcase with the rubles hidden in every other book, passing the trunk with the false bottom in the attic, the coal pile hiding the samovar in the cellar, the lace in the samovar . . .

"Russia is ridden by Jews," the sergeant said, grinning. "It is this country's great plague. I fought at Tannenburg, I'm entitled to have opinions."

Sara started screaming outside in the living room and I heard my father start to pray.

"We will kill the Jews," the sergeant said, "and then the Bolsheviks. I suppose you're a Bolshevik."

"I'm a painter," I said. I said it proudly, even then.

"Well," said the sergeant, speaking loudly, because Sara was screaming, "a little boy like you." He picked up my hand and saw my wrist watch. "That's just what I've been looking for," he said. He tore it off my wrist and dropped it into his pocket. "Thank you, little one." He grinned.

I felt very bad. That wrist watch made me a gentleman, a citizen of the world.

He took out a pack of cigarettes, took one, automatically offered the pack to me. I had never smoked before, but I took one. I smoked it, feeling suddenly a man, thinking of what my father would say if he saw me now, smoking. None of us smoked in our house, not even my uncle. Well, I thought, no matter what, I know what it is to smoke. I didn't inhale the smoke. I pushed it around my mouth and hurriedly blew it out.

"The painter," the sergeant said, "the little artist. Are you having a good time, Mr. Artist?"

He was a very cruel man, that sergeant.

"Maybe they're opening a closet door downstairs," the sergeant said, patting my knee, "and maybe they see candlesticks there, gold candlesticks."

"They don't see anything," I said, crying all of a sudden because the smoke whirled up in my eyes. "There's nothing to see."

"Little artist, little Jew painter." He cut the buttons off my coat one by one with the bayonet. He was having a very good time. Hester and Sara were both screaming in the living room. The door opened and two of the searchers came in.

"Nothing," said one of them, "not a stinking button."

"Lucky little boy," the sergeant said to me. He leaned over, smiling, and hit me on the temple, with his fist. I fell over and the room and the noise went far, far away.

When I came to, my head was in my mother's lap, and the men had gone. I opened my eyes and saw Sara in my uncle Samuel's arms, with the blood still coming slowly from the wound in his head and staining their clothes and they not noticing it all, but just standing there, clutched together without tears, their hands digging into each other's shoulders. The baby was lying on the chair next to them sleeping. My mother's face was calm over me and her voice came down distantly, "Daniel, little Daniel, lion-hearted Daniel, everything is all right, sweetheart, everything is all right."

In the distance I heard my father. "The most profound mistake of my life," he was saying. "I had an opportunity to go to America in 1910. Why didn't I go? Why in the name of the Almighty God, didn't I go?"

"Don't move, baby," my mother said softly. "Lie there and close your eyes."

"I ought to be ashamed of myself," I heard my brother Eli's voice, bitter, full of tears, "I am the oldest son. And he stepped forward. I'm nineteen and he's sixteen and I stayed behind. God forgive me."

"Little Daniel," my mother crooned, her hand going lightly over my forehead, "little Daniel with the brains of a philosopher." She was chuckling. In the middle of all the blood and tears she was chuckling. I sat up and laughed, too, and she kissed me.

Outside, from the other side of the city, we heard shots and nearer a man screamed and we heard horses galloping down the next street.

"Maybe it's the Bolsheviks," my mother said. "Maybe we're saved."

"Let us pray," said my father. Everyone arranged himself for prayer, even my uncle Samuel. He gently took Sara's arms down from his shoulders and kissed her hands. He bent down and picked up his hat and put it on. Sara sat with the child in her arms, the fright draining from her eyes. The men hadn't really hurt her.

My father started to pray. I didn't believe in my father's prayers. My father was always at the side of God and he neglected life. I hated this insane holiness, this neglect of flesh, the denial of the present for eternity.

I stood up and went to the window when my father began, "Blessed Father, God Almighty . . ."

He stopped. "Daniel," he called. "We are praying."

"I know," I said. My brothers and sisters looked nervously at me. "I want to look out the window. I don't want to pray."

I could hear the breath whistle into the lungs of my brothers.

My father's lip twisted. "Daniel," he began . . . then he stopped and shrugged and looked up at his angels. "Blessed Father," he started the prayer, "God Almighty . . ."

My brothers chimed in with the responses.

I smiled to myself at the window. This was the first time I had ever refused my father. "The oldest son," they had asked, and I had stepped out and said, "What?" Now I could announce to my father, "I don't want to pray."

I listened to the shots in the distance and the shrieks and the solid noise of the crowds and I smiled at the window.

In the next two days the mobs came to our house nineteen times. In the middle of all the screams, all the laughter, all the terror and devastation, I kept a careful, crazy account. They have been here nine times, here they come again, there are still two silver candy dishes in the cellar we can give them, this makes the tenth time, will they kill somebody this time, ten, remember ten, the next time will be the eleventh.

The house was completely gutted. All the windows were broken, all the doors had been torn off to make fires in the streets, all the mirrors had been smashed, the carpets ripped up and carried out with the furniture. The last bit of hidden food had been found and stolen, the last blanket and loose piece of clothing. The mobs had broken into liquor stores by the second night and the men came rushing in reeking of alcohol, louder, more and more violent. Death came nearer and nearer with each visit, the eleventh time, the twelfth time, the heavy muddy boots, the shouts, the drunken songs, the men standing, swaying a little in front of my father and my uncle, prodding them with bayonets, waiting for a sign of resistance, of violence, a call of encouragement from their friends, to start the business of killing. They played joyously with death, always on the thin edge of it, sniffing it as the ultimate satisfaction of the carnival, calling it near, allowing it to retreat, postponing it for another time, the way a child postpones a sweet.

They twice stripped my aunt Sara and my oldest sister Rachel completely of their clothes and made them stand there, upright, in the broken-windowed house, on the glass-strewn floor, with all to see, but they went no further and we wrapped Sara and Rachel in rags and for the first time my mother wept.

All night we saw the flare of burning houses outside our windows and all night we heard the sounds of scattered shots and all night, the screams.

The women huddled in the cold, on the floor, and cried and the children sobbed and my brother David kept walking up and down yelling, "The next time, I'll kill one of them! I swear to God!"

"Sssh," said my father. "You'll kill no one. That's not your business. Let them kill, not you."

"I'd like them to kill me," David shouted. "Let me kill one of them first, then let them kill me! It's better than this."

"Sssh," said my father. "God's will be done. They will suffer finally."

"Oh, my God!" David said.

"Why didn't I go to America in 1910?" my father asked, rocking back and forth. "Why didn't I?"

My uncle Samuel sat by the window holding his child, looking first down the street for new mobs, then at his wife Sara, stretched in the corner, in her rags, her face turned hopelessly to the wall. The blood had dried on Samuel's face and he had neglected to wipe it off and it made a pattern on his cheek like rivers on a map. His beard was coming out heavily on his face and his eyes had gone deep into his head and his cheeks had collapsed along the bones of his jaw. Occasionally he bent over and kissed his child, sleeping in his arms.

I sat with my arms around my brother Eli, with Hester between us, to keep warm. They had taken my jacket and I was stiff with cold and I lay there with my eyes wide open remembering, listening, tonight's tears, yesterday's, tomorrow's.

"Go to sleep, Hester, little Hester," I said softly from time to time when Hester would awake. Every time she woke she began to sob, immediately, as though that were the way nature had made little children, sleep quiet, awake weeping.

Vengeance, I thought, listening to the women of my family cry; feeling the bruises stiffen where I had been beaten, sighing, as I moved and cuts opened and bled into my clotted clothes, vengeance, vengeance.

"They're coming again," my uncle Samuel said, from his place at the window, just before daybreak. We heard the well-recognized sound of the mob coming nearer. "I'm not going to stay here," Samuel said. "The hell with it. Sara, Sara, darling," he said more gently than any man I have ever heard use a woman's name. "Come, Sara . . ."

Sara stood up and took his arm.

"What should we do?" my mother asked.

My father looked up at his angels. "Come," I said, taking my place in command, "let's try the streets."

We filed out through the back door, twelve of us walking, Samuel carrying the child in his arms. We trailed through the icy mud, keeping close to walls, walking, walking, avoiding the sounds of life, fleeing from lights, halting every five minutes to allow the children to rest, running across open streets like rabbits across a bare field.

Vengeance, I thought, leading the march along back alleys, behind fences, death, fire and torture. I held my mother's hand. "Keep going, Momma, please, Momma," I yelled at her as she stumbled in the mud. "You must, Momma."

"Yes, Daniel, of course, Daniel," she said, gripping my hand in her calloused, work-scarred hands. "Excuse me for going so slow, kindly excuse me."

"Cleveland," my father said, as the sun came up. "I could have gone to Cleveland. My uncle invited me."

"Keep quiet, Poppa! Please, please don't talk about America!" David said.

"Yes," said my father. "Of course. What's done is . . . God's will. Who am I," he said, leaning against a wall as we stopped for a moment, "who am I to question . . . ? Still, in America these things do not happen and I had the opportunity . . ."

David didn't say any more.

It became harder to keep out of the mobs' way as it grew lighter. Nobody in Kiev seemed to sleep all those two days and our escapes became closer and closer. Twice we were shot at from windows and we ran slithering in the mud, with the children screaming, to take protection behind the corners of houses. The third time we were shot at my brother David turned around with his mouth open and sat down in the mud.

"In the knee," he said. "My knee . . ."

My mother and I ripped the sleeve off my father's jacket and tied it around David's leg above the knee. My father stood there, watching us, looking lopsided and peculiar, standing there with one sleeve. I put David over my back and we started back to the house. He tried to keep from yelling by pounding me in the back with his fists as I lurched and the knee knocked against me.

When we got back to the house we sat once more in the destroyed living room. The sun streamed in and it looked mad and unfamiliar and impossible, with all of us sitting there on the floor in the broad daylight, with Rachel and Sara wrapped in rags like mummies, and my father with one sleeve and David with the sleeve knotted around his leg and the sweat coming off him and making little pools on the floor. The children sat all together in a corner, terribly quiet, watching each movement of the adults with quick movements of their eyes.

All day long the mobs kept coming and each time they brought death a little closer, each time the bayonet prods went a little deeper, each time more blood was shed. David became hysterical late in the afternoon and fell into trances and rigid fits and there was nothing to do but sit there and listen to him and look at each other like insane animals in a lunatic zoo.

"You can blame this on me," my father kept saying. "I had the opportunity and I was not the man to grasp it. The truth. I am not a strong man. I'm a scholar. I did not want to cross the ocean to a country with a foreign language. Blame me. Everybody blame me."

At four o'clock Eli got up. "I'm going out," he said. "I can't stand it here."

Before he could be stopped he turned and ran down the street.

Just at nightfall a mob came with torches. They filled the house. They were in dangerous high spirits, full of whisky and blood.

They ranged the house, came back to the living room disappointed because there was nothing left to be looted.

They held all the men, two to each one of us and stood in front of us, trying to devise new pleasures. This was the time, I thought, this is where we die, there is nothing left. I didn't want to die.

And this time we nearly did die, but one of the members of the mob spoke up, "Shave him, shave the old holy bastard!"

The mob met this with roars of approval and two men pulled my father out to the center of the room and in the flaring light of the torches a little fat man began to shave him with a bayonet. The fat man did it with elaborate comic flourishes, holding my father's chin in arched fingers and standing off with cocked head to admire his handi-work while the men behind him laughed uproariously.

Finally, my father wept. The tears streamed down his cheeks and gleamed on the bayonet that was shaving his soft trim black beard off his face.

When the job was done, they threw my father to the floor and left in good spirits, singing.

My father sat in the new silence on the floor, bleeding and strangely naked in my eyes, with his suddenly girlish mouth and soft chin and his eyes staring wild and frightened and helpless, imploring the angels now, not regarding them any longer as magnificent equals.

"The next time," I said, trying to sound very businesslike and un-emotional among these wild and feverish animals of my family, "the next time they will kill us. Let's get into the streets in the dark. Please . . . Please . . ."

I carried David and my mother led my father by the hand as we stepped out of our house.

As we started down the street, the door of the tailor's shop across the street opened and our neighbor, Kirov, the tailor, came out. He was not a Jew and his shop hadn't been touched. He was a big fat man of thirty-two or three, already bald. He crossed the street to us and silently shook my father's hand.

"Terrible," he said. "Wild animals. The times, the times, who would ever have thought we would see times like this in Kiev?"

My father kept pumping his hand again and again, unable to talk.

"Where're you going?" Kirov asked.

"No place," I told him. "We're going to walk up and down in the streets."

"Jesus Christ!" Kirov said, stroking Hester's head. "Impossible! I can't believe, I can't . . . Come, come with me, all of you. In my house no-body'll bother you and you can wait until this has blown over. Come. Not another word!"

My mother looked at me and I looked at her and we smiled crookedly at each other.

Kirov helped me with David and in five minutes we were all in his house, lying once more on the floor in the dark, but for the first time in two days with a feeling of safety.

I even fell asleep and awoke only for an instant when I heard a door open and close in the house. I slept without dreams, without the past, the future, without vengeance, or wonder that I was still alive or might survive this time. I slept and the children slept and my mother slept next to me in my father's arms and Sara slept in Samuel's arms, with their child beside them.

Somebody kicked me and I opened my eyes and looked up in the light and there was Kirov and there was the mob and Kirov was smiling and I realized suddenly that he had lived for eight years as a neighbor across the street from us, saying "Good morning" every day and "Isn't this a wonderful spring day?" and mending our clothes and for eight years he had nursed a secret hatred and the last two days had touched it off in him and here he was with a mob he had collected himself, and this was going to be the worst.

I sat up. The lights were on in the room and I saw my family awakening, deep out of the pit of sleep, bit by bit take in the silent grinning men standing around us, bit by bit awaken to terror and hopelessness.

Kirov had brought all the men of his family, his two brothers, big heavy men, and even his old father, toothless, limping, grinning like the rest of them.

"Mr. Kirov," my mother said. "What do you want from us? We have nothing left. Nothing but rags. You have been our neighbor for eight years and we have never had a harsh word . . ."

One of Kirov's brothers grabbed Sara and ripped the rags off her and I saw what the men had come for, what we had left. Kirov himself grabbed my sister Rachel, seventeen years old, but slim and unformed, like a child.

My uncle Samuel sprang at Kirov's brother and hit him across the face and a man standing behind him stabbed Samuel through with a bayonet. Samuel's hand clutched Sara, then relaxed and the man behind him pulled the bayonet out and Samuel fell down. He got up to one knee again and Kirov's brother took the bayonet and put it through Samuel's throat and left it there as Samuel fell.

I saw what happened after that. Everybody else closed his eyes, my mother, my father, David, even the children. My father's lips moved in prayer and he kept his eyes tightly shut, but I saw what happened.

I kept alive by planning, with cold reason and ingenuity, torture, mutilation, horror, for the men in that room. Torture by knife and fire and whip, applied with my own hands, making sure to hurt each man most in his most vulnerable spot. I marked each man in that room and remembered each man in that room.

I don't know how long the men would have stayed but soon from the streets came cries of, "Bolsheviks! The Reds! They're coming! They're entering the city! The Reds! They're coming! They're entering the city! The Reds! Long live the Soviets!"

Kirov put out the lights hurriedly and there was a confused scurrying and trampling around. I opened a window and dropped to the ground and went running toward the cries. Soon I was among a whole crowd of men and women, running, running to greet the victorious army. I felt the tears flow bitterly, like iron, down my cheeks as I ran and I saw that in that crowd of people there were many others weeping as they ran.

We turned a corner and there was the vanguard of the triumphant Red Army, marching into Kiev. They were in rags, many of them, and bearded and cheerful and some of them were in uniform and some weren't and some had shoes and some didn't and there was one soldier in a butcher's apron who carried only a huge cavalry saber for armament and they were all eating fruit compote out of cans from a grocery store they had passed on the way into town, but they marched in, fighting men who had won the town fairly, and men and women alike flung themselves at the soldiers and kissed them as they marched.

"Captain!" I stopped the man who seemed to be in command. He was a small man who looked like a clerk. He was very busy as he walked along, spearing a peach with his bayonet out of the can. "Captain, please . . ."

"What do you want?" He started walking again, after stopping for a moment, still fishing for the peach.

"I want a gun, Captain, I must have a gun, and some soldiers!" I was crying and I dug my fingers into his arm. "Listen to me, for God's sake, listen to me!"

"How old are you, comrade?" He kept walking, eating the peach now.

"Sixteen. Please, please give me a gun and some soldiers . . ."

"Go home, little comrade," he said, patting me on the head, "go home to your momma and tomorrow when we've all had some sleep and everything is nicely organized you come around to headquarters and everything will be . . ."

"I can't wait until tomorrow!" The tears kept coming. "Now! Tonight! I must have the gun tonight!"

"Whom do you want to shoot?" He stopped and examined me for the first time.

"There are fifteen men I . . ."

"God almighty, comrade!" He laughed.

"What're you laughing at?" I yelled. "What the hell do you mean by laughing?"

He wiped his face wearily. "I'm so tired, comrade. We've been fighting for two weeks and I want to lie down."

"Goddamn you!" I cried. "Why don't you listen to me?"

He sighed and put his arm around me and we walked close together. "All right, little boy," he said. "Is it as bad as you think?"

I told him. His face became very grave and he threw away the compote can and gripped my shoulder twice. He took me to a very large man with a uniform jacket but ordinary pants who was marching a few paces back. This was the Cheka officer who was to set up police in Kiev immediately.

The Captain talked to him, still holding me by the shoulder. The Cheka officer sighed. "I can give you one man," he said. "I hope he can keep awake long enough to get to the house."

"And a gun! I want a gun!" I yelled. "A rifle for me, don't forget that!"

Both the men looked queerly at me, then at each other. "He's sixteen years old," the Captain said. "Sure," the Cheka officer said softly, "we'll give you a rifle. Now, for Christ's sake, will you stop bawling?"

"Yes," I said, though the tears didn't stop. "Don't mind that. Where's the gun?"

The Cheka officer gave me his rifle and called to a soldier. "Go with this young man," the Cheka officer said. "There is a little police work to be done. He knows what to do, the young man. Please stop crying . . . what's your name?"

"Daniel," I said. "I'm not crying. Thank you very much."

We started off, the soldier and I. He was a very tall, wide soldier, a very young one, too. His eyes were almost closed and there were dark circles under them as though he had been punched neatly there.

"Long live the revolution, Daniel!" the Captain yelled after me. "Long live Lenin!"

"Yes," I called back. Then, to the soldier, "Please, comrade, walk faster!"

"I'm very sleepy," the soldier said. "I want very much to lie down."

When we got back to Kirov's house, only my family were there, grouped silently around my uncle Samuel's body. Sara and Rachel lay face down on the floor with two of Kirov's blankets over them. Rachel was sobbing, but Sara lay without a sound, without movement, clutching her baby. The men had disappeared.

"Where are they?" I asked as I came through the door. "Where're the Kirovs?"

My father looked soberly at the rifle in my hand.

"Daniel," he said, "what are you doing with a gun?"

"Where're the Kirovs?" I yelled.

My father shook his head. Already the distant light of God and His angels was coming back into his eyes.

"Tell me! Tell me!" I screamed.

"They are not here," my father said. "That is sufficient. They will not bother us any more. The trouble is over. God has punished us and He has lifted the punishment. Let that be enough. It is not our part to punish."

"You damned fool!" I screamed.

"Listen," said the soldier, "I've got to get some sleep."

"Momma!" I appealed to my mother. "Momma, I got a gun, tell me where they are!"

My mother looked at my father. He shook his head. My mother took my hand. "They're in the cellar of our house. Six of them. The old man couldn't run, he has a bad leg, old man Kirov."

"Shame!" said my father. "What're you doing?"

"All the Kirovs?" I asked. "Are they there?"

My mother nodded.

"Come on," I said to the soldier. We ran down the steps and across the street to my own house. I found a candle in the kitchen and the soldier lit it and held it for me. I threw open the door of the cellar and went down the steps. There, against the far wall, crouched six men. The four Kirovs, a cousin of theirs, and the man who had stabbed my uncle Samuel, still holding his bayonet.

When he saw us standing there with guns he threw his bayonet down. It made a dry, shuffling noise on the dirt floor.

"We didn't do anything," Kirov the tailor cried to the soldier. "As Jesus is my Judge!"

"We were just hiding here to avoid getting caught in the fighting," old man Kirov said. His nose was running but he paid no attention to it.

"We're Reds," the owner of the bayonet cried. "Long live Lenin!"

"Long live Lenin!" they all shouted.

Their voices abruptly dropped when my mother and father and Sara appeared and came down the steps.

The soldier just stood there, his eyes almost closed, holding his rifle loosely, yawning, wide tremendous yawns from time to time.

My mother and father and Sara stood behind us silently. Sara held her baby at her throat. Her eyes were dry.

"Long live the Revolution!" old man Kirov called finally, his voice thin and quavery in the wet cellar.

"Well," said the soldier, "these the ones?"

"Yes," I said.

"We didn't do anything!" Kirov the tailor cried. "So help me, Jesus!"

"These are not the men," my father said. "These are old friends. The men you want ran away."

"Who's this?" the soldier asked.

"My father."

"Well, who's right?" The soldier looked blearily at my father.

"The old man!" Kirov the tailor shouted. "We have been neighbors for eight years!"

"Those are the men," my mother said quietly.

Old man Kirov finally wiped his nose. I laughed.

"Idiot!" my father said bitterly to my mother. "You are storing up more trouble. 'Those're the men' you say. Today they're arrested. To-morrow the Whites come in, they are free. Then what'll happen to us?"

"Those're the men," my mother said.

"Who's she?" The soldier yawned.

"My mother."

"Those're the men," Sara said. Her voice was very low and broken, as though these were her last words and after them she would discard forever the instrument of speech.

"Well?" I asked the soldier. "Are you satisfied?"

"I'm satisfied," he said.

I fired the gun into the dirt wall of the cellar.

All heads but the soldier's jerked with the noise, immense in that small low room. The smell of the powder was sharp in our noses. I sneezed.

"What're you going to do?" my father asked, his voice trembling.

I pulled the bolt of the gun, throwing the spent cartridge, putting in the fresh one. "Is that how you do it?" I asked.

"That's how," the soldier answered. He stood there impersonally, ragged, spent, just.

"What are you going to do?" Kirov the tailor asked.

I shot him through the head. He died as he fell. He was only eleven feet away.

The other men shrank against the wall, but separately, trying to put as much space as possible between themselves and the next man.

"Daniel!" my father shouted. "I forbid you! You must not have their blood on your hands! Daniel!"

I shot the tailor's older brother.

The old man Kirov began to cry. He fell to his knees and put his hands out toward me and said, "Daniel, Daniel, little boy . . ." I remembered what I had seen in the lighted room in his son the tailor's house, I remembered the old man, toothless and chuckling and my aunt Sara. I shot him as he kneeled.

My father started to sob and ran up the steps. Sara and my mother stood behind me. The soldier rubbed his eyes to keep them open. I felt, in a way, happy, though bitterly happy.

I pulled the bolt.

"Forgive me, forgive me," wept the youngest Kirov. "I didn't know what I . . ."

I pressed the trigger. He wheeled around and fell across his father.

I pulled the bolt and aimed carefully at the next man. He was standing there, calmly, rubbing his nose, looking at the ceiling. I pressed the trigger, but nothing happened.

"You need a new clip," the soldier said. He gave me a new clip and opened the magazine for me and I put the clip in and aimed once more at the next man. He was still rubbing his nose and looking at the ceiling and it was a little surprising to see him die.

The bayonet owner rushed at me as I was pulling the bolt for the last shot and brushed past me and ran up the steps. I ran after him and out into the street. I fired at him and somehow hit him and he fell. He got up again and ran again and I ran after him and shot again. Once more he fell. More slowly this time, he reeled to his feet and stumbled on. I had plenty of time to go after him and take careful aim. This was the most satisfactory moment, the wavering, bloody figure, arms out directly in the rifle's sights. This time he fell, raised himself once on his hand, then dropped into the mud for good.

I stood there with the rifle getting warm in my hand. I felt disappointed and cold and let down. This had not been the deep pleasure I had imagined in Kirov's room. The balances were not even. They had died too easily. They had not suffered enough pain. They had come off best in the bargain, finally.

The soldier came over and I gave him the rifle. Then I began to cry again. He patted me on the head. "All right, little comrade," he said. Then he trudged off with the two rifles to get some sleep.

My mother and Sara came and let me into the house.

My father wouldn't talk to me after that, and after we had buried my uncle Samuel and sat for a week in proper mourning, during which my father didn't look at me once, I decided to move on. I was restless and changed anyway and I couldn't live in my father's home any more as a schoolboy and I left.

The Reds lost Kiev again and it was a long time before the war was over and before I saw any of my family again and by that time my father was dead.

WEEP IN YEARS TO COME

THEY CAME OUT of the movie house and started slowly eastward in the direction of Fifth Avenue. "Hitler!" a newsboy called. "Hitler!"

"That Fletcher," Dora said, "the one that played her father. Remember him?"

"Uh huh," Paul said, holding her hand, as they walked slowly up the dark street.

"He's got stones in his kidney."

"That's the way he acts," Paul said. "Now I know how to describe the way that man acts—he acts like a man who has stones in his kidney."

Dora laughed. "I X-rayed him last winter. He's one of Dr. Thayer's best patients. He's always got something wrong with him. He's going to try to pass the stones out of his kidney this summer."

"Good luck, Fletcher, old man," Paul said.

"I used to massage his shoulder. He had neuritis. He makes fifteen hundred dollars a week."

"No wonder he has neuritis."

"He asked me to come to his house for dinner." Dora pulled her hand out of Paul's and slipped it up to his elbow and held on, hard. "He likes me."

"I bet he does."

"What about you?"

"What about me what?" Paul asked.

"Do you like me?"

They stopped at Rockefeller Plaza and leaned over the marble wall and looked down at the fountain and the statue and the people sitting out at the tables, drinking, and the waiters standing around, listening to the sound of the fountain.

"I can't stand you," Paul said. He kissed her hair.

"That's what I thought," Dora said. They both laughed.

They looked down at the Plaza, at the thin trees with the light-green leaves rustling in the wind that came down between the buildings. There were pansies, yellow and tight, along the borders of the small pools with the bronze sea statues, and hydrangeas, and little full trees, all shaking in the wind and the diffuse, clear light of the flood lamps above. Couples strolled slowly down from Fifth Avenue, talking amiably in low, calm, week-end voices, appreciating the Rockefeller frivolity and extravagance which had carved a place for hydrangeas and water and saplings and spring and sea-gods riding bronze dolphins out of these austere buildings, out of the bleak side of Business.

Paul and Dora walked up the promenade, looking in the windows. They stopped at a window filled with men's sports clothes—gabardine slacks and bright-colored shirts with short sleeves and brilliant handkerchiefs to tie around the throat.

"I have visions," Paul said, "of sitting in my garden, with two Great Danes, dressed like that, like a Hollywood actor in the country."

"Have you got a garden?" Dora asked.

"No."

"Those're nice pants," Dora said.

They went on to the next window. "On the other hand," Paul said, "there are days when I want to look like that. A derby hat and a stiff blue shirt with a pleated bosom and a little starched white collar and a five-dollar neat little necktie and a Burberry overcoat. Leave the office at five o'clock every day to go to a cocktail party."

"You go to a cocktail party almost every afternoon anyway," Dora said. "Without a derby hat."

"A different kind of cocktail party," Paul said. He started her across Fifth Avenue. "The kind attended by men with starched blue pleated bosoms. Some day."

"Oh, Lord," Dora said as they ran to escape a bus, "look at those dresses."

They stood in front of Saks.

"Fifth Avenue," Paul said. "Street of dreams."

"It's nice to know things like that exist," Dora murmured, looking into the stage-lit window at the yellow dress and the sign that said "Tropical Nights in Manhattan" and the little carved-stone fish that for some reason was in the same window. "Even if you can't have them."

"Uptown?" Paul asked. "Or to my house?"

"I feel like walking." Dora looked up at Paul and grinned. "For the moment." She squeezed his arm. "Only for the moment. Uptown."

They started uptown.

"I love those models," Paul said. "Each and every one of them. They're superior, yet warm; inviting, yet polite. Their breasts are always tipped at the correct angle for the season."

"Sure," Dora said, "papier-mâché. It's easy with papier-mâché. Look. Aluminum suitcases. Travel by air."

"They look like my mother's kitchen pots."

"Wouldn't you like to own a few of them?"

"Yes." Paul peered at them. "Fly away. Buy luggage and depart. Leave for the ends of the earth."

"They got a little case just for books. A whole separate little traveling bookcase."

"That's just what I need," Paul said, "for my trips on the Fifth Avenue bus every morning."

They passed St. Patrick's, dark and huge, with the moon sailing over it.

"Do you think God walks up Fifth Avenue?" Paul asked.

"Sure," said Dora. "Why not?"

"We are princes of the earth," Paul said. "All over the world men slave to bring riches to these few blocks for us to look at and say 'Yes, very nice' or 'Take it away, it stinks.' I feel very important when I walk up Fifth Avenue."

They stopped at the window of the Hamburg-American Line. Little dolls in native costumes danced endlessly around a pole while other dolls in native costume looked on. All the dolls had wide smiles on their faces. "Harvest Festival in Buckeburg, Germany," a small sign said.

A private policeman turned the corner and stood and watched them. They moved to the next window.

"'A suggestion to passengers to promote carefree travel,'" Paul read off a booklet. "Also, Hapag-Lloyd announces a twenty-per-cent reduction for all educators on sabbatical leave. They are 'Masters in the Art of Travel,' they say."

"I used to want to go to see Germany," Dora said. "I know a lot of Germans and they're nice."

"I'll be there soon," Paul said as they passed the private policeman.

"You're going to visit it?"

"Uh huh. At the expense of the government. In a well-tailored khaki uniform. I'm going to see glamorous Europe, seat of culture, at last.

From a bombing plane. To our left we have the Stork Club, seat of culture for East Fifty-third Street. Look at the pretty girls. A lot of them have breasts at the correct angle, too. See how nature mimics art. New York is a wonderful city."

Dora didn't say anything. She hung onto him tightly as they went down the street. They turned at the corner and walked down Madison Avenue. After a while they stopped at a shop that had phonographs and radios in the window. "That's what I want." Paul pointed at a machine. "A Capehart. It plays two symphonies at a time. You just lie on your back and out come Brahms and Beethoven and Prokofieff. That's the way life should be. Lie on your back and be surrounded by great music, automatically."

Dora looked at the phonograph, all mahogany and doors and machinery. "Do you really think there's going to be a war?" she said.

"Sure. They're warming up the pitchers now. They're waiting to see if the other side has right-handed or left-handed batters before they nominate their starting pitchers."

They continued walking downtown.

"But it's in Europe," Dora said. "Do you think we'll get into it?"

"Sure. Read the papers." He glanced at the window they were passing. "Look at those nice tables. Informal luncheons on your terrace. Metal and glass for outdoor feeding. That would be nice, eating out on a terrace off those wonderful colored plates, rich food with green salads. With a view of mountains and a lake, and inside, the phonograph."

"That sounds good," Dora said quietly.

"I could get an extra speaker," Paul said, "and wire it out to the terrace, so we could listen as we ate. I like Mozart with dinner." He laughed and drew her to a bookstore window.

"I always get sad," Dora said, "when I look in a bookshop window and see all the books I'm never going to have time to read."

Paul kissed her. "What did you think the first time you saw me?" he asked.

"What did *you* think?"

"I thought, 'I must get that girl!'"

Dora laughed, close to him.

"What did you think?" Paul asked.

"I thought"—she giggled—"I thought, 'I must get that man!'"

"Isn't New York marvelous?" Paul said. "Where did you say you come from?"

"Seattle," Dora said. "Seattle, Washington."

"Here we are on Madison Avenue, holding hands, shopping for the future . . ."

"Even if there was a war," Dora said after a while, "why would you have to get mixed up in it? Why would the United States have to get mixed up in it?"

"They got into the last one, didn't they?" Paul said. "They'll get into this one."

"They were gypped the last time," Dora said. "The guys who were killed were gypped."

"That's right," said Paul. "They were killed for six-per-cent interest on bonds, for oil wells, for spheres of influence. I wish I had a sphere of influence."

"Still," said Dora, "you'd enlist this time?"

"Yop. The first day. I'd walk right up to the recruiting office and say, 'Paul Triplett, twenty-six years old, hard as nails, good eyes, good teeth, good feet, give me a gun. Put me in a plane, so I can do a lot of damage.'"

They walked a whole block in silence.

"Don't you think you'd be gypped this time, too?" Dora said. "Don't you think they'd have you fighting for bonds and oil wells all over again?"

"Uh huh."

"And even so, you'd sign up?"

"The first day."

Dora pulled her hand away from him. "Do you *like* the idea of killing people?"

"I hate the idea," Paul said slowly. "I don't want to hurt anybody. I think the idea of war is ridiculous. I want to live in a world in which everybody sits on a terrace and eats off a metal-and-glass table off colored plates and the phonograph inside turns Mozart over automatically and the music is piped out to an extra loudspeaker on the terrace. Only Hitler isn't interested in that kind of world. He's interested in another kind of world. I couldn't stand to live in his kind of world, German or home-made."

"You wouldn't kill Hitler," Dora said. "You'd just kill young boys like yourself."

"That's right."

"Do you like that?"

"I'm really not interested in killing Hitler, either," Paul said. "I want to kill the idea he represents for so many people. In years to come I'll cry over the young boys I've killed and maybe if they kill me, they'll cry over me."

"They're probably just like you." They were walking fast now.

"Sure," Paul said. "I'm sure they'd love to go to bed with you tonight. I bet they'd love to walk along the fountains with the bronze statues in Rockefeller Plaza, holding hands with you on a spring Saturday evening and looking at the sports clothes in the windows. I bet a lot of them like Mozart, too, but still I'll kill them. Gladly."

"Gladly?"

"Yes, gladly." Paul wiped his eyes with his hands, suddenly tired. "Gladly today. I'll weep for them in years to come. Today they're guns aimed at me and the world I want. Their bodies protect an idea I have to kill to live. Hey!" He stretched out his hands and caught hers. "What's the sense talking about things like this tonight?"

"But it's all a big fraud," Dora cried. "You're being used and you know it."

"That's right," Paul said. "It's all a big fraud, the whole business. Even so, I got to fight. I'll be gypped, but by a little bit I'll do something for my side, for Mozart on a terrace at dinner. What the hell, it's not even heroism. I'll be dragged in, whatever I say."

"That's too bad," Dora said softly, walking by herself. "It's too bad."

"Sure," Paul said. "Some day maybe it'll be better. Maybe some day the world'll be run for people who like Mozart. Not today."

They stopped. They were in front of a little art store. There was a reproduction of the Renoir painting of a boating party on the river. There was the woman kissing the Pekinese, and the man in his underwear with a straw hat and his red beard, solid as earth, and the wit with his cocked derby hat whispering to the woman with her hands to her ears, and there was the great still life in the foreground, of wine and bottles and glasses and grapes and food.

"I saw it in Washington," Paul said. "They had it in Washington. You can't tell why it's a great picture from the print. There's an air of pink immortality hanging over it. They got it in New York now and I go look at it three times a week. It's settled, happy, solid. It's a picture of a summertime that vanished a long time ago." Paul kissed her hand. "It's getting late, darling, the hours're dwindling. Let's go home."

They got into a cab and went downtown to his apartment.

BOROUGH OF CEMETERIES

DURING THE COCKTAIL HOUR, in Brownsville, the cab drivers gather in Lammanawitz's Bar and Grill and drink beer and talk about the world and watch the sun set slowly over the elevated tracks in the direction of Prospect Park.

"Mungo?" they say. "Mungo? He got a fish for a arm. A mackerel. He will pitch Brooklyn right into the first division of the International League."

"I saw the Mayor today. His Honor, himself. The Little Flower. What this country needs . . ."

"Pinky, I want that you should trust me for a glass of beer."

Pinky wiped the wet dull expanse of the bar. "Look, Elias. It is against the law of the State of New York," he said nervously, "to sell intoxicating liquors on credit."

"One glass of beer. Intoxicatin'!" Elias' lips curled. "Who yuh think I am, Snow White?"

"Do you want me to lose my license?" Pinky asked plaintively.

"I stay up nights worryin' Pinky might lose his license. My wife hears me cryin' in my sleep," Elias said. "One beer, J. P. Morgan."

Regretfully, Pinky drew the beer, with a big head, and sighed as he marked it down in the book. "The last one," he said, "positively the last one. As God is my witness."

"Yeah," Elias said. "Keep yer mouth closed." He drank the beer in one gulp, with his eyes shut. "My God," he said quietly, his eyes still shut, as he put the glass down. "Fer a lousy dime," he said to the room in general, "yuh get somethin' like that! Fer a lousy dime! Brooklyn is a wonderful place."

"Brooklyn stinks," said another driver, down the bar. "The borough of cemeteries. This is a first class place for graveyards."

"My friend Palangio," Elias said. "Il Doochay Palangio. Yuh don't like Brooklyn, go back to Italy. They give yuh a gun, yuh get shot in the behind in Africa." The rest of the drivers laughed and Elias grinned at his own wit. "I seen in the movies. Go back t' Italy, wit' the fat girls. Who'll buy me a beer?"

Complete silence fell over the bar, like taps over an army camp.

"My friends," Elias said bitterly.

"Brooklyn is a wonderful place," Palangio said.

"All day long," Elias said, reflectively rubbing his broken nose, "I push a hack. Eleven hours on the street. I now have the sum of three dollars and fifty cents in my pocket."

Pinky came right over. "Now, Elias," he said, "there is the small matter of one beer. If I'd knew you had the money . . ."

Elias impatiently brushed Pinky's hand off the bar. "There is somebody callin' for a beer down there, Pinky," he said. "Attend yer business."

"I think," Pinky grumbled, retreating, "that a man oughta pay his rightful debts."

"He thinks. Pinky thinks," Elias announced. But his heart was not with Pinky. He turned his back to the bar and leaned on his frayed elbows and looked sadly up at the tin ceiling. "Three dollars and fifty cents," he said softly. "An' I can't buy a beer."

"Whatsamatta?" Palangio asked. "Yuh got a lock on yuh pocket?"

"Two dollars an' seventy-fi' cents to the Company," Elias said. "An' seventy-fi' cents to my lousy wife so she don't make me sleep in the park. The lousy Company. Every day for a year I give 'em two dollars an' seventy-fi' cents an' then I own the hack. After a year yuh might as well sell that crate to Japan to put in bombs. Th' only way yuh can get it to move is t' drop it. I signed a contract. I need a nurse. Who wants t' buy me a beer?"

"I signed th' same contract," Palangio said. A look of pain came over his dark face. "It got seven months more to go. Nobody shoulda learned me how to write my name."

"If you slobs would only join th' union," said a little Irishman across from the beer spigots.

"Geary," Elias said. "The Irish hero. Tell us how you fought th' English in th' battle of Belfast."

"O.K., O.K.," Geary said, pushing his cap back excitably from his red hair. "You guys wanna push a hack sixteen hours a day for beans, don' let me stop yuh."

"Join a union, get yer hair parted down the middle by the cops," Elias said. "That is my experience."

"O.K., boys," Geary pushed his beer a little to make it foam. "Property-owners. Can't pay for a glass a beer at five o'clock in th' afternoon. What's the use a' talkin' t' yuh? Lemme have a beer, Pinky."

"Geary, you're a red," Elias said. "A red bastidd."

"A Communist," Palangio said.

"I want a beer," Geary said loudly.

"Times're bad," Elias said. "That's what's th' trouble."

"Sure," Geary drained half his new glass. "Sure."

"Back in 1928," Elias said, "I averaged sixty bucks a week."

"On New Year's Eve, 1927," Palangio murmured, "I made thirty-six dollars and forty cents."

"Money was flowin'," Elias remembered.

Palangio sighed, rubbing his beard bristles with the back of his hand. "I wore silk shirts. With stripes. They cost five bucks a piece. I had four girls in 1928. My God!"

"This ain't 1928," Geary said.

"Th' smart guy," Elias said. "He's tellin' us somethin'. This ain't 1928, he says. Join th' union, we get 1928 back."

"Why the hell should I waste my time?" Geary asked himself in disgust. He drank in silence.

"Pinky!" Palangio called. "Pinky! Two beers for me and my friend Elias."

Elias moved, with a wide smile, up the bar, next to Palangio. "We are brothers in misery, Angelo," he said. "Me and th' Wop. We both signed th' contract."

They drank together and sighed together.

"I had th' biggest pigeon flight in Brownsville," Elias said softly. "One hundred and twelve pairs of pedigreed pigeons. I'd send 'em up like fireworks, every afternoon. You oughta've seen 'em wheelin' aroun' an' aroun' over th' roofs. I'm a pigeon fancier." He finished his glass. "I got fifteen pigeons left. Every time I bring home less than seventy-five cents, my wife cooks one for supper. A pedigreed pigeon. My lousy wife."

"Two beers," Palangio said. He and Elias drank with grave satisfaction.

"Now," Elias said, "if only I didn't have to go home to my lousy wife. I married her in 1929. A lot of things've changed since 1929." He sighed. "What's a woman?" he asked. "A woman is a trap."

"You shoulda seen what I seen today," Palangio said. "My third fare. On Eastern Parkway. I watched her walk all th' way acrost Nostrand Avenue, while I was waitin' on the light. A hundred-and-thirty pound girl. Blonde. Swingin' her hips like orchester music. With one of those little straw hats on top of her head, with the vegetables on it. You never saw nothin' like it. I held onto the wheel like I was drownin'. Talkin' about traps! She went to the St. George Hotel."

Elias shook his head. "The tragedy of my life," he said, "is I was married young."

"Two beers," Palangio said.

"Angelo Palangio," Elias said, "yer name reminds me of music."

"A guy met her in front of the St. George. A big fat guy. Smilin' like he just seen Santa Claus. A big fat guy. Some guys . . ."

"Some guys . . ." Elias mourned. "I gotta go home to Annie. She yells at me from six to twelve, regular. Who's goin' to pay the grocer? Who's goin' to pay the gas company?" He looked steadily at his beer for a moment and downed it. "I'm a man who married at the age a' eighteen."

"We need somethin' to drink," Palangio said.

"Buy us two whiskys," Elias said. "What the hell good is beer?"

"Two Calverts," Palangio called. "The best for me and my friend Elias Pinsker."

"Two gentlemen," Elias said, "who both signed th' contract."

"Two dumb slobs," said Geary.

"Th' union man," Elias lifted his glass. "To th' union!" He downed the whisky straight. "Th' hero of th' Irish Army."

"Pinky," Palangio shouted. "Fill 'em up to the top."

"Angelo Palangio," Elias murmured gratefully.

Palangio soberly counted the money out for the drinks. "Now," he said, "the Company can jump in Flushing Bay. I am down to two bucks even."

"Nice," Geary said sarcastically. "Smart. You don't pay 'em one day, they take yer cab. After payin' them regular for five months. Buy another drink."

Palangio slowly picked up his glass and let the whisky slide down his throat in a smooth amber stream. "Don't talk like that, Geary," he said. "I don't want to hear nothin' about taxicabs. I am busy drinkin' with friends."

"You dumb Wop," Geary said.

"That is no way to talk," Elias said, going over to Geary purposefully. He cocked his right hand and squinted at Geary. Geary backed off, his hands up. "I don't like to hear people call my friend a dumb Wop," Elias said.

"Get back," Geary shouted, "before I brain yuh."

Pinky ran up excitably. "Lissen, boys," he screamed, "do you want I should lose my license?"

"We are all friends," Palangio said. "Shake hands. Everybody shake hands. Everybody have a drink. I hereby treat everybody to a drink."

Elias lumbered back to Palangio's side. "I am sorry if I made a commotion. Some people can't talk like gentlemen."

"Everybody have a drink," Palangio insisted.

Elias took out three dollar bills and laid them deliberately on the bar. "Pass the bottle around. This is on Elias Pinsker."

"Put yer money away, Elias," Geary pushed his cap around on his head with anger. "Who yuh think yuh are? Walter Chrysler?"

"The entertainment this afternoon is on me," Elias said inexorably. "There was a time I would stand drinks for twenty-five men. With a laugh, an' pass cigars out after it. Pass the bottle around, Pinky!"

The whisky flowed.

"Elias and me," Palangio said. "We are high class spenders."

"You guys oughta be fed by hand," Geary said. "Wards of the guvment."

"A man is entitled to some relaxation," Elias said. "Where's that bottle?"

"This is nice," Palangio said. "This is very nice."

"This is like the good old days," Elias said.

"I hate to go home." Palangio sighed. "I ain't even got a radio home."

"Pinky!" Elias called. "Turn on the radio for Angelo Palangio."

"One room," Palangio said. "As big as a toilet. That is where I live."

The radio played. It was soft and sweet and a rich male voice sang, "I Married an Angel."

"When I get home," Elias remembered, "Annie will kill a pedigreed pigeon for supper. My lousy wife. An' after supper I push the hack five more hours and I go home and Annie yells some more and I get up tomorrow and push the hack some more." He poured himself another drink. "That is a life for a dog," he said. "For a Airedale."

"In Italy," Palangio said, "they got donkeys don't work as hard as us."

"If the donkeys were as bad off as you," Geary yelled, "they'd have sense enough to organize."

"I want to be a executive at a desk." Elias leaned both elbows on the bar and held his chin in his huge gnarled hands. "A long distance away from Brownsville. Wit' two thousand pigeons. In California. An' I should be a bachelor. Geary, can yuh organize *that*? Hey, Geary?"

"You're a workin' man," Geary said, "an' you're goin' to be a workin' man all yer life."

"Geary," Elias said. "You red bastidd, Geary."

"All my life," Palangio wept, "I am goin' to push a hack up an' down Brooklyn, fifteen, sixteen hours a day an' pay th' Company forever an' go home and sleep in a room no bigger'n a toilet. Without a radio. Jesus!"

"We are victims of circumstance," Elias said.

"All my life," Palangio cried, "tied to that crate!"

Elias pounded the bar once with his fist. "Th' hell with it! Palangio!" he said. "Get into that goddamn wagon of yours."

"What do yuh want me to do?" Palangio asked in wonder.

"We'll fix 'em," Elias shouted. "We'll fix those hacks. We'll fix that Company! Get into yer cab, Angelo. I'll drive mine, we'll have a chicken fight."

"Yuh drunken slobs!" Geary yelled. "Yuh can't do that!"

"Yeah," Palangio said eagerly, thinking it over. "Yeah. We'll show 'em. Two dollars and seventy-fi' cents a day for life. Yeah. We'll fix 'em. Come on, Elias!"

Elias and Palangio walked gravely out to their cars. Everybody else followed them.

"Look what they're doin'!" Geary screamed. "Not a brain between the both of them! What good'll it do to ruin the cabs?"

"Shut up," Elias said, getting into his cab. "We oughta done this five months ago. Hey, Angelo," he called, leaning out of his cab. "Are yuh ready? Hey, Il Doochay!"

"Contact!" Angelo shouted, starting his motor. "Boom! Boom!"

The two cars spurted at each other, in second, head-on. As they hit, glass broke and a fender flew off and the cars skidded wildly and the metal noise echoed and re-echoed like artillery fire off the buildings.

Elias stuck his head out of his cab. "Are yuh hurt?" he called. "Hey, Il Doochay!"

"Contact!" Palangio called from behind his broken windshield. "The Dawn Patrol!"

"I can't watch this," Geary moaned. "Two workin' men." He went back into Lammanawitz's Bar and Grill.

The two cabs slammed together again and people came running from all directions.

"How're yuh?" Elias asked, wiping the blood off his face.

"Onward!" Palangio stuck his hand out in salute. "Sons of Italy!"

Again and again the cabs tore into each other.

"Knights of the Round Table," Palangio announced.

"Knights of Lammanawitz's Round Table," Elias agreed, pulling at the choke to get the wheezing motor to turn over once more.

For the last time they came together. Both cars flew off the ground at the impact and Elias's toppled on its side and slid with a harsh grating noise to the curb. One of the front wheels from Palangio's cab rolled calmly and decisively toward Pitkin Avenue. Elias crawled out of his cab before anyone could reach him. He stood up, swaying, covered with blood, pulling at loose ends of his torn sweater. He shook hands soberly with Palangio and looked around him with satisfaction at the torn fenders and broken glass and scattered headlights and twisted steel. "Th' lousy Company," he said. "That does it. I am now goin' to inform 'em of th' accident."

He and Palangio entered the Bar and Grill, followed by a hundred men, women, and children. Elias dialed the number deliberately.

"Hullo," he said, "hullo, Charlie? Lissen, Charlie, if yuh send a wreckin' car down to Lammanawitz's Bar and Grill, yuh will find two of yer automobiles. Yuh lousy Charlie." He hung up carefully.

"All right, Palangio," he said.

"Yuh bet," Palangio answered.

"Now we oughta go to the movies," Elias said.

"That's right," Palangio nodded seriously.

"Yuh oughta be shot," Geary shouted.

"They're playin' Simone Simon," Elias announced to the crowd. "Let's go see Simone Simon."

Walking steadily, arm in arm, like two gentlemen, Elias and Angelo Palangio went down the street, through the lengthening shadows, toward Simone Simon.

THE EIGHTY-YARD RUN

THE PASS was high and wide and he jumped for it, feeling it slap flatly against his hands, as he shook his hips to throw off the halfback who was diving at him. The center floated by, his hands desperately brushing Darling's knee as Darling picked his feet up high and delicately ran over a blocker and an opposing linesman in a jumble on the ground near the scrimmage line. He had ten yards in the clear and picked up speed, breathing easily, feeling his thigh pads rising and falling against his legs, listening to the sound of cleats behind him, pulling away from them, watching the other backs heading him off toward the sideline, the whole picture, the men closing in on him, the blockers fighting for position, the ground he had to cross, all suddenly clear in his head, for the first time in his life not a meaningless confusion of men, sounds, speed. He smiled a little to himself as he ran, holding the ball lightly in front of him with his two hands, his knees pumping high, his hips twisting in the almost girlish run of a back in a broken field. The first halfback came at him and he fed him his leg, then swung at the last moment, took the shock of the man's shoulder without breaking stride, ran right through him, his cleats biting securely into the turf. There was only the safety man now, coming warily at him, his arms crooked, hands spread. Darling tucked the ball in, spurted at him, driving hard, hurling himself along, his legs pounding, knees high, all two hundred pounds bunched into controlled attack. He was sure he was going to get past the safety man. Without thought, his arms and legs working beautifully together, he headed right for the safety man, stiff-armed him, feeling blood spurt instantaneously from the man's nose onto his hand, seeing his face go awry, head turned, mouth pulled to one side. He pivoted away, keeping the arm locked, dropping the safety man as he ran easily toward the goal line, with the drumming of cleats diminishing behind him.

How long ago? It was autumn then, and the ground was getting hard because the nights were cold and leaves from the maples around the stadium blew across the practice fields in gusts of wind, and the girls were beginning to put polo coats over their sweaters when they came to watch practice in the afternoons. . . . Fifteen years. Darling walked slowly over the same ground in the spring twilight, in his neat shoes, a man of thirty-five dressed in a double-breasted suit, ten pounds heavier in the fifteen years, but not fat, with the years between 1925 and 1940 showing in his face.

The coach was smiling quietly to himself and the assistant coaches were looking at each other with pleasure the way they always did when one of the second stringers suddenly did something fine, bringing credit to them, making their $2,000 a year a tiny bit more secure.

Darling trotted back, smiling, breathing deeply but easily, feeling wonderful, not tired, though this was the tail end of practice and he'd run eighty yards. The sweat poured off his face and soaked his jersey and he liked the feeling, the warm moistness lubricating his skin like oil. Off in a corner of the field some players were punting and the smack of leather against the ball came pleasantly through the afternoon air. The freshmen were running signals on the next field and the quarterback's sharp voice, the pound of the eleven pairs of cleats, the "Dig, now *dig!*" of the coaches, the laughter of the players all somehow made him feel happy as he trotted back to midfield, listening to the applause and shouts of the students along the sidelines, knowing that after that run the coach would have to start him Saturday against Illinois.

Fifteen years, Darling thought, remembering the shower after the workout, the hot water steaming off his skin and the deep soapsuds and all the young voices singing with the water streaming down and towels going and managers running in and out and the sharp sweet smell of oil of wintergreen and everybody clapping him on the back as he dressed and Packard, the captain, who took being captain very seriously, coming over to him and shaking his hand and saying, "Darling, you're going to go places in the next two years."

The assistant manager fussed over him, wiping a cut on his leg with alcohol and iodine, the little sting making him realize suddenly how fresh and whole and solid his body felt. The manager slapped a piece of adhesive tape over the cut, and Darling noticed the sharp clean white of the tape against the ruddiness of the skin, fresh from the shower.

He dressed slowly, the softness of his shirt and the soft warmth of his wool socks and his flannel trousers a reward against his skin after the harsh pressure of the shoulder harness and thigh and hip pads. He drank three glasses of cold water, the liquid reaching down coldly inside of him, soothing the harsh dry places in his throat and belly left by the sweat and running and shouting of practice.

Fifteen years.

The sun had gone down and the sky was green behind the stadium and he laughed quietly to himself as he looked at the stadium, rearing above the trees, and knew that on Saturday when the 70,000 voices roared as the team came running out onto the field, part of that enormous salute would be for him. He walked slowly, listening to the gravel crunch satisfactorily under his shoes in the still twilight, feeling his clothes swing lightly against his skin, breathing the thin evening air, feeling the wind move softly in his damp hair, wonderfully cool behind his ears and at the nape of his neck.

Louise was waiting for him at the road, in her car. The top was down and he noticed all over again, as he always did when he saw her, how pretty she was, the rough blonde hair and the large, inquiring eyes and the bright mouth, smiling now.

She threw the door open. "Were you good today?" she asked.

"Pretty good," he said. He climbed in, sank luxuriously into the soft leather, stretched his legs far out. He smiled, thinking of the eighty yards. "Pretty damn good."

She looked at him seriously for a moment, then scrambled around, like a little girl, kneeling on the seat next to him, grabbed him, her hands along his ears, and kissed him as he sprawled, head back, on the seat cushion. She let go of him, but kept her head close to his, over his. Darling reached up slowly and rubbed the back of his hand against her cheek, lit softly by a street lamp a hundred feet away. They looked at each other, smiling.

Louise drove down to the lake and they sat there silently, watching the moon rise behind the hills on the other side. Finally he reached over, pulled her gently to him, kissed her. Her lips grew soft, her body sank into his, tears formed slowly in her eyes. He knew, for the first time, that he could do whatever he wanted with her.

"Tonight," he said. "I'll call for you at seven-thirty. Can you get out?"

She looked at him. She was smiling, but the tears were still full in her eyes. "All right," she said. "I'll get out. How about you? Won't the coach raise hell?"

Darling grinned. "I got the coach in the palm of my hand," he said. "Can you wait till seven-thirty?"

She grinned back at him. "No," she said.

They kissed and she started the car and they went back to town for dinner. He sang on the way home.

Christian Darling, thirty-five years old, sat on the frail spring grass, greener now than it ever would be again on the practice field, looked thoughtfully up at the stadium, a deserted ruin in the twilight. He had started on the first team that Saturday and every Saturday after that for the next two years, but it had never been as satisfactory as it should have been. He never had broken away, the longest run he'd ever made was thirty-five yards, and that in a game that was already won, and then that kid had come up from the third team, Diederich, a blank-faced German kid from Wisconsin, who ran like a bull, ripping lines to pieces Saturday after Saturday, plowing through, never getting hurt, never changing his expression, scoring more points, gaining more ground than all the rest of the team put together, making everybody's All-American, carrying the ball three times out of four, keeping everybody else out of the headlines. Darling was a good blocker and he spent his Saturday afternoons working on the big Swedes and Polacks who played tackle and end for Michigan, Illinois, Purdue, hurling into huge pile-ups, bobbing his head wildly to elude the great raw hands swinging like meat-cleavers at him as he went charging in to open up holes for Diederich coming through like a locomotive behind him. Still, it wasn't so bad. Everybody liked him and he did his job and he was pointed out on the campus and boys always felt important when they introduced their girls to him at their proms, and Louise loved him and watched him faithfully in the games, even in the mud, when your own mother wouldn't know you, and drove him around in her car keeping the top down because she was proud of him and wanted to show everybody that she was Christian Darling's girl. She bought him crazy presents because her father was rich, watches, pipes, humidors, an icebox for beer for his room, curtains, wallets, a fifty-dollar dictionary.

"You'll spend every cent your old man owns," Darling protested once when she showed up at his rooms with seven different packages in her arms and tossed them onto the couch.

"Kiss me," Louise said, "and shut up."

"Do you want to break your poor old man?"

"I don't mind. I want to buy you presents."

"Why?"

"It makes me feel good. Kiss me. I don't know why. Did you know that you're an important figure?"

"Yes," Darling said gravely.

"When I was waiting for you at the library yesterday two girls saw you coming and one of them said to the other, 'That's Christian Darling. He's an important figure.'"

"You're a liar."

"I'm in love with an important figure."

"Still, why the hell did you have to give me a forty-pound dictionary?"

"I wanted to make sure," Louise said, "that you had a token of my esteem. I want to smother you in tokens of my esteem."

Fifteen years ago.

They'd married when they got out of college. There'd been other women for him, but all casual and secret, more for curiosity's sake, and vanity, women who'd thrown themselves at him and flattered him, a pretty mother at a summer camp for boys, an old girl from his home town who'd suddenly blossomed into a coquette, a friend of Louise's who had dogged him grimly for six months and had taken advantage of the two weeks that Louise went home when her mother died. Perhaps Louise had known, but she'd kept quiet, loving him completely, filling his rooms with presents, religiously watching him battling with the big Swedes and Polacks on the line of scrimmage on Saturday afternoons, making plans for marrying him and living with him in New York and going with him there to the night clubs, the theaters, the good restaurants, being proud of him in advance, tall, white-teethed, smiling, large, yet moving lightly, with an athlete's grace, dressed in evening clothes, approvingly eyed by magnificently dressed and famous women in theater lobbies, with Louise adoringly at his side.

Her father, who manufactured inks, set up a New York office for Darling to manage and presented him with three hundred accounts, and they lived on Beekman Place with a view of the river with fifteen thousand dollars a year between them, because everybody was buying everything in those days, including ink. They saw all the shows and went to all the speakeasies and spent their fifteen thousand dollars a year and in the afternoons Louise went to the art galleries and the matinees of the more serious plays that Darling didn't like to sit through and Darling slept with a girl who danced in the chorus of *Rosalie* and with the wife of a man who owned three copper mines. Darling played squash three times a week and remained as solid as a stone barn and Louise never took her eyes off him when they were in the same room together, watching him with a secret, miser's smile, with a trick of coming over to him in the middle of a crowded room and saying gravely, in a low voice, "You're the handsomest man I've ever seen in my whole life. Want a drink?"

Nineteen twenty-nine came to Darling and to his wife and father-in-law, the maker of inks, just as it came to everyone else. The father-in-law waited until 1933 and then blew his brains out and when Darling went to Chicago to see what the books of the firm looked like he found out all that was left were debts and three or four gallons of unbought ink.

"Please, Christian," Louise said, sitting in their neat Beekman Place apartment, with a view of the river and prints of paintings by Dufy and Braque and Picasso on the wall, "please, why do you want to start drinking at two o'clock in the afternoon?"

"I have nothing else to do," Darling said, putting down his glass, emptied of its fourth drink. "Please pass the whisky."

Louise filled his glass. "Come take a walk with me," she said. "We'll walk along the river."

"I don't want to walk along the river," Darling said, squinting intensely at the prints of paintings by Dufy, Braque and Picasso.

"We'll walk along Fifth Avenue."

"I don't want to walk along Fifth Avenue."

"Maybe," Louise said gently, "you'd like to come with me to some art galleries. There's an exhibition by a man named Klee. . . ."

"I don't want to go any art galleries. I want to sit here and drink Scotch whisky," Darling said. "Who the hell hung those goddam pictures up on the wall?"

"I did," Louise said.

"I hate them."

"I'll take them down," Louise said.

"Leave them there. It gives me something to do in the afternoon. I can hate them." Darling took a long swallow. "Is that the way people paint these days?"

"Yes, Christian. Please don't drink any more."

"Do you like painting like that?"

"Yes, dear."

"Really?"

"Really."

Darling looked carefully at the prints once more. "Little Louise Tucker. The middle-western beauty. I like pictures with horses in them. Why should you like pictures like that?"

"I just happen to have gone to a lot of galleries in the last few years . . ."

"Is that what you do in the afternoon?"

"That's what I do in the afternoon," Louise said.

"I drink in the afternoon."

Louise kissed him lightly on the top of his head as he sat there squinting at the pictures on the wall, the glass of whisky held firmly in his hand. She put on her coat and went out without saying another word. When she came back in the early evening, she had a job on a woman's fashion magazine.

They moved downtown and Louise went out to work every morning and Darling sat home and drank and Louise paid the bills as they came up. She made believe she was going to quit work as soon as Darling found a job, even though she was taking over more responsibility day by day at the magazine, interviewing authors, picking painters for the illustrations and covers, getting actresses to pose for pictures, going out for drinks with the right people, making a thousand new friends whom she loyally introduced to Darling.

"I don't like your hat," Darling said, once, when she came in in the evening and kissed him, her breath rich with martinis.

"What's the matter with my hat, Baby?" she asked, running her fingers through his hair. "Everybody says it's very smart."

"It's too damned smart," he said. "It's not for you. It's for a rich, sophisticated woman of thirty-five with admirers."

Louise laughed. "I'm practicing to be a rich, sophisticated woman of thirty-five with admirers," she said. He stared soberly at her. "Now, don't look so grim, Baby. It's still the same simple little wife under the hat." She took the hat off, threw it into a corner, sat on his lap. "See? Homebody Number One."

"Your breath could run a train," Darling said, not wanting to be mean, but talking out of boredom, and sudden shock at seeing his wife curiously a stranger in a new hat, with a new expression in her eyes under the little brim, secret, confident, knowing.

Louise tucked her head under his chin so he couldn't smell her breath. "I had to take an author out for cocktails," she said. "He's a boy from the Ozark Mountains and he drinks like a fish. He's a Communist."

"What the hell is a Communist from the Ozarks doing writing for a woman's fashion magazine?"

Louise chuckled. "The magazine business is getting all mixed up these days. The publishers want to have a foot in every camp. And anyway, you can't find an author under seventy these days who isn't a Communist."

"I don't think I like you to associate with all those people, Louise," Darling said. "Drinking with them."

"He's a very nice, gentle boy," Louise said. "He reads Ernest Dowson."

"Who's Ernest Dowson?"

Louise patted his arm, stood up, fixed her hair. "He's an English poet."

Darling felt that somehow he had disappointed her. "Am I supposed to know who Ernest Dowson is?"

"No, dear. I'd better go in and take a bath."

After she had gone, Darling went over to the corner where the hat was lying and picked it up. It was nothing, a scrap of straw, a red flower, a veil, meaningless on his big hand, but on his wife's head a signal of something . . . big city, smart and knowing women drinking and dining with men other than their husbands, conversation about things a normal man wouldn't know much about, Frenchmen who painted as though they used their elbows instead of brushes, composers who wrote whole symphonies without a single melody in them, writers who knew all about politics and women who knew all about writers, the movement of the proletariat, Marx, somehow mixed up with five-dollar dinners and the best-looking women in America and fairies who made them laugh and half-sentences immediately understood and secretly hilarious and wives who called their husbands "Baby." He put the hat down, a scrap of straw and a red flower, and a little veil. He drank some whisky straight and went into the bathroom where his wife was lying deep in her bath, singing to herself and smiling from time to time like a little girl, paddling the water gently with her hands, sending up a slight spicy fragrance from the bath salts she used.

He stood over her, looking down at her. She smiled up at him, her eyes half closed, her body pink and shimmering in the warm, scented water. All over again, with all the old suddenness, he was hit deep inside him with the knowledge of how beautiful she was, how much he needed her.

"I came in here," he said, "to tell you I wish you wouldn't call me 'Baby.'"

She looked up at him from the bath, her eyes quickly full of sorrow, half-understanding what he meant. He knelt and put his arms around her, his sleeves plunged heedlessly in the water, his shirt and jacket soaking wet as he clutched her wordlessly, holding her crazily tight, crushing her breath from her, kissing her desperately, searchingly, regretfully.

He got jobs after that, selling real estate and automobiles, but somehow, although he had a desk with his name on a wooden wedge on it, and he went to the office religiously at nine each morning, he never managed to sell anything and he never made any money.

Louise was made assistant editor, and the house was always full of strange men and women who talked fast and got angry on abstract subjects like mural painting, novelists, labor unions. Negro short-story writers drank Louise's liquor, and a lot of Jews, and big solemn men with scarred faces and knotted hands who talked slowly but clearly about picket lines and battles with guns and leadpipe at mine-shaft-heads and in front of factory gates. And Louise moved among them all, confidently, knowing what they were talking about, with opinions that they listened to and argued about just as though she were a man. She knew everybody, condescended to no one, devoured books that Darling had never heard of, walked along the streets of the city, excited, at home, soaking in all the million tides of New York without fear, with constant wonder.

Her friends liked Darling and sometimes he found a man who wanted to get off in the corner and talk about the new boy who played fullback for Princeton, and the decline of the double wing-back, or even the state of the stock market, but for the most part he sat on the edge of things, solid and quiet in the high storm of words. "The dialectics of the situation . . . The theater has been given over to expert jugglers . . . Picasso? What man has a right to paint old bones and collect ten thousand dollars for them? . . . I stand firmly behind Trotsky . . . Poe was the last American critic. When he died they put lilies on the grave of American criticism. I don't say this because they panned my last book, but . . ."

Once in a while he caught Louise looking soberly and consideringly at him through the cigarette smoke and the noise and he avoided her eyes and found an excuse to get up and go into the kitchen for more ice or to open another bottle.

"Come on," Cathal Flaherty was saying, standing at the door with a girl, "you've got to come down and see this. It's down on Fourteenth Street, in the old Civic Repertory, and you can only see it on Sunday nights and I guarantee you'll come out of the theater singing." Flaherty was a big young Irishman with a broken nose who was the lawyer for a longshoreman's union, and he had been hanging around the house for six months on and off, roaring and shutting everybody else up when he got in an argument. "It's a new play, *Waiting for Lefty*; it's about taxi-drivers."

"Odets," the girl with Flaherty said. "It's by a guy named Odets."

"I never heard of him," Darling said.

"He's a new one," the girl said.

"It's like watching a bombardment," Flaherty said. "I saw it last Sunday night. You've got to see it."

"Come on, Baby," Louise said to Darling, excitement in her eyes already. "We've been sitting in the Sunday *Times* all day, this'll be a great change."

"I see enough taxi-drivers every day," Darling said, not because he meant that, but because he didn't like to be around Flaherty, who said things that made Louise laugh a lot and whose judgment she accepted on almost every subject. "Let's go to the movies."

"You've never seen anything like this before," Flaherty said. "He wrote this play with a baseball bat."

"Come on," Louise coaxed, "I bet it's wonderful."

"He has long hair," the girl with Flaherty said. "Odets. I met him at a party. He's an actor. He didn't say a goddam thing all night."

"I don't feel like going down to Fourteenth Street," Darling said, wishing Flaherty and his girl would get out. "It's gloomy."

"Oh, hell!" Louise said loudly. She looked coolly at Darling, as though she'd just been introduced to him and was making up her mind about him, and not very favorably. He saw her looking at him, knowing there was something new and dangerous in her face and he wanted to say something, but Flaherty was there and his damned girl, and anyway, he didn't know what to say.

"I'm going," Louise said, getting her coat. "I don't think Fourteenth Street is gloomy."

"I'm telling you," Flaherty was saying, helping her on with her coat, "it's the Battle of Gettysburg, in Brooklynese."

"Nobody could get a word out of him," Flaherty's girl was saying as they went through the door. "He just sat there all night."

The door closed. Louise hadn't said good night to him. Darling walked around the room four times, then sprawled out on the sofa, on top of the Sunday *Times*. He lay there for five minutes looking at the ceiling, thinking of Flaherty walking down the street talking in that booming voice, between the girls, holding their arms.

Louise had looked wonderful. She'd washed her hair in the afternoon and it had been very soft and light and clung close to her head as she stood there angrily putting her coat on. Louise was getting prettier every year, partly because she knew by now how pretty she was, and made the most of it.

"Nuts," Darling said, standing up. "Oh, nuts."

He put on his coat and went down to the nearest bar and had five drinks off by himself in a corner before his money ran out.

The years since then had been foggy and downhill. Louise had been nice to him, and in a way, loving and kind, and they'd fought only once, when he said he was going to vote for Landon. ("Oh, Christ," she'd said, "doesn't *anything* happen inside your head? Don't you read the papers? The penniless Republican!") She'd been sorry later and apologized for hurting him, but apologized as she might to a child. He'd tried hard, had gone grimly to the art galleries, the concert halls, the bookshops, trying to gain on the trail of his wife, but it was no use. He was bored, and none of what he saw or heard or dutifully read made much sense to him and finally he gave it up. He had thought, many nights as he ate dinner alone, knowing that Louise would come home late and drop silently into bed without explanation, of getting a divorce, but he knew the loneliness, the hopelessness, of not seeing her again would be too much to take. So he was good, completely devoted, ready at all times to go anyplace with her, do anything she wanted. He even got a small job, in a broker's office, and paid his own way, bought his own liquor.

Then he'd been offered the job of going from college to college as a tailor's representative. "We want a man," Mr. Rosenberg had said, "who as soon as you look at him, you say, 'There's a university man.'" Rosenberg had looked approvingly at Darling's broad shoulders and well-kept waist, at his carefully brushed hair and his honest, wrinkle-less face. "Frankly, Mr. Darling, I am willing to make you a proposition. I have inquired about you, you are favorably known on your old campus, I understand you were in the backfield with Alfred Diederich."

Darling nodded. "Whatever happened to him?"

"He is walking around in a cast for seven years now. An iron brace. He played professional football and they broke his neck for him."

Darling smiled. That, at least, had turned out well.

"Our suits are an easy product to sell, Mr. Darling," Rosenberg said. "We have a handsome, custom-made garment. What has Brooks Brothers got that we haven't got? A name. No more."

"I can make fifty, sixty dollars a week," Darling said to Louise that night. "And expenses. I can save some money and then come back to New York and really get started here."

"Yes, Baby," Louise said.

"As it is," Darling said carefully, "I can make it back here once a month, and holidays and the summer. We can see each other often."

"Yes, Baby." He looked at her face, lovelier now at thirty-five than it had ever been before, but fogged over now as it had been for five years with a kind of patient, kindly, remote boredom.

"What do you say?" he asked. "Should I take it?" Deep within him he hoped fiercely, longingly, for her to say, "No, Baby, you stay right here," but she said, as he knew she'd say, "I think you'd better take it."

He nodded. He had to get up and stand with his back to her, looking out the window, because there were things plain on his face that she had never seen in the fifteen years she'd known him. "Fifty dollars is a lot of money," he said. "I never thought I'd ever see fifty dollars again." He laughed. Louise laughed, too.

Christian Darling sat on the frail green grass of the practice field. The shadow of the stadium had reached out and covered him. In the distance the lights of the university shone a little mistily in the light haze of evening. Fifteen years. Flaherty even now was calling for his wife, buying her a drink, filling whatever bar they were in with that voice of his and that easy laugh. Darling half-closed his eyes, almost saw the boy fifteen years ago reach for the pass, slip the halfback, go skittering lightly down the field, his knees high and fast and graceful, smiling to himself because he knew he was going to get past the safety man. That was the high point, Darling thought, fifteen years ago, on an autumn afternoon, twenty years old and far from death, with the air coming easily into his lungs, and a deep feeling inside him that he could do anything, knock over anybody, outrun whatever had to be outrun. And the shower after and the three glasses of water and the cool night air on his damp head and Louise sitting hatless in the open car with a smile and the first kiss she ever really meant. The high point, an eighty-yard run in the practice, and a girl's kiss and everything after that a decline. Darling laughed. He had practiced the wrong thing, perhaps. He hadn't practiced for 1929 and New York City and a girl who would turn into a woman. Somewhere, he thought, there must have been a point where she moved up to me, was even with me for a moment, when I could have held her hand, if I'd known, held tight, gone with her. Well, he'd never known. Here he was on a playing field that was fifteen years away and his wife was in another city having dinner with another and better man, speaking with him a different, new language, a language nobody had ever taught him.

Darling stood up, smiled a little, because if he didn't smile he knew the tears would come. He looked around him. This was the spot. O'Connor's pass had come sliding out just to here . . . the high point. Darling put up his hands, felt all over again the flat slap of the ball. He shook his hips to throw off the halfback, cut back inside the center, picked his knees high as he ran gracefully over two men jumbled on the ground at the line of scrimmage, ran easily, gaining speed, for ten yards, holding the ball lightly in his two hands, swung away from the halfback diving at him, ran, swinging his hips in the almost girlish manner of a back in a broken field, tore into the safety man, his shoes drumming heavily on the turf, stiff-armed, elbow locked, pivoted, raced lightly and exultantly for the goal line.

It was only after he had sped over the goal line and slowed to a trot that he saw the boy and girl sitting together on the turf, looking at him wonderingly.

He stopped short, dropping his arms. "I . . ." he said, gasping a little, though his condition was fine and the run hadn't winded him. "I—once I played here."

The boy and the girl said nothing. Darling laughed embarrassedly, looked hard at them sitting there, close to each other, shrugged, turned and went toward his hotel, the sweat breaking out on his face and running down into his collar.

MAIN CURRENTS
OF AMERICAN THOUGHT

"FLACKER: All right now, Kid, now you'd better talk," Andrew dictated. "Business: Sound of the door closing, the slow turning of the key in the lock. Buddy: You're never going to get me to talk, Flacker. Business: Sound of a slap. Flacker: Maybe that'll make you think different, Kid. Where is Jerry Carmichael? Buddy: (Laughing) Wouldn't you like to know, Flacker? Flacker: Yeah. (Slowly, with great threat in his voice) And I'm going to find out. One way or another. See? Business: Siren fades in, louder, fades out. Announcer: Will Buddy talk? Will Flacker force him to disclose the whereabouts of the rescued son of the railroad king? Will Dusty Blades reach him in time? Tune in Monday at the same time, et cetera, et cetera . . ."

Andrew dropped onto the couch and put his feet up. He stretched and sighed as he watched Lenore finish scratching his dictation down in the shorthand notebook. "Thirty bucks," he said. "There's another thirty bucks. Is it the right length?"

"Uhuh," Lenore said. "Eleven and a half pages. This is a very good one, Andy."

"Yeah," Andrew said, closing his eyes. "Put it next to *Moby Dick* on your library shelf."

"It's very exciting," Lenore said, standing up. "I don't know what they're complaining about."

"You're a lovely girl." Andrew put his hands over his eyes and rubbed around and around. "I have wooden hinges on my eyelids. Do you sleep at night?"

"Don't do that to your eyes." Lenore started to put on her coat. "You only aggravate them."

"You're right." Andrew dug his fists into his eyes and rotated them slowly. "You don't know how right you are."

"Tomorrow. At ten o'clock?" Lenore asked.

"At ten o'clock. Dig me out of the arms of sleep. We shall leave Dusty Blades to his fate for this week and go on with the further adventures of Ronnie Cook and His Friends, forty dollars a script. I always enjoy writing Ronnie Cook much better than Dusty Blades. See what ten dollars does to a man." He opened his eyes and watched Lenore putting her hat on in front of the mirror. When he squinted, she was not so plain-looking. He felt very sorry for Lenore, plain as sand, with her flat-colored face and her hair pulled down like rope, and never a man to her name. She was putting on a red hat with a kind of ladder arrangement going up one side. It looked very funny and sad on her. Andrew realized that it was a new hat. "That's a mighty fine hat," he said.

"I thought a long time before I bought this hat," Lenore said, flushing because he'd noticed it.

"Har-*riet!*" The governess next door screamed in the alley to the next-door neighbor's little girl. "Harriet, get away from there this minute!"

Andrew turned over on his stomach on the couch and put a pillow over his head. "Have you got any ideas for Ronnie Cook and His Friends for tomorrow?" he asked Lenore.

"No. Have you?"

"No." He pulled the pillow tight around his head.

"You'll get them by tomorrow," Lenore said. "You always do."

"Yeah," said Andrew.

"You need a vacation," Lenore said.

"Get out of here."

"Good-bye." Lenore started out. "Get a good night's sleep."

"Anything you say."

Andrew watched her with one eye as she went off the porch on which he worked and through the living room and dining room, toward the stairs. She had nice legs. You were always surprised when a girl with a face like that had nice legs. But she had hair on her legs. She was not a lucky girl. "Oh, no," Andrew said as the door closed behind her, "you are not a lucky girl."

He closed his eyes and tried to sleep. The sun came in through the open windows and the curtains blew softly over his head and the sun was warm and comforting on his closed eyes. Across the street, on the public athletic field, four boys were shagging flies. There would be the neat pleasant crack of the bat and a long time later the smack of the ball in the fielder's glove. The tall trees outside, as old as Brooklyn, rustled a little from time to time as little spurts of wind swept across the baseball field.

"Harriet!" the governess called. "Stop that or I will make you stand by yourself in the corner all afternoon! Harriet! I demand you to stop it!" The governess was French. She had the only unpleasant French accent Andrew had ever heard.

The little girl started to cry, "Mamma! Mamma! Mamma, she's going to hit me!" The little girl hated the governess and the governess hated the little girl, and they continually reported each other to the little girl's mother. "Mamma!"

"You are a little liar," the governess screamed. "You will grow up, and you will be a liar all your life. There will be no hope for you."

"Mamma!" wailed the little girl.

They went inside the house and it was quiet again.

"Charlie," one of the boys on the baseball field yelled, "hit it to me, Charlie!"

The telephone rang, four times, and then Andrew heard his mother talking into it. She came onto the porch.

"It's a man from the bank," she said. "He wants to talk to you."

"You should've told him I wasn't home," Andrew said.

"But you are home," his mother said. "How was I to know that . . . ?"

"You're right." Andrew swung his legs over and sat up. "You're perfectly right."

He went into the dining room, to the telephone, and talked to the man at the bank.

"You're a hundred and eleven dollars overdrawn," said the man at the bank.

Andrew squinted at his mother, sitting across the room, on a straight chair, with her arms folded in her lap, her head turned just a little, so as not to miss anything.

"I thought I had about four hundred dollars in the bank," Andrew said into the phone.

"You are a hundred and eleven dollars overdrawn," said the man at the bank.

Andrew sighed. "I'll check it." He put the phone down.

"What's the matter?" his mother asked.

"I'm a hundred and eleven dollars overdrawn," he said.

"That's shameful," his mother said. "You ought to be more methodical."

"Yes." Andrew started back to the porch.

"You're awfully careless." His mother followed him. "You really ought to keep track of your money."

"Yes." Andrew sat down on the couch.

"Give me a kiss," his mother said.

"Why?"

"No particular reason." She laughed.

"O.K." He kissed her and she held him for a moment. He dropped down on the couch. She ran her finger under his eye.

"You've got rings under your eyes," she said.

"That's right."

She kissed him again and went to the rear of the house. He closed his eyes. From the rear of the house came the sound of the vacuum cleaner. Andrew felt his muscles getting stiff in protest against the vacuum cleaner. He got up and went to her bedroom, where she was running the machine back and forth under the bed. She was down on one knee and was bent over, looking under the bed.

"Hey!" Andrew yelled. "Hey, Mom!"

She turned off the machine and looked up at him. "What's the matter?"

"I'm trying to sleep," he said.

"Well, why don't you sleep?"

"The vacuum cleaner. It's shaking the house."

His mother stood up, her face setting into stern lines. "I've got to clean the house, don't I?"

"Why do you have to clean the house while I'm trying to sleep?"

His mother bent down again. "I can't use it while you're working. I can't use it while you're reading. I can't use it until ten o'clock in the morning because you're sleeping." She started the machine. "When am I supposed to clean the house?" she called over the noise of the cleaner. "Why don't you sleep at night like everybody else?" And she put her head down low and vigorously ran the machine back and forth.

Andrew watched her for a moment. No arguments came to him. The sound of the cleaner so close to him made his nerves jump. He went out of the room, closing the door behind him.

The telephone was ringing and he picked it up and said, "Hello."

"Ahndrew?" his agent's voice asked. His agent was from Brooklyn, too, but he had a very broad A, with which he impressed actors and sponsors.

"Yes, this is Ahndrew." Andrew always made this straight-faced joke with his agent, but the agent never seemed to catch on. "You didn't have to call. The Dusty Blades scripts are all through. You'll get them tomorrow."

"I called about something else, Ahndrew," his agent said, his voice very smooth and influential on the phone. "The complaints're piling up on the Blades scripts. They're as slow as gum. Nothing ever happens. Ahndrew, you're not writing for the *Atlantic Monthly*."

"I know I'm not writing for the *Atlantic Monthly*."

"I think you've rather run out of material," his agent said lightly, soothingly. "I think perhaps you ought to take a little vacation from the Blades scripts."

"Go to hell, Herman," Andrew said, knowing that Herman had found somebody to do the scripts more cheaply for him.

"That's hardly the way to talk, Ahndrew," Herman said, his voice still smooth, but hurt. "After all, I have to stand in the studio and listen to the complaints."

"Sad, Herman," Andrew said. "That's a sad picture," and hung up.

He rubbed the back of his neck reflectively, feeling again the little lump behind his ear.

He went into his own room and sat at his desk looking blankly at the notes for his play that lay, neatly piled, growing older, on one side. He took out his checkbook and his last month's vouchers and arranged them in front of him.

"One hundred and eleven dollars," he murmured, as he checked back and added and subtracted, his eyes smarting from the strain, his hands shaking a little because the vacuum cleaner was still going in his mother's room. Out on the athletic field more boys had arrived and formed an infield and were throwing the ball around the bases and yelling at each other.

Dr. Chalmers, seventy-five dollars. That was for his mother and her stomach.

Eighty dollars rent. The roof over his head equaled two Ronnie Cooks and His Friends. Five thousand words for rent.

Buddy was in the hands of Flacker. Flacker could torture him for six pages. Then you could have Dusty Blades speeding to the rescue with Sam, by boat, and the boat could spring a leak because the driver was in Flacker's pay, and there could be a fight for the next six pages. The driver could have a gun. You could use it, but it wouldn't be liked, because you'd done at least four like it already.

Furniture, and a hundred and thirty-seven dollars. His mother had always wanted a good dining-room table. She didn't have a maid, she said, so he ought to get her a dining-room table. How many words for a dining-room table?

"Come on, Baby, make it two," the second baseman out on the field was yelling. "Double 'em up!"

Andrew felt like picking up his old glove and going out there and joining them. When he as still in college he used to go out on a Saturday at ten o'clock in the morning and shag flies and jump around the in-field and run and run all day, playing in pickup games until it got too dark to see. He was always tired now and even when he played tennis he didn't move his feet right, because he was tired, and hit flat-footed and wild.

Spain, one hundred dollars. Oh, Lord.

A hundred and fifty to his father, to meet his father's payroll. His father had nine people on his payroll, making little tin gadgets that his father tried to sell to the dime stores, and at the end of every month Andrew had to meet the payroll. His father always gravely made out a note to him.

Flacker is about to kill Buddy out of anger and desperation. In bursts Dusty, alone. Sam is hurt. On the way to the hospital. Buddy is spirited away a moment before Dusty arrives. Flacker, very smooth and oily. Confrontation. "Where is Buddy, Flacker?" "You mean the little lad?" "I mean the little lad, Flacker!"

Fifty dollars to Dorothy's piano teacher. His sister. Another plain girl. She might as well learn how to play the piano. Then one day they'd come to him and say, "Dorothy is ready for her debut. All we're asking you to do is rent Town Hall for a Wednesday evening. Just advance the money." She'd never get married. She was too smart for the men who would want her and too plain for the men she'd want herself. She bought her dresses in Saks. He would have to support, for life, a sister who would only buy her dresses in Saks and pay her piano teacher fifty dollars a month every month. She was only twenty-four, she would have a normal life expectancy of at least forty years, twelve times forty, plus dresses at Saks and Town Hall from time to time . . .

His father's teeth—ninety dollars. The money it cost to keep a man going in his losing fight against age.

The automobile. Nine hundred dollars. A nine-hundred-dollar check looked very austere and impressive, like a penal institution. He was going to go off in the automobile, find a place in the mountains, write a play. Only he could never get himself far enough ahead on Dusty Blades and Ronnie Cook and His Friends. Twenty thousand words a week, each week, recurring like Sunday on the calendar. How many words was *Hamlet*? Thirty, thirty-five thousand?

Twenty-three dollars to Best's. That was Martha's sweater for her birthday. "Either you say yes or no," Martha said Saturday night. "I want to get married and I've waited long enough." If you married you paid rent in two places, light, gas, telephone twice, and you bought stockings, dresses, toothpaste, medical attention, for your wife.

Flacker plays with something in his pocket. Dusty's hand shoots out, grabs his wrist, pulls his hand out. Buddy's little penknife, which Dusty had given him for a birthday present, is in Flacker's hand. "Flacker, tell me where Buddy Jones is, or I'll kill you with my bare hands." A gong rings. Flacker has stepped on an alarm. Doors open and the room fills with his henchmen.

Twenty dollars to Macy's for books. Parrington, *Main Currents in American Thought*. How does Dusty Blades fit into the *Main Currents of American Thought*?

Ten dollars to Dr. Farber. "I don't sleep at night. Can you help me?"

"Do you drink coffee?"

"I drink one cup of coffee in the morning. That's all."

Pills, to be taken before retiring. Ten dollars. We ransom our lives from doctors' hands.

If you marry, you take an apartment downtown because it's silly to live in Brooklyn this way; and you buy furniture, four rooms full of furniture, beds, chairs, dishrags, relatives. Martha's family was poor and getting no younger and finally there would be three families, with rent and clothes and doctors and funerals.

Andrew got up and opened the closet door. In it, stacked in files, were the scripts he had written in the last four years. They stretched from one end of a wide closet across to another, bridge from one wall to another of a million words. Four years' work.

Next script. The henchmen close in on Dusty. He hears the sounds of Buddy screaming in the next room . . .

How many years more?

The vacuum cleaner roared.

Martha was Jewish. That meant you'd have to lie your way into some hotels, if you went at all, and you never could escape from one particular meanness of the world around you; and when the bad time came there you'd be, adrift on that dangerous sea.

He sat down at his desk. One hundred dollars again to Spain. Barcelona had fallen and the long dusty lines were beating their way to the French border with the planes over them, and out of a sense of guilt at not being on a dusty road, yourself, bloody-footed and in fear of death, you gave a hundred dollars, feeling at the same time that it was too much and nothing you ever gave could be enough. Three-and-a-third The Adventures of Dusty Blades to the dead and dying of Spain.

The world loads you day by day with new burdens that increase on your shoulders. Lift a pound and you find you're carrying a ton. "Marry me," she says, "marry me." Then what does Dusty do? What the hell can he do that he hasn't done before? For five afternoons a week now, for a year, Dusty has been in Flacker's hands, or the hands of somebody else who is Flacker but has another name, and each time he has escaped. How now?

The vacuum roared in the hallway outside his room.

"Mom!" he yelled. "Please turn that thing off!"

"What did you say?" his mother called.

"Nothing."

He added up the bank balances. His figures showed that he was four hundred and twelve dollars overdrawn instead of one hundred and eleven dollars, as the bank said. He didn't feel like adding the figures over. He put the vouchers and the bank's sheet into an envelope for his income-tax returns.

"Hit it out, Charlie!" a boy called on the field. "Make it a fast one!"

Andrew felt like going out and playing with them. He changed his clothes and put on a pair of old spikes that were lying in the back of the closet. His old pants were tight on him. Fat. If he ever let go, if anything happened and he couldn't exercise, he'd blow up like a house, if he got sick and had to lie in bed and convalesce . . . Maybe Dusty has a knife in a holster up his sleeve . . . How plant that? The rent, the food, the piano teacher, the people at Saks who sold his sister dresses, the nimble girls who painted the tin gadgets in his father's shop, the teeth in his father's mouth, the doctors, the doctors, all living on the words that would have to come out of his head. See here, Flacker, I know what you're up to. Business: Sound of a shot. A groan. Hurry, before the train gets to the crossing! Look! He's gaining on us! Hurry! will he make it? Will Dusty Blades head off the desperate gang of counterfeiters and murderers in the race for the yacht? Will I be able to keep it up? The years, the years ahead . . . You grow fat and the lines become permanent under your eyes and you drink too much and you pay more to the doctors because death is nearer and there is no stop, no vacation from life, in no year can you say, "I want to sit this one out, kindly excuse me."

His mother opened the door. "Martha's on the phone."

Andrew clattered out in his spiked shoes, holding the old, torn fielder's glove. He closed the door to the dining room to show his mother this was going to be a private conversation.

"Hello," he said. "Yes." He listened gravely. "No," he said. "I guess not. Good-bye. Good luck, Martha."

He stood looking at the phone. His mother came in and he raised his head and started down the steps.

"Andrew," she said, "I want to ask you something."

"What?"

"Could you spare fifty dollars, Andrew?"

"Oh, God!"

"It's important. You know I wouldn't ask you if it wasn't important. It's for Dorothy."

"What does she need it for?"

"She's going to a party, a very important party, a lot of very big people're going to be there and she's sure they'll ask her to play. . . ."

"Do the invitations cost fifty dollars apiece?" Andrew kicked the top step and a little piece of dried mud fell off the spiked shoes.

"No, Andrew." His mother was talking in her asking-for-money voice. "It's for a dress. She can't go without a new dress, she says. There's a man there she's after."

"She won't get him, dress or no dress," Andrew said. "Your daughter's a very plain girl."

"I know." His mother's hands waved a little, helpless and sad. "But it's better if she at least does the best she can. I feel so sorry for her, Andrew . . ."

"Everybody comes to me!" Andrew yelled, his voice suddenly high. "Nobody leaves me alone! Not for a minute!"

He was crying now and he turned to hide it from his mother. She looked at him, surprised, shaking her head. She put her arms around him. "Just do what you want to, Andrew, that's all. Don't do anything you don't want to do."

"Yeah," Andrew said. "Yeah. I'm sorry. I'll give you the money. I'm sorry I yelled at you."

"Don't give it to me if you don't want to, Andrew." His mother was saying this honestly, believing it.

He laughed a little. "I want to, Mom, I want to."

He patted her shoulder and went down toward the baseball field, leaving her standing there puzzled at the top of the steps.

The sun and the breeze felt good on the baseball field, and he forgot for an hour, but he moved slowly. His arm hurt at the shoulder when he threw, and the boy playing second base called him Mister, which he wouldn't have done even last year, when Andrew was twenty-four.

WELCOME TO THE CITY

As HE DREW NEARER to it, Enders looked up at his hotel through the black drizzle of the city that filled the streets with rain and soot and despair. A small red neon sign bloomed over the hotel entrance, spelling out CIRCUS HOTEL, REASONABLE, turning the drizzle falling profoundly around it into blood.

Enders sighed, shivered inside his raincoat, and walked slowly up the five steps to the entrance and went in. His nostrils curled, as they did each time he opened the door of the hotel, and his nose was hit by the ancient odor of ammonia and lysol and old linoleum and old beds and people who must depend on two bathrooms to the floor, and over the other odors the odor of age and sin, all at reasonable rates.

Wysocki was at the desk, in his gray suit with the markings of all the cafeteria soup in the city on it, and the pale face shaven down to a point where at any moment you half-expected to see the bone exposed, gleaming and green. Wysocki stood against the desk with the thirty-watt bulb shining down on his thinning hair and his navy-blue shirt and the solid orange tie, bright as hope in the dark hotel lobby, gravely reading the next morning's *Mirror*, his pale, hairy hands spread importantly, with delicate possessiveness, on the desk in front of him.

Josephine was sitting in one of the three lobby chairs, facing Wysocki. She wore a purple tailored suit with a ruffled waist, and open-toed red shoes, even though the streets outside were as damp and penetratingly cold as any marsh, and Enders could see the high red polish under her stockings, on her toenails. She sat there, not reading, not talking, her face carved out of powder and rouge under the blonde hair whose last surge of life had been strangled from it a dozen years before by peroxide and small-town hairdressers and curling irons that could have been used to primp the hair of General Sherman's granite horse.

"The English," Wysocki was saying, without looking up from his paper. "I wouldn't let them conduct a war for me for one million dollars in gilt-edged securities. Debaters and herring-fishermen," he said. "That's what they are."

"I thought Jews ate herring," Josephine said. Her voice scraped in the lobby, as though the Circus Hotel itself had suddenly broken into speech in its own voice, lysol and ammonia and rotting ancient wood finally put into sound.

"Jews eat herring," Wysocki said. "And the English eat herring."

Enders sighed again and walked up to the desk. In the chair near the stairway, he noticed, a girl was sitting, a pretty girl in a handsome green coat trimmed with lynx. He watched her obliquely as he talked to Wysocki, noticed that her legs were good and the expression cool, dignified, somehow hauntingly familiar.

"Hello, Wysocki," Enders said.

"Mr. Enders." Wysocki looked up pleasantly from the newspaper. "So you decided to come in out of the rain to your cozy little nest."

"Yes," said Enders, watching the girl.

"Did you know," Josephine asked, "that the English eat herring?"

"Yes," Enders said, digging into his mind for the face the girl reminded him of.

"That's what Wysocki said." Josephine shrugged. "I was living in happy ignorance."

Enders leaned over so that he could whisper into Wysocki's ear. "Who is she?" Enders asked.

Wysocki peered at the girl in the green coat, his eyes sly and guilty, as a thief might peer at a window at Tiffany's through which he intended to heave a brick later in the evening. "Zelinka," Wysocki whispered. "Her name's Bertha Zelinka. She checked in this afternoon. You could do worse, couldn't you?" He chuckled soundlessly, his bone-shaven face creasing without mirth, green and gleaming under the thirty-watt bulb.

"I've seen her someplace," Enders whispered, looking at the girl over his shoulder. She sat remote, cold, her legs crossed beautifully under the green coat, looking under heavy lids at the scarred and battered clock over Wysocki's head. "I know that face," Enders said. "But from where?"

"She looks like Greta Garbo," Wysocki said. "That's where you know her from."

Enders stared at the girl in the green coat. She did look like Greta Garbo, the long pale face, the long eyes, the wide, firm mouth, the whole thing a mirror of passion and pain and deep, Northern melancholy and bony, stubborn beauty. Suddenly Enders realized that he was a stranger in a strange city, a thousand miles from home, that it was raining out, that he had no girl, and that no one in this huge and wrangling seven-million town had ever said anything more tender to him than "Pass the mustard." And here, before him, solid as his hand, in a green coat with a lynx collar, sat a tall, melancholy girl who looked enough like Greta Garbo, pain and passion and beauty and understanding all mixed on the bony, pale face, to be her twin sister. His voice charged at his throat, leaping to say the first tender word in this rat-eaten, roach-claimed hotel lobby.

"Enders!" His name as spoken gaily, warmly. He turned from looking at Bertha Zelinka, wrenching his soul. "Mr. Enders, I was waiting for your appearance." It was Bishop, the owner of the hotel, a little fat, gray-faced man with wet mustaches. He was rubbing his hands jovially now. "You were just the person I wanted to see tonight," he said.

"Thanks," said Enders.

"Wait!" Bishop's voice trilled. "Don't move an inch from the spot! I have a treat in store for you."

He darted back of the desk through the door into his office. Enders turned and looked at Bertha Zelinka, sitting there as calmly, as remotely, as Garbo herself.

"Observe!" Bishop darted out again from his office. "Look!" He held his hand high above his head. From it dangled a dead, wet chicken. "See what I've saved for you. I am willing to give you this chicken for sixty cents, Mr. Enders."

Enders looked politely at the chicken, hanging sadly in death from Bishop's proud hand.

"Thanks, Mr. Bishop," Enders said. "But I have no place to cook a chicken."

"Take it to your home." Bishop whirled the chicken lovingly, giving it a spruce and electric appearance of life, the wings spreading, the feathers ruffling. "Your mother would be delighted with this bird."

"My mother's in Davenport, Iowa," Enders said.

"You must have some relatives in the city." Bishop pushed it lovingly under his nose, spreading the limp wings for inspection. "They'll receive you with open arms with this chicken. This is a guaranteed Plymouth

Rock chicken. Birds like this are exhibited in poultry shows from coast to coast. Sixty cents, Mr. Enders," Bishop said winningly. "Can you go wrong for sixty cents?"

Enders shook his head. "I have no relatives in the city," he said. "Thanks a lot, but I can't use it."

Bishop looked at him coldly. He shrugged. "I could've sold this chicken five times already," he said, "but I was saving it for you because you looked so pale. You gained my sympathy." He shrugged again, and holding the Plymouth Rock by the neck, he went into his office.

"Well," said Enders loudly, looking squarely at Bertha Zelinka. "I guess I'll turn in for the night."

"Want some company, Baby?" Josephine asked, in her voice the first note of hope she had allowed to sound there all evening.

"No, thank you," Enders said, embarrassedly, glad that Miss Zelinka wasn't looking at him at the moment.

"You certainly are a great ladies' man," Josephine said, her voice rasping through the lobby. "Don't you know you'll go crazy, you go so long without a woman? You been here two weeks, you haven't had a woman all that time. They face that problem in Sing Sing, the convicts climb on the walls."

Enders looked uneasily at Miss Zelinka. He didn't want a girl who looked like Greta Garbo to hear him mixed up in that kind of a conversation. "Good night," he said, and walked past Miss Zelinka, down the hallway to his own room, which was on the ground floor, at the bottom of an airwell, three dollars a week. He looked back regretfully. Miss Zelinka's legs were visible, jutting out, like a promise of poetry and flowers, past the grime and gloom of the hallway. Sadly he opened the door and went into his room, took off his hat and coat and fell on the bed. He could hear Josephine talking, as though the walls, the vermin, the old and wailing plumbing, the very rats hurrying on their gloomy errands between the floors, had at last found a voice.

"The papers are full of boys like him," Josephine was saying. "Turning the gas on and stuffing their heads into the oven. What a night! What a stinking whore of a night! They'll find plenty of bodies in the river tomorrow morning."

"Josephine," Wysocki's voice floated down the hallway. "You ought to learn to talk with more cheerfulness. You're ruining your business, Josephine. The wholesale butchers from Tenth Avenue, the slaughterhouse workers, your whole regular clientele, they're all avoiding you. Should I tell you why?"

"Tell me why," Josephine said.

"Because you're gloomy!" Wysocki said. "Because you depress them with your talk. People like a woman to be cheerful. You can't expect to succeed in your line if you walk around like the last day of the world is beginning in two and three-quarter hours, Bulova watch time."

"The butchers from Tenth Avenue!" Josephine snarled. "Who wants them? I give them to you as a gift."

Enders lay on the bed, regretting that a proud and beautiful woman like Bertha Zelinka had to sit in one of the three chairs of the lobby of the Circus Hotel on a rainy night and listen to a conversation like that. He put on the light and picked up the book he was reading.

> *I was neither at the hot gates*
> *Nor fought in the warm rain*
> *Nor knee deep in the salt marsh, heaving a cutlass,*
> *Bitten by flies, fought . . .*

"What a night!" Josephine's voice scraped down the hallway. "The river will be stuffed with bodies in the morning."

Enders put down T. S. Eliot. It was hard to read T. S. Eliot in the Circus Hotel without a deep feeling of irony. Enders got up and looked around the doorpost, down the hall. The proud, poetic legs were still there, lean, muscular, beautifully shaped, aristocratic, stemming down into slim ankles and narrow feet. Enders leaned dreamily against the doorpost, regarding Miss Zelinka's legs. Music played from a well-known orchestra in a night club lit by orange lamps, where no dish cost less than a dollar seventy-five, even tomato juice, and he danced with Bertha Zelinka, both of them dressed beautifully, shiningly, and he made those deep, long eyes, charged with Northern melancholy, crinkle with laughter, and later grow sober and reflective as he talked swiftly of culture, of art, of poetry. " 'Nor fought in the warm rain,' in the phrase of T. S. Eliot, a favorite of mine, 'nor knee deep in the salt marsh . . .' "

He walked quickly down the hallway, looking neither to right nor left until he stopped at the desk. "Have there been any telephone calls for me today?" he asked Wysocki, carefully avoiding looking at Miss Zelinka.

"No," said Wysocki. "Not a thing."

Enders turned and stared full at Miss Zelinka, trying, with the deep intensity of his glance, to get her to look at him, smile at him . . .

"Heads like yours, my friend," Josephine said, "they find in ovens."

Miss Zelinka sat passionless, expressionless, heedless, looking at a point twenty-five feet over Wysocki's shoulder, patiently, but coolly, in the attitude of a woman who is expecting a Lincoln to drive up at any moment and a uniformed chauffeur to spring from it and lead her fastidiously to the heavy, upholstered door, rich with heavy hardware.

Enders walked slowly back to his room. He tried to read some more. "April is the cruellest month . . ." He thumbed through the book. "Here, said she, is your card, the drowned Phoenician Sailor . . ." Enders put the book down. He couldn't read tonight. He went to the door and looked out. The legs, silk and skin and firm muscle, were still there. Enders took a deep breath and walked back toward the desk.

"Look," said Josephine, "the shuttle's back."

"I forgot to ask." He looked straight at Wysocki. "Is there any mail for me?"

"No mail," said Wysocki.

"I'll tell you frankly, friend," Josephine said. "You should've stayed in Davenport, Iowa. That's my honest opinion. New York City will break you like a peanut shell."

"Nobody asked for your opinion," Wysocki said, noticing Enders peering uneasily at Miss Zelinka to see what impression Josephine's advice had made on her. "He's a nice boy, he's educated, he's going to go a long way. Leave him alone."

"I'm only giving him my honest opinion," Josephine said. "I've been in New York a dozen years. I see them begin and I see them wind up in the river."

"Will you, for Christ's sake, stop talking about the river?" Wysocki slammed his hand on the desk.

Gratefully, Enders noticed that Miss Zelinka was listening to the conversation, that her head tilted just a little, a shade went across her disdainful, beautiful eyes.

"I come from Fall River," Josephine said. "I should've stayed there. At least when you're dead in Fall River they bury you. Here they leave you walk around until your friends notice it. Why did I ever leave Fall River? I was attracted by the glamor of the Great White Way." She waved her red and white umbrella ironically, in salute to the city.

Enders noticed that a hint, a twitch of a smile, played at the corner of Miss Zelinka's mouth. He was glad that she'd heard Wysocki say he was educated, he was going to go a long way.

"If you'd like," he heard his voice boom out suddenly in the direction of Miss Zelinka, "if you'd like, if you're waiting for someone, you can wait in my room. It's not so noisy there."

"No, thank you," Miss Zelinka said, speaking curiously, her lips together, not showing her teeth. Her voice, behind the closed, beautiful lips, was deep and hoarse and moving, and Enders felt it grip at his throat like a cool, firm hand. He turned to Wysocki, determined now that he was not going back to his room.

"I was curious," he said. "Where did Bishop get that chicken he wants to sell me?"

Wysocki looked behind him carefully. "Don't buy those chickens, Enders," he said in a low voice. "I advise you as a good friend. Bishop picks them up on Tenth Avenue, alongside the railroad tracks."

"What're they doing there?" Enders asked.

"The trains bring them in from the farms, from the country," Wysocki said. "The ones that died on the trip for one reason or another, the trainmen throw them off the cars and they're piled up alongside the tracks and Bishop picks out the ones that look as though they died most peaceful and he tries to sell them." Wysocki slid back to the office door, listened guiltily for a moment for Bishop, like a spy in the movies. "I advise you not to buy them. They're not the most nourishing articles of food in the world."

Enders smiled. "Bishop ought to be in Wall Street," he said. "With talent like that."

Miss Zelinka laughed. Feeling twice as tall as he had felt a moment before, Enders noticed that Miss Zelinka was laughing, quietly, and without opening her mouth, but true laughter. He laughed with her and their eyes met in friendly, understanding amusement.

"May I buy you a cup of coffee?" hurled out of his throat, at Miss Zelinka's head, like a hand grenade.

The light of thought, consideration, appeared in the large gray eyes, while Enders waited. Then Miss Zelinka smiled. "All right," she said. She stood up, five feet six inches tall, graceful as a duchess.

"I'll be right back," Enders said, quickly. "Just have to get my coat."

He fled lightly down the hall toward his room.

"That's what keeps me poor," Josephine said. "Girls like that. What a night, what a dirty whore of a night!"

"I'm a dancer," Bertha Zelinka was saying two hours later, her coat off, in Enders' room, as she drank the whisky straight in one of the two water tumblers the room boasted. "Specialty dancing." She put the whisky down, suddenly sank beautifully to the floor in a split. "I'm as supple as a cat."

"I see," Enders said, his eyes furious with admiration for Miss Zelinka, full-breasted, flat-bellied, steel-thighed, supple as a cat, spread magnificently on the dirty carpet. It was more pleasant to look at her body, now that he had seen her eating, mouth opened to reveal the poor, poverty-stricken, ruined teeth jagged and sorrowful in her mouth. "That looks very hard to do."

"My name's been in lights," Miss Zelinka said, from the floor. "Please pass the whisky. From one end of the country to another. I've stopped show after show. I've got an uncanny sense of timing." She stood up, after taking another draught of her whisky, closing her eyes with a kind of harsh rapture as the Four Roses went down past the miserable teeth, down inside the powerful, long white throat. "I'm an actress, too, you know, Mr. Enders."

"I'm an actor," Enders said shyly, feeling the whisky beat in his blood, keeping his eyes fiercely and wonderingly on Miss Zelinka. "That's why I'm in New York. I'm an actor."

"You ought to be a good actor," Miss Zelinka said. "You got the face for it. It's refined." She poured herself another drink, watching the amber liquor pour into her glass with a brooding, intense expression in her face. "I had my name in lights from coast to coast. Don't you believe it?"

"I believe it," Enders said sincerely, noting that half the bottle was already gone.

"That's why I'm here now," she said. She walked beautifully around the small, flaky-walled room, her hands running sorrowfully over the warped bureau, the painted bedstead. "That's why I'm here now." Her voice was faraway and echoing, hoarse with whisky and regret. "I'm very much in demand, you know. I've stopped shows for ten minutes at a time. They wouldn't let me get off the stage. Musicals that cost one hundred and fifty thousand to ring the curtain up. That's why I'm here now," she said mysteriously, and drained her glass. She threw herself on the bed next to Enders, stared moodily through almost closed eyes, at the stained and beaten ceiling. "The Shuberts're putting on a musical. They want me for it. Rehearsals are on Fifty-second Street, so I thought I'd move close by for the time being." She sat up, silently reached for the bottle, poured with the fixed expression, brooding and infatuate, which she reserved for the distillers' product. Enders, too full for words, sitting on the same bed with a woman who looked like Greta Garbo, who had stopped musical shows with specialty dancing from coast to coast, who got drunk with the assured yet ferocious grace of a young society matron, watched her every move, with hope, admiration, growing passion.

"You might ask," Miss Zelinka said, "what is a person like myself doing in a rat-hole like this." She waited, but Enders merely gulped silently at his whisky. She chuckled and patted his hand. "You're a nice boy. Iowa, you said? You come from Iowa?"

"Iowa."

"Corn," Miss Zelinka said. "That's what they grow in Iowa." She nodded, having placed Iowa and Enders firmly in her mind. "I passed through Iowa on my way to Hollywood." Half the whisky in her glass disappeared.

"Have you acted in pictures?" Enders asked, impressed, sitting on the same bed with a woman who had been in Hollywood.

Miss Zelinka laughed moodily. "Hollywood!" She finished her drink. "Don't look for my footprints in front of Grauman's Chinese." She reached fluently for the bottle.

"It seems to me," Enders said seriously, breathing deeply because Miss Zelinka was leaning across him for the moment. "It seems to me you'd do very well. You're beautiful and you've got a wonderful voice."

Miss Zelinka laughed again. "Look at me," she said.

Enders looked at her.

"Do I remind you of anybody?" Miss Zelinka asked.

Enders nodded.

Miss Zelinka drank moodily. "I look like Greta Garbo," she said. "Nobody could deny that. I'm not being vain when I tell you when I photograph you couldn't tell me apart from the Swede." She sipped her whisky, ran it lovingly around in her mouth, swallowed slowly. "A woman who looks like Greta Garbo in Hollywood is like the fifth leg on a race horse. Do you understand what I mean?"

Enders nodded sympathetically.

"It's my private curse," Miss Zelinka said, tears looming in her eyes like mist over the ocean. She jumped up, shaking her head, walked lightly and dramatically around the room. "I have no complaints," she said. "I've done very well. I live in a two-room suite on the twentieth floor of a hotel on Seventy-fifth Street. Overlooking the park. All my trunks and bags are up there. I just took a few things with me, until the rehearsals are over. Seventy-fifth Street, on the East Side, is too far away; when you're rehearsing a musical comedy, you've got to be on tap twenty-four hours a day for the Shuberts. A very luxurious two-room suite in the Hotel Chalmers. It's very exclusive, but it's too far from Fifty-second Street." She poured some more whisky for herself, and Enders noticed that the bottle was almost empty. "Oh, yes," she said, crooning to the glass in her hand, "I've done very well. I've danced all over the country. In the most exclusive nightspots, I was the featured entertainment. I'm very greatly in demand." She sat down, close to him, her body moving gently and rhythmically as she spoke. "Seattle, Chicago, Los Angeles, Detroit." She gulped her whisky and her eyes clouded with a final, deep, vague mist and her voice suddenly got very throaty and hoarse. "Miami, Florida." She sat absolutely still and the cloud dissolved into tears and the tears coursed slowly down her face.

"What's the matter?" Enders asked anxiously. "Did I do something?"

Miss Zelinka threw the empty tumbler against the opposite wall. It broke heavily and sullenly, scattered over the carpet. She threw herself back on the bed, wept. "Miami, Florida," she sobbed. "Miami, Florida . . ."

Enders patted her shoulder consolingly.

"I danced in The Golden Horn in Miami, Florida," she cried. "It was a Turkish night club. Very exclusive."

"Why're you crying, darling?" Enders asked, feeling sorry for her, but elated, too, because he had said "darling."

"Every time I think of Miami, Florida," Miss Zelinka said, "I cry."

"Can I do anything to help?" Enders held her hand softly.

"It was January, 1936." Miss Zelinka's voice throbbed with old, hopeless, broken tragedy, forlorn as the story of a siege of a lost and ruined village. "I was dressed in Turkish garments: a brassiere, and veils around my legs and nothing around the middle. At the end of the dance I had to do a back-bend. I leaned back and touched the floor with my hands, with my hair falling down to the floor. There was a bald man. There was a convention of the Metal-Trades Union in Miami, Florida. He had on a badge. The whole night club was full of them." The tears and the anguish pulled at her face. "I'll remember that bald son of a bitch until the day I die. There was no music at that part of the dance. Drums and tambourines. He leaned over and put an olive in my navel and sprinkled it with salt." Miss Zelinka rolled suddenly over on her face and, clutching the bedspread, her shoulders heaving, burrowed into the grayish cotton. "It was a cartoon. He saw it in a cartoon in a magazine. It's funny in a magazine, but wait until it happens to you! The humiliation," she wept. "Every time I think of the humiliation I want to die. Miami, Florida."

Enders watched the bedspread stain with tears, mascara and rouge. With genuine sympathy, he put his arm around her. "I want to be treated with respect," Miss Zelinka wailed. "I was brought up in a good family, why shouldn't I be treated with respect? That fat, bald man, with the badge from the Metal-Trades Union Convention. He leaned over and put the olive in my navel like an egg in an egg cup and sprinkled salt like he was starting breakfast and everybody laughed and laughed, including the orchestra. . . ." Her voice went wailing up the air well, lost, despairing, full of an ancient and irreparable sorrow.

She sat up and threw her arms around Enders, digging her grief-torn head into his shoulder, clutching him with strong hands, both of them rocking back and forth like Jews praying, on the enameled bed that squeaked and wailed in the little room.

"Hold me tight," she wept, "hold me tight. I haven't got a two-room suite on East Seventy-fifth Street. I got no trunks in the Hotel Chalmers, hold me tight." Her hands dug into him and her tears and rouge and mascara stained his coat. "The Shuberts aren't giving me a job. Why do I lie, why do I always lie?" She lifted her head, kissed his throat fiercely. He shook at the soft, violent pressure, at the wetness of her lips and the tragic and exhilarating trickle of her tears under his chin, knowing that he was going to have this woman, this Bertha Zelinka. Lonely, far from home, on a rainy night, the city was pulling him in, making a place in its wild and ludicrous life for him. As he kissed her, this woman who looked like Greta Garbo, the century's dream of passion and tragedy and beauty, this woman whom he had met in a rat-tenanted lobby off Columbus Circle, among whores thinking of death and a Pole in an orange tie checking in each night's transients, age and sin, at reasonable rates, Enders felt suddenly at home, accounted for. The city had produced for him a great beauty, supple as a cat, full of lies and whisky and ancient, shadowy victories, a woman with magnificent, proud legs and deep, stormy eyes who wept bitterly behind the frail, warped door because once, in 1936, a bald man from a Metal-Trades Union had put an olive in her navel. Enders held Bertha Zelinka's head in his two hands, looked intently at the bony, drunken, beautiful, tear-stained face. Bertha Zelinka peered longingly and sadly at him through half-closed classic lids, her mouth hanging softly open in passion and promise, her poor jagged teeth showing behind the long, heart-breaking lips. He kissed her, feeling deep within him, that in its own way, on this rainy night, the city had put out its hand in greeting, had called, in its own voice, wry and ironic, "Welcome, Citizen."

Gratefully, near tears, hating himself, his hands shaking exultantly, Enders bent to his knees and took the scraped, year-worn shoes, swollen with the streets' rain, from the long and handsome feet of Bertha Zelinka.

SEARCH THROUGH THE STREETS
OF THE CITY

WHEN HE finally saw her, he nearly failed to recognize her. He walked behind her for a half block, vaguely noticing that the woman in front of him had long legs and was wearing a loose, college-girl polo coat and a plain brown felt hat.

Suddenly something about the way she walked made him remember —the almost affected rigidity of her back and straightness of throat and head, with all the movement of walking, flowing up to the hips and stopping there, like Negro women in the South and Mexican and Spanish women carrying baskets on their heads.

For a moment, silently, he watched her walk down Twelfth Street, on the sunny side of the street, in front of the little tired gardens behind which lay the quiet, pleasantly run-down old houses. Then he walked up to her and touched her arm.

"Low heels," he said. "I never thought I'd live to see the day."

She looked around in surprise, then smiled widely, took his arm. "Hello, Paul," she said. "I've gone in for health."

"Whenever I think of you," he said, "I think of the highest heels in New York City."

"The old days," Harriet said. They walked slowly down the sunny street, arm in arm, toward Sixth Avenue. "I was a frivolous creature."

"You still walk the same way. As though you ought to have a basket of laundry on your head."

"I practiced walking like that for six months. You'd be surprised how much attention I get walking into a room that way."

"I wouldn't be surprised," Paul said, looking at her. She had black hair and pale, clear skin and a long, full body, and her eyes were deep gray and always brilliant, even after she'd been drinking for three days in a row.

Harriet closed her coat quickly and walked a little faster. "I'm going to Wanamaker's," she said. "There're a couple of things I have to buy. Where are you going?"

"Wanamaker's," Paul said. "I've been dying to go to Wanamaker's for three years."

They walked slowly, in silence, Harriet's arm in his.

"Casual," Paul said. "I bet to the naked eye we look casual as hell. How do you feel?"

Harriet took her arm away. "Casual."

"O.K. Then that's how I feel, too." Paul whistled coldly to himself. He stopped and looked critically at her and she stopped, too, and turned toward him, a slight puzzled smile on her face. "What makes you dress that way?" he asked. "You look like Monday morning in Northampton."

"I just threw on whatever was nearest," Harriet said. "I'm just going to be out about an hour."

"You used to look like a nice big box of candy in your clothes." Paul took her arm again and they started off. "Viennese bonbons. Every indentation carefully exploited in silk and satin. Even if you were just going down to the corner for a pint of gin, you'd look like something that ought to be eaten for dessert. This is no improvement."

"A girl has different periods in clothes. Like Picasso," Harriet said. "And if I'd known I was going to meet you, I'd've dressed differently."

Paul patted her arm. "That's better."

Paul eyed her obliquely as they walked: the familiar, long face, the well-known wide mouth with always a little too much lipstick on it, the little teeth that made her face, when she smiled, look suddenly like a little girl's in Sunday school.

"You're getting skinny, Paul," Harriet said.

Paul nodded. "I'm as lean as a herring. I've been leading a fevered and ascetic life. What sort of life have you been leading?"

"I got married." Harriet paused a moment. "Did you hear I got married?"

"I heard," Paul said. "The last time we crossed Sixth Avenue together the L was still up. I feel a nostalgic twinge for the Sixth Avenue L." They hurried as the light changed. "On the night of January ninth, 1940," Paul said, holding her elbow, "you were not home."

"Possible," Harriet said. "I'm a big girl now; I go out at night."

"I happened to pass your house, and I noticed that the light wasn't on." They turned down toward Ninth Street. "I remembered how hot you kept that apartment—like the dahlia greenhouse in the Botanical Gardens."

"I have thin blood," Harriet said gravely. "Long years of in-breeding in Massachusetts."

"The nicest thing about you," Paul said, "was you never went to sleep."

"Every lady to her own virtue," Harriet said. "Some women're beautiful, some're smart—me—I never went to sleep. The secret of my great popularity. . . ."

Paul grinned. "Shut up."

Harriet smiled back at him and they chuckled together. "You know what I mean," he said. "Any time I called you up, two, three in the morning, you'd come right over, lively and bright-eyed, all the rouge and mascara in the right places. . . ."

"In my youth," said Harriet, "I had great powers of resistance."

"In the morning we'd eat breakfast to Beethoven. The Masterwork Hour. WNYC. Beethoven, by special permission of His Honor, the Mayor, from nine to ten." Paul closed his eyes for a moment. "The Little Flower, Mayor for Lovers."

Paul opened his eyes and looked at the half-strange, half-familiar woman walking lightly at his side. He remembered lying close to her, dreamily watching the few lights of the towers of the night-time city, framed by the big window of his bedroom against the black sky, and one night when she moved sleepily against him and rubbed the back of his neck where the hair was sticking up in sharp little bristles because he had had his hair cut that afternoon. Harriet had rubbed them the wrong way, smiling, dreamily, without opening her eyes. "What a delicious thing a man is . . ." she'd murmured. And she'd sighed, then chuckled a little and fallen asleep, her hand still on the shaven back of his neck.

Paul smiled, remembering.

"You still laughing at my clothes?" Harriet asked.

"I remembered something I heard someplace . . ." Paul said. " 'What a delicious thing a man is . . .' "

Harriet looked at him coldly. "Who said that?"

Paul squinted suspiciously at her. "Oswald Spengler."

"Uhuh," Harriet said soberly. "It's a famous quotation."

"It's a well-turned phrase," said Paul.

"That's what I think, too." Harriet nodded agreeably and walked a little faster.

They passed the little run-down bar where they'd sat afternoons all winter drinking martinis and talking and talking, and laughing so loud the people at the other tables would turn and smile. Paul waited for Harriet to say something about the bar, but she didn't even seem to notice it. "There's Eddie's Bar," Paul said.

"Uhuh." Harriet nodded briskly.

"He's going to start making his martinis with sherry when all the French vermouth runs out," Paul said.

"It sounds horrible." Harriet made a face.

"Is that all you have to say?" Paul said loudly, remembering all the times he'd looked in to see if she was there.

"What do you want me to say?" Harriet looked honestly puzzled, but Paul had never known when she was lying to him or telling the truth, anyway, and he hadn't improved in the two years, he discovered.

"I don't want you to say anything. I'll take you in and buy you a drink."

"No, thanks. I've really got to get to Wanamaker's and back home in a hurry. Give me a raincheck."

"Yeah," Paul said sourly.

They turned up Ninth Street toward Fifth Avenue.

"I knew I'd meet you someplace, finally," Paul said. "I was curious to see what would happen."

Harriet didn't say anything. She was looking absently at the buildings across the street.

"Don't you ever talk any more?" Paul asked.

"What *did* happen?"

"Every once in a while," he started, "I meet some girl I used to know . . ."

"I bet the country's full of them," Harriet said.

"The country's full of everybody's ex-girls."

Harriet nodded. "I never thought of it that way, but you're right."

"Most of the time I think, isn't she a nice, decent person? Isn't it wonderful I'm no longer attached to her? The first girl I ever had," Paul said, "is a policewoman now. She subdued a gangster single-handed in Coney Island last summer. Her mother won't let her go out of the house in her uniform. She's ashamed for the neighbors."

"Naturally," Harriet said.

"Another girl I used to know changed her name and dances in the Russian Ballet. I went to see her dance the other night. She has legs like a Fordham tackle. I used to think she was beautiful. I used to think you were beautiful, too."

"We were a handsome couple," Harriet said. "Except you always needed a shave. That electric razor . . ."

"I've given it up."

They were passing his old house now and he looked at the doorway and remembered all the times he and Harriet had gone in and come out, the rainy days and the early snowy mornings with the milkman's horse silent on the white street behind them. They stopped and looked at the old red house with the shabby shutters and the window on the fourth floor they had both looked out of time and time again to see what the weather was and Paul remembered the first time, on a winter's night, when he and Harriet had gone through that door together.

"I was so damn polite," Paul said softly.

Harriet smiled, knowing what he was talking about. "You kept dropping the key and saying, 'Lord, Lord,' under your breath while you were looking for it."

"I was nervous. I wanted to make sure you knew exactly how matters stood—no illusions. Good friends, everybody understanding everybody else, another girl coming in from Detroit in six weeks, no claims on me, no claims on you . . ." Paul looked at the window on the fourth floor and smiled. "What a fool!"

"It's a nice, quiet street," Harriet said, looking up at the window on the fourth floor, too. She shook her head, took Paul's arm again. "I've got to get to Wanamaker's."

They started off.

"What're you buying at Wanamaker's?" Paul asked.

Harriet hesitated for a moment. "Nothing much. I'm looking at some baby clothes. I'm going to have a baby." They crowded over to one side to let a little woman with four dachshunds pass them in a busy tangle. "Isn't it funny—me with a baby?" Harriet smiled. "I lie around all day and try to imagine what it's going to be like. In between, I sleep and drink beer to nourish us. I've never had such a good time in all my life."

"Well," said Paul, "at least it'll keep your husband out of the army."

"Maybe. He's a raging patriot."

"Good. When he's at Fort Dix I'll meet you in Washington Square Park when you take the baby out for an airing in its perambulator. I'll put on a policeman's uniform to make it proper. I'm not such a raging patriot."

"They'll get you anyway, won't they?"

"Sure. I'll send you my picture in a lieutenant's suit. From Bulgaria. I have a premonition I'm going to be called on to defend a strategic point in Bulgaria."

"How do you feel about it?" For the first time Harriet looked squarely and searchingly at him.

Paul shrugged. "It's going to happen. It's all damned silly, but it isn't as silly now as it was ten years ago."

Suddenly Harriet laughed.

"What's so funny?" Paul demanded.

"My asking you how you felt about something. I never used to have a chance . . . You'd let me know how you felt about everything. Roosevelt, James Joyce, Jesus Christ, Gypsy Rose Lee, Matisse, Yogi, liquor, sex, architecture . . ."

"I was full of opinions in those days." Paul smiled a little regretfully. "Lust and conversation. The firm foundations of civilized relations between the sexes."

He turned and looked back at the window on the fourth floor. "That was a nice apartment," he said softly. "Lust and conversation . . ."

"Come on, Paul," Harriet said. "Wanamaker's isn't going to stay open all night."

Paul turned up his collar because the wind was getting stronger as they neared Fifth Avenue. "You were the only girl I ever knew I could sleep in the same bed with."

"That's a hell of a thing to say to a girl." Harriet laughed. "Is that your notion of a compliment?"

Paul shrugged. "It's an irrelevant fact. Or a relevant fact. Is it polite to talk to a married lady this way?"

"No."

Paul walked along with her. "What do you think of when you look at me?" he asked.

"Nothing much," Harriet said carefully.

"What're you lying about?"

"Nothing much," Harriet said flatly.

"Don't you even think, 'What in the name of God did I ever see in him?'"

"No." Harriet put her hands deep in her pockets and walked quickly along the railings.

"Should I tell you what I think of when I look at you?"

"No."

"I've been looking for you for two years," Paul said.

"My name's been in the telephone book." Harriet hurried even more, wrapping her coat tightly around her.

"I didn't realize I was looking for you until I saw you."

"Please, Paul . . ."

"I would walk along the street and I'd pass a bar we'd been in together and I'd go in and sit there, even though I didn't want a drink, not knowing why I was sitting there. Now I know. I was waiting for you to come in. I didn't pass your house by accident."

"Look, Paul," Harriet pleaded. "It was a long time ago and it was fine and it ended. . . ."

"I was wrong," Paul said. "Do you like hearing that? I was wrong. You know, I never did get married, after all."

"I know," Harriet said. "Please shut up."

"I walk along Fifth Avenue and every time I pass St. Patrick's I half look up to see if you're passing, because I met you that day right after you'd had a tooth pulled, and it was cold; you were walking along with the tears streaming from your eyes and your eyes red and that was the only time I ever met you by accident anyplace. . . ."

Harriet smiled. "That certainly sounds like a beautiful memory."

"Two years . . ." Paul said. "I've gone out with a lot of girls in the last two years." He shrugged. "They've bored me and I've bored them. I keep looking at every woman who passes to see if it's you. All the girls I go out with bawl the hell out of me for it. I've been walking around, following girls with dark hair to see if it'll turn out to be you, and girls with a fur jacket like that old one you had and girls that walk in that silly, beautiful way you walk. . . . I've been searching the streets of the city for you for two years and this is the first time I've admitted it even to myself. That little Spanish joint we went the first time. Every time I pass it I remember everything—how many drinks we had and what the band played and what we said and the fat Cuban who kept winking at you from the bar and the very delicate way we landed up in my apartment. . . ."

They were both walking swiftly now, Harriet holding her hands stiffly down at her sides.

"There is a particular wonderful way you are joined together . . ."

"Paul, stop it." Harriet's voice was flat but loud.

"Two years. In two years the edge should be dulled off things like that. Instead . . ." How can you make a mistake as big as that? Paul thought, how can you deliberately be as wrong as that? And no remedy. So long as you live, no remedy. He looked harshly at Harriet. Her face was set, as though she weren't listening to him and only intent on getting across the street as quickly as possible. "How about you?" he asked. "Don't you remember . . . ?"

"I don't remember anything," she said. And then, suddenly, the tears sprang up in her eyes and streamed down the tight, distorted cheeks. "I don't remember a goddamn thing!" she wept. "I'm not going to Wanamaker's. I'm going home! Good-bye!" She ran over to a cab that was parked at the corner and opened the door and sprang in. The cab spurted past Paul and he had a glimpse of Harriet sitting stiffly upright, the tears bitter and unheeded in her eyes.

He watched the cab go down Fifth Avenue until it turned. Then he turned the other way and started walking, thinking, I must move away from this neighborhood. I've lived here long enough.

NIGHT, BIRTH AND OPINION

"TENTS!" LUBBOCK was saying, gloomily swishing his beer around in his glass, his voice echoing hoarsely in the empty shadows of Cody's bar, dark and almost deserted now, deep in the heel of the winter night. "Yuh join the army, yuh sit in a tent and freeze yer tail all winter. I'm a civilized man, I'm used to living in steam-heated apartments."

He looked around him challengingly. He was a big man, with huge longshoreman's hands and a long neat scar down one side of his face. The other two men at the bar looked carefully into their beer.

"National defense," the bartender said. The bartender was a pale little man in a vest and apron, with pale, hairy arms and a long, nervous nose. "Everybody has to make certain sacrifices."

"The trouble with this country," Lubbock said loudly, "is there are too goddamn many patriots walking the streets."

"Don't say anything against patriotism," said the man nearest Lubbock. "Not in my presence."

Lubbock looked consideringly at him. "What's *your* name?" he asked.

"Dominic di Calco," the man said clearly, showing that he was not to be bullied. "I don't see anything wrong with being a patriot."

"He doesn't see anything wrong with being a patriot," Lubbock said. "An Italian patriot."

"They need you," said Sweeney, the man on the other side of Lubbock. "They need you bad—in Greece."

The others laughed. Sweeney looked around him proudly, his little creased red face beery and complacent.

"I'm an American citizen," Di Calco shouted. "After you boys get through laughing."

"You know what I'd like to see?" Sweeney waved his arms, laughing. "I'd like to see the Italian army try to invade Red Hook."

"I'm not in favor of Mussolini," Di Calco shouted. "But keep yer trap shut about the Italian army!"

"Three Irishmen," Sweeney said. "It would take three Irishmen about a half hour. The Italians're wonderful when they fight other Italians."

"Would you like to step outside, whatever yer name is?" Di Calco asked quietly.

"Boys!" the bartender spread his hands pacifically. "Remember, we're in America."

"Remember," Di Calco said, "I offered you satisfaction, whatever yer name is."

"My name is Sweeney!" Sweeney shouted. "I got two cousins in the Royal Air Force!"

"That's a hot one," Lubbock said. "A man by the name of Sweeney with two cousins in the English army. Yuh can just about imagine" —Lubbock spoke reasonably to the bartender—"what type of Irishman yuh could get to fight in the English army."

"What do you want?" the bartender asked. "You want to disagree with every patron of this saloon?"

"That must be some family, the Sweeneys," Lubbock went over and clapped Sweeney on the back.

"They're fightin' for you and me," Sweeney said coldly. "They're fightin' to preserve our way of life."

"I agree," said Di Calco.

"Yeah," said the bartender.

Lubbock turned on the bartender. "What's *your* name?"

"Cody," said the bartender. "William Cody."

Lubbock glared at him. "You kidding me?"

"I swear to God," said the bartender.

"They got a statue in Wyoming. Buffalo Bill. Any relation?" Lubbock asked.

"It's a pure coincidence," the bartender said.

"Beer, Buffalo Bill," Lubbock said. He watched the bartender draw the beer and place it before him. "From the very hand," Lubbock marveled. "A man with a statue in Wyoming. No wonder you're so patriotic. If I had a statue in Wyoming, I'd be patriotic too."

"Pure coincidence," protested the bartender.

Lubbock drank half his glass of beer, leaned back, spoke quietly and reflectively. "I just love to think of two Sweeneys in England protecting my way of life. I just love it. I feel safer already." He smacked the bar savagely. "Tents! We'll be sitting in tents in the middle of winter!"

"What do you want?" Di Calco said. "You want Hitler to come over here and clean up?"

"I hate him; I hate the bastard," Lubbock said. "I'm a Dutchman myself, but I hate the Germans."

"Give the Dutchman a beer," Sweeney said. "On me."

"I hate the Germans," Lubbock went on, "and I hate the English and I hate the French and I hate the Americans . . ."

"Who do you like?" the bartender asked.

"The Italians. You can't get them to fight. They're civilized human beings. A man comes up to them with a gun, they run like antelopes. I admire that."

Di Calco tapped warningly on the bar. "I'm not going to stand here and have the Italian army insulted."

Lubbock ignored him. "The whole world should be full of Italians. That's my program. My name is Lubbock, boys. I come from a long line of Dutchmen, but I hate them all. If the British're defending my way of life, they can stop right now. My way of life stinks."

"Boys," the bartender said. "Talk about something else, boys."

"The truth is," Sweeney said, "I wouldn't mind if there was a war. I make eleven dollars a week. Any change would be an improvement."

"This is the war of the Hotel Pee-yeah," Lubbock said.

"What do you mean by that?" Di Calco looked at him suspiciously, sensing a new insult to the Italian army.

"On Fifth Avenue and Sixtieth Street. They tea-dance." Lubbock scowled. "They tea-dance for the Empiuh."

"What's objectionable about *that?*" the bartender asked.

"Yuh ever see the people that go into the Hotel Pee-yeah?" Lubbock leaned over the bar and scowled at the bartender. "The little fat rabbits in the mink coats?"

"The best people," the bartender said defiantly.

"Yeah." Lubbock smiled mirthlessly. "If they're for anything, it must be wrong."

"I'm speaking carefully," Di Calco said in measured tones. "I don't want to be misconstrued, but to a neutral ear you sound like a Communist."

Lubbock laughed, drained his beer. "I hate the Communists," he said. "They are busy slitting their own throats seven days a week. Another beer, Buffalo Bill."

"I wish you wouldn't call me Buffalo Bill." The bartender filled

Lubbock's glass. "You start something like that, you can wind up making life intolerable." He flipped the head off the glass and pushed it in front of Lubbock.

"A statue in Wyoming . . ." Lubbock shook his head wonderingly. "Today they tea-dance for the Empiuh, tomorrow we get shot for the Empiuh."

"It don't necessarily follow." Sweeney moved closer, earnestly.

"Mr. Sweeney, of the flying Sweeneys." Lubbock patted him gently on the wrist. "The reader of the *New York Times*. I'll put a lily on yer grave in the Balkans."

"It may be necessary," Di Calco said. "It may be necessary to supply soldiers; it may be necessary for Sweeney to get shot."

"Don't make it so personal," Sweeney said angrily.

"Before we get through, Mr. Sweeney," Lubbock put his arm confidentially around him, "this war is going to be very personal to you and me. It will not be very personal to the rabbits from the Hotel Pee-yeah."

"Why can't you leave the Hotel Pierre out of this discussion?" the bartender complained.

"The snow will fall," Lubbock shouted, "and we'll be sitting in tents!" He turned on Di Calco. "The Italian patriot. I'd like to ask yuh a question."

"Always remember," Di Calco said coldly, "that I'm an American citizen."

"How will you feel, George Washington, sitting behind a machine gun with Wops running at you?"

"I'll do my duty," Di Calco said doggedly. "And don't use the term 'Wop.'"

"What do you mean running *at* him?" Sweeney roared. "The Italian army don't run at anything but the rear."

"Remember," Di Calco shouted at Sweeney, "I have a standing invitation to meet you outside."

"Boys," the bartender cried. "Talk about other matters. Please . . ."

"One war after another," Lubbock marveled. "One after another, and they get poor sons of bitches like you into tents in the wintertime, and yuh never catch on."

"I'm overlooking the language." Sweeney took a step back and spoke dispassionately, like a debater. "But I'd like to hear your solution. Since you're so clear on the subject."

"I don't want to overlook the language," Di Calco said hotly.

"Let him talk." Sweeney waved his hand majestically. "Let's hear everybody's point of view. Let the Dutchman talk."

"Well . . ." Lubbock started.

"Don't be insulting," the bartender said. "It's late and I'm ready to close up the bar anyway, so don't insult the patrons."

Lubbock rinsed his mouth with beer, let it slide slowly down his throat. "Don't yuh ever clean the pipes?" he asked the bartender. "Yuh know, that's the most important thing about beer—the pipes."

"He's got a comment on everything!" Di Calco said angrily. "This country's full of them!"

"They are dividing up the world," Lubbock said. "I got eighty-five cents to my name. No matter which way they finish dividing, I'll be lucky to still have eighty-five cents when it's all over."

"That's not the way to approach the problem," said Sweeney. "Your eighty-five cents."

"Will I get Greece?" Lubbock pointed his huge finger threateningly at Sweeney. "Will Di Calco get China?"

"Who wants China?" Di Calco asked triumphantly.

"We get one thing," Lubbock said soberly. "You and me and Sweeney and Buffalo Bill . . ."

"Please," said the bartender.

"We get trouble. The workingman gets trouble." Lubbock sighed and looked sadly up at the ceiling, and the other men silently drank their beer. "Military strategists agree," Lubbock said, his tongue going proudly over the phrase, "that it takes four men to attack a position defended by one man."

"What's that got to do with it?" Sweeney demanded.

"This war is going to be fought in Europe, in Africa, in Asia," Lubbock chanted. "It is not going to be fought in William Cody's Bar."

"Sorry I can't oblige you," the bartender said sarcastically.

"I've studied the situation," Lubbock said, "and I've decided that there's going to be four times as many Americans killed as anybody else. It stands to reason. They're not going to attack us here, are they? We're going to take the offensive. Four to one!" He banged the bar with savage certainty. "Us four poor dumb yokels'll get it just to put one lousy Dutchman out of the way. Military strategy guarantees!"

"Don't yell so loud," the bartender said nervously. "The people upstairs don't like me."

"The worst thing is," Lubbock shouted, glaring wildly around him, "the worst thing is I look around and I see the world full of poor dumb stupid bastards like Sweeney and Di Calco and William Cody!"

"The language," Di Calco snarled. "Watch the language."

"Hitler has to be beaten!" Sweeney yelled. "That's a fundamental fact."

"Hitler has to be beaten!" Lubbock's voice sank to a significant, harsh whisper. "Why does Hitler have to be beaten? Because poor ignorant bastards like you put him there in the first place and left him there in the second place and went out to shoot him down in the third place and in the meantime just drank yer beer and argued in bars!"

"Don't accuse me," said Sweeney. "I didn't put Hitler anyplace."

"Sweeneys all over the world!" Lubbock shouted. "And now I got to get shot for it. I got to sit in tents in the wintertime!" Suddenly he grabbed Sweeney by the collar with one hand. "Say . . ." Sweeney gasped. Lubbock's other hand shot out, grasped Di Calco by his collar. Lubbock drew the two men close to his face and stared with terrible loathing at them. "I would like to mash yer stupid thick heads," he whispered.

"Now, lissen," Di Calco gasped.

"Boys," said the bartender, reaching for the sawed-off baseball bat he kept under the counter.

"If I get shot it's your fault!" Lubbock shook the two men fiercely. "I oughta kill yuh. I feel like killin' every dumb slob walkin' the streets . . ."

Di Calco reached back for a beer bottle and Sweeney grabbed the big hand at his throat and the bartender lifted the sawed-off baseball bat. The door swung open and a girl stepped through it and looked blankly at them.

"Go right ahead," she said, the expression on her face not surprised or worried or amused. "Don't let me interrupt."

"Boys . . ." the bartender said and put the baseball bat away. Lubbock gave Sweeney and Di Calco a last little push and released them and turned back to his beer.

"People like you," Sweeney murmured, outraged, "people like you they ought to commit to asylums."

Di Calco straightened his tie and tried to smile gallantly through his rage at the girl, who was still standing by the open door, hatless, her dirty blonde hair falling straight down to her shoulders. She was a thin girl, with the bones showing plainly in her face, and her hands skinny and rough coming out of the sleeves of the light old gray coat she was wearing. Her face was very tired, as though she had been working too long, too many nights.

"Would you like to close the door, Miss?" the bartender asked. "It's getting awfully cold."

The girl wearily closed the door and stood against it for a moment, wearily surveying the four men.

"I need some help," she said.

"Now, Miss . . ." the bartender started.

"Oh, shut up!" she snapped at him. Her voice was flat and worn. "I'm not bumming anything. My sister's just had a kid and she's laying in a stinking little hospital and she was bleeding all day and they gave her two transfusions and that's all they got and they just told me maybe she's dyin'. I been walkin' past this saloon for the last half hour watchin' you four guys talkin', gettin' up nerve to come in. She needs blood. Any you guys got some blood you don't need?" The girl smiled a little.

The men carefully avoided looking at each other.

"We're busted," the girl said, her tone as flat as ever. "The kid came out seven months and her husband's a sailor; he's on his way to Portugal and there's nobody in this whole goddamned, freezin' town I can turn to." She shrugged. "My blood's the wrong type." She took a step nearer the bar. "She's only nineteen years old, my sister. She had to go marry a sailor . . ." Lubbock turned and looked at her.

"All right," Lubbock said. "I'll go with yuh."

"Me, too," said Di Calco.

Sweeney opened his mouth, closed it, opened it again. "I hate hospitals," he said. "But I'll come along."

Lubbock turned and looked slowly at the bartender.

"It's late anyway," the bartender said, nervously drying the bar with a towel. "I might as well come along, just in case. . . . My type blood might . . . Yes." He nodded vigorously, and started taking off his apron.

Lubbock reached over the bar and brought up a bottle of rye and a glass and silently poured it and pushed it in front of the girl. The girl took it without smiling and drained it in one gulp.

They all sat in the dreary hospital clinic room with the old dead light of the hospital on them and all the weary sorrowful smells of the hospital swelling around them. They sat without talking, waiting for the interne to come and tell them which one of them had the right type of blood for the transfusion. Lubbock sat with his hands between his knees, occasionally glancing sharply at Sweeney and Di Calco and Cody, all of them nervously squirming on their benches. Only the girl walked slowly back and forth down the middle of the room, smoking a cigarette, the smoke curling slowly over her lank, blonde hair.

The door opened and the interne came in and touched Lubbock on the arm. "You're elected," he said.

Lubbock took a deep breath and stood up. He looked around him, at Di Calco, at Sweeney, at Cody, triumphantly, smiled at the girl, and followed the interne out of the room.

When he was through, when the blood had poured out of his veins, slowly and delicately, into the veins of the pale, quiet girl on the table next to him, Lubbock got up and bent over her and whispered, "You're going to be all right," and she smiled weakly at him.

Then he put on his coat and went back into the clinic room. The others were still there. They stood there, scowling at him in the blue hospital light. He smiled widely at them.

"Everything all right?" Di Calco asked solemnly.

"Everything's fine," Lubbock said cheerfully. "My blood is singing in her system like whisky."

Di Calco looked at Sweeney, Sweeney at Cody, each with doubt and hesitancy in his eye.

"Say, Dutchman," Sweeney said loudly, "we'll buy you a drink. What d'yuh say?"

They waited, tense, almost ready for attack.

Lubbock looked consideringly at them. Cody put up the collar of his coat.

"Sure," Lubbock said, putting his arm around the girl. "It'll be an honor."

They walked out through the hospital doors together.

THE CITY
WAS IN TOTAL DARKNESS

DUTCHER STOOD at the bar, feeling clean after his shower and still thirsty, looking at the girls, glad that he was alone, listening with one ear to the conversation around him. "The British and French," a man in a hound's-tooth-check jacket was saying, "will shuttle back and forth over Germany from Paris to Warsaw. And besides, he has no oil. Everybody knows Hitler has no oil."

"'Darling,' she says to me," a large blonde woman said loudly to another large blonde woman, "'darling, I haven't seen you in for*ever*. Where've you been—in the summer theater?' She knows goddamn well I just finished two pictures for Fox!"

"It's a bluff," the man in the hound's-tooth-check said. "He's going to back down, Russia or no Russia. He has no oil. Where are you today without oil?"

"Mr. Dutcher." The barman brought over a phone and plugged it in. "For you."

It was Machamer on the phone. "What're you doing tonight, Ralph?" Machamer asked, his voice, as always, grating and noisy.

"I'm drinking tonight," Dutcher said. "I'm drinking and waiting for something good to happen to me."

"We're going to Mexico," Machamer said. "Want to come along?"

"Who's we?"

"Dolly and me. Want to come along?"

"What part of Mexico?" Dutcher asked. "What distant part of that verdant land? Vera Cruz, Mexico City . . . ?"

Machamer laughed. "Tia Juana. I got to be back on Tuesday to look for a job. Just overnight. For the races. Want to go?"

"Without oil," the man in the check was saying, "a war is absolutely impractical." Dutcher looked gravely at him, considering whether or not he wanted to go to Mexico. He had avoided people after playing tennis in the afternoon, because he'd wanted to be alone, by himself, with the decks clear for something special and significant to happen to him on this special and significant week end.

"Have they got bullfights in Tia Juana?" he asked Machamer.

"Maybe," Machamer said. "They have them sometimes. Come on, this is Labor Day, there's nobody in Hollywood."

"I'm tired," Dutcher said. "I've been listening to the radio for seven nights and I played tennis and I'm thirsty."

"You can lie down in the back of the car, with a bottle," Machamer said. Machamer was a young writer and very impressed with Dutcher's two novels and constantly was after him. "I'll drive."

"I never saw a bullfight," Dutcher said. "Did you ever see one there?"

"Oh, nuts!" Machamer said. "Dolly and I'll be over in fifteen minutes to pick you up."

"Tonight," Dutcher said, "I would like to have a startling adventure."

"Oh, nuts," Machamer said. "Fifteen minutes."

Dutcher gravely put the phone back on its pedestal. "I've got to find another bar," he said to the barman. "Whenever people want to find me they call me here. It's bad for the reputation. In two years nobody'll give me a job." The barman grinned. "Another Rum Collins," Dutcher said, looking steadfastly at a slender girl down the bar who had long thick black hair and tremendous full breasts that jutted out like pennants in front of her. The barman looked too. "Doesn't it break your heart?" the barman said.

"California," Dutcher said. "Specialty of the country."

"That cameraman," one of the blonde ladies was saying, "he made me look like William S. Hart's mother. I told him, too, but *loud!*"

In Poland, now, the tanks were roaring over the dusty plains. German boys were climbing into bombers now, Dutcher thought, fiddling with the controls, peering at the instruments, thinking in this one minute when they were waiting and there was nothing to do, "Is this the last time?" and then getting the signal and sweeping off the field toward Warsaw. Cavalry, Dutcher remembered, the Poles had wonderful cavalry. He could just see a wonderful Polish cavalryman sitting heavily on his plodding mount, retreating, sleepless, from the border, stinking from the horse, listening to the bombers overhead, thinking of sleep and home and the English air force, kicking his horse wearily, saying, "Son of a bitch." And the rich and their women, like the rich and their women everywhere, leaving quietly out the back way, while the dawn broke and the light came up and the boy in the bomber could get a good clear view of the cavalryman on the long, open road below.

Dutcher looked at the girl with breasts like pennants. He sat at the bar, making believe he was staring blankly ahead, making believe nothing was happening inside him, feeling lust rise within him as definitely as water rising in a filling glass. General, non-particular lust, he thought, looking at the girl, pretty, with her black hair and long throat and bright print dress and that amazing bosom. I ought to be ashamed, Dutcher thought. The reader of Spinoza, the admirer of John Milton, the advocate of moral and economic reforms, a sufferer from general and indiscriminate lust ten times daily at the sight of a face, a ruffle, at the sound of a woman's laugh.

"We live on two planes," Dutcher said to the bartender. The bartender smiled weakly.

Hollywood, Dutcher thought, Hollywood had a great deal to do with it. It was the product of the neighborhood, and everywhere you went it was pushed in your face like cheese in Wisconsin, and you tried to keep yourself from thinking about *Murder at Midnight* and sex rushed in to fill the vacuum. *Murder at Midnight* was the picture he was writing. It had a long complicated story about a night-club singer who got drunks to spend money on her but who was genuine, all the way through, as everyone always said in the conferences. She had a small son from whom she bravely tried to conceal the tawdriness of her profession, and she got mixed up in a murder and she fled town in the rain with the son and the cops picked up an innocent man. . . . Dutcher shook his head. He never could get the story straight. Anyway, this was the week end. And he'd be through in two weeks and have enough money for eight months in New York. Why'm I kidding myself? he thought. I look at them in New York, too.

Hollywood, you could always blame everything on Hollywood. That was the nicest thing about Hollywood.

"Sacred and profane," he told the bartender. "That's the whole explanation."

Machamer came in with Dolly. "On to Mexico," Machamer said.

"Sit down," Dutcher said, "and give me some good arguments. Dolly, you look beautiful." Dolly looked as thin and as plain and nervous as ever, and Dutcher was always very careful, in this city of magnificent

women, to be gallant and flattering to her. "Give me Dolly," he said
to Machamer, "and I'll go to Mexico."

Dolly laughed. Her laugh was high and very nervous and always
made Dutcher a little uncomfortable.

"Poor Dutcher," Dolly said. "Poor lonesome Dutcher."

"Get me a girl," Dutcher said, suddenly, not thinking about it or
why he was saying it, "and I'll go with you."

"Now, Dutcher," Machamer protested. "Eight o'clock Saturday night,
Labor Day week end . . ."

"On a high moral plane," Dutcher said. "I just want to have somebody to talk to."

"You have plenty of girls," Machamer said.

"I'm tired of them," Dutcher said. "Tonight I'm tired of them. War,
Murder at Midnight, the fickleness of the male character, I'm tired of
them. Tonight I'm in the mood for a new face." Dutcher waved his
hands elaborately, embroidering on the theme, although already half-
sorry that he'd said anything about a girl. "A face moody, passionate,
with the eyes cynical and despairing, the mouth lost and contemptuous
and stormy, the hair tossed and black . . ."

"He wants a character out of Thomas Wolfe," Machamer said.

"A face for the week end," Dutcher said, his tongue sliding joyfully
in his mouth after the Rum Collins, "a face tragic and tortured by
the guilt of a slaughtering and slaughtered world . . ."

Dolly jumped off her stool. "I'm going to call Maxine," she said.

"Who's Maxine?" Dutcher asked, warily.

"She's very pretty," Dolly said. "She's an actress at Republic."

"Oh, God," Dutcher said.

"Don't be such a snob," said Dolly. "Give me a nickel."

"What do you expect at eight o'clock Saturday night?" Machamer
gave her a nickel. "Hedy Lamarr?"

"She's very pretty," Dolly repeated. "She just got in from New
York and she may not be busy . . ." She started toward the phone.

"On a high moral plane!" Dutcher shouted after her. "Remember!"

Dolly strode out of sight toward the telephone booth. Dutcher
watched her and then turned to Machamer. "When you read the
papers," he said, "and you read about airplanes bombing people and
then being shot down, do you ever think about what it's like up there,
with the bullets coming at you and the plane bucking and all of a sudden just air below . . . ?"

"All the time," Machamer said soberly.

"During the Spanish War I used to dream about being machine-gunned by airplanes. I'd run and run along alleyways between garages and the planes would always come back and get me from an open side." Dutcher finished his drink. "I wonder what garages had to do with it. The trouble with the human race is it's too brave. You can get people to do anything—fly around and get shot at twenty thousand feet up, walk into hand grenades, fight naval battles. If the human race wasn't so damn courageous, this would be a much better world to live in. That's the sum total of my thinking in two months in Hollywood."

"Einstein is resting easy," Machamer said. "He's still got a good lead."

"I know," said Dutcher. "But he doesn't have to think in this climate."

Dolly slipped in between them. "It's all settled," she said. "Maxine is dying to go. She's heard about you."

"Good or bad?" Dutcher asked.

"She's just heard about you. She says you mustn't get fresh."

Dutcher wrinkled his nose. "Did she say 'fresh'?"

"Yes," Dolly said.

"I don't like Maxine."

"Nuts," Machamer said, and pulled him away from the bar and out to his car.

The big car sped toward Mexico. Dutcher sprawled luxuriously on the back seat with his head in Maxine's lap. Occasionally he moved his head lazily because Maxine was wearing a suit trimmed all the way down the front with red fox and the fur got into his nose and tickled him.

"He was an Italian," Maxine was saying. "He had large estates in Italy and he had a good job in New York, fifteen thousand a year, but he didn't like Mussolini."

"A character," Dutcher said softly. "A beautiful character."

"We were engaged to be married," Maxine said, speaking loudly, talking to Dolly, "but two weeks later he gave up his job. He relaxed; my little Wop relaxed." She laughed a little sadly, stroked Dutcher's head absently. "As soon as I meet a man he relaxes."

Machamer turned on the radio, and a man in London said that Hitler had not as yet answered Chamberlain's ultimatum and an orchestra played, "I May Be Wrong, But I Think You're Wonderful."

Dutcher looked thoughtfully up at Maxine's face. It was a round, full face, with a little full mouth that looked as though it had been created in God's mind with a careful brilliant smear of lipstick already on it. "You're very pretty," he said seriously.

Maxine smiled. "I'm not so bad." She patted him in appreciation. "I'm a little fat at the moment. I drank too much wine in New York. Dolly, I heard that Gladys is marrying Eddie Lane. Is that true?"

"In October," Dolly said.

Maxine sighed. "That Gladys. Eddie Lane's old man is good for five hundred thousand a year. She was in my class at high school. Oil. Old man Lane is up to his navel in oil. Eddie Lane chased me for two years like a kid after a fire truck. What a goddamn fool I was to go to New York."

Dutcher laughed, looking up at her. "You have a nice, refreshing outlook on finance."

Maxine laughed with him. "Money is money," she said. "I'll get a little fatter and even Republic won't have me, and then where'll I be?"

"I'll write a play," Machamer said, at the wheel, "and you can act in it in New York. They like them fat in New York."

"I tried that, too," Maxine said grimly. "I thought of another way out. I had my step-father insured . . ."

"Holy God!" Dutcher said. "For how much?"

"Fifty thousand."

"We're in the dough," Dutcher said. "Stop and buy me a Lincoln."

"Hah," said Maxine. "I paid his insurance three years then he went and got married on me. A little Irish biddy he saw waiting on table in San Luis Obispo."

They all laughed. "You're wonderful," Dutcher said. He pulled her down and kissed her. She kissed politely, with reserve, carefully, yet with a hint of vulgar accomplishment.

Unsatisfactory, Dutcher thought, letting his head fall back, yet . . . Reader of Spinoza, admirer of John Milton . . .

"This is Berlin," a voice said on the radio. "The city is in total darkness. The Fuehrer has not replied as yet to the English ultimatum. There is constant troop movement at the Berlin railroad stations and trains are pouring toward the Polish frontier."

A band played "Begin the Beguine," and Maxine talked to Dolly about another friend of theirs who had married a seventy-year-old man with fourteen blocks of real estate in downtown Cleveland.

"The city is in total darkness," Dutcher murmured. He lay back comfortably. This wasn't so bad, racing through the night to a new country, with a new girl, even though it was only Tia Juana and only an ordinarily pretty girl, getting a little fat, and a little hard and not exactly the girl you'd pick to take with you on a visit to your old Professor of Ethics at Amherst. Still it was better than sitting at a bar all alone, thinking, "I'll wait another ten minutes and then go out and buy another paper, see what *they* have to say."

He turned and buried his face in the red fox. There was a heavy smell of perfume, which was pleasant over the old smell of leather and gasoline in the back of the car. "Prince Matchabelli," Dutcher said. "This fox fell into a well of Prince Matchabelli and drowned. A beautiful death. Machamer, did I ever tell you about Cynthia Messmore, who was a classmate of mine at PS 99 and Miss Finch's? She married old Shamus Goonan, from the eleventh assembly district . . ."

"No!" Machamer said, in tones of wonder.

"A brilliant match," Dutcher said. "He was on the WPA three days a week and he was good for seven hundred and sixty dollars a year, as long as he stayed sober. Sewer construction, he was a sewer construction magnate, he was up to his navel in . . ."

"Are you making fun of me?" Maxine's voice was hard, and Dutcher knew he ought to stop, but he couldn't. He sat up.

"I never should've left PS 99," he said sadly. "Sex is the opium of the people. Turn on the radio, Machamer."

Dolly was shaking her head at him, but Dutcher made believe he was looking out the window. Mean, he thought, I've been mean. And I liked it. Tonight I want to be everything . . . mean, angry, noble, gracious, lordly, docile, everything. I want my emotions to be engaged. I can't love her, I can't make her love me, but I can make her angry at me and then win her over, then . . .

"This is Paris," a voice said. "All the lights are out. The Cabinet has been in conference since seven o'clock this evening."

Machamer turned the radio off.

Dutcher felt Maxine eyeing him. He turned and looked pleasantly at her. After all, he thought, regarding her, she *is* a pretty girl, with a fine figure and we *are* going to be together until tomorrow night . . .

"Is that how you're going to the races tomorrow?" Maxine asked. "Without a tie?"

Dutcher felt at his collar. He was wearing a polo shirt, open at the throat. "I guess so," he said. "It's awfully hot."

"I won't go with you," Maxine said, "unless you wear a tie."

"I haven't got a tie."

"I won't go with you," Maxine said firmly.

"We live in a tropical climate," Dutcher said. "We mustn't ever forget that. I'm a Northern man, I sweat like . . ."

"I have an extra tie," Machamer said. "You can wear that."

Dutcher nodded. "If it'll make Maxine happy . . ." He smiled at her.

"I wouldn't be seen in front of all those people with a man who wasn't wearing a tie."

"You're right," Dutcher said, smiling pleasantly at her. "Now that I think of it, you're absolutely right."

Maxine smiled back at him. At least, he thought, I haven't thought of *Murder at Midnight* since the trip began. At least, she's done that.

They stopped in San Diego and drank at a bar among a lot of sailors from the naval base. Dolly took some of the pills she was always taking and for a moment gripped Machamer's arm and leaned over and kissed his neck. It was nearly two o'clock and the bar was closing and the sailors were drunk.

"The United States will not get into any war," a big blond farm boy jutting out of his flimsy blue uniform announced. "I have the guarantee of my congressman."

"Where you from?" Dutcher asked.

"Arkansas."

Dutcher nodded as though this convinced him. The sailor gulped down what was left of his beer.

"Let the Japs come over," he called. "We'll sweep 'em from the seas. I'd like to see the Japs just try and come over. I'd just like to see . . ."

Maxine was smiling at the sailor.

"I'm hungry," Dutcher said, herding Maxine and Dolly toward the door. "I hate discussions of relative naval strength."

"That was heartening," Machamer said, as they walked toward the bright lights of a waffle shop down the street. "An official representative of the United States armed forces says we won't get into a war."

"He was a nice-looking boy," Maxine said, as they entered the waffle shop. "If you took him out of that sailor suit."

The waffle shop was crowded, and they sat at a table that had not been cleared. Maxine and Dolly went to the ladies' room and Machamer and Dutcher were left at the table, looking at each other in the garish waffle-room light, across the dirty dishes and spilled coffee on the table.

"She's all right," Machamer said loudly, grinning at Dutcher. "Dolly did all right for you, didn't she? She's got a wonderful figure."

"Machamer," Dutcher said, "if I had a cement mixer and I wanted somebody to make a speech while it was going, I would pick you."

Machamer looked around him apologetically. "Isn't it funny, how loud I talk?"

"Everybody in the Square Deal Waffle Shop now knows you think Maxine has a wonderful figure."

The waitress, very pale and harried-looking at two in the morning, rattled the dishes between them as she cleared the table.

"You're having a good time, aren't you?" Machamer asked. "She makes you laugh, doesn't she?"

"She makes me laugh," Dutcher said.

Dolly and Maxine came back. Dutcher watched Maxine walk down the aisle between the tables, her red fox shaking down the front of her suit and all the men in the place watching her. That suit, Dutcher thought, is one-half inch too tight, in all directions. Everything she wears, always, I bet, is one-half inch too tight. Even her nightgowns.

"You know what I'm thinking of?" Dutcher said to Maxine as she sat down.

"What?" Maxine asked, all newly powdered and rouged.

"Your nightgowns."

Maxine frowned. "That's not a nice thing to say."

"Dutcher's a very vulgar man," Machamer said. "You ought to read his books."

"The English," Maxine said, "just declared war on the Germans. The woman in the ladies' room told us."

That's how I found out, Dutcher thought. In the ladies' room in a waffle shop in San Diego, a woman told an actress from Republic, who drank too much wine in New York, that the English declared war on Germany, and that's how I found out.

"This fork is dirty," Maxine said loudly to the waitress, who was putting their waffles down on the table. "You have some nerve giving us dirty forks."

The waitress sighed and put down a clean fork.

"They'll get away with murder," Maxine said, "if you let them."

All through the room, people knifed slabs of butter and poured syrup and ate waffles, Dutcher noted, as he started on his. There was no change, just the usual restaurant noise of voices and plates.

"This waffle stinks," Maxine said. "That's my honest opinion. And they make a specialty of them! San Diego!"

Dutcher put his hand gently on hers to calm her.

"You got the hand of a day-laborer," Maxine said. "What do you do, hammer in nails with them at the studio?"

"It's the disgraceful heritage of my wasted youth," Dutcher said.

Maxine turned his hand over and carefully examined the palm. "You got a heart line that's branched many times," she said.

"Tell me more," said Dutcher.

"You're fickle, jealous, selfish." Maxine leaned over his hand very seriously. "And in the long run, you're not going to be very successful."

"What a catch!" Dolly said.

"Tell me more," said Dutcher.

"You're moody." Maxine ran her finger lightly over his palm. "You're a very moody man."

"They don't come any moodier," said Dutcher.

"Your life line is short."

Dutcher took his hand back gravely. "Thank you very much," he said, his hand still aware of the soft promising feel of Maxine's fingers. "Now I'm all cleared up about myself. I certainly am glad I brought you down to San Diego."

"It's all there in the palm," Maxine said defensively. "I didn't put it there." She drew her collar around her. "Let's get out of this joint." She walked toward the door, with all the men in the room watching her.

"You're not her type," Dolly whispered to Dutcher. "She told me in the ladies' room. She likes you, but you're not her type."

Dutcher shrugged. "Palmists don't like me. It's something I've always noticed."

He caught up with Maxine and held her elbow as they walked toward the car. "Now," he said, "we come to a most delicate point. We—uh . . . We have to go to a hotel—and—I . . ."

"I want my own room," Maxine said firmly.

"I just thought I'd ask." Dutcher shrugged.

"A gentleman doesn't ask," Maxine said.

"What does a gentleman do for girls?" Dutcher asked.

"He doesn't talk about it! It just happens."

"It never occurred to me before," Dutcher said as they got into the car. "But you're absolutely right."

They could only get a two-room suite at the hotel, because it was all filled up, and there were some other people from Hollywood in the lobby and Dutcher tried to appear as though he were in no way connected with Maxine. If only she didn't have that red fox, he thought. And all day tomorrow, at the races, there would be people he knew, and he'd have to try to be eight paces in front of her or at the betting windows or at the bar . . .

Upstairs, Maxine primly put her bag down next to Dolly's in one of the two rooms. Machamer looked at Dutcher.

"We have the west wing," Dutcher said, and walked into the next room.

"Look." Machamer followed him. "This was supposed to be a holiday for Dolly and me. She lives at home and her mother prays to God every night to save her sinful daughter's soul." Dolly came in and looked at them. Then she giggled.

"Go in and talk to Maxine," Machamer shouted to Dutcher.

Dutcher shrugged. "I see my duty," he said.

He went into the next room. Maxine was sitting neatly on the bed, her hands folded, her eyes reflectively on the ceiling. "Maxine, old girl," Dutcher said.

"Don't make fun of me."

"I'm tired," Dutcher said wearily. "There's a war on. I give up. There're two beds inside. I promise not to touch you. For Machamer and Dolly . . ."

"Let Machamer be a gentleman!" Maxine said loudly. "For one night."

Dutcher went back into the other room. "She says let Machamer be a gentleman for one night," he said. He took off one shoe. "I'm going to sleep."

Dolly kissed Machamer. She hung on, her arms wound around his neck and Dutcher made a big business of carefully arranging his shoes neatly in line under a chair. Dolly came over and kissed Dutcher lightly. "You sure make a big hit with the girls," she said, and went in.

Machamer and Dutcher put on their pajamas and turned off the light and Machamer got into bed. Dutcher went to the door of the girls' room. "Latest bulletin," he announced. "Machamer has promised not to lay a hand on me. Good night."

The girls laughed and Machamer roared and Dutcher joined them, the two rooms resounding wildly with laughter, as Dutcher climbed into bed.

Outside, the newsboys, far off along the dark streets of San Diego, cried that England had declared war.

Dutcher lay in his bed and listened to the newsboys' cries, swelling and wailing in the streets, and looked up at the dark ceiling; and the hour and the war, which had been kept off all night by drink and speed and laughter and lust, like lions warded off by a trainer's chair, now closed in on him. The cavalryman in Poland now lay across the dusty Polish road, his mouth open in surprise and death and his dead horse beside him and the boy in the German bomber flew back from Warsaw saying to himself, "One more time. I came back one more time."

"It's for Dolly's sake," Machamer's voice came across the small dark abyss between the beds, grating, but young and sorrowful. "It's nothing to me, but she's crazy to grab every hour. Do you want to go to sleep, Ralph?"

"No."

"She wants to grab everything. Everything. She hates to go to sleep. She always has her hands on me. She's going to die." Dutcher heard Machamer sigh and the bedsprings click gently and the newsboys coming nearer. "She's sick; the doctors can't cure her; she has Bright's disease. She gets numb, she feels as though an eye is falling out, an ear . . . That's why she takes those pills. She doesn't tell anybody except me. Her family doesn't know, and her boss . . ."

Dutcher lay rigid in his bed, looking up at the ceiling.

"I don't love her." Machamer's voice was harsh but small. "I tell her I do, but . . . I like other girls. . . . I tell her I do. She doesn't want to lose an hour."

"Sssh," Dutcher said gently. "Don't talk so loud."

"Even now," Machamer marveled. "Even now my voice would break down a wall. Are you sad, Dutcher?"

"Yes," said Dutcher.

"It came funny, didn't it?" Machamer asked.

"You hardly felt it." Dutcher talked with his eyes closed, his head straight back on the pillow. "You were waiting for it for six years and expecting it, and each time a shot was fired you'd say, 'Here it is,' but it wasn't, and you read the papers every day, and by the time it came you didn't feel it at all. We'll feel it later, we'll feel it later . . ."

"What're you going to do now?"

Dutcher laughed. "Go to sleep."

"Good night," Machamer said.

"Good night."

The bomber was coming down to a landing and the boy banked and looked down to see that the landing gear was out and he, Dutcher, was on his way with a fat citizen in a red fox-trimmed suit to a rat-eaten Mexican racetrack, where the youngest horse running was at least nine years old, where the Hollywood people in their scarves and dark glasses and buckskin shoes, with their agents and beauty-contest winners for the week end gambled their crazy easy money in the dusty Mexican heat, talking of sex and dollars, saying over and over, "Colossal, terrific, he's hot this year, it lost Metro a million." The war was on, and it was on here, too, among these idle, unbombed, frivolous people. I'd stay here, in Hollywood, Dutcher thought, if I could bear *Murder at Midnight* and all the Murders at Midnight to come. I don't want to write any more books. An honest book is a criticism. Why should I torture myself into criticizing this poor, corrupt, frantic, tortured, agony-stricken world? Later, later, let the criticism come later. . . .

The newsboys wailed in the streets below.

Here I am, Dutcher thought, in a hotel room far from home, with a dying and unloved girl, cheated of an hour, and a movie writer who wanders like a refugee from studio to studio, week in, week out, beggary plain on his face, looking for a job, and a palm-reader who could have been bought for the night with three compliments and ten minutes of polite charade. Fickle, jealous, selfish, moody, not successful, short of life.

"England, England . . ." The boys' voices, wavering in the night wind, came faintly through the window. I'm ashamed of myself, Dutcher thought. I met the tragic hour in a mournful and ludicrous costume.

Now is the time, Dutcher thought, for some noble and formidable act. Who will supply me with a noble and formidable act?

"I would like to speak to the continent of Europe," Dutcher said aloud.

"Huh?" Machamer murmured.

"Nothing." Dutcher pulled the covers up to his chin. "You know what I'm going to do?"

"Huh?"

"I'm going to get married. I'm going to have a wife and live on a farm and grow corn and wheat and grapes and watch the snow fall and slaughter pigs and become involved with the seasons. For a little while I want to become involved in an eternal motion."

"Sure," said Machamer. "I just dreamed Mervyn LeRoy was offering me a job. Isn't it too bad, isn't it too, too bad . . ." His voice trailed off.

"Involved with the seasons," Dutcher said, rolling it on his tongue. "Involved with the seasons." He closed his eyes.

Now the bomber stopped and the boy jumped out, feeling the ground solid under his feet and cold in the early morning. The boy grinned and the sweat of relief ran down under his arms and he said, "I made it, I made it again," as he went off across the field to report to his commanding officer.

HAMLETS OF THE WORLD

THE CAPTAIN was getting more and more remote every moment. He kept stuffing papers into a heavy saddle-leather bag, whistling tunelessly under his breath. From time to time he looked out over the windy plain, swirling with dust in the late afternoon sun. He would peer thoughtfully into the eye-burning distance, then shake himself a little and resume his packing, a little more quickly each time. He never looked at Lieutenant Dumestre.

Lieutenant Dumestre sat on the edge of the desk, very neat in his expensive uniform. He was a tall, fairish man, who looked too young to be in his lieutenant's uniform, too young to be so serious, too young to be in a war.

He never took his eyes off the Captain. The Captain was a round, solid man, who had been very jovial when they had met in Algiers and had paid for the wine and had sighed gallantly over all the pretty women in the café. There was nothing jovial or gallant about the Captain now, as he prepared in a businesslike way to disappear, each moment seeming more and more remote.

"Do you expect to come back, sir?" Lieutenant Dumestre finally asked, because the silence in the orderly room broken only by the low bumble of the Captain's humming was at last too much to bear.

The Captain stopped his packing and looked thoughtfully out over the plain again, as though there, in the dust and scrub, some answer to a profound although somewhat vague question was to be found. He stood silently, even forgetting to hum.

"Do you expect to come back, sir?" the Lieutenant asked loudly.

The Captain at last turned and looked at the Lieutenant. His eyes were very cool and you would never have thought from looking at him in this moment that he had ever bought a bottle of wine for a lieutenant in his life. "Come back?" the Captain said. He turned away and sturdily buckled his bag. "Who can tell?"

"What do I do with the Americans?" The Lieutenant's voice, he noticed angrily, was much higher than it should have been. At Saint Cyr they had been after him all the time to pitch his voice lower. "An order given in the soprano register, Mister, is not calculated to drive troops to impossible glories." "What happens when the Americans arrive?"

The Captain was putting his helmet on very carefully in front of a mirror. "That is just what I hope to discover," he said.

"In the meantime?"

"In the meantime your orders are to resist. Naturally."

The Lieutenant peered out over the plain, hoping painfully that over the rim of the horizon the Americans would appear before the Captain could leave on his personal retreat. But the only movement to be seen was a corporal hurrying to the battery observation post.

"They'll arrive tomorrow morning, at the latest," the Lieutenant said.

"Quite possibly." The Captain picked up his bag decisively, marched out and into the command car. The Lieutenant followed him and saluted. The Captain saluted and the car started and the Captain drove down the road.

The Lieutenant plodded slowly up the road toward the forward gun, thinking of the Captain, in the command car, speeding over a macadam road to Algiers, where there would be other men to make the decisions, other men to say, "We will move to the left, we will move to the right . . ." and the Captain would have to make no decisions himself. No matter how things turned out, he would not be committed and would be a fine fellow with whichever side turned up on top, and would jovially buy wine for his new lieutenants at the second-best restaurant in town. . . .

The Lieutenant made his way to the aimless little mud house they used as an observation post and climbed the ladder and stood under the umbrella next to the red-eyed little corporal and peered through his glasses at the plain. He looked until his eyes ached, but aside from the blowing dust there was nothing.

The men who served the forward gun had rigged up a tarpaulin to one side and lay under it, out of the wind. Usually they slept all the afternoon, but today no one was sleeping.

Sergeant Fourier even went so far as to get up and look out across the plain.

"Anything?" Labat asked.

The Sergeant squinted anxiously. "Nothing."

"Waiting, everything is waiting," Labat said. He was a long, ugly man, with a big nose and large ears. He was from Paris and excitable and given to throwing his arms around in rage and was a great patriot of the French Republic. "In a war you wait for everything! Even the Americans! At last, I thought, things will finally move. The Americans are famous for their briskness. . . . We're still waiting. . . ."

"Only a day," said Boullard. Boullard was a big, quiet man, over forty, with a wrinkled, brown, farmer's face. "They'll be here soon enough."

"I can't wait," Labat said. He stood up and peered out. "For a year I sat in the Maginot Line. Now for two years I sit here. I am finally impatient. A day is too much."

"Shut up," Boullard said calmly. "You'll get us all nervous."

Labat lay down and put his hands behind his head and looked up at the tarpaulin angrily. Sergeant Fourier came back and sat down.

"More of the same," Sergeant Fourier said. "More nothing."

"It must be worse for Americans," Corporal Millet said. He was a man who, although he was nearly thirty-five, was still plagued by pimples. His face had raging red blots on it all the time and he suffered meanly under his affliction, taking his misfortune out on the work details in his charge. "It must be unbearable for Americans."

"Why?" Labat asked angrily. "What's wrong with the Americans?"

"They are not a military people," Corporal Millet said. He had a lawyer's voice, smooth and reasonable and superior, and on bad days it made men want to kill Corporal Millet. "They are used to sitting back and pushing buttons."

"Corporal," Labat said calmly, "you are perhaps the biggest idiot in the French Army of 1942."

"The jokes," Corporal Millet said. "We can do without the jokes. It is a fact that war is harder on some races than on others. The Americans must be suffering the tortures of the damned."

"I repeat," Labat said. "The biggest."

Corporal Millet was a devotee of Vichy, and Labat enjoyed making him angry.

"Push buttons," Boullard said reflectively. "I could use a few push buttons at the moment."

"See," Corporal Millet gestured to Boullard. "Boullard agrees."

"See," Boullard said. "Boullard does not agree."

There was silence for a moment, while the men thought of the wind and the ugliness of the men around them and the possibility of dying tomorrow.

"This war," the Sergeant said. "This disease of a war."

"Somebody talk about a woman," Private Jouvet said. "I'm tired of the war. I am in the mood for breasts and hips." Private Jouvet was twenty years old and made a desperate effort to keep on an equal footing with these sun-stricken veterans of bed and battle.

"It can't be," Labat said, "that the Americans will appear and we will be asked to shoot at them. It's impossible."

"In the French Army," Boullard said, "nothing is impossible."

"Why not?" Corporal Millet asked in his bland voice. "An invasion of French soil . . ."

"I am very tired of those two words," Boullard said. "French soil."

Labat opened his canteen and took a mouthful. He closed the canteen over the precious water and then thought that perhaps he would be shot by morning, and said, "Hell," and opened the canteen and took another mouthful.

"The problem is," Private Jouvet said, "are the Americans to be regarded as friends, enemies, or tourists?"

"What a war!" Sergeant Fourier sighed. He had just married three months before, a masseuse with a good clientele in Algiers, and he was by and large as comfortable as a sergeant could hope to be in this foul year. "What a disease of a war!"

"Lafayette," Boullard said, "we are here."

"We will be given our orders," Corporal Millet said loudly.

"That's what we're afraid of," said Labat.

"After all," said Corporal Millet, tenderly touching his current most blazing pimple, "we are soldiers. We have officers. They have their instructions."

"Please, Corporal," said Labat. "Quiet. Such official sentiments have a tendency to make me throw up."

"The Americans." Sergeant Fourier sighed again. "Things were going as well as could be expected. This wasn't good, but a man could bear it. They are crazy with anxiety to make a landing someplace. . . . They have all Europe to make a landing on. No! They must choose Africa! We will all be dead."

"Be more cheerful," Boullard said, "or kindly keep quiet."

The men sat silently for a moment, everyone heavy and gloomy because the word death had finally been mentioned.

"It will be a ridiculous thing," Labat said. "To be killed by an American." Labat had fought at Sedan and made his way bitterly down the length of France, cursing the politicians, cursing the officers, cursing the Germans and English and Italians and Americans. At last he had stowed away aboard a freighter to Algiers and without losing a day had joined up all over again and had since then sat, full of pent-up vengeance, in the gloom of Africa, waiting to fight the Germans once more.

"I refuse," Labat said. "I refuse to be killed by an American."

"You will be told what your orders are," Corporal Millet said, "and you will follow them."

Labat stared gloomily and dangerously at Corporal Millet. His face, which was ugly but usually pleasant enough, now was harsh and his eyes were squinted balefully. "Corporal," he said, "Corporal of the pimples, do you know what our orders are?"

"No."

"Does anybody know?" Labat looked around, his face still flushed and glowering, angry at Corporal Millet and the government of France and his position in the world that afternoon.

Sergeant Fourier cleared his throat professionally. "The Lieutenant. He must know. The Captain's gone . . ."

"What a wonderful thing," Boullard said, "to be a captain. . . ."

"Let us ask the Lieutenant," Labat said.

"Sergeant Fourier, we make you a committee of one."

Sergeant Fourier looked around him uneasily, pulling in his round little belly nervously, uncomfortable at the thought of any action that would make him conspicuous, endanger his pleasant anonymous future with the masseuse in Algiers. "Why me?" he asked.

"Highest non-commissioned officer present," Labat chanted. "Channels of communication with the commissioned personnel."

"I haven't said two words to him," Sergeant Fourier protested. "After all, he just got here five days ago. And he's reserved. . . . All he's said to me in five days is, 'Make sure the men do not smoke in the open at night.'"

"Enough," Labat said cheerfully. "It's obvious he likes you."

"Don't joke," Boullard said sharply. "We have no more time to joke."

"I'm only joking," Labat said soberly, "because I am willing to slit my throat."

He got up and went to the edge of the tarpaulin and stood there, his back to the men, watching across the enigmatic plain for the first fateful dust cloud.

"What sort of man is this Lieutenant Dumestre?" Boullard asked.

"It's hard to tell," Sergeant Fourier said, with the caution born of three years in an army where a hasty approval of a man, before all the facts of courage, sense and rectitude were in, might one day cause your death. "He's very quiet. Stiff . . ."

"A bad sign," said Boullard.

"Very rich in the uniform department."

"Another bad sign."

"It doesn't pay to be too hurried," Sergeant Fourier protested.

"It's the Americans," Boullard said. "They're in a hurry, not me. Well, there's only one thing to be done." He rubbed his cheek absently with the back of his hand, like a man determining whether or not he needs a shave. The other men watched him silently, anxious and curious about a definite plan that might have finally bloomed on this last nervous afternoon. "One thing," Boullard repeated. "We kill him."

Lieutenant Dumestre stood in the observation post and felt the headache coming on like an express train. Every afternoon the boredom and misery of the day accumulated in his brain pan and punished him for still living. He stared painfully over the darkening plain, which was silently enveloping itself in blue and purple folds, intangible and deceptive, in which the shapes of men and machines might be capriciously and dangerously lost. . . .

Lieutenant Dumestre shook his head and closed his eyes, measuring gloomily the exact extent of the pain in his skull.

How do you do it? he asked himself. How does a first lieutenant hand a battery over to an advancing army, without orders? How does a first lieutenant save his life in a situation like this? In the distance there is a puff of dust and soon the first shell dropping somewhere near you, and all around you doubtful and uncertain men whom you do not know but who, for the lack of a better word, are under your command. Why had he left his post in Algiers? In this one, crazy, fateful week, his transfer had to be granted, this transfer to dilemma, this transfer to death. . . . In the days of Napoleon it was said that every French private had a marshal's baton in his knapsack. Today every French soldier had in his knapsack a fatal and insoluble conundrum.

Lieutenant Dumestre had asked to be transferred from Algiers because he had been spending too much money there. It was as simple as that. The bills came in, the monthly reckonings were made, the deductions for the money sent home to his mother and father, who were lean and ailing in Paris, and it became clear that on a lieutenant's salary you could not save money in a gay town, especially if you had been rich all your life and your family rich before you and certain habits of eating and drinking and generosity ingrained in you, war or no war. . . .

So, it was too expensive, Algiers. So, the desert would prove to be even more expensive.

. . . Back in Algiers he knew the men of his battery had mimicked him behind his back—his slow, painful way of delivering orders, full of agonized pauses, as he tried to remember to keep his voice down, tried not to sound like a young idiot imposing callously on these veterans of a war that had passed him by. . . . They had mimicked him, but he knew them and even felt they liked him, and if he were with them now in this tragedy of a situation he would be able to go to them, talk to them, draw strength and resolution, one way or another from the men who would have to bear the burden of living and dying with him.

But here he was, on the one important day of the last two years, with a group of sullen and bearded strangers, who regarded him only with steady and cool hostility, a newcomer and an officer in an army where newcomers were automatically suspect and officers automatically hated. . . .

Lieutenant Dumestre walked slowly out toward the west across the dusty scrub. The sun had set and the wind had died and the walking, he felt, might help somehow. Perhaps, he thought, smiling a little to himself, there will be an American patrol and I am unavoidably captured and there's an end to the problem. . . . It's like a child, he thought, hoping that by morning he will have a sore throat so he does not have to go to school and take his examination in arithmetic. What an arithmetic was being imposed upon him now! What a savage and pitiless calculation! He looked toward the last blur of the horizon beyond which the Americans were marching. How simple it was to be an American! In their arithmetic there was an answer to all problems. How merry and dashing a lieutenant in the artillery in the American army must feel tonight, marching beside men whom he could trust, who trusted him, who all believed the same thing, who knew an enemy when they saw one, whose parents were well-fed and healthy, in no one's power, three thousand sweet miles from all battlefields. . . .

What a tragic thing to be a Frenchman this year! Hamlet, sword out, killing Polonius and uncle in blind unprofitable lunges. . . . Frenchmen, Hamlets of the world . . .

Lieutenant Dumestre stopped and sat down like a little boy on the dark earth and put his head in his hands and wept. He stopped suddenly and bit his lips and neglected to dry the tears from his cheeks. Nonsense, he thought, a grown man . . . There must be an answer to this, too. After all, I am not the only Frenchman afloat on this continent. The thing is, the men. If I knew what they wanted . . . If there was only some way to be present, without being seen. Armies have surrendered before. Detachments have surrendered before. Officers have appeared under a flag of truce and offered their services to their official enemies. The Captain was in Algiers, there was no one to stop him. "Dear sir, is there anyone here who speaks French? Dear sir, Lieutenant Dumestre, Battery C, wishes to state that he desires to join forces with the American Army in North Africa and put himself under the flag of the United States for the duration against the common enemy. . . ." There must be a technique to surrender, just the way there was a technique for everything else in the army. His mother and father would have to look out for themselves. Now, if only the men . . .

Lieutenant Dumestre slapped his thigh briskly as he stood up. At last he had reached a decision. He had faced the arithmetic and at least he knew what answer he wanted. There only remained going in frankly to the men and putting the situation up to them, in words of one syllable, simply. . . . He started back toward the forward gun, walking more swiftly than he had walked for a week.

"Men," he would say, remembering to keep his voice pitched low, "this is the way it is. You may or may not know it, but tomorrow an American army will appear." You never knew how much the men knew, what rumors had reached them, what facts confirmed, what punishments and discharges and prophecies and movements were peddled at the latrine or over a morning cigarette. "I am under orders to resist," he would say. "Personally, I do not believe we are bound by those orders, as I believe all Frenchmen to be on the side for which the Americans are now fighting." Perhaps that was too heroic, but it was impossible to fight a war without sounding from time to time a little heroic. "I intend to go out under a flag of truce and give over the guns of this battery." Now the question of dissenters. "Anyone who does not wish to join me in this action is free to leave toward the rear. . . ." No, they'd go back and talk and by morning a troop of cavalry would come up and Lieutenant Dumestre would be finished in thirty minutes. Keep them with him? How do that? Supposing they were all Vichy men?

After all, they were being paid by Vichy and there were thousands of Frenchmen in Africa who had staked their lives on a German victory. They'd shoot him in cold blood.

Once more he cursed the trick that had landed him at this moment among two hundred strangers. In his old company he would have been able to take Sergeant Goubille aside and talk honestly and get an honest answer. Sergeant Goubille was forty-five years old and there was something fatherly and tolerant of young officers in his bearing, and a man like that would be worth a man's life on this harsh and doubtful plain tonight. Well, there was no Sergeant Goubille at hand. . . . Perhaps that Breton, that farmer, Boullard. He was an older man and he looked honest and pleasant.

He took a deep breath and walked swiftly, not knowing exactly what he would do but knowing he had to do something, toward the forward gun. . . .

Under the tarpaulin, Boullard was talking, his voice low and harsh, all the kindly, old countryman's lines somehow vanished from the set, desperate face. "There will be a token resistance," he was saying to the men, who were all sitting up, looking at the ground most of the time, looking up only occasionally at Boullard with a kind of deep embarrassment. "In a token resistance there are token deaths." He looked around him calmly from face to face, his thought plain in his eyes. "A token corpse feeds as many worms as any other. . . ."

Jouvet, the young one, was the only one who could not manage to sit still. He rubbed his heels back and forth, making marks in the sand, and studying them intensely.

"Kill the pretty lieutenant," Boullard said, "and we have our own lives in our own hands. We dispose of them as we see fit."

"Let us look at it from the political angle," Labat said. "Politically, we are fried if the Germans win. . . ."

"Perhaps," Sergeant Fourier said uneasily, his voice full of the nagging pain of having to make a decision. "Perhaps we ought to wait and see what happens."

"We will wait and see ourselves buried," Boullard said.

"At least," said Labat, "we ought to talk to the Lieutenant. Sound him out."

"I was on the Meuse," said Boullard. "I know better than to talk to a lieutenant. I'll take the responsibility. If you're all afraid . . ." He looked around him with savage, peasant contempt. "There're a lot of men still to be killed in this war. I don't mind making it one more or less, personally. . . ."

"We have to talk to him first," Labat said stubbornly.

"Why?" Boullard asked loudly.

"Maybe he's with us. Maybe he wants to fight with the Americans, too. . . ."

Boullard laughed harshly. Then he spat. "I'm surrounded by children," he said. "If he's still an officer in the French Army after two years, he is not fond of the Americans. I am. At this moment, I am crazy about Americans. If there is any hope for anybody in this stinking year, it is in the Americans. I'm forty-four years old and I've fought in two wars. The third one, I want to pick my own side. . . ."

"Still," Labat said, his voice low and persistent, "still, we ought to talk to him."

"For myself," Corporal Millet said briskly, standing up, "I am on duty at the observa—"

He let his hands fall gently to his sides as Boullard brought his rifle up and touched his chest lightly with the bayonet.

"You are on duty here, Corporal." Boullard moved the bayonet tenderly on a breast button. "There is a question before the house that must be decided by a full membership."

Corporal Millet sat down carefully.

"I don't care," Labat was saying, grinning at Corporal Millet, "what you do to the fighting corporal, but nothing happens to the Lieutenant until we talk to him." He patted Boullard's shoulder, in a small, reassuring gesture. Boullard slowly took his eyes off Millet and the Corporal sighed.

Boullard looked around him searchingly at the men caught in this hour on this desert with him. Sergeant Fourier, haunted by dreams of a pension and his masseuse and still troubled by some obscure, painful sense of patriotism and honor, refused to look at him. Jouvet, faced at the age of twenty with the ancient, tangled threads of a bloody and complex century, looked ready to weep. Labat was smiling but stubborn. Corporal Millet was sweating, and was making a great effort to look like a man who did not intend to rush to the nearest officer and announce a mutiny.

"All right," Boullard said wearily, "if that's what you want. Although I tell you, two words too many and we are all against a wall, looking at a firing squad."

Jouvet fumbled with his handkerchief quickly and Boullard looked at him curiously and impersonally.

"It is not necessary to commit ourselves," said Labat. His long, workman's arms waved in argument. "We approach the subject, we skirt it, we take soundings like a boat coming into a harbor . . ."

"Better!" Sergeant Fourier said loudly, happy at all deferment. "Excellent! Much better!"

Boullard stared at him coldly and Sergeant Fourier became quiet and nervously took out a pack of cigarettes.

"It's possible," Labat was saying, convincing Boullard, "to judge a man without a direct question. . . ."

"Possibly," Boullard said with no enthusiasm. "Possibly."

"I'll do the talking," Labat said. "I'm used to things like this. I have talked at union meetings for seven years and nothing could be more delicate . . ." He looked around him anxiously, hoping for a little laughter to take some of the deadly tension away, but only little Jouvet, who was always polite, smiled nervously because he realized Labat had meant it as a little joke.

"All right," Boullard said. He fingered his rifle gently and let it dip almost imperceptibly toward Corporal Millet. "I will judge. And you . . ." The rifle dipped very clearly toward Corporal Millet. "You will not open your mouth. Is that clear?"

Corporal Millet sat up stiffly at attention, feeling sorrowfully within him that his honor demanded some show of resistance and that his life would not be worth a great deal if he was incorporated in the army of the United States. He looked at Boullard's huge crushing hands, calm on the rifle. "It is your affair," he said faintly. "I wash my hands of it."

Boullard laughed.

Sergeant Fourier lighted his cigarette, gift of his plump wife the masseuse, eating her dinner comfortably, all unknowing, in the curtainy little apartment in Algiers with three exposures. He sighed and stood up and walked between Boullard and the limp Corporal Millet and stood at the edge of the tarpaulin in the full darkness, pulling with small comfort at his cigarette, while behind him, under the tarpaulin, there was no sound from the waiting men.

Lieutenant Dumestre made his way slowly across the rough black ground toward the gun position, turning over in his mind his possible opening sentences to the gun crew. "Men," he could say, "I am going to be absolutely honest with you. I am putting a white flag up beside this gun and I am delivering this battery over to . . ." Or he could say, "There is a possibility that tomorrow morning American troops will appear. Hold your fire until I give the word . . ." while silently swearing to himself that the word would never be given. There was much to be said for this method, as it was indefinite and seemed less dangerous and didn't tip his hand until the last moment, when it would probably be too late for anyone to do anything about it. Of course there was always the possibility that he could stand up in front of the men and pour his heart out to them, remind them in ringing words of their country's shame, call upon them with blood and passion to forget themselves, forget their families in France, remember only honor and final victory. . . . He could see himself, pale and fluent, in the dim light of the moon, roaring, whispering, his voice singing in the quiet night air, the men listening entranced, the tears starting down their cheeks. . . . He shook himself, smiled wryly at the dream, remembering his harsh, slow way of speaking, plain, indefinite, without the power to move men to the nearest café, much less throw themselves grandly and thoughtlessly upon a doubtful and possibly fatal cause. . . .

Oh, Lord, he thought, I am the wrong man for this, the wrong man, the wrong man. . . .

He turned the corner of the tarpaulin, seeing the watchful, hateful shape of the gun outlined stubbornly against the starlit sky.

Sergeant Fourier was smoking pensively in the open and the other men were sitting, strangely quiet, under cover. When Sergeant Fourier saw him he started guiltily and threw his cigarette away as unostentatiously as possible. He stood at attention and saluted and with his right heel tried to douse the glowing speck in the dirt. Somehow, the sight of the small man with the comfortable little pot belly trying to pretend, like a vaudeville comedian, that he hadn't been smoking, irritated Lieutenant Dumestre, who all morning and all afternoon had been grappling bitterly with war and fratricide and tragic, bloody policy. . . .

He returned the Sergeant's salute curtly. "What's wrong with you?" he asked sharply, his high voice making all the men in the tarpaulin turn their heads coldly and automatically to watch him. "You know there's to be no smoking."

"Please, sir," Sergeant Fourier said stupidly, "I was not smoking."

"You were smoking," Lieutenant Dumestre said, weeping inside because inside he knew how ridiculous this charge and countercharge was.

"I was not smoking, sir." Sergeant Fourier stood very straight and formal and stupid with the problem of the evening, almost happy to have a simple little idiotic argument to worry about at least for ten minutes. . . .

"You've been told, you've been told!" Lieutenant Dumestre shrieked in his highest voice, mourning deep within himself for that womanly timber, for his military insistence upon form and truth at this unmilitary hour, but somehow unable, with the Captain's departure and the imminence, potent and desperate, of the Americans over the horizon, to stop the high noise of his tongue. "At any moment we may be bombed. A cigarette glows like a lighthouse in a black desert at ten thousand feet! Why don't you draw a map of the gun position and publish it in the morning newspapers?" He saw Labat look at Boullard and shrug coldly and turn away with an air of dangerous significance and something within him clutched at his throat, but now there was no stopping that high, silly tongue, freed for a moment from the locked agony and doubt of the day's decision making. Here at least was familiar ground. Troops disobeying orders. Troops endangering security of the post or station. Troops slightly insubordinate, lying. . . . His weary, ragged mind, terribly grateful to be relieved of its unaccustomed task of painful exploration, relapsed into the formal, years-long grooves of Saint Cyr, of countless garrisons, countless lectures. . . . "There will be double security tonight, two-hour watches for everyone," the voice still high, but with the three-thousand-year-old bite of military command. "An extra half day's ammunition will be drawn up from the battery dump by three this morning." He saw the men's faces bleakly collapse and also something else in them, although he couldn't tell in the rush of his commands what it was. Even as he spoke he hated himself for what he was doing, knowing that a better man would have ignored the cigarette or joked about it. . . . He hated Sergeant Fourier, standing there, pained and stupid and impassive, but in a way he was grateful to him, because he had given him the opportunity at this late hour once more for postponement.

He turned on his heel and strode away. Later, perhaps at midnight, he would come back, he told himself, and finally get this question of the Americans settled. He pulled his shoulders high in disgust as the sound of his own voice squalling about the cigarette sounded in his ears, but there was nothing to be done about it and he walked without looking back. Midnight, he thought, midnight is still time. . . .

Back under the tarpaulin, Boullard looked around him at the men. Their faces were grave, but except for Millet, there was consent in all of them.

Boullard walked out from under the tarpaulin with his rifle.

Midnight, Lieutenant Dumestre was thinking, when the bullet struck, midnight is still time. . . .

They buried him quickly without marking the grave and sat down in front of the gun to wait for the army of the Americans.

WALKING WOUNDED

HE WONDERED what had happened to the curtains. He lay stiffly on the bed, listening, with the old, irritated tightening of the nerves, to the wild and grating hubbub of the Cairo street outside his window, the insane wailing of newsboys, the everlasting iron drip of garry-horses' hooves, the pained yelps of peddlers. The sun, bright and hurtful as hot nickel, cut in through the open windows. On the floor lay the curtains, torn, with bits of cord still running from them to the top of the windows, like a ruptured spider web.

"What happened to the curtains?" he asked. His voice felt dry and sandy in his throat, and the right side of his head began to ache.

Mac was shaving at the washstand. His beard made a crinkly, Spartan sound against the razor. "Last night," Mac said, without turning. "In the excitement."

"What excitement?"

"You pulled the curtains down."

"Why?"

Mac shaved quietly and intently around the short, soldierly mustache. "Don't know," he said. "Either you wanted to throw me out, or throw yourself out, or just tear down the curtains."

"Oh, God!"

Mac scrubbed his face with water. "Pretty drunk, Peter," he said.

"What else did I do?"

"Two lieutenants and a major. In the lounge. Ten minutes of insults."

"A major! Christ!" Peter closed his eyes.

"I think you hit a lieutenant." Mac's voice was muffled in a towel. "Anyway, you hit something. Your hand's all cut up."

Peter opened his eyes and looked at his hand. Across the back of it there was a wide, ugly wound, just beginning to puff up around the edges. As he looked at it, he realized that it was hurting him.

"I poured iodine over it," Mac said. "You won't die."

"Thanks." Peter let his hand drop, licked his dry lips. "What did I say to the major?"

" 'Base wallah.' 'Imperial vulture.' 'Gezira bloodsucker.' 'Headquarters hangman.' "

"That's enough." The right side of Peter's head hurt very strongly for a moment.

"You were a little unfair," Mac said calmly. "He was a nice type. Been in the desert three years. Just come back from Sicily with dysentery. Wounded twice. Been attached to headquarters four days."

"Oh, Christ," Peter said. "Oh, Christ."

The room was silent as Mac put on his shirt and combed his hair.

"Get his name?" Peter asked finally.

"Major Robert Lewis. Might be a good idea to say good morning."

"How about the lieutenants?"

Mac took out his notebook. "MacIntyre and Clark," he read. "They await your pleasure."

Peter sat up and swung his legs over the side of the bed. The room faded and glittered for a moment, and he had to hold on to the bed when he stood up.

"Some day, soon," he said, "I have to stop drinking."

"A little whisky," Mac said kindly, "is good for the soul. Anything I can do for you?"

"No, thanks."

Mac stood at the door.

"Mac . . ."

"Yes, Captain . . . ?" Tiny, astringent, helpful mockery in the title.

"Mac, this is the first time anything like this ever happened to me."

"I know," Mac said softly. He went quietly out of the room.

Peter walked slowly over to the wash basin, looked at himself in the mirror. The familiar long, thin face, the uneven dotted crenelation of his wound across his forehead, the strange dark mark in the eye that had been blind for three weeks, all seeming to tremble slightly now in the bitter sunlight, as it had trembled for two months.

He shaved carefully and went to take a shower. He came back, feeling better, and put on fresh clothes. He switched his tabs with the three pips to his clean shirt, looking absently and automatically to see if there was any lipstick on them. Three and a half years ago, at Arras, there had been lipstick one morning, and he had walked around all day long, ignorant, wondering why smiles hid on sergeants' lips.

Then he went down to apologize to the major.

He sat at his desk, sweating. The heat of Egypt was like the inside of a balloon. The balloon was being constantly filled; the pressure getting greater and greater. Typewriters clicked dryly in the swelling air, and flies, the true owners of Egypt, whirled cleverly and maliciously before his eyes.

Sergeant Brown, his thick glasses clouded with sweat, clumped in and put a stack of papers on his desk, clumped out again. The back of Sergeant Brown's shirt was soaked where he had been pressing against the back of a chair, and sweat ran in trickles down his infantryman legs to the heavy wool socks and gaiters.

Peter stared at the stack of papers. Ruled forms and tiny and intricate notations that had to be gone over slowly, corrected, signed.

Outside, a donkey brayed painfully. It sounded like an immense wooden machine in agony, wood grating against wood, incredibly loud. It made the little, paper-stacked room seem hotter than ever.

Peter reread the letter he had received that morning from Italy. ". . . I am taking the liberty of answering your letter to Col. Sands, who was badly wounded last week. I am afraid there is nothing we can do about requesting your being posted to this regiment, as there is no provision in our establishment for medically graded officers."

The donkey brayed again outside. It sounded like the death of all the animals of Egypt on this hot morning.

Peter stared at the papers on his desk. Three flies danced over them, lighted, swept off. The typewriters rattled flatly in the heat. He took the top paper off the pile, looked at it. The figures leapt and wavered in the heat, and a drop of sweat fell from his forehead and mistily covered a 3, a 7, an 8. His hands glistened in little sick beads, and the paper felt slippery under his fingers. Hobnails sounded on the marble floor in the corridor, ostentatious and overmilitary among the clerks and filing cabinets. His throat burned dryly with the fifteenth cigarette of the morning.

He stood up jerkily and took his hat and went out. In the corridor he passed Mrs. Burroughs. She was a tall, full-bodied girl who wore flowered prints and always seemed to manage silk stockings. She was going home to England to divorce her husband, who was a lieutenant in India. She was going to marry an American air-force major who had been switched to London from Cairo. She was very pretty and she had a soft, hesitant voice, and her bosom was always oppressively soft and noticeable under the flowered prints.

She smiled at him, hesitant, polite, gentle. She had two rosebuds clasped in her dark hair. "Good morning," she said, stopping, her voice cool, shy, inviting in the drab corridor. She always tried to stop him, talk to him.

"Good morning," Peter said stiffly. He never could look squarely at her. He looked down. No silk stockings this morning. The pretty legs bare, the skin firm and creamy. He had a sudden, hateful vision of Mrs. Burroughs landing in London, running to be crushed in the arms of the American major in the press of Waterloo Station, her eyes bright with tears of love and gratitude, her husband, used and forgotten, in India. . . .

"I'm going to Groppi's," he heard himself say, surprisingly. "Tea. Would you like to join me?"

"Sorry," Mrs. Burroughs said, her voice sounding genuinely sorry. "So much work. Some other time. I'd be delighted. . . ."

Peter nodded awkwardly, went out. He hated Mrs. Burroughs.

The street was full of heat, beggars, dirt, children with fly-eaten eyes, roaring army lorries. He put on his hat, feeling his forehead, wet and warm, rebel under the wool. A drunken New Zealander, at eleven o'clock in the morning, wobbled sorrowfully in the full glare of the sun, hatless, senseless, reft of dignity, 7,000 miles from his green and ordered island.

Groppi's was cooler, dark and shaded. The red-fezzed waiters in the long white gaballiehs moved quietly through the pleasant gloom. Two American sergeants with gunners' wings on their shirts solemnly were drinking two ice-cream sodas apiece.

Peter had tea and read the morning paper. The birth rate had gone up in England, and an American magazine had suggested that Princess Elizabeth marry an American. The *Egyptian Mail* reprinted it with approval in a flood of Anglo-American feeling. After six years, somebody said in Parliament, men in the forces were to be sent home. The Russians were pouring across the Dnieper. Peter always saved the Russian news for last. Every step the Russians took was that much nearer home, nearer the rugged and manly weather of Scotland, near Anne. . . .

He tried to think of Anne, what she looked like, what her skin felt like. He looked up at the ceiling and half closed his eyes to shut out the tea and ice-cream shop, to close out Egypt, summer, war, army, distance, absence, close out everything but his wife. But he couldn't remember what she looked like. He remembered the dress she wore when they were married and the inn they'd stayed at after Dunkirk and what they'd played at the concert the last night in London, and he remembered that he loved her. But her face, the sound of her voice . . . lost. She refused to have photographs taken of her. Some whim or female superstition, far away in England. . . .

He paid and went out and started back to his office. But when he stood in front of the peeling, ornately balconied, sand-bagged building and thought of the small, hot office, the endless papers, the sweat and hobnails, he couldn't go in. He turned and walked slowly down the street. He looked at his watch. Still an hour before the bars opened. He walked on the shady side, erect and soldierly, slowly, like a man with a grave purpose. A horribly dirty woman with a horribly dirty child, as dirty and street-worn as only Egyptians can be, followed him, whining, for half a block. Peter didn't walk any faster, although he felt his nerves jerking at the sound of the woman's voice.

The woman left him finally, and he walked deliberately through the crowded streets, stopping from time to time to peer into shop windows. French perfume, women's dresses, mangoes, books, photographs, his mind recorded heavily. He went into the photographer's and had his picture taken, refusing to smile, looking soberly square into the camera, intimidating the photographer. He would send the picture to Anne. Three years. How long could a woman be expected to remember a man? His face would stare solemnly at her morning, noon, and night, crying, "Remember me, remember your husband. . . ."

Out in the street again he resumed his grave pacing down the shady side of the street. Fifteen minutes more and the bars would open. He grinned crookedly to himself as he thought of his pose before the camera, frozen Scotch passion grimly and puritanically peering across three years and two oceans. Anne would probably giggle at the absurdly stern, accusing face.

"Officer, wanna lady, wanna lady?"

Peter looked down. A tiny, filthy ten-year-old boy, barefooted, in a torn, bag-like single garment, was smiling up at him conspiratorially, pulling at his blouse.

"French lady," the boy whispered wickedly. "Fine French lady."

Peter stared at him disbelievingly, then broke into a roar of laughter. The boy, after a moment of doubt, also laughed.

"No, thank you, sir," Peter said.

The boy shrugged, grinned up at him. "Officer," he said, "cigarette?"

Peter gave him a cigarette and lit it for him, and the boy darted off, to try the French lady on a Polish corporal.

The bar had a nice beery smell and was dark and cool and the bartender drew eight glasses at a time, letting the foam settle whitely on the glass rims.

"The two lieutenants," Peter was saying, "were a little stuffy, but the major was fine."

"I knew he would be," Mac said. "I talked to him last night."

"I had breakfast with him"—Peter waved for two more beers—"and he said he guessed he'd be doing the same thing himself if he had to hang around this town five months."

Mac comfortably drained his beer.

"The birth rate in England," Peter said, "has gone up. I read it in the *Mail* this morning. There're three million Englishmen out of the country and the birth rate's rocketing. . . ." He heard his own voice loud and angry and humorless. "How in the name of God do they dare print things like that?" He saw Mac grinning widely, but he couldn't stop. "Who're the fathers? Where're the fathers? Bloody damned newspaper!"

"My," Mac said, "you have it bad today."

Suddenly Peter realized that Mac, placid and tolerant, was bearing a great deal of the burden of Peter's nerves.

"Mac," he said quietly, "forgive me."

"Uh?" Mac looked at him, surprised.

"Wailing Wall Chrome. Agony, Cairo division." Peter shook his head in disgust. "I keep feeding it to you seven days a week."

"Oh, shut up. I've lived with lots worse."

"Any time I get on your nerves, sing out, will you?"

"Sure thing. Drink your beer." Mac was embarrassed.

"I must be going a little crazy." Peter looked at his hands, which had taken to trembling in the last few months. The cigarette jerked minutely between his fingers, in a spasmodic rhythm. "This town. When I was with the regiment . . . Oh, hell . . ." The truth was that out in the desert, under the guns, on a pint of water a day, and the sudden air often dire with Stukas, he had been much happier. There were no women in the desert, no reminders of a civilized and normal life. There was clean, sterile sand, the noise of armor, thousands of grumbling, good-humored men intimate with an equal death, and above all there was the sense of immense and hardy effort and accomplishment, as first they had held the Afrika Corps and then driven it back. Cairo then had been a beautiful town, two days at a time, a hot bath and unlimited

Scotch, and sweet, clean sheets and relief from the guns. But now, under the dry flood of paper, under the stiffness and pettiness of headquarters politics, under the cheap weight of men who had clung to soft jobs for three years, with the streets full of bare-legged girls, with the war on another continent a thousand miles away . . .

Now the regiment, what was left of it, was broken up. Most of them were in graves on the road to Tunis, others were in hospitals, the rest scattered among other units, after the four years that had started in France. Mac, who had been his platoon sergeant at Arras, calmly instructing the untrained men how to load and fire the guns they had never used before, then taking them out into the fresh May fields of France hunting for parachutists. Himself, who had crawled through the German lines to Dunkirk, who had entered Tripoli the first hour, who had blown up in the jeep outside Mareth, with his driver dead in the air beside him . . . Now, both of them clerks in small offices, chained to paper and civil servants.

"Six years," he said, "some bloody MP said we'd be sent home after six years. What do you think a woman thinks when she reads that she'll get her man back in only six years?"

"Always remember," Mac grinned, "what Monty said. 'The war can't last more than seven years. We'll run out of paper.'"

"If only I could get back to England," Peter said, "and sleep with my wife for two nights, everything would be all right. Just two nights."

Mac sighed. He was a quiet, efficient, small, matter-of-fact man, noticeably graying, and sighing was strange and incongruous to him. "Peter," he said, "can I talk plainly?"

Peter nodded.

"Peter, you ought to get yourself a girl."

They sat in silence. Peter played somberly with his beer. In France, even though he had just been married, he had been the gay young officer. Handsome and debonair, he had played joyfully and thoughtlessly with the pretty ladies of the country towns at which he'd been stationed, and in Paris, when he'd had a month there, a charming, beautifully dressed wife of a French captain stationed in Algiers.

But when he'd got back to England with the gray-faced remnants of his regiment, after the hideous, bloody days of the break-through, and had taken his wife silently into his arms, all frivolity, all smallness and lack of faith had seemed wanton and irreligious in the face of so much ruin, such agony. Leaving England for Africa, he had felt that behind him he had to leave the best part of his life orderly and decent.

"Maybe," he said to Mac. "Maybe . . ."

"A man's got to be practical," Mac said. "Three years. Oh, my God!"

Peter had to smile at the drastic expression on the practical man's face.

"You'll just explode," Mac said, "and blow away."

Peter laughed loudly, nervously. "Whisky," he said, "provides certain compensations."

"Whisky," Mac said grimly, "will send you home a doddering wreck. You'll do no one any good that way."

"Maybe. Maybe . . ." Peter shrugged. "Anyway, I hate these women out here. Having the best time of their lives. Ugly, impossible girls no one would ever look at in peacetime, just because there are a hundred men for every woman . . . Snobbish, overconfident . . . Bitches, all of them. A man has to sacrifice all decent, male pride to chase after one of these. . . ." He talked faster and faster, all the bitter observation of the past years flooding to his tongue. "They demand abasement, homage, the ugliest, most horrible and meanest of them. Women," he said, "have been among the most horrible of the war's casualties. All humility's gone, all normal value, all friendship. They're man-greedy. They're profiteering on the war, like the worst usurer and manufacturer of machine tools, except that their profits are lieutenants and generals, not cash. After the war," he said, "we should have rehabilitation hospitals for women who have been in troop areas, just like the hospitals for maimed men, to teach them how to live normal lives again. . . ."

Mac was laughing by now, helplessly, into his beer. "Enough," he said. "Enough, John Knox! All I wanted to say is that I have a date tonight, and my girl has a friend who's just come from Jerusalem, and it might do you a world of good just to have dinner with a woman for once. Do you want to go?"

Peter flushed, looked down at the beer-ringed table. "I won't even know how to talk to a woman any more."

"Do you want to go?"

Peter opened his mouth, closed it. "All right," he said. "All right."

"Jerusalem is nice enough . . ." It was on the dance floor at the Auberge des Pyramides, under the stars, with the three great tombs standing huge and a rebuke to time in the darkness just outside the lights and the music. Joyce was talking as they went slowly and painfully around the dance floor. "The city's clean, and the King David's an amusing hotel, but the people're simply dreadful." She had a brittle, drawling voice, pitched just high enough so that everyone near by could hear clearly what she was saying. "There," she said brightly, as Peter managed a full turn, "we're doing much better, aren't we?"

"Yes," Peter said, sweating in the heavy Nile heat, only slightly tempered by night, as he tried to concentrate on the beat of the music. Joyce's voice distracted him and put him off, and somehow she never seemed to stop talking. She worked in the consular service, and by nine-thirty Peter had a full store of information on the doings of the consulate in Jerusalem for the last year and a half, at which time Joyce had come out from England. He had hardly said a word all night, stammering, half finishing sentences, suffering, feeling like the clumsiest farmer. Still, she was pretty, most desirable in a full white evening gown ("We always dress in Jerusalem"), with full, sleek shoulders bare and daring under the gay lights.

"That's King Farouk. . . ." For the first time all evening her voice dropped a bit. "Isn't it?"

Peter looked. "Yes," he said.

"Isn't he attractive? What an original beard!"

Peter looked at King Farouk. "He looks like a fat, self-satisfied young man," Peter said, the first full sentence he had got out all evening. "And I understand he grew the beard because he has a terrible case of acne."

"Dance around the edge of the dance floor," Joyce whispered. "I'd like people to see me."

Dutifully and heavily Peter danced around the edge of the floor until the music stopped. He followed Joyce to the table. Joyce smiled vivaciously at seven or eight officers seated at various tables throughout the establishment.

"It's amazing," she said, brightly and loudly, "how many men I know in Cairo." They sat down. There was an awful silence while Peter wondered where in the name of God Mac was, and his girl, and Joyce smiled prettily first at one table, then another.

"Are you married?" Peter heard his voice, crooked and rasping, asking inexplicably. For the first time that evening Joyce gave him her undivided attention.

"Why," she said, looking at him queerly and coldly, "what a strange question!"

"It's just that there's a girl around my office," Peter said, almost dazedly. "Married to a lieutenant in India. Marrying an American major in London . . ." The expression on Joyce's face became more and more strained. "I don't know what made me think of her," Peter said lamely.

"No," Joyce said coldly, "I'm not married."

"I am," Peter said, despairingly.

"Really." Joyce smiled automatically at a colonel four tables away.

"My wife," said Peter, not knowing why he was talking, feeling his tongue too loose from the drinking that had been continuous since six that evening, "my wife is a woman of admirable character, although I can't remember what she looks like. Her name is Anne. She works for the Air Ministry in Manchester. After Dunkirk, I was stationed on the beach at Dover for five months. I used to manage to get away week ends. We'd just stay in one room and just look at each other. After France . . . I felt as though my wife had healed me of a dreadful disease. She healed me of mud and death and friends dying on all sides. She's most beautiful, but I don't remember what she looks like. She's very calm and simple and her voice is low, although I don't remember that, either. I sent her my photograph today. Six years is too long for a man to expect a woman to remember him. Someone ought to tell Parliament that. . . . Don't you think?"

Joyce was staring at him, her mouth frozen to one side. "Yes," she said.

"If I could only see her for two nights . . ." Well, finally, the thought crossed his consciousness, the lady from Jerusalem is listening to me. "Right before I came out here, I was moved to another beach. It was raining. Autumn and miserable and barbed wire at the high-tide marks and mines all over the beaches. I called her long-distance and she told me she had a week and asked me if she should come down. I told her no. It was so miserable. Cheap little shacks waiting for the Germans in the rain. I knew we were leaving for Africa and I didn't want our last days together to be dreary, in that abominable place. I told her no, but she said, 'You wait right there. I'm coming down tonight.'" Suddenly, above the dance music in the Valley of the Nile, Peter remembered what his wife's voice had sounded like, merry and sensual and confidently commanding over the faulty wires on that autumn night on a wet beach on the English Channel. "She came down and we had the week together, and the rain and the barbed wire made no difference at all. I've never been so gay, and it was early in the war, and we always had a coal fire and hot rum and lovely heavy breakfasts, with the curtains still drawn. And never a tear when she left. And I started for Africa singing in my heart." He was talking straight ahead to the Pyramids in the ancient desert darkness now, not to the silly, bare-shouldered girl across the table. "I haven't heard from her in two months. Not a letter in two months." He shrugged. "After the war," he said, "I'm going to go in for politics. I'm going to stand for Parliament. There must be somebody in Parliament who knows what a war is like,

WALKING WOUNDED 243

who knows that one war is enough, six years is too much . . ."

"Why, Joyce, how nice!" It was the colonel, standing gallantly at the table. "Dance?"

Joyce looked doubtfully at Peter. Peter stood up, a little unsteadily. "Delighted," he said ambiguously. Without looking at Peter, Joyce went off with the colonel, smiling impartially at dozens of officers in Sam Browne belts as she danced on the edge of the floor.

Peter hazily watched the flashing plump white dress among the brave khaki and brass pips. He passed his hand over his eyes, thinking, as he remembered his outburst, God, I must be going crazy.

He saw a captain step in and dance with Joyce, then an American major. "The world," he said softly to himself, "is full of American majors." He laughed gently to himself, stood up, walked slowly out of the night club. Outside, with the music thin and distant in his ears, the Pyramids loomed, crumbling in the darkness, in memory of the un-remembered dead.

He got into a cab and started for Cairo.

When the cab got to Gezira Island, he tapped the driver on the shoulder. "Sporting Club," he said.

The old, wheezing taxi laboriously turned. "I need a drink," Peter told himself seriously. "I need a drink very badly." He thought of old Mac caught there with two girls and the tremendous bill. He felt bad about it, but he'd pay his share, although it would mean considerably less drinking for the rest of the month. But he couldn't stay with that damned girl. The truth was he couldn't stay with any girl. Anne, un-photographed, in Manchester . . . Still, she should write more often than once every two months. . . .

The bar at Gezira was still open. There were some South Africans and some American fliers lounging against it. One of the American fliers was singing, in a soft Southern voice, "Oh, Susannah, don't you cry for me . . ."

"Scotch," Peter said to the bartender, feeling for the first time that evening a cessation of loneliness, his constant climate.

"Fo' Ah'm gawn' t' Alabama, with mah banjo on mah knee . . ." the American pilot sang sweetly and happily.

"Gin and lime," said one of the South Africans, a gigantic captain with huge, bare arms, whom the others called Lee. "Gin and lime all around." He turned to Peter. "What're you drinking, Captain?"

"I've ordered, thanks." Peter smiled at him.

"Man says he's ordered," the American pilot sang. "What do you know about that? British captain says he's ordered. Order again and order again, oh, Captain, order again. . . ."

The bartender put two Scotches in front of Peter, grinning. The huge South African captain poured it all into one glass. They lifted their glasses.

"To South Africa," one of the Americans said.

They drank.

"To sergeants." The American who had been singing grinned at a large South African lieutenant with a mustache. The lieutenant looked around him uneasily. "Quiet, please," he said. "I'll be in jail five years."

"This gentleman looks like a gentleman." Lee put his arm around the lieutenant with the mustache. "Doesn't he?"

"Yes," said Peter.

"Jail," said the lieutenant with the mustache.

"He's not a gentleman. He is a sergeant. He is my bloody sergeant from my bloody company."

"Ten years," said the lieutenant with the mustache.

"We're all AWOL, Sergeant Monks, lieutenant for the evening, Lieutenant Fredericks . . ." He waved to a slightly smaller red-headed South African down the bar. "And myself. We're farmers. Independent men. When the bloody O.C. said 'no leaves,' we said farewell. Sixty miles out on the desert for three weeks. Miserable little clerk of an O.C. Sergeant, I said, here's a pip. Take off those bloody stripes. We wish to show you the glories of Shepheard's and Gezira, so that you can come back and dazzle the poor bastards in the other ranks with tales of the high life in Cairo."

"I've been talking to brigadiers all afternoon and evening," Monks complained. "Wearing on the nerves."

"If the O.C. shows up, it's all taped," Lee said. "I grab Monks by one arm, Freddy grabs him by the other. 'We've just arrested the bugger, sir,' we say. 'Impersonating an officer.'"

"Ten years," Monks said, grinning. "This round is on me."

Peter laughed. He lifted his glass. "To sergeants everywhere." They all drank.

"On my right," said Lee, "is the American Air Force."

The American Air Force raised its glasses at Peter and the pilot who sang started in on "Chattanooga Choo-choo." There were two lieutenants and a twenty-four-year-old major.

"The American Air Force is going home," said Lee. "Their tour is over. Home by way of England. The infantry's tour is never over. Oh, the poor, stinking, bloody infantry, their tour is never over . . ."

"Unskilled labor," one of the pilots said calmly. "We're delicate and highly sensitive mechanisms. We are war-weary. Our Schneiders are low as an Egyptian whore. We've bombed too many places. We've seen too much flak. We are lopsided from wearing ribbons. We are going home now to instruct the young how to shoot."

"I am going home to play with my wife," the twenty-four-year-old major said soberly.

"The infantry is not under the same Awful Strain," said the pilot who had been singing. "All they have to do is walk in and be shot. Their nerves are not stretched to the breaking point like ours. Captain," he said, leaning back and talking to Peter, "you look a little war-weary yourself."

"I'm pretty war-weary," Peter said.

"He looks sensitive," the major said. "He looks fine and sensitive enough to be at least a navigator. He looks like Hamlet on a rough night."

"I was in the tanks," Peter said.

"It's possible," said the major, "to get war-weary in a tank, too, I suppose."

"It's possible," Peter said, grinning.

". . . breakfast in Carolina . . ." sang the musical pilot.

"When're you leaving for home?" Peter asked.

"6 A.M. tomorrow. 0600 hours, as they say in the army," said the major.

"Five or six glorious days in London among our brave English Allies and cousins," said the other pilot, "and then the Stork Club, the Harvard-Yale football game, all the blonde, full-bosomed, ribbon-conscious, lascivious American girls . . ."

"London," said Peter. "I wish I were going with you."

"Come along," said the major expansively. "We have a nice empty Liberator. Pleased to have you. Closer relations with our British comrades. Merely be at the airport at 0600 hours, as they say in the army."

"Did you see," asked the singing pilot, "in the *Mail* today? Some idiot wants Princess Elizabeth to marry an American."

"Excellent idea," said the major. "Some upstanding representative citizen of the Republic. Post-war planning on all fronts. My nomination for Prince Escort is Maxie Rosenbloom."

Everyone considered the suggestion gravely.

"You could do worse," the pilot said.

"In fusion of sturdy American stock into an aging dynasty," the major said. "The issue would be strongly built, with good left hands. . . ."

"Do you mean it?" Peter asked. "You really could take me?"

"Delighted," the major said.

The singing pilot started in on "All Alone," and everyone but Peter joined him. Peter stared unseeingly at the glasses and bottles behind the bar. In three days he could be home. Three days and he could walk into Anne's room, quietly, unannounced, smiling a little tremulously as she looked up unsuspectingly. Maybe it was possible. He had had no leave since he'd come to Africa, except for two weeks' convalescence. He could go immediately to Colonel Foster's apartment, explain to him. Colonel Foster liked him, was very sympathetic. If he gave him a written order, releasing him from duty for twenty-one days, he, Peter, would undertake to get transportation back. Somehow, somehow . . . He would take all the responsibility himself. He was sure that Colonel Foster, who was a good soul, would do it.

Peter stood up straight. He spoke to the American major. "Perhaps I'll see you at six o'clock."

"Fine," the major said heartily. "It's going to be a great trip. We're loaded with Scotch." He waved as Peter turned and left the bar.

"All alone, by the telephone . . ." the wailing, mocking voices quavered in the night. Peter got into a taxicab and gave Colonel Foster's address.

He felt he was trembling. He closed his eyes and leaned back. It was all absolutely possible. England was only three days away. Two weeks there and the desert and the guns and the dying and ruled paper and heat and loneliness and insane expanding tension would disappear. He could face the rest of the war calmly, knowing that he would not explode, would not lose his reason. It was possible. Men were going home to their wives. That American major. All so cheerful and matter-of-fact about it. England in three days, after the three years . . . Colonel Foster would most certainly say yes. Peter was sure of it as the taxi drove up to the dark building where Colonel Foster lived. Peter paid the driver and looked up. The colonel's window was alight, the only one in the entire building. Peter felt his breath coming fast. It was a symbol, an omen. The man was awake. His friend, who could give him England tonight with five strokes of a pen, by luck was wakeful in the quiet night, when all the rest of the city slept around him. It would be irregular, and Colonel Foster would be running some risk, but he had rank enough and was independent enough to take the chance. . . .

Peter rang the night-bell to the side of the locked doors of the apartment building. Far in the depths of the sleeping stone and brick, a forlorn and distant bell sang weirdly.

As he waited for the hall-boy to open the doors, Peter hastily rehearsed his story. No leave in three years. The tension getting worse and worse. Medically graded, no chance of getting to an active unit. Regiment disbanded. Work deteriorating. Given to sudden fits of temper and what could only be described as melancholia, although a doctor wouldn't believe it until it was too late. He knew the British Army couldn't provide transportation, but here were these Americans with an empty Liberator. He'd get back somehow.

As he went over it, in the darkness, with the faraway bell sounding as though it were ringing at the bottom of a troubled sea, Peter was sure the logic was irrefutable; Foster couldn't refuse.

When the hall-boy finally opened the door, Peter sprang past him, raced up the steps, too impatient to take the elevator.

He was panting when he rang Colonel Foster's bell, and the sweat was streaming down the sides of his face. He rang the bell sharply, twice. He heard his breath whistling into his lungs, and he tried to compose himself, so that Colonel Foster would think him absolutely calm, absolutely lucid. . . .

The door opened. The figure at the door was silhouetted against the yellowish light behind it.

"Colonel," Peter said, panting, "I'm so glad you're up. I must talk to you. I hate to disturb you, but . . ."

"Come in." The door was opened wider and Peter strode down the hall, into the living room. He heard the door close and turned around. "I . . ." he began. He stopped. The man who was standing there was not Colonel Foster. It was a large, red-faced man, bald, in a tattered red bathrobe. He had a mustache and tired eyes and he was holding a book in his hand. Peter looked at the book. *The Poems of Robert Browning.*

The man stood there, waiting, pulling his bathrobe a little tighter, a curious little smile on his weary face.

"I . . . I saw the light, sir," Peter said. "I thought Colonel Foster would be up and I took the liberty of . . . I had some business with . . ."

"Colonel Foster doesn't live here," the man said. His voice was clipped and military, but tired, aging. "He moved out a week ago."

"Oh," Peter said. He suddenly stopped sweating. He swallowed, made a conscious effort to speak quietly. "Do you know where he lives, sir?"

"I'm afraid not. Is there anything I can do, Captain? I'm Colonel Gaines." He smiled, false teeth above the old robe. "That's why when you said Colonel, at the door, I . . ."

"No, sir," Peter said. "Nothing, sir. I'm dreadfully sorry. This time of night . . ."

"Oh, that's all right." The man waved a little embarrassedly. "I never go to sleep. I was reading."

"Well . . . Thank you, sir. Good night."

"Uh . . ." The man looked hesitantly at him, as though he felt that somehow Peter should be helped in some dubious, obscure way. "Uh—perhaps a drink. I have some whisky I was just going to—for my-self . . ."

"No, thank you, sir," Peter said. "I'd better be getting along."

Clumsily, they went down the passage together to the door. The man opened the door. He stood there, red-faced, huge, British, like a living Colonel Blimp, lonely and tired, with Robert Browning in the foreign night.

"Good night, sir."

"Good night. . . ."

The door closed and Peter walked slowly down the dark stairs.

Peter started toward his hotel, but the thought of the disordered room and Mac lying there, steadily asleep, steadily and slightly snoring in the next bed, was impossible.

He walked slowly past the dark policemen standing quietly with their rifles on the street corners. Down the street garry-lights, small and flickering and lonesome, wandered past, and the sound of the horses' hooves was deliberate and weary.

He came to the English Bridge and stood on the banks of the river, looking at the dark water swirling north toward the Mediterranean. Down the river a felucca, its immense sail spread in a soaring triangle, slowly made its way among the shadows from the trees along the shore.

Across the river a minaret, poignant with faith, shone sharp and delicate in the moonlight.

Peter felt spent and drained. A nervous and hysteric pulse pulled at his bad eye and a gigantic sob seemed wedged into his throat.

Overhead, far away, there was the sound of a plane. It came nearer, passed across the stars, died away, going somewhere.

The wedge dislodged and the sob broke out like tears and blood.

Peter closed his eyes, and when he opened them again the wild pulse had stopped, his throat was clear. He stared across the river at the minaret, faithful and lovely in the light of the moon, by the side of the old river.

Tomorrow, he thought, tomorrow there may be a letter from home. . . .

GUNNERS' PASSAGE

"IN BRAZIL," Whitejack was saying, "the problem was girls. American girls."

They were lying on the comfortable cots with the mosquito netting looped gracefully over their heads and the barracks quiet and empty except for the two of them and shaded and cool when you remembered that outside the full sun of Africa stared down.

"Three months in the jungle, on rice and monkey meat." Whitejack lit a large, long, nickel cigar and puffed deeply, squinting up at the tin roof. "When we got to Rio, we felt we deserved an American girl. So the Lieutenant and Johnny and myself, we got the telephone directory of the American Embassy, and we went down the list, calling up likely names—secretaries, typists, interpreters, filing clerks. . . ." Whitejack grinned up at the ceiling. He had a large, sunburned, rough face that was broken into good looks by the white teeth of his smile, and his speech was Southern, but not the kind of Southern that puts a Northerner's teeth on edge.

"It was the Lieutenant's idea, and by the time we got to the Q's he was ready to give up but we hit pay dirt on the S's." Slowly he blew out a long draught of cigar smoke. "Uh-uh," he said, closing his eyes reflectively. "Two months and eleven days of honey and molasses. Three tender and affectionate American girls as loving as the day is long, with their own flat. Beer in the icebox from Sunday to Sunday, steaks big enough to saddle a mule with, and nothing to do, just lie on the beach in the afternoon and go swimmin' when the mood seized yuh. On per diem."

"How were the girls?" Stais asked. "Pretty?"

"Well, Sergeant," Whitejack paused and pursed his lips with thoughtful honesty. "To tell you the truth, Sergeant, the girls the Lieutenant and Johnny Moffat had were as smart and pretty as chipmunks. Mine . . ." Once more he paused. "Ordinarily, my girl would find herself hard put to collect a man in the middle of a full division of infantry soldiers. She was small and runty and she had less curves than a rifle barrel, and she wore glasses. But from the first time she looked at me, I could see she wasn't interested in Johnny or the Lieutenant. She looked at me and behind her glasses her eyes were soft and hopeful and humble and appealing." Whitejack flicked the cigar ash off into the little tin can on his bare chest he was using as an ash tray. "Sometimes," he said slowly, "a man feels mighty small if he just thinks of himself and turns down an appeal like that. Let me tell you something, Sergeant, I was in Rio two months and eleven days and I didn't look at another woman. All those dark-brown women walkin' along the beach three-quarters out of their bathing suits, just wavin' it in front of your face. . . . I didn't look at them. This runty, skinny little thing with glasses was the most lovin' and satisfactory and decent little person a man could possibly conceive of, and a man'd just have to be hog-greedy with sex to have winked an eye at another woman." Whitejack doused his cigar, took his ash tray off his chest, rolled over on his belly, adjusted the towel properly over his bare buttocks. "Now," he said, "I'm going to get myself a little sleep. . . ."

In a moment Whitejack was snoring gently, his tough mountaineer's face tucked childishly into the crook of his arm. Outside the barracks the native boy hummed low and wild to himself as he ironed a pair of suntan trousers on the shady side of the building. From the field, two hundred yards away, again and again came the sliding roar of engines climbing or descending the afternoon sky.

Stais closed his eyes wearily. Ever since he'd got into Accra he had done nothing but sleep and lie on his cot, day-dreaming, listening to Whitejack talk.

"Hi," Whitejack had said, as Stais had come slowly into the barracks two days before, "which way you going?"

"Home," Stais had said, smiling wearily as he did every time he said it. "Going home. Which way you going?"

"Not home." Whitejack had grinned a little. "Not home at all."

Stais liked to listen to Whitejack. Whitejack talked about America, about the woods of the Blue Ridge Mountains where he had been in the forestry service, about his mother's cooking and how he had owned great dogs which had been extraordinary at finding a trail and holding it, about how they had tried hunting deer in the hills from the medium bomber, no good because of the swirling winds rising from the gorges, about pleasant indiscriminate week-end parties in the woods with his friend Johnny Moffat and the girls from the mill in the next town. . . . Stais had been away from America for nineteen months now and Whitejack's talk made his native country seem present and pleasantly real to him.

"There was a man in my town by the name of Thomas Wolfe," Whitejack had said irrelevantly that morning. "He was a great big feller and he went away to New York to be an author. Maybe you heard of him?"

"Yes," said Stais. "I read two books of his."

"Well, I read that book of his," said Whitejack, "and the people in town were yellin' to lynch him for a while, but I read that book and he got that town down fair and proper, and when they brought him back dead I came down from the hills and I went to his funeral. There were a lot of important people from New York and over to Chapel Hill down for the funeral and it was a hot day, too, and I'd never met the feller, but I felt it was only right to go to his funeral after readin' his book. And the whole town was there, very quiet, although just five years before they were yellin' to lynch him, and it was a sad and impressive sight and I'm glad I went."

And another time, the slow deep voice rolling between sleep and dreams in the shaded heat. . . . "My mother takes a quail and bones it, then she scoops out a great big sweet potato and lays some bacon on it, then she puts the quail in and cooks it slow for three hours, bastin' it with butter all the time. . . . You got to try that some time. . . ."

"Yes," said Stais, "I will."

Stais did not have a high priority number and there seemed to be a flood of colonels surging toward America, taking all the seats on the C-54's setting out westward, so he'd had to wait. It hadn't been bad. Just to lie down, stretched full-out, unbothered, these days, was holiday enough after Greece, and anyway he didn't want to arrive home, in front of his mother, until he'd stopped looking like a tired old man. And the barracks had been empty and quiet and the chow good at the transient mess and you could get Coca-Cola and chocolate milk at the PX. The rest of the enlisted men in Whitejack's crew were young and ambitious and were out swimming all day and going to the movies or playing poker in another barracks all night, and Whitejack's talk was smooth and amusing in the periods between sleep and dreams. Whitejack was an aerial photographer and gunner in a mapping-and-survey squadron and he'd been in Alaska and Brazil and back to the States and now was on his way to India, full of conversation. He was in a Mitchell squadron and the whole squadron was supposed to be on its way together, but two of the Mitchells had crashed and burned on the take-off at Natal, as Whitejack's plane had circled the field, waiting to form up. The rest of the squadron had been held at Natal and Whitejack's plane had been sent on to Accra across the ocean, by itself.

Vaguely and slowly, lying on the warm cot, with the wild song of the Negro boy outside the window, Stais thought of the two Mitchells burning between sea and jungle three thousand miles away, and other planes burning elsewhere, and what it was going to be like sitting down in the armchair in his own house and looking across the room at his mother, and the pretty Viennese girl in Jerusalem, and the DC-3 coming down slowly, like an angel in the dusk to the rough secret pasture in the Peloponesian hills. . . .

He fell asleep. His bones knit gently into dreams on the soft cot, with the sheets, in the quiet barracks, and he was over Athens again, with the ruins pale and shining on the hills, and the fighters boring in, and Lathrop saying, over the intercom, as they persisted in to a hundred, fifty yards, twisting, swiftly and shiftily in the bright Greek sky, "They grounded all the students today. They have the instructors up this afternoon. . . ." And, suddenly, and wildly, fifty feet over Ploesti, with Liberators going down into the filth in dozens, flaming. . . . Then swimming off the white beach at Bengasi with the dead boys playing in the mild, tideless swell, then the parachute pulling at every muscle in his body, then the green and forest blue of Minnesota woods and his father, fat and small, sleeping on pine needles on his Sunday off, then Athens again, Athens . . .

"I don't know what's come over the Lieutenant," a new voice was saying as Stais came out of his dream. "He passes us on the field and he just don't seem to see us."

Stais opened his eyes. Novak, a farm boy from Oklahoma, was sitting on the edge of Whitejack's bed, talking. "It has all the guys real worried." He had a high, shy, rather girlish voice. "I used to think they never came better than the Lieutenant. . . . Now . . ." Novak shrugged. "If he does see you, he snaps at you like he was General George Patton."

"Maybe," Whitejack said, "maybe seeing Lieutenant Brogan go down in Natal . . . He and Brogan were friends since they were ten years old. Like as if I saw Johnny Moffat go down . . ."

"It's not that." Novak went over to his own cot and got out his writing pad. "It began back in Miami four weeks ago. Didn't you notice it?"

"I noticed it," Whitejack said slowly.

"You ought to ask him about it." Novak started writing a letter. "You and him are good friends. After all, going into combat now, it's bad, the Lieutenant just lookin' through us when he passes us on the field. You don't think he's drunk all the time, do you?"

"He's not drunk."

"You ought to ask him."

"Maybe I will." Whitejack sat up, tying the towel around his lean middle. "Maybe I will." He looked forlornly down at his stomach. "Since I got into the Army, I've turned pig-fat. On the day I took the oath, I was twenty-eight and one-half inches around the waist. Today I'm thirty-two and three-quarters, if I'm an inch. The Army . . . Maybe I shouldn't've joined. I was in a reserved profession, and I was the sole support of an ailing mother."

"Why did you join?" Stais asked.

"Oh," Whitejack smiled at him, "you're awake. Feeling any better, Sergeant?"

"Feeling fine, thanks. Why did you join?"

"Well . . ." Whitejack rubbed the side of his jaw. "Well . . . I waited and I waited. I sat up in my cabin in the hills and I tried to avoid listenin' to the radio, and I waited and I waited, and finally I went downtown to my mother and I said, 'Ma'am, I just can't wait any longer,' and I joined up."

"When was that?" Stais asked.

"Eight days . . ." Whitejack lay down again, plumping the pillow under his head. "Eight days after Pearl Harbor."

"Sergeant," Novak said, "Sergeant Stais, you don't mind if I tell my girl you're a Greek, do you?"

"No," Stais said gravely. "I don't mind. You know, I was born in Minnesota."

"I know," said Novak, writing industriously. "But your parents came from Greece. My girl'll be very interested, your parents coming from Greece and you bombing Greece and being shot down there."

"What do you mean, your girl?" Whitejack asked. "I thought you said she was going around with a Technical Sergeant in Flushing, Long Island."

"That's true," Novak said apologetically. "But I still like to think of her as my girl."

"It's the ones that stay at home," said Whitejack darkly, "that get all the stripes and all the girls. My motto is: Don't write to a girl once you get out of pillow-case distance from her."

"I like to write to this girl in Flushing, Long Island," Novak said, his voice shy but stubborn. Then to Stais, "How many days were you in the hills before the Greek farmers found you?"

"Fourteen," said Stais.

"And how many of you were wounded?"

"Three. Out of seven. The others were dead."

"Maybe," Whitejack said, "he doesn't like to talk about it, Charley."

"Oh, I'm sorry." Novak looked up, his young, unlined face crossed with concern.

"That's all right," Stais said. "I don't mind."

"Did you tell them you were a Greek, too?" Novak asked.

"When one finally showed up who could speak English."

"That must be funny," Novak said reflectively. "Being a Greek, bombing Greece, not speaking the language . . . Can I tell my girl they had a radio and they radioed to Cairo . . . ?"

"It's the girl of a Technical Sergeant in Flushing, Long Island," Whitejack chanted. "Why don't you look facts in the face?"

"I prefer it this way," Novak said with dignity.

"I guess you can tell about the radio," Stais said. "It was pretty long ago. Three days later, the DC-3 came down through a break in the clouds. It'd been raining all the time and it just stopped for about thirty minutes at dusk and that plane came down throwin' water fifteen feet in the air. . . . We cheered, but we couldn't get up from where we were sitting, any of us, because we were too weak to stand."

"I got to write that to my girl," Novak said. "Too weak to stand."

"Then it started to rain again and the field was hip-deep in mud and when we all got into the DC-3, we couldn't get it started." Stais spoke calmly and thoughtfully, as though he were alone, reciting to himself. "We were just bogged down in that Greek mud. Then the pilot got out—he was a captain—and he looked around, with the rain coming down and all those farmers just standing there, sympathizing with him, and nothing anyone could do and he just cursed for ten minutes. He was from San Francisco and he really knew how to curse. Then everybody started breaking branches off the trees in the woods around that pasture, even two of us who couldn't stand one hour before, and we just covered that big DC-3 complete with branches and waited for the rain to stop. We just sat in the woods and prayed no German patrols would come out in weather like that. In those three days I learned five words of Greek."

"What are they?" Novak asked.

"*Vouno*," Stais said. "That means mountain. *Vrohi*: Rains. *Theos*: God. *Avrion*: Tomorrow. And *Yassov*: That means farewell."

"*Yassov*," Novak said. "Farewell."

"Then the sun came out and the field started to steam and nobody said anything. We just sat there, watching the water dry off the grass, then the puddles started to go here and there, then the mud to cake a little. Then we got into the DC-3 and the Greeks pushed and hauled for a while and we broke loose and got out. And those farmers just standing below waving at us, as though they were seeing us off at Grand Central Station. Ten miles farther on we went right over a German camp. They fired at us a couple of times, but they didn't come anywhere close. The best moment of my whole life was getting into that hospital bed in Cairo, Egypt. I just stood there and looked at it for a whole minute, looking at the sheets. Then I got in very slow."

"Did you ever find out what happened to those Greeks?" Novak asked.

"No," said Stais. "I guess they're still there, waiting for us to come back some day."

There was silence, broken only by the slow scratching of Novak's pen. Stais thought of the thin, dark mountain faces of the men he had last seen, fading away, waving, standing in the scrub and short silver grass of the hill pasture near the Aegean Sea. They had been cheerful and anxious to please, and there was a look on the faces that made you feel they expected to die.

"How many missions were you on?" Novak asked.

"Twenty-one and a half," Stais said. He smiled. "I count the last one as half."

"How old are you?" Novak was obviously keeping the Technical Sergeant's girl carefully posted on all points of interest.

"Nineteen."

"You look older," said Whitejack.

"Yes," said Stais.

"A lot older."

"Yes."

"Did you shoot down any planes?" Novak peered at him shyly, his red face uncertain and embarrassed, like a little boy asking a doubtful question about girls. "Personally?"

"Two," Stais said. "Personally."

"What did you feel?"

"Why don't you leave him alone?" Whitejack said. "He's too tired to keep his eyes open, as it is."

"I felt—relieved," Stais said. He tried to think of what he'd really felt when the tracers went in and the Focke-Wolfe started to smoke like a crazy smudge pot and the German pilot fought wildly for half a second with the cowling and then didn't fight wildly any more. There was no way of telling these men, no way of remembering, in words, himself. "You'll find out," he said. "Soon enough. The sky's full of Germans."

"Japs," Whitejack said. "We're going to India."

"The sky's full of Japs."

There was silence once more, with the echo of the word "Japs" rustling thinly in the long, quiet room, over the empty rows of cots. Stais felt the old waving dizziness starting behind his eyes that the doctor in Cairo had said came from shock or starvation or exposure or all of these things, and lay back, still keeping his eyes open, as it became worse and waved more violently when he closed his eyes.

"One more question," Novak said. "Are—are guys afraid?"

"You'll be afraid," Stais said.

"Do you want to send that back to your girl in Flushing?" Whitejack asked sardonically.

"No," said Novak quietly. "I wanted that for myself."

"If you want to sleep," said Whitejack, "I'll shut this farmer up."

"Oh, no," said Stais, "I'm pleased to talk."

"If you're not careful," Whitejack said, "he'll talk about his girl in Flushing."

"I'd be pleased to hear it," said Stais.

"It's only natural I should want to talk about her," Novak said defensively. "She was the best girl I ever knew in my whole life. I'd've married her if I could."

"My motto," said Whitejack, "is never marry a girl who goes to bed with you the first time out. The chances are she isn't pure. The second time—that, of course, is different." He winked at Stais.

"I was in Flushing, Long Island, taking a five-weeks' course in aerial cameras," Novak said, "and I was living at the YMCA. . . ."

"This is where I leave." Whitejack got off the bed and put on his pants.

"The YMCA was very nice. There were bathrooms for every two rooms, and the food was very good," said Novak, talking earnestly to Stais, "but I must confess, I was lonely in Flushing, Long Island. . . ."

"I will be back," Whitejack was buttoning up his shirt, "for the ninth installment."

"As long as you're going out," Novak said to him, "I wish you'd talk to the Lieutenant. It really makes me feel queer passing him, and him just looking through me like I was a window pane."

"Maybe I'll talk to the Lieutenant. And leave the Sergeant alone. Remember he's a tired man who's been to the war and he needs his rest." Whitejack went out.

Novak stared after him. "There's something wrong with him, too," he said. "Just lying on his back here for ten days, reading and sleeping. He never did that before. He was the liveliest man in the United States Air Force. Seeing those two planes go down . . . It's a funny thing, you fly with fellers all over the world, over America, Brazil, Alaska; you watch them shoot porpoises and sharks in gunnery practice over the Gulf Stream, you get drunk with them, go to their weddings, talk to them over the radio with their planes maybe a hundred feet away, in the air—and after all that flying, in one minute, for no reason, two planes go down. Fourteen fellers you've been livin' with for over a year. . . ." Novak shook his head. "There was a particular friend of Whitejack's in one of those planes. Frank Sloan. Just before we left Miami, they had a big fight. Frank went off and married a girl that Whitejack's been going with off and on for a year, every time we hit Miami. Whitejack told him he was crazy, half the squadron had slept with the lady, and that was true, too, and just to teach him a lesson he'd sleep with her himself after they'd been married. And he did, too. . . ." Novak sighed. "A lot of funny things happen in the army, when fellers've been together a long time and get to know each other real well. And then, one minute, the Mitchell goes down. I guess Whitejack must've felt sort of queer, watching Frankie burn." Novak had put his writing pad down and now he screwed the top on his fountain pen. "The truth is," he said, "I don't feel so solid myself. That's why I like to talk. Especially to you . . . You've been through it. You're young, but you've been through it. But if it's any bother to you, I'll keep quiet. . . ."

"No," said Stais, still lying back, abstractedly wondering whether the waving would get worse or better, "not at all."

"This girl in Flushing, Long Island," Novak said slowly. "It's easy for Whitejack to make fun of me. The girls fall all over themselves chasing after him; he has no real conception of what it's like to be a man like me. Not very good-looking. Not much money. Not an officer. Not humorous. Shy."

Stais couldn't help grinning. "You're going to have a tough time in India."

"I know," Novak said. "I have resigned myself to not having a girl until the armistice. How did you do with the girls in the Middle East?" he asked politely.

"There was a nice Viennese girl in Jerusalem," Stais said dreamily. "But otherwise zero. You have to be very good unless you're an officer in the Middle East."

"That's what I heard," Novak said sorrowfully. "Well, it won't be so different to me from Oklahoma. That was the nice thing about this girl in Flushing, Long Island. She saw me come into the jewelry store where she worked and . . . I was in my fatigues and I was with a very smooth feller who made a date with her for that night. But she smiled at me, and I knew if I had the guts I could ask her for a date, too. But of course I didn't. But then later that night I was sitting in my room in the YMCA and my phone rang. It was this girl. The other feller had stood her up, she said, and would I take her out." Novak smiled dimly, thinking of that tremulous moment of glory in the small hotel room far away. "I got my fatigues off in one minute and shaved and showered and I picked her up. We went to Coney Island. It was the first time in my entire life I had ever seen Coney Island. It took three and a half weeks for me to finish my course and I went out with that girl every single night. Nothing like that ever happened to me before in my life—a girl who just wanted to see me every night of the week. Then the night before I was due to leave to join my squadron she told me she had got permission to take the afternoon off and she would like to see me off if I let her. I called at the jewelry shop at noon and her boss shook my hand and she had a package under her arm and we got into the subway and we rode to New York City. Then we went into a cafeteria and had a wonderful lunch and she saw me off and gave me the package. It was Schrafft's candy, and she was crying at the gate there, crying for me, and she said she would like me to write, no matter what . . ." Novak paused and Stais could tell that the scene at the gate, the hurrying crowds, the package of Schrafft's chocolates, the weeping young girl, were as clear as the afternoon sunlight to Novak there on the coast of Africa. "So I keep writing," Novak said. "She's written me she has a Technical Sergeant now, but I keep writing. I haven't seen her in a year and a half and what's a girl to do? Do you blame her?"

"No," said Stais, "I don't blame her."

"I hope I haven't bored you," Novak said.

"Not at all." Stais smiled at him. Suddenly the dizziness had gone and he could close his eyes. As he drifted down into that weird and

ever-present pool of sleep in which he half-lived these days, he heard
Novak say,

"Now I have to write my mother."

Outside, the Negro boy sang and the planes grumbled down from
the Atlantic and laboriously set out across the Sahara Desert.

Dreams again. Arabs, bundled in rags, driving camels along the
perimeter of the field, outlined against the parked Liberators and waiting bombs, two Mitchells still burning on the shores of Brazil and
Frank Sloan burning there and circling above him, Whitejack, who
had told him he'd sleep with his wife and had, the hills around Jerusalem, gnarled, rocky, dusty, with the powdered green of olive groves
set on slopes here and there, clinging against the desert wind,
Mitchells slamming along the gorges of the Blue Ridge Mountains,
bucking in the updraughts, their guns going, hunting deer, the Mediterranean, bluer than anything in America, below them on the way
home from Italy, coming down below oxygen level, with the boys
singing dirty songs over the intercom and leave in Alexandria ahead of
them. The girl from Flushing, Long Island, quietly going hand in hand
with Novak to Coney Island on a summer's night. . . .

It was Whitejack who awakened him. He woke slowly. It was dark
outside and the electric light was shining in his eyes and Whitejack
was standing over him, shaking him gently.

"I thought you'd like to know," Whitejack was saying, "your name's
on the bulletin board. You're leaving tonight."

"Thanks," Stais said, dimly grateful at being shaken out of the broken
and somehow sorrowful dreams.

"I took the liberty of initialing it for you, opposite your name,"
Whitejack said. "Save you a trip up to the field."

"Thanks," said Stais. "Very kind of you."

"Also," said Whitejack, "there's fried chicken for chow."

Stais pondered over the fried chicken. He was a little hungry, but
the effort of getting up and putting on his shoes and walking the
hundred yards to the mess hall had to be weighed in the balance.
"Thanks. I'll just lie right here," he said. "Any news of your boys?"
he asked.

"Yes," said Whitejack. "The squadron came in."

"That's good."

"All except one plane." Whitejack sat down on the end of Stais' cot.
His voice was soft and expressionless, under the bright electric light.
"Johnny Moffat's plane."

In all the months that Stais had been in the air force, on fields to which planes had failed to return, he had learned that there was nothing to say. He was only nineteen years old, but he had learned that. So he lay quiet.

"They got separated in clouds on the way out of Ascension, and they never picked them up again. There's still a chance," Whitejack said, "that they'll drop in any minute." He looked at his watch. "Still a chance for another hour and forty minutes . . ."

There was still nothing to say, so Stais lay silent.

"Johnny Moffat," said Whitejack, "at one time looked as though he was going to marry my sister. In a way, it's a good thing he didn't. It'd be a little hard, being brothers-in-law, on some of the parties the air force goes on in one place and another." Whitejack fell silent, looked down at his belly. Deliberately, he let his belt out a notch. He pulled it to, with a severe little click. "That fried chicken was mighty good," he said. "You sure you want to pass it up?"

"I'm saving my appetite," Stais said, "for my mother's cooking."

"My sister," said Whitejack, "was passing fond of Johnny, and I have a feeling when he gets home from the war and settles down, she's going to snag him. She came to me right before I left and she asked me if I would let her have ten acres on the north side of my property and three acres of timber to build their house. I said it was OK with me." He was silent again, thinking of the rolling ten acres of upland meadow in North Carolina and the three tall acres of standing timber, oak and pine, from which it would be possible to build a strong country house. "There's nobody in the whole world I'd rather have living on my property than Johnny Moffat. I've known him for twenty years and I've had six fist fights with him and won them all, and been alone with him in the woods for two months at a time, and I still say that. . . ." He got up and went over to his own cot, then turned and came back. "By the way," he said softly, "this is between you and me, Sergeant."

"Sure," said Stais.

"My sister said she'd murder me for my hide and taller if I ever let Johnny know what was in store for him." He grinned a little. "Women're very confident in certain fields," he said. "And I never did tell Johnny, not even when I was so drunk I was singing 'Casey Jones' naked in the middle of the city of Tampa at three o'clock in the morning." He went over to his musette bag and got out a cigar and thoughtfully lit it. "You'd be surprised," he said, "how fond you become of nickel cigars in the Army."

"I tried smoking," said Stais. "I think I'll wait until I get a little older."

Whitejack sat heavily on his own cot. "Do you think they'll send you out to fight again?" he asked.

Stais stared up at the ceiling. "I wouldn't be surprised," he said. "There's nothing really wrong with me. I'm just tired."

Whitejack nodded, smoking slowly. "By the way," he said, "you heard us talking about the Lieutenant, didn't you?"

"Yes."

"I went out to the field and had a little conversation with him. He's just been sittin' there all day and most of the night since we got here, outside the Operations room, just lookin' and starin' across at the planes comin' in. Him and me, we've been good friends for a long time and I asked him point-blank. I said, 'Freddie,' I said, 'there's a question the boys're askin' themselves these days about you.' And he said, 'What's the matter?' And I said, 'The boys're asking if you've turned bad. You pass 'em and you don't even look at them as though you recognize 'em. What is it, you turn GI after a year?' I said. He looked at me and then he looked at the ground and he didn't say anything for maybe a minute. Then he said, 'I beg your pardon, Arnold. It never occurred to me.' Then he told me what was on his mind." Whitejack looked at his watch, almost automatically, then lifted his head again. "Ever since we got the order to go overseas he's been worrying. About the waist gunner and his navigator."

"What's he worrying about?" For a moment a crazy list of all the thousand things you can worry about in the crew of one airplane flashed through Stais' head.

"They're not fighting men," Whitejack said slowly. "They're both good fellers, you wouldn't want better, but the Lieutenant's been watchin' 'em for a long time on the ground, in the air, at their guns, and he's convinced they won't measure. And he feels he's responsible for taking the Mitchell in and getting it out with as many of us alive as possible and he feels the waist gunner and the navigator're dangerous to have in the plane. And he's makin' up his mind to put in a request for two new men when we get to India, and he can't bear to think of what it'll do to the gunner and the navigator when they find out he's asked to have 'em grounded, and that's why he just sits there outside Operations, not even seein' us when we go by. . . ." Whitejack sighed. "He's twenty-two years old, the Lieutenant. It's a strain, something like that, for a man twenty-two years old. If you see Novak, you won't tell him anything, will you?"

"No," said Stais.

"I suppose things like this come up all the time in any army."

"All the time," said Stais.

Whitejack looked at his watch. Outside there was the growing and lapsing roar of engines that had been the constant sound of both their lives for so many months.

"Ah," said Whitejack, "they should've put me in the infantry. I can hit a rabbit at three hundred yards with a rifle; they put me in the Air Force and give me a camera. . . . Well, Sergeant, I think it's about time you were movin'."

Slowly, Stais got up. He put on his shoes and put his shaving kit into his musette bag and slung it over his shoulder.

"You ready?" asked Whitejack.

"Yes," said Stais.

"That all the baggage you got—that little musette bag?"

"Yes," said Stais. "I was listed as missing, presumed dead, and they sent all my stuff into the supply room and all my personal belongings home to my mother."

Stais looked around the barracks. It shone in the harsh army light of barracks at night all over the world, by now familiar, homelike, to all the men who passed through them. He had left nothing.

They walked out into the soft, engine-filled night. A beacon flashed nervously across the sky, dimming the enormous pale twinkle of Southern stars for a moment. They walked slowly, stepping cautiously over the ditches dug for the flood rains of the African West Coast.

As they passed the Operations room, Stais saw a young lieutenant slumped down in a wobbly old wicker chair, staring out across the field.

"They come yet?" Whitejack asked.

"No," said the Lieutenant, without looking up.

Stais went into the building and into the room where they had the rubber raft and the patented radio and the cloth painted blue on one side and yellow on the other. A fat middle-aged ATC captain wearily told them about ditching procedure. There were more than thirty people in the room, all passengers on Stais's plane. There were two small, yellow Chinese who were going to be airsick and five bouncing fat Red Cross women, and three sergeants with a lot of Air Force medals, trying not to seem excited about going home, and two colonels in the Engineers, looking too old for this war. Stais only half listened as the fat captain explained how to inflate the raft, what strings to pull, what levers to move, where to find the waterproofed Bible. . . .

Whitejack was standing outside when Stais started for his plane. He gave Stais a slip of paper. "It's my home address," he said. "After the war, just come down sometime in October and I'll take you hunting."

"Thank you very much," said Stais gravely. Over Whitejack's

shoulder he saw the Lieutenant, still slumped in the wicker chair, still staring fixedly and unrelievedly out across the dark field.

Whitejack walked out to the great plane with Stais, along the oil-spattered concrete of the runway, among the Chinese and loud Red Cross women and the sergeants. They stopped, without a word, at the steps going up to the doorway of the plane and the other passengers filed past them.

They stood there, silently, with the two days of random conversation behind them and Brazil and Athens behind them, and five hundred flights behind them, and Jerusalem and Miami behind them, and the girls from Vienna and the American Embassy and Flushing, Long Island, behind them, and the Greek mountaineers behind them and Thomas Wolfe's funeral, and friends burning like torches, and dogs under treed raccoons in the Blue Ridge Mountains behind them, and a desperate twenty-two-year-old Lieutenant painfully staring across a dusty airfield for ten days behind them, and the Mediterranean and the hospital bed in Cairo and Johnny Moffat wandering that night over the Southern Atlantic, with ten acres of meadow and three acres of timber for his house, and Whitejack's sister waiting for him, all behind them. And, ahead of Stais, home and a mother who had presumed him dead and wept over his personal belongings, and ahead of Whitejack the cold bitter mountains of India and China and the tearing dead sound of the fifties and the sky full of Japs. . . .

"All right, Sergeant," the voice of the Lieutenant checking the passengers. "Get on."

Stais waved, a little broken wave, at Whitejack standing there. "See you," he said, "in North Carolina."

"Some October." Whitejack smiled a little in the light of the flood-lamps.

The door closed and Stais sat down in the seat in front of the two Chinese.

"I think these planes are absolutely charming," one of the Red Cross women was saying loudly. "Don't you?"

The engines started and the big plane began to roll. Stais looked out of the window. A plane was landing. It came slowly into the light of the runway lamps and set down heavily, bumping wearily. Stais stared. It was a Mitchell. Stais sighed to himself. As the big C-54 wheeled at the head of the runway, then started clumsily down, Stais put the slip of paper with Arnold Whitejack written on it, and the address, in scrawling, childlike handwriting, into his pocket. And as he saw the Mitchell pull to a stop near the Operations room, he felt for the moment a little less guilty for going home.

MEDAL FROM JERUSALEM

"THE QUESTION that haunts me," Schneider was saying in his high, soft voice, "is, my jazz, is it real jazz or is it merely European jazz?" He was leaning against the bar of the Patio restaurant between Tel Aviv and Jaffa, which used to be the old German consulate, and speaking to Lieutenant Mitchell Gunnison in short, gaspy bursts of talk, smiling a little sadly and a little archly at Mitchell, and occasionally touching his sleeve lightly with the tips of his fingers. "I mean," he said, "I know it's good enough for Palestine, but in America what would they say about a pianist like me?"

"Well," said Gunnison gravely, "I'd say they'd think it was real jazz." He was young and he spoke slowly and he seemed to think very hard before he answered a question.

"You don't know," Schneider said, sighing, "how you've encouraged me. I listen to the records, of course, but they're old, and you never know what actually is going on in America and, after all, we all know there *is* no other jazz, no place, and with a war like this, and God knows how long it's going to last, a musician gets out of touch. And once you are out of touch, you might as well die. Just die."

"You have nothing to worry about," Mitchell said. "You'll be a sensation in America."

"If I ever get there." Schneider smiled sadly and shrugged a little. "Anyway, you must come tomorrow. I'm working on a new arrangement with the drummer. A rumba, Viennese style. It's ridiculous, but I think you'll like it."

"I'm sorry," Mitchell said. "I won't be here tomorrow."

"Then next night," said Schneider.

"I won't be here then, either," Mitchell said. "I'm going tomorrow. Leave's up."

There was a little silence and Schneider looked down at the bar and flicked his beer glass with his fingernail, making a frail musical sound in the dark oak barroom. "Some more fighting?" Schneider asked.

"A little more fighting." Mitchell nodded soberly.

"You fly, no doubt," said Schneider. "I have no wish to intrude on military information, but the wings on the chest . . ."

"I'm a navigator." Mitchell smiled at him.

"It must be an interesting profession. Measuring the distance between one star and another star." Schneider finished his beer slowly. "Well, *sholom aleichem* . . . That's good luck. Or, to be more exact, peace be with you."

"Thank you," Mitchell said.

"Hebrew," said Schneider. "I'm ashamed to talk Hebrew to anybody who knows it. The accent, they tell me, is frightful. But you don't mind, do you?"

"No," said Mitchell. He turned to the bartender. "Mr. Abrams," he said, "another beer please, for Mr. Schneider."

"No, no." Schneider waved his hands in protest. "The artist should not drink before the performance. After . . . Another matter . . . Ah," he said, bowing elaborately, *"Fräulein,* we are enchanted."

Mitchell turned around. Ruth was standing there, looking a little hurried and out of breath, but smiling, and as pretty as ever in a light cotton dress, with her skin burned dark by the sun and her eyes full of welcome and pleasure at seeing him.

"I was afraid," she said, coming over to him and taking his hand, "I was afraid you were going to be angry and leave."

"I wasn't going to leave," Mitchell said. "Not until they closed the doors on me and threw me out."

"I am delighted." Ruth laughed and squeezed his arm. "I am so absolutely delighted."

"My presence," Schneider said, bowing, "I no longer consider necessary. A hundred thanks for the beer, Lieutenant. Now I play or Mr. Abrams will start complaining he is not getting his money's worth out of me. Listen, carefully, if it is not too much of a bore, to my version of 'Stardust.'"

"We'll listen very carefully," Mitchell said.

Schneider went outside to the patio, and a moment later preliminary erratic runs and fragments of melody came floating into the bar as he warmed up for the night's work.

"So." Ruth faced him, looking at him with an expression that was half ownership, half amusement. "So. What have we been doing all day?"

"Well," Mitchell started, "we . . ."

"You are the most beautiful lieutenant in the American army," Ruth said, grinning.

"Well, we went swimming," Mitchell said, pleased and embarrassed, pretending she'd said nothing. "And we hung around on the beach. And we flew a couple of barroom missions. Gin and grapefruit juice."

"Isn't Palestinian grapefruit wonderful?" Ruth asked loyally.

"Sensational," Mitchell said. "Nothing like it in America."

"You're such a liar." Ruth leaned over and kissed him lightly.

"There was an Eighth Air Force pilot down from England," Mitchell said, "and he told us how tough it was over Wilhelmshaven and we told the lies about Ploesti and then it was time to shave and come to see you."

"What did you think while you were shaving? Were you sad because you had to leave your interesting friends and see me?"

"Broken-hearted," Mitchell said.

"You've got such a nice, skinny face," Ruth touched the line of his jaw. "You're as pretty as an English lieutenant. I'm not fond of the English, but they have the prettiest lieutenants of any army."

"We send our pretty ones to the Pacific," said Mitchell. "Guadalcanal. We preserve them for American womanhood."

Ruth signaled Mr. Abrams for a drink. "I was in Jerusalem today. I told my boss I was sick and went there. It's so bad—we never got to see Jerusalem together."

"Some other time," Mitchell said. "I'll come back and we'll see Jerusalem."

"Don't lie to me," Ruth said, seriously. "Please don't lie. You won't come back. You won't see me again. Absolutely no lies, please."

Mitchell felt very young. He felt there was something to be said, and an older man would know how to say it, but he felt dumb and bereaved and clumsy, and it must have showed on his face as he peered at his glass, because Ruth laughed and touched his lips with her fingers and said, "You have such a tragic face for an American. Where do you come from in America?"

"Vermont," Mitchell said.

"Has everybody got a face like yours in Vermont?"

"Everybody."

"I will visit there," Ruth drained her glass, "at some later date."

"I'll give you my address," Mitchell said.

"Of course," said Ruth politely. "You must write it down some time."

They went out into the patio and sat down at a table on the old flagstones under a palm tree, with the blue blackout lights shining dimly over the uniforms and pale dresses, and the moon riding over the Mediterranean and casting flickering shadows over the dancers who now claimed the spot where the German consul had lived well in days gone by. Mitchell ordered champagne because it was his last night. It was Syrian champagne, but not bad, and to both of them it gave an air of festivity and importance to the evening, as it rocked in its silver bucket of ice. Eric, the waiter with the limp, ceremoniously took Ruth's ration tickets, and Schneider, seated with the drummer across the patio, with the drum dimly lit from inside by an orange light of which Schneider was very proud, played "Summertime" because he had decided that was the song Mitchell liked best. The old song, played trickily and well in the soft, echoing patio, somehow sounded, by some ineradicable stamp in Schneider's blood, like Carolina and Vienna and the Balkans, with here and there chords of an old Hebrew chant, quite just and indigenous here between the heavy stone walls on the edge of the Sinai desert.

"I'm jealous of him," said Ruth, speaking over the edge of her glass.

"Who?"

"Schneider."

"Why?" Mitchell asked.

"Because of the way he looks at you. He's crazy about you. Has he asked you to come to tea with him and his mother?"

"Yes," said Mitchell, trying not to smile.

"I'll tear his eyes out," Ruth said. "I'm jealous of anybody who looks at you that way. The girls back in Vermont and those Red Cross girls."

"You have nothing to worry about," Mitchell said. "Nobody looks at me that way. Not even Schneider or you."

"That's the nicest thing about you," Ruth said. "You don't know anything. I'm so used to men who know just how many steps out of bed each look a woman gives them measures. I must visit America after the war. . . ."

"Where will you really go?" Mitchell asked. "Back to Berlin?"

"No." Ruth stared reflectively down at her plate. "No, not back to Berlin. Never back to Berlin. The Germans have made clear their feeling about me. A little thing like a war will not change them. The lamb does not go back to the slaughterhouse. Anyway, I have nobody there. There was a young man . . ." She leaned over and picked up the bottle and absently poured for Mitchell and herself. "I don't know what happened to him. Stalingrad, maybe, Alamein . . . who knows?"

Four men came into the patio and walked through the brief illumination of the blue lights. Three of them were Arabs in European dress, and the fourth was a man in the uniform of the American Army with the civilian technical adviser patch on his shoulder. They stopped at the table. The three Arabs bowed a little, ceremoniously, to Ruth, and the American said, "I thought you were sick."

"This is Mr. Carver," Ruth said to Mitchell, with a wave to the American. "He's my boss."

"Hi, Lieutenant," said Carver. He was a big, fat man, with a weary, puffy, intelligent face. He turned back to Ruth. "I thought you were sick," he repeated in a pleasant, loud, slightly drunken voice.

"I was sick," Ruth said, cheerfully. "I had a miraculous recovery."

"The American Army," Carver said, "expects every civilian worker to do her duty."

"Tomorrow," said Ruth. "Now please go away with your friends. The lieutenant and I are having an intimate talk."

"Lieutenant . . ." It was one of the Arabs, the shortest of the three, a slight, dark man, with a round face and liquid, veiled eyes. "My name is Ali Khazen. Permit me to introduce myself, as no one here seems to remember his manners well enough to do so."

Mitchell stood up. "Mitchell Gunnison," he said, putting out his hand.

"Forgive me," Carver said. "I'm suffering from drink. This is Sayed Taif . . ." He indicated the tallest of the Arabs, a middle-aged man with a severe, handsome, tight-lipped face. Mitchell shook hands with him.

"He doesn't like Americans," Carver said loudly. "He's the leading journalist of the local Arab world and he writes for thirty-five papers in the United States and he doesn't like Americans."

"What was that?" Taif asked politely, inclining his head in a reserved, small gesture.

"Also, he's deaf," said Carver. "Most useful equipment for any journalist."

Nobody bothered to introduce the third Arab, who stood a little to one side, watching Taif with a fierce, admiring stare, like a boxer dog at his master's feet.

"Why don't you all go away and eat your dinner?" Ruth said.

"Lieutenant," Carver said, ignoring her, "take the advice of a veteran of the Middle East. Do not become involved with Palestine."

"He's not becoming involved with Palestine," Ruth said. "He's becoming involved with me."

"Beware Palestine." Carver weaved a little as he spoke. "The human race is doomed in Palestine. For thousands of years. They chop down the forests, burn down the cities, wipe out the inhabitants. This is no place for an American."

"You drink too much, Mr. Carver," Ruth said.

"Nevertheless," Carver shook his big head heavily, "it is no accident that they picked this place to crucify Christ. You couldn't pick a better place to crucify Christ if you scoured the maps of the world for five hundred years. I'm a Quaker myself, from the city of Philadelphia, Pennsylvania, and all I see here is the blood of bleeding humanity. When this war is over I'm going back to Philadelphia and wait until I pick up the morning newspaper and read that everybody in Palestine has exterminated everybody else in Palestine the night before." He walked unsteadily over to Ruth's chair and bent over and peered intently into her face. "Beautiful girl," he said, "beautiful, forlorn girl." He straightened up. "Gunnison, I admonish you, as an officer and gentleman, do not harm one hair on this beautiful girl's head."

"Every hair," Mitchell said, gravely, "is safe with me."

"If you must drink," Ruth said to Carver sharply, "why don't you do it with Americans? Why do you have to go around with bandits and murderers like these?" She waved her hand toward the Arabs. The journalist smiled, his handsome face frosty and amused in the wavering light.

"Impartiality," Carver boomed. "American impartiality. We are famous for it. We are nobody's friend and nobody's enemy. We merely build airfields and pipelines. Impartially. Tomorrow I lunch with the President of the Jewish Agency."

Ruth turned to the journalist. "Taif," she said, loudly, "I read your last piece."

"Ah, yes," he said, his voice a little dead and without timbre. "Did you like it?"

"You'll be responsible for the death of thousands of Jews," said Ruth.

"Ah, thank you," he said. He smiled. "It is my fondest hope." He turned to Mitchell. "Naturally, Lieutenant," he said, "our charming little Ruth is biased in the matter. It is necessary to give the Arab side of the proposition." He began to speak more seriously, with a severe, oratorical emphasis, like an evangelical preacher. "The world is dazzled by the Jewish accomplishment in Palestine. Fine, clean cities, with plumbing. Industries. Where once was desert, now the rose and the olive bloom. Et cetera."

"Taif, old boy," Carver pulled at his arm, "let's eat and you can lecture the lieutenant some other time."

"No, if you please." The journalist pulled his arm politely away from Carver's hand. "I welcome the opportunity to talk to our American friends. You see, my good Lieutenant, you may be very pleased with the factory and the plumbing, and perhaps, even, from one point of view, they may be good things. But they have nothing to do with the Arab. Perhaps the Arab prefers the desert as it was. The Arab has his own culture. . . ."

"When I hear the word 'culture,'" Carver said, "I reach for my pistol. What famous American said that?"

"To Americans and Europeans," the journalist went on, in his singsong, dead voice, "the culture of the Arab perhaps seems backward and dreadful. But, forgive us, the Arab prefers it. The virtues which are particularly Arab are kept alive by primitive living. They die among the plumbing."

"Now," said Ruth, "we have heard a new one. Kill the Jew because he brings the shower bath."

The journalist smiled indulgently at Ruth, as at a clever child. "Personally," he said, "I have nothing against the Jews. I swear that I do not wish to harm a single Jew living in Palestine today. But I will fight to the death to keep even one more Jew from entering the country. This is an Arab state, and it must remain an Arab state."

"Gunnison," Carver said, "aren't you glad you came?"

"Six million Jews have died in Europe," Ruth said, her voice harsh and passionate, and surprising to Mitchell. "Where do you want the survivors to go?" She and the journalist had forgotten the rest of them and were locked with each other across the table.

The journalist shrugged and looked for a moment up above the palm fronds at the dark sky. "That," he said, "is a question for the world to decide. Why must the poor Arab have the whole decision? We've taken in much more than our share. If the rest of the world really wants to see the Jewish race survive let them take them in. America, Britain, Russia . . . I do not notice those large countries taking in great masses of Jews."

"There are no great masses," Ruth said. "There is only a handful."

Taif shrugged. "Even so. The truth may be, perhaps," he paused, a little doubtfully, reminding Mitchell of an old Latin teacher in a class in Cicero, shrewdly hesitating for effect, before telling the class whether the word in question was in the ablative or dative absolute, "the truth may be that the rest of the world really wants to see the Jewish race die out." He turned and smiled warmly at Mitchell. "It is an interesting supposition, Lieutenant. It might be most interesting to examine it before talking any more about Palestine." He walked over to Ruth and leaned over and kissed her fleetingly on the forehead. "Good night, little Ruth," he said, and went to a table across the patio, with the silent, adoring Arab behind him.

"If I see you with that man once more," Ruth spoke to the man who had introduced himself to Mitchell, and who had remained standing at their table, "I'll never talk to you again."

The Arab looked swiftly at Mitchell, a veiled, probing flick of the eyes, and said something to Ruth in Arabic.

"No," said Ruth, her voice clipped and sharp. "Definitely no."

The Arab bowed slightly, put out his hand to Mitchell and, as they shook hands, said, "Very pleasant meeting you, Lieutenant," and went off to join his friends at their table.

"Thé dansants in old Tel Aviv," said Carver. "Bring the kiddies. Good night." He waddled over to the other table.

"Ruth," Mitchell started to talk.

"Lieutenant Gunnison . . ." It was the soft, apologetic voice of Schneider at his elbow. "I am so anxious for your opinion. What did you think of 'Stardust'?"

Mitchell turned slowly from staring at Ruth, who was sitting tense and upright in her chair. "Great, Schneider," Mitchell said. "I thought it was sensational."

Schneider beamed with pleasure. "You are too kind," he said. "I will play you 'Summertime' once more."

"Thanks a lot," said Mitchell. He put out his hand and covered Ruth's, lying on the table. "You all right?" he asked.

She smiled up at him. "Sure," she said. "I am an admirer of abstract political discussions." Her face grew serious. "Do you want to know what Khazen asked when he spoke to me in Arabic?"

"Not if you don't want to tell me."

"I want to tell you." Ruth absently caressed his fingers. "He asked me if I would meet him later."

"Yes," said Mitchell.

"I told him no."

"I heard you." Mitchell grinned at her. "They probably heard you in Cairo."

"I didn't want you to feel disturbed or doubtful," Ruth said, "your last night."

"I feel fine," Mitchell said.

"I've been going with him for four years." She played for a moment with the food on the plate that the waiter had put before her. "When I came here in the beginning I was frightened and lonely and he was very decent. He's a contractor for the Americans and British and he's made a fortune during the war. But when Rommel was outside Alexandria he and his friends used to celebrate in secret. I can't stand him any more. I tell him when I take up with other men. But he hangs on. Ah, finally, I suppose he'll get me to marry him. I'm not strong enough any more." She looked up at Mitchell and tried to smile. "Don't be shocked, darling," she said. "Americans can't understand how tired the human race can get." She stood up suddenly. "Let's dance."

They went onto the floor and Schneider broke into "Summertime" when he saw them and smiled fondly at them as they danced. She danced very well, lightly and passionately, and Mitchell knew as he danced that he was going to remember this for a long time, at odd moments, swinging away from targets with the flak falling off behind him, and later, if he made it, in the snowy hills of his home state, the light, soft pressure of the bright cotton dress, the dark, curved, delicate face below his, the hushed sound of their feet on the old floor under the palms, the clever, rich music of the piano under the small blue lights strung out from the stone building. There were a million things that crowded his throat that he wanted to tell her, and there was no way of saying them. He kissed her cheek as the music ended, and she glanced up at him, and smiled and said, "There, that's better," and they were laughing by the time they got back to their table.

He paid the bill and they went out, saying good night to Schneider, not looking back at the table where Carver and the three Arabs sat, but hearing Carver's deep voice rolling through the music and the darkness, calling, "Does anyone want an airfield? I'll build it for him. Does anyone want a crown of thorns? I'll build it for him."

There was an old carriage waiting outside the restaurant, its driver dozing and its lights dimmed, and they climbed in and sat close together as the driver clucked to the horse and they rattled slowly back toward town. The breeze had gone down as it did at nine o'clock every night, and there was a small, warm breath of salt off the Mediterranean and every once in a while a jeep rushed past in a whistle of American wind, with its slits of cat's-eye lights cutting a darting, frail, skidding pattern in the darkness, making the creakings and rustlings of the old carriage older and dearer and more private as they sat there holding on to each other in silence.

They got off a block from where Ruth lived because the people from whom she rented her room were intensely moral and did not approve of their boarder going out with soldiers. They walked past the corner where the Italian bombers had killed a hundred and thirty people on a Friday morning the year before, and turned into Ruth's street. From a darkened window came the sound of someone practicing the third movement of the Brahms violin concerto, and Mitchell couldn't help smiling and realizing that one of his strongest memories of Tel Aviv would be the strains of Tschaikovsky and Brahms and Beethoven coming through the opened windows on every street of the town, as the furiously cultured inhabitants practiced runs and cadenzas with never-ending zeal.

All the houses were blacked out, but there was a tiny sliver of light along one of the windows in the third-floor apartment in which Ruth lived, and they stopped in dismay when they saw it.

"She's up," Ruth said.

"Doesn't she ever sleep?" Mitchell asked angrily.

Ruth giggled and kissed him. "She can't stay up forever," Ruth said. "We'll take a little walk and by the time we get back she'll be asleep."

Mitchell took her arm and they walked slowly down toward the sea. Soldiers and whores and fat, placid couples strolled on the concrete walk along the beach, and the Mediterranean heaved gently under the moon and broke in small white rolls of foam against the beach, with a steady, foreign grumble, not like the roar of the Atlantic on the cold northern beaches of home. From a café a hundred yards away came the sound of a string quartet playing a Strauss waltz as though Vienna had never been taken, the waltz never lost to the enemy.

Mitchell and Ruth went down the steps to the beach. A weaving British lance-corporal, coming up the steps with a girl, stiffened and saluted rigidly, his hand quivering with respect for authority, and Mitchell saluted back, and Ruth giggled.

"What're you laughing at?" Mitchell asked, when they had passed the lance-corporal.

"I laugh," Ruth said, "every time I see you salute."

"Why?"

"I don't know why. I just laugh. Forgive me." She took off her shoes and walked barefoot in the sand up to the water's edge. The sea swept softly in from Gibraltar and Tunis and Cyrene and Alexandria and lapped at her toes.

"The Mediterranean," Ruth said. "I hate the Mediterranean."

"What's the matter with it?" Mitchell stared out at the flickering silver path of the moon over the water.

"I was on it," Ruth said, "for thirty-three days. In the hold of a Greek steamer that used to carry cement. Maybe I oughtn't to tell you things like that. You're a tired boy who's been sent here to have a good time so he can go back and fight well. . . ."

"You tell me anything you want to tell me," Mitchell said. "I'll fight all right."

"Should I tell you about Berlin, too? Do you want to hear about Berlin?" Ruth's voice was hard and cold, and somehow a little sardonic, not at all like her voice as he had heard it in the whole week he had known her. The meeting with the journalist at the restaurant had started something stirring within her, something that he hadn't seen before, and he felt that before he left he should see that side of her too.

"Tell me about Berlin," Mitchell said.

"I worked for a newspaper," Ruth said, her toes digging lightly in the sand, "even after the Nazis came in, and I was in love with the man who wrote the Economics column and he was in love with me. . . ."

"Economics?" Mitchell was puzzled.

"The stock exchange. The prophecies and excuses."

"Oh," said Mitchell, trying to picture what a man who wrote stock-exchange tips in Berlin in 1934 would look like.

"He was very gay," Ruth said. "Very young, but elegant, with check-ered vests, and he wore a monocle and he lost all his money at the races. His name was Joachim. He used to take me to the races and to the cafés and it used to drive my mother crazy, because if they ever found out I was a Jewish girl out with a Gentile man, they would have sentenced me to death for polluting the blood stream of the German nation. They'd have sent him to a concentration camp, too, but he was always easy and laughing, and he said, 'The important thing is to be brave,' and we were never questioned, and I went to every night club in Berlin, even nights that Goering and Goebbels were in the same room.

"My father was taken to a concentration camp and we decided it was time for me to leave, and Joachim got together all the money he could lay his hands on and gave it to me and I went to Vienna. I was supposed to go to Palestine, if I could, and send for my mother, and for my father, too, if he ever got out of the concentration camp. There was an office in Vienna, and it was filled with refugees from all over Germany, and we collected money to buy transportation and bribe the nations of the world to let some of us in. I slept in the bathtub and talked to sailors and thieves and murderers and crooked shipowners, and finally we got a Greek steamer that was supposed to put in at Genoa and pick us up if we managed to get there. We gave the man 75,000 dollars in cash in advance because that's the only way he would do it, and somehow we got the Austrian government and the Italian government to look the other way, at a price, and they piled us into freight cars, eight hundred of us, and locked us in, men, women and children, lying one on top of another, and the trip took a week and a day to Genoa, and when we got there the ship never arrived. The Greek took the 75,000 dollars and disappeared. There are all kinds of Greeks, and I have nothing against them, but this was a bad one. Then the Italian government sent us back to Vienna and six people committed suicide because they couldn't bear it, and we started in all over again."

Mitchell stared out at the dark line of the sea where it blended in the western distance with the purple of the sky. He tried to think of what it would have been like for his sister and mother if they had been locked into freight cars at Rutland and forced to travel for eight days up to Quebec, say, to wait for an illegal ship to an unknown country. His mother was tall and white-haired and unruffled and pleasant, and his sister was cool and pretty and had some irritating superior mannerisms that she had picked up when she had been foolishly sent for a year to a fancy girls' finishing school in Maryland.

"Let's start home," Ruth said. "If my landlady's still up, we'll shoot her."

They turned their backs on the quiet, white churn of the waves and walked, hand in hand, across the heavy sand of the beach toward the black pile of the buildings of the city.

"Well," Mitchell said, "I want to hear the rest of it."

"No, you don't," Ruth said. "Forgive me for telling you so much. It's too dreary."

"I want to hear," Mitchell said. In the week he had known Ruth, she had been gay and light-hearted, and had helped him to forget the planes spinning out of control and the dying men lying in their frozen blood on the tangled wires and broken aluminum of the Liberator floors, and now he felt as though he owed it to himself and to Ruth to take back with him some of her agony, too, not only the laughter and the tender jokes and the self-effacing merriment. Suddenly, tonight, she had become terribly dear to him, and he felt responsible to her in a way he had never felt responsible to a girl before.

"Tell me," he said.

Ruth shrugged. "Back in Vienna," she said, "we did it all over again. It took two months and the police caught a lot of us, and it meant hiding and running most of the time, but we collected the money again, and we found ourselves another Greek, and this time he turned out to be honest. Or at least as honest as people were to Jews without passports in those days in Europe. We got down to Genoa in only five days this time, and we boarded the steamer at night and they locked the hatch doors on us after we had paid every cent of the money in advance, and we set sail before dawn. The steamer had been built in 1887." They were at the edge of the beach now, and Ruth leaned on Mitchell's shoulder as she put on her shoes. "Nobody can have any idea," Ruth said, as they went up the steps to the concrete walk above, "of what dirt is like until he has been locked into the hold of a fifty-year-old Greek ship with 700 people for over a month. People died every day, and the ship captain would let a rabbi and three other people up on deck at night to perform the burial service and dump the body overboard. The only thing we got to eat was biscuit and canned beef, and there were always worms in everything, even the water we got to drink, and everybody got sores all over their bodies, and the old people got too weak to move and the children wept all day, and the relatives of the people who died screamed a good deal of the time, and it is impossible to tell anyone who was not on that boat what it smelled like, in the middle of the summer in the Mediterranean, with a ventilating system that had been installed in Salonika in 1903."

They turned off the beach walk and climbed slowly up the hill toward the center of the town, past the clean, white, very modernistic apartment houses with gardens and fountains and balconies that faced the sea.

"We were supposed to be let off in Turkey," Ruth went on, her voice almost without inflection and emotion, as though she were reciting from a ledger the business accounts of an importing firm for the year 1850. "And we had given the Greek money to pay off every officer of the port, but something went wrong and we had to put out to sea again, and we started toward Palestine, although the British had patrols along every mile of coastline. But there was no place else to go. People started to get hallucinations about food, and the sailors would sell a sandwich or a lemon for twenty dollars or a bowl of soup for a gold candlestick. And three of the girls couldn't stand it any more and allowed themselves to be taken up every night to be used by the sailors in exchange for regular meals. It was hard to blame them, but they were cursed by the older people as they walked through the crowd each night toward the ladder, and once a Polish woman with two small daughters knocked one of the girls down with an iron pin and tried to stab her with a kitchen knife she had in her bag."

They turned into Ruth's street and looked up at the window just in time to see the thin edge of light under the blind disappear. They stopped and leaned against a stucco fence in front of a plain, shining white house with cactus plants and a fig tree in the front yard.

"We were on that ship for thirty-five days," Ruth said, "and we came to the coast of Palestine between Haifa and Rehovoth, at night, and maybe someone had been bribed, and maybe it was just lucky, but people were waiting for us in rowboats and in eight hours we were all off. There was one woman, who looked as strong as anyone, a solid, sensible-looking woman, and she seemed cheerful and healthy when she got into the little boat with me, but she suddenly died ten feet off the coast, when the water was so shallow a child could have stepped out and walked ashore. Luckily, it was a dark night, and there were no patrols, and we were taken in cars to a movie theater in a little town near Haifa and put inside. The theater had been playing Betty Grable in 'Campus Confessions,' a musical picture, and there were signs with her in tights and ostrich plumes all over it, and the management had written all over the posters, 'Closed This Week for Repairs.'"

"I saw the picture," Mitchell said. He had seen it one night in Cambridge, and he remembered how some of the boys in the audience had whistled when Miss Grable had kissed the leading man.

"We were all told to keep absolutely quiet," Ruth said, "because the British had patrols going through every town. They must have known something, because that week three men high up in the police force were suspended and investigated. It wasn't so hard to keep the older people quiet, but it was awful with the children, and one man really proposed that a little girl who kept crying all day be strangled for the good of the others. We sat there for a week, whispering, making a noise like thousands of mice in a cupboard, and each night cars would come and some people would be taken away to a collective farm somewhere in the hills. Finally, my turn came and I stayed on that farm for two years, working in the fields and teaching children how to read and write German.

"After two years, the British gave you papers, if you managed to dodge them all that time, and I got my papers and started to work for a canning factory outside Tel Aviv. My father was let out of concentration camp in 1938, but his ship was turned back at Haifa, and he was put back in concentration camp in Germany, and for all I know he's still there now, although he's probably dead.

"Joachim wrote me, and my mother, from Berlin. They became good friends once I was gone, and he brought her food, and on Friday nights would come and watch her light the candles. My mother wrote me he told her he had a girl, but he was dissatisfied, he guessed he'd gotten the taste for Jewish girls." Ruth smiled slightly, thinking of the boy with the checkered vest and the monocle many years ago, and Mitchell wondered if he had dropped a bomb near the market-analyzer somewhere in Africa, or in Sicily or Italy.

"He helped my mother get out of Germany," Ruth went on, staring up at the window of her home, which was now secure and dark. "She came out in a Portuguese boat, and I heard she was coming and I was on the shore at Haifa Harbor when it came in. But the British wouldn't let it dock, and after six days they insisted that it turn back, and there were thousands of people on the shore, relatives and friends of the people on the boat, and the worst sound I've ever heard in the world was the sound those people on the shore made when the boat turned around and started to steam toward the Haifa breakwater. But the boat never got out of the harbor." Ruth paused and licked her lips, and spoke very matter of factly. "There was an explosion. We saw the puff of dirty black smoke first, then a long time later we heard the noise, and people on shore were screaming and laughing and crying. Then there was fire and the boat started to go down, and everybody grabbed at any kind of boat they could find and started out toward the steamer, and there were people who couldn't find boats who just jumped into the water, clothes and all, and started to swim, and nobody ever found out how many people drowned that way, because bodies were washed in to shore for three weeks afterward. My mother was drowned and five hundred other people on the boat, but 700 were saved, and then the British had to let them in, and I suppose that's what the people who set the bomb figured would happen. Some people would die, but some would be saved. If the boat went back to Europe, everybody would be killed. Of course, they bungled it somewhat, and they didn't figure on the fire, and they thought the boat would sink more slowly and only a few people would be killed, but even so it was a pretty fair bargain." Ruth lit a cigarette calmly and held the light for Mitchell. "My mother was washed up a week later, and at least her grave is in Palestine. I couldn't tell my father she was dead, so when I wrote to him in concentration camp, I forged letters from my mother, because I had a lot of her letters and I learned how to make good copies. Even now, through the Red Cross, I write him notes in my mother's handwriting, and if he's alive he thinks my mother is living on a farm with a family near Rehovoth."

Ruth pulled at her cigarette and inhaled deeply and in the increased glow Mitchell looked at her and thought again, as he'd thought so many times before, that it was a wonderful and terrible thing that the human race covered its scars so completely, so that Ruth, standing there, with the torture and smuggling and burning and drowning and hiding and dying behind her, looked, with her lipstick and fluffy, cleverly combed hair, and her soft, fragile, print dress, like any one of a thousand girls at a dance in America, with nothing more behind them than a weekly allowance from father, and two proms a season at New Haven or Cambridge.

"Ah," Ruth said, throwing her cigarette away, "she must be asleep by now. Come." She smiled at him, dry-eyed and pleasant, and took his hand, and they walked quietly up through the dim hallways to the apartment in which she lived. She opened the door silently and waved him in, her finger to her lips, and when they were safely in her room, with the door locked behind them, she giggled like a child who has pulled some sly trick on the grown-up world, then kissed him hungrily in the dark room, and whispered, "Mitchell, Mitchell," making the name somehow foreign and tender by the way she said it.

He held her tight, but she pulled away. "Not yet, Lieutenant," she said, grinning, "not yet." She put on a light and went over to a chest of drawers in a corner and started to rummage under some scarves. "I have something for you. Sit down and wait, like a polite boy."

Mitchell sat on the low day bed, blinking in the light. The room was small and painted white and very clean. There was a large piece of Egyptian batik in red and dark green on the wall over the bed and there were three photographs on a dressing table. Mitchell looked at the photographs—a round, smiling woman, with a healthy, simple face, Ruth's mother, the picture taken long before the morning when the ship went down in Haifa Harbor. The other two photographs were of men. There was a man who looked like Ruth, obviously her father, a studious, humorous, rather weak face, with frail, delicate bones and shy, childish eyes. And there was the young man in the checkered vest, slender and laughing and proud of himself, with the monocle in his eye like a burlesque of a German general or a British actor.

"Here." Ruth came over to him and sat down beside him. She had a soft chamois bag, and there was a little rich clinking as she put it in his hand. "To take with you," she said.

Mitchell slowly opened the bag. A heavy silver medal on a chain, glittering dully in the lamplight, fell into his hand. Ruth was crouched on her knees on the couch beside him, looking anxiously at his face to see if her present would meet with favor. Mitchell turned it over. It was a Saint Christopher, old and irregular, of heavy silver, with the Saint awkward and angular and archaic and very religious in the loving workmanship of a silversmith who had died a long time before.

"It's for voyages," Ruth said, hurriedly. "For a navigator, I thought, it might be quite—quite useful. . . ." She smiled uncertainly at him. "Of course," she said, "it is not in my religion, but I don't think it would do any harm to give it to you. That's why I went to Jerusalem. Something like this, something holy, might have a tendency to be more effective if it comes from Jerusalem, don't you think?"

"Of course," Mitchell said. "It's bound to be."

"Will you wear it?" Ruth glanced quickly and shyly at him, sitting there, dangling the medal on its chain.

"All the time," Mitchell said. "Day and night, every mission, every jeep-ride, year in, year out."

"May I put it on for you?"

Mitchell opened his collar and gave the medal to Ruth. She stood up and he bowed his head and she slipped it on, then leaned over and kissed the back of his neck where the chain lay against the flesh.

She stepped back. "Now," she said matter-of-factly. "There we are." She went over to the lamp. "We don't need this any more." She put the light out and went over to the window and threw back the blackout blinds, and a faint breeze carrying salt and the scent of gardens came into the room. She stood at the window, looking out, and Mitchell got up and crossed over to her, feeling the unfamiliar cool jewelry of the medal dangling against his chest. He stood behind her, silently, holding her lightly, looking out over the city. The white buildings shone in the heavy moonlight machined and modern and Biblical all at once, and from the west came the faint sound of the sea. Mitchell wanted to tell her that he would remember her, remember everything about her, her drowned mother and imprisoned father, her old, courageous lover, drinking champagne with her at the Nazi cafés; he wanted to tell her that he would remember the dealings with the Greek sailor and the hold of the ship that had been built in 1887 and the dying Jews buying a lemon with a gold candlestick; he wanted to tell her that flying over the Germans in Europe or watching the first snow fall at Stowe he would remember the small boat grating on the sand in the darkness outside Rehovoth and the week in the closed movie theater with the British patrols outside; he wanted to tell her that the terror and courage would not be forgotten, but he didn't know how to say it, and besides, being honest with himself, he knew it would be difficult to remember, and finally, back in Vermont, it would blur and cloud over and seem unreal as a story in a child's book, read many years ago and now almost forgotten. He held her more tightly, but he said nothing.

"There he is," Ruth said, her voice casual and unimpressed. "See him standing down there next to the house with the picket gate. . . ."

Mitchell looked over Ruth's shoulder. Down on the street, thirty yards from the entrance of Ruth's house, was a small dark figure, almost completely lost in shadow.

"Ali Khazen," Ruth said. "He comes and waits outside my window. Ah . . ." she sighed, "I suppose finally he'll kill me."

She turned away from the window and led him back to the couch across the strip of moonlight that divided the room. She looked up at him gravely, then suddenly pushed him gently down to the couch and fell beside him, holding onto him. She held him and kissed his cheek and chuckled a little. "Now, Lieutenant," she said, "tell me about Vermont."

ACT OF FAITH

"PRESENT IT in a pitiful light," Olson was saying, as they picked their way through the mud toward the orderly room tent. "Three combat-scarred veterans, who fought their way from Omaha Beach to—what was the name of the town we fought our way to?"

"Konigstein," Seeger said.

"Konigstein." Olson lifted his right foot heavily out of a puddle and stared admiringly at the three pounds of mud clinging to his overshoe. "The backbone of the army. The noncommissioned officer. We deserve better of our country. Mention our decorations in passing."

"What decorations should I mention?" Seeger asked. "The marksman's medal?"

"Never quite made it," Olson said. "I had a cross-eyed scorer at the butts. Mention the bronze star, the silver star, the Croix de Guerre, with palms, the unit citation, the Congressional Medal of Honor."

"I'll mention them all." Seeger grinned. "You don't think the CO'll notice that we haven't won most of them, do you?"

"Gad, sir," Olson said with dignity, "do you think that one Southern military gentleman will dare doubt the word of another Southern military gentleman in the hour of victory?"

"I come from Ohio," Seeger said.

"Welch comes from Kansas," Olson said, coolly staring down a second lieutenant who was passing. The lieutenant made a nervous little jerk with his hand as though he expected a salute, then kept it rigid, as a slight superior smile of scorn twisted at the corner of Olson's mouth. The lieutenant dropped his eyes and splashed on through the mud. "You've heard of Kansas," Olson said. "Magnolia-scented Kansas."

"Of course," said Seeger. "I'm no fool."

"Do your duty by your men, Sergeant." Olson stopped to wipe the rain off his face and lectured him. "Highest ranking noncom present took the initiative and saved his comrades, at great personal risk, above and beyond the call of you-know-what, in the best traditions of the American army."

"I will throw myself in the breach," Seeger said.

"Welch and I can't ask more," said Olson, approvingly.

They walked heavily through the mud on the streets between the rows of tents. The camp stretched drearily over the Rheims plain, with the rain beating on the sagging tents. The division had been there over three weeks by now, waiting to be shipped home, and all the meager diversions of the neighborhood had been sampled and exhausted, and there was an air of watchful suspicion and impatience with the military life hanging over the camp now, and there was even reputed to be a staff sergeant in C Company who was laying odds they would not get back to America before July Fourth.

"I'm redeployable," Olson sang. "It's so enjoyable . . ." It was a jingle he had composed to no recognizable melody in the early days after the victory in Europe, when he had added up his points and found they only came to 63. "Tokyo, wait for me . . ."

They were going to be discharged as soon as they got back to the States, but Olson persisted in singing the song, occasionally adding a mournful stanza about dengue fever and brown girls with venereal disease. He was a short, round boy who had been flunked out of air cadets' school and transferred to the infantry, but whose spirits had not been damaged in the process. He had a high, childish voice and a pretty baby face. He was very good-natured, and had a girl waiting for him at the University of California, where he intended to finish his course at government expense when he got out of the army, and he was just the type who is killed off early and predictably and sadly in motion pictures about the war, but he had gone through four campaigns and six major battles without a scratch.

Seeger was a large, lanky boy, with a big nose, who had been wounded at Saint Lô, but had come back to his outfit in the Siegfried Line, quite unchanged. He was cheerful and dependable, and he knew his business and had broken in five or six second lieutenants who had been killed or wounded and the CO had tried to get him commissioned in the field, but the war had ended while the paperwork was being fumbled over at headquarters.

They reached the door of the orderly tent and stopped. "Be brave, Sergeant," Olson said. "Welch and I are depending on you."

"O.K.," Seeger said, and went in.

The tent had the dank, army-canvas smell that had been so much a part of Seeger's life in the past three years. The company clerk was reading a July, 1945, issue of the *Buffalo Courier-Express,* which had just reached him, and Captain Taney, the company CO, was seated at a sawbuck table he used as a desk, writing a letter to his wife, his lips pursed with effort. He was a small, fussy man, with sandy hair that was falling out. While the fighting had been going on, he had been lean and tense and his small voice had been cold and full of authority. But now he had relaxed, and a little pot belly was creeping up under his belt and he kept the top button of his trousers open when he could do it without too public loss of dignity. During the war Seeger had thought of him as a natural soldier, tireless, fanatic about detail, aggressive, severely anxious to kill Germans. But in the past few months Seeger had seen him relapsing gradually and pleasantly into a small-town wholesale hardware merchant, which he had been before the war, sedentary and a little shy, and, as he had once told Seeger, worried, here in the bleak champagne fields of France, about his daughter, who had just turned twelve and had a tendency to go after the boys and had been caught by her mother kissing a fifteen-year-old neighbor in the hammock after school.

"Hello, Seeger," he said, returning the salute in a mild, off-hand gesture. "What's on your mind?"

"Am I disturbing you, sir?"

"Oh, no. Just writing a letter to my wife. You married, Seeger?" He peered at the tall boy standing before him.

"No, sir."

"It's very difficult," Taney sighed, pushing dissatisfiedly at the letter before him. "My wife complains I don't tell her I love her often enough. Been married fifteen years. You'd think she'd know by now." He smiled at Seeger. "I thought you were going to Paris," he said. "I signed the passes yesterday."

"That's what I came to see you about, sir."

"I suppose something's wrong with the passes." Taney spoke resignedly, like a man who has never quite got the hang of army regulations and has had requisitions, furloughs, requests for court-martial returned for correction in a baffling flood.

"No, sir," Seeger said. "The passes're fine. They start tomorrow. Well, it's just . . ." He looked around at the company clerk, who was on the sports page.

"This confidential?" Taney asked.

"If you don't mind, sir."

"Johnny," Taney said to the clerk, "go stand in the rain someplace."

"Yes, sir," the clerk said, and slowly got up and walked out.

Taney looked shrewdly at Seeger, spoke in a secret whisper. "You pick up anything?" he asked.

Seeger grinned. "No, sir, haven't had my hands on a girl since Strasbourg."

"Ah, that's good." Taney leaned back, relieved, happy he didn't have to cope with the disapproval of the Medical Corps.

"It's—well," said Seeger, embarrassed, "it's hard to say—but it's money."

Taney shook his head sadly. "I know."

"We haven't been paid for three months, sir, and . . ."

"Damn it!" Taney stood up and shouted furiously. "I would like to take every bloody chair-warming old lady in the Finance Department and wring their necks."

The clerk stuck his head into the tent. "Anything wrong? You call for me, sir?"

"No," Taney shouted. "Get out of here."

The clerk ducked out.

Taney sat down again. "I suppose," he said, in a more normal voice, "they have their problems. Outfits being broken up, being moved all over the place. But it is rugged."

"It wouldn't be so bad," Seeger said. "But we're going to Paris tomorrow. Olson, Welch and myself. And you need money in Paris."

"Don't I know it." Taney wagged his head. "Do you know what I paid for a bottle of champagne on the Place Pigalle in September . . . ?" He paused significantly. "I won't tell you. You won't have any respect for me the rest of your life."

Seeger laughed. "Hanging," he said, "is too good for the guy who thought up the rate of exchange."

"I don't care if I never see another franc as long as I live." Taney waved his letter in the air, although it had been dry for a long time.

There was silence in the tent and Seeger swallowed a little embarrassedly, watching the CO wave the flimsy sheet of paper in regular sweeping movements. "Sir," he said, "the truth is, I've come to borrow some money for Welch, Olson and myself. We'll pay it back out of the first pay we get, and that can't be too long from now. If you don't want to give it to us, just tell me and I'll understand and get the hell out of here. We don't like to ask, but you might just as well be dead as be in Paris broke."

Taney stopped waving his letter and put it down thoughtfully. He peered at it, wrinkling his brow, looking like an aged bookkeeper in the single gloomy light that hung in the middle of the tent.

"Just say the word, Captain," Seeger said, "and I'll blow . . ."

"Stay where you are, son," said Taney. He dug in his shirt pocket and took out a worn, sweat-stained wallet. He looked at it for a moment. "Alligator," he said, with automatic, absent pride. "My wife sent it to me when we were in England. Pounds don't fit in it. However . . ." He opened it and took out all the contents. There was a small pile of francs on the table in front of him. He counted them. "Four hundred francs," he said. "Eight bucks."

"Excuse me," Seeger said humbly. "I shouldn't have asked."

"Delighted," Taney said vigorously. "Absolutely delighted." He started dividing the francs into two piles. "Truth is, Seeger, most of my money goes home in allotments. And the truth is, I lost eleven hundred francs in a poker game three nights ago, and I ought to be ashamed of myself. Here . . ." he shoved one pile toward Seeger. "Two hundred francs."

Seeger looked down at the frayed, meretricious paper, which always seemed to him like stage money, anyway. "No, sir," he said, "I can't take it."

"Take it," Taney said. "That's a direct order."

Seeger slowly picked up the money, not looking at Taney. "Some time, sir," he said, "after we get out, you have to come over to my house and you and my father and my brother and I'll go on a real drunk."

"I regard that," Taney said, gravely, "as a solemn commitment."

They smiled at each other and Seeger started out.

"Have a drink for me," said Taney, "at the Café de la Paix. A small drink." He was sitting down to write his wife he loved her when Seeger went out of the tent.

Olson fell into step with Seeger and they walked silently through the mud between the tents.

"Well, *mon vieux?*" Olson said finally.

"Two hundred francs," said Seeger.

Olson groaned. "Two hundred francs! We won't be able to pinch a whore's behind on the Boulevard des Capucines for two hundred francs. That miserable, penny-loving Yankee!"

"He only had four hundred," Seeger said.

"I revise my opinion," said Olson.

They walked disconsolately and heavily back toward their tent.

Olson spoke only once before they got there. "These raincoats," he said, patting his. "Most ingenious invention of the war. Highest saturation point of any modern fabric. Collect more water per square inch, and hold it, than any material known to man. All hail the quartermaster!"

Welch was waiting at the entrance of their tent. He was standing there peering excitedly and short-sightedly out at the rain through his glasses, looking angry and tough, like a big-city hack-driver, individual and incorruptible even in the ten-million-colored uniform. Every time Seeger came upon Welch unexpectedly, he couldn't help smiling at the belligerent stance, the harsh stare through the steel-rimmed GI glasses, which had nothing at all to do with the way Welch really was. "It's a family inheritance," Welch had once explained. "My whole family stands as though we were getting ready to rap a drunk with a beer glass. Even my old lady." Welch had six brothers, all devout, according to Welch, and Seeger from time to time idly pictured them standing in a row, on Sunday mornings in church, seemingly on the verge of general violence, amid the hushed Latin and Sabbath millinery.

"How much?" Welch asked loudly.

"Don't make us laugh," Olson said, pushing past him into the tent.

"What do you think I could get from the French for my combat jacket?" Seeger said. He went into the tent and lay down on his cot.

Welch followed them in and stood between the two of them, a superior smile on his face. "Boys," he said, "on a man's errand."

"I can just see us now," Olson murmured, lying on his cot with his hands clasped behind his head, "painting Montmartre red. Please bring on the naked dancing girls. Four bucks worth."

"I am not worried," Welch announced.

"Get out of here." Olson turned over on his stomach.

"I know where we can put our hands on sixty-five bucks." Welch looked triumphantly first at Olson, then at Seeger.

Olson turned over slowly and sat up. "I'll kill you," he said, "if you're kidding."

"While you guys are wasting your time," Welch said, "fooling around with the infantry, I used my head. I went into Reems and used my head."

"Rance," Olson said automatically. He had had two years of French in college and he felt, now that the war was over, that he had to introduce his friends to some of his culture.

"I got to talking to a captain in the air force," Welch said eagerly. "A little fat old paddle-footed captain that never got higher off the ground than the second floor of Com Z headquarters, and he told me that what he would admire to do more than anything else is take home a nice shiny German Luger pistol with him to show to the boys back in Pacific Grove, California."

Silence fell on the tent and Welch and Olson looked tentatively at Seeger.

"Sixty-five bucks for a Luger, these days," Olson said, "is a very good figure."

"They've been sellin' for as low as thirty-five," said Welch hesitantly. "I'll bet," he said to Seeger, "you could sell yours now and buy another one back when you get some dough, and make a clear twenty-five on the deal."

Seeger didn't say anything. He had killed the owner of the Luger, an enormous SS major, in Coblenz, behind some paper bales in a warehouse, and the major had fired at Seeger three times with it, once knicking his helmet, before Seeger hit him in the face at twenty feet. Seeger had kept the Luger, a long, heavy, well-balanced gun, very carefully since then, lugging it with him, hiding it at the bottom of his bedroll, oiling it three times a week, avoiding all opportunities of selling it, although he had been offered as much as a hundred dollars for it and several times eighty and ninety, while the war was still on, before German weapons became a glut on the market.

"Well," said Welch, "there's no hurry. I told the captain I'd see him tonight around 8 o'clock in front of the Lion D'Or Hotel. You got five hours to make up your mind. Plenty of time."

"Me," said Olson, after a pause. "I won't say anything."

Seeger looked reflectively at his feet and the other two men avoided looking at him. Welch dug in his pocket. "I forgot," he said. "I picked up a letter for you." He handed it to Seeger.

"Thanks," Seeger said. He opened it absently, thinking about the Luger.

"Me," said Olson, "I won't say a bloody word. I'm just going to lie here and think about that nice fat air force captain."

Seeger grinned a little at him and went to the tent opening to read the letter in the light. The letter was from his father, and even from one glance at the handwriting, scrawly and hurried and spotted, so different from his father's usual steady, handsome, professorial script, he knew that something was wrong.

"Dear Norman," it read, "sometime in the future, you must forgive me for writing this letter. But I have been holding this in so long, and there is no one here I can talk to, and because of your brother's condition I must pretend to be cheerful and optimistic all the time at home, both with him and your mother, who has never been the same since Leonard was killed. You're the oldest now, and although I know we've never talked very seriously about anything before, you have been through a great deal by now, and I imagine you must have matured considerably, and you've seen so many different places and people. . . . Norman, I need help. While the war was on and you were fighting, I kept this to myself. It wouldn't have been fair to burden you with this. But now the war is over, and I no longer feel I can stand up under this alone. And you will have to face it some time when you get home, if you haven't faced it already, and perhaps we can help each other by facing it together. . . ."

"I'm redeployable," Olson was singing softly, on his cot. "It's so enjoyable, In the Pelilu mud, With the tropical crud . . ." He fell silent after his burst of song.

Seeger blinked his eyes, at the entrance of the tent, in the wan rainy light, and went on reading his father's letter, on the stiff white stationery with the University letterhead in polite engraving at the top of each page.

"I've been feeling this coming on for a long time," the letter continued, "but it wasn't until last Sunday morning that something happened to make me feel it in its full force. I don't know how much you've guessed about the reason for Jacob's discharge from the Army. It's true he was pretty badly wounded in the leg at Metz, but I've asked around, and I know that men with worse wounds were returned to duty after hospitalization. Jacob got a medical discharge, but I don't think it was for the shrapnel wound in his thigh. He is suffering now from what I suppose you call combat fatigue, and he is subject to fits of depression and hallucinations. Your mother and I thought that as time went by and the war and the army receded, he would grow better. Instead, he is growing worse. Last Sunday morning when I came down into the living room from upstairs he was crouched in his old uniform, next to the window, peering out . . ."

"What the hell," Olson was saying, "if we don't get the sixty-five bucks we can always go to the Louvre. I understand the Mona Lisa is back."

"I asked Jacob what he was doing," the letter went on. "He didn't turn around. 'I'm observing,' he said. 'V-1's and V-2's. Buzz-bombs and rockets. They're coming in by the hundreds.' I tried to reason with him and he told me to crouch and save myself from flying glass. To humor him I got down on the floor beside him and tried to tell him the war was over, that we were in Ohio, 4,000 miles away from the nearest spot where bombs had fallen, that America had never been touched. He wouldn't listen. 'These're the new rocket bombs,' he said, 'for the Jews.'"

"Did you ever hear of the Pantheon?" Olson asked loudly.

"No," said Welch.

"It's free."

"I'll go," said Welch.

Seeger shook his head a little and blinked his eyes before he went back to the letter.

"After that," his father went on, "Jacob seemed to forget about the bombs from time to time, but he kept saying that the mobs were coming up the street armed with bazookas and Browning automatic rifles. He mumbled incoherently a good deal of the time and kept walking back and forth saying, 'What's the situation? Do you know what the situation is?' And he told me he wasn't worried about himself, he was a soldier and he expected to be killed, but he was worried about Mother and myself and Leonard and you. He seemed to forget that Leonard was dead. I tried to calm him and get him back to bed before your mother came down, but he refused and wanted to set out immediately to rejoin his division. It was all terribly disjointed and at one time he took the ribbon he got for winning the Bronze star and threw it in the fireplace, then he got down on his hands and knees and picked it out of the ashes and made me pin it on him again, and he kept repeating, 'This is when they are coming for the Jews.'"

"The next war I'm in," said Olson, "they don't get me under the rank of colonel."

It had stopped raining by now and Seeger folded the unfinished letter and went outside. He walked slowly down to the end of the company street, and facing out across the empty, soaked French fields, scarred and neglected by various armies, he stopped and opened the letter again.

"I don't know what Jacob went through in the army," his father wrote, "that has done this to him. He never talks to me about the war and he refuses to go to a psychoanalyst, and from time to time he is his own bouncing, cheerful self, playing in tennis tournaments, and going around with a large group of girls. But he has devoured all the concentration camp reports, and I have found him weeping when the newspapers reported that a hundred Jews were killed in Tripoli some time ago.

"The terrible thing is, Norman, that I find myself coming to believe that it is not neurotic for a Jew to behave like this today. Perhaps Jacob is the normal one, and I, going about my business, teaching economics in a quiet classroom, pretending to understand that the world is comprehensible and orderly, am really the mad one. I ask you once more to forgive me for writing you a letter like this, so different from any letter or any conversation I've ever had with you. But it is crowding me, too. I do not see rockets and bombs, but I see other things.

"Wherever you go these days—restaurants, hotels, clubs, trains—you seem to hear talk about the Jews, mean, hateful, murderous talk. Whatever page you turn to in the newspapers you seem to find an article about Jews being killed somewhere on the face of the globe. And there are large, influential newspapers and well-known columnists who each day are growing more and more outspoken and more popular. The day that Roosevelt died I heard a drunken man yelling outside a bar, 'Finally, they got the Jew out of the White House.' And some of the people who heard him merely laughed and nobody stopped him. And on V-E Day, in celebration, hoodlums in Los Angeles savagely beat a Jewish writer. It's difficult to know what to do, whom to fight, where to look for allies.

"Three months ago, for example, I stopped my Thursday night poker game, after playing with the same men for over ten years. John Reilly happened to say that the Jews were getting rich out of this war, and when I demanded an apology, he refused, and when I looked around at the faces of the men who had been my friends for so long, I could see they were not with me. And when I left the house no one said good night to me. I know the poison was spreading from Germany before the war and during it, but I had not realized it had come so close.

"And in my economics class, I find myself idiotically hedging in my lectures. I discover that I am loath to praise any liberal writer or any liberal act and find myself somehow annoyed and frightened to see an article of criticism of existing abuses signed by a Jewish name. And I hate to see Jewish names on important committees, and hate to read of Jews fighting for the poor, the oppressed, the cheated and hungry. Somehow, even in a country where my family has lived a hundred years, the enemy has won this subtle victory over me—he has made me disfranchise myself from honest causes by calling them foreign, Communist, using Jewish names connected with them as ammunition against them.

"And, most hateful of all, I find myself looking for Jewish names in the casualty lists and secretly being glad when I discover them there, to prove that there at least, among the dead and wounded, we belong. Three times, thanks to you and your brothers, I have found our name there, and, may God forgive me, at the expense of your blood and your brother's life, through my tears, I have felt that same twitch of satisfaction. . . .

"When I read the newspapers and see another story that Jews are still being killed in Poland, or Jews are requesting that they be given back their homes in France, or that they be allowed to enter some country where they will not be murdered, I am annoyed with them, I feel they are boring the rest of the world with their problems, they are making demands upon the rest of the world by being killed, they are disturbing everyone by being hungry and asking for the return of their property. If we could all fall through the crust of the earth and vanish in one hour, with our heroes and poets and prophets and martyrs, perhaps we would be doing the memory of the Jewish race a service. . . .

"This is how I feel today, son. I need some help. You've been to the war, you've fought and killed men, you've seen the people of other countries. Maybe you understand things that I don't understand. Maybe you see some hope somewhere. Help me. Your loving father."

Seeger folded the letter slowly, not seeing what he was doing because the tears were burning his eyes. He walked slowly and aimlessly across the dead autumn grass of the empty field, away from the camp.

He tried to wipe away his tears, because with his eyes full and dark, he kept seeing his father and brother crouched in the old-fashioned living room in Ohio and hearing his brother, dressed in the old, discarded uniform, saying, "These're the new rocket bombs. For the Jews."

He sighed, looking out over the bleak, wasted land. Now, he thought, now I have to think about it. He felt a slight, unreasonable twinge of anger at his father for presenting him with the necessity of thinking about it. The army was good about serious problems. While you were fighting, you were too busy and frightened and weary to think about anything, and at other times you were relaxing, putting your brain on a shelf, postponing everything to that impossible time of clarity and beauty after the war. Well, now, here was the impossible, clear, beautiful time, and here was his father, demanding that he think. There are all sorts of Jews, he thought, there are the sort whose every waking moment is ridden by the knowledge of Jewishness, who see signs against the Jew in every smile on a streetcar, every whisper, who see pogroms in every newspaper article, threats in every change of the weather, scorn in every handshake, death behind each closed door. He had not been like that. He was young, he was big and healthy and easy-going and people of all kinds had seemed to like him all his life, in the army and out. In America, especially, what was going on in Europe had seemed remote, unreal, unrelated to him. The chanting, bearded old men burning in the Nazi furnaces, and the dark-eyed women screaming prayers in Polish and Russian and German as they were pushed naked into the gas chambers had seemed as shadowy and almost as unrelated to him as he trotted out onto the Stadium field for a football game, as they must have been to the men named O'Dwyer and Wickersham and Poole who played in the line beside him.

They had seemed more related in Europe. Again and again in the towns that had been taken back from the Germans, gaunt, gray-faced men had stopped him humbly, looking searchingly at him, and had asked, peering at his long, lined, grimy face, under the anonymous helmet, "Are you a Jew?" Sometimes they asked it in English, sometimes French, or Yiddish. He didn't know French or Yiddish, but he learned to recognize the phrase. He had never understood exactly why they had asked the question, since they never demanded anything from him, rarely even could speak to him, until, one day in Strasbourg, a little bent old man and a small, shapeless woman had stopped him, and asked, in English, if he was Jewish.

"Yes," he said, smiling at them.

The two old people had smiled widely, like children. "Look," the old man had said to his wife. "A young American soldier. A Jew. And so large and strong." He had touched Seeger's arm reverently with the tips of his fingers, then had touched the Garand he was carrying. "And such a beautiful rifle . . ."

And there, for a moment, although he was not particularly sensitive, Seeger got an inkling of why he had been stopped and questioned by so many before. Here, to these bent, exhausted old people, ravaged of their families, familiar with flight and death for so many years, was a symbol of continuing life. A large young man in the uniform of the liberator, blood, as they thought, of their blood, but not in hiding, not quivering in fear and helplessness, but striding secure and victorious down the street, armed and capable of inflicting terrible destruction on his enemies.

Seeger had kissed the old lady on the cheek and she had wept and the old man had scolded her for it, while shaking Seeger's hand fervently and thankfully before saying good-bye.

And, thinking back on it, it was silly to pretend that, even before his father's letter, he had been like any other American soldier going through the war. When he had stood over the huge dead SS major with the face blown in by his bullets in the warehouse in Coblenz, and taken the pistol from the dead hand, he had tasted a strange little extra flavor of triumph. How many Jews, he'd thought, has this man killed, how fitting it is that I've killed him. Neither Olson nor Welch, who were like his brothers, would have felt that in picking up the Luger, its barrel still hot from the last shots its owner had fired before dying. And he had resolved that he was going to make sure to take this gun back with him to America, and plug it and keep it on his desk at home, as a kind of vague, half-understood sign to himself that justice had once been done and he had been its instrument.

Maybe, he thought, maybe I'd better take it back with me, but not as a memento. Not plugged, but loaded. America by now was a strange country for him. He had been away a long time and he wasn't sure what was waiting for him when he got home. If the mobs were coming down the street toward his house, he was not going to die singing and praying.

When he was taking basic training he'd heard a scrawny, clerklike-looking soldier from Boston talking at the other end of the PX bar, over the watered beer. "The boys at the office," the scratchy voice was saying, "gave me a party before I left. And they told me one thing. 'Charlie,' they said, 'hold onto your bayonet. We're going to be able to use it when you get back. On the Yids.'"

He hadn't said anything then, because he'd felt it was neither possible nor desirable to fight against every random overheard voice raised against the Jews from one end of the world to another. But again and again, at odd moments, lying on a barracks cot, or stretched out trying to sleep on the floor of a ruined French farmhouse, he had heard that voice, harsh, satisfied, heavy with hate and ignorance, saying above the beery grumble of apprentice soldiers at the bar, "Hold onto your bayonet. . . ."

And the other stories—Jews collected stories of hatred and injustice and inklings of doom like a special, lunatic kind of miser. The story of the naval officer, commander of a small vessel off the Aleutians, who, in the officers' wardroom, had complained that he hated the Jews because it was the Jews who had demanded that the Germans be beaten first and the forces in the Pacific had been starved in consequence. And when one of his junior officers, who had just come aboard, had objected and told the commander that he was a Jew, the commander had risen from the table and said, "Mister, the Constitution of the United States says I have to serve in the same navy with Jews, but it doesn't say I have to eat at the same table with them." In the fogs and the cold, swelling Arctic seas off the Aleutians, in a small boat, subject to sudden, mortal attack at any moment . . .

And the two young combat engineers in an attached company on D Day, when they were lying off the coast right before climbing down into the landing barges. "There's France," one of them had said.

"What's it like?" the second one had asked, peering out across the miles of water toward the smoking coast.

"Like everyplace else," the first one had answered. "The Jews've made all the dough during the war."

"Shut up!" Seeger had said, helplessly thinking of the dead, destroyed, wandering, starving Jews of France. The engineers had shut up, and they'd climbed down together into the heaving boat, and gone into the beach together.

And the million other stories. Jews, even the most normal and best adjusted of them, became living treasuries of them, scraps of malice and bloodthirstiness, clever and confusing and cunningly twisted so that every act by every Jew became suspect and blameworthy and hateful. Seeger had heard the stories, and had made an almost conscious effort to forget them. Now, holding his father's letter in his hand, he remembered them all.

He stared unseeingly out in front of him. Maybe, he thought, maybe it would've been better to have been killed in the war, like Leonard. Simpler. Leonard would never have to face a crowd coming for his mother and father. Leonard would not have to listen and collect these hideous, fascinating little stories that made of every Jew a stranger in any town, on any field, on the face of the earth. He had come so close to being killed so many times, it would have been so easy, so neat and final.

Seeger shook his head. It was ridiculous to feel like that, and he was ashamed of himself for the weak moment. At the age of twenty-one, death was not an answer.

"Seeger!" It was Olson's voice. He and Welch had sloshed silently up behind Seeger, standing in the open field. "Seeger, *mon vieux*, what're you doing—grazing?"

Seeger turned slowly to them. "I wanted to read my letter," he said.

Olson looked closely at him. They had been together so long, through so many things, that flickers and hints of expression on each other's faces were recognized and acted upon. "Anything wrong?" Olson asked.

"No," said Seeger. "Nothing much."

"Norman," Welch said, his voice young and solemn. "Norman, we've been talking, Olson and me. We decided—you're pretty attached to that Luger, and maybe—if you—well . . ."

"What he's trying to say," said Olson, "is we withdraw the request. If you want to sell it, O.K. If you don't, don't do it for our sake. Honest."

Seeger looked at them, standing there, disreputable and tough and familiar. "I haven't made up my mind yet," he said.

"Anything you decide," Welch said oratorically, "is perfectly all right with us. Perfectly."

They walked aimlessly and silently across the field, away from camp. As they walked, their shoes making a wet, sliding sound in the damp, dead grass, Seeger thought of the time Olson had covered him in the little town outside Cherbourg, when Seeger had been caught going down the side of a street by four Germans with a machine gun on the second story of a house on the corner and Olson had had to stand out in the middle of the street with no cover at all for more than a minute, firing continuously, so that Seeger could get away alive. And he thought of the time outside Saint Lô when he had been wounded and had lain in a minefield for three hours and Welch and Captain Taney had come looking for him in the darkness and had found him and picked him up and run for it, all of them expecting to get blown up any second.

And he thought of all the drinks they'd had together and the long marches and the cold winter together, and all the girls they'd gone out with together, and he thought of his father and brother crouching behind the window in Ohio waiting for the rockets and the crowds armed with Browning automatic rifles.

"Say," he stopped and stood facing them. "Say, what do you guys think of the Jews?"

Welch and Olson looked at each other, and Olson glanced down at the letter in Seeger's hand.

"Jews?" Olson said finally. "What're they? Welch, you ever hear of the Jews?"

Welch looked thoughtfully at the gray sky. "No," he said. "But remember, I'm an uneducated fellow."

"Sorry, Bud," Olson said, turning to Seeger. "We can't help you. Ask us another question. Maybe we'll do better."

Seeger peered at the faces of his friends. He would have to rely upon them, later on, out of uniform, on their native streets, more than he had ever relied on them on the bullet-swept street and in the dark minefield in France. Welch and Olson stared back at him, troubled, their faces candid and tough and dependable.

"What time," Seeger asked, "did you tell that captain you'd meet him?"

"Eight o'clock," Welch said. "But we don't have to go. If you have any feeling about that gun . . ."

"We'll meet him," Seeger said. "We can use that sixty-five bucks."

"Listen," Olson said, "I know how much you like that gun and I'll feel like a heel if you sell it."

"Forget it," Seeger said, starting to walk again. "What could I use it for in America?"

AGE OF REASON

HE HAD the dream only once—in December. He thought about it for a few moments the next morning, and forgot about it until one evening in April, ten minutes before his plane was scheduled to take off. Then, suddenly, it returned to him. Always, when he was about to board a plane, there was a slight tremor; an awareness of risk, however small and controlled; a slight, subconscious realization that each flight might end with death; a hidden knowledge that there was a small, lurking fatality in winds and cloud and valves and wings, and that no amount of airline skill and care and advertising could ever absolutely dispel it. It was that usual minute, buried twinge of disaster that made him remember the dream as he stood at the gate with his wife and sister, looking out at the dark field and the huge, substantial plane and the flickering lights that marked the runways.

The dream had been a simple one. In it, somehow, his sister Elizabeth had died, and he had, in a resigned and hopeless way, followed the coffin to the cemetery and watched with dry eyes as it was lowered into the ground, and then he had returned home. And somehow, in the dream, it had all happened on May 14th. The date had been absolutely clear and definite and had given the dream a real, tragic sense that it might not otherwise have had. When he woke, he tried to figure out why May 14th, an obscure day five months in the future, had been chosen so relentlessly and specifically by his dreaming mind, but it was no use. There were no birthdays in his family in May, no anniversaries, and nothing in particular had ever happened to him or anyone he knew on that day. He had laughed a little, sleepily, to himself, gently touched Alice's bare shoulder in the bed beside him, and had risen and gone to work, in the sensible, everyday atmosphere of drafting boards and blueprints, without saying a word then or later to her or anyone else about the dream.

And then—laughing at the way his five-year-old daughter had sleepily and carelessly said good-bye when he had left the apartment, standing there with the noise of engines filling the fresh April evening air, kissing his sister Elizabeth good-bye—the dream came back. Elizabeth was as rosy and sturdy as ever, a cheerful, pretty girl who looked as though she had just come triumphantly off a tennis court or from a swimming meet, and if there was any touch of doom hanging over her, it was very well hidden.

"Bring me back Cary Grant," Elizabeth said as she brushed his cheek.

"Of course," Roy said.

"I now leave you two to say a fond farewell," Elizabeth said. "Alice, give him his last-minute instructions. Tell him to behave himself."

"I've already briefed him for this mission," Alice said. "No girls. No more than three Martinis before dinner. Telephone me and report twice weekly. Get on the plane and get home the minute the job is done."

"Two weeks," Roy said. "I swear I'll be back in two weeks."

"Don't have too good a time." Alice was smiling but on the verge of tears, as she always was every time he went anyplace without her, even overnight to Washington.

"I won't," Roy said. "I promise to be miserable."

"Good enough." Alice laughed.

"No old telephone numbers secreted on your person?" Elizabeth asked.

"No." There had been a period in Roy's life, just before he married Alice, when he had been quite lively, and during the war some of his friends had come back from Europe with lurid and highly fictionized tales of wild times in Paris and London, and to the women of his family he seemed more dashing and unstable than was the fact.

"God," he said, "it'll be a relief getting away from this female board of directors for a few days."

He and Alice went up to the gate.

"Take care of yourself, darling," Alice said softly.

"Don't worry." He kissed her.

"I hate this," Alice said, holding onto him. "We're always saying good-bye. This is the last time. From now on, no matter where you go, I'm going with you."

"All right." Roy smiled down at her.

"Even if you only go to Yankee Stadium."

"Couldn't be more pleased." He held her tightly for a moment, dear and familiar and forlorn, left behind this way. Then he walked out to the plane. He turned as he started to climb into it, and waved. Alice and Elizabeth waved back, and he noticed again how much alike they looked, standing together, like two sisters in a pretty family, both of them blond and fair, trim, with little tricks of movement and holding themselves that were almost identical.

He turned and went into the plane, and a moment later the door was shut behind him and the plane started rolling toward the end of the runway.

Ten days later, over the phone between Los Angeles and New York, Roy told Alice she would have to come West. "Munson says it's going to take six months," Roy said, "and he's promised me a place to live, and you are hereby invited."

"Thanks," Alice said. "Tell Munson I would like to kick him in the teeth."

"Can't be helped, baby," Roy said. "Commerce above all. You know."

"Why couldn't he have told you before you went out? Then you could've helped me close up the apartment and we could've gone out together."

"He didn't know before I came out," Roy said patiently. "The world is very confused these days."

"I would like to kick him in the teeth."

"O.K." Roy grinned. "You come out and tell him yourself. When do you arrive? Tomorrow?"

"There's one thing you've got to learn, Roy," Alice said. "I am not a troop movement. You can't say, 'Civilian Alice Gaynor will report three thousand miles from here at 4 P.M. tomorrow,' and expect it to happen."

"O.K., you're not a troop movement. When?"

Alice chuckled. "You sound nice and anxious."

"I *am* nice and anxious."

"That's good."

"When?"

"Well"—Alice hesitated thoughtfully—"I have to get Sally out of school, I have to send some things to storage, I have to rent the apartment, I have to get plane reservations—"

"When?"

"Two weeks," Alice said, "if I can get the reservations all right. Can you wait?"

"No," Roy said.

"Neither can I." They both laughed. "Have you been very gay out there?"

Roy recognized the tentative, inquiring tone and sighed to himself. "Dull as mud," he said. "I stay in in the evenings and read. I've read six books and I'm halfway through General Marshall's report on the conduct of the war."

"There was one evening you didn't read." Alice's voice was careful and purposely light.

"All right," Roy said flatly. "Let's hear it."

"Monica came in from the Coast Tuesday and she called me. She said she saw you with a beautiful girl at a fancy restaurant."

"If there was any justice," Roy said, "they would drop Monica on Bikini Atoll."

"She had long black hair, Monica said."

"She was absolutely right," Roy said. "The girl had long black hair."

"Don't shout. I can hear perfectly well."

"What Monica neglected to say was that it was Charlie Lewis's wife—"

"She said you were alone."

"—and Charlie Lewis was twenty feet away, in the men's room."

"Are you sure?"

"No. Maybe he was in the ladies' room."

"It may be funny to you, but with your history—"

"I will match my history with any husband's," Roy said.

"I hate your sense of humor on this subject." Alice's voice began to tremble a little, and Roy relented.

"Listen, baby," he said softly. "Get out here quick. Quick as you can. Then we can stop this nonsense."

"I'm sorry." Alice's voice was soft and repentant. "It's just that we've been away from each other for so long in these last few years. I'm foolish and jittery. Who's paying for this call?"

"The company."

"That's good." Alice chuckled. "I'd hate to fight on our own money. Do you love me?"

"Get out here quick."

"Do you consider that an answer to my question?"

"Yes."

"O.K.," Alice said. "So do I. Good-bye, darling. See you soon."

"Kiss Sally for me," said Roy.

"I will. Good-bye."

Roy hung up. First he shook his head a little wearily, remembering the argument; then he smiled, remembering the end of the conversation. He got up from his chair and went over to the calendar on the desk, to try to figure what day he could expect his wife and child.

The telegram came three days later: "RESERVATIONS ON 2 O'CLOCK FLIGHT MAY 14. WILL ARRIVE BURBANK AT 10 P.M. YOUR TIME. PLEASE SHAVE. LOVE, ALICE."

Roy grinned as he reread the telegram, then became conscious of a sensation of uneasiness that refused to be crystallized or pinned down. He walked around all that day with that undefined sense of trouble, and it wasn't until he was dozing off to sleep that night that it suddenly became clear to him. He woke and got out of bed and read the telegram again. May 14th. He kept the lamp on and lit a cigarette and sat up in the narrow bed in the impersonal hotel room and slowly allowed the thing to take control.

He had never been a superstitious man, or even a religious man, and he had always laughed at his mother, who had a fund of dreams and predictions and omens of good and evil at her command. Alice had one or two superstitious habits—like not talking about anything that she wanted to have happen, because she was sure it wouldn't happen if it were mentioned or hoped for too much—but he had always scorned them, too. During the war, when every magazine assured the world that there were no atheists in foxholes, he had never prayed, even in the most gloomy and dangerous times. He had never, in all his adult life, done anything as a result of superstition or premonition. He looked around him at his efficiently furnished, bright, twentieth-century room and felt foolish to be awake now in the heel of the night, chasing phantoms and echoing warnings and scraps of old dreams through the sensible channels of his engineer's mind.

The dream, of course, had been explicit. His sister was to die on May 14th. But dreams never were what they seemed to be, and Elizabeth and Alice looked so much alike, and they were always together and such good friends. . . . He knew enough about dreams to understand that it would be a simple transference in that shadowy, whimsical world—a wife for a sister, a sister for a wife. And now, of all the days in the year, his wife and child had picked May 14th to fly the three thousand miles over the rivers and mountains of the continent from New York to California.

He put out the light much later, with nothing decided, and tried to sleep. He stared up at the dark ceiling, listening to the occasional swift swhoosh of a car on the street outside, hurrying home through the waning night. For a man who didn't believe in Fate, he thought, who saw the world in terms of simple cause and effect; who felt that no act was inevitable, that what was going to happen tomorrow or the next second was in no place determined and was everlastingly variable; who felt that no man's death or burial place was fixed, that no event was recorded in any future book, that the human race got hints or warnings from no supernatural source—this was a ludicrous and profitless way to spend a night. For a man who walked under ladders, cheerfully broke mirrors, never had his palm read or his fortune told from cards, he felt that he was behaving idiotically, and yet he couldn't sleep.

In the morning he called New York.

"Alice," he said, "I want you to come by train."

"What's the matter?" she said.

"I'm afraid of the plane." He heard her laugh incredulously over the phone. "I'm afraid of the plane," he repeated stubbornly.

"Don't be silly," Alice said. "They haven't had an accident with that plane yet, and they won't start now."

"Even so—"

"And I'm not going to try to keep Sally amused for three days in a roomette," Alice said. "It would take me the whole summer to recover."

"Please," Roy said.

"And I couldn't get train reservations for weeks," Alice said, "and the apartment's rented and everything. What's come over you?" Her voice sounded suspicious and wary.

"Nothing," Roy said. "It's just that I'm worried about flying."

"Good God!" Alice said. "You've flown two hundred thousand miles in all sorts of contraptions."

"I know," Roy said. "That's why I'm worried."

"Are you drunk?" Alice asked.

"Alice, darling," Roy sighed. "It's eight o'clock in the morning out here."

"Well, you sound queer."

"I've been up all night, worrying."

"Well, stop worrying. I'll see you on the fourteenth. Are you sure you're all right?"

"Yes."

"This is a very strange telephone call, I must say."

"I'm sorry."

They talked for a moment more, but quite coldly, and Roy hung up feeling dissatisfied and defeated.

He called again two days later and tried once more.

"Don't ask any questions," he said. "Just do this for me, and I'll explain when you get out here. If you want to come on the plane, that's all right, but don't come on the fourteenth. Come on the fifteenth or sixteenth or seventeenth. Any other day. But not on the fourteenth."

"Roy," Alice said, "you've got me terribly worried. What's come over you? I've asked Elizabeth and she says that this doesn't sound like you at all."

"How is she?" Roy asked.

"Elizabeth is fine. She tells me to ignore you and come out as scheduled."

"Tell her to mind her own damned business." Roy had been working hard and sleeping badly and his voice was raw and nervous, and Alice reacted to it.

"I think I know what's going on," she said coldly. "Monica told me there's a big party at the Condons' on the fourteenth, and you've probably promised to take someone else, and a wife would be a big handicap—"

"Oh, God, will you stop that!" Roy shouted into the phone.

"I haven't been married to you for seven years for nothing," Alice said. "I'm not blind."

"Come out today!" Roy shouted. "Come out tomorrow! Come out the thirteenth! Only not the fourteenth!"

"You know as well as I do that if I give up my reservations, I won't get another until June. If you don't want to see me any more, tell me. You don't have to go through all this rigmarole."

"Alice, darling," Roy pleaded, "I assure you I want to see you."

"Well, then, stop this nonsense or tell me what it's all about."

"Alice, it's this way," he began, resolved to tell her, no matter how much of an idiot it made him feel, but there was a click on the wire and then three thousand miles of whispering silence. By the time he got Alice back on the phone, ten minutes later, he felt too ridiculous, felt that he could not live with himself or his wife if he at this late date exposed himself as a silly, undependable man with a brain gone soft and nervous and irresponsible after all the sane, dependable years.

"I haven't anything else to say," he told Alice when the operator finally made the connection, "except that I love you very much and I couldn't bear it if anything ever happened to you."

He heard Alice crying softly at the other end of the wire. "We have to be together soon," she said. "This is awful. And please don't call me any more, Roy, darling. You're acting so strangely, and after I talk to you, the most miserable ideas grab hold of me. Will it be all right when I get out there?"

"It'll be wonderful, darling," Roy said.

"And you'll never go away without me again? Never?"

"Never." He could close his eyes and see her crouched like a little girl over the phone in the bedroom of their quiet, pleasant home, both her hands on the instrument, her pretty, clever face screwed up with grief and longing, and it was hard to say anything more. "Good night," he said. "Be careful."

He hung up and stared wildly at the blank wall on the other side of the room, knowing he wouldn't sleep again that night.

There was an early fog on the morning of May 14th, and Roy stared at it, hot-eyed and lightheaded from lack of sleep, and went out and walked along the quiet, gray streets, with only police cars and milk-delivery carts disturbing the soft, thick dawn.

California, he thought; it's always foggy in the morning, fog is general in California before eight, and it's a different time and a different weather on the coast of the Atlantic, and her plane isn't due to leave for hours yet.

It must be the war, he thought. This would never have happened to me before the war. I thought I came out all right, but maybe I was overconfident. All the cemeteries, with the young men tucked away in the sand and spring grass, and the old ladies in black lace dresses dying on the next street in London in the air raids. A man's imagination was bound to take a morbid turn, finally. I must take hold of myself, he told himself reasonably. I'm the man who always felt sane, balanced, healthy in all situations, who always scorned mediums and table tappers, priests and psychoanalysts.

The fog was beginning to lift, and he stopped to stare at the distant smudge of mountains that stood guard over the eastern approaches of the city. Planes had to come in steeply over them and circle the city and land from the westward side. A strip of blue appeared above the mountains and widened and widened, and the fog melted away in wisps among the ugly, fat palm trees that lined the street, and soon the sun was shining on the dewy lawns, and the sky looked clear and blue from Beverly Hills to Scotland.

He went back to his hotel and lay down without even taking his shoes off. Some time later he woke up. Vaguely, in the moment before waking, there was a confusion of planes going down in puffs of smoke, like the newsreel of an air battle, and Sally's voice over it, regretfully saying, as she always did at bedtime, "Do I *really* have to go to sleep now? I'm terribly wide-awake."

He looked at the clock. It was one-forty in New York. They were at the airport now, and the big plane was waiting on the field, with the mechanics fiddling on it and the men checking the gas tanks. The hell with it, he thought. I don't care how foolish I seem.

He picked up the phone. "La Guardia Field, New York," he said.

"There will be a slight delay," the operator sang. "I will call you."

"This is very important," Roy said. "Urgent."

"There will be a slight delay," the operator said in exactly the same tones. "I will call you."

He hung up and went to the window and stared out. The sky stretched, radiant and clear, over the hills toward New York. I'll tell her the whole thing, he thought, idiotic or not. Forbid her to get on the plane. We can laugh about it later. I'll take the first plane back myself and fly back with them. That'll prove to her it has nothing to do with anything here.

He went and got out his valise and put three shirts in it, then picked up the phone again. Five minutes later he got the airport, but it took another five minutes to get through to the station manager for the airline.

"My name is Gaynor"—Roy's voice was high and hurried—"and this is a very unusual request, so please listen carefully."

"What was that name, sir?"

"Gaynor. G-a-y-n-o-r."

"Oh, yes, Gaynor. Like the dive." The distant voice laughed politely at its own joke. "What can I do for you, sir?"

"My wife and child—"

"You will have to speak louder, please."

"My wife and child!" Roy shouted. "Mrs. Alice Gaynor, on the two-o'clock flight to Los Angeles. I want you to stop them—"

"What did you say?"

"I said I wanted you to stop them. They are not to take the plane. My wife and child. Mrs. Alice Gaynor. The two-o'clock flight to Los Angeles—"

"I'm afraid that's impossible, Mr. Gaynor." The voice was puzzled but polite.

"It can't be impossible. All you have to do is announce it over the public-address system and—"

"Impossible, sir. The two-o'clock flight is just taking off at this moment. I'm terribly sorry. Is there anything else I can do for you?"

"No," Roy said flatly, and put the phone down. He sat on the edge of his bed for a moment, then got up and went to the window. He looked out at the bright sky and the green-and-yellow mountains. He remained standing there, staring at the mountains, waiting for the call from the airline.

MIXED DOUBLES

As JANE COLLINS walked out onto the court behind her husband, she felt once more the private, strong thrill of pride that had moved her again and again in the time she had known him. Jane and Stewart had been married six years, but even so, as she watched him stride before her in that curious upright, individual, half-proud, half-comic walk, like a Prussian drill sergeant on his Sunday off, Jane felt the same mixture of amusement and delight in him that had touched her so strongly when they first met. Stewart was tall and broad and his face was moody and good-humored and original, and Jane felt that even at a distance of five hundred yards and surrounded by a crowd of people, she could pick him out unerringly. Now, in well-cut white trousers and a long-sleeved Oxford shirt, he seemed elegant and a little old-fashioned among the other players, and he looked graceful and debonair as he hit the first few shots in the preliminary rallying.

Jane was sensibly dressed, in shorts and tennis shirt, and her hair was imprisoned in a bandanna, so that it wouldn't get into her eyes. She knew that the shorts made her look a little dumpy and that the handkerchief around her head gave her a rather skinned and severe appearance, and she had a slight twinge of female regret when she looked across the net and saw Eleanor Burns soft and attractive in a prettily cut tennis dress and with a red ribbon in her hair, but she fought it down and concentrated on keeping her eye on the ball as Mr. Croker, Eleanor's partner, sliced it back methodically at her.

Mr. Croker, a vague, round, serious little man, was a neighbor of the Collinses' hosts. His shorts were too tight for him, and Jane knew, from having watched him on previous occasions, that his face would get more serious and more purple as the afternoon wore on, but he played a steady, dependable game and he was useful when other guests were too lazy or had drunk too much at lunch to play in the afternoon.

Two large oak trees shaded part of the court, and the balls flashed back and forth, in light and shadow, making guitarlike chords as they hit the rackets, and on the small terrace above the court, where the other guests were lounging, there was the watery music of ice in glasses and the bright flash of summer colors as people moved about.

How pleasant this was, Jane thought—to get away from the city on a week end, to this cool, tree-shaded spot, to slip all the stiff bonds of business and city living and run swiftly on the springy surface of the court, feeling the country wind against her bare skin, feeling youth in her legs, feeling, for this short Sunday hour at least, free of desks and doors and weekday concrete.

Stewart hit a tremendous overhead smash, whipping all the strength of his long body into it, and the ball struck the ground at Eleanor's feet and slammed high in the air. He grinned. "I'm ready," he said.

"You're not going to do that to me in the game, are you?" Eleanor asked.

"I certainly am," Stewart said. "No mercy for women. The ancient motto of the Collins family."

They tossed for service, and Stewart won. He served and aced Eleanor with a twisting, ferocious shot that spun off at a sharp angle.

"Jane, darling," he said, grinning, as he walked to the other side, "we're going to be sensational today."

They won the first set with no trouble. Stewart played very well. He moved around the court swiftly and easily, hitting the ball hard in loose, well-coached strokes, with an almost exaggerated grace. Again and again, the people watching applauded or called out after one of his shots, and he waved his racket, smiling at them, and said, "Oh, we're murderous today." He kept humming between shots—a tuneless, happy composition of his own—like a little boy who is completely satisfied with himself, and Jane couldn't help smiling and adoring him as he lightheartedly dominated the game and the spectators and the afternoon, brown and dashing and handsome in his white clothes, with the sun flooding around him like a spotlight on an actor in the middle of the stage.

Occasionally, when Stewart missed a shot, he would stand, betrayed and tragic, and stare up at the sky and ask with mock despair, "Collins, why don't you just go home?" And then he would turn to Jane and say, "Janie, darling, forgive me. Your husband's just no good."

And even as she smiled at him and said, "You're so right," she could sense the other women, up on the terrace, looking down at him, their eyes speculative and veiled and lit with invitation as they watched.

Jane played her usual game, steady, unheroic, getting almost everything back quite sharply, keeping the ball in play until Stewart could get his racket on it and kill it. They were a good team. Jane let Stewart poach on her territory for spectacular kills, and twice Stewart patted her approvingly on the behind after she had made difficult saves, and there were appreciative chuckles from the spectators at the small domestic vulgarity.

Stewart made the last point of the set on a slamming deep backhand that passed Eleanor at the net. Eleanor shook her head and said, "Collins, you're an impossible man," and Croker said stolidly, "Splendid. Splendid," and Stewart said, grinning, "Something I've been saving for this point, old man."

They walked off and sat down on a bench in the shade between sets, and Croker and Jane had to wipe their faces with towels and Croker's alarming purple died a little from his cheeks.

"That overhead!" Eleanor said to Stewart. "It's absolutely frightening. When I see you winding up, I'm just tempted to throw away my poor little racket and run for my life."

Jane lifted her head and glanced swiftly at Stewart to see how he was taking it. He was taking it badly, smiling a little too widely at Eleanor, being boyish and charming. "It's nothing," he said. "Something I picked up on Omaha Beach."

That, too, Jane thought bitterly. Foxhole time, too. She ducked her head into her towel to keep from saying something wifely. This is the last time, she thought, feeling the towel sticky against her sweaty forehead, the last time I am coming to any of these week-end things, always loaded with unattached or semi-attached, man-hungry, half-naked, honey-mouthed girls. She composed her face, so that when she looked up from the towel she would look like a nice, serene woman who merely was interested in the next set of tennis.

Eleanor, who had wide green eyes, was staring soberly and unambiguously over the head of her racket at Stewart, and Stewart, fascinated, as always, and a little embarrassed, was staring back. Oh, God, Jane thought, the long stare, too.

"Well," she said briskly, "I'm ready for one more set."

"What do you say," Stewart asked, "we divide up differently this time? Might make it more even. Croker and you, Jane, and the young lady and me."

"Oh," said Eleanor, "I'd be a terrible drag to you, Stewart. And besides, I'm sure your wife loves playing on your side."

"Not at all," Jane said stiffly. The young lady! How obvious could a man be?

"No," said Croker surprisingly. "Let's stay the way we are." Jane wanted to kiss the round purple face, a bleak, thankful kiss. "I think we'll do better this time. I've been sort of figuring out what to do with you, Collins."

Stewart looked at him briefly and unpleasantly, then smiled charmingly. "Anything you say, old man. I just thought . . ."

"I'm sure we'll do better," Croker said firmly. He stood up. "Come on, Eleanor."

Eleanor stood up, lithe and graceful in her short dress, which whipped around her brown legs in the summer wind. Never again, Jane thought, will I wear shorts. Dresses like that, even if they cost fifty dollars apiece, and soft false bosoms to put in them, too, and no bandanna, even if I'm blinded on each shot.

Stewart watched Eleanor follow Croker onto the court, and Jane could have brained him for the buried, measuring glint in his eye.

"Let's go," Stewart said, and under his breath, as they walked to their positions on the base line. He added, "Let's really show the old idiot this time, Jane."

"Yes, dear," Jane said, and pulled her bandanna straight and tight around her hair.

The first three games were ludicrously one-sided. Stewart stormed the net, made sizzling, malicious shots to Croker's feet, and purposely made him run, so that he panted pitifully and grew more purple than ever, and from time to time muttered to Jane, "Ridiculous old windbag," and "I thought he had me figured out," and "Don't let up, Janie, don't let up."

Jane played as usual, steady, undeviating, as predictably and sensibly as she always played. She was serving in the fourth game and was at 40-15 when Stewart dropped a shot just over the net, grinning as Croker galloped heavily in and barely got his racket on it. Croker's return wobbled over Stewart's head and landed three inches beyond the base line.

"Nice shot," she heard Stewart say. "Just in."

She looked at him in surprise. He was nodding his head emphatically at Croker.

Eleanor was at the net on the other side, looking at Stewart. "It looked out to me," she said.

"Not at all," Stewart said. "Beautiful shot. Serve them up, Janie."

Oh, Lord, Jane thought, now he's being sporting.

Jane made an error on the next point and Croker made a placement for advantage and Stewart hit into the net for the last point, and it was Croker's and Eleanor's game. Stewart came back to receive the service, not humming any more, his face irritable and dark.

Croker suddenly began to play very well, making sharp, sliding, slicing shots that again and again forced Stewart and Jane into errors. As they played, even as she swung at the ball, Jane kept remembering the shot that Stewart had called in, that had become the turning point of the set. He had not been able to resist the gallant gesture, especially when Eleanor had been standing so close, watching it all. It was just like Stewart. Jane shook her head determinedly, trying to concentrate on the game. This was no time to start dissecting her husband. They had had a lovely week end till now and Stewart had been wonderful, gay and funny and loving, and criticism could at least be reserved for weekdays, when everything else was dreary, too. But it *was* just like Stewart. It was awful how everything he did was all of a piece. His whole life was crowded with gestures. Hitting his boss that time in the boss's own office with three secretaries watching, because the boss had bawled him out. Giving up his R.O.T.C. commission and going into the Army as a private, in 1942. Giving five thousand dollars, just about the last of their savings, to Harry Mather, for Mather's business, just because they had gone to school together, when everyone knew Mather had become a hopeless drunk and none of his other friends would chip in. To an outsider, all these might seem the acts of a generous and rather noble character, but to a wife, caught in the consequences . . .

"Damn these pants," Stewart was muttering after hitting a ball into the net. "I keep tripping over them all the time."

"You ought to wear shorts, like everyone else," Jane said.

"I will. Buy me some this week," Stewart said, taking time out and rolling his cuffs up slowly and obviously. Jane had bought him three pairs of shorts a month before, but he always pretended he couldn't find them, and wore the long trousers. His legs are surprisingly skinny, Jane thought, hating herself for thinking it, and they're hairy, and his vanity won't let him. . . . She started to go for a ball, then stopped when she saw Stewart going for it.

He hit it out to the backstop. "Janie, darling," he said, "at least stay out of my way."

"Sorry," she said. Stewie, darling, she thought, Stewie, be careful. Don't lay it on. You're not really like this. I know you're not. Even for a moment, don't make it look as though you are.

Stewart ended the next rally by hitting the ball into the net. He stared unhappily at the ground. "The least they might do," he said in a low voice to Jane, "is roll the court if they invite people to play on it."

Please, Stewie, Jane begged within herself, don't do it. The alibis. The time he forgot to sign the lease for the apartment and they were put out and he blamed it on the lawyer, and the time he lost the job in Chicago and it was because he had gone to the wrong college, and the time . . . By a rigorous act of will, Jane froze her eyes on the ball, kept her mind blank as she hit it back methodically again and again.

Eleanor and Croker kept winning points. Croker had begun to chop every ball, spinning soft, deceptive shots that landed in mid-court and hardly bounced before they fell a second time. The only way that Jane could return them was to hit them carefully, softly, just getting them back. But Stewart kept going in on them furiously, taking his full, beautiful swing, sending the ball whistling into the net or over the court into the backstop. He looked as pretty and expert as ever as he played, but he lost point after point.

"What a way to play tennis," he grumbled, with his back to his opponents. "Why doesn't he play ping-pong or jacks?"

"You can't slam those dinky little shots like that," Janie said. "You have to get them back soft."

"You play your game," Stewart said, "and I'll play mine."

"Sorry," Jane said. Oh, Stewart, she mourned within her.

Stewart went after two more of Croker's soft chops, each time whipping his backhand around in his usual, slightly exaggerated, beautiful stroke, and each time knocking the ball into the net.

I can't help it, Jane thought. That is the way he is. Form above everything. If he were hanging over a cliff, he'd let himself fall to the rocks below rather than risk being ungraceful climbing to safety to save his life. He always has to pick up the check in bars and restaurants, no matter whom he is with or how many guests there are at the table, always with the same lordly, laughing, slightly derisive manner, even if we are down to our last fifty dollars. And when they had people in to dinner, there had to be two maids to wait on table, and French wines, and there always had to be those special bottles of brandy that cost as much as a vacation in the country. And he became so cold and remote when Jane argued with him about it, reminding him they were not rich and there was no sense in pretending they were. And his shoes. She blinked her eyes painfully, getting a sudden vision, there in the sun and shadow, of the long row of exquisite shoes, at seventy dollars a pair, that he insisted upon having made to his order. How ridiculous, she thought, to allow yourself to be unnerved at your husband's taste in shoes, and she loyally reminded herself how much a part of his attraction it had been in the beginning that he was always so beautifully dressed and so easy and graceful and careless of money.

The score was 4-3 in favor of Eleanor and Croker. Stewart's shots suddenly began to work again, and he and Jane took the next game with ease. Stewart's grin came back then, and he cheerfully reassured Jane, "Now we're going to take them." But after winning the first two points of the next game he had a wild streak and missed the base line by a few inches three times in a row, and they eventually lost the game.

I will make no deductions from this, Jane told herself stonily as she went up to the net for Stewart's serve. Anybody is liable to miss a few shots like that—anybody. And yet, how like Stewart! Just when it was most important to be steady and dependable. . . . The time she'd been so sick and the maid had quit, and Jane lay, broken and miserable, in bed for three weeks, with no one to take care of her except Stewart . . . He had been charming and thoughtful for the first week, fixing her meals, reading to her, sitting at her side for hours on end, cheerful and obliging, making her illness gently tolerable. And then he had suddenly grown nervous and abrupt, made vague excuses to leave her alone, and vanished for hours at a time, only to come back and hastily attend her for a few moments and vanish again, leaving her there in the rumpled bed, staring, lonely and shaken, at the ceiling as dusk faded into night and night into morning. She had been sure there was another girl then and she had resolved that when she was well and able to move around again, she would come to some decision with him, but as unpredictably as his absences had begun, they stopped. Once more he was tender and helpful, once more he sat at her side and nursed her and cheered her, and out of gratitude and love she had remained quiet and pushed her doubts deep to the back of her mind. And here they were again, in the middle of a holiday afternoon, foolishly, in this most unlikely place, during this mild, pointless game, with half a dozen people lazily watching, laughing and friendly, over their drinks.

She looked at him a few moments later, handsome and dear and familiar at her side, and he grinned back at her, and she was ashamed of herself for the thoughts that had been flooding through her brain.

It was that silly girl on the other side of the net who had started it all, she thought. That practiced, obvious, almost automatic technique of flattering the male sex. That meaningless, rather pitiful flirtatiousness. It was foolish to allow it to throw her into the bitter waters of reflection. Marriage, after all, was an up-and-down affair and in many ways a fragile and devious thing, and was not to be examined too closely. Marriage was not a bank statement or a foreign policy or an X-ray photograph in a doctor's hand. You took it and lived through it, and maybe, a long time later—perhaps the day before you died—you totaled up the accounts, if you were of that turn of mind, but not before. And if you were a reasonable, sensible, mature woman, you certainly didn't do your additions and subtractions on a tennis court every time your husband hit a ball into the net. Jane smiled at herself and shook her head.

"Nice shot," she said warmly to Stewart as he swept a forehand across court, past Croker, for a point.

But it was still set point. Croker placed himself to receive Stewart's service, tense and determined and a little funny-looking, with his purple face and his serious round body a little too tight under his clothes. The spectators had fallen silent, and the wind had died, and there was a sense of stillness and expectancy as Stewart reared up and served.

Jane was at the net and she heard the sharp twang of Stewart's racket hitting the ball behind her and the rifle-like report as it hit the tape and fell away. He had just missed his first service.

Jane didn't dare look around. She could feel Stewart walking into place, in that stiff-backed, pleasant way of his, and feel him shuffling around nervously, and she couldn't look back. Please, she thought, please get this one in. Helplessly, she thought of all the times when, just at the crucial moment, he had failed. Oh, God, this is silly, she thought. I mustn't do this. The time he had old man Sawyer's account practically in his hands and he got drunk. On the sporting pages, they called it coming through in the clutch. There were some players who did and some players who didn't, and after a while you got to know which was which. If you looked at it coldly, you had to admit that until now Stewart had been one of those who didn't. The time her father died, just after her sister had run off with the vocalist in that band, and if there had been a man around, taking hold of things, her father's partner wouldn't've been able to get away with most of the estate the way he did, and the vocalist could have been frightened off. One day's strength and determination, one day of making the right move at the right time . . . But after the funeral, Stewart had pulled out and gone to Seattle on what he had said was absolutely imperative business, but that had never amounted to anything anyway, and Jane's mother and sister, and Jane, too, were still paying for that day of failure.

She could sense Stewart winding up for his service behind her back. Somewhere in her spine she felt a sense of disaster. It was going to be a double fault. She knew it. No, she thought, I mustn't. He isn't really like that. He's so intelligent and talented and good, he can go so far. She must not make this terrible judgment on her husband just because of the way he played tennis. And yet, his tennis was so much like his life. Gifted, graceful, powerful, showy, flawed, erratic . . .

Please, she thought, make this one good. Childishly, she felt, If this one is good it will be a turning point, a symbol, his whole life will be different. She hated herself for her thoughts and stared blankly at Eleanor, self-consciously alert and desirable in her pretty dress.

Why the hell did she have to come here this Sunday? Jane thought despairingly.

She heard the crack of the racket behind her. The ball whistled past her, hit the tape, rolled undecidedly on top of the net for a moment, then fell back at her feet for a double fault and the set.

"Too bad." She turned and smiled at Stewart, helplessly feeling herself beginning to wonder how she would manage to find the six weeks it would take in Reno. She shook her head, knowing that she wasn't going to Reno, but knowing, too, that the word would pass through her thoughts again and again, more and more frequently, with growing insistence, as the days went by.

She walked off the court with Stewart, holding his hand.

"The shadows," Stewart was saying. "Late in the afternoon, like this. It's impossible to see the service line."

"Yes, dear," Jane said.

THE CLIMATE OF INSOMNIA

CAHILL LET HIMSELF into the silent house, softly closing the door behind him. He hung up his hat and coat, noticing the pleasant, frail smell of damp and night that came up from the cloth. Then he saw the note on the telephone table. It was scrawled in the maid's grave, childish handwriting, which always amused him a little when he saw it. "Mr. Reeves called," the message read. "He must talk to you. Very important, he says."

Cahill started to take up the phone under the mirror. Then he glanced at his watch. It was past one. Too late, he decided; it will have to wait till morning. He looked at himself in the dim glass, noting with satisfaction that his face was still thin and rather young-looking and that his eyes, despite the three drinks after the meeting that night, were not bloodshot. With dissatisfaction, he noted also that the gray was gaining over the black at his temples and that the lines under his eyes were now permanent. He sighed with agreeable melancholy, thinking gently: Older, older . . .

He put out the light and started upstairs. He was a large, bulky man, but he moved gracefully up the carpeted steps of his home. He touched the smooth wood of the banister, smelling the mixed but orderly aromas of living that the house breathed into the still darkness—the lemony fragrance of furniture polish, the autumnal dust of chrysanthemums from the living room, the hint of his wife's perfume, lingering here after the day's comings and goings.

He walked past the adjoining doors behind which slept his son and his daughter. He thought of the dark-haired, seventeen-year-old girl

lying neatly in the quilted bed, the almost womanly mouth relaxed back
into childishness by sleep. He brushed the door with his fingertips sentimentally. As he passed his son's door, he could hear a low, dreamy mumble, then, more clearly, Charlie's voice calling, "Intercept! Intercept!"
Then the voice stopped. Cahill grinned, reflecting on what vigorous,
simple dreams of green fields and sunny afternoons visited the sleep of
his fifteen-year-old son. Cahill, the miser, he thought, quietly going past
the closed doors, counting his treasures at midnight.

He went into the bathroom and undressed there, so as not to wake his
wife. After he had put on his pajamas and slippers, he stood for a moment in front of the medicine chest, debating whether or not to take the
sedative for his stomach that Dr. Manners had prescribed for him on
Tuesday. He patted his stomach thoughtfully. It bulged a little, as it
had been doing for seven or eight years now, but it felt relaxed and
healthy. The hell with it, he thought. I am going to break the tyranny
of the Pill.

Unmedicined, he put out the bathroom light and padded into the
bedroom. He sat carefully on the edge of his bed and silently took off
his slippers, moving with domestic caution, watching his wife, in the
next bed. She did not stir. A little moonlight filtered in through the cur-
tained windows and softly outlined the head against the pillows. She
slept steadily, not moving even when Cahill inadvertently knocked
against the base of the lamp on the bed table, making a resonant metal-
lic noise. She looked young, pretty, defenseless in the obscure light, although Cahill noticed, with a grimace, that she had her hair up in
curlers, leaving only a small bang loose in front as a sop to marital at-
tractions. A woman must be awfully certain of her husband, he thought,
to appear in bed night after night in those grim ringlets. He grinned to
himself as he got under the covers, amused at his strong feelings on the
subject.

As the warmth of the blankets slowly filled in around him, he
stretched, enjoying the softness of the bed, his muscles luxuriously delivering him over to the long weariness of the day. The curtains, folded
in moonlight, rustled gently at the windows. A fragile, tenuous sense of
peace settled drowsily upon him. His son and his daughter slept youthfully and securely beyond the bedroom wall. His first class the next
morning was not until ten o'clock. His wife confidently clamped her
hair in ludicrous curls, knowing nothing could disturb her marriage.
At the meeting, he had spoken quite well, and Professor Edwards, who
was the head of the department, had come over afterward and approved
of it. In the next morning's second class, Philosophy 12, there were three

of the brightest young people in the college—two boys and a girl, and the girl was rather pretty, too—and they had all made it plain that they admired him enormously, and were constantly quoting him in the classes of other instructors. Cahill moved softly under the covers as the pleasant, half-formed images of contentment drifted across his brain. Tomorrow, he thought, will be clear and warmer—that's what the paper says. I'll wear my new brown tweed suit.

Just before he dozed off, he thought of the message from Joe Reeves. Important, he thought a little irritably, important—now, what could that be? He twitched a little, uneasily, nearly coming back to wakefulness. Then, with the steady breathing of his wife sounding from the next bed, he dropped off to sleep.

The siren must have been wailing for some time before Cahill woke, because it entered harshly into his dream, and somehow he was back in London, in the cold billet, and the planes were overhead and the guns were going off, and he had the old feeling that neighbors were dying by chance in burning buildings on the street outside his window. He could feel himself moaning softly and shivering under the blankets and hoping he would be alive in the morning, and then he awoke.

He gazed blindly at the dark ceiling, feeling the cold, unreasonable sweat come out on his body. What is it? he thought. What is it? Then he realized that he was at home, in his own bed, and that the war was over. The noise of the siren howled down the quiet street outside—a police car going to investigate a burglary or pick up a drunk—echoing among the untouched homes, behind their undamaged lawns. He shook his head, irritated with himself for his nervousness. He looked across at his wife. She slept, unperturbed, her breath coming evenly, her arms primly down at her sides, her captured hair untossed on the pillow, happily beyond the reach of sirens and the memory of sirens.

He felt tremblingly awake. Every sound now reached him clearly and with individual significance: the wind troubling the curtains in a starched rhythm; the insubstantial creak of the stairs reacting to the obscure strain that years put upon old houses; the distant crashing of a truck's gears past a faraway street corner, attacking all insomniacs within a radius of a mile; the even intake and exhalation of his wife's breath, too mild to be called a snore but now as annoying as a suddenly loud clock, holding the hours of the night too strictly to account, reminding the would-be sleeper that every moment of wakefulness now would be answered by weariness tomorrow.

Cahill looked at the low radium gleam of the clock on the bed table. Four-thirty. He fell back onto his pillow heavily. Too late to take a sleeping pill. If he took a pill now, he'd be doped all day; he wouldn't have time to sleep it off. The ubiquitous problem of modern civilization, he thought: Is it too late for a pill? Too early? Which way will it be worse tomorrow? All over the country, sleepy, nervous hands reaching out for the clock, troubled heads calculating, It will wear off in six hours, but I have to get up in four. Sleep, he thought, the first great natural resource to be exhausted by modern man. The erosion of the nerves, not to be halted by any reclamation project, private or public.

He lay rigid in his bed, conscious now of various dull, unpleasant sensations in his body. His eyelids felt harsh and granular and seemed to scrape his eyeballs when he blinked. He was too warm, but a damp breeze from the window felt cold and uncomfortable on his forehead. The muscles of his right leg felt cramped, and he had a curious sensation that the tendon running up from his ankle had grown too short during the night. His stomach, just under the diaphragm, was moving in little spasms. He put his hand on the spot and felt the sick, erratic fluttering. He could taste the whiskey he had drunk, high and sour in his throat. That damned siren, he thought. I was feeling so well . . .

Then Cahill remembered the message. It must be something really pressing, he thought, for Joe Reeves to call like that. Cahill couldn't recall another occasion, in all the time he'd known Joe, when Joe had left that sort of a message for him. Early in his college career, Joe had decided to be urbane, debonair, off-hand, and his manner of treating all matters light-handedly and without urgency had become, if anything, more pronounced with the years. And there was nothing off-handed about leaving a disturbing note like that waiting for a man to pick up at one o'clock in the morning. After all, he saw Joe almost every day, at lunch. You'd think a man could wait until noon the next day. Unless it was a matter of the most drastic importance . . .

Cahill twisted restlessly in his bed, trying to keep his eyes closed, sullenly inviting sleep. I will think about this tomorrow, he thought. I will think about this tomorrow. But the restful emptiness of mind he sought evaded him. Unpleasantly, he remembered that Joe had good reason to call him. Subconsciously, he realized, he had been waiting for just such a message, and dreading it. For the twentieth time, he wondered if Joe had heard what he, Cahill, had said about him at the Faculty Club two weeks before. He had felt guilty about it ever since, and ashamed of himself. Even giving himself the excuse that he had drunk a little too much had not helped. In a discussion about teaching techniques, the subject of Joe's popularity with his classes had come up, and Cahill had said cruelly, "Joe Reeves charms his classes into believing they're learning a great deal about economics when what they're really learning is how charming Joe Reeves can be." It was a stupid thing to say, even though it was partly true, and Lloyd and Evarts, who had been listening to him, had chuckled maliciously. Reeves had seemed rather cool for the last two weeks, and Cahill was almost certain that the remark had got back to him, as was almost inevitable in the narrow companionship of a college town. It was too bad. He and Joe Reeves had been close friends for over twenty years, and even though the relationship by now had more the form than the substance of the earlier friendship (how really remain friendly with any man after you are married?), it was silly to risk it for a light and mischievous judgment over a glass of whiskey. And it didn't even represent what Cahill really felt about Reeves. True, there was a superficiality about Reeves, especially in recent years, that came with his easy success with everyone—university presidents, faculty wives, students—but buried beneath that were the shrewdness, the good sense, the honorable instincts that had attracted Cahill to him in the first place. Jealousy, Cahill thought, ashamed of himself. How can a grown man give himself to it so easily? Probably, Cahill thought, Reeves had heard about the remark the very next morning and had mulled it over for the last two weeks, growing angrier and angrier, until this evening, when he had decided to have a showdown with Cahill about it. And Cahill couldn't deny having said it, or disguise in any way the envy and criticism that had called it forth, and that would be the end of the friendship. Joe, for all his easy assurance, was terribly touchy, vain, unforgiving. Cahill pondered on what it would be like not to be friendly with Joe. They had gone through college together, traveled through Europe together, lent each other money, books, opinions, neckties, celebrated together, mourned, exulted together. Even now, they and their wives had dinner together once or twice a week and made free of each other's homes in a carefully preserved informality that was pleasant, if not quite honest, and that kept alive for them a kind of gentle memory of their exciting younger days. And now, for a phrase, for a drop of wanton acid, to lose it all.

Cahill stared bitterly at the ceiling. The tongue, he thought, grows looser and more destructive with the years. Give a talkative man enough listeners and he will bring down stone with his indiscretions.

The curtains scraped in their humble starch at the windows, rasping across his consciousness. Of course, Cahill thought, it is possible that Joe did not hear what I said about him. The message could be about a dozen other things. What things? Joe was so intimately connected with his life, with the people and events of his past, with the problems and promises of the present, that the message might be concerned with his wife, his children, his job, his health, his finances, anything.

Edith moved a little in the next bed, sighing—a forlorn, sleep-bound, homeless, unremembered intake of breath—then settled back into that steady almost snore. Cahill looked over at her shadowed face. She slept, resting, secure, masked, giving no information, volunteering no help. Suddenly, he disliked and mistrusted her. Just to be so calmly and happily unconscious at a moment like this, when her husband lay awake, remorseful and torn by doubt, was a kind of willful absence, a tacit infidelity, a form of uncaring callousness.

Cahill considered his wife coldly. Her face looked surprisingly young. Twenty-eight, you might say—thirty. Frivolity, he thought, has preserved her youth. Age needed some assistance from thought and feeling to carve lines into a face, and in Edith's case age had had to work unaided. Still, she looked pretty, attractive, despite the net and curlers. Why was she so finickingly careful about the way she looked? Not for his sake, that was sure. Another man? How could anyone ever possibly know? Lectures in other towns took him away from home quite often. And then there were the whole long days that were hers to spend unquestioned. Maybe Joe had something to say on this subject—something that couldn't wait.

Unwillingly, Cahill remembered the evening, the week before, at the Crowells', when he'd gone out onto the darkened porch and come upon Joe and Edith sitting close to each other, both of them speaking in low, urgent whispers. They'd seemed embarrassed when they saw Cahill, and Edith had looked startled. And Joe's rather heavy standard joke about being caught in the act had not served to clear the air. Cahill had been troubled for a moment; then he had dismissed it from his mind. There could be a hundred reasons, all innocent, for Joe and Edith to be talking secretly together. They'd always been friendly, right from the beginning. They kissed each time they met, Cahill suddenly recalled. Why was that? He, Cahill, never kissed Joe's wife, except ceremonially, on New Year's Eve and birthdays. The whole modern world, Cahill thought with distaste, kisses too damned much. Sly, without innocence, full of subtle invitation and hidden implication, these public embraces of the married. And, considered coldly, Joe was ripe for experiment. He and his wife didn't get along at all well. She bored Joe; that was plain enough. He was impatient with her in discussions, and she often gave the impression that she had been crying before guests arrived. And she was one of those women who are always going off on long visits to their families, in the Midwest. No woman who had a happy married life remained that attached to her mother and father. And in those bachelor-like periods God knew what Joe did with himself. Also, Cahill remembered, Joe had not been spectacularly celibate in his youth, and in his speech, at least, gave no indication that he had reformed. Another thing: Edith, Cahill remembered, always laughed at Joe's jokes. Damaging, Cahill thought, very damaging. She laughed markedly seldom at his. Well, the truth was he wasn't terribly witty, and a woman might be expected to catch on in eighteen years of marriage. He mourned briefly over the fact that he was not witty, and mourned even more bitterly because now, at the age of forty, he realized it. When he was younger, he had had a higher opinion of himself. Edith had laughed at his jokes then, and so had other people, but now he knew that it was not wit so much as the good humor and vitality of youth that had created an air of cheerfulness about him. That was gone, there was no doubt about that, and it would be unseemly and embarrassing to pretend it wasn't. I must turn, as gracefully as possible, he thought, into a grave old man. Let people like Joe Reeves, who had the talent, say the bright things. He thought of Reeves, with his arched, actor's eyebrows and his dry, knowing delivery, at the center of things at parties, surrounded by eagerly listening, easily laughing people. Of course, Cahill thought bleakly, that's bound to be attractive to women. Also, Reeves wasn't fat. He had never exercised in all his life, but he was still as thin and straight and young-looking as ever. God has a vicious habit, Cahill thought, of putting all the gifts in one basket. Weighing the matter objectively, a woman would have to be crazy to prefer Cahill to Joe Reeves. Cahill thought of all the stories he'd heard, through the years, of good friends who had switched wives. And of the man he had met during the war who had arrived back from Europe to find his brother and his wife waiting for him on the dock with the brave, honorable, up-to-date news that they were in love with each other and wanted to marry, but not without his permission. What permission would he be able to give Joe Reeves and his sleeping wife, and what permission had they already given themselves?

Hating Edith, Cahill twitched under the rumpled covers and groaned softly. I should have taken the pill when I woke up, regardless of the time, he thought.

It might not be Edith, Cahill thought, violently keeping his eyes shut; it might be about the Mitchell girl. There was no doubt about it, he'd been a fool about that, and trouble waited there inevitably. Dora Mitchell had been in one of his classes the year before and had decided that she was in love with him. She was nineteen years old, with a dark, unstable look to her and a kind of solemn, uncertain beauty that Cahill thought most attractive. They had met several times out of class, by accident. (At least, Cahill had thought it was by accident until Dora had told him that she waited for him outside his classroom and on the steps of the library building.) And then, more times than he wished to remember, Cahill had met her in quiet bars and had taken her on drives to the country and to a small inn for tea, fifteen miles out of town. He had been flattered by her devotion, and some obscure, middle-aged hunger in him had fed on her youth and her ingenuous high estimate of him. He had known enough, of course, never to touch her. In fact, he had never even kissed her. But who, seeing them together in a clandestine corner of the Red Wheel Inn—the animated, unaccustomedly high-spirited man and the tall, adoring girl—would ever believe that? And he knew they'd been observed several times. And, besides that, Dora had once or twice wept and rather hysterically declared she could not go on this way and had even suggested, with the melodrama born of a hundred movies full of Other Women, that she have a heart-to-heart talk with Edith.

Cahill shuddered in his bed. It was all too possible that Dora had gone to Reeves, whom she knew, and unburdened herself to him, sobbing and overflowing with grandiose, youthful passion. Perhaps she had been to see Reeves that very night, and that's why Reeves had been so anxious to have Cahill call him. Tenderness, Cahill thought, the blind, many-edged weapon for the cutting down of fools. Bitterly, he made himself imagine what it would be like the day his own daughter, Elizabeth, herself only two years younger than Dora, found out (from a malicious sorority sister, a newspaper report, from a process server for divorce proceedings, from Dora herself over ice-cream sodas after a basketball game). Grotesque, he thought, for a few hours of gentle conversation, for an illusory, ephemeral buttressing of the vanity, for the titillating suggestion of sin without the sin itself, to risk so much! Maybe, he thought despairingly, I should go to a psychoanalyst; the urge for self-destruction has overcome me.

That, of course, was out of the question. He couldn't afford it. He could be as mad as Peter the Great, or as any lunatic screaming in a padded cell, and he couldn't pay the first bill of the rawest young practitioner, just past his initial reading of Freud and Jung. Absolutely sane or raving like an ape in a tree, he would still have to conduct classes in Philosophy 22, Philosophy 12, Philosophy 53A, for Students in Pre-Educational Courses. Money. He thought about money and groaned again. Still three payments on the car. Elizabeth's tuition, due in two weeks. Butter, how many cents a pound? Roast beef once a week, eighty cents a pound, and Charles, his son, and Margaret, the maid, between them devoured four whole ribs each time. Insurance, he calculated in the darkness, in a well-remembered, dreadful nighttime litany, taxes, clothes, dentist, doctor, gifts to his wife's large family, amusement. Perhaps, he thought, Reeves had called him to tell him about promotion. God knew he was up for it, and Old Man Edwards was almost due to retire, and that would leave some room near the top. Reeves was very friendly with the president. Dinner there once a month. First names and private confidences. Reeves had been in to see the president that afternoon. Cahill knew because Lloyd, in his own department, who had all the gossip of the university at his fingertips, had told him so. Perhaps Reeves had been given the good word and wanted to pass it on. Cahill played luxuriously with the idea of promotion. Twelve, fifteen hundred more a year. No more Philosophy 53A, the dullest course in the curriculum. No eight-o'clock classes. Then the glow passed. Probably, he thought, it's the other way around. The president had never been any more than polite to him, and it was to be remembered that he had been passed over twice on the promotion lists, for Kennedy and O'Rourke, younger men than he. It wouldn't be too surprising, all things considered, if they had decided to get rid of him. He was far from being the most popular instructor on the campus. To be absolutely honest, he wouldn't blame them for firing him. Ever since he'd come back from the war, the job had bored him. Not that there was anything else that he particularly wanted to do. Just sit, perhaps, and stare into an open fire. Drink more whiskey than was good for him. Not pretend to anyone that he knew anything much, or not pretend he thought it was valuable that anyone learn anything much. Dangerous doctrine for professors, assistant professors, instructors, tutors. Probably others had caught on. Come to think of it, the last time he had seen the president at a faculty meeting, the president had been . . . frosty. That was the word—frosty. Purge by frost. Execution, university style. The polite death among the library shelves. He could almost hear Joe Reeves' troubled voice on the phone, warning him, trying to break it to him gently, trying to cheer him up with lies about other jobs, in other colleges.

Cahill lay in bed thinking about what it would be like not to have a job. Rent, taxes, roast beef, tuition, clothes. The advantage of marrying a rich wife. Nothing, finally, was crucial. There was always the net of fat relatives to fall back on, like a high-wire artist who slipped in the circus. Edith's father had worked for the Pennsylvania Railroad and had retired on a pension of a hundred and thirty-five dollars a month. Not much of a net there. Cahill thought of the rich wives he might have married. Rowena . . . Rowena what? Twenty years ago, in Chicago. Shipping. Father in Lake steamers. How could a man be expected to marry a girl named Rowena? Also, she had weighed a hundred and seventy pounds. No exaggeration. Maybe a hundred and eighty. Amorous as the gilded fly, too. Who wanted a wife like that, Lake steamers or no Lake steamers, especially at that weight? Anyway, that had been his one chance of marrying into wealth. Some people were lucky, of course. They met pretty girls, very nice, whose fathers controlled the Chase National Bank or owned mining empires in Central America. Still, if he had married Rowena—Rowena Grumman, that was it; good God, what a name—he wouldn't be trembling like this tonight. Seven hundred dollars in the bank, debts three fifty-five, and that was that. One month and then relief. For this relief, very little thanks. He supposed that nine-tenths of the people in the country walked, as he did, on this thin edge of disaster all their lives, smiling, dissembling, not sleeping some nights, hoping their nerve would hold out as they saw the edge crumbling, crumbling. And then the people in China, scouring sidewalks for lost grains of rice, running before the armies with two pans and a blanket on their backs, dying politely, with Oriental good manners, of starvation. Maybe Reeves ought to call them up, too. Perhaps he had an important message for the Chinese as well. Still, all the philosophical identification in the world would not help if the frost set in. Somehow, he thought regretfully, I should have arranged things better. Somewhere, I missed a chance, was too lazy, too stupid, too complacent.

Of course, Reeves might be calling him about something entirely different. Maybe Elizabeth. Reeves had a nephew, name of Richard, and he and Elizabeth had been seeing a good deal of each other recently. Fact was, last Saturday night Cahill had surprised them kissing at the door. Quite a shock. Item: What do you do when you see your seventeen-year-old daughter kissing the nephew of your best friend? Bringing up a daughter was a little like sitting over one of those dud bombs that had been dropped into cellars during the war. A year might go by, two years. Nothing might happen. Or, the world was full of women who had gone bad, and at one time they had all been seventeen and some father's dewy darling. Ministers' daughters, admirals' daughters, daughters of the leaders of society. How could any father know what obscure, shameful invitations of the flesh his daughter was accepting and succumbing to among the college pennants and dimity and framed photographs in the next room? And Elizabeth was no help. She had always been a secretive, self-willed child, going her own way, disdainful of help or advice, not lying, exactly, but never telling any more of the truth than she was forced to. He tried to think of her as someone else's daughter, in order to get an objective impression of her. Handsomely developed, prematurely womanly, he would have to say, with a promising, challenging look in her eye, a hidden, guarded sensuality, very much like her mother's. Oh, God, he thought torturedly, I hope the message isn't about her!

Or Reeves might want to talk to him about Charlie. Cahill considered the question of Charlie. In addition to eating an enormous amount of expensive roast beef when he got the chance, Charlie did very badly in his studies (was it possible that he was fundamentally stupid?) and got into trouble regularly with all authorities. A smooth-tongued truant, a brawler in schoolyards, a mischievous vandal in locker rooms, Charlie had been the occasion, again and again, for long visits of apology on the part of Cahill to parents of broken-nosed children, angry and insulted teachers, even, once, to the police station, when Charlie had broken into the country-club tennis shop and stolen a dozen cans of balls and two lengths of chrome twist. At what moment did the high-spirited schoolboy turn into the juvenile delinquent? Cahill thought of Charlie's sly, blond, unruly face. Consider your son objectively. What did you see? The insolence of the radio-and-comic-book age. The violence and irresponsibility of the double- and triple-featured generation of movie gangsters and movie sensualists. The restless superficiality of the book haters, who slid into whiskey, divorce courts, bankruptcy, worse, as the years wore on. Cahill had a vision of himself at the age of seventy, supporting his son, paying various blonde women alimony for him, bailing him out of magistrates' courts, and trying to hush up charges of drunken driving and cop-fighting. Tomorrow, he thought gloomily, I am going to have a serious talk with that young man. Though who knew what good it might do? John Dillinger's father probably had several talks with his son on the farm back in Indiana, and old Mr. Capone no doubt had the parish priest in to talk sternly to his dark-eyed boy in the crowded home in Brooklyn.

Cahill hoped that Reeves was not going to talk to him about Charlie when they finally met the next day.

The bed now seemed intolerably warm, and Cahill could feel the sweat collecting in the crease of his chest. He threw back the covers.

They made a loud, electric crackle and static electricity from the friction jumped in strange blue flashes around him. Edith stirred a little at the noise but did not wake. Cahill glared gloomily at her, listening to her breathe. If she had been home, as she had said she was going to be, that evening, it would have been she who had talked to Reeves. He'd have given her some inkling of what it was he wanted to talk to Cahill about and he'd have been spared this agonizing night of conjecture. Tomorrow, Cahill thought, I'm going to damn well ask her a question or two, too. No, he thought, I'll be sly. If I seem to be quizzing her, she'll get suspicious or angry and sulk for days, and there'll be hell to pay around the house, and I'll have to give in to her on everything from now to Easter Sunday. I'll be nonchalant, elaborately offhand—pretend to be reading the paper, mix it up with questions about the kids, surprise her into revelations, if there are any. Then he was ashamed of himself for plotting this way against his wife, sleeping so trustfully and innocently in the next bed. He had an impulse to go over to her and hold her in his arms. He even sat up, tentatively. Then he thought better of it. Edith was terribly grouchy when he woke her in the middle of the night, and could be depended on to make him suffer for it the next day. He stared at her, resenting her. The business of the two beds, now. Until the war, they'd slept in one big old bed, as married people should. You felt really married, two people defending themselves as a unit against the world, if each night you retired into the warm fortress of the marital bed. Two beds brought with them the inevitable warning of division, oneness, loneliness, rejection. And when he'd come back from the war, Edith had said she couldn't sleep that way any more, she'd got too used to sleeping alone. And, like a fool, he'd consented. The two beds, with the extra mattresses and blankets, had cost nearly three hundred dollars, too. All his terminal-leave pay. Your bonus for fighting the war was that your wife made you sleep alone. Beds fit for heroes to sleep in—singularly.

It was silly to worry about that any more. It was a battle he'd lost, definitely, a long time ago. Each night to its own insomnia. Tonight, he thought—by now a little light-headed and oratorical, even in his thoughts—we take up the problem of the message of Joseph Reeves.

The thing was to systematize it, attack the problem scientifically. Like *Time* magazine: Business, Politics, National Affairs, Science, Religion, Sex. Everything in its neat, crisp department. Two minutes with each one and you're ready with enough facts and opinions to carry you until the next publication date.

National Affairs. In the twentieth century, Reeves had said at lunch three days before, National Affairs had become a euphemism for butchery. Butchery accomplished, butchery in progress, butchery contemplated. Slaughter in three tenses, with a corresponding rise in the budget. In the last few months, Reeves had become more and more obsessed with the idea of war. At the same lunch, they'd had a gloomy conversation about the possibility that it would break out soon. Reeves, so optimistic about other things, somberly dug around in newspapers and magazines to find new and disturbing items about the imminence of conflict and the dreadful new tools that might be employed. Cahill had even tried to avoid Reeves recently, because it was a subject he preferred not to reflect on. And his friend's dark flood of statistics about the range of atomic missiles and the mortal potential of biologic agents was not calculated to improve the delicate lunchtime appetite. Also, Reeves had made an unpleasant survey of the various and all too frequent occasions in history on which whole nations and, in fact, whole civilizations had committed suicide, deducing from that that it was entirely possible, and, indeed, probable, that in the next few years just such a widespread immolation would take place. To preserve his sanity, Cahill thought, resentfully trying to crowd Reeves' apocalyptic arguments out of his mind, a man must keep himself from speculating on these matters. Impotent and haunted, frozen in the slow, massive tide of events beyond his control, the night waker could only hope to ignore the question, or at least think about it in daylight, when the nerves were steadier. War, he thought angrily and helplessly, war. He remembered the cemeteries of Normandy and the sound shells made going over his head. At this moment, in a dozen places on the crust of the earth, machine guns were flicking and men were joyfully and devotedly putting other men to death and inviting the Americans, the Russians, the Berbers, the Malayans, the Yugoslavs, the Finns, and the Bulgars to join them.

Read a newspaper, listen to a news broadcast, wake for a quarter hour in your own bed some time before dawn, and death came familiarly to hand. When he'd come home in 1945, he'd thought all that was behind him. My limit, he always said—not seriously, but meaning it, too—is one war. But other people, of more influence, seemed to have other limits. It was one thing, at the age of thirty-three, bravely to don the uniform and sail off to a relatively old-fashioned war, in which comprehensible weapons like machine guns and bombs were being used. It was quite another, seven years later, a sedentary forty, to contemplate exposing yourself to the atom and the microbe, feeling, too, all the while, that your well-run home, enclosing your wife and children, might at any moment dissolve in radioactive dust or become the harbor for the germs of plague. He looked over at his wife, comfortably at rest. How, he wondered, does anyone sleep this year?

The dim light of dawn was washing through the curtains now. God, Cahill thought, his hot eyes resentfully taking it in, I am going to be a wreck today. Masochistically, he continued with his list. Politics. There we have a subject, he reflected, to keep a man's eyes open a night or two. According to Lloyd again, after Reeves had visited the president's office that afternoon, he had been called into a secret session of the committee of state senators who were down from the capital investigating Communist influence on the campus. Lloyd, who had been active in several questionable organizations for years, and who didn't trust Reeves, had been none too happy about that. "A company man," Lloyd had said resentfully, in Cahill's presence. "He'd sell his best friend for a smile from the stockholders." Lloyd had peered meaningfully at Cahill when he said it, too, and Cahill was sure that the phrase "his best friend" had not been a random choice of words. Cahill thought of various things that Reeves might have told the committee and twitched uneasily. Back in the years before the war, when Communism was an almost respectable doctrine, Cahill had been on various committees with people he was sure belonged to the Party, and had let his name be used again and again on a flood of well-meaning petitions and statements that, if not promulgated by the Communists, certainly had their endorsement. Once, he and Reeves had even gone to a kind of polite, open Party meeting, at which several people he knew had made amorphous speeches about Communism's being twentieth-century Americanism, and stuff like that. He had even been invited to join, he remembered, although he couldn't remember who had actually come up to him and spoken the fateful words. He hadn't joined, and he'd never gone to another meeting, but what if the committee, armed with informers' information, demanded of him whether he had ever attended a meeting and if he had ever been asked to join. What would he do? Perjure himself, and say he had never gone, or tell the truth, and leave himself open to the next question. Was Professor Kane there? Did Mr. Ryan, instructor in chemistry, make a speech about the working of the Communist Party? Will you kindly look over this list of names and check off the ones you can swear were present? What do you do in a situation like that? Professor Kane had been there and had made a speech, but Cahill knew that he had quietly resigned from the Party at the time of the Pact and had had no more to do with it. Still, who knew what Kane had told the committee? Kane was a friend of his, and needed the job. And if Cahill told the truth, Kane would be out of his job, disgraced, in a month. And poor Ryan. He'd been suspended on suspicion already, and his wife was sick, and he'd had to pay a lawyer to defend him. And, Communist or no, he'd always seemed to Cahill to be a very decent, shy, undangerous man. Cahill had given Ryan fifty dollars toward his defense, secretly, in cash. It was hard to understand just why. He was opposed to Ryan's politics, but he liked Ryan and felt sorry for him, and fifty dollars was not much, one way or another. Cahill had told Reeves about the fifty dollars and had even asked Reeves to help, too. Reeves, coldly, saying Ryan had it coming to him, had refused. What if Reeves had been trapped into saying something about the fifty dollars to the committee? What could Cahill tell them when he was questioned? How would he act? Would he be brave, considered, honorable? Just what was honorable in a situation like this? Was there honor in perjury? Or did honor lie in destroying your friends? Or destroying yourself? Did he actually believe that Ryan, for example, was an innocent, idealistic fellow, or did he believe that Ryan, the soft-voiced, scholarly, shyly smiling family man Ryan, was a potential traitor, a patient murderer, a dangerous conspirator against all the values that he, Cahill, held dear? I am too weary, Cahill thought pettishly, to decide this this morning. What if they asked about the meeting? What day was it? What year? Who invited you? The mists of memory shifted thickly around the fact. Whatever you answered was bound to be wrong. And if you said honestly, "I don't remember," how would that look on the record and in the newspapers? Like evasion, guilt, worthy only of disbelief and disdain.

So much for the crisp, neat two minutes of Politics. It was simpler in a magazine, where another issue was coming out in seven days, with another capsule of highly polished, anonymous, streamlined facts. A new man, Cahill thought, should be published every week, under a different title, anonymously. Each issue built around a different fact. The honorable man. The perjured man. The sensual man. The devout man. The economic man. Fifty-two times a year, something new and interesting in each copy. No irreconcilable facts to be found in any single volume. For Christmas, we plan to give you the friendly man, to be followed shortly by the betraying man, all in fine, unlimited editions. And, as a dividend to our subscribers, bound in blood, stitched with nerve ends, and illustrated by the leading artists of the age, with copious notes, the doubtful man, on which our editors have been working continuously for three hundred years at great personal expense.

There was a soft, sighing sound at the window, and Cahill saw that the wind had grown stronger and that it had begun to snow. A thin shower of snow sifted in through the open window, making a pale pattern on the floor. Fair and warmer, Cahill thought angrily, that's what the forecasters said. The liars of science, portentously surrounded by inaccurate instruments, confidently deluding you with false visions of the future. Like Dr. Manners, armed with stethoscope and X ray, patting him heartily on the back last Tuesday, telling him of course he occasionally must expect to feel a twinge here, a pain there; he was not as young as he used to be. How many men died on Sunday who had been told during the week by their doctors that they were not as young as they used to be? The breezy assumption on the part of the medical profession that agony was the ordinary condition of life. Manners, he thought resentfully, would be considerably less breezy with himself if it were his chest that trembled to the tone of pain, secret and until now distant, but there, warning, definite. Experimentally, Cahill lifted his left arm and stretched it. Again, as always in the last few months, there was the small answering pressure, dull, lurking, across his chest, across his heart. "A slight irregularity," Manners had said. "Just nerves. Nothing to worry about." Nothing for Manners to worry about, perhaps. And the constriction across the stomach; that, too, according to Manners, was nerves. Nerves, the modern equivalent for Fate, the substitute for the medieval Devil, which attacked mankind in the form of obscure, and often mortal, ills. Nerves, the perfect formula for the lazy diagnostician. Or—and Cahill could feel his breath catching in his throat at the thought—perhaps Manners, out of kindness, was hiding the true information from him. A hearty clap on the back, an innocuous prescription for sugar water and belladonna, and, after the door had closed, a thoughtful, sorrowful shrug, and the fateful entry in the case history of Philip Cahill "Prognosis negative."

Cahill put the palm of his hand under his pajama jacket, on the warm skin of his abdomen, as though by the touch of flesh on flesh he might discover the dreadful secret that lay there. Within him, under his hand, he could feel a faint, erratic quivering. Not good, he thought, not good at all. His mind touched regretfully on the edge of the word he was afraid to say. The papers were so damned full of it, the posters on the buses, even the radio. And if it occurred in the stomach, it was fatal at least eighty per cent of the time, and you almost never found out about it before it was too late. Maybe that was what Reeves had called about. Maybe Manners had gone to Reeves and explained to him and asked what Reeves thought should be done. The services that friends had to do for each other. You start out as gay children, playing tennis with each other, racing each other across the lakes of summer, roaring jubilantly together on your first drunks, and twenty years later, all that far in the past, you have to go in and announce to your friend that his death is at hand.

Ridiculous, Cahill thought. I'm not going to lie here any longer. He got out of bed and stood up. His legs felt weary and uncertain, and there was the tense, stretched sensation in his stomach as he put on his robe and slippers. He looked over at Edith. She still slept, the rhythm of her breathing unchanged. Walking slowly, his slippers shuffling across the rug, he went silently out of the bedroom. He descended the stairs, holding the banister, shivering a little in the night-frozen house. In the hall below, he went over to the telephone, on the table under the mirror. He hesitated, staring at the phone. The clock in the living room said ten minutes to seven. He picked up the phone and dialed Joe Reeves' number. While he listened to the long succession of buzzes in the receiver, he stared at himself in the mirror. His face was haggard, his eyes thick and glazed and encircled completely by muddy blue shadows. His rumpled hair looked slack and lustreless, his face exhausted and—hunted. He looked for a moment, then turned his back on the mirror.

Finally, there was the sound of someone picking up the receiver at the other end. Whoever it was fumbled a long time with the instrument, and Cahill said impatiently, "Hello! Hello!" Then he heard a sleepy, dark voice mumbling irritatedly, "Mr. Reeves' residence. Who that calling?"

"Hello," Cahill said eagerly. "Violet?"

"Yes. This Violet. Who calling?"

"Violet," Cahill said, making his voice even and clear, because he remembered with what suspicion Violet regarded the telephone, "this is Mr. Cahill."

"Who?"

"Cahill. Mr. Cahill."

"It's an awful early hour of the mawnin', Mr. Cahill," Violet said aggrievedly.

"I know," Cahill said, "but Mr. Reeves has a message for me. He especially asked me to call him as soon as I could. Is he up yet?"

"I dunno, Mr. Cahill," said Violet. He could hear her yawn enormously at the other end of the wire. "He's not here."

"What's that?"

"He's gone. Went last night. He and Mis' Reeves. They gone for the weekend. I'm the only livin' soul in the house. And"—her voice took on a tone of impatient complaint—"I'm freezin' here in my nightshirt in this drafty old hall."

Cahill could sense that Violet was on the verge of hurling the receiver down on the hook—an amusing trick of hers, with which she concluded telephone conversations in mid-message. It was not amusing now. "Violet," he said urgently, "don't hang up. Where did they go?"

"Don't ask me," Violet said. "They didn't tell me. You know Mr. Reeves. He was sittin' around the house last night, real restless, like he is, and all of a sudden he jumped up and said to Mis' Reeves, 'Let's get into the car and get away from here for a couple of days.' They just packed one little bag. Mis' Reeves was wearing slacks and she didn't even bother to change 'em. They just gone for a ride, I guess. They'll be back by Monday, never you worry."

Slowly, Cahill put the receiver down. He looked up and saw that Elizabeth was standing at the foot of the stairs, in an almost transparent nightgown, her bathrobe carelessly open and hanging loose from her shoulders. Her dark hair was down, flowing thickly around her throat. Her face was creamy with sleep and her eyes were half closed in an amused, almost condescending smile. "Daddy," she said, "who on earth are you calling at this fantastic hour? One of your other girls?"

Cahill stared dully at her. Through the frail rayon of her nightdress, he could see, very plainly, the swell of her breasts, rising generously from the exposed, rich skin of her bare bosom. "None of your business," he said harshly. "Now go upstairs. And when you come down again, make sure you're decently covered! This is your home. It is not a burlesque house! Is that clear?"

He could see the incredulous, hurt grimace gripping her features, and then the blush, rising from her bosom, flaming on her cheeks. "Yes," she said faintly. "Yes, Daddy." She turned, hugging her robe around her ashamedly. Cahill watched her walk slowly and painfully up the stairs. He wanted to say something, call her back, but by now he knew there was nothing to say and that the child would not come back.

He went into the living room and sank into a chair, feeling cold. Wildly, he contemplated the thought of living until Monday.

THE GREEN NUDE

As a young man, Sergei Baranov, although he preferred painting large still lifes of red apples, green pears and very orange oranges, joined the Red Army and did a mild amount of damage in several engagements against the Whites around Kiev. He was a sturdy, good-humored, dreamy youth who did not like to refuse anyone anything, and since all his friends were joining the Revolution he went along and served faithfully and cheerfully, eating the soldier's black bread, sleeping on the soldier's straw, pulling the trigger of his ancient rifle when the people around him ordered him to do so, advancing bravely when everyone else was advancing and running in fear of his life when that seemed like the necessary thing to do. When the Revolution was over, he retired from the military, equipped with a modest decoration for an action at which he was not present, and took up quarters in Moscow and began once more to paint red apples, green pears, and very orange oranges. All his friends were enthusiastically convinced that the Revolution was an excellent thing, and Sergei, never one to strike out on his own, amiably and decorously concurred. The truth was that he was only really interested in his highly colored fruits and vegetables and when, in his studio or in the café which he frequented, discussions would start about Lenin and Trotsky or the new economic program, he would laugh his hearty and agreeable laugh and say, bashfully, "Eh, who knows? It is for the philosophers." Besides, being a decorated hero of the Revolution and an artist to boot, he was treated well, and was assigned an excellent studio with a skylight and permitted heavy laborer's rations. His paintings, too, were warmly approved by everyone, since he had the trick of making all his garden products seem marvelously edible. They sold without delay and his work was to be seen in the homes and offices of many quite-important officials of the new regime, warm and appetizing globs of color on the otherwise bleak and functional walls.

When, in 1923, he met and conquered an ample and beautiful young lady from Soviet Armenia, his painting took a new turn. He began to paint nudes. Since his technique remained the same, despite the change in subject matter, his success increased in leaps and bounds. As edible as ever, his paintings now combined the most satisfactory features of the orchard and the harem, and examples of his work, rosy, healthy, and very round, were much sought after by even more important officials of the regime.

He undoubtedly would have continued thus to this day, happily producing a succession of canvases of hearty, lightly clad, appetizing girls, alternating with piled heaps of oversized purple grapes and bananas, going from success to success, honor to honor, if he had not met, at a literary party, the woman who was finally to become his wife.

Anna Kronsky was one of those sharp-featured and overpoweringly energetic women that the liberation of women from the nursery and kitchen has turned loose on the male world. Angular, voracious, and clever, with a tongue like an iron clapper in a new bell, racked by indigestion and a deep contempt for the male sex, she was the sort of woman who in this country would run a department store or report wars for the Luce publications. As one of her friends said of her, in attempting to put his finger on the exact difference between Anna and her more gentle contemporaries, "Anna does not make up her face when she goes out in the morning—she hones it."

In Moscow, at the time Sergei met her, she had gravitated inexorably into the education system. With twenty-three day nurseries for the children of working parents under her supervision, and a staff of over five hundred cowed men and women, she had already made her mark on the new population of the growing state. The children under her care were known as the cleanest and most precocious in the Soviet Union, and it was not until 1938 that a routine survey of neurotic diseases disclosed the fact that the graduates of Anna Kronsky's immaculate creches led all other population groups of the nation by three to one in absolute nervous breakdowns.

In a necessarily incomplete study, prepared by a thoughtful Artillery Colonel during a slow month on the Southern front in 1944, the estimate was made that the ministrations of Anna Kronsky to the rising generation had cost the Red Army more manpower than a full armored brigade of the Nazi 9th Army. However, the study was accepted with a grain of salt by the Colonel's superiors, since his OGPU dossier revealed that he had been the lover of Miss Kronsky between the dates of August third and August seventh, 1922, and had sent into headquarters a fervent request for transfer to Archangel on August eighth of the same year.

It was this lady, who, flanked by a heroic poet and an aging test-pilot, set her eyes on the sturdy Baranov as he came through the door, and, in one moment of iron speculation, made the decision that was to transform the painter's life. Her carborundum eyes glittering, she crossed the room, introduced herself to her prey, ignored the beautiful girl from Soviet Armenia who had come with Baranov, and started the necessary process which resulted three months later in marriage. Just what it was that made Baranov so immediately attractive to her, none of her friends could decide. Perhaps she saw, in the painter's simple docility and good-humored health, evidence of a fine digestion and an uncomplicated nervous system, excellent attributes for the husband of a busy lady executive who came home each night jangled and worried with the day's thousand cares. Whatever the reasons, Anna left no escape possible for Sergei. He had a tearful scene with his beloved Soviet Armenian, painted one last, pink, fruity nude, and helped carry the poor girl's meager belongings to the new room Anna had managed to find for her in a slum section three-quarters of an hour away from the center of town. Then Anna moved in, bringing with her a new bed-spread, three packing cases of pamphlets and reports, and a large goose-neck lamp.

The marriage seemed from the beginning to be a thoroughly happy one, and there was only one noticeable change in Baranov, outside of a subtle, but growing tendency toward silence in company. He no longer painted nudes. Not one painting, not one sketch, not even a wash from the waist up, of the ripe, unclad female form, came from his studio. Confined once more entirely to the vegetable world, he seemed to have mastered a new understanding of the problems of the apple, the orange, and the pear. As edible as ever, a new dust seemed to be powdered over his work, a haunting and melancholy fragrance, as though the fruit he chose to paint came now from autumnal boughs, the last sweet bounty of the closing year, the final, nostalgic yield of trees and vines through whose dying leaves and frozen branches the cruel winds of winter were already moaning.

This new development in Baranov's work was greeted with respectful praise by critics and public alike and examples of the new phase were hung in many museums and public places. Success did not change him, however. More silent than ever, he painted steadily, experimenting with beets and pumpkins in ever darker reds and yellows, going everywhere with his sallow and brilliant wife, listening with model attention night after night as she monopolized conversations in literary, artistic, political, educational, and industrial circles. Once, it is true, at the request of his wife, he went to one of her nurseries and started a painting of a group of children he saw there. He painted for about an hour, then put his brush down, tore the canvas in half and had it burned in the stove, and went into the men's room, where he was reported sobbing uncontrollably. This story was not believed by anyone, as it was retailed by a young teacher who had crossed swords with Anna Kronsky and who was removed later at her instigation as unreliable. Whatever the truth of the matter was, Baranov returned to his studio and went back to his beets and pumpkins.

It was about this time that he took to painting at night, using the gooseneck lamp that Anna had brought with her as part of her dowry. They had their own apartment by now, as a result of their double importance, more than a mile away from the studio, and the sturdy though now slightly bent figure of the painter, trudging through the snow late at night was a common sight on the almost deserted streets between his home and his studio. He became very secretive, locking his door at all times, and when friends asked him about his current work, he would merely smile vaguely and politely and change the subject. Anna, of course, never asked him about his work, as she was a very busy woman, and it was not until the opening of his one-man show, an affair attended by many of the intellectual élite of the government and the arts, that she saw for the first time the painting that had engaged her husband for the past many months.

It was a nude. But it was like no nude that Baranov had painted before. There was no touch of pink anywhere on the enormous and frightening canvas. The prevailing color was green, that green that lurks in the sky before cyclones and hurricanes, sallow, lurid, oppressive to the eye. The figure itself, of a slack-breasted and lank-haired woman with a wrinkled abdomen and stringy but somehow violent loins, was also done in mottled green, and the staring and demonic eyes under the dry brow were another shade of the dominant hue. The mouth, the most fearful feature of the work, was done in dead black and somehow gave the startling impression of howling speech, as though the painter had caught his model in a full flood of maniac oratory. The mouth seemed to fill the canvas, indeed the entire room, with a tumbling, morbid, glittering torrent of horrid rhetoric, and it was to be noticed that the viewers attempted, uneasily, to avoid, as much as possible, looking at that particular section of the work. The background, so different from Baranov's usual arrangement of carefully painted, richly figured materials, was spume and wreckage, jagged stony ruins of temples and tenements against a green and charcoal sky. The only recognizable link with Baranov's past work was a cherry tree in the right foreground. But the tree was stunted and uprooted; a green fungus ate at the branches; a thick and snakelike vine wound murderously around the suffering trunk, and minutely painted green worms munched among the unripe fruit. The entire effect was of madness, genius, energy, disaster, sorrow, and despair.

When Anna Kronsky Baranov entered the room, people were standing in muted groups, staring with horrid fascination at the new painting. "Great," she heard Suvarnin, the critic for *The Sickle,* mutter. And, "Incredible," whispered Levinoff, the painter, as she passed him.

Baranov himself was standing in a corner, shyly and excitedly accepting the awed congratulations of friends. Anna stared incredulously at the painting, then again at her husband, who, with his rosy complexion and pleasantly smiling, obedient face, looked not one whit different from the man she had known all these years. She started to go over to congratulate him, although the painting seemed very unlifelike to her, but she was intercepted by two men who ran a tractor factory in Rostov, and she became so interested in lecturing to them about tractor manufacture that she forgot to mention anything about the painting to Baranov until much later in the evening.

From time to time, various of the guests stole sidelong and speculative glances at Anna, especially when she happened to be standing in front of her husband's masterpiece. Although Anna was conscious of their regard and also conscious of something vaguely disturbing in their eyes, she dismissed the feeling, since she was well-used by now to glances of varying intensity from her subordinates in the halls and offices of the nurseries under her command. The real reason for the hurried, measuring appraisals of the people in the gallery she never discovered and no one in the Soviet Union had the courage to apprise her of it. The wild and nightmare face that topped the terrible body of the green nude bore a family resemblance to Anna Kronsky that no amount of stylization on the part of the artist could erase. Sisters, twin souls, the painted and the living woman existed in a hideous relationship that escaped the notice of none. The only other person in Moscow who did not know that the artist had painted his wife's portrait was the man who went home obediently each night with her. Ignorant and happy in his new glory, Sergei Baranov took his wife to the ballet that night to celebrate and later ordered three bottles of champagne at a café, most of which was drunk by the two tractor men from Rostov.

The week following the opening of the show marked the highpoint of Sergei Baranov's early life. Feted, pointed out wherever he went, especially when accompanied by his wife, saluted in the press, urged to create murals to cover acres of walls, he swam in a bright stream of praise. The critic Suvarnin, who had barely acknowledged his greeting before this, even deigned to come to Baranov's studio to interview him, and, breaking all precedent, appeared sober.

"Tell me," said Suvarnin, squinting at Baranov through his pale, cold eyes, those eyes which had riddled holes in so many canvases before this, "tell me how a man who has only painted fruit before this comes to do such a painting."

"Well," said Baranov, who had recaptured some of his early loquacity and expansiveness in the past week, "Well, it happened something like this. As you know, if you have seen any of my painting recently, my work has become more and more melancholy."

Suvarnin nodded thoughtfully, agreeing.

"The palette became more and more subdued. Brown, dark brown, entered increasingly into the canvases. The fruit . . . well, the truth is, the fruit began to be withered, frostbitten, sad. I would come here to my studio and I would sit down and cry. For an hour. Two hours at a time. All by myself. I began to dream every night. Dreams of death, dreams of trains going out of stations, dreams of boats leaving me on the dock, in the rain, dreams of being buried alive and being sniffed at by dark brown foxes and other small animals . . ." Baranov spoke with lively animation, as a perfectly healthy man might describe symptoms of a dreadful disease which he has suffered and proudly conquered. "The worst dream, and one that I had over and over again, was that I was in a small room and it was crowded with women, only women. All the women could talk, but I couldn't. I tried. I moved my lips. My tongue quivered between my teeth. The conversation around me filled the air deafeningly like locomotive whistles and French horns. And I could not make a sound. You have no idea how terrible this simple thing can be. It was like being committed each night to a new kind of awful prison. I began to fear going to bed. I would come and stare at the blank canvas on my easel, at the arrangement of potatoes and eggplants on which I intended to work, and I could not move my fingers to the brushes. An artist, as you know, must create out of his emotions. How could I transfer how I felt into the image of an eggplant, into potatoes? I felt I was lost. I felt I would never be able to paint again. I contemplated suicide."

Suvarnin nodded. He even thought of making notes, something he hadn't done for twenty years, since he was of the firm opinion that accuracy in reporting was the foe of creative criticism. He put his hand into his pocket for a pencil, but discovered he had neglected to bring one along with him. He took his hand out of his pocket and gave up the thought of taking notes.

"Suicide," Baranov repeated, flushed with joy at having the redoubtable Suvarnin pay such close attention to his confession. "I moaned. I shrieked." Baranov knew that he had done no such thing, and had, in fact, merely gloomed silently in front of the easel, but he felt that these active expressions of passion would sit well with the critic, as indeed they did. "I cried out. I despaired." Suvarnin moved restively, glancing instinctively at the vodka bottle on the table, and licking the corner of his mouth, and Baranov hurried on, feeling anxiously that he had perhaps gone a little far with his synonyms. "I slashed out blindly at the canvas. I did not guide my hand. I did not search for colors. I did not look at the potatoes or the eggplant. My terrors painted through me. I was the instrument of my dreams. I hardly looked to see what I was doing. I painted all night long, one night after another. I did not know what I was doing . . ." By now Baranov had forgotten that he was trying to make an impression. By now he was letting the simple truth pour out. "All I knew was, that as the painting grew, a great weight was being lifted from me. My subconscious was being delivered from its prison. When I slept, I no longer dreamed of being struck dumb or being nosed by dark brown foxes. Now my dreams were of vineyards in the springtime and large-breasted young women I wished to approach on the streets. Finally, when I was finished, and I sat back and looked at the green nude and the ruins, I was as surprised by what I had done as if I had come into my studio and found that another man, a complete stranger, had used my easel while I was away on holiday. And I was grateful to him, whoever he was. And I was grateful to the green lady on the canvas. Between them," Baranov said simply, "they had delivered me from Hell."

Suvarnin stood up and silently shook the painter's hand. "Out of anguish," he said finally, "comes the great art. Out of the depths of despair only can we reach to the skies. Look at Dostoyevsky."

Baranov nodded, although a little uneasily, as he had tried to read

The Brothers Karamazov three times and had never got past page 165. But Suvarnin did not press the point. "Read my article on Saturday," he said modestly. "I think you will be pleased."

"Thank you," Baranov said humbly, resolving to call Anna immediately Suvarnin left to impart to her the heady news. "I am in your debt."

"Nonsense," said Suvarnin, with the concision and gift for a phrase that had made his reputation secure in a dozen cities. "Art is in your debt. And now," he asked, "what is the next painting going to be?"

Baranov smiled happily. "Cherries," he said. "Six kilos of red cherries in a wicker basket. They are being delivered here at two o'clock from the market."

"Good," said Suvarnin. They shook hands once more and the critic departed, with only one tentative glance at the vodka bottle.

Baranov sat down, waiting dreamily for the arrival of the cherries, thinking, as he sat there, Perhaps it is time that I started a scrapbook for my reviews.

On Saturday, Baranov opened the magazine with trembling fingers. There, on the page with Suvarnin's photograph, was a streaming black title, "FILTH IN THE GALLERIES." Baranov blinked. Then he began to read. "Last week," Suvarnin had written, "the Counter-Revolution struck one of its most audacious blows at Russian Art. From the bestial brushes of one, Sergei Baranov, who has until now concealed his heretical infamies under bushels of rotten fruit, and who now feels that he can come out boldly and shamelessly in his true colors, we have received a nauseating sample of decadent, bourgeois 'art.'"

Baranov sat down, trying to get air into his aching lungs. Then he forced himself to read on. "In this gangrenous excrescence," Suvarnin continued, using what Baranov, even in his extremity, recognized as a pet phrase, "the dying world of Capitalism, allied with the Trotskyist bandits, has served notice on the Soviet Union that its minions and agents have wormed their way into the heart of the fatherland's cultural life. By what treachery and corruption the notorious Baranov managed to get his monstrosity hung on a gallery wall, we shall leave to the public prosecutor to discover. But while waiting for the reports on the investigation that will surely take place, we of the art world must join ranks to defend ourselves. We must not permit the insidious Baranov and others of his ilk, slavishly devoted to the fads and aberrations of their plutocratic masters, to desecrate our walls with these samples of dada-istic despair, reactionary cubism, retrogressive abstractionism, surrealistic archaism, aristocratic individualism, religiostic mysticism, materialistic Fordism."

Baranov put the magazine down carefully. He did not have to read further. He had read it often enough before so that he could have recited the rest of the piece without glancing once more at the page. He sat on his stool, his world in ruins, staring unhappily at the six kilos of bright red cherries, arranged prettily in their wicker basket.

There was a knock on the door. Before he could say, "Come in," the door opened and Suvarnin came in. The critic went directly to the table and poured himself five fingers of vodka and drained it. Then he turned to Baranov. "I see," he said, gesturing toward the still-open magazine, "that you've read the piece."

"Yes," said Baranov hoarsely.

"Here," said Suvarnin, taking some manuscript pages out of his pocket. "You might be interested in reading what I wrote originally."

Baranov numbly took the sheets and stared at them. Suvarnin poured himself another drink while Baranov read through swimming eyes, ". . . a great new unfolding of talent . . . a courageous grappling with the problems of doubt and disillusionment which are the beginning of understanding . . . a blazing display of technical ability . . . a pioneering plunge into the depths of the modern psyche in paint . . ."

Baranov pushed the pages aside. "What . . . what happened?" he asked dimly.

"The Committee," Suvarnin said. "They saw your painting. Then they saw my review. They asked me to make certain changes," he said delicately. "That Klopoyev, the president of the Committee, the one who has made eighty-four portrait heads of Stalin, he was especially anxious."

"What's going to happen to me now?"

Suvarnin shrugged. "Nothing good," he said. "As a friend, I advise you . . . leave the country." He went over and picked up the manuscript sheets of his first review. He tore them into small pieces, made a little pile of them on the floor and put a match to them. He watched until the flame had burnt itself out, then carefully scattered the ashes with his foot. He finished the vodka, drinking this time directly from the bottle, and went out.

Baranov did not dream that night. He was up all night listening to his wife.

She spoke vigorously from eight in the evening until eight the next morning, a full-length address in which every relevant topic was stated and developed with a balance and fullness which Edmund Burke, in

another country and a more leisurely century, would have wholeheart-
edly admired. She had been notified that afternoon that their apartment
was being taken over by a cellist with a cousin on the Central Committee and she had been removed from her position as head of the
nursery system at five P.M. and relegated to the post of assistant
dietician at a ward for backward and criminally inclined children in
a penal camp some thirty kilometers outside Moscow. With these facts
as a springboard and with her audience of one wanly rooted against the
bedpillows, she ran through her eloquent twelve hours of recrimina-
tion without noticeably pausing for breath and without repeating herself.

"Ruined," she said clearly, with no sign of hoarseness, as the eight
o'clock factory whistles sounded outside, "we are completely ruined.
And for what? For an idiotic, senseless daub that no one can make
head or tail of! A man wants to be a painter. All right! It is childish
—but all right, I do not complain. A man wants to paint apples. Silly?
All right. But apples can be understood. Apples do not have political
implications. Apples do not turn into bombshells. But this . . . this
naked witch . . . Why? Why have you done this to me? Why?"

Dumbly, Baranov leaned against the pillows, staring at his wife.

"Come," Anna called. "Come, you must have something to say. You
can't sit without speaking forever. Say something. Say one word."

"Anna," Baranov said brokenly, "Anna . . . please . . ." He hesitated.
He wanted to say, "Anna, I love you," but he thought better of it.

"Well," Anna demanded. "Well?"

"Anna," Baranov said, "let us have hope. Maybe it will all blow
over."

Anna glared at him coldly. "Nothing," she said, "nothing blows
over in Moscow."

Then she got dressed and went out to the penal camp to report to
her new job in the kitchen there.

Anna's prediction proved only too well-founded. Attacks which made
Suvarnin's article seem like an unrestrained paean of praise by com-
parison, were loosed on him in newspapers and magazines all over the
Soviet Union. *The New Masses*, in New York City, which had never
before mentioned his name, printed, opposite a full page pen and ink
drawing of Stalin by Klopoyev, a heated diatribe which called him,
among other things, a "traitor to the working class of the world, a
lecher after Western fleshpots, a Park Avenue sensationalist, a man
who would be at home drawing cartoons for *The New Yorker*." In a

follow-up article, a writer who later joined the Catholic Church and went to work for Metro-Goldwyn-Mayer preparing scenarios for a dog star, used the Baranov case to point out that Michelangelo had been the first proponent of Socialist-realism. In Moscow, a painters' congress, led by the fiery Klopoyev, dropped Baranov from the Painters' Union by the customary vote of 578 to nothing. On one morning, between the hours of ten and twelve, every painting of Baranov's disappeared from every wall in Russia on which they had been hanging. Baranov's studio, which he had held for ten years, was taken from him and given to a man who drew signs for the Moscow subway. Two large plainclothesmen appeared and followed Baranov day and night for three months. His mail was always late and always opened. Anna Kronsky discovered a dictaphone under the sink in the kitchen in which she now worked. Old friends crossed over to the other side of the street when they spotted Baranov in the distance and he no longer found it possible to get tickets for the ballet or the theater. A woman he had never seen before claimed that he was the father of her illegitimate child and when the case came to trial he lost and was ordered to pay 90 rubles a week for her support and only barely avoided being sent to a work-camp.

Sensing which way the wind was blowing, Baranov put an old camel's brush and the gooseneck lamp into a bag, and haggard and thin, with Anna at his side, fled the country.

Six months later, in the summer of 1929, Baranov and Anna were established in Berlin. The climate of the German capital at that time was most propitious for artists, and Baranov, who had set to work industriously painting oranges, lemons, and apples, in his early edible style, enjoyed an immediate success. "We will be very happy here," Anna prophesied, correctly. "You will paint only fruits and vegetables. You will use dark colors very sparingly. You will avoid nudes and political implications. You will keep your mouth shut and permit me to do all the talking."

Baranov was only too happy to obey these simple and salutary injunctions. Aside from a certain vagueness of outline, a kind of subtle mist, which seemed to arise from the artist's subconscious hesitancy to come out too definitely on any subject, even the exact location of a lemon on a tablecloth, his work compared very favorably with the first canvases he had done when he returned from the Revolution. He prospered. His cheeks filled out and grew rosy again and he developed a little paunch. He took a small chalet for the summer in Bavaria and rented a superb studio near the Tiergarten. He learned to sit in raths-kellers and drink Munich beer and say, with a hearty laugh, when politics was discussed, as it often was in those days, "Eh, who knows? That is for the philosophers."

When Suvarnin, who had slid from official suspicion to official ostracism in Moscow, as a result of his first, unpublished tribute to Baranov, appeared in Berlin, looking somewhat the worse for wear, Baranov generously took him in and let the critic live in the spare room under the studio, even managing a warm, reminiscent chuckle when Suvarnin told him that the green nude had the most conspicuous place in a new museum for decadent art in Leningrad.

Anna found herself a position as a physical-training instructress in one of the new organizations for young women that were springing up at the time and soon became noted for the vigor of her programs. She turned out battalions of iron-thewed females with enormous hips who could march eighteen hours a day through plowed country and who could, bare-handed, disarm strong men equipped with rifles and bayo-nets. When Hitler came to power, she was called into the government and given command of the entire women's training program for Prussia and Saxony. Much later, the Bureau of Statistics for the Women's Motherhood-and-National-Honor-Front put out a report disclosing that the graduates of Anna's classes led all other Germans in incidence of miscarriage and death in childbirth seven to one, but by that time, of course, the Baranovs had left the country.

Between 1933 and 1937, the life the Baranovs led was very much as it had been in the good days in Moscow. Baranov painted steadily, and his ripe fruit was hung on many famous walls, including, it was said, the Fuehrer's private gas-proof bomb shelter under the Chancel-lery, where it considerably brightened the otherwise rather austere atmosphere. Much in demand socially because of Anna's prominence and Baranov's good humor, the couple attended a constant round of parties, at which Anna, as usual, monopolized the conversation, holding forth at great length and with her famous clarity and sharpness on such matters as military tactics, steel production, diplomacy and the upbringing of children.

It was during this period, friends later recalled, that Baranov seemed to grow more and more silent. At parties, he would stand near Anna, listening attentively, munching on grapes and almonds, answering ques-tions with absent-minded monosyllables. He began to fall off in weight, too, and his eyes had the look about them of a man who slept poorly and had bad dreams. He began to paint at night, locking his door, pulling down the blinds, his studio lit by the functional glare of the gooseneck lamp.

It came as a complete surprise, both to Anna and the Baranovs' friends when the green nude was discovered. Suvarnin, who had seen both the original and the Berlin canvas, has said that, if possible, the second was even better than the first, although the main figure was, in conception at least, almost identical in the two paintings. "The anguish," said Suvarnin, who at that time was employed by the government as a roving critic of official architecture, a post, he sensibly figured, in which errors of judgment could not be as spectacular and dangerous as those that might be made in the field of easel painting, "the anguish by now in the painting seemed intolerable. It was heroic, gigantic, god-size. Baranov had plunged to the sub-cellars of despair. [Perhaps it was because I knew of Baranov's nightmares, particularly the one in which he could not say a word in a roomful of conversing women, that I got so strong an impression that this was all humanity, locked in dumbness, protesting, wordlessly and hopelessly, against the tragic predicament of life.] I liked especially the nice new touch of the dwarf hermaphrodite nude, done in pink, being nosed in the left foreground by a brace of small dark brown animals."

It is doubtful that Baranov was rash enough to contemplate showing the painting publicly. [Whatever necessity drove him to re-creating his masterpiece was adequately served by its completion and his memories of the damage he had suffered in Moscow must have been too fresh to allow him to court disaster in Berlin by unveiling his work.] But the matter was taken out of his hands, by the Gestapo, who, in their routine weekly search of the homes and offices of all people who read foreign newspapers (a habit to which Baranov was foolishly addicted) came upon the green nude on the very day Baranov had finished it. The two detectives were simple fellows, but they were well-enough imbued with National Socialist culture to sense defection and heresy here. Arranging for reinforcements and throwing a cordon around the building, they called the chief of the bureau which dealt in these matters. One hour later, Baranov was under arrest and Anna had been removed from her post and sent to work as an assistant dietician in a home for unwed mothers near the Polish border. As was the case in Moscow, no one, not even a fire-eating Colonel in an SS Armored division with whom Anna had quite an intimate relationship, ever dared point out to Anna that her husband had not gone out of his home for his model.

Baranov was questioned by the Gestapo for one month. The questioning, more or less routine, during the course of which Baranov lost three teeth and was twice condemned to death, was aimed largely at getting Baranov to deliver over his lists of accomplices and fellow-conspirators and to confess to certain acts of sabotage in nearby airplane factories which had been committed in the past several months. While he was in the hands of the Gestapo, Baranov's painting was put on public view in a large exhibition arranged by the Propaganda Ministry to acquaint the population with the newest trends in decadent and un-German art. The exhibition was enormously successful and was attended by a hundred thousand more people than had ever witnessed a showing of paintings in Berlin until that time.

On the day that Baranov was released from jail, considerably stooped and doomed to eat soft foods for some months to come, the leading critic of the Berlin *Tageblatt* came out with the official judgment on the painting. Baranov bought a paper and read, "This is Judaeo-Anarchism at its most insolent peak. Egged on by Rome (there was a new addition in the background of the ruins of a village church), with the connivance of Wall Street and Hollywood, under orders from Moscow, this barbaric worm of a Baranov, né Goldfarb, has insinuated himself into the heartland of German culture in an attempt to bring discredit on our German health and our German institutions of justice. It is a pacifistic attack on our Army, Navy and Air Force, a vile Oriental slander of our glorious German women, a celebration of the lecherous so-called psychology of the Viennese ghetto, a noxious fume from the Paris sewers of the French degenerates, a sly argument from the British Foreign office for their bloodthirsty Imperialism. With our usual reticent dignity, we Germans of the German art world, we monitors of the proud and holy German soul, must band together and demand, in respectful, firm, reserved tones that this gangrenous excrescence on our national life be expunged. Heil Hitler!"

That night, in bed with Anna, who had luckily managed to get a three-day leave to welcome her husband home, listening to what was now a standard twelve-hour lecture on his wife's part, Baranov looked back with something like fondness on the comparatively delicate phrasing of the *Tageblatt* critic.

The next morning he saw Suvarnin. Suvarnin noted that despite the physical ravages of the past month, his friend seemed to have regained some secure inner peace, some great lessening of the weight of an impalpable but soul-destroying burden. Also, despite the night of oratory he had just passed through and the thirty days of police handling, he seemed rested, as if he had been sleeping well recently.

"You shouldn't have done it," Suvarnin said with mild reproach.

"I know," said Baranov. "But I couldn't help it. It just came out."

"Do you want some advice?"

"Yes."

"Leave the country," Suvarnin said. "Fast."

But Anna, who liked Germany and was convinced that she could win her way up the ladder once more, refused. And it was inconceivable to Baranov that he go without her. But in the next three months, he was twice beaten up severely on the street by SA gangs and a man who lived three blocks away who resembled him slightly was kicked to death by five young men by mistake; all his paintings were collected and officially burned; he was accused by his janitor of homosexuality and was given a suspended sentence after a trial of four days; he was arrested and questioned for twenty-four hours when he was caught carrying a camera past the Chancellery on the way to a pawnshop and the camera was confiscated. All this would not have shaken Anna in her determination to remain in Germany, but when proceedings were put under way to have Baranov sterilized as a threat to the German bloodstream, she crossed the border with him into Switzerland in the middle of a snowstorm.

It took the Baranovs more than a year to get to America, but as Sergei walked down 57th Street in New York City, staring at the windows of the art galleries, in which the most extreme styles of painting, from lurid surrealism to sugary naturalism were peacefully on display, he felt that all his trials and troubles had been worthwhile because they had eventually brought him to this harbor. Gratefully and emotionally he made application within the first week for citizenship for Anna and himself. As further demonstration of his new-born allegiance he even took to watching the Giants play at the Polo Grounds, although it never became quite clear to him what, exactly, the players were doing around second base, and he patriotically developed a taste for Manhattan cocktails, which he rightly assumed to be the native drink.

The next few years were the happiest of the Baranovs' lives. Critics and patrons alike found that the soft-voiced Russian brought a mysterious European flavor, melancholy and classic, to homely American tomatoes and cucumbers, and his shows almost invariably sold out at good prices. A large wine company used Baranov grapes on all their labels and advertising and a large Baranov still life of a basket of oranges was bought by a California packing company and blown up into twenty-four sheets and plastered on billboards from one end of the country to the other. Baranov bought a small house in Jersey, not far from New York, and when Suvarnin turned up, having left Germany with a price on his head because he had been overheard, in his cups, saying that the German Army could not reach Moscow in three weeks, Baranov gladly invited the critic to live with them.

Heady with his new sense of freedom, Baranov even went so far as to paint a nude, very pink and firm-fleshed, from memory. But Anna, who by this time was attached to a nationally circulated news magazine as an authority on Communism and Fascism, was very firm in her handling of the situation. She ripped the painting to shreds with a breadknife and dismissed the robust, apple-cheeked Czech girl who did their cooking, although the girl went to the rather extreme length of having a reputable physician testify to her virginity in an attempt to retain her position.

Anna's success in America, where men have long been conditioned to listen to women, and where her particular brand of crisp, loquacious efficiency was regarded with stunned fascination by her male colleagues, was even more dazzling than any she had enjoyed in Europe. By the end of the war the magazine for which she worked had put her in charge of the departments of Political Interpretation, Medicine for Women, Fashion, Books, and, of course, Child Care. She even got a job for Suvarnin on the magazine, reviewing motion pictures, a job he held until the autumn of '47, when he lost his eyesight.

Anna became a well-known figure in Washington, testifying at great length as a friendly witness before several important committees, discoursing on such varied subjects as the sending of subversive literature through the mails and the effect of sex education in the public school systems of several Northern states. She even had the exhilarating experience of having her girdle pinched in an elevator by a senior Senator from the West. As was inevitable, she was invited to countless dinners, receptions, congresses, and parties, and to all of them Baranov faithfully escorted her. In the beginning, living in the free atmosphere of literary and artistic America, Baranov had seemed to shed the taciturnity that had set in during the last part of his years in Moscow. He laughed frequently, he sang old Red Army songs without much urging, he insisted on mixing Manhattans at the homes of his friends, he spoke up on all subjects with disarming and agreeable gusto. But after a while he began to sink back into his old silences. Munching peanuts, occasionally muttering a monosyllable, he would stand by Anna's side at parties, watching her closely, listening with strange concentration as she spoke out, clearly and fully, on the destiny of the Republican Party, trends in the theater, and the intricacies of the American Constitution. It was at this time, too, that Baranov began to have trouble sleeping. His weight fell off and he began to work at night.

Half-blind as he was, Suvarnin saw what was happening. Excitedly, he waited for the great day. In advance, he composed once more the stirring tribute to his friend's genius that he had first written so long ago in Moscow. Suvarnin was one of those writers who hates to see any word of his go unpublished and the fact that nearly twenty years had passed since he had been forced to jettison his appreciation only made him more eager to get it finally into print. Also, it was a great relief to write about painting again, after the long months of Betty Grable and Van Johnson.

On the morning that, Anna being in the city and the house quiet, Baranov came to him and said, "I would like you to come into my studio," Suvarnin found himself trembling. Stumbling a little, he hurried out of the house and followed Baranov across the driveway to the barn which had been converted into a studio. He peered through his darkening eyes for a long time at the enormous canvas. "This," he said humbly, "this is the great one. Here," he took out some manuscript papers from his pocket, "here, read what I have to say about it."

When he had finished reading his friend's eulogy, Baranov wiped a tear from his eye. Then he went over to Suvarnin and kissed him. There was no question this time about hiding the masterpiece. Baranov rolled it up carefully, put it in a case, and with Suvarnin at his side, drove in with it to his dealer. However, by silent agreement, he and Suvarnin tactfully refrained from telling Anna anything about the matter.

Two months later Sergei Baranov was the new hero of the world of art. His dealer had to put up velvet ropes to contain the crowds who came to see the green nude. Suvarnin's tribute now seemed pale and insubstantial in the torrent of adjectives poured out by the other critics. Picasso was mentioned in the same sentence as Baranov countless times and several writers brought up the name of El Greco. Bonwit Teller had six green nudes in their windows, wearing lizard shoes and draped with mink. A Baranov Grapes and Local Cheese, which the painter had sold in 1940 for two hundred dollars brought 5600 dollars at an auction. The Museum of Modern Art sent a man around to arrange about a retrospective show. The World Good Will Association, whose letterhead boasted the names of many dozen legislators and leaders of industry, requested it as the leading item in a show of American art which they proposed to send, at government expense, to fourteen European countries. Even Anna, to whom, as usual, no one dared mention the interesting resemblance of painter's wife and painter's model, seemed pleased, and for a whole evening allowed Baranov to speak without interrupting once.

At the opening of the show of American art, which was being revealed in New York preliminary to its trip overseas, Baranov was the center of attention. Photographers took his picture in all poses, toying with a Manhattan, munching on a smoked salmon canapé, talking to the wife of an Ambassador, looking up gravely at his masterpiece, surrounded by admirers. It was the crowning moment of his life and if he had been struck dead that midnight he would have expired happily. In fact, later on, looking back at that evening, from the vantage point of the events that followed, Baranov often bitterly wished that he *had* died that night.

For, one week later, on the floor of Congress, an economy-minded representative, enraged at what he called the irresponsible money-squandering proclivities of the Administration, which had put up good American dollars to send this sinister travesty on America to our late allies, demanded a thorough investigation of the entire enterprise. The lawmaker went on to describe the main exhibit, a green nude by a Russian foreigner, as sickening twaddle, Communist-inspired, an insult to American womanhood, a blow to White Supremacy, atheistic, psychological, un-American, subversive, Red-Fascistic, not the sort of thing he would like his fourteen-year-old daughter to see either alone or accompanied by her mother, decadent, likely to inspire scorn for the Republic of the United States in foreign breasts, calculated aid to Stalin in the cold war between America and the Soviet Union, a slap in the face to the heroes of the Berlin air lift, injurious to trade, an offense to our neighbors to the South, artistic gangsterism, a natural result of our letting down our immigration barriers, proof of the necessity of Federal censorship of the press, the radio, and the movies, and a calamitous consequence of the Wagner Labor Relations Act.

Other developments followed quickly. A conservative, mellow-voiced radio commentator, broadcasting from Washington, announced that he had warned the country over and over again that New Deal paternalism would finally spawn just such monstrosities and hinted darkly that the man responsible for the painting had entered the United States illegally, being put ashore from a submarine by night with a woman he alleged to be his wife.

Several newspaper chains took up the matter in both their editorial and news columns, sending their least civil employees down to the Baranov farm to question the culprit and reporting that a samovar stood in a place of honor in the Baranov living room and that the outside of the studio was painted red. One editor demanded to know why no cover from the *Saturday Evening Post* was included in the collection of paintings. Leaders of the American Legion filed a formal protest against sending the paintings in question over to the lands where our boys had fought so bravely so shortly before and pointing out that Baranov was not a veteran.

The House Committee on un-American Activities served a subpoena on both Baranovs and put a tap on their telephone wires, hiring a man who knew Russian to monitor it. At the hearing, it was brought out that Baranov in 1917, 1918, and 1919, had served in the Red Army and the Bureau of Immigration was publicly denounced for allowing such doubtful human material into the country. Ministers of all three religions circulated a petition calling upon the government to halt the shipment of the paintings to Europe, a place which all knew was badly shaken in the department of religious faith as it was. A well-known jurist was quoted as saying he was tired of modern art experts and that he could paint a better picture than the green nude with a bucket of barn paint and a paperhanger's brush. A psychiatrist, quoted in a national magazine, said that the painting in question had obviously been done by a man who felt rejected by his mother and who had unstable and violent tendencies which were bound to grow worse with the years. The FBI threw in a squad of investigators who conducted interviews with seventy-five friends of the Baranovs and discovered that the couple had subscriptions to the Book-of-the-Month Club, *House and Garden,* and the *Daily News,* and that they often spoke Russian in front of their servants.

A cross was burned on the Baranov lawn on a rainy evening, but even so, wind-blown sparks ignited a privy on a neighbor's property and reduced it to the ground. Irate, the neighbor fired a shotgun at the Baranovs' Siamese cat, nicking it twice in the rear.

The local Chamber of Commerce petitioned the Baranovs to move away, as they were giving the town a bad name, just at a time when they were trying to attract a plumbing factory to set up business there.

A Communist civil-liberties group held a mass meeting to raise funds for Baranov, who denounced them. They, in turn, denounced the Baranovs and demanded that they be deported to Russia.

The Treasury Department, attracted by the commotion, went over Baranov's last five income-tax returns and disallowed several items and sent in a bill for an additional eight hundred and twenty dollars. The Baranovs' citizenship papers were carefully scanned and it was revealed that Mrs. Baranov had lied about her age.

At a radio forum on the subject "What Should We Do with the Green Nude" Baranov's name was hissed by the audience every time it was mentioned and the next day the postmaster in a small Massachusetts town announced that a mural of cranberry pickers and fishermen that Baranov had painted for the postoffice in the days of the WPA, would be torn down.

Anna Baranov, due to the unwelcome publicity given her, was deprived by her editor first of the Department of Political Interpretation, then of Medicine for Women, then of Books and Fashion, and finally, of Child Care, after which she was allowed to resign.

Baranov moved through all this in a dull haze, dreading more than anything else the long hours of mounting rhetoric which were loosed on him by his wife between midnight and eight each morning. Occasionally, huddled for disguise into the turned-up collar of his overcoat, he would go to the gallery where the disputed painting still hung, and would stare mournfully and puzzledly at it. When, one day, the director of the gallery took him aside, and told him, not unkindly, that in response to certain pressures, the authorities had decided to disband the show and not send it to Europe after all, he wept.

That night, he was sitting alone, slumped in a wooden chair in the middle of his cold studio. The blinds were drawn because of the habit the small boys of the neighborhood had developed of hurling rocks through the windows at any moving shadows they saw within. In Baranov's hand he held a small world atlas, opened to a map of the Caribbean and Central America, but he did not look at it.

The door opened and Suvarnin came in. He sat down without a word.

Finally, Baranov spoke, without looking at his friend. "I was at the gallery today," he said, his voice low and troubled. "I looked at the painting for a long time. Maybe it's my imagination," he said, "but I thought I noticed something."

"Yes?"

"Suddenly," Baranov said, "the painting reminded me of someone. I thought and thought who it could be. Just now I remembered. Suvarnin," he twisted anxiously in his chair to face the critic, "Suvarnin, have you ever noticed that there was any resemblance there to my wife, Anna?"

Suvarnin said nothing for a while. He closed his movie-destroyed eyes thoughtfully and rubbed his nose. "No," he said, finally. "Not the slightest."

Baranov smiled wanly. "Oh, what a relief," he said. "It would be a terrible shock to her." He spread the book on his knees and stared down at the small red and blue countries of the warm middle Atlantic. "Suvarnin," he said, "have you ever been to the Caribbean?"

"No," said Suvarnin.

"What sort of fruit," Baranov asked, peering at the map, "do you think a man could find to paint in Costa Rica?"

Suvarnin sighed and stood up. "I will go pack my things," he said heavily, and went out, leaving Baranov alone in the cold studio, staring at his brightly colored, repetitious map.

TIP ON A DEAD JOCKEY

LLOYD BARBER was lying on his bed reading *France-Soir* when the phone rang. It was only two o'clock in the afternoon, but it was raining for the fifth consecutive day and he had no place to go anyway. He was reading about the relative standing of the teams in the Rugby leagues. He never went to Rugby games and he had no interest in the relative standings of Lille and Pau and Bordeaux, but he had finished everything else in the paper. It was cold in the small, dark room, because there was no heat provided between ten in the morning and six in the evening, and he lay on the lumpy double bed, his shoes off, covered with his overcoat.

He picked up the phone, and the man at the desk downstairs said, "There is a lady waiting for you here, M. Barber."

Barber squinted at himself in the mirror above the bureau across from the bed. He wished he was better-looking. "Did she give her name?" he asked.

"No, Monsieur. Should I demand it?"

"Never mind," Barber said. "I'll be right down."

He hung up the phone and put on his shoes. He always put the left one on first, for luck. He buttoned his collar and pulled his tie into place, noticing that it was frayed at the knot. He got into his jacket and patted his pockets to see if he had cigarettes. He had no cigarettes. He shrugged, and left the light on vindictively, because the manager was being unpleasant about the bill, and went downstairs.

Maureen Richardson was sitting in the little room off the lobby, in one of those age-colored plush chairs that fourth-rate Parisian hotels furnished their clientele to discourage excessive conviviality on the ground floor. None of the lamps was lit, and a dark, dead, greenish light filtered in through the dusty curtains from the rainy street outside. Maureen had been a young, pretty girl with bright, credulous blue eyes when Barber first met her, during the war, just before she married Jimmy Richardson. But she had had two children since then and Richardson hadn't done so well, and now she was wearing a worn cloth coat that was soaked, and her complexion had gone, and in the greenish lobby light she seemed bone-colored and her eyes were pale.

"Hello, Beauty," Barber said. Richardson always called her that, and while it had amused his friends in the squadron, he had loyally stuck to it, and finally everyone had picked it up.

Maureen turned around quickly, almost as though he had frightened her. "Lloyd," she said, "I'm so glad I found you in."

They shook hands, and Barber asked if she wanted to go someplace for a coffee.

"I'd rather not," Maureen said. "I left the kids with a friend for lunch and I promised I'd collect them at two-thirty and I don't have much time."

"Sure," Barber said. "How's Jimmy?"

"Oh, Lloyd . . ." Maureen pulled at her fingers, and Barber noticed that they were reddened and the nails were uneven. "Have you seen him?"

"What?" Barber peered through the gloom at her, puzzled. "What do you mean?"

"Have you seen him?" Maureen persisted. Her voice was thin and frightened.

"Not for a month or so," Barber said. "Why?" He asked it, but he almost knew why.

"He's gone, Lloyd," Maureen said. "He's been gone thirty-two days. I don't know what I'm going to do."

"Where did he go?" Barber asked.

"I don't know." Maureen took out a pack of cigarettes and lit one. She was too distracted to offer the pack to Barber. "He didn't tell me." She smoked the cigarette avidly but absently. "I'm so worried. I thought maybe he'd said something to you—or that you'd bumped into him."

"No," Barber said carefully. "He didn't say anything."

"It's the queerest thing. We've been married over ten years and he never did anything like this before," Maureen said, trying to control her voice. "He just came to me one night and he said he'd got leave of absence from his job for a month and that he'd be back inside of thirty days and he'd tell me all about it when he got back, and he begged me not to ask any questions."

"And you didn't ask any questions?"

"He was acting so strangely," Maureen said. "I'd never seen him like that before. All hopped up. Excited. You might even say happy, except that he kept going in all night to look at the kids. And he's never given me anything to worry about in the—the girl department," Maureen said primly. "Not like some of the other boys we know. And if there was one thing about Jimmy, it was that you could trust him. So I helped him pack."

"What did he take?"

"Just one Valpak," Maureen said. "With light clothes. As though he was going off on a summer vacation. He even took a tennis racket."

"A tennis racket," Barber nodded, as though it were the most natural thing in the world for husbands to take tennis rackets along when disappearing. "Did you hear from him at all?"

"No," Maureen said. "He told me he wouldn't write. Did you ever hear of anything like that?" Even in her anguish, she permitted herself a tone of wifely grievance. "I knew we shouldn't have come to Europe. It's different for you. You're not married and you were always kind of wild anyway, not like Jimmy—"

"Did you call his office?" Barber asked, interrupting. He didn't want to hear how wild people thought he was, or how unmarried.

"I had a friend call," Maureen said. "It would look too fishy—his wife calling to ask where he was."

"What did they say?"

"They said that they had expected him two days ago but he hadn't come in yet."

Barber took one of Maureen's cigarettes and lit it. It was the first one in four hours and it tasted wonderful. He had a little selfish twinge of gratitude that Maureen had come to his hotel.

"Lloyd, do you know anything?" Maureen asked, worn and shabby in her damp, thin coat in the foggy green light.

Barber hesitated. "No," he said. "But I'll put in a couple of calls and I'll telephone you tomorrow."

They both stood up. Maureen pulled on gloves over her reddened hands. The gloves were worn and greenish black. Looking at them, Barber suddenly remembered how neat and shining Maureen had been when they first met, in Louisiana, so many years before, and how healthy and well-dressed he and Jimmy and the others had been in their lieutenants' uniforms with the new wings on their breasts.

"Listen, Beauty," Barber said. "How are you fixed for dough?"

"I didn't come over for that," Maureen said firmly.

Barber took out his wallet and peered judiciously into it. It wasn't necessary. He knew exactly what was there. He took out a five-thousand-franc note. "Here," he said, handing it to her. "Try this on for size."

Maureen made a motion as though to give it back to him. "I really don't think I should . . ." she began.

"Sh-h-h, Beauty," Barber said. "There isn't an American girl in Paris who couldn't use five *mille* on a day like this."

Maureen sighed and put the bill in her pocketbook. "I feel terrible about taking your money, Lloyd."

Barber kissed her forehead. "In memory of the wild blue yonder," he said, pocketing the wallet, with its remaining fifteen thousand francs, which, as far as he knew, would have to last him for the rest of his life. "Jimmy'll give it back to me."

"Do you think he's all right?" Maureen asked, standing close to him.

"Of course," Lloyd said lightly and falsely. "There's nothing to worry about. I'll call you tomorrow. He'll probably be there, answering the phone, getting sore at me for sucking around his wife when he's out of town."

"I bet." Maureen smiled miserably. She went through the cavelike murk of the lobby, out into the rainy street, on her way to pick up the two children, who had been sent out to lunch at the home of a friend.

Barber went to his room and picked up the phone and waited for the old man downstairs to plug in. There were two suitcases standing open on the floor, with shirts piled in them, because there wasn't enough drawer space in the tiny bureau supplied by the hotel. On top of the bureau there were: a bill, marked overdue, from a tailor; a letter from his ex-wife, in New York, saying she had found an Army pistol of his in the bottom of a trunk and asking him what he wanted her to do with it, because she was afraid of the Sullivan Law; a letter from his mother, telling him to stop being a damn fool and come home and get a regular job; a letter from a woman in whom he was not interested, inviting him to come and stay with her in her villa near Eze, where it was beautiful and warm, she said, and where she needed a man around the house; a letter from a boy who had flown as his waist-gunner during the war and who insisted that Barber had saved his life when he was hit in the stomach over Palermo, and who, surprisingly, had written a book since then. Now he sent long, rather literary letters at least once a month to Barber. He was an odd, intense boy, who had been an excitable gunner, and he was constantly examining himself to find out whether he and the people he loved, among whom he rather embarrassingly included Barber, mostly because of the eight minutes over Palermo, where living up to their promise. "Our generation is in danger," the boy had typed in the letter on the bureau, "the danger of diminution. We have had our adventures too early. Our love has turned to affection, our hate to distaste, our despair to melancholy, our passion to preference. We have settled for the life of obedient dwarfs in a small but fatal sideshow."

The letter had depressed Barber and he hadn't answered it. You got enough of that sort of thing from the French. He wished the ex-waist-gunner would stop writing him, or at least write on different subjects. Barber hadn't answered his ex-wife, either, because he had come to Europe to try to forget her. He hadn't answered his mother, because he was afraid she was right. And he hadn't gone down to Eze, because no matter how broke he was, he wasn't selling that particular commodity yet.

Stuck into the mirror above the bureau was a photograph of himself and Jimmy Richardson, taken on the beach at Deauville the summer before. The Richardsons had taken a cottage there, and Barber had spent a couple of weekends with them. Jimmy Richardson was another one who had attached himself to Barber during the war. Somehow, Barber was always being presented with the devotion of people whose devotion he didn't want. "People hang on to you," a girl who was angry at him once told him, "because you're an automatic hypocrite. As soon as somebody comes into the room, you become gay and confident."

Jimmy and he had been in bathing trunks when the picture was snapped, and Barber was tall and blessed with a blond, California kind of good looks next to Jimmy, who seemed like a fat, incompetent infant, standing there with the sunny sea behind him.

Barber peered at the photograph. Jimmy didn't look like the sort of man who would ever be missing from anywhere for thirty-two days. As for himself, Barber thought wryly, he looked automatically gay and confident.

He leaned over and took the picture down and threw it into a drawer. Then, holding the phone loosely, he stared around him with distaste. In the glare of the unshaded lamp, the dark woodwork looked gloomy and termite-ridden, and the bed, with its mottled velours spread, the color of spoiled pears, looked as though it had been wallowed on by countless hundreds of obscenely shaped men and women who had

rented the room for an hour at a time. For a second, he was piercingly
homesick for all the rooms of all the Hotel Statlers he had slept in and
all the roomettes on trains between New York and Chicago, and St.
Louis and Los Angeles.

There was a whistling, static-like sound in the phone, and he shook
himself and gave the number of the George V. When he got the George
V, he asked for M. Smith, M. Bert Smith. After a while, the girl said
M. Smith was no longer at the hotel. Barber asked hurriedly, before the
girl could cut him off, whether M. Smith was expected to return shortly
or if he had left a forwarding address. No, the girl said after a long
wait, he was not expected to return and there was no forwarding
address.

Barber hung up. He was not surprised about Bert Smith. He was a
man who wandered mysteriously from hotel to hotel, and he might have
used a half-dozen names besides Smith since Barber had spoken to him
last.

With a conscious effort, Barber tried not to think about Jimmy
Richardson or his wife, who was called, as a friendly squadron joke,
Beauty, or about Jimmy Richardson's two small sons.

Scowling, Barber went over to the window. The winter rain of Paris
was seeping down into the narrow street, blurring it with the unpro-
ductive malice of city rain, chipping colorlessly at the buildings opposite, making it impossible to imagine what they had looked like
when they were new. A workman was unloading cases of wine from a
truck, looking persecuted by the weather, the Paris sound of clinking
bottles muted and made hollow and mournful by the flow of gray
water from the skies and from window ledges and signs and rolled
awnings. It was not a day for a husband to be missing, for a friend to
be missing. It was not a day to be alone or to have only fifteen thousand
francs in your pocket or to be in a narrow hotel room where the heat
was off from ten in the morning till six at night. It was not a day to be
without a job or cigarettes or lunch. It was not a day on which to
examine yourself and realize that no matter how many excuses you
gave yourself, you were going to wind up knowing that, finally, you
were responsible.

Barber shook himself again. There was no sense in just staying in
the room all day. If he was going to do any good, he would have to find
Bert Smith. He looked at his watch. It was nearly two-thirty. He tried
to remember all the places he had ever seen Bert Smith at two-thirty in
the afternoon. The fancy restaurant near the Rond-Point, where the
movie people and the French newspaper owners and the rich tourists

ate; the bistro on the Boulevard Latour-Maubourg, on the Left Bank; the restaurants at Auteuil and Longchamp and St. Cloud. Barber looked at the newspaper. They were running at Auteuil today.

If he was not at the races and if he was still in Paris, Bert Smith was likely to be in one art gallery or another in the middle of the afternoon. Bert Smith was an art lover, or at least he bought pictures, shrewdly and knowingly. Since Smith lived in hotel rooms, which were unlikely places for a collection, it was probable that he bought paintings on speculation or as an agent or, when they were important ones that the government did not wish to have leave the country, to be smuggled out of France.

Barber had also seen Smith late in the afternoons in the steam room at Claridge's, a small, round man with surprisingly well-shaped legs, sitting in the vapor, wrapped in a sheet, growing pinker and pinker, smiling luxuriously in the steam, sweating off the fat that he had accumulated in many years of eating in the best restaurants in Europe.

He had also seen Smith several times around six o'clock in the evening in the barbershop at the George V getting shaved, and after that in the bar upstairs, and in the bar at the Relais Plaza and the English bar downstairs at the Plaza-Athénée. And late at night he had seen him at various night clubs—L'Eléphant Blanc, Carroll's, La Rose Rouge . . .

Barber thought unhappily of the last fifteen thousand francs in his wallet. It was going to be a long, wet, hard, expensive day. He put on his hat and coat and went out. It was still raining, and he hailed a taxi and gave the driver the address of the restaurant near the Rond-Point.

It had started about two months before, in the stand at Auteuil just before the sixth race. The day was misty and there weren't many spectators, and Barber had not been doing very well, but he had got a tip on the sixth race, on an eight-to-one shot. He put five thousand down on the nose and climbed high up in the stand to get a good view of the race.

There was only one other spectator near him in the stand, a small, round man wearing an expensive-looking velours hat, and carrying a pair of binoculars and a rolled umbrella, like an Englishman. He smiled at Barber and nodded. As Barber smiled back politely, he realized that he had seen the man many times before, or his brother, or a half-dozen other men who looked like him, in restaurants and in bars and on the street, usually with tall girls who might have been lower-class mannequins or upper-class tarts.

The man with the umbrella moved over to him along the damp concrete row of seats. He had little, dapper feet and a bright necktie, and he had a well-cared-for, international kind of face, with large, pretty dark eyes, fringed by thick black lashes. He had what Barber had come to call an import-export face. It was a face that was at the same time bland, cynical, self-assured, sensual, hopeless, and daring, and its owner might be Turkish or Hungarian or Greek or he might have been born in Basra. It was a face you might see in Paris or Rome or Brussels or Tangier, always in the best places, always doing business. It was a face, you felt somehow, that was occasionally of interest to the police.

"Good afternoon," the man said, in English, tipping his hat. "Are you having a lucky day?" He had an accent, but it was difficult to place it. It was as though as a child he had gone to school everywhere and had had ten nurses of ten different nationalities.

"Not bad," Barber said carefully.

"Which do you like in this one?" The man pointed with his umbrella at the track, where the horses were gingerly going up to the distant starting line on the muddied grass.

"Number Three," Barber said.

"Number Three." The man shrugged, as though he pitied Barber but was restrained by his good breeding from saying so. "How is the movie business these days?" the man asked.

"The movie business went home a month ago," Barber said, slightly surprised that the man knew anything about it. An American company had been making a picture about the war, and Barber had had four lucky, well-paid months as a technical expert, buckling leading men into parachutes and explaining the difference between a P-47 and a B-25 to the director.

"And the blond star?" the man asked, taking his glasses away from his eyes. "With the exquisite behind?"

"Also home."

The man moved his eyebrows and shook his head gently, indicating his regret that his new acquaintance and the city of Paris were now deprived of the exquisite behind. "Well," he said, "at least it leaves you free in the afternoon to come to the races." He peered out across the track through the glasses. "There they go."

No. 3 led all the way until the stretch. In the stretch, he was passed rapidly by four other horses.

"Every race in this country," Barber said as the horses crossed the finish line, "is a hundred metres too long." He took out his tickets and tore them once and dropped them on the wet concrete.

He watched with surprise as the man with the umbrella took out some tickets and tore them up, too. They were on No. 3, and Barber could see that they were big ones. The man with the umbrella dropped the tickets with a resigned, half-amused expression on his face, as though all his life he had been used to tearing up things that had suddenly become of no value.

"Are you staying for the last race?" the man with the umbrella asked as they started to descend through the empty stands.

"I don't think so," Barber said. "This day has been glorious enough already."

"Why don't you stay?" the man said. "I may have something."

Barber thought for a moment, listening to their footsteps on the concrete.

"I have a car," the man said. "I could give you a lift into town, Mr. Barber."

"Oh," Barber said, surprised, "you know my name."

"Of course," the man said, smiling. "Why don't you wait for me at the bar? I have to go and cash some tickets."

"I thought you lost," Barber said suspiciously.

"On Number Three," the man said. From another pocket he took out some more tickets and waved them gently. "But there is always the insurance. One must always think of the insurance," he said. "Will I see you at the bar?"

"O.K.," Barber said, not because he hoped for anything in the way of information on the next race from the man with the umbrella but because of the ride home. "I'll be there. Oh—by the way, what's your name?"

"Smith," the man said. "Bert Smith."

Barber went to the bar and ordered a coffee, then changed it to a brandy, because coffee wasn't enough after a race like that. He stood there, hunched over the bar, reflecting sourly that he was one of the category of people who never think of the insurance. Smith, he thought, Bert Smith. More insurance. On how many other names, Barber wondered, had the man lost before he picked that one?

Smith came to the bar softly, on his dapper feet, smiling, and laid a hand lightly on Barber's arm. "Mr. Barber," he said, "there is a rumor for the seventh race. Number Six."

"I never win on Number Six," Barber said.

"It is a lovely little rumor," Smith said. "At present, a twenty-two-to-one rumor."

Barber looked at the man doubtfully. He wondered briefly what there was in it for Smith. "What the hell," he said, moving toward the seller's window. "What have I got to lose?"

He put five thousand francs on No. 6 and superstitiously remained at the bar during the race, drinking brandy. No. 6 won, all out, by half a length, and, although the odds had dropped somewhat, paid eighteen to one.

Barber walked through the damp twilight, across the discarded newspapers and the scarred grass, with its farmlike smell, patting his inside pocket with the ninety thousand francs in a comforting bulge there, pleased with the little man trotting beside him.

Bert Smith had a Citroën, and he drove swiftly and well and objectionably, cutting in on other cars and swinging wide into the outside lane to gain advantage at lights.

"Do you bet often on the races, Mr. Barber?" he was saying as they passed a traffic policeman, forlorn in his white cape on the gleaming street.

"Too often," Barber said, enjoying the warmth of the car and the effects of the last brandy and the bulge in his pocket.

"You like to gamble?"

"Who doesn't?"

"There are many who do not like to gamble," Smith said, nearly scraping a truck. "I pity them."

"Pity them?" Barber looked over at Smith, a little surprised at the word. "Why?"

"Because," Smith said softly, smiling, "in this age there comes a time when everyone finds that he is forced to gamble—and not only for money, and not only at the seller's window. And when that time comes, and you are not in the habit, and it does not amuse you, you are most likely to lose."

They rode in silence for a while. From time to time, Barber peered across at the soft, self-assured face above the wheel, lit by the dashboard glow. I would like to get a look at his passport, Barber thought—at all the passports he's carried for the last twenty years.

"For example," Smith said, "during the war . . ."

"Yes?"

"When you were in your plane," Smith said, "on a mission. Weren't there times when you had to decide suddenly to try something, to depend on your luck for one split second, and if you hesitated, if you balked at the act of gambling—sssszt!" Smith took one hand from the wheel and made a gliding, falling motion, with his thumb down. He smiled across at Barber. "I suppose you are one of the young men who were nearly killed a dozen times," he said.

"I suppose so," Barber said.

"I prefer that in Americans," Smith said. "It makes them more like Europeans."

"How did you know I was in the war?" Barber said. For the first time, he began to wonder if it was only a coincidence that Smith had been near him in the stand before the sixth race.

Smith chuckled. "You have been in Paris how long?" he said. "A year and a half?"

"Sixteen months," Barber said, wondering how the man knew *that*.

"Nothing very mysterious about it," Smith said. "People talk at bars, at dinner parties. One girl tells another girl. Paris is a small city. Where shall I drop you?"

Barber looked out the window to see where they were. "Not far from here," he said. "My hotel is just off the Avenue Victor Hugo. You can't get in there with a car."

"Oh, yes," Smith said, as though he knew about all hotels. "If it doesn't seem too inquisitive," he said, "do you intend to stay long in Europe?"

"It depends."

"On what?"

"On luck." Barber grinned.

"Did you have a good job in America?" Smith asked, keeping his eyes on the traffic ahead of him.

"In thirty years, working ten hours a day, I would have been the third biggest man in the company," Barber said.

Smith smiled. "Calamitous," he said. "Have you found more interesting things to do here?"

"Occasionally," Barber said, beginning to be conscious that he was being quizzed.

"After a war it is difficult to remain interested," Smith said. "While it is on, a war is absolutely boring. But then when it is over, you discover peace is even more boring. It is the worst result of wars. Do you still fly?"

"Once in a while."

Smith nodded. "Do you maintain your license?"

"Yes."

"Yes, that's wise," Smith said.

He pulled the car sharply in to the curb and stopped, and Barber got out.

"Here you are," Smith said. He put out his hand, smiling, and Barber shook it. Smith's hand was softly fleshed, but there was a feeling of stone beneath it.

"Thanks for everything," Barber said.

"Thank you, Mr. Barber, for your company," Smith said. He held Barber's hand for a moment, looking across the seat at him. "This has been very pleasant," he said. "I hope we can see each other again soon. Maybe we are lucky for each other."

"Sure," Barber said, grinning. "I'm always at home to people who can pick eighteen-to-one shots."

Smith smiled, relinquishing Barber's hand. "Maybe one of these days we'll have something even better than an eighteen-to-one shot," he said.

He waved a little and Barber closed the car door. Smith spurted out into the traffic, nearly causing two *quatre chevaux* to pile up behind him.

It had taken two weeks for Smith to declare himself. From the beginning, Barber had known that something was coming, but he had waited patiently, curious and amused, lunching with Smith in the fine restaurants Smith patronized, going to galleries with him and listening to Smith on the subject of the Impressionists, going out to the race tracks with him and winning more often than not on the information Smith picked up from tight-lipped men around the paddocks. Barber pretended to enjoy the little, clever man more than he actually did, and Smith, on his part, Barber knew, was pretending to like *him* more than he actually did. It was a kind of veiled and cynical wooing, in which neither party had yet committed himself. Only, unlike more ordinary wooings, Barber for the first two weeks was not sure in just which direction his desirability, as far as Smith was concerned, might lie.

Then, late one night, after a large dinner and a desultory tour of the night clubs, during which Smith had seemed unusually silent and abstracted, they were standing in front of Smith's hotel and he made his move. It was a cold night, and the street was deserted except for a prostitute with a dog, who looked at them without hope as she passed them on the way to the Champs-Elysées.

"Are you going to be in your hotel tomorrow morning, Lloyd?" Smith asked.

"Yes," Barber said. "Why?"

"Why?" Smith repeated absently, staring after the chilled-looking girl and her poodle walking despairingly down the empty, dark street. "Why?" He chuckled irrelevantly. "I have something I would like to show you," he said.

"I'll be in all morning," Barber said.

"Tell me, my friend," Smith said, touching Barber's sleeve lightly with his gloved hand. "Do you have any idea why I have been calling you so often for the last two weeks, and buying you so many good meals and so much good whiskey?"

"Because I am charming and interesting and full of fun," Barber said, grinning. "And because you want something from me."

Smith chuckled, louder this time, and caressed Barber's sleeve. "You are not absolutely stupid, my friend, are you?"

"Not absolutely," said Barber.

"Tell me, my friend," Smith said, almost in a whisper. "How would you like to make twenty-five thousand dollars?"

"What?" Barber asked, certain that he had not heard correctly.

"Sh-h-h," Smith said. He smiled, suddenly gay. "Think about it. I'll see you in the morning. Thank you for walking me home." He dropped Barber's arm and started into the hotel.

"Smith!" Barber called.

"Sh-h-h." Smith put his finger playfully to his mouth. "Sleep well. See you in the morning."

Barber watched him go through the glass revolving doors into the huge, brightly lit, empty lobby of the hotel. Barber took a step toward the doors to follow him in, then stopped and shrugged and put his collar up, and walked slowly in the direction of his own hotel. I've waited this long, he thought, I can wait till morning.

Barber was still in bed the next morning when the door opened and Smith came in. The room was dark, with the curtains drawn, and Barber was lying there, half asleep, thinking drowsily, Twenty-five thousand, twenty-five thousand. He opened his eyes when he heard the door open. There was a short, bulky silhouette framed in the doorway against the pallid light of the corridor.

"Who's that?" Barber asked, without sitting up.

"Lloyd. I'm sorry," Smith said. "Go back to sleep. I'll see you later."

Barber sat up abruptly. "Smith," he said. "Come in."

"I don't want to disturb—"

"Come in, come in." Barber got out of bed and, barefooted, went over to the window and threw back the curtains. He looked out at the street. "By God, what do you know?" he said, shivering and closing the window. "The sun is shining. Shut the door."

Smith closed the door. He was wearing a loose gray tweed overcoat, very British, and a soft Italian felt hat, and he was carrying a large manila envelope. He looked newly bathed and shaved, and wide awake.

Barber, blinking in the sudden sunshine, put on a robe and a pair of moccasins and lit a cigarette. "Excuse me," he said. "I want to wash." He went behind the screen that separated the washbasin and the *bidet* from the rest of the room. As he washed, scrubbing his face and soaking his hair with cold water, he heard Smith go over to the window. Smith was humming, in a soft, true, melodious tenor voice, a passage from an opera that Barber knew he had heard but could not remember. Aside from everything else, Barber thought, combing his hair roughly, I bet the bastard knows fifty operas.

Feeling fresher and less at a disadvantage with his teeth washed and his hair combed, Barber stepped out from behind the screen.

"Paris," Smith said, at the window, looking out. "What a satisfactory city. What a farce." He turned around, smiling. "Ah," he said, "how lucky you are. You can afford to put water on your head." He touched his thin, well-brushed hair sadly. "Every time I wash my hair, it falls like the leaves. How old did you say you are?"

"Thirty," Barber said, knowing that Smith remembered it.

"What an age." Smith sighed. "The wonderful moment of balance. Old enough to know what you want, still young enough to be ready for anything." He came back and sat down and propped the manila envelope on the floor next to the chair. "Anything." He looked up at Barber, almost coquettishly. "You recall our conversation, I trust," he said.

"I recall a man said something about twenty-five thousand dollars," Barber said.

"Ah—you do remember," Smith said gaily. "Well?"

"Well what?"

"Well, do you want to make it?"

"I'm listening," Barber said.

Smith rubbed his soft hands together gently in front of his face, his fingers rigid, making a slight, dry, sliding sound. "A little proposition has come up," he said. "An interesting little proposition."

"What do I have to do for my twenty-five thousand dollars?" Barber asked.

"What do you have to do for your twenty-five thousand dollars?" Smith repeated softly. "You have to do a little flying. You have flown for considerably less, from time to time, haven't you?" He chuckled.

"I sure have," Barber said. "What else do I have to do?"

"Nothing else," Smith said, sounding surprised. "Just fly. Are you still interested?"

"Go on," said Barber.

"A friend of mine has just bought a brand-new single-engine plane. A Beechcraft, single engine. A perfect, pleasant, comfortable, one-hundred-per-cent dependable aircraft," Smith said, describing the perfect little plane with pleasure in its newness and its dependability. "He himself does not fly, of course. He needs a private pilot, who will be on tap at all times."

"For how long?" Barber asked, watching Smith closely.

"For thirty days. Not more." Smith smiled up at him. "The pay is not bad, is it?"

"I can't tell yet," Barber said. "Go on. Where does he want to fly to?"

"He happens to be an Egyptian," Smith said, a little deprecatingly, as though being an Egyptian were a slight private misfortune, which one did not mention except among friends, and then in lowered tones. "He is a wealthy Egyptian who likes to travel. Especially back and forth to France. To the South of France. He is in love with the South of France. He goes there at every opportunity."

"Yes?"

"He would like to make two round trips from Egypt to the vicinity of Cannes within the next month," Smith said, peering steadily at Barber, "in his private new plane. Then, on the third trip, he will find that he is in a hurry and he will take the commercial plane and his pilot will follow two days later, alone."

"Alone?" Barber asked, trying to keep all the facts straight.

"Alone, that is," Smith said, "except for a small box."

"Ah," Barber said, grinning. "Finally the small box."

"Finally." Smith smiled up at him delightedly. "It has already been calculated. The small box will weigh two hundred and fifty pounds. A comfortable margin of safety for this particular aircraft for each leg of the journey."

"And what will there be in the small two-hundred-and-fifty-pound box?" Barber asked, cool and relieved now that he saw what was being offered to him.

"Is it absolutely necessary to know?"

"What do I tell the customs people when they ask me what's in the box?" Barber said. " 'Go ask Bert Smith'?"

"You have nothing to do with customs people," Smith said. "I assure you. When you take off from the airport in Cairo, the box is not on board. And when you land at the airport at Cannes, the box is not on board. Isn't that enough?"

Barber took a last pull at his cigarette and doused it. He peered thoughtfully at Smith, sitting easily on the straight-backed chair in the rumpled room, looking too neat and too well-dressed for such a place at such an hour. Drugs, Barber thought, and he can stuff them . . .

"No, Bertie boy," Barber said roughly. "It is not enough. Come on. Tell."

Smith sighed. "Are you interested up to now?"

"I am interested up to now," Barber said.

"All right," Smith said regretfully. "This is how it will be done. You will have established a pattern. You will have been in and out of the Cairo airport several times. Your papers always impeccable. They will know you. You will have become a part of the legitimate routine of the field. Then, on the trip when you will be taking off alone, everything will be perfectly legitimate. You will have only a small bag with you of your personal effects. Your flight plan will show that your destination is Cannes and that you will come down at Malta and Rome for refueling only. You will take off from Cairo. You will go off course by only a few miles. Some distance from the coast, you will be over the desert. You will come down on an old R.A.F. landing strip that hasn't been used since 1943. There will be several men there. . . . Are you listening?"

"I'm listening." Barber had walked to the window and was standing there, looking out at the sunny street below, his back to Smith.

"They will put the box on board. The whole thing will not take more than ten minutes," Smith said. "At Malta, nobody will ask you anything, because you will be in transit and you will not leave the plane and you will stay only long enough to refuel. The same thing at Rome. You will arrive over the south coast of France in the evening, before the moon is up. Once more," Smith said, speaking as though he was savoring his words, "you will be just a little off course. You will fly low over the hills between Cannes and Grasse. At a certain point, you will see an arrangement of lights. You will throttle down, open the door, and push the box out, from a height of a hundred feet. Then you will close the door and turn toward the sea and land at the Cannes airport. Your papers will be perfectly in order. There will have been no deviations from your flight plan. You will have nothing to declare. You will walk away from the airplane once and for all, and we will pay you the twenty-five thousand dollars I have spoken of. Isn't it lovely?"

"Lovely," Barber said. "It's just a delicious little old plan, Bertie boy."
He turned away from the window. "Now tell me what will be in the
box."

Smith chuckled delightedly, as though what he was going to say was
too funny to keep to himself. "Money," he said. "Just money."

"How much money?"

"Two hundred and fifty pounds of money," Smith said, his eyes
crinkled with amusement. "Two hundred and fifty pounds of tightly
packed English notes in a nice, strong, lightweight metal box. Five-
pound notes."

At that moment, it occurred to Barber that he was speaking to a
lunatic. But Smith was sitting there, matter-of-fact and healthy, obviously a man who had never for a minute in all his life had a single
doubt about his sanity.

"When would I get paid?" Barber asked.

"When the box was delivered," Smith said.

"Bertie boy . . ." Barber shook his head reprovingly.

Smith chuckled. "I have warned myself that you were not stupid," he
said. "All right. We will deposit twelve thousand five hundred dollars in
your name in a Swiss bank before you start for the first time to Egypt."

"You trust me for that?"

Fleetingly the smile left Smith's face. "We'll trust you for that," he
said. Then the smile reappeared. "And immediately after the delivery
is made, we will deposit the rest. A lovely deal. Hard currency. No
income tax. You will be a rich man. Semi-rich." He chuckled at his
joke. "Just for a little plane ride. Just to help an Egyptian who is fond
of the South of France and who is naturally a little disturbed by the
insecurity of his own country."

"When will I meet this Egyptian?" Barber asked.

"When you go to the airfield to take off for your first flight," Smith
said. "He'll be there. Don't you worry. He'll be there. Do you hesitate?"
he asked anxiously.

"I'm thinking," Barber said.

"It's not as though you were involved in your own country," Smith
said piously. "I wouldn't ask a man to do that, a man who had fought
for his country in the war. It isn't even as though it had anything to do
with the English, for whom it is possible you have a certain affection.
But the Egyptians . . ." He shrugged and bent over and picked up the
manila envelope and opened it. "I have all the maps here," he said, "if
you would like to study them. The route is all marked out, but, of

course, it would be finally in your hands, since it would be you who was doing the flying."

Barber took the thick packet of maps. He opened one at random. All it showed was the sea approaches to Malta and the location of the landing strips there. Barber thought of twenty-five thousand dollars and the map shook a little in his hands.

"It is ridiculously easy," Smith said, watching Barber intently. "Fool-proof."

Barber put the map down. "If it's so easy, what are you paying twenty-five thousand bucks for?" he said.

Smith laughed. "I admit," he said, "there may be certain little risks. It is improbable, but one never knows. We pay you for the improbability, if you want to put it that way." He shrugged. "After all, after a whole war you must be somewhat hardened to risks."

"When do you have to know?" Barber asked.

"Tonight," Smith said. "If you say no, naturally we have to make other plans. And my Egyptian friend is impatient."

"Who is we?" Barber asked.

"Naturally," Smith said, "I have certain colleagues."

"Who are they?"

Smith made a small regretful gesture. "I am terribly sorry," he said, "but I cannot tell you."

"I'll call you tonight," said Barber.

"Good." Smith stood up and buttoned his coat and carefully put the soft Italian felt hat on his head, at a conservative angle. He played gently and appreciatively with the brim. "This afternoon, I will be at the track. Maybe you would like to join me there."

"Where're they running today?"

"Auteuil," Smith said. "Jumping today."

"Have you heard anything?"

"Perhaps," Smith said. "There is a mare who is doing the jumps for the first time. I have spoken to the jockey and I have been told the mare has responded in training, but I'll hear more at three o'clock."

"I'll be there."

"Good," Smith said enthusiastically. "Although it is against my interests, of course, to make you too rich in advance." He chuckled. "However, for the sake of friendship . . . Should I leave the maps?"

"Yes," said Barber.

"Until three o'clock," Smith said as Barber opened the door. They shook hands, and Smith went out into the corridor, a rich, tweedy, perfumed figure in the impoverished light of the pallid hotel lamps.

Barber locked the door behind him and picked up the packet of maps and spread them on the bed, over the rumpled sheets and blankets. He hadn't looked at aerial maps for a long time. Northern Egypt. The Mediterranean. The island of Malta. Sicily and the Italian coast. The Gulf of Genoa. The Alpes-Maritimes. He stared at the maps. The Mediterranean looked very wide. He didn't like to fly over open water in a single-engined plane. In fact, he didn't like to fly. Since the war, he had flown as little as possible. He hadn't made any explanations to himself, but when he had had to travel, he had gone by car or train or boat whenever he could.

Twenty-five thousand dollars, he thought.

He folded the maps neatly and put them back into the envelope. At this point, the maps weren't going to help.

He lay down on the bed again, propped against the pillows, with his hands clasped behind his head. Open water, he thought. Five times. Even that wouldn't be too bad. But what about the Egyptians? He had been in Cairo briefly during the war. He remembered that at night the policemen walked in pairs, carrying carbines. He didn't like places where the policemen carried carbines. And Egyptian prisons . . .

He moved uneasily on the bed.

Who knew how many people were in on a scheme like this? And it would only take one to cook you. One dissatisfied servant or accomplice, one greedy or timid partner . . . He closed his eyes and almost saw the fat, dark uniformed men with their carbines walking up to the shiny, new little plane.

Or suppose you blew a tire or crumpled a wheel on the landing strip? Who knew what the strip was like, abandoned in the desert since 1943?

Twenty-five thousand dollars.

Or you would think you were making it. The box would be on the seat beside you and the coast of Egypt would be falling off behind you and the sea stretching blue below and ahead and the engine running like a watch—and then the first sign of the patrol. The shimmering dot growing into . . . What did the Egyptian Air Force fly? Spitfires, left over from the war, he supposed. Coming up swiftly, going twice as fast as you, signaling you to turn around . . . He lit a cigarette. Two hundred and fifty pounds. Say the box alone—it would have to be really solid—weighed a hundred and fifty pounds. How much did a five-pound note weigh? Would there be a thousand to a pound? Five thousand multiplied by a hundred, with the pound at two-eighty. Close to a million and a half dollars.

His mouth felt dry, and he got up and drank two glasses of water.

Then he made himself sit down on the chair, keeping his hands still. If there was an accident, if for any reason you failed to come through with it . . . If the money was lost, but you were saved. Smith didn't look like a murderer, although who knew what murderers looked like these days? And who knew what other people he was involved with? My colleagues, as Smith called them, who would then be your colleagues. The wealthy Egyptian, the several men at the old R.A.F. landing strip in the desert, the people who were to set out the lights in the certain arrangement in the hills behind Cannes— How many others, sliding across frontiers, going secretly and illegally from one country to another with guns and gold in their suitcases, the survivors of war, prison, denunciation— How many others whom you didn't know, whom you would see briefly in the glare of the African sun, as a running figure on a dark French hillside, whom you couldn't judge or assess and on whom your life depended, who were risking prison, deportation, police bullets for their share of a box full of money . . .

He jumped up and put on his clothes and went out, locking the door. He didn't want to sit in the cold, disordered room, staring at the maps.

He walked around the city aimlessly for the rest of the morning, looking blindly into shopwindows and thinking of the things he would buy if he had money. Turning away from a window, he saw a policeman watching him incuriously. Barber looked speculatively at the policeman, who was small, with a mean face and a thin mustache. Looking at the policeman, Barber remembered some of the stories about what they did to suspects when they questioned them in the back rooms of the local prefectures. An American passport wouldn't do much good if they picked you up with five hundred thousand English pounds under your arm.

This is the first time in my life, Barber thought curiously, walking slowly on the crowded street, that I have contemplated moving over to the other side of the law. He was surprised that he was considering it so calmly. He wondered why that was. Perhaps the movies and the newspapers, he thought. You get so familiar with crime it becomes humanized and accessible. You don't think about it, but then, suddenly, when it enters your life, you realize that subconsciously you have been accepting the idea of crime as an almost normal accompaniment of everyday life. Policemen must know that, he thought, all at once seeing things from the other side. They must look at all the shut, ordinary faces going past them and they must know how close to theft, murder, and defaulting everyone is, and it must drive them crazy. They must want to arrest everybody.

While Barber was watching the horses move in their stiff-legged, trembling walk around the paddock before the sixth race, he felt a light tap on his shoulder.

"Bertie boy," he said, without turning around.

"I'm sorry I'm late," Smith said, coming up to the paddock rail beside Barber. "Were you afraid I wouldn't come?"

"What's the word from the jock?" Barber asked.

Smith looked around him suspiciously. Then he smiled. "The jockey is confident," Smith said. "He is betting himself."

"Which one is it?"

"Number Five."

Barber looked at No. 5. It was a light-boned chestnut mare with a delicate, gentle head. Her tail and mane were braided, and she walked alertly but not too nervously, well-mannered and with a glistening coat. Her jockey was a man of about forty, with a long, scooped French nose. He was an ugly man, and when he opened his mouth, you saw that most of his front teeth were missing. He wore a maroon cap, with his ears tucked in, and a white silk shirt dotted with maroon stars.

Barber, looking at him, thought, It's too bad such ugly men get to ride such beautiful animals.

"O.K., Bertie boy," he said. "Lead me to the window."

Barber bet ten thousand francs on the nose. The odds were a comfortable seven to one. Smith bet twenty-five thousand francs. They walked side by side to the stands and climbed up together as the horses came out on the track. The crowd was small and there were only a few other spectators that high up.

"Well, Lloyd?" Smith said. "Did you look at the maps?"

"I looked at the maps," Barber said.

"What did you think?"

"They're very nice maps."

Smith looked at him sharply. Then he decided to chuckle. "You want to make me fish, eh?" he said. "You know what I mean. Did you decide?"

"I . . ." Barber began, staring down at the cantering horses. He took a deep breath. "I'll tell you after the race," he said.

"Lloyd!" The voice came from below, to the right, and Barber turned in that direction. Toiling up the steps was Jimmy Richardson. He had always been rather round and baby-plump, and Parisian food had done nothing to slim him down, and he was panting, his coat flapping open, disclosing a checkered vest, as he hurried toward Barber.

"How are you?" he said breathlessly as he reached their level. He clapped Barber on the back. "I saw you up here and I thought maybe you had something for this race. I can't figure this one and they've been murdering me all day. I'm lousy on the jumps."

"Hello, Jimmy," Barber said. "Mr. Richardson. Mr. Smith."

"Pleased to meet you," Richardson said. "How do you spell it?" He laughed loudly at his joke. "Say, really, Lloyd, do you know anything? Maureen'll murder me if I go home and tell her I went into the hole for the afternoon."

Barber looked across at Smith, who was watching Richardson benignly. "Well," he said, "Bertie boy, here, thinks he heard something."

"Bertie boy," Richardson said, "please . . ."

Smith smiled thinly. "Number Five looks very good," he said. "But you'd better hurry. They're going to start in a minute."

"Number Five," Richardson said. "Roger. I'll be right back." He went galloping down the steps, his coat flying behind him.

"He's a trusting soul, isn't he?" Smith said.

"He was an only child," Barber said, "and he never got over it."

Smith smiled politely. "Where do you know him from?"

"He was in my squadron."

"In your squadron." Smith nodded, looking after Richardson's hurrying, diminishing figure on the way to the seller's window. "Pilot?"

"Uh-huh."

"Good?"

Barber shrugged. "Better ones got killed and worse ones won every medal in the collection."

"What is he doing in Paris?"

"He works for a drug company," Barber said.

The bell rang and the horses raced toward the first jump.

"Your friend was too late, I'm afraid," Smith said, putting his binoculars to his eyes.

"Yep," Barber said, watching the bunched horses.

No. 5 fell on the fourth jump. She went over with two other horses, and suddenly she was down and rolling. The pack passed around her. The fourth jump was far off down the track, and it was hard to see what, exactly, was happening until, a moment later, the mare struggled to her feet and cantered after the pack, her reins broken and trailing. Then Barber saw that the jockey was lying there motionless, crumpled up clumsily on his face, with his head turned in under his shoulder.

"We've lost our money," Smith said calmly. He took his binoculars from his eyes and pulled out his tickets and tore them and dropped them.

"May I have those, please?" Barber reached over for the binoculars.

Smith lifted the strap over his head, and Barber trained the glasses on the distant jump where the jockey was lying. Two men were running out to him and turning him over.

Barber adjusted the binoculars, and the figures of the two men working on the motionless figure in the maroon-starred shirt came out of the blur into focus. Even in the glasses, there was something terribly urgent and despairing in the movements of the distant men. They picked the jockey up between them and started running clumsily off with him.

"Damn it!" It was Richardson, who had climbed up beside them again. "The window closed just as I—"

"Do not complain, Mr. Richardson," Smith said. "We fell at the fourth jump."

Richardson grinned. "That's the first bit of luck I had all day."

Down below, in front of the stands, the riderless mare was swerving and trotting off down the track to avoid a groom who was trying to grab the torn reins.

Barber kept the glasses on the two men who were carrying the jockey. Suddenly, they put him down on the grass, and one of the men bent down and put his ear against the white silk racing shirt. After a while, he stood up. Then the two men started to carry the jockey again, only now they walked slowly, as though there was no sense in hurrying.

Barber gave the glasses back to Smith. "I'm going home," he said. "I've had enough of the sport for one day."

Smith glanced at him sharply. He put the glasses to his eyes and stared at the men carrying the jockey. Then he put the glasses into their case and hung the case by its strap over his shoulder. "They kill at least one a year," he said in a low voice. "It is to be expected in a sport like this. I'll take you home."

"Say," Richardson said. "Is that fellow dead?"

"He was getting too old," Smith said. "He kept at it too long."

"Holy man!" Richardson said, staring down the track. "And I was sore because I came too late to bet on him. That was some tip." He made a babyish grimace. "A tip on a dead jock."

Barber started down toward the exit.

"I'll come with you," Richardson said. "This isn't my lucky day."

The three men went down under the stands without speaking. People were standing in little groups, and there was a queer rising, hissing sound of whispering all over the place, now that the news was spreading.

When they reached the car, Barber got into the back, allowing Richardson to sit next to Smith, on the front seat. He wanted to be at least that much alone for the time being.

Smith drove slowly and in silence. Even Richardson spoke only once. "What a way to get it," he said as they drove between the bare, high trees. "In a lousy, three-hundred-thousand-franc claiming race."

Barber sat in the corner, his eyes half closed, not looking out. He kept remembering the second time the two men had picked up the jockey. Smith's selection for the afternoon, Barber thought. He closed his eyes altogether and saw the maps spread out on the bed in his room. The Mediterranean. The wide reaches of open water. He remembered the smell of burning. The worst smell. The smell of your dreams during the war. The smell of hot metal, smoldering rubber. Smith's tip.

"Here we are," Smith was saying.

Barber opened his eyes. They were stopped at the corner of the dead-end street down which was the entrance to his hotel. He got out.

"Wait a minute, Bertie boy," Barber said. "I have something I want to give you."

Smith looked at him inquiringly. "Can't it wait, Lloyd?" he asked.

"No. I'll just be a minute." Barber went into his hotel and up to his room. The maps were folded in a pile on the bureau, except for one, which was lying open beside the others. The approaches to Malta. He folded it quickly and put all the maps into the manila envelope and went back to the car. Smith was standing beside the car, smoking, nervously holding on to his hat, because a wind had come up and dead leaves were skittering along the pavement.

"Here you are, Bertie boy," Barber said, holding out the envelope.

Smith didn't take it. "You're sure you know what you're doing?" he said.

"I'm sure."

Smith still didn't take the maps. "I'm in no hurry," he said softly. "Why don't you hold on to them another day?"

"Thanks, no."

Smith looked at him silently for a moment. The fluorescent street lamps had just gone on, hard white-blue light, and Smith's smooth face looked powdery in the shadows under his expensive hat, and his pretty eyes were dark and flat under the curled lashes.

"Just because a jockey falls at a jump—" Smith began.

"Take them," Barber said, "or I'll throw them in the gutter."

Smith shrugged. He put out his hand and took the envelope. "You'll never have a chance like this again," he said, running his finger caressingly over the envelope edge.

"Good night, Jimmy." Barber leaned over the car and spoke to Richardson, who was sitting there watching them, puzzled. "Give my love to Maureen."

"Say, Lloyd," Richardson said, starting to get out. "I thought maybe we could have a couple of drinks. Maureen doesn't expect me home for another hour yet and I thought maybe we could cut up some old touches and—"

"Sorry," Barber said, because he wanted, more than anything else, to be alone. "I have a date. Some other time."

Smith turned and looked thoughtfully at Richardson. "He always has a date, your friend," Smith said. "He's a very popular boy. I feel like a drink myself, Mr. Richardson. I would be honored if you'd join me."

"Well," Richardson said uncertainly, "I live way down near the Hôtel de Ville and—"

"It's on my way," Smith said, smiling warmly.

Richardson settled back in his seat, and Smith started to get into the car. He stopped and looked up at Barber. "I made a mistake about you, didn't I, Lloyd?" he said contemptuously.

"Yes," Barber said. "I'm getting too old. I don't want to keep at it too long."

Smith chuckled and got into the car. They didn't shake hands. He slammed the door, and Barber watched him pull sharply away from the curb, making a taxi-driver behind him jam on his brakes to avoid hitting him.

Barber watched the big black car weave swiftly down the street, under the hard white-blue lights. Then he went back to the hotel and up to his room and lay down, because an afternoon at the races always exhausted him.

An hour later, he got up. He splashed cold water on his face to wake himself, but even so he felt listless and empty. He wasn't hungry and he wasn't thirsty and he kept thinking about the dead jockey in his soiled silks. There was no one he wanted to see. He put on his coat and went out, hating the room as he closed the door behind him.

He walked slowly toward the Etoile. It was a raw night and a fog was moving in from the river, and the streets were almost empty, because everybody was inside eating dinner. He didn't look at any of the lighted windows, because he wasn't going to buy anything for a long time. He passed several movie houses, neon in the drifting fog. In the movies, he thought, the hero would have been on his way to Africa by now. He would nearly be caught several times in Egypt, and he would fight his way out of a trap on the desert, killing several dark men just in time on the airstrip. And he would develop engine trouble over the Mediter-ranean and just pull out, with the water lapping at the wing tips, and he would undoubtedly crash, without doing too much damage to himself, probably just a photogenic cut on the forehead, and would drag the box out just in time. And he would turn out to be a Treasury agent or a member of British Intelligence and he would never doubt his luck and his nerve would never fail him and he would not end the picture with only a few thousand francs in his pocket. Or, if it was an artistic pic-ture, there would be a heavy ground mist over the hills and the plane would drone on and on, desperate and lost, and then, finally, with the fuel tanks empty, the hero would crash in flames. Battered and stagger-ing as he was, he would try to get the box out, but he wouldn't be able to move it, and finally the flames would drive him back and he would stand against a tree, laughing crazily, his face blackened with smoke, watching the plane and the money burn, to show the vanity of human aspiration and greed.

Barber grinned bleakly, rehearsing the scenarios in front of the giant posters outside the theatres. The movies do it better, he thought. They have their adventures happen to adventurers. He turned off the Champs-Elysées, walking slowly and aimlessly, trying to decide whether to eat now or have a drink first. Almost automatically, he walked toward the Plaza-Athénée. In the two weeks that he had been wooed by Smith, they had met in the English bar of the Plaza-Athénée almost every evening.

He went into the hotel and downstairs to the English bar. As he came into the room, he saw, in the corner, Smith and Jimmy Richardson.

Barber smiled. Bertie boy, he thought, are you whatever wasting your time. He stood at the bar and ordered a whiskey.

". . . fifty missions," he heard Richardson say. Richardson had a loud, empty voice that carried anywhere. "Africa, Sicily, Italy, Yugo—"

Then Smith saw him. He nodded coolly, with no hint of invitation. Richardson swiveled in his chair then, too. He smiled uncomfortably at Barber, getting red in the face, like a man who has been caught by a friend with his friend's girl.

Barber waved to them. For a moment, he wondered if he ought to go over and sit down and try to get Richardson out of there. He watched the two men, trying to figure out what they thought of each other. Or, more accurately, what Smith thought of Richardson. You didn't have to speculate about Jimmy. If you bought Jimmy a drink, he was your friend for life. For all that he had been through—war and marriage and being a father and living in a foreign country—it had still never occurred to Jimmy that people might not like him or might try to do him harm. When you were enjoying Jimmy, you called it trustfulness. When he was boring you, you called it stupidity.

Barber watched Smith's face carefully. By now, he knew Smith well enough to be able to tell a great deal of what was going on behind the pretty eyes and the pale, powdered face. Right now, Barber could tell that Smith was bored and that he wanted to get away from Jimmy Richardson.

Barber turned back to his drink, smiling to himself. It took Bertie boy just about an hour, he thought, an hour of looking at that good-natured empty face, an hour of listening to that booming, vacant voice, to decide that this was no man to fly a small box of five-pound notes from Cairo to Cannes.

Barber finished his drink quickly and went out of the bar before Smith and Richardson got up from the table. He had nothing to do for the evening, but he didn't want to get stuck with Jimmy and Maureen Richardson for dinner.

And now it was almost two months later and nobody had heard from Jimmy Richardson for thirty-two days.

In the whole afternoon of searching, Barber had not come upon any trace of Bert Smith. He had not been at the restaurants or the track or the art galleries, the barbershop, the steam bath, the bars. And no one had seen him for weeks.

It was nearly eight o'clock when Barber arrived at the English bar of the Plaza-Athénée. He was wet from walking in the day's rain, and tired, and his shoes were soggy and he felt a cold coming on. He looked around the room, but it was almost empty. Indulging himself, thinking unhappily of all the taxi fares he had paid that day, he ordered a whiskey.

Barber sipped his whiskey in the quiet room, thinking circularly, I should have said something. But what could I have said? And Jimmy wouldn't have listened. But I should have said something. *The omens are bad, Jimmy, go on home. . . . I saw a plane crashing at the fourth jump, I saw a corpse being carried across dead grass by Egyptians, Jimmy, I saw silks and maps stained by blood.*

I had to be so damned superior, Barber thought bitterly. I had to be so damned sure that Jimmy Richardson was too stupid to be offered that much money. I had to be so damned sure that Bert Smith was too clever to hire him.

He hadn't said any of the things he should have said, and it had all wound up with a frantic, husbandless, penniless girl pleading for help that could only be too late now. Penniless. Jimmy Richardson had been too stupid even to get any of the money in advance.

He remembered what Jimmy and Maureen had looked like, smiling and embarrassed and youthfully important, standing next to Colonel Sumners, the Group Commander, at their wedding in Shreveport. He remembered Jimmy's plane just off his wing over Sicily; he remembered Jimmy's face when he landed at Foggia with an engine on fire; he remembered Jimmy's voice singing drunkenly in a bar in Naples; he remembered Jimmy the day after he arrived in Paris, saying, "Kid, this is the town for me, I got Europe in my blood."

He finished his drink and paid and went upstairs slowly. He went into a phone booth and called his hotel to see if there were any messages for him.

"Mme. Richardson has been calling you all day," the old man at the switchboard said. "Ever since four o'clock. She wanted you to call her back."

"All right," Barber said. "Thank you." He started to hang up.

"Wait a minute, wait a minute," the old man said irritably. "She called an hour ago to say she was going out. She said that if you came in before nine o'clock, she would like you to join her at the bar of the Hotel Bellman."

"Thanks, Henri," Barber said. "If she happens to call again, tell her I'm on my way." He went out of the hotel. The Bellman was nearby, and he walked toward it slowly, even though it was still raining. He was in no hurry to see Maureen Richardson.

When he reached the Bellman, he hesitated before going in, feeling too tired for this, wishing Maureen could be put off at least until the next day. He sighed, and pushed the door open.

The bar was a small one, but it was crowded with large, well-dressed men who were taking their time over drinks before going out to dinner. Then he saw Maureen. She was sitting in a corner, half turned away from the room, her shabby, thin coat thrown back over her chair. She was sitting alone and there was a bottle of champagne in a bucket in a stand beside her.

Barber went over to her, irritated by the sight of the champagne. Is that what she's doing with my five thousand francs, he thought, annoyed. Women are going crazy, too, these days.

He leaned over and kissed the top of her head. She jumped nervously, then smiled when she saw who it was. "Oh, Lloyd," she said, in a funny kind of whisper. She jumped up and kissed him, holding him hard against her. There was a big smell of champagne on her breath and he wondered if she was drunk. "Lloyd, Lloyd . . ." she said. She pushed him away a little, holding on to both his hands. Her eyes were smeary with tears and her mouth kept trembling.

"I came as soon as I got your message," Lloyd said, trying to sound practical, afraid Maureen was going to break down in front of all the people in the bar. She kept standing there, her mouth working, her hands gripping his avidly. He looked down, embarrassed, at her hands. They were still reddened and the nails were still uneven, but there was an enormous ring glittering, white and blue, on her finger. It hadn't been there when she came to his hotel, and he knew he had never seen her with a ring like that before. He looked up, almost frightened, thinking, What the hell has she started? What has she got herself into?

Then he saw Jimmy. Jimmy was making his way among the tables toward him. He was smiling broadly and he had lost some weight and he was dark brown and he looked as though he had just come from a month's vacation on a southern beach.

"Hi, kid," Jimmy said, his voice booming across the tables, across the barroom murmur of conversation. "I was just calling you again."

"He came home," Maureen said. "He came home at four o'clock this afternoon, Lloyd." She sank suddenly into her chair. Whatever else had happened that afternoon, it was plain that she had had access to a bottle. She sat in her chair, still holding on to one of Barber's hands, looking up, with a shimmering, half-dazed expression on her face, at her husband.

Jimmy clapped Barber on the back and shook hands fiercely. "Lloyd," he said. "Good old Lloyd. *Garçon!*" he shouted, his voice reverberating through the whole room. "Another glass. Take your coat off. Sit down. Sit down."

Lloyd took his coat off and sat down slowly.

"Welcome home," he said quietly. He blew his nose. The cold had arrived.

"First," Jimmy said, "I have something for you." Ceremoniously he dug his hand into his pocket and brought out a roll of ten-thousand-franc notes. The roll was three inches thick. He took off one of the notes. "Maureen told me," he said seriously. "You were a damn good friend, Lloyd. Have you got change of ten?"

"I don't think so," Barber said. "No."

"*Garçon*," Jimmy said to the waiter, who was putting down a third glass, "get me two fives for this, please." When he spoke French, Jimmy had an accent that made even Americans wince.

Jimmy filled the three glasses carefully. He lifted his glass and clinked it first against Barber's and then against Maureen's. Maureen kept looking at him as though she had just seen him for the first time and never hoped to see anything as wonderful again in her whole life.

"To crime," Jimmy said. He winked. He made a complicated face when he winked, like a baby who has trouble with a movement of such subtlety and has to use the whole side of its face and its forehead to effect it.

Maureen giggled.

They drank. It was very good champagne.

"You're having dinner with us," Jimmy said. "Just the three of us. The victory dinner. Just Beauty and me and you, because if it hadn't been for you . . ." Suddenly solemn, he put his hand on Barber's shoulder.

"Yes," said Barber. His feet were icy and his trousers hung soddenly around his wet socks and he had to blow his nose again.

"Did Beauty show you her ring?" Jimmy asked.

"Yes," Barber said.

"She's only had it since six o'clock," Jimmy said.

Maureen held her hand up and stared at her ring. She giggled again.

"I know a place," Jimmy said, "where you can get pheasant and the best bottle of wine in Paris and . . ."

The waiter came back and gave Jimmy the two five-thousand-franc notes. Dimly, Barber wondered how much they weighed.

"If ever you're in a hole," Jimmy said, giving him one of the notes, "you know where to come, don't you?"

"Yes," Barber said. He put the note in his pocket.

He started to sneeze then, and ten minutes later he said he was sorry but he didn't think he could last the evening with a cold like that. Both Jimmy and Maureen tried to get him to stay, but he could tell that they were going to be happier without him.

He finished a second glass of champagne, and said he'd keep in touch, and went out of the bar, feeling his toes squish in his wet shoes. He was hungry and he was very fond of pheasant and actually the cold wasn't so bad, even if his nose kept running all the time. But he knew he couldn't bear to sit between Maureen and Jimmy Richardson all night and watch the way they kept looking at each other.

He walked back to his hotel, because he was through with taxis, and went up and sat on the edge of his bed in his room, in the dark, without taking his coat off. I better get out of here, he thought, rubbing the wet off the end of his nose with the back of his hand. This continent is not for me.

IN THE FRENCH STYLE

BEDDOES GOT in from Egypt in the middle of the morning. He went to his hotel and shook hands with the concierge and told him that the trip had been fine but that Egyptians were impossible. From the concierge he found out that the city was crowded, as usual, and that the price of the room had gone up once more, as usual.

"The tourist season now lasts twelve months a year," the concierge said, giving Beddoes his key. "Nobody stays home any more. It is exhausting."

Beddoes went upstairs and told the porter to put his typewriter in the closet, because he didn't want to see it for a while. He opened the window and looked out with pleasure at the Seine flowing past. Then he took a bath and put on fresh clothes and gave Christina's number over the telephone to the woman at the switchboard. The woman at the switchboard had an insulting habit of repeating numbers in English, and Beddoes noticed, with a smile, that that had not changed. There was the familiar hysteria on the wires as the woman on the switchboard got Christina's number. The telephone in Christina's hotel was down the hall from her room, and Beddoes had to spell the name slowly—Mlle. "T" for Théodore, "A" for André, "T" for Théodore, "E" for Edouard—before the man on the other end understood and went away to tell Christina an American gentleman demanded her on the telephone.

Beddoes heard Christina's footsteps coming down the hall toward the telephone and he thought he could tell from the sound that she was wearing high heels.

"Hello," Christina said. There was a sudden crackle on the wire as Christina spoke, but even so Beddoes could recognize the breathless, excited tone of her voice. Christina answered the phone as though she expected each call to be an invitation to a party.

"Hi, Chris," Beddoes said.

"Who's this?"

"The voice of Egypt," said Beddoes.

"Walter!" Christina said happily. "When did you get in?"

"This minute," Beddoes said, lying by an hour to please her. "Are you wearing high heels?"

"What?"

"You're wearing high heels, aren't you?"

"Wait a minute while I look," Christina said. Then, after a pause, "Did you turn psychic in Cairo?"

Beddoes chuckled. "Semi-Oriental fakery," he said. "I brought back a supply. Where're we going for lunch?"

"Walter!" Christina said. "I'm in despair."

"You have a date."

"Yes. When are you going to learn to cable?"

"That's O.K.," Beddoes said carelessly. He made a point of never sounding disappointed. He had a feeling that if he asked Christina to break the date she would, but he also made a point of never pleading for anything. "We'll make it later."

"How about a drink this afternoon?"

"We can start with that," Beddoes said. "Five?"

"Make it five-thirty," Christina said.

"Where're you going to be?" Beddoes asked, minutely annoyed at the postponement.

"Near the Etoile," Christina said.

"Alexandre's?"

"Fine," Christina said. "Will you be on time for once?"

"Be more polite," Beddoes said, "the first day the man comes to town."

"*A tout à l'heure,*" Christina said.

"What did you say, Ma'am?"

"All the kids are speaking French this year." Christina laughed. "Isn't it nice to have you back in town."

There was a click as she hung up. Beddoes put the phone down slowly and went over to the window. He stared at the river, thinking that this was the first time in a long while that Christina hadn't come over immediately when he arrived in Paris. The river appeared cold and the trees were bare and the sky looked as though it had been gray for months. But with all that, the city looked promising. Even the sunless, snowless winter weather couldn't prevent Paris from looking promising.

He had lunch with a man from the A.P. who had just come back from America. The man from the A.P. said that things were in unholy shape in America and that even if you ate in drugstores it cost at least a dollar and a half for lunch and Beddoes ought to be damned glad he wasn't there.

Beddoes got to the café a little late, but Christina hadn't arrived. He sat on the glass-enclosed terrace, next to the huge window, feeling it cold from the winter afternoon against his sleeve. The terrace was crowded with women drinking tea and men reading the evening newspapers. Outside, under the trees, a little parade was forming, the veterans of some World War I unit, huddling, middle-aged, and chilled in their overcoats, with their flags and decorations, preparing to walk behind an Army band up to the Arch and put a wreath on the tomb in memory of comrades who had fallen in battles that no one any longer remembered. The French, Beddoes thought sourly, because Christina was late and the afternoon had failed its promise, are always finding occasions to block traffic. They have an endless supply of dead to celebrate.

He ordered a beer, because he had drunk too much at lunch. He had also eaten too much, in the first wave of gluttony after Egyptian food. His stomach felt uncomfortable, and he was suddenly very tired from all the miles he had traveled in the past twenty-four hours. After the age of thirty-five, he thought, in evening melancholy, no matter how swift the plane, how calm the air, how soft the cushion, the bones record the miles inexorably. He had turned thirty-five three months before and he had begun to reflect uneasily upon age. He stared at his face in mirrors, noticing wrinkles under his eyes and gray in his beard when he shaved. He remembered hearing that aging ballplayers shaved two and three times a day to keep managers and sportswriters from seeing the telltale flecks in beard stubble. Maybe, he thought, career men in the foreign service ought to do the same thing. Seventy minus thirty-five leaves thirty-five, he thought. It was an equation that came ominously to mind, especially late in the afternoon, more and more often after the midway anniversary. He stared out through the cold glass at the shuffling veterans, ranked shabbily behind their flags, their breath, mingled with cigarette smoke, rising in little clouds above their heads. He wished they'd start marching and get away from there. "Veteran" was a word that suddenly fell on his ear with an unpleasant sound.

He also wished that Christina would arrive. It wasn't like her to be late. She was one of those rare girls who always got to places exactly on the appointed hour. Irrelevantly, he remembered that she also dressed with great speed and took only a minute or two to comb her hair. She had blond hair, cut in the short Parisian manner, which left the back of her neck bare. Beddoes thought about the back of Christina's neck and felt better.

They would give themselves a gay evening, he thought. One should not permit himself to feel tired or old in Paris. If the feeling ever gets chronic, he told himself, I'll move away for good.

He thought about the evening ahead of him. They'd wander around to a couple of bars, avoiding their friends and not drinking too much, and go to a *bistro* in the markets where there were thick steaks and a heavy red wine, and after that maybe they'd go to the night club where there was a queer, original puppet show and three young men who sang funny songs that, unlike so many night-club songs, really did turn out to be funny. When you came out into the street after their act you were charmed and amused and you had the sense that this was the way a man should feel in Paris at two o'clock in the morning.

The night before he left for Cairo, he had taken Christina there. The prospect of going back on this first night home gave him an unexplained but pleasant feeling of satisfactory design. Christina had looked very pretty, the prettiest girl in the room full of handsome women, he'd thought, and he had even danced, for the first time in months. The music was supplied by a pianist and a man who got quivering, rich sounds from an electric guitar, and they played those popular French songs that always made you feel how sweet was love in the city, how full of sorrow and tempered regret.

The music had made Christina a little moony, he remembered, which was strange for her, and she had held his hand during the show, and kissed him when the lights went out between numbers. Her eyes had filled with tears for a moment and she had said, "What am I going to do without you for two months?" when he spoke of his departure the next morning. He had felt, a little warily, because he was affected, too, that it was lucky he was leaving, if she was moving into that phase. That was the pre-yearning-for-marriage phase, and you had to be on guard against it, especially late at night, in Paris, in darkened rooms where pianists and electric guitars played songs about dead leaves and dead loves and lovers who were separated by wars.

Beddoes had been married once, and he felt, for the time being, that that was enough. Wives had a tendency to produce children, and sulk and take to drink or other men when their husbands were called away to the other side of the earth for three or four months at a time on jobs.

He had been a little surprised at Christina. Yearning was not in her line. He had known her, although until recently not very well, almost from the time she arrived from the States four years before. She did some modeling for photographers and was pretty enough to have done very well at it, except that, as she said, she felt too silly making the fashionable languorous, sexy grimaces that were demanded of her. She knew how to type and take dictation and she found odd jobs with American businessmen who had work for a month or two at a time in Paris. She had picked up French immediately, and drove a car, and from time to time she got curious little jobs as a companion for old American ladies who wanted to tour through the château country or into Switzerland. She never seemed to need any sleep (even now she was only about twenty-six) and she would stay up all night with any-body and she went to all the parties and had had, to Beddoes' knowl-edge, affairs with two friends of his—a free-lance photographer and an Air Transport Command pilot who had been killed in a crash outside Frankfurt. You could telephone her at any hour of the day or night without making her angry and you could introduce her into any group and be pleased with the way she behaved. She always knew which *bistro* was having a rage at the moment and who was singing at which night club and which new painter was worth seeing and who was in town and who was going to arrive next week and which little hotels outside Paris were pleasant for lunch or a weekend. She obviously didn't have much money, but she dressed charmingly, French enough to amuse her French friends and not so French that she made Ameri-cans feel she was trying to pretend she was European. All in all, while she was not a girl of whom your grandmother was likely to approve, she was, as Beddoes had once told her, an ornament to the wandering and troubled years of the second half of the twentieth century.

The veterans started to move off, the banners flapping a little in the dusk as the small parade turned past the TWA office and up the Champs-Elysées. Beddoes watched them, thinking vaguely of other parades, other banners. Then he saw Christina striding diagonally across the street, swift and sure of herself in the traffic. She could live in Europe the rest of her life, Beddoes thought, smiling as he watched her, and all she'd have to do would be to walk ten steps and everybody would know she had been born on the other side of the ocean.

He stood when she opened the door into the terrace. She was hatless,

and Beddoes noticed that her hair was much darker than he remembered and she was wearing it longer. He kissed her on both cheeks as
she came up to the table. "Welcome," he said. "In the French style."

She hugged him momentarily. "Well, now," she said, "here's the man
again."

She sat down, opening her coat, and smiled across the table at him.
Her cheeks were flushed from the cold and her eyes were shining and
she looked glitteringly young.

"The spirit of Paris," Beddoes said, touching her hand on the table.
"American division. What'll it be to drink?"

"Tea, please. I'm so glad to see you."

"Tea?" Beddoes made a face. "Anything wrong?"

"No." Christina shook her head. "I just want tea."

"That's a hell of a drink to welcome a traveler home on," Beddoes
said.

"With lemon, please," Christina said.

Beddoes shrugged, and ordered one tea from the waiter.

"How was Egypt?" Christina asked.

"Was I in Egypt?" Beddoes stared at Christina, enjoying her face.

"That's what it said in the papers."

"Oh, yes," Beddoes said. "A new world struggling to be born," he
said, his voice deep and expert. "Too late for feudalism, too early for
democracy . . ."

Christina made a face. "Lovely phrases for the State Department
archives," she said. "I mean over a drink how is Egypt?"

"Sunny and sad," Beddoes said. "After two weeks in Cairo you feel
sorry for everybody. How is Paris?"

"Too late for democracy," Christina said, "too early for feudalism."

Beddoes grinned and leaned across the little table and kissed her
gently. "I mean over a kiss," he said, "how is Paris?"

"The same," Christina said. She hesitated. "Almost the same."

"Who's around?"

"The group," Christina said carelessly. "The usual happy exiles.
Charles, Boris, Anne, Teddy . . ."

Teddy was the free-lance photographer. "You see much of him?"
Beddoes asked, very lightly.

"Uh?" Christina smiled, just a little, at him.

"Merely checking." Beddoes grinned.

"No, I haven't," Christina said. "His Greek's in town."

"Still the Greek?"

"Still the Greek," Christina said.

The waiter came and placed the tea in front of her. She poured it into the cup and squeezed the lemon. She had long, competent fingers, and Beddoes noticed that she no longer used bright nail polish.

"Your hair," he said. "What happened?"

Christina touched her hair absently. "Oh," she said. "You noticed?"

"Where're the blondes of yesteryear?"

"I decided to go natural." Christina stirred her tea. "See what that was like for a change. Like it?"

"I haven't decided yet. It's longer, too."

"Uh-huh. For the winter. The back of my neck was cold. People say it makes me look younger."

"They're absolutely right," Beddoes said. "You now look exactly eleven."

Christina smiled and lifted her cup to him. "To those who return," she said.

"I don't accept toasts in tea," Beddoes said.

"You're a finicky, liquor-loving man," Christina said, and placidly sipped at her tea.

"Now," Beddoes said, "the evening. I thought we might skip our dear friends and go to that place in the markets for dinner, because I'm dying for a steak, and after that—" He stopped. "What's the matter? Can't we have dinner together?"

"It's not that, exactly." Christina kept her head down and stirred her tea slowly. "I have a date—"

"Cancel him," Beddoes said promptly. "Cancel the swine."

"I can't really." Christina looked soberly up at him. "He's coming to meet me here any minute now."

"Oh." Beddoes nodded. "That makes it different, doesn't it?"

"Yes."

"Can't we shake him?"

"No," Christina said. "We can't shake him."

"The man doesn't live who can't be shaken," said Beddoes. "Old friend, you say, who just arrived from the horrors of the desert, just escaped dysentery and religious wars by the skin of his teeth, needs soothing, you say, and tender attention for his shattered nerves, et cetera."

Christina was smiling, but shaking her head. "Sorry," she said. "It can't be done."

"Want me to do it?" Beddoes said. "Man to man. See here, old fellow, we're all grown-up, civilized human beings— That sort of thing?"

"No," Christina said.

"Why not?" Beddoes asked, conscious that he was breaking a long-standing and until now jealously adhered-to rule about not pleading for anything. "Why can't we?"

"Because I don't want to," Christina said.

"Oh," said Beddoes. "The wind is in that direction."

"Variably," Christina said softly, "in that direction. We could all have dinner together. The three of us. He's a very nice man. You'd like him."

"I never like any man the first night I'm in Paris," Beddoes said.

They sat in silence for a moment while Beddoes remembered all the times that Christina had said over the phone, "O.K., it's sinful, but I'll brush him. Meet you at eight." It was hard to believe, sitting across from her, noticing that there was no obvious change in the way she looked at him, in the way she touched his hand, that she wouldn't say it in the next minute or so.

"Two months is a long time, isn't it?" Beddoes said. "In Paris?"

"No," Christina said. "It's not a long time. In Paris or anywhere else."

"Hello, Christina." It was a tall, rather heavy-set young man, smiling and blond, who was standing, holding a hat, next to the table. "I found the place all right." He leaned over and kissed her forehead.

Beddoes stood up.

"Jack," Christina said, "this is Walter Beddoes. John Haislip. Dr. Haislip."

The two men shook hands.

"He's a surgeon," Christina said as Haislip gave his hat and coat to the attendant and sat down beside her. "He nearly had his picture in *Life* last year for something he did with kidneys. In thirty years he's going to be enormously famous."

Haislip chuckled. He was a big, placid, self-confident-looking man, with the air of an athlete, who was probably older than he looked. And just with one glance Beddoes could tell how the man felt about Christina. Haislip wasn't hiding anything in that department.

"What'll you drink, Doctor?" Beddoes asked.

"Lemonade, please."

"*Un citron pressé*," Beddoes said to the waiter. He peered curiously at Christina, but she was keeping her face straight.

"Jack doesn't drink," Christina said. "He says it isn't fair for people who make a living out of cutting other people up."

"When I retire," Haislip said cheerfully, "I'm going to soak it up and let my hands shake like leaves in the wind." He turned to Beddoes.

You could tell that it took a conscious wrench for him to stop looking at Christina. "Did you have a good time in Egypt?" he asked.

"Oh," Beddoes said, surprised. "You know about my being in Egypt?"

"Christina's told me all about you," Haislip said.

"I swore a solemn oath that I was going to forget Egypt for a month once I got here," Beddoes said.

Haislip chuckled. He had a low, unforced laugh and his face was friendly and unself-conscious. "I know how you feel," he said. "The same way I feel about the hospital sometimes."

"Where is the hospital?" Beddoes asked.

"Seattle," Christina said quickly.

"How long have you been here?" Beddoes saw Christina glance at him obliquely as he spoke.

"Three weeks," said Haislip. He turned back toward Christina, as though he could find comfort in no other position. "The changes that can take place in three weeks. My Lord!" He patted Christina's arm and chuckled again. "One more week and back to the hospital."

"You here for fun or for business?" Beddoes asked, falling helplessly into the pattern of conversation of all Americans who meet each other abroad for the first time.

"A little of both," Haislip said. "There was a conference of surgeons I was asked to attend, and I moseyed around a few hospitals on the side."

"What do you think of French medicine now you've had a chance to see some of it?" Beddoes asked, the investigator within operating automatically.

"Well"—Haislip managed to look away from Christina for a moment —"they function differently from us over here. Intuitively. They don't have the equipment we have, or the money for research, and they have to make up for it with insight and intuition." He grinned. "If you're feeling poorly, Mr. Beddoes," he said, "don't hesitate to put yourself in their hands. You'll do just about as well here as anyplace else."

"I feel all right," Beddoes said, then felt that it had been an idiotic thing to say. The conversation was beginning to make him uncomfortable, not because of anything that had been said but because of the way the man kept looking, so openly and confessingly and completely, at Christina. There was a little pause and Beddoes had the feeling that unless he jumped in, they would sit in silence forever. "Do any sightseeing?" he asked lamely.

"Not as much as I'd like," Haislip said. "Just around Paris. I'd've loved to go down south this time of the year. That place Christina keeps talking about. St. Paul de Vence. I guess that's about as different from Seattle as a man could wish for and still get running water and Christian nourishment. You've been there, haven't you, Mr. Beddoes?"

"Yes," Beddoes said.

"Christina told me," said Haislip. "Oh, thank you," he said to the waiter who put the lemonade down in front of him.

Beddoes stared at Christina. They had spent a week together there early in the autumn. He wondered what, exactly, she had told the Doctor.

"We'll make it the next trip," Haislip said.

"Oh," said Beddoes, noting the "we" and wondering whom it included. "You planning to come over again soon?"

"In three years." Haislip carefully extracted the ice from his lemonade and put it on the saucer. "I figure I can get away for six weeks in the summer every three years. People don't get so sick in the summertime." He stood up. "Pardon me," he said, "but I have to make a couple of telephone calls."

"Downstairs and to the right," Christina said. "The woman'll put the calls through for you. She speaks English."

Haislip laughed. "Christina doesn't trust my French," he said. "She says it's the only recognizable Puget Sound accent that has ever been imposed upon the language." He started away from the table, then stopped. "I sincerely hope you'll be able to join us for dinner, Mr. Beddoes."

"Well," Beddoes said, "I made a tentative promise I'd meet some people. But I'll see what I can do."

"Good." Haislip touched Christina's shoulder lightly, as though for some obscure reassurance, and walked away between the tables.

Beddoes watched him, thinking unpleasantly, Well, one thing, I'm better-looking, anyway. Then he turned to Christina. She was stirring the tea leaves at the bottom of her cup absently with her spoon. "That's why the hair is long and natural," Beddoes said. "Isn't it?"

"That's why." Christina kept stirring the tea leaves.

"And the nail polish."

"And the nail polish."

"And the tea."

"And the tea."

"What did you tell him about St. Paul de Vence?"

"Everything."

"Look up from that damned cup."

Slowly Christina put down the spoon and raised her head. Her eyes were glistening, but not enough to make anything of it, and her mouth was set, as with an effort.

"What do you mean by everything?" Beddoes demanded.

"Everything."

"Why?"

"Because I don't have to hide anything from him."

"How long have you known him?"

"You heard," Christina said. "Three weeks. A friend of mine in New York asked him to look me up."

"What are you going to do with him?"

Christina looked directly into his eyes. "I'm going to marry him next week and I'm going back to Seattle with him."

"And you'll come back here three years from now for six weeks in the summertime, because people don't get so sick in the summertime," Beddoes said.

"Exactly."

"And that's O.K.?"

"Yes."

"You said that too defiantly," Beddoes said.

"Don't be clever with me," Christina said harshly. "I'm through with all that."

"Waiter!" Beddoes called. "Bring me a whiskey, please." He said it in English, because for the moment he had forgotten where he was. "And you," he said to Christina. "For the love of God, have a drink."

"Another tea," Christina said.

"Yes, Madame," said the waiter, and went off.

"Will you answer some questions?" Beddoes asked.

"Yes."

"Do I rate straight answers?"

"Yes."

Beddoes took a deep breath and looked through the window. A man in a raincoat was walking past, reading a newspaper and shaking his head.

"All right," Beddoes said. "What's so great about him?"

"What can I be expected to say to that?" Christina asked. "He's a gentle, good, useful man. And now what do you know?"

"What else?"

"And he loves me." She said it in a low voice. In all the time they'd been together, Beddoes hadn't heard her use the word before. "He loves me," Christina repeated flatly.

"I saw," said Beddoes. "Immoderately."

"Immoderately," Christina said.

"Now let me ask another question," Beddoes said. "Would you like to get up from this table and go off with me tonight?"

Christina pushed her cup away, turning it thoughtfully. "Yes," she said.

"But you won't," said Beddoes.

"No."

"Why not?"

"Let's talk about something else," said Christina. "Where're you going on your next trip? Kenya? Bonn? Tokyo?"

"Why not?"

"Because I'm tired of people like you," Christina said clearly. "I'm tired of correspondents and pilots and promising junior statesmen. I'm tired of all the brilliant young men who are constantly going someplace to report a revolution or negotiate a treaty or die in a war. I'm tired of airports and I'm tired of seeing people off. I'm tired of not being allowed to cry until the plane gets off the ground. I'm tired of being so damned prompt. I'm tired of answering the telephone. I'm tired of all the spoiled, hung-over international darlings. I'm tired of sitting down to dinner with people I used to love and being polite to their Greeks. I'm tired of being handed around the group. I'm tired of being more in love with people than they are with me. That answer your question?"

"More or less," Beddoes said. He was surprised that no one at any of the other tables seemed to be paying any special attention to them.

"When you left for Egypt," Christina went on, her voice level, "I decided. I leaned against that wire fence watching them refueling all those monstrous planes, with the lights on, and I dried the tears and I decided. The next time, it was going to be someone who would be shattered when I took off."

"And you found him."

"I found him," Christina said flatly. "And I'm not going to shatter him."

Beddoes put out his hands and took hers. They lay limp in his grasp. "Chris . . ." he said. She was looking out the window. She sat there, outlined against the shining dusk beyond the plate glass, scrubbed and youthful and implacable, making him remember, confusedly, the first time he had met her, and all the best girls he had ever known, and what she had looked like next to him in the early-morning autumnal sunlight that streamed, only three months before, into the hotel room in the south, which overlooked the brown minor Alps and the distant sea.

Holding her hands, with the familiar touch of the girlish fingers against his, he felt that if he could get her to turn her head everything would be different.

"Chris . . ." he whispered.

But she didn't turn her head. "Write me in Seattle," she said, staring out the window, which was streaked with moisture and in which the lights from within the café and the lights from the restaurant across the street were reflected and magnified and distorted.

Beddoes let her hands go. She didn't bother to move them. They lay before her, with their pale nail polish glistening dully, on the stained wood table. Beddoes stood up. "I'd better go." It was difficult to talk, and his voice sounded strange to him inside his head, and he thought, God, I'm getting senile, I'm tempted to cry in restaurants. "I don't want to wait for the check," he said. "Tell your friend I'm sorry I couldn't join you for dinner and that I apologize for leaving him with the check."

"That's all right," Christina said evenly. "He'll be happy to pay."

Beddoes leaned over and kissed her, first on one cheek, then on the other. "Good-bye," he said, thinking he was smiling. "In the French style."

He got his coat quickly and went out. He went past the TWA office to the great boulevard and turned the corner, where the veterans had marched a half hour before. He walked blindly toward the Arch, where the laurel leaves of the wreath were already glistening in the evening mist before the tomb and the flame.

He knew that it was a bad night to be alone and that he ought to go in somewhere and telephone and ask someone to have dinner with him. He passed two or three places with telephones, and although he hesitated before each one, he didn't go in. Because there was no one in the whole city he wanted to see that night.

VOYAGE OUT, VOYAGE HOME

CONSTANCE SAT IMPATIENTLY in the little chair in the first-class cabin, taking occasional sips of the champagne that Mark had sent. Mark had been called out of town and hadn't been able to come, but he'd sent champagne. She didn't like champagne, but she didn't know what else to do with it, so she drank it. Her father stood in front of the porthole, drinking, too. From his expression, Constance could guess that he didn't like champagne either. Or perhaps he didn't like this particular vintage. Or he didn't like it because Mark had sent it. Or maybe it wasn't the champagne at all but just that he was embarrassed.

Constance knew that she was looking sullen, and she tried to change the set of her face, because she also knew that she looked younger, childish, sixteen, seventeen, when she was sullen. She was sure that everything she did with her face at that moment made her look more sullen than ever, and she wished the horn would blow and her father would get off the ship.

"You'll probably drink a lot of this," her father said. "In France."

"I don't expect to stay in France long," she said. "I'm going to look for someplace quiet." Her voice sounded to her as though it were coming out of the nursery, wailing and spiteful and spoiled. She tried to smile at her father. The last few weeks in the apartment, while the argument had been going on and the hostility had been so close to the surface, had been painful to her, and now, in the last ten minutes before the ship pulled away, she wanted to recapture an earlier, easier relationship as far as she could. So she smiled, but she had the impression that the smile was crafty and cold and coquettish. Her father turned around and looked vaguely out the porthole at the covered wharf. It was rainy and there was a cold wind blowing and the men on the dock waiting to throw off the lines looked miserable.

"It's going to be a choppy night," her father said. "Have you got the Dramamine?"

The hostility returned, because he asked about the Dramamine. At a moment like that. "I won't need Dramamine," Constance said shortly. She took a long drink of the champagne. The label on the bottle was impeccable, like all Mark's gifts, but the wine was sourish and acidy.

Her father turned back toward her. He smiled at her, and she thought, bitterly, This is the last time he's going to get away with patronizing me. He stood there, a robust, confident, healthy, youngish-seeming man, looking privately amused, and Constance thought, How would you like it if I just got out of here and walked off this precious boat—how would you ever like it?

"I envy you," her father said. "If someone had only sent me to Europe when I was twenty . . ."

Twenty, twenty, Constance thought. He's always harping on twenty. "Please, Father, let's cut that out," she said. "I'm here and I'm going and it's all settled, but let's spare ourselves the envy."

"Every time I happen to remind you that you're twenty," her father said mildly, "you react as though I'd insulted you."

He smiled, pleased with himself that he was so damned perceptive, that he understood her so well, that he was not one of those fathers whose children slide irrevocably away from them into mysterious, modern depths.

"Let's not discuss it," Constance said, pitching her voice low. When she remembered, she always made a point of pitching her voice low. It sometimes made her sound forty years old on the telephone, or like a man.

"Have a great time," her father said. "Go to all the bright places. And if you decide you want to stay on, just let me know. Maybe I'll be able to come over and join you for a few weeks—"

"Three months from now," Constance said crisply, "to this day, I'll be coming up the harbor."

"Whatever you say, my dear."

When he said "my dear," Constance knew he was humoring her. She couldn't bear being humored there in the ugly little cabin, with the weather bad outside, and the ship ready to leave, and the sounds of people saying good-bye, laughing loudly, in the next room. If she had been on better terms with her father, she would have cried.

The horn blew for visitors to go ashore, and her father came and kissed her, holding her for an extra second, and she tried to be polite. But when he said, very seriously, "You'll see—three months from now you'll thank me for this," she pushed him back, furious with him for his obnoxious assurance, and mournful at the same time that they, who had been so close to each other, were no longer friends.

"Good-bye," she said, her voice choked and not pitched low. "The whistle's blowing. Good-bye."

He picked up his hat, patted her shoulder, hesitated a moment at the door, looking thoughtful but not disturbed, and went out into the corridor and disappeared among the other visitors who were streaming up toward the gangplank and the shore.

When she was sure her father was off, Constance went up to the boat deck and stood there, alone in the sharp, blowy rain, watching the tugs pull the ship into the stream. As the ship went slowly downriver into the harbor and then headed into open water, she shivered in the wintry air, and, approving of herself a little for the grandeur of the sentiment, thought, I am approaching a continent to which I have no connection.

Constance braced herself against the crossbar of the lift as she approached the mid-point of the hill. She made sure that her skis were firmly in the ruts as she came up onto the flat section of packed snow where there was a short line of skiers who had come down only halfway and were waiting to pick up empty hooks and go back to the top. She always felt a little uncertain here, because if you were alone on one side of the T bar, the first person in the line would swing into place alongside you and there would be an extra, sudden pull as the new weight caught that could throw you off balance. She saw that there was a man waiting for the place next to her, and she concentrated on keeping erect gracefully as he settled into place beside her. He did it smoothly, and they skidded easily past the waiting line. She was conscious that he was looking across at her, but she was too occupied for the moment with the terrain in front of her to turn her head.

"Oh, I know you," the man said as they started safely up the hill again, leaning against the pull of the bar, their skis bumping a little in the ruts. "You're the grave young American."

Constance looked at him for the first time. "And you," she said, because everybody talked to everybody else on the hills, "you're the gay young Englishman."

"Half right," he said. He smiled. His face was a skier's brown, with an almost girlish flush of blood along the cheekbones. "At least, one-third right." She knew his name was Pritchard, because she had heard people talking to him in the hotel. She remembered hearing one of the ski teachers say about him, "He is too reckless. He thinks he is better than he actually is. He does not have the technique for so much speed." She glanced across at him and decided he *did* look reckless. He had a long nose—the kind that doesn't photograph well but that looks all right just the same, especially in a long, thin face. Twenty-five, Constance thought, twenty-six. No more. He was leaning easily against the bar, not holding on with his hands. He took off his gloves and fished a package of cigarettes out of his pockets and offered them to Constance. "Players," he said. "I hope you won't hate me."

"No, thank you," Constance said. She was sure that if she tried to light a cigarette she would fall off the lift.

He lit his cigarette, bending over a little and squinting over his cupped hands as the smoke twisted up past his eyes. He had long, thin hands, and ordinarily you had the feeling that people with hands like that were nervous and easily upset. He was tall and slender, and his ski pants were very downhill, Constance noted, and he wore a red sweater and a checked scarf. He had the air of a dandy, but a dandy who was amused at himself. He moved easily on his skis, and you could tell he was one of the people who weren't afraid of falling.

"I never see you in the bar," he said, tossing the match into the snow and putting on his gloves.

"I don't drink," she said, not quite telling the truth.

"They have Coca-Cola," he said. "Switzerland, the forty-ninth state."

"I don't like Coca-Cola."

"Used to be one of the leading British colonies," he said, grinning. "Switzerland. But we lost it, along with India. Before the war, in this town, the English covered the hills like the edelweiss. If you wanted to find a Swiss between January 1st and March 13th, you had to hunt with dogs."

"Were you here before the war?" Constance asked, surprised.

"With my mother. She broke a leg a year."

"Is she here now?"

"No," he said. "She's dead."

I must be careful, Constance thought, avoiding looking at the man beside her, not to ask people in Europe about their relatives. So many of them turn out to be dead.

"It used to be very gay," he said, "the hotels swarming, and dances every night, and everybody dressing for dinner, and singing 'God Save the King' on New Year's. Did you know it was going to be this quiet?"

"Yes," Constance said. "I asked the man at the travel bureau in Paris."

"Oh. What did he say?"

"He said everybody was a serious skier here and went to bed by ten o'clock."

The Englishman glanced at her momentarily. "You're not a serious skier, are you?"

"No. I've only been two or three times before."

"You're not one of the delicate ones, are you?"

"Delicate?" Constance looked at him, puzzled. "What do you mean?"

"You know," he said, "the advertisements. Schools for delicate children. Swiss for t.b."

Constance laughed. "Do I look as though I have t.b.?"

He regarded her gravely, and she felt plump and unaustere and a little too bosomy in her tight clothes. "No," he said. "But you never can tell. Did you ever read *The Magic Mountain?*"

"Yes," she said, feeling proud that she could show she was not completely uncultured, although American and very young, and remembering that she had skipped the philosophic discussions and cried over the death of the cousin. "I read it. Why?"

"The sanitarium it was written about isn't far from here," Pritchard said. "I'll show it to you someday when the snow's bad. Do you think this place is sad?"

"No," she said, surprised. "Why?"

"Some people do. The mixture. The pretty mountains and the healthy types walloping down the hills, risking their necks and feeling marvelous, and the people with the bad lungs hanging on, watching them and wondering if they're ever going to leave here alive."

"I guess I didn't think about it," Constance admitted honestly.

"It was worse right after the war," he said. "There was a boom here right after the war. All the people who hadn't eaten enough or had been living underground or in prison and who had been frightened so long—"

"Where're they now?"

Pritchard shrugged. "Dead, discharged, or destitute," he said. "Is it true that people refuse to die in America?"

"Yes," she said. "It would be an admission of failure."

He smiled and patted her gloved hand, which was clutching tightly onto the middle bar. "You mustn't be angry that we're jealous," he said.

"It's the only way we can show our gratitude." Gently, he loosened her fingers from the wood. "And you mustn't be so tight when you ski. Not even with your fingers. You mustn't even frown until you go in for tea. The drill is—loose, desperate, and supremely confident."

"Is that how you are?"

"Mostly desperate," he said.

"What are you doing on this little beginners' slope, then?" Constance asked. "Why didn't you take the *téléphérique* up to the top?"

"I twisted my ankle yesterday," Pritchard said. "Overrated myself. The February disease. Out of control and into a gully, with a great deal of style. So today I can only do slow, majestic turns. But tomorrow we attack that one once more—" He gestured up toward the peak, half closed in by fog, with the sun a wet, pale ball above it, making it look forbidding and dangerous. "Come along?" He looked at her inquiringly.

"I haven't been up there yet," Constance said, regarding the mountain respectfully. "I'm afraid it's a little too much for me so far."

"You must always do things that are a little too much for you," he said. "On skis. Otherwise, where's the fun?"

They were silent for several moments, moving slowly up the hill, feeling the wind cut across their faces, noticing the quiet and the queer, fogged mountain light. Twenty yards ahead of them, on the preceding bar, a girl in a yellow parka moved evenly upward like a bright, patient doll.

"Paris?" Pritchard said.

"What's that?" He jumps around entirely too much, Constance thought, feeling heavy.

"You said you came from Paris. Are you one of those nice people who come here to give us your government's money?"

"No," said Constance. "I just came over on a—well, on a vacation. I live in New York, really. And French food makes me break out."

He looked at her critically. "You look completely unbroken out now," he said. "You look like the girls who advertise soap and beer in American magazines." Then he added hastily, "If that's considered insulting in your country, I take it back."

"And the men in Paris," she said.

"Oh. Are there men in Paris?"

"Even in the museums. They follow you. With homburg hats. Looking at you as though they're weighing you by the pound. In front of religious pictures and everything."

"Girl I knew, English girl," Pritchard said, "was followed from Prestwick, Scotland, to the tip of Cornwall by an American gunner in 1944. Three months. No religious pictures, though, as far as I know."

"You know what I mean. It's an impolite atmosphere," she said primly, knowing he was making fun of her in that straight-faced English way but not knowing whether to be offended or not.

"Were you brought up in a convent?"

"No."

"It's amazing how many American girls sound as though they were brought up in a convent. Then it turns out they drink gin and roar in bars. What do you do at night?"

"Where? At home?"

"No. I know what people do at night in America. They look at television," he said. "I mean here."

"I—I wash my hair," she said defensively, feeling foolish. "And I write letters."

"How long are you staying up here?"

"Six weeks."

"Six weeks." He nodded, and swung his poles to his outside hand, because they were nearing the top. "Six weeks of shining hair and correspondence."

"I made a promise," she said, thinking, I might as well let him know now, just in case he's getting any ideas. "I promised someone I'd write him a letter a day while I was gone."

Pritchard nodded soberly, as though sympathizing with her. "Americans," he said as they came to the top and slid out from the T bar onto the flat place. "Americans baffle me."

Then he waved his poles at her and went straight down the hill, his red sweater a swift, diminishing gay speck against the blue-shadowed snow.

The sun slipped between the peaks, like a gold coin in a gigantic slot, and the light got flat and dangerous, making it almost impossible to see the bumps. Constance made her last descent, falling twice and feeling superstitious, because it was always when you said, "Well, this is the last one," that you got hurt.

Running out and coming to a stop on the packed snow between two farmhouses at the outskirts of the town, she kicked off her skis with a sense of accomplishment and relief. Her toes and fingers were frozen, but she was warm everywhere else and her cheeks were bright red and she breathed the thin, cold air with a mountain sense of tasting something delicious. She felt vigorous and friendly, and smiled at the other skiers clattering to a stop around her. She was brushing the snow of the last two falls off her clothes, so that she would look like a good skier as she walked through the town, when Pritchard came down over the last ridge and flicked to a stop beside her.

"I see you," he said, bending to unlock his bindings, "but I won't tell a soul."

Constance gave a final, self-conscious pat to the icy crystals on her parka. "I only fell four times all afternoon," she said.

"Up there, tomorrow"—he made a gesture of his head toward the mountain—"you'll crash all day."

"I didn't say I was going up there." Constance buckled her skis together and started to swing them up to her shoulder. Pritchard reached over and took them from her. "I can carry my own skis," she said.

"Don't be sturdy. American girls are always being sturdy about inessential points." He made a big V out of the two pairs of skis on his shoulders, and they started walking, their boots crunching on the stained, hard snow of the road. The lights came on in the town, pale in the fading light. The postman passed them, pulling his sled with his big dog yoked beside him. Six children in snowsuits on a linked whip of sleds came sliding down out of a steep side street and overturned in front of them in a fountain of laughter. A big brown horse with his belly clipped to keep the ice from forming there slowly pulled three huge logs toward the station. Old men in pale-blue parkas passed them and said "Grüezi," and a maid from one of the houses up the hill shot out on a little sled, holding a milk can between her knees as she rocketed around the turns. They were playing a French waltz over at the skating rink, and the music mingled with the laughter of the children and the bells on the horse's bridle and the distant, old-fashioned clanging of the gong at the railroad station, announcing a train's departure.

"Departure," the station bell said, insistent among the other sounds.

There was a booming noise far off in the hills, and Constance looked up, puzzled. "What's that?" she asked.

"Mortars," said Pritchard. "It snowed last night, and the patrols have been out all day firing at the overhangs. For the avalanches."

There was another shot, low and echoing, and they stopped and listened. "Like old times," Pritchard said as they started walking again. "Like the good old war."

"Oh," said Constance, feeling delicate, because she had never heard guns before. "The war. Were you in it?"

"A little." He grinned. "I had a little war."

"Doing what?"

"Night fighter," he said, shifting the yoke of skis a little on his shoulders. "I flew an ugly black plane across an ugly black sky. That's the wonderful thing about the Swiss—the only thing they shoot is snow."

"Night fighter," Constance said vaguely. She had been only twelve years old when the war ended, and it was all jumbled and remote in her memory. It was like hearing about the graduating class two generations before you in school. People were always referring to names and dates and events that they expected you to recognize, but which you could never quite get straight. "Night fighter. What was that?"

"We flew interceptor missions over France," Pritchard said. "We'd fly on the deck to avoid the radar and flak, and hang around airfields making the Hun miserable, waiting for planes to come in slow, with their wheels down."

"Oh, I remember now," Constance said firmly. "You're the ones who ate carrots. For night vision."

Pritchard laughed. "For publication we ate carrots," he said. "Actually, we used radar. We'd locate them on the screen and fire when we saw the exhuast flares. Give me a radar screen over a carrot any day."

"Did you shoot down many planes?" Constance asked, wondering if she sounded morbid.

"*Grüezi,*" Pritchard said to the owner of a *pension* who was standing in front of his door looking up at the sky to see if it was going to snow that night. "Twenty centimetres by morning. Powder."

"You think?" the man said, looking doubtfully at the evening sky.

"I guarantee," Pritchard said.

"You're very polite," the man said, smiling. "You must come to Switzerland more often." He went into his *pension,* closing the door behind him.

"A couple," Pritchard said carelessly. "We shot down a couple. Should I tell you how brave I was?"

"You look so young," Constance said.

"I'm thirty," said Pritchard. "How old do you have to be to shoot down a plane? Especially poor, lumbering transports, running out of gas, full of clerks and rear-echelon types, wiping their glasses and being sorry the airplane was ever invented."

In the hills, there was the flat sound of the mortars again. Constance wished they'd stop. "You don't look thirty," she said to Pritchard.

"I've led a simple and salutary life. Here," he said. They were in front of one of the smaller hotels, and he put the skis in the rack and jammed the poles into the snow beside them. "Let's go in here and get a simple and salutary cup of tea."

"Well," said Constance, "I really—"

"Make the letter two pages shorter tonight, and more intense." He took her elbow gently, barely touching it, as he guided her toward the door. "And polish your hair some other night."

They went into the bar and sat down at a heavy, carefully carved wood table. There were no other skiers in the bar—just some village men sitting under the chamois antlers on the wall, quietly playing cards on felt cloths and drinking coffee out of small stemmed glasses.

"I told you," Pritchard said, taking off his scarf. "This country is being overrun by the Swiss."

The waitress came over, and Pritchard ordered, in German.

"What did you ask for?" Constance asked, because she could tell it wasn't only tea.

"Tea and lemon and black rum," said Pritchard.

"Do you think I ought to have rum?" she asked doubtfully.

"Everybody in the whole world should have rum," he said. "It will keep you from committing suicide in the twilight."

"You speak German, don't you?"

"I speak all the dead languages of Europe," he said. "German, French, Italian, and English. I was carefully educated for a world of interchangeable currency." He sat back, rubbing the knuckles of one hand against the palm of the other, to warm them. His head was leaning against the wood-paneled wall and he was smiling at her and she couldn't tell whether she was uncomfortable or not. "Let me hear you say 'Hi-ho, Silver.'"

"What?" she asked, puzzled.

"Isn't that what people say in America? I want to perfect my accent for the next invasion," he said.

"They stopped that," she said, thinking, My, he's a jumpy boy, I wonder what happened to him to make him that way. "They don't say it any more. It's out of date."

"All the best things go out of date so quickly in your country," he said regretfully. "Observe the Swiss." He gestured with his head toward where the men were playing. "That game has been going on since 1910," he said. "Living among the Swiss is so placid. It's like living alongside a lake. Many people can't stand it, of course. You remember that joke about the Swiss in that film about Vienna?"

"No," Constance said. "What film?" This is the first time, she thought, I've ever called a movie a film. I must be careful.

"One of the characters says, 'The Swiss haven't had a war in a hundred and fifty years and what have they produced? The cuckoo clock.'

I don't know." Pritchard shrugged. "Maybe it's better to live in a country that invents the cuckoo clock than one that invents radar. Time is nothing serious to a cuckoo clock. A little toy that makes a silly, artificial sound every half hour. For people who invent radar, time is ominous, because it's the difference between the altitude of a plane and the location of the battery that's going to bring it down. It's an invention for people who are suspicious and are thinking of ambush. Here's your tea. As you see, I'm making a serious effort to amuse you, because I've been watching you for five days and you give the impression of a girl who cries herself to sleep several times a week."

"How much of this stuff do I put in?" Constance asked, confused by the flood of talk, holding up the glass of rum, and carefully making sure not to look at Pritchard.

"Half," he said. "You have to have something in reserve for the second cup."

"It smells good," Constance said, sniffing the fragrance that rose from the cup after she had measured out half the glass of rum and squeezed the lemon into it.

"Perhaps"—Pritchard prepared his own cup—"perhaps I'd better talk only on impersonal subjects."

"Perhaps that would be better," Constance said.

"The chap who receives all those letters," Pritchard said. "Why isn't he here?"

Constance hesitated for a moment. "He works," she said.

"Oh. That vice." He sipped his tea, then put down his cup and rubbed his nose with his handkerchief. "Hot tea does that to you, too?"

"Yes."

"Are you going to marry him?"

"You said impersonal."

"So. The marriage is arranged."

"I didn't say that."

"No. But you would have said no if it wasn't."

Constance chuckled. "All right," she said. "Arranged. Anyway, approximately arranged."

"When?"

"When the three months're up," she said, without thinking.

"Is that a law in New York?" Pritchard asked. "That you have to wait three months? Or is it a private family taboo?"

Constance hesitated. Suddenly, she felt that she hadn't really talked to anyone in a long time. She had ordered meals and asked directions in railroad stations and said good morning to the people in shops, but everything else had been loneliness and silence, no less painful because she had imposed it on herself. Why not, she thought, selfishly and gratefully. Why not talk about it, for once?

"It's my father," she said, twisting her cup. "It's his idea. He's against it. He said wait three months and see. He thinks I'll forget Mark in three months in Europe."

"America," Pritchard said. "The only place left where people can afford to act in an old-fashioned manner. What's the matter with Mark? Is he a fright?"

"He's beautiful," Constance said. "Melancholy and beautiful."

Pritchard nodded, as though noting all this down. "No money, though," he said.

"Enough," said Constance. "At least, he has a good job."

"What's the matter with him, then?"

"My father thinks he's too old for me," Constance said. "He's forty."

"A grave complaint," Pritchard said. "Is that why he's melancholy?"

Constance smiled. "No. He was born that way. He's a thoughtful man."

"Do you only like forty-year-old men?" Pritchard asked.

"I only like Mark," said Constance. "Although it's true I never got along with the young men I knew. They—they're cruel. They make me feel shy—and angry with myself. When I go out with one of them, I come home feeling crooked."

"Crooked?" Pritchard looked puzzled.

"Yes. I feel I haven't behaved like me. I've behaved the way I think the other girls they've gone out with have behaved. Coquettish, cynical, amorous. Is this too complicated?"

"No."

"I hate the opinions other people have of me," Constance said, almost forgetting the young man at the table with her, and talking bitterly, and for herself. "I hate being used just for celebrations, when people come into town from college or from the Army. Somebody for parties, somebody to maul on the way home in the taxi. And my father's opinion of me." She was getting it out for the first time. "I used to think we were good friends, that he thought I was a responsible, grown-up human being. Then when I told him I wanted to marry Mark, I found out it was all a fraud. What he really thinks of me is that I'm a child. And a child is a form of idiot. My mother left him when I was ten and we've been very close since then, but we weren't as close as I thought we were. He was just playing a game with me. Flattering me. When the first real issue came up, the whole thing collapsed. He wouldn't let me have my own opinion of me at all. That's why I finally said all right to the three months. To prove it to him once and for all." She looked suddenly, distrustfully, at Pritchard, to see whether he was smiling. "Are you being amused at me?"

"Of course not," he said. "I'm thinking of all the people I've known who've had different opinions of me than I've had of myself. What a frightening idea." He looked at her speculatively, but it was hard for her to tell how serious he was. "And what's your opinion of yourself?"

"It's not completely formed yet," she said slowly. "I know what I want it to be. I want to be responsible and I don't want to be a child and I don't want to be cruel—and I want to move in a good direction." She shrugged, embarrassed now. "That's pretty lame, isn't it?"

"Lame," Pritchard said, "but admirable."

"Oh, I'm not admirable yet," she said. "Maybe in ten years. I haven't sorted myself out completely yet." She laughed nervously. "Isn't it nice," she said, "you're going away in a few days and I'll never see you again, so I can talk like this to you."

"Yes," he said. "Very nice."

"I haven't talked to anyone for so long. Maybe it's the rum."

Pritchard smiled. "Ready for your second cup?"

"Yes, thank you." She watched him pour the tea and was surprised to notice that his hand shook. Perhaps, she thought, he's one of those young men who came out of the war drinking a bottle of whisky a day.

"So," he said. "Tomorrow we go up to the top of the mountain."

She was grateful to him for realizing that she didn't want to talk about herself any more and switching the conversation without saying anything about it.

"How will you do it—with your ankle?" she asked.

"I'll get the doctor to put a shot of Novocain in it," he said. "And for a few hours my ankle will feel immortal."

"All right," she said, watching him pour his own tea, watching his hand shake. "In the morning?"

"I don't ski in the morning," he said. He added the rum to his tea and sniffed it appreciatively.

"What do you do in the morning?"

"I recover, and write poetry."

"Oh." She looked at him doubtfully. "Should I know your name?"

"No," he said. "I always tear it up the next morning."

She laughed, a little uncertainly, because the only other people she had ever known who wrote poetry had been fifteen-year-old boys in prep school. "My," she said, "you're a queer man."

"Queer?" He raised his eyebrows. "Doesn't that mean something a little obscene in America? Boys with boys, I mean."

"Only sometimes," Constance said, embarrassed. "Not now. What sort of poetry do you write?"

"Lyric, elegiac, and athletic," he said. "In praise of youth, death, and anarchy. Very good for tearing. Shall we have dinner together tonight?"

"Why?" she asked, unsettled by the way he jumped from one subject to another.

"That's a question that no European woman would ever ask," he said.

"I told the hotel that I was going to have dinner up in my room."

"I have great influence at the hotel," he said. "I think I may be able to prevent them from taking the tray up."

"Besides," Constance said, "what about the lady you've been having dinner with all week—the French lady?"

"Good." He smiled. "You've been watching me, too."

"There're only fifteen tables in the whole dining room," Constance said uncomfortably. "You can't help . . ." The French lady was at least thirty, with a short, fluffed haircut and a senselessly narrow waist. She wore black slacks and sweaters and very tight, shiny belts, and she and Pritchard always seemed to be laughing a great deal together over private jokes in the corner in which they sat every night. Whenever Constance was in the room with the French lady, she felt young and clumsy.

"The French lady is a good friend," Pritchard said, "but Anglo-Saxons are not *nuancé* enough for her, she says. The French are patriots down to the last bedsheet. Besides, her husband is arriving tomorrow."

"I think I'd really rather stick to my plan," Constance said formally. She stood up. "Are we ready to go?"

He looked at her quietly for a moment. "You're beautiful," he said. "Sometimes it's impossible to keep from saying that."

"Please," she said. "Please, I do have to go now."

"Of course," he said. He stood up and left some money on the table. "Whatever you say."

They walked the hundred yards to their hotel in silence. It was completely dark now, and very cold, and their breath crystallized in little clouds before their mouths as they walked.

"I'll put your skis away," he said, at the door of the hotel.

"Thank you," she said in a low voice.

"Good night. And write a nice letter," he said.

"I'll try," she said. She turned and went into the hotel.

In her room, she took off her boots but didn't bother changing her clothes. She lay down on her bed, without putting on the lights, and stared at the dark ceiling, thinking, Nobody ever told me the English were like that.

"Dearest," she wrote. "Forgive me for not writing, but the weather has been glorious and for a little while I've just devoted myself to making turns and handling deep snow. . . . There's a young man here, an Englishman," she wrote conscientiously, "who's been very nice, who has been good enough to act as an instructor, and even if I say it myself, I'm really getting pretty good. He was in the R.A.F. and his father went down with the Hood and his mother was killed in a bombing—"

She stopped. No, she thought, it sounds tricky. As though I'm hiding something, and putting in the poor, dead, patriotic family as artful window dressing. She crumpled the letter and threw it in the wastebasket. She took out another sheet of paper. "Dearest," she wrote.

There was a knock on the door, and she called "Ja."

The door opened and Pritchard came in. She looked up in surprise. In all the three weeks, he'd never come to her room. She stood up, embarrassed. She was in her stocking feet, and the room was littered with the debris of the afternoon's skiing—boots standing near the window, sweaters thrown over a chair, gloves drying on the radiator, and her parka hanging near the bathroom door, with a little trickle of melting snow running down from the collar. The radio was on, and an American band was playing "Bali Ha'i" from an Armed Forces station in Germany.

Pritchard, standing in front of the open door, smiled at her. "Ah," he said, "some corner of a foreign room that is forever Vassar."

Constance turned the radio off. "I'm sorry," she said, waving vaguely and conscious that her hair was not combed. "Everything's such a mess."

Pritchard went over to the bureau and peered at Mark's picture, which was standing there in a leather frame. "The receiver of letters?" he asked.

"The receiver of letters." There was an open box of Kleenex on the bureau, and an eyelash curler, and a half-eaten bar of chocolate, and Constance felt guilty to be presenting Mark so frivolously.

"He's very handsome." Pritchard squinted at the photograph.

"Yes," Constance said. She found her moccasins and put them on, and felt a little less embarrassed.

"He looks serious." Pritchard moved the Kleenex to get a better view.

"He *is* serious," said Constance. In all the three weeks that she had been skiing with Pritchard, she had said hardly anything about Mark. They had talked about almost everything else, but somehow, by a tacit agreement, they had avoided Mark. They had skied together every after-noon and had talked a great deal about the necessity of leaning forward at all times, and about falling relaxed, and about Pritchard's time in public school in England, and about his father, and about the London theatre and American novelists, and they had talked gravely about what it was like to be twenty and what it was like to be thirty, and they had talked about Christmastime in New York and what football weekends were like at Princeton, and they had even had a rather sharp discussion on the nature of courage when Constance lost her nerve in the middle of a steep trail late one afternoon, with the sun going down and the mountain deserted. But they had never talked about Mark.

Pritchard turned away from the picture. "You didn't have to shoe yourself for me," he said, indicating her moccasins. "One of the nicest things about skiing is taking those damned heavy boots off and walking around on a warm floor in wool socks."

"I'm engaged in a constant struggle not to be sloppy," Constance said.

They stood there, facing each other in silence for a moment. "Oh," Constance said. "Sit down."

"Thank you," Pritchard said formally. He seated himself in the one easy chair. "I just came by for a minute. To say good-bye."

"Good-bye," Constance repeated stupidly. "Where're you going?"

"Home. Or at least to England. I thought I'd like to leave you my ad-dress," Pritchard said.

"Of course."

He reached over and picked up a piece of paper and her pen and wrote for a moment. "It's just a hotel," he said. "Until I find a place of my own." He put the paper down on the desk but kept the pen in his hand, playing with it. "Give you somebody else to write to," he said. "The English receiver of letters."

"Yes," she said.

"You can tell me what the snow's like," he said, "and how many times you came down the mountain in one day and who got drunk at the bar the night before."

"Isn't this sudden?" Constance asked. Somehow, after the first few days, it had never occurred to her that Pritchard might leave. He had been there when she arrived and he seemed to belong there so thor-oughly, to be so much a part of the furniture of the place, that it was hard to conceive of being there without him.

"Not so sudden," Pritchard said. He stood up. "I wanted to say good-bye in private," he said. She wondered if he was going to kiss her. In all the three weeks, he hadn't as much as held her hand, and the only times he had touched her had been when he was helping her up after a particularly bad fall. But he made no move. He stood there, smiling curiously, playing with the pen, unusually untalkative, as though waiting for her to say something. "Well," he said, "will I see you later?"

"Yes," she said.

"We'll have a farewell dinner. They have veal on the menu, but I'll see if we can't get something better, in honor of the occasion." He put the pen down carefully on the desk. "Until later," he said, and went out, closing the door behind him.

Constance stared at the closed door. Everybody goes away, she thought. Unreasonably, she felt angry. She knew it was foolish, like a child protesting the end of a birthday party, but she couldn't help feeling that way. She looked around the room. It seemed cluttered and untidy to her, like the room of a silly and careless schoolgirl. She shook her head impatiently and began to put things in place. She put the boots out in the hall and hung the parka in the closet and carried the box of Kleenex into the bathroom and gave the half bar of chocolate to the chambermaid. She straightened the coverlet of the bed and cleaned the ashtray and, on a sudden impulse, dropped the eyelash curler into the wastebasket. It's too piddling, she thought, to worry about curling your eyelashes.

Pritchard ordered a bottle of Burgundy with dinner, because Swiss wine, he said, was too thin to say farewell on. They didn't talk much during dinner. It was as though he had already departed a little. Once or twice, Constance almost started to tell him how grateful she was for his patience with her on the hills, but somehow it never came out, and the dinner became more and more uncomfortable for both of them. Pritchard ordered brandy with the coffee, and she drank it, although it gave her heartburn. The three-piece band began to play for the evening's dancing while they were drinking their brandy, and then it was too noisy to talk.

"Do you want to dance?" he asked.

"No," she said.

"Good," he said. "I despise dancing."

"Let's get out of here," Constance said. "Let's take a walk."

They went to their rooms to get some warm clothes, and Pritchard was waiting for her outside the hotel door when she came down in her snow boots and the beaver coat her father had given her the year before. Pritchard was leaning against a pillar on the front porch and she stared at him for a moment before he turned around, and she was surprised to see how tired and suddenly old he seemed when he was unaware that he was being watched.

They walked down the main street, with the sounds of the band diminishing behind them. It was a clear night, and the stars shone above the mountains, electrically blue. At the top of the highest hill, at the end of the *téléphérique*, a single light glittered from the hut there, where you could warm yourself before the descent, and buy spiced hot wine and biscuits.

They walked down to the bottom of the street and crossed over onto the path alongside the dark skating rink. The ice reflected the stars dimly and there was the noise of water from the brook that ran along one side of the rink and scarcely ever froze.

They stopped at a small, snow-covered bridge, and Pritchard lit a cigarette. The lights of the town were distant now and the trees stood around them in black silence. Pritchard put his head back, with the smoke escaping slowly from between his lips, and gestured up toward the light on top of the mountain.

"What a life," he said. "Those two people up there. Night after winter night alone on top of the hills, waiting for the world to arrive each morning." He took another puff of the cigarette. "They're not married, you know," he said. "Only the Swiss would think of putting two people who weren't married on top of a hill like that. He's an old man and she's a religious fanatic and they hate each other, but neither of them will give the other the satisfaction of taking another job." He chuckled as they both looked at the bright pinpoint above them. "Last year there was a blizzard and the *téléphérique* didn't run for a week and the power lines were down and they had to stay up there for six days and nights, breaking up chairs for firewood, living off chocolate and tins of soup, and not talking to each other." He stared reflectively at the faraway high light. "It will do as a symbol this year for this pretty continent," he said softly.

Suddenly Constance knew what she had to say. "Alan"—she moved squarely in front of him—"I don't want you to go."

Pritchard flicked at his cigarette. "Six days and six nights," he said. "For their hardness of heart."

"I don't want you to go."

"I've been here for a long time," he said. "I've had the best of the snow."

"I want you to marry me," Constance said.

Pritchard looked at her. She could see he was trying to smile. "That's the wonderful thing about being twenty years old," he said. "You can say things like that."

"I said I want you to marry me."

He tossed away his cigarette. It glowed on the snow. He took a step toward her and kissed her. She could taste the fumed grape of the brandy faint on his lips. He held her for a moment, then stepped back and buttoned her coat, like a nurse being careful with a little girl. "The things that can happen to a man," he said. He shook his head slowly.

"Alan," Constance said.

"I take it all back," Pritchard said. "You're not at all like the girls who advertise soap and beer."

"Please," she said. "Don't make it hard."

"What do you know about me?" He knocked the snow off the bridge railing and leaned against it, brushing the snow off his hands with a dry sound. "Haven't you ever been warned about the young men you're liable to meet in Europe?"

"Don't confuse me," she said. "Please."

"What about the chap in the leather frame?"

Constance took a deep breath. She could feel the cold tingling in her lungs. "I don't know," she said. "He's not here."

Pritchard chuckled, but it sounded sad. "Lost," he said. "Lost by an ocean."

"It's not only the ocean," she said.

They walked in silence again, listening to the sound of their boots on the frozen path. The moon was coming up between the peaks and reflecting milkily off the snow.

"You ought to know one bit of information," Pritchard said in a low voice, looking down at the long shadow the moon cast on the path ahead of him. "I've been married."

"Oh," Constance said. She was very careful to walk in the footprints of the others who had tamped the path down before her.

"Not gravely married," Pritchard said, looking up. "We were divorced two years ago. Does that make a difference to you?"

"Your business," Constance said.

"I must visit America someday," Pritchard said, chuckling. "They are breeding a new type."

"What else?" Constance asked.

"The next thing is unattractive," Pritchard said. "I don't have a pound. I haven't worked since the war. I've been living off what was left of my mother's jewelry. There wasn't much and I sold the last brooch in Zurich last week. That's why I have to go back, even if there were no other reasons. You can see," he said, grinning painfully, "you've picked the prize of the litter."

"What else?" Constance asked.

"Do you still want to hear more?"

"Yes."

"I would never live in America," Pritchard said. "I'm a weary, poverty-stricken, grounded old R.A.F. type, and I'm committed to another place. Come on." He took her elbow brusquely, as though he didn't want to talk any more. "It's late. We'd better get to the hotel."

Constance hung back. "You're not telling me everything," she said.

"Isn't that enough?"

"No."

"All right," he said. "I couldn't go with you to America if I wanted to."

"Why not?"

"Because they wouldn't let me in."

"Why not?" Constance asked, puzzled.

"Because I am host to the worm," Pritchard said.

"What're you talking about?"

"Swiss for delicate," he said harshly. "They kicked D. H. Lawrence out of New Mexico and made him die along the Riviera for it. You can't blame them. They have enough diseases of their own. Now let's go back to the hotel."

"But you seem so healthy. You ski—"

"Everybody dies here in the best of health," Pritchard said. "It goes up and down with me. I almost get cured, then the next year"—he shrugged and chuckled soundlessly—"the next year I get almost uncured. The doctors hold their heads when they see me going up in the lift. Go home," he said. "I'm not for you. I'm oppressed. And you're not oppressed. It is the final miscegenation. Now shall we go back to the hotel?"

Constance nodded. They walked slowly. The town on the hill ahead of them was almost completely dark now, but they could hear the music of the dance band, thin and distant in the clear night air.

"I don't care," Constance said as they came to the first buildings. "I don't care about anything."

"When I was twenty—" Pritchard said. "When I was twenty I once said the same thing."

"First, we'll be practical," Constance said. "You'll need money to stay here. I'll give it to you tomorrow."

"I can't take your money."

"It's not mine," Constance said. "It's my father's."

"England is forever in your debt," Pritchard said. He was trying to smile. "Be careful of me."

"What do you mean?"

"I am beginning to feel as though I can be consoled."

"What's wrong with that?"

"It can prove to be mortal," Pritchard whispered, taking her clumsily and bulkily in his arms, "for those of us who are inconsolable."

When they woke in the morning, they were solemn at first, and disconnectedly discussed the weather, which was revealed through the not quite closed curtains to be gray and uncertain. But then Pritchard asked, "How do you feel?" and Constance, taking her time and wrinkling her eyebrows in a deep attempt to be accurate, said, "I feel *enormously* grown up." Pritchard couldn't help roaring with laughter, and all solemnity was gone. They lay there comfortably discussing themselves, going over their future like misers, and Constance was worried, although not too seriously, about scandalizing the hotel people, and Pritchard said that there was nothing to worry about—nothing that foreigners could do could scandalize the Swiss—and Constance felt more comfortable than ever at being in such a civilized country.

They made plans about the wedding, and Pritchard said they'd go to the French part of Switzerland to get married, because he didn't want to get married in German, and Constance said she was sorry she hadn't thought of it herself.

Then they decided to get dressed, because you could not spend the rest of your life in bed, and Constance had a sorrowful, stinging moment when she saw how thin he was, and thought, conspiratorially, Eggs, milk, butter, rest. They went out of the room together, bravely determined to brazen it out, but there was no one in the corridor or on the stairway to see them, so they had the double pleasure of being candid and being unobserved at the same time, which Constance regarded as an omen of good luck. They discovered that it was almost time for lunch, so they had some kirsch first, and then orange juice and bacon and eggs and wonderful, dark coffee in the scrubbed, wood-paneled dining room, and in the middle of it tears came into Constance's eyes and Pritchard asked why she was crying and she said, "I'm thinking of all the breakfasts we're going to eat together." Pritchard's eyes got a little wet then, too, as he stared across the table at her, and she said, "You must cry often, please."

"Why?" he asked.

"Because it's so un-English," she said, and they both laughed.

After breakfast, Pritchard said he was going up the hill to make a few runs and asked if she wanted to go with him, but she said she felt too melodious that day to ski, and he grinned at the "melodious."

She said she was going to write some letters, and he grew thoughtful. "If I were a gentleman, I'd write your father immediately and explain everything," he said.

"Don't you dare," she said, meaning it, because she knew her father would be over on the next plane if he got a letter like that.

"Don't worry," he said. "I'm not that much of a gentleman."

She watched him stride off between the snowbanks with his red sweater and his skis, looking boyish and jaunty, and then went to her room and wrote a letter to Mark, saying that she had thought it over and that she was sorry but she had decided it was a mistake. She wrote the letter calmly, without feeling anything, cozy in her warm room. She didn't mention Pritchard, because that was none of Mark's business.

Then she wrote a letter to her father and told him that she had broken off with Mark. She didn't mention Pritchard in the letter to her father, either, because she didn't want him over on the next plane, and she didn't say anything about coming home. All that could wait.

She sealed the letters, then lay down dreamily to nap, and slept without dreaming for more than an hour. She dressed for the snow and went to the post office to mail the letters and walked down to the skating rink to watch the children on the ice, and on her way back to the hotel she stopped at the ski shop and bought Pritchard a light-weight yellow sweater, because soon the sun would be very hot all day and the clothes of winter would all be too warm.

She was in the bar, waiting unhurriedly for Pritchard, when she heard that he was dead.

Nobody had come to tell her, because there was no particular reason for anybody to come to tell her.

There was an instructor with whom Pritchard had sometimes skied talking in the bar to some Americans, and he was saying, "He was out of control and he miscalculated and he went into a tree and he was dead in five minutes. He was a jolly fine fellow"—the ski teacher had learned his English from his British pupils before the war—"but he went too fast. He did not have the technique to handle the speed."

The ski teacher did not sound as though it were routine to die on skis, but he did not sound surprised. He himself had had many of his bones broken, as had all his friends, crashing into trees and stone walls and from falls in the summertime, when he was a guide for climbers, and he sounded as though it were inevitable, and even just, that from time to time people paid up to the mountain for faults of technique.

Constance stayed for the funeral, walking behind the black-draped sled to the churchyard and the hole in the snow and the unexpected dark color of the earth after the complete white of the winter. No one came from England, because there was no one to come, although the ex-wife telegraphed flowers. A good many of the villagers came, but merely as friends, and some of the other skiers, who had known Pritchard casually, and as far as anyone could tell, Constance was just one of them.

At the grave, the ski teacher, with the professional habit of repetition common to teachers, said, "He did not have the technique for that much speed."

Constance didn't know what to do with the yellow sweater, and she finally gave it to the chambermaid for her husband.

Eight days later, Constance was in New York. Her father was waiting for her on the pier and she waved to him and he waved back, and she could tell, even at that distance, how glad he was to see her again. They kissed when she walked off the gangplank, and he hugged her, very hard, then held her off at arm's length and stared at her delightedly, and said, "God, you look absolutely wonderful! See," he said, and she wished he hadn't said it, but she realized he couldn't help himself. "See—wasn't I right? Didn't I know what I was talking about?"

"Yes, Father," she said, thinking, How could I ever have been angry with him? He's not stupid or mean or selfish or uncomprehending—he is merely alone.

Holding her hand the way he used to do while they took walks together when she was a little girl, he led her into the customs shed, to wait for her trunk to come off the ship.

THE SUNNY BANKS
OF THE RIVER LETHE

HUGH FORESTER always remembered everything. He remembered the dates of the Battle of New Cold Harbor (May 31-June 12, 1864); he remembered the name of his teacher in the first grade (Webel; red-haired; weight, one-forty-five; no eyelashes); he remembered the record number of strikeouts in one game in the National League (Dizzy Dean, St. Louis Cards, July 30, 1933, seventeen men, against the Cubs); he remembered the fifth line of "To a Skylark" (Shelley: "In profuse strains of unpremeditated art"); he remembered the address of the first girl he ever kissed (Prudence Collingwood, 248 East South Temple Street, Salt Lake City, Utah; March 14, 1918); he remembered the dates of the three partitions of Poland and the destruction of the Temple (1772, 1793, 1795, and 70 A.D.); he remembered the number of ships taken by Nelson at the Battle of Trafalgar (twenty), and the profession of the hero of Frank Norris's novel *McTeague* (dentist); he remembered the name of the man who won the Pulitzer Prize for history in 1925 (Frederic L. Paxson), the name of the Derby winner at Epsom in 1923 (Papyrus); and the number he drew in the draft in 1940 (4726); he remembered the figures for his blood pressure (a hundred and sixty-five over ninety; too high), his blood type (O), and his vision (forty over twenty for the right eye and thirty over twenty for the left); he remembered what his boss told him when he was fired from his first job ("I'm getting a machine to do the job"), and what his wife said when he proposed to her ("I want to live in New York"); he remembered the correct name of Lenin (Vladimir Ilyich Ulyanov), and what caused the death of Louis XIV (gangrene of the leg). He also remembered the species of birds, the mean depths of the navigable rivers of America; the names, given and assumed, of all the Popes, including the ones at Avignon; the batting averages of Harry Heilmann and Heinie Groh; the dates of the total eclipses of the sun since the reign of Charlemagne; the speed of sound; the location of the tomb of D. H. Lawrence; all of the *Rubáiyát* of Omar Khayyámm; the population of the lost settlement of Roanoke; the rate of fire of the Browning automatic rifle; the campaigns of Caesar in Gaul and Britain; the name of the shepherdess in *As You Like It* and the amount of money he had in the Chemical Bank & Trust on the morning of December 7, 1941 ($2,367.58).

Then he forgot his twenty-fourth wedding anniversary (January 25th). His wife, Narcisse, looked at him strangely over breakfast that morning, but he was reading the previous night's newspaper and thinking, They will never get it straight in Washington, and he didn't pay much attention. There was a letter from their son, who was at the University of Alabama, but he put it in his pocket without opening it. It was addressed only to him, so he knew it was a request for money. When Morton wrote his dutiful, familial notes they were addressed to both his parents. Morton was at Alabama because his marks had not been high enough to get him into Yale, Dartmouth, Williams, Antioch, the College of the City of New York, or the University of Colorado.

Narcisse asked if Hugh wanted fish for dinner and he said yes, and Narcisse said that fish was criminally expensive, too, and he said yes, and she asked if anything was the matter and he said no and kissed her and walked out of the apartment to the 242nd Street subway station and stood all the way down to the office, reading the morning newspaper. Narcisse's parents had lived in France for some time and that was where the name came from; by now he was used to it. As he read his newspaper in the crowded car he wished, mildly, that most of the people whom people wrote about in the newspapers would vanish.

Hugh was the first one in the office, and he went to his cubbyhole and sat at his desk, leaving the door open, enjoying the empty desks and the sound of silence. He remembered that Narcisse's nose had twitched at the breakfast table and that she had seemed about to cry. He wondered briefly why, but knew that he would be told in good time, and dismissed it. Narcisse cried between five and eight times a month.

The company for which he worked was putting out a one-volume encyclopedia, absolutely complete, on Indian paper, with seven hundred and fifty illustrations. There was some talk of its being called the Giant

Pocket Encyclopedia, but no final decision had as yet been reached. Hugh was working on the "S"s. Today he had Soap, Sodium, Sophocles, and Sorrento before him. He remembered that Maxim Gorki had lived in Sorrento, and that of the hundred and twenty-three plays that Sophocles wrote, only seven had been discovered. Hugh was not actually unhappy at his work except when Mr. Gorsline appeared. Mr. Gorsline was the owner and editor-in-chief of the house, and believed in standing behind the backs of his employees, silently watching them at their labors. Whenever Mr. Gorsline came into the room, Hugh had the curious feeling that blood was running slowly over his groin.

Mr. Gorsline was gray-haired, wore tweed suits, had the face and figure of a picador, and had started with calendars. The house still put out a great variety of calendars—pornographic, religious and occasional. Hugh was very useful on calendars because he remembered things like the death of Oliver Cromwell (September 3, 1658) and the date on which Marconi sent the first wireless message across the Atlantic (December 12, 1901) and the date of the first steamboat run from New York to Albany (August 17, 1807).

Mr. Gorsline appreciated Hugh's peculiar talents and was relentlessly paternal about his welfare. Mr. Gorsline was a believer in homeopathic medicines and the health-giving properties of raw vegetables, particularly eggplant. He was also opposed to glasses, having thrown his away in 1944 after reading a book about a series of exercises for the muscles of the eyes. He had persuaded Hugh to discard his glasses for a period of seven months in 1948, during which time Hugh had suffered from continual headaches, for which Mr. Gorsline had prescribed minute doses of a medicine from a homeopathic pharmacy which made Hugh feel as though he had been hit in the skull with bird shot. Now whenever Mr. Gorsline stood behind Hugh, he stared at Hugh's glasses with the stubborn, Irredentist expression of an Italian general surveying Trieste. Hugh's health, while not actively bad, was shabby. He had frequent, moist colds, and his eyes had a tendency to become bloodshot after lunch. There was no hiding these lapses or the fact that in cold weather he had to make several trips an hour to the men's room. At such times, Mr. Gorsline would break his customary silence to outline diets designed to improve the tone of the nasal passages, the eyes and the kidneys.

During the morning, Mr. Gorsline came into Hugh's room twice. The first time, he stood behind Hugh's chair without saying a word for five minutes, then said, "Still on sodium?" and left. The next time, he stood silently for eight minutes, then said, "Forester, you're putting on weight. White bread," and left. Each time, Hugh had the familiar feeling in the groin.

Just before lunch, Hugh's daughter came into his office. She kissed him and said, "Many happy returns of the day, Daddy," and gave him a small oblong package with a bow of colored ribbon on top of it. Clare was twenty-two and had been married four years but she refused to stop saying "Daddy." Hugh opened the package, feeling confused. There was a gold-topped fountain pen in it. It was the fourth fountain pen Clare had given him in the last six years, two on birthdays and the third on Christmas. She had not inherited her father's memory.

"What's this for?" Hugh asked.

"Daddy!" Clare said. "You're kidding."

Hugh stared at the pen. He knew it wasn't his birthday (June 12th). And it certainly wasn't Christmas (December 25th).

"It can't be," Clare said incredulously. "You didn't *forget!*"

Hugh remembered Narcisse's face at breakfast, and the twitching of her nose. "Oh, my," he said.

"You better load yourself with flowers before you set foot in the house tonight," Clare said. She peered anxiously at her father. "Daddy, are you all right?" she asked.

"Of course I'm all right," Hugh said, annoyed. "Everybody forgets an anniversary once in a while."

"Not you, Daddy."

"Me, too. I'm human, too," he said, but he felt shaken. He unscrewed the top of the pen and wrote TWENTY-FOUR YEARS, in capitals, on a pad, keeping his head down. He now owned eight fountain pens. "It's just what I needed, Clare," he said, and put it in his pocket. "Thank you very much."

"You haven't forgotten that you promised to take me to lunch, have you?" Clare had phoned the day before to make the appointment for lunch, because, she told Hugh, she had some serious problems to discuss.

"Of course not," Hugh said briskly. He put on his overcoat, and they went out together. Hugh ordered sole, then changed to a lamb chop, because he remembered that Narcisse had said at breakfast they were to have fish for dinner. Clare ordered roast chicken and Waldorf salad, and a bottle of wine, because, she said, the afternoons became less sad after a bottle of wine. Hugh didn't understand why a pretty twenty-two-year-old girl needed wine to keep her from being sad in the afternoons, but he didn't interfere.

While Clare was going over the wine card, Hugh took Morton's letter out of his pocket and read it. Morton was asking for two hundred and fifty dollars. It seemed that he had borrowed a fraternity brother's Plymouth and gone into a ditch with it after a dance and the repairs had come to a hundred and twenty-five dollars. There had been a girl with him, too, and her nose had been broken and the doctor had charged a hundred dollars for the nose and Morton had promised to pay. Then, there was ten dollars for two books in a course on ethics and fifteen dollars just, as Morton phrased it, to make it a round number. Hugh put the letter back in his pocket without saying anything about it to Clare. At least, Hugh thought, it wasn't as bad as last year, when it looked as though Morton was going to be kicked out of school for cheating on a calculus examination.

As Clare ate her chicken and drank her wine, she told her father what was troubling her. Mostly, it was Freddie, her husband. She was undecided, she said as she ate away steadily at her chicken, whether to leave him or have a baby. She was sure Freddie was seeing another woman, on East Seventy-eighth Street, in the afternoons, and before she took a step in either direction she wanted Hugh to confront Freddie man to man and get a statement of intentions from him. Freddie wouldn't talk to her. Whenever she brought the subject up, he left the house and went to a hotel for the night. If it was to be a divorce, she would need at least a thousand dollars from Hugh for the six weeks in Reno, because Freddie had already told her he wouldn't advance a cent for any damn thing like that. Besides, Freddie was having a little financial trouble at the moment. He had overdrawn against his account at the automobile agency for which he worked, and they had clamped down on him two weeks ago. If they had the baby, the doctor Clare wanted would cost eight hundred dollars, and there would be at least another five hundred for the hospital and nurses, and she knew she could depend on Daddy for that.

She drank her wine and talked on as Hugh ate silently. Freddie, she said, was also five months behind in his dues and greens fees at the golf club, and they were going to post his name if he didn't pay by Sunday, and that was *really* urgent, because of the disgrace, and Freddie had behaved like an absolute savage around the house ever since he received the letter from the club secretary.

"I told him," Clare said, with tears in her eyes and eating steadily, "I told him I would gladly go out and work, but he said he'd be damned if he'd let people say he couldn't support his own wife, and, of course, you have to respect a feeling like that. And he told me he wouldn't

come to you for another cent, either, and you can't help admiring him
for that, can you?"

"No," Hugh said, remembering that his son-in-law had borrowed
from him, over a period of four years, three thousand eight hundred
and fifty dollars and had not paid back a cent. "No, you can't. Did he
know you were going to come and talk to me today?"

"Vaguely," Clare said, and poured herself another glass of wine. As
she carefully harvested the last bits of apple and walnut from her salad,
Clare said she didn't really like to burden him with her problems but
he was the only one in the whole world whose judgment she really
trusted. He was so solid and sensible and smart, she said, and she didn't
know any more whether she really loved Freddie or not and she was
so confused and she hated to see Freddie so unhappy all the time about
money and she wanted to know whether Hugh honestly felt she was
ready for motherhood at the age of twenty-two. By the time they finished
their coffee, Hugh had promised to talk to Freddie very soon about the
woman on Seventy-eighth Street and to underwrite either the trip to
Reno or the obstetrician, as the case might be, and he had made a half
promise about the back dues and the greens fees.

On the way to the office, Hugh bought an alligator handbag for
Narcisse for sixty dollars and worried sharply, for a moment, about in-
flation as he wrote out the check and handed it to the salesgirl.

It was a little difficult to work after lunch, because he kept thinking
about Clare and what she had been like as a little girl (measles at
four, mumps the year after, braces from eleven to fifteen, acne between
fourteen and seventeen). He worked very slowly on Sorrento. Mr.
Gorsline came in twice during the afternoon. The first time he said,
"Still on Sorrento?" and the second time he said, "Who the hell cares if
that Communist Russian wrote a book there?"

In addition to the usual sensation in the groin, Hugh noticed a
quickening of his breath, which was almost a gasp, when Mr. Gorsline
stood behind him during the afternoon.

After work, he went into the little bar on Lexington Avenue where
he met Jean three times a week. She was sitting there, finishing her
first whisky, and he sat down beside her and squeezed her hand in
greeting. They had been in love for eleven years now, but he had
kissed her only once (V-E Day), because she had been a classmate of
Narcisse's at Bryn Mawr and they had decided early in the game to be
honorable. She was a tall, majestic woman who, because she had led
a troubled life, still looked comparatively young. They sat sadly and

secretly in sad little bars late in the afternoon and talked in low, nostalgic tones about how different everything could have been. In the beginning, their conversation had been more animated, and for a half hour at a time Hugh had recovered some of the optimism and confidence that he had had as a young man who had taken all the honors at college, before it had become apparent that a retentive memory and talent and intelligence and luck were not all the same thing.

"I think, very soon," Jean said while he was sipping his drink, "we'll have to give this up. It isn't going anywhere, really, is it, and I just don't feel right about it. I feel guilty. Don't you?"

Until then, it hadn't occurred to Hugh that he had done anything to feel guilty about, with the possible exception of the kiss on V-E Day. But now that Jean had said it, he realized that he probably would feel guilty from now on, every time he entered the bar and saw her sitting there.

"Yes," he said sadly. "I suppose you're right."

"I'm going away for the summer," Jean said. "In June. When I come back I'm not going to see you any more."

Hugh nodded miserably. The summer was still five months away, but behind him he had a sense of something slipping, with a rustling noise, like a curtain coming down.

He had to stand in the subway all the way home, and the car was so crowded that he couldn't turn the pages of his newspaper. He read and reread the front page, thinking, I certainly am glad I wasn't elected President.

It was hot in the train, and he felt fat and uncomfortable jammed among the travelers, and he had a new, uneasy feeling that his flesh was overburdening him. Then, just before he came to Two hundred and forty-second Street, he realized that he had left the alligator bag on his desk in the office. He felt a little tickle of terror in his throat and knees. It was not so much that, empty-handed, he faced an evening of domestic sighs, half-spoken reproaches, and almost certain tears. It was not even so much the fact that he mistrusted the cleaning woman who did his office every night and who had once (November 3, 1950), he was sure, taken a dollar and thirty cents' worth of airmail stamps from the upper right-hand drawer. But, standing there in the now uncrowded car, he had to face the fact that twice in one day he had forgotten something. He couldn't remember when anything like that had ever happened to him before. He touched his head with his fingertips, as though there might be some obscure explanation to be found that way. He decided to give up drinking. He drank only five or six whiskies a week, but the induction of partial amnesia by alcohol was a well-established medical principle, and perhaps his level of tolerance was abnormally low.

The evening passed as he had expected. He bought some roses at the station for Narcisse, but he couldn't tell her about the alligator bag left on his desk, because he figured, correctly, that that would only compound the morning's offense. He even suggested that they return to the city for an anniversary dinner, but Narcisse had had the whole day alone to augment her self-pity and brood upon her martyrdom, and she insisted on eating the fish, which had cost ninety-three cents a pound. By ten-thirty she was crying.

Hugh slept badly and got to the office early the next morning, but even the sight of the alligator bag, left squarely in the middle of the desk by the cleaning woman, did not raise his spirits. During the day he forgot the names of three of Sophocles' plays (*Oedipus at Colonus, Trachiniae,* and *Philoctetes*) and the telephone number of his dentist.

It started that way. Hugh began to make more and more frequent trips to the reference library on the thirteenth floor, dreading the trip through the office, because of the way his fellow-workers commenced to look at him, curious and puzzled, as he traversed the room again and again in the course of an hour. One day he forgot the titles of the works of Sardou, the area of Santo Domingo, the symptoms of silicosis, the definition of syndrome, and the occasion of the mortification of Saint Simeon Stylites.

Hoping it would pass, he said nothing about it to anyone—not even to Jean, in the little bar on Lexington Avenue.

Mr. Gorsline took to standing for longer and longer periods behind Hugh's desk, and Hugh sat there, pretending to be working, pretending he didn't look haggard, his jowls hanging from his cheekbones like gallows ropes, his brain feeling like a piece of frozen meat that was being nibbled by a wolf. Once, Mr. Gorsline muttered something about hormones, and once, at four-thirty, he told Hugh to take the afternoon off. Hugh had worked for Mr. Gorsline for eighteen years and this was the first time Mr. Gorsline had told him to take an afternoon off. When Mr. Gorsline left his office, Hugh sat at his desk, staring blindly into terrifying depths.

One morning, some days after the anniversary, Hugh forgot the name of his morning newspaper. He stood in front of the news dealer, staring down at the ranked *Times* and *Tribunes* and *News* and *Mirrors,* and they all looked the same to him. He knew that for the past twenty-five years he had been buying the same paper each morning, but now there was no clue for him in their makeup or in their headlines as to which one it was. He bent down and peered more closely at the papers. The President, a headline announced, was to speak that night. As Hugh straightened up, he realized he no longer remembered the President's name or whether he was a Republican or a Democrat. For a moment, he experienced what could be described only as an exquisite pang of pleasure. But he knew it was deceptive, like the ecstasy described by T. E. Lawrence on the occasion when he was nearly beaten to death by the Turks.

He bought a copy of *Holiday*, and stared numbly at the colored photographs of distant cities all the way down to the office. That morning, he forgot the date on which John L. Sullivan won the heavyweight championship of the world, and the name of the inventor of the submarine. He also had to go to the reference library because he wasn't sure whether Santander was in Chile or Spain.

He was sitting at his desk that afternoon, staring at his hands, because for an hour he had had the feeling that mice were running between his fingers, when his son-in-law came into the office.

"Hi, Hughie, old boy," his son-in-law said. From the very first night his son-in-law had appeared at the house, he had been unfalteringly breezy with Hugh.

Hugh stood up and said "Hello—" and stopped. He stared at his son-in-law. He knew it was his son-in-law. He knew it was Clare's husband. But he couldn't remember the man's name. For the second time that day he experienced the trilling wave of pleasure that he had felt at the newsstand when he realized he had forgotten the name and political affiliations of the President of the United States. Only this time it seemed to last. It lasted while he shook hands with his son-in-law and all during the trip down in the elevator with him, and it lasted in the bar next door while he bought his son-in-law three Martinis.

"Hughie, old boy," his son-in-law said during the third Martini, "let's get down to cases. Clare said you had a problem you wanted to talk to me about. Spit it out, old boy, and let's get it over with. What have you got on your mind?"

Hugh looked hard at the man across the table. He searched his brain conscientiously, but he couldn't think of a single problem that might possibly involve them. "No," Hugh said slowly. "I have nothing in particular on my mind."

His son-in-law kept looking at Hugh belligerently while Hugh was paying for the drinks, but Hugh merely hummed under his breath, smiling slightly at the waitress. Outside, where they stood for a moment, his son-in-law cleared his throat once and said, "Now, look here, old boy, if it's about—" but Hugh shook his hand warmly and walked briskly away, feeling deft and limber.

But back in his office, looking down at his cluttered desk, his sense of well-being left him. He had moved on to the "T"s by now, and as he looked at the scraps of paper and the jumble of books on his desk, he realized that he had forgotten a considerable number of facts about Tacitus and was completely lost on the subject of Taine. There was a sheet of notepaper on his desk with the date and the beginning of a salutation: "Dear . . ."

He stared at the paper and tried to remember who it was he had been writing to. It was five minutes before it came to him; the letter was to have been to his son, and he had meant, finally, to enclose the check for the two hundred and fifty dollars, as requested. He felt in his inside pocket for his checkbook. It wasn't there. He looked carefully through all the drawers of his desk, but the checkbook wasn't there, either. Shaking a little, because this was the first time in his life that he had misplaced a checkbook, he decided to call up his bank and ask them to mail him a new book. He picked up the phone. Then he stared at it blankly. He had forgotten the telephone number of the bank. He put the phone down and opened the classified telephone directory to "B." Then he stopped. He swallowed dryly. He had forgotten the name of his bank. He looked at the page of banks. All the names seemed vaguely familiar to him, but no one name seemed to have any special meaning for him. He closed the book and stood up and went over to the window. He looked out. There were two pigeons sitting on the sill, looking cold, and across the street a bald man was standing at a window in the building opposite, smoking a cigarette and staring down as though he were contemplating suicide.

Hugh went back to his desk and sat down. Perhaps it was an omen, he thought, the thing about the checkbook. Perhaps it was a sign that he ought to take a sterner line with his son. Let him pay for his own mistakes for once. He picked up his pen, resolved to write this to Alabama. "Dear . . ." he read. He looked for a long time at the word. Then he carefully closed his pen and put it back in his pocket. He no longer remembered his son's name.

He put on his coat and went out, although it was only three-twenty-five. He walked all the way up to the Museum, striding lightly, feeling better and better with each block. By the time he reached the Museum, he felt like a man who has just been told that he has won a hundred-dollar bet on a fourteen-to-one shot. In the Museum, he went and looked at the Egyptians. He had meant to look at the Egyptians for years, but he had always been too busy.

When he got through with the Egyptians, he felt wonderful. He continued feeling wonderful all the way home in the subway. He no longer made any attempt to buy the newspapers. They didn't make any sense to him. He didn't recognize any of the people whose names appeared in the columns. It was like reading the Karachi *Sind Observer* or the Sonora *El Mundo*. Not having a paper in his hands made the long ride much more agreeable. He spent his time in the subway looking at the people around him. The people in the subway seemed much more interesting, much more pleasant, now that he no longer read in the newspapers what they were doing to each other.

Of course, once he opened his front door, his euphoria left him. Narcisse had taken to looking at him very closely in the evenings, and he had to be very careful with his conversation. He didn't want Narcisse to discover what was happening to him. He didn't want her to worry, or try to cure him. He sat all evening listening to the phonograph, but he forgot to change the record. It was an automatic machine and it played the last record of the second Saint-Saëns piano concerto seven times before Narcisse came in from the kitchen and said, "I'm going out of my mind," and turned it off.

He went to bed early. He heard Narcisse crying in the next bed. It was the third time that month. There were between two and five more times to go. He remembered that.

The next afternoon, he was working on Talleyrand. He was bent over his desk, working slowly but not too badly, when he became conscious that there was someone standing behind him. He swung in his chair. A gray-haired man in a tweed suit was standing there, staring down at him.

"Yes?" Hugh said curtly. "Are you looking for someone?"

The man, surprisingly, turned red, then went out of the room, slamming the door behind him. Hugh shrugged incuriously and turned back to Talleyrand.

The elevator was crowded when he left for the day, and the hall downstairs was thronged with clerks and secretaries hurrying out of the building. Near the entrance, a very pretty girl was standing, and she smiled and waved at Hugh over the heads of the homeward-bound office workers. Hugh stopped for an instant, flattered, and was tempted to smile back. But he had a date with Jean, and anyway he was too old for anything like that. He set his face and hurried out in the stream of people. He thought he heard a kind of wail, which sounded curiously like "Daddy," but he knew that was impossible, and didn't turn around.

He went to Lexington Avenue, enjoying the shining winter evening, and started north. He passed two bars and was approaching a third when he slowed down. He retraced his steps, peering at the bar fronts. They all had chromium on them, and neon lights, and they all looked the same. There was another bar across the street. He went and looked at the bar across the street, but it was just like the others. He went into it, anyway, but Jean wasn't there. He ordered a whisky, standing at the bar, and asked the bartender, "Have you seen a lady alone in here in the last half hour?"

The bartender looked up at the ceiling, thinking. "What's she look like?" he asked.

"She—" Hugh stopped. He sipped his drink. "Never mind," he said to the bartender. He laid a dollar bill on the counter and went out.

Walking over to the subway station he felt better than he had felt since he won the hundred-yard dash at the age of eleven at the annual field day of the Brigham Young Public School in Salt Lake City on June 9, 1915.

The feeling lasted, of course, only until Narcisse put the soup on the table. Her eyes were puffed, and she had obviously been crying that afternoon, which was curious, because Narcisse never cried when she was alone. Eating his dinner, conscious of Narcisse watching him closely across the table, Hugh began to feel the mice between his fingers again. After dinner, Narcisse said, "You can't fool me. There's another woman." She also said, "I never thought this would happen to me."

By the time Hugh went to bed, he felt like a passenger on a badly loaded freighter in a winter storm off Cape Hatteras.

He awoke early, conscious that it was a sunny day outside. He lay in bed, feeling warm and healthy. There was a noise from the next bed, and he looked across the little space. There was a woman in the next bed. She was middle-aged and was wearing curlers and she was snoring and Hugh was certain he had never seen her before in his life. He got out of bed silently, dressed quickly, and went out into the sunny day.

Without thinking about it, he walked to the subway station. He watched the people hurrying toward the trains and he knew that he probably should join them. He had the feeling that somewhere in the city to the south, in some tall building on a narrow street, his arrival was expected. But he knew that no matter how hard he tried he would never be able to find the building. Buildings these days, it occurred to him suddenly, were too much like other buildings.

He walked briskly away from the subway station in the direction of the river. The river was shining in the sun and there was ice along the banks. A boy of about twelve, in a plaid mackinaw and a wool hat, was sitting on a bench and regarding the river. There were some schoolbooks, tied with a leather strap, on the frozen ground at his feet.

Hugh sat down next to the boy. "Good morning," he said pleasantly.

"Good morning," said the boy.

"What're you doing?" Hugh asked.

"I'm counting the boats," the boy said. "Yesterday I counted thirty-two boats. Not counting ferries. I don't count ferries."

Hugh nodded. He put his hands in his pockets and looked down over the river. By five o'clock that afternoon he and the boy had counted forty-three boats, not including ferries. He couldn't remember having had a nicer day.

THEN WE WERE THREE

MUNNIE BROOKS was awakened by the sound of two shots outside the window. He opened his eyes and looked at the ceiling. By the quality of the light, even through the drawn curtains, he could tell that it was sunny outside. He turned his head. In the other bed Bert was still asleep. He slept quietly, the blankets neat, in control of his dreams. Munnie got out of his bed and, barefooted, in his pajamas, went over to the window and parted the curtains.

The last mists of morning were curling up from the fields, and far off and below, the sea was smooth in the October sunlight. In the distance, along the curve of the coast, the Pyrenees banked back in green ridges toward a soft sky. From behind a haystack more than a hundred yards away, beyond the edge of the hotel terrace, a hunter and his dog appeared, walking slowly, the hunter reloading. Watching him, Munnie remembered, with mild, gluttonous pleasure, that he had had partridge, newly killed and plump with the summer's feeding, for dinner the night before.

The hunter was an old man, dressed in fisherman's blue and wearing fisherman's rubber boots. He moved solidly and carefully behind his dog, through the cut stubble. When I am an old man, thought Munnie, who was twenty-two, I hope I look and feel like that on an October morning.

He opened the curtains wider and looked at his watch. It was after ten o'clock. They had been up late the night before, all three of them, at the casino in Biarritz. Earlier in the summer, when they had been on the Côte d'Azur, a paratroop lieutenant on leave had showed them a fool-proof system for beating the roulette table, and whenever they could, they frequented casinos. The system took a lot of capital and they had never made more than 8000 francs in one night among them on it, and sometimes it meant sitting up till three o'clock in the morning following the wheel, but they hadn't lost yet, either, since they met the lieutenant. It had made their trip unexpectedly luxurious, especially when they got to places where there was a casino. The system ignored the numbers and concentrated on the red and the black and involved a rather complicated rhythm of doubling. The night before they had won only 4500 francs and it had taken them until two o'clock, but still, waking late, with the weather clear and an old man hunting birds outside your window, the thousand-franc notes on the dresser added a fillip of luck and complacency to the morning.

Standing there, feeling the sun warm on his bare feet and smelling the salt and hearing the distant calm mutter of the surf, remembering the partridge and the gambling and everything else about the summer that had just passed, Munnie knew he didn't want to start home that morning as they had planned. Staring down at the hunter following his dog slowly across the brown field on the edge of the sea, Munnie knew that when he was older he would look back upon the summer and think, Ah, it was wonderful when I was young. This double ability to enjoy a moment with the immediacy of youth and the reflective melancholy of age had made Bert say to him, half seriously, half as a joke, "I envy you, Munnie. You have a rare gift—the gift of instantaneous nostalgia. You get twice your investment out of everything."

The gift had its drawbacks. It made moving away from places he liked difficult for Munnie and packed all endings and farewells with emotion, because the old man who traveled within him was always saying, in his autumnal whisper, It will never be like that again.

But putting an end to this long summer, which had stretched into October, was going to be more painful than any other finish or departure that Munnie had known. These were the last days of the last real holiday of his life, Munnie felt. The trip to Europe had been a gift from his parents upon his graduation from college and now when he went back, there they would all be on the dock, the kind, welcoming, demanding faces, expecting him to get to work, asking him what he intended to do, offering him jobs and advice, settling him lovingly and implacably into the rut of being a grownup and responsible and tethered adult. From now on all holidays would be provisional, hurried interludes of gulped summertime between work and work. The last days of your youth, said the old man within. The boat docks in seven days.

Munnie turned and looked at his sleeping friend. Bert slept tranquilly, extended and composed under his blankets, his sunburned long thin nose geometrically straight in the air. This would change, too, Munnie thought. After the boat docked they would never be as close again. Never as close as on the rocks over the sea in Sicily or climbing through the sunny ruins at Paestum or chasing the two English girls through the Roman nightclubs. Never as close as the rainy afternoon in Florence when they talked, together, for the first time, to Martha. Never as close as on the long, winding journey, the three of them packed into the small open car, up the Ligurian coast toward the border, stopping whenever they felt like it for white wine or a swim at the little beach pavilions with all the small, brightly colored pennants whipping out in the hot Mediterranean afternoon. Never as close as the conspiratorial moment over the beers with the paratrooper in the bar of the casino at Juan-les-Pins, learning about the unbeatable system. Never as close as in the lavender, hilarious dawns, driving back to their hotel gloating over their winnings, with Martha dozing between them. Never as close as on the blazing afternoon at Barcelona, sitting high up on the sunny side, sweating and cheering and shading their eyes as the matador walked around the ring holding up the two bull's ears, with the flowers and the wineskins sailing down around him. Never as close as Salamanca and Madrid and on the road through the straw-colored, hot, bare country up to France, drinking sweet, raw Spanish brandy and trying to remember how the music went that the gypsies danced to in the caves. Never so close, again, finally, as here in this small whitewashed Basque hotel room, with Bert still asleep, and Munnie standing at the window watching the old man disappear with his dog and his shotgun, and upstairs in the room above them, Martha, sleeping, as she always did, curled like a child, until they came in, as they always did, together, as though they didn't trust themselves or each other to do it alone, to wake her and tell her what they planned to do for the day.

Munnie threw the curtains wide open and let the sun stream in. If there's one boat that I have a right to miss in my life, he thought, it's the one that's sailing from Le Havre the day after tomorrow.

Munnie went over to Bert's bed, stepping carefully over the clothes that were crumpled on the floor. He poked Bert's bare shoulder with his finger. "Master," he said, "rise and shine." The rule was that whoever lost in tennis between them had to call the other Master for twenty-four hours. Bert had won the day before 6-3, 2-6, 7-5.

"It's after ten." Munnie poked him again.

Bert opened both eyes and stared coldly at the ceiling. "Do I have a hangover?" he asked.

"We only had one bottle of wine amongst us for dinner," said Munnie, "and two beers after."

"I do not have a hangover," Bert said, as if the news depressed him. "But it's raining outside."

"It's a bright, hot sunny morning," Munnie said.

"Everybody always told me it rained all the time on the Basque coast," said Bert, lying still, complaining.

"Everybody is a liar," Munnie said. "Get the hell out of bed."

Bert swung his legs slowly over the side of the bed and sat there, thin, bony and bare from the waist up, in his pajama pants that were too short for him and from which his big feet dangled loosely. "Do you know why American women live longer than American men, Fat Man?" he asked, squinting at Munnie in the sunlight.

"No."

"Because they sleep in the morning. My ambition," Bert said, lying back on the bed again, but with his legs still over the side, "is to live as long as the American Woman."

Munnie lit a cigarette and tossed one to Bert, who managed to light it without lifting his head from the blanket. "I had an idea," Munnie said, "while you were wasting the precious hours of your childhood sleeping."

"Put it in the suggestion box." Bert yawned and closed his eyes. "The management will give a buffalo-hide saddle to every employee who presents us with an idea that is put into practice by the . . ."

"Listen," Munnie said eagerly. "I think we ought to miss that damned boat."

Bert smoked in silence for a moment, narrowing his eyes and pointing his nose at the ceiling. "Some people," he said, "are born boat-missers and train-missers and plane-missers. My mother, for example. She once saved herself from getting killed by ordering a second dessert at lunch. The plane left just as she got to the field and came down in flames thirty-five minutes later. Not a single survivor. It was ice cream, with crushed fresh strawberries . . ."

"Come on, Bert." Sometimes Munnie got very impatient with Bert's habit of going off on tangents while he was making up his mind. "I know all about your mother."

"In the springtime," Bert said, "she goes mad for strawberries. Tell me, Munnie, have you ever missed anything in your life?"

"No," Munnie said.

"Do you think it's wise," Bert asked, "at this late stage, to fiddle with the patterns of a lifetime?"

Munnie went into the bathroom and filled a glass with water. When he came back into the bedroom, Bert was still lying on the bed, his legs dangling over the side, smoking. Munnie stood over him, then slowly tipped the glass over Bert's bare brown chest. The water splashed a little and ran in thin trickles over Bert's ribs onto the sheets.

"Ah," Bert said, still smoking. "Refreshing."

They both laughed and Bert sat up.

"All right, Fat Man," Bert said. "I didn't know you were serious."

"My idea," said Munnie, "is to stay here until the weather changes. It's too sunny to go home."

"What'll we do about the tickets?"

"We'll send a telegram to the boat people and tell them we'll take passage later. They've got a waiting list a mile long. They'll be delighted."

Bert nodded judiciously. "What about Martha?" he asked. "Maybe she has to get to Paris today."

"Martha doesn't have to go anyplace. Anytime," Munnie said. "You know that."

Bert nodded again. "The luckiest girl in the world," he said.

Outside the window there was the sound of the shotgun again. Bert turned his head, listening. There was a second report. "My," Bert said, running his tongue over his teeth, "that was wonderful partridge last night." He stood up, looking, in his flapping pajama pants like a boy who would be a good prospect for the college crew if he could be induced to eat heavily for a year. He had been chubby until he went into the Army, but by the time he got out in May, he was long and stringy and his ribs showed. When she wanted to make fun of him, Martha told him he looked like an English poet in his bathing trunks. He went to the window and Munnie crossed over and stood beside him, looking out over the mountains and the sea and the sunlight.

"You're right," Bert said. "Only an idiot would dream of starting home on a day like this. Let's go tell Martha the party's still on."

They dressed quickly, in espadrilles and cotton trousers and tennis shirts and went upstairs together and into Martha's room, without knocking. The wind was making one of the shutters rap against the window, but Martha was still asleep, curled around herself, only the top of her head showing above the blanket, the hair dark and tangled and short. The pillow was on the floor.

Munnie and Bert stood in silence for a moment, looking down at the curled, blanketed figure and the dark head, each of them convinced that the other did not know what he was thinking.

"Awake," Bert said softly. "Awake to glory." He went over to the bed and touched the top of Martha's head. Watching him, Munnie could feel the tips of his own fingers twitching electrically.

"Please," Martha said, her eyes still closed. "It's the middle of the night."

"It's nearly noon," Munnie said, lying by nearly two hours, "and we have to tell you something."

"Tell it to me," said Martha, "and get out of here."

"The Fat Man here," said Bert, standing at her head, "has come up with an idea. He wants us to stay here until it begins to rain. How do you feel about it?"

"Of course," Martha said.

Bert and Munnie smiled at each other, because they felt they understood her so well. "Martha," said Bert, "you're the only perfect girl alive."

Then they went out of the room to give her a chance to get dressed.

They had met Martha Holm in Florence. They seemed to have the same ideas about which museums and which churches to go to and they kept bumping into her and she was alone and obviously American and as Bert said, they didn't come prettier, and finally they started talking to each other. Maybe it was because they had first seen her in the Uffizi Gallery among the Botticellis that gave Munnie the idea, but he thought, privately, that, aside from the fact that her hair was short and dark and irregularly cut, she looked like the Primavera, tall, slender, and girlish, with a long narrow nose and deep, brooding, dangerous eyes. He felt extravagant and embarrassed to be thinking things like this about a twenty-one-year-old American girl who wore slacks and had gone for a year to Smith, but he couldn't help himself. He never told Martha about it and, of course, he never said a word on the subject to Bert.

Martha knew a lot of people in and around Florence (later on, it turned out that she knew a lot of people in and around everyplace) and she got them invited to a tea in Fiesole at a villa where there was a swimming pool and to a party at which Munnie found himself dancing with a Contessa. Martha had been in Europe for nearly two years and she was wonderful at telling you what places to go to and what places were traps, and she spoke Italian and French, and she was ready when you told her to be ready, and she didn't scream for pity when she had to walk a few blocks on her own two feet, and she laughed at Bert's and Munnie's jokes and made some of her own, and she didn't giggle, weep or sulk, which put her several notches above every other girl Munnie had ever known. After they had been together for three days in Florence and were due to start for Portofino and France, it seemed unbearable just to leave her behind. As far as Munnie and Bert could tell, she had no plans of her own. "I tell my mother," Martha explained, "that I'm taking courses at the Sorbonne, and it's almost true, at least in the wintertime."

Martha's mother lived in Philadelphia, after three divorces, and every once in awhile, Martha said, she sent back a photograph, so that when she finally did arrive back home, there wouldn't be an embarrassing moment on the dock when her mother wouldn't recognize her.

So Munnie and Bert talked it over very seriously and sat at a café table with Martha in the Piazza del Signoria and ordered coffee and put it up to her.

"What we've decided," Bert said, with Munnie sitting beside him, silently agreeing, "is that the Brooks-Carboy unguided tour of Europe could use you, as interpreter, hotel-finder, and chief taster of foreign foods. Aside from supplying a welcome feminine touch. Are you interested?"

"Yes," Martha said.

"We'd like to know if we could mesh schedules, more or less," Munnie said.

Martha smiled. "I'm on a schedule of drift," she said. "Didn't you know?"

"Does that mean," Munnie asked, because he liked to have everything absolutely clear, "that you want to come along?"

"It means that I want to come along very much," said Martha, "and I was hoping you'd ask me." She looked at each of them for exactly the same number of seconds, cheerful, grateful, ready for anything.

"Now," said Bert, "Munnie and I have talked it over and we're going to lay it on the line. Something like this has to be planned out in advance or there comes a dark and hideous night of disaster. We've thought up a good, workable set of rules and if you agree, off we go tomorrow. If not—no harm done—and we hope you spend a pleasant summer."

"Get to it, Bert," Munnie said, impatiently. "Don't recite the preamble to the Constitution."

"Rule Number One," Bert said, with Martha sitting still, nodding, gravely listening, "rule number one is basic. No entanglements. Munnie and I're old friends and we've planned this summer for years and we've been having a wonderful time and we don't want to wind up fighting

duels with each other or anything like that. Now, I know women . . ."
He paused, daring either of them to smile. They didn't smile.

"He wouldn't have said that," Munnie explained, "before the Army."

"What do you know about women?" Martha asked, being serious.

"What I know is that women're always busy choosing," Bert went on.
"They come into a room and if there're five men present, their minds get
to work like a business machine, punching holes. First Choice, Second
Choice, Acceptable, Perhaps, Impossible."

"Oh, my." Martha began to laugh. She covered her mouth with her
hand apologetically and tried to straighten her face. "Forgive me. Munnie . . . do you believe this?"

"I don't know," he said embarrassedly. "I haven't had Bert's advan-
tages. I wasn't in the Army."

"I'll even tell you how you'd choose," Bert said, "between Munnie and
me, so you won't have to wonder or waste your time."

"Tell me," Martha said. "Do tell me."

"In the beginning," said Bert, "the tendency is to choose me. I'll go
into the reasons some other time. Then, after awhile, the switch sets in,
and Munnie gets the final decision."

"Poor Bert," Martha said, chuckling. "How awful for you! Only winning the opening game of the season all the time. Why are you telling
me all this?"

"Because you've got to promise not to choose anybody," Bert said.
"And if you *do* choose, you have to go to the grave with your secret."

"To the grave," Martha repeated, trying to be solemn.

"Until the boat sails," Bert said, "we treat each other like brothers
and sister, and that's all. *D'accord?*"

"*D'accord*," Martha said.

"Good." Bert and Munnie nodded at each other, pleased with how
reasonable everybody was.

"Rule Number Two," Bert said, "if after awhile we get to feel you're
a nuisance—we say farewell and you leave. No tears. No recriminations.
No scenes. Just a friendly shake of the hand and off to the nearest railroad station. *D'accord?*"

"*D'accord* two times," Martha said.

"Rule Number Three—everybody pays exactly one-third of the expenses."

"Of course," said Martha.

"Rule Number Four," Bert went on, like the director of a company
explaining a plan of operations to his board, "everybody is free to go
wherever he or she wants to, and with anyone else whoever, and no

questions asked. We are not an inseparable unit, because inseparable units are boring. O.K.?"

"A free, loose confederation of sovereign states," Martha said. "I got it. Whomever."

They all shook hands on it, surrounded by the looming oversized statues, and started out together early the next morning, after figuring out a way to squeeze Martha into the car and strap her baggage onto the back, and it all couldn't have worked out better. There hadn't been a single argument all summer, although they had discussed, among other things, sex, religion, politics, marriage, the choice of careers, the position of women in modern society, the theatre in New York and Paris, and the proper size of bathing costumes for young girls on the beaches of Italy, France and Spain. And when Bert had taken up with a plump little blonde American girl in St. Tropez for a week or so, it hadn't seemed to disturb Martha for a minute, even when the girl moved into the hotel they were staying at and frankly installed herself in the room next to Munnie's and Bert's.

The truth was, nothing seemed to disturb Martha very much. She greeted the events of each day with a strange and almost dreamlike placidity. She seemed to make no decisions herself and whatever decisions the others made, regardless of how they turned out, she accepted with exactly the same good-natured, smiling, rather vague approval. Linked in Munnie's mind with this pleasant will-lessness was Martha's extraordinary talent for sleeping. If nobody went in to awaken her in the morning, she would sleep on till noon, till two o'clock in the afternoon, even if she had gone to bed early the evening before. It wasn't anything physical, either, because she didn't need the sleep and never suggested, herself, that it was time to go to bed, no matter how late they stayed up at night or at what hour she had arisen in the morning. She never wrote any letters and rarely received any, since she hardly ever remembered to leave a forwarding address when they moved. When she needed money she would wire the bank in Paris that handled her allowance, and when it came she spent it carelessly. She took almost no interest in clothes and the reason she cut her hair short the way she did, she told Bert and Munnie, was that she didn't want to be bothered having to comb it all the time.

When the three of them talked about what they would like to do with their lives, she was vaguer than ever. "I don't know," she said, shrugging, smiling, seeming to be mildly and indulgently puzzled about herself. "I suppose I'll just hang around. Wait and see. For the moment, I'm on a policy of float. I don't see anybody else our age doing anything so damned attractive. I'm waiting for a revelation to send me in a permanent direction. I'm in no hurry to commit myself, no hurry at all . . ."

In a curious way, Martha's lack of direction made her much more interesting to Munnie than all the other girls he had ever known, the positive but limited girls who knew they wanted to be married and have babies and join a country club, the girls who wanted to go on the stage and be famous, the girls who wanted to become editors or deans of women's colleges. Martha hadn't settled for anything yet, Munnie felt, because nothing good enough had come up. And there was always the chance, he believed, that when she finally did commit herself it would be for something huge, original and glorious.

The only way that the plans hadn't worked out as outlined in Florence had been that, except for the week of the plump blonde in St. Tropez, they had been an inseparable unit, but that was only because all three of them enjoyed being with one another better than being with anyone else. It wouldn't have worked if Martha had been a different kind of girl, if she had been a coquette or greedy or foolish, and it wouldn't have worked if Munnie and Bert hadn't been such good friends and hadn't trusted each other so completely, and finally, it wouldn't have worked if they had all been a little older. But it *had* worked, at least up until the first week of October, and with luck, it would continue to work, until they kissed Martha good-bye and got on the boat train, and started for home.

They lay on the deserted beach until nearly two o'clock and then took a swim. They had a race, because the water was cold, and it was the best way to keep warm. The race was a short one, only about fifty yards, and Munnie was completely out of breath by the time he finished, trying to keep up with Martha. Martha won easily and was floating serenely on her back when Munnie came up to her, blowing heavily and fighting to get air in his lungs.

"It would be a different story," Munnie said, grinning, but a little ashamed, "if I didn't have asthma."

"Don't be gloomy about it," Martha said, kicking her legs gently. "Women're more naturally buoyant."

They both stood up and watched Bert plowing doggedly up toward them.

"Bert," Martha said, as he reached them and stopped, "you're the only man I know who looks like an old lady driving an electric automobile when he swims."

"My talents," said Bert, with dignity, "run in another direction."

They went in then, shouting and pink from the cold water and waving their arms. They dressed on the beach, under the big towel, one after another, for modesty's sake. Martha wore slacks that came down only to the middle of her calf and a fisherman's jersey, striped blue and white. Watching her arrange her clothes with light, careless movements, Munnie felt that never in his life would he see again anything so gay and obscurely touching as Martha Holm, dressed in a sailor's striped shirt, on a sunny beach, shaking the sea water out of her short, dark hair.

They decided to have a picnic rather than to go to a restaurant for lunch and they got into the little two-seater MG that Munnie's brother had left for him, when he had had his summer in Europe the year before. With Martha sitting on the cushioned brake in the middle they went into town and bought a cold chicken and a long loaf of bread and a piece of Gruyère cheese. They borrowed a basket from the fruit dealer from whom they bought a huge bunch of blue grapes and picked up two bottles of pink wine and got back into the car and drove all around the harbor to the old fort, which had been besieged and which had fallen at other times but which was used now in the summertime as a school to teach young people how to sail. They parked the car and walked out along the broad, bleached top of the sea wall, carrying the basket and the wine and the big, slightly damp towel, to serve as a tablecloth.

From the wall they could see the wide stretch of the oval harbor, empty now except for a dory with a homemade sail heading toward the point of Sainte Barbe, and the deserted beach and the white and red buildings of Saint Jean de Luz. The boatyard near the fort was crammed with small blue Snipe-class boats, lashed down and on blocks for the winter, and from somewhere in the distance came the faint sound of hammering, lonely and out-of-season, where a single workman was putting new planks into the bow of a small fishing vessel. Out at sea, almost lost against the gray-blue wash of the horizon, the boats of the tuna fleet bobbed in the swell. The tide was out and the waves rolled in, white and spumy, but not ominous, over the slanting uncovered rocks on which the sea wall was built. Close to the wall, on the bay side, the ruined, circular bastions of the old wall, which the sea had broken in another century, loomed out of the quiet water, irregular, crumbling, useless, looking somehow Roman and reminding Munnie of aqueducts that had brought mountain water to cities that had long since vanished and dungeons in which the last prisoners had died five hundred years before.

They didn't go all the way out to the end of the wall, which was separated from the middle section of the breakwater by a wide channel through which the shipping entered and left the harbor. Even on the calmest day, Munnie felt something wild and dangerous out there on the flat point of stone, where the full force of the unbroken ocean probed, however quietly, at the guarded waters of the bay and the land beyond. Munnie suffered a little from vertigo and when he looked down the sheer sides of the wall into the shifting green depths and the fringe of foam he had a helpless picture of himself caught there below, or plunging down to fight against the tides and the rocks and the waves coming and going and crossing each other with upcurling tips of spray. He didn't say anything about it, of course, but he was grateful when Martha said, "This is good enough," before they had gone very far, and he carefully helped weight the towel down as a tablecloth squarely in the middle of the wall.

There was a little wind, capricious and sporadically chilly, but Bert took off his shirt, to maintain his tan. Munnie, who had a soft, rather full growth of fuzzy reddish hair on his chest, and who was embarrassed by it, said that the wind was too cold for undressing. Bert glanced at him ironically, because he knew how Munnie felt about his chest, but he didn't say anything.

As Martha cut up the chicken and arranged the cheese and bread and grapes on pieces of paper in the center of the towel, where they could all get at them neatly, Bert cocked his head, listening to the distant, slow, rhythmic hammering from the boatyard. "Whenever I hear that noise in a place like this," he said, "it reminds me of the end of *The Cherry Orchard*. Everything melancholy and closed up and ready to die and the autumn setting in . . ."

"Whenever I hear it," Martha said, arranging the grapes, "I think, 'Divorce, divorce.' "

"That's the difference," said Bert, "between Russia and America." He walked over to the edge of the wall and stood there, his toes dangerously over the brink, staring out at the horizon, a tall, spare, loose-limbed figure, reciting, his arms ritually upraised, "Break, break, break, On thy cold gray stones, Oh, sea, And I would that my heart could utter, The thoughts that arise in me . . ."

"Lunch is on," Martha said, sitting cross-legged and pushing her sleeves above the elbows, her bare arms, under the bunched jersey, brown and surprisingly full and solid for such a slender girl. She took a piece of chicken and bit into it and said, "It's the only kind of picnic that makes picnics worth while. And no ants."

Munnie drank some of the wine from the bottle, because they had neglected to bring glasses, and broke a piece of bread off the long loaf and took some of the dark meat. Bert sat on the other side of Martha, folding his long legs down in slow motion. He reached for a piece of chicken, and said, as he munched at it, "Do you think a bright, sober young American would make a fortune setting up a factory in France to manufacture paper plates and paper cups?"

"It would spoil all the ineffable medieval charm," Martha said.

"Oh, that old, lowdown, ineffable, medieval, greasy-paper charm," Bert said. "Trust a woman to notice things like that, eh, Munnie?" He lifted his eyebrow in an exaggerated, theatrical leer. "God, isn't it lucky we walked into that gallery in Florence and found Martha? Otherwise, you know what our summer would've been like? We'd have been de- livered over to all the female riffraff of Europe—all those Italian movie starlets, bursting out of their shirtwaists, all those skinny French models, all those hungry-eyed, golden-brown American divorcees, smelling from Arpège. God, Munnie, doesn't it make you feel as though Something was watching over you that day in the museum? Tell me the truth, Fat Man, doesn't it make you feel supernaturally serene?"

"Where did you ever learn to talk like that?" Martha asked, sitting cross-legged, placidly lifting the wine bottle to her lips.

"My grandfather was a Baptist preacher in Memphis, Tennessee," Bert said, "and he taught me to fear the Lord, read the Bible, relish corn, and speak in balanced sentences." He stood up and waved the drum- stick of the chicken at the Atlantic Ocean. "Repent, ye sinners, because ye have swum in the warm waters, and ogled the virgins . . ." He made a bow in Martha's direction. "And ye have played at the tables and ye have neglected to send postcards home. Repent, because ye have found pleasure and ye have missed the boat."

"Do you want some cheese?" Martha asked.

"With mustard." Bert sat down again. He peered thoughtfully at Munnie. "What do you think, Munnie?" he asked. "Are we really as happy as we feel or do we only *think* we're this happy? The philoso- pher's everlasting cud—illusion or reality. Is this wall stone?" he de- manded oratorically. "Is this ocean blue, this water wet? Is this girl beautiful? Is this money we have in our pockets or is it really coupons for prizes that were given away in Duluth in 1922 by a tobacco company that went bankrupt the first Thursday after the crash? Is this the good wine of France we're drinking or is it vinegar spiked with blood and seawater? Rosé de Béarn," he said, reading the label on the bottle. "It seems real, doesn't it, but *is* it? Are we three over-privileged, white-toothed, splendid young American princes, visiting our greatest colony, or are we, without knowing it, pitiful refugees, in flight, with our backs to the sea? . . . Have you read a newspaper this morning, do you know the answer? Are we friends and brothers, or will we betray each other by sunset? Search the lady for daggers."

"Holy man," Martha said, "the self-starter got loose."

Munnie smiled dreamily, in appreciation of Bert's performance. He himself was literal and direct and always said exactly what he meant and no more. But he was entertained by Bert's flights of rhetoric and appreciated Bert much the way a man with no talent, but a love for music, appreciates a friend who is a skillful pianist and who generously performs at just the right moments, without being asked. It went all the way back to the time when they were both sixteen and in school together and Bert used to make scandalous improvisations in blank verse about the assumed sexual habits of the middle-aged and slightly bald lady who taught them chemistry. It got Bert into trouble from time to time because he was recklessly brave and once he started he let himself be carried away and say outrageous things, no matter who was listening. Just this summer, they had had to fight four young Germans in a *brasserie* in Nice and run from the police because of one of his performances. Bert had struck up a conversation with the young men and asked them where they came from and they had said, after a little hesitation, that they were Swiss. "What part of Switzerland?" Bert had asked blandly. "Düsseldorf? Hamburg?"

The Germans, who were large, solid men, had looked uncomfortable and turned away from him toward the beers that were standing on the bar in front of them, but Bert wouldn't leave it alone. "The part of Switzerland I find most charming," Bert said loudly, "is Belsen. So rural, so cosy, so full of memories. What I always have said is that Switzerland would have won the war if it hadn't been stabbed in the back by the watchmakers. And a good thing, too."

"Cut it out," Munnie had whispered, and Martha had shaken her head warningly too, and pulled at Bert's arm. "There're four of them. They'll murder us."

But Bert had gone right on. "I'm proud to tell you gentlemen," he had said, smiling broadly, "that I have always been a believer in a Greater Switzerland and there are plenty of good, red-blooded Americans who go right along with me." The Germans were muttering among themselves by now and Munnie took off his watch and slipped it into his pocket because he didn't want it broken when the fight began.

"Shut up, Bert," Martha said. "They're going to hit you with a beermug."

"Now, boys," Bert went on, lifting his glass, "I'd like you to join me in a toast to the greatest little old Swiss of them all, that kindly, sweet old lovable fellow, Adolf Hitler, and after that we'll all join in singing Switzerland Über Alles. I'm sure you know the words . . ."

Munnie had edged around by now and when the first German swung, he grabbed the man's arm and clubbed him twice with his right hand. The Germans were slow, but strong, and very angry, and by the time Munnie dragged Bert to the door, he had a bloody nose and Bert's coat collar was half torn off and all the waiters were screaming for the police.

The three of them ran through the back streets of Nice, hearing confused shouting dying down behind them. Bert was chuckling as he ran, and shaking his right hand, which was numb from a German skull, and he kept saying to Munnie, "What part of Switzerland you from, Bud? Leipzig? Nuremberg?"

A half hour later, when they were sitting safely in a bar along the Promenade des Anglais, it had begun to seem funny to Martha and Munnie, too, and for the rest of the summer, whenever any one of them did something that seemed objectionable or foolish, the others would ask, incredulously, "What part of Switzerland are *you* from?"

Now Bert was sitting, waving the wine bottle gently, beaming out at the bay. "I think I am going to start a new kind of travel service. Out-of-season tours to slightly rundown resorts. I'll write a brochure, entitled 'Know bliss! Be Unfashionable! Get Away from Your Fellow Man on Your Next Vacation!' Do you think your father would be inclined to put up the dough to get us started, Munnie?"

Bert had an unshakable belief that Munnie's father was enormously wealthy and avid for unusual business opportunities, which Bert was happy to find for him. The opportunities had included the planting of an avocado grove near Grasse, and the building of a 4000-foot téléphérique for skiing in a village of twenty-two houses in the Spanish Pyrenees. All of Bert's projects, aside from involving great outlays of capital on the part of Munnie's father, also included the necessity of Bert's remaining permanently in Europe as manager.

"Munnie," Bert said, "don't you think we ought to send your father a cable?"

"No," said Munnie.

"The chance of a lifetime," Bert said. "What does he want to hold onto all that money for? The inheritance people'll just take it from him in the hideous end. Well, I'll find something. That's not the only way to turn a dollar." He peered speculatively at Martha, who was eating the grapes by now. "Martha," he said, "do you know that you represent a source of vast potential income?"

"I'm going to donate my body to science," Martha said, "at the age of eighty-five."

"The essential thing," said Bert, "is not to marry an American."

"Report that man to a committee," Martha said.

"America is not the place for a pretty woman," Bert went on. "The houses're getting too small, the help too expensive, a beauty suddenly finds herself in a cosy little nest in Scarsdale surrounded by television sets and labor-saving devices and invitations to join the Parent-Teachers Association. A beautiful woman does better in a country which is decaying a little, and rather uneconomically run—like France. You could marry a nice forty-five-year-old man with a clean mustache and large, rolling feudal estates on the banks of the Loire. Wonderful shooting in the autumn and good, light wines grown on the property and dozens of servants taking off their caps and bowing when the station wagon went by. Your husband would adore you and invite all your friends down to keep you happy and he'd leave you alone a good deal of the time when he went up to Paris to attend to his affairs and have his doctor probe his liver."

"Where do you fit into this picture?" Martha asked.

"He'd be one of the friends invited to keep you happy," Munnie said. He wasn't enjoying the conversation. Even though Bert was joking, Munnie knew that actually Bert would approve if Martha *did* go out and marry an old man with a lot of money. Just the other day, when they had been talking about the careers that might lie ahead of them, Bert had said, "The important thing is to recognize your gift and then use it. And the best way to use it is to keep you from the insufferable boredom of work. Now your gift—" he had grinned at Martha "—your gift is beauty. That's easy. You use it on a man and the sky's the limit. My gift is a double one, but in the long run less hopeful. I have charm . . ." He grinned more widely, making fun of himself, "and I don't give a damn. Still, if I'm clever enough and don't rise to the wrong bait, I may go a long way on it. As for Munnie . . ." He shook his head doubtfully. "His gift is virtue. Poor sod. What can he do with that?"

Now, sitting on the corner of the towel, picking the grapes appreciatively off their stems, one by one, Bert was shaking his head. "No," he said, "I won't be one of the invited friends. I'm a permanent fixture. I'm the overseer of the estates, the curious American with no ambition who likes to live in France on the banks of the pretty river. I walk around in an old tweed jacket smelling a little from horses and new wine barrels, loved by one and all, making wry comments on the state of the world, playing backgammon in front of the fire with the mistress of the house when her husband is away, and going up the stairs later, with the last glass of Armagnac in my hand, to entertain her in my wry, American way in the ancestral bed . . ."

"Ah," Martha said, "how idyllic!"

"Every age," Bert said gravely, "to its own particular idyll. This is this year, among the wars."

Munnie felt very uncomfortable and when he looked over at Martha he felt even more uncomfortable, because she was laughing. They had laughed together at a lot of things since Florence, and they had covered all the subjects, but Munnie didn't want to hear Martha laughing now at this.

He stood up. "I think I'm going down the wall a way," he said, "and take a siesta. Wake me when you want to go."

He walked about thirty yards, carrying a sweater to use as a pillow, and as he stretched out on the smooth sun-warmed stone, he heard Martha and Bert laughing together, the laughter private and small in the wide, bright emptiness.

Closing his eyes against the glare of the sun, listening to the distant laughter, Munnie realized that he was in pain. The pain was not localized and it had a curious, evasive quality. Just when Munnie felt, *There, I've got it, it's in my throat*, it slipped away, not to disappear, but to put vague, sharp, almost detectable fingers somewhere else. Then, lying there, with the curtain of heat on his eyelids, Munnie understood that what he was feeling was not pain, but sorrow.

The sorrow was deep and complex, and was composed of many elements—a sense of deprivation, a shadow of impending departure, a nostalgia for memories that were moving irrevocably away from innocence, a confusion of emotion more profound than anything he had ever experienced before in his life. Engulfed and shaken as he was, Munnie also knew that if, telepathically affected, Martha would stop laughing with Bert and get up and walk the thirty yards along the wall to where he lay, and if she were to sit down beside him and touch his hand, all would instantaneously be well.

But she didn't move, and he heard her laugh more loudly at something that Bert had said and which Munnie couldn't hear.

Suddenly, Munnie knew what he was going to do. As soon as he was on the boat, and all bargains were over, all rules no longer in effect, he was going to write Martha and ask her to marry him. Clumsily, he began to compose the letter in his mind. *This will come as a surprise to you, I suppose, because all summer long I never said a word, but I didn't realize for a long time what had been happening to me, and besides there was the arrangement you and Bert and I made in Florence to keep everything on a purely friendly basis, which I am happy we did. But now I'm on the boat and I feel free to tell you how I feel about you. I love you and I want to marry you. I don't know how you feel about me, but maybe the arrangement kept you from saying anything, just the way it did me. Anyway, I hope so. I am going to get a job and get settled just as soon as I get home, and then you could come back and meet my family and all that . . ."*

The letter stopped writing itself inside his head. He thought of his mother sitting down having tea with Martha, saying, "You say your mother lives in Philadelphia? And your father . . . oh . . . Do try one of these cakes. And you say you met Munnie in Florence and then just you and he and Bert went all around Europe for the rest of the summer all together . . . Lemon, cream?"

Munnie shook his head. He'd handle his mother when the time came. He went back to writing the imaginary letter.

You said once that you didn't know what you wanted to do with yourself, that you were waiting for some kind of revelation to send you in a permanent direction. Maybe you'll laugh at me for offering myself as a revelation, but maybe you'll feel that marrying me will . . .

Munnie shook his head disgustedly. God, even if she was crazy in love with him, he thought, a sentence like that would queer it forever.

I don't know about you and other men, he went on jumpily in his head. *You never seemed interested in anybody else while you were with us and you never mentioned anybody else in any particular way and as far as I could tell you never showed any preference between Bert and me . . .*

Munnie opened his eyes and turned his head to look at Bert and Martha. They were sitting close together, almost head to head, facing each other, talking in low, serious voices.

He remembered Bert's description of what he called his gift. I have charm and I don't give a damn. Well, Munnie thought, with satisfaction, even if she overlooked the egotism, that can't have attracted her so much. And besides, there was that open and avowed blonde in St. Tropez. If Bert had planned to do anything with Martha, or if Martha, as Bert had predicted, was interested in making a choice, that certainly would have put an end to it, wouldn't it? Bert, Munnie decided, could be the amusing, bachelor friend of the family. The best kind.

Munnie dozed a little, a succession of warm and delicious images pouring through his mind. Martha coming off the airplane at Idlewild, because after getting his letter the boat was too slow, and walking away from the runway into his arms. Martha and he waking late on a Sunday morning in their own apartment and deciding to doze for another hour and then go out to breakfast. Martha coming into a party on his arm and a slight, approving, envious, subtle hush sweeping the room for a moment, because she was so beautiful. Martha . . .

Someone was shouting. Far off, someone was shouting.

Munnie opened his eyes and blinked, thinking, puzzled. Now, why did anyone shout in my dream?

The cry came again and Munnie stood up and looked out at the bay. In the water, at least three hundred yards away, was a small boat. It was the dory they had seen before. It had capsized and it was low in the water and there were two figures clinging to it. As he watched, he heard the cry again, wordless, desperate. A hand and arm flashed in the sunlight, waving.

Munnie turned and looked over at Bert and Martha. They were stretched out, their heads together on the towel, their bodies making a wide V, sleeping.

"Bert!" Munnie called. "Martha! Get up!"

Bert stirred, then sat up, rubbing his eyes. The shout came again, wailing, from the bay.

"Out there," Munnie said, pointing. Bert swung around, still sitting, and looked at the capsized boat and the two almost-submerged figures clinging to it, a man and a woman. "Good God," Bert said. "What do they think they're doing there?" He nudged Martha. "Wake up," he said, "and watch the shipwreck."

The boat lay almost motionless in the water, only shifting a little as the two figures moved, changing their positions. As Munnie watched, he saw the man push off from the boat and start to swim toward the beach. The man swam slowly and every thirty seconds he stopped and shouted and waved. After each stop he slid under, then reappeared, splashing and frantic.

"Oh, my," Bert said. "He's leaving her out there!"

Bert was standing by now, with Martha at his side, peering across the bay. The man had a good three hundred yards to go before he could touch down on the beach and with his screaming and waving and going under twice a minute, it didn't look as though he was going to make it. The woman who had been left hanging onto the boat shouted from time to time, too, and her voice sounded shrill and angry as it floated across the glittering quiet water.

Finally, Munnie could make out what the swimmer was shouting. *"Au secours! Je noye, je noye!"* Munnie felt a little flicker of annoyance with him. It seemed melodramatic and overdone to be shouting "I'm drowning," especially in such a powerful voice, on a peaceful afternoon in the calm, sunny bay. He went over to the edge of the wall, joining Bert and Martha.

"He seems to be doing all right," Bert said. "He's got a nice, strong stroke there."

"He's going to have to do a little explaining later," Martha said, "leaving his girl friend out there like that."

As they watched, the man went under again. He seemed to stay under a long time and Munnie began to feel his mouth get very dry, watching the spot where the man had disappeared. Then the man surfaced again, this time with his shoulders and arms bare, white and glistening against the deep blue water. He had taken off his shirt underwater and a moment later the shirt came up and floated away, billowing soddenly. The man shouted again. By now it was plain that he was calling directly to the three of them, standing on the wall. The man started swimming again, thrashing heavily.

Munnie scanned the beach and the wharf on which the Snipes were put up on blocks for the winter. There wasn't a boat of any kind he could use, or even a length of rope. He listened for the sound of the hammer they had heard when they had first come onto the wall. Then he realized it had stopped a long time ago, while they were still eating. Far across, on the other side of the bay, there was no movement in front of the houses that faced the water and there were no swimmers or fishermen or children playing anywhere in sight. The entire world of stone, sand and sea that afternoon seemed to be given over to the three of them standing on the wall, and the woman clinging to the bottom of the capsized boat calling shrilly and angrily to the half-naked man struggling in the water and moving slowly and painfully away from her.

Why couldn't this have happened in August? Munnie thought irritably. He looked down at the water rippling in gentle regular swells against the base of the wall. It wasn't very deep now, with the tide out, four or five feet at the most, and huge chunks of rock and concrete broke the surface irregularly. If you jumped it was a drop of at least fifteen feet and there would be no avoiding the rocks.

Munnie looked, almost embarrassedly, across at Martha and Bert.

Martha was squinting and there were lines on her forehead. She was biting her thumbnail absently like a little girl puzzling over a problem in school. Bert seemed critical and mildly interested, as though he were watching the performance of an acrobat in a third-rate circus.

"The damn fool," Bert said mildly. "If he couldn't handle a boat any better than that you'd think he'd have had the sense to stick close to the shore."

"Frenchmen," Martha said. "They think they can do anything." She went back to chewing on her nail.

The man called again, aiming it at them.

"What're we going to do?" Munnie asked.

"Bawl the stupid bastard out," Bert said, "when he comes ashore, for being such a lousy sailor."

Munnie peered at the swimmer. He was going more slowly now and he seemed to be settling deeper in the water after each stroke. "I don't think he's going to make it," Munnie said.

"Well," said Bert, "that'll be too bad."

Martha said nothing.

Munnie swallowed dryly. Later on, he thought, I won't be able to bear remembering today, standing here, watching a man drown.

Then another picture flicked before his eyes. It was sharp and clear and there was nothing missing. It was of Bert and Martha and himself standing in front of a French policeman, seated at a desk, with his cap on, scratching away with a leaking fountain pen in a little black book.

"So," the policeman was saying, "you wish to report a drowning?"

"Yes."

"So—you saw this gentleman, some distance from the shore, waving at you, and then he disappeared?"

"Yes."

"And the lady?"

"The last we saw of her she was still holding onto the boat, floating out to sea."

"Ah. And—uh—what steps did you take, personally?"

"We . . . we came here and reported it."

"Oh, yes. Of course." More scratching in the book. A hand reaching out. "Your passports, please." A quick riffling through the pages and one short, coldly smiling glance as the policeman tossed them on the desk. "Ah, Americans, all of you . . ."

The man out in the water went under again for a second.

Munnie tried to swallow again. This time he couldn't manage it.

"I'm going to go get him," he said. But for a moment he didn't move, as though, somehow, just saying it would fix everything, put the man on dry land, right the boat, stop the screams.

"It's two hundred and fifty yards at least from the beach," Bert said, very calmly. "And then two hundred and fifty yards back, or a little less, with a crazy Frenchman holding onto your neck."

Munnie listened gratefully. "Yes," he said. "At least."

"You never swam five hundred yards in your life," Bert said, sounding friendly and reasonable.

The man screamed again and now his voice was hoarse and terrified.

Munnie started walking swiftly along the wall, back to where there was a narrow flight of steps leading down to the little beach in front of the fort. He didn't run because he didn't want to be out of breath when he went into the water.

"Munnie!" he heard Bert call behind him. "Don't be a damn fool!"

Even as he started down the steep flight of steps, slippery with moss, Munnie noticed that Martha hadn't said anything. When he got down to the beach he trotted across it, at the water line, to get to the point nearest the man. He stopped, breathing heavily, and waved at the swimmer, encouraging him. Now, down at water level, it looked a good deal more than two hundred and fifty yards. He kicked off his shoes and tore off his shirt. The wind felt cold on his skin. He took off his pants, tossing them to one side on the sand, and stood there in his shorts. He hesitated. They were old shorts and they had torn at the crotch and he had mended them, clumsily, himself. He had a sudden picture of his body washed ashore and people noticing the shabby mending job and smiling a little. He unbuttoned the shorts, his fingers fumbling thickly at the buttons and let the shorts drop to the sand. As he walked deliberately into the water, he thought, She's never seen me naked, I wonder what she thinks.

He scraped his toes on a rock and the pain made the tears come into his eyes. He kept walking until the water was up to his chest, then pushed off and began to swim. The water was cold and his skin felt tight and frozen almost at once. He tried not to swim too fast, so that he would have some strength left when he reached the drowning man. Whenever he looked up to see how far he'd gone it seemed to him that he had hardly moved at all, and it was hard to keep going in a straight line. Somehow he always seemed to be veering to his left, in the direction of the wall, and he had to keep correcting himself all the time. Once, he looked up at the wall, searching for Bert and Martha. He couldn't see them and he had a moment of panic. What the hell have they done? he thought. They've left. He turned over on his back, losing precious seconds, and saw them on the beach, standing at the water's edge, watching him. Of course, he thought.

He turned over and kept on swimming methodically toward the Frenchman. Whenever he picked his head out of the water, the Frenchman seemed to be screaming, and just as far away as ever. He decided not to look again for awhile. It was too discouraging.

Then his arms began to feel tired. It can't be, he thought. I haven't even gone fifty yards yet. Still, the muscles between his shoulders and his elbows seemed to be contracted, twisting his bones, and there was a deep ache of weariness in the back of his arms. His right hand began to cramp a little, too, and he let it flutter loosely through the water, which slowed him down, but he didn't know what else to do about it. The cramp reminded him that he had eaten not very long before and had a lot of wine and grapes and cheese. As he swam, with the water a green blur in his eyes and the slow, steady push of it going past his ears, he remembered his mother, in all the summers of his boyhood, on the shores of the lake in New Hampshire, saying, "No swimming for at least two hours after meals." Sitting on a little wooden chair, under a striped umbrella, watching the children play on the narrow, pebbly beach.

The back of his neck and the base of his skull started to ache now, and his thoughts wavered across his consciousness, disconnected and slippery. He had never liked swimming much, he remembered. He just went in to cool off and play around. Swimming had always seemed like a boring sport. The same old thing, over and over again, lift one arm, lift the other arm, kick, lift one arm, lift the other arm, kick, never really get anyplace. And he had never learned to keep the water out of his ears and sometimes he'd feel deaf for hours and the water wouldn't come out until he'd gone to bed and slept on one side for a long time.

His arms began to feel numb and he rolled more and more, in an effort to get his shoulders into the job, and he seemed to be swimming lower in the water than he ever had before. There's no sense in wasting time, he thought, making himself worry about something else besides his arms, I might as well figure out what to do once I get there. Laboriously, he tried to phrase what he would say to the man in French when he approached him. *Monsieur, J'y suis. Doucement. Doucement.* He would stay off from the man and try to calm him down before grabbing him. Dimly, he remembered having seen a demonstration of life-saving at a pool when he was fourteen years old. He hadn't paid much attention, because the boy behind him had surreptitiously kept flicking at him with a wet towel. But there was something about letting yourself sink if the drowning man put his arms around your neck, then twisting and putting your hand under his chin and pushing back. He hadn't believed it when he was fourteen years old and he didn't believe it now. It was one of those things that looked good in practice, on dry land. Then there were all the stories about hitting people on the chin and knocking them out. More dry land. He had never knocked anybody out in his whole life. His mother hated fighting. *Monsieur, soyez tranquille. Roulez sur votre dos, s'il vous plaît.* Then he'd go in and grab him by the hair and start towing him, sidestroke. If the man understood him. He had an awful lot of trouble getting Frenchmen to understand his accent, especially here in the Basque country. Martha had no trouble at all. They all said what a charming accent she had. Well, why not, after all that time at the Sorbonne? She should have come with him as an interpreter, if for nothing else. *Tournez sur votre dos.* That was better.

He swam heavily and slowly, his eyes beginning to smart from the salt water. When he lifted his head there were white and silver spots before his eyes and everything seemed to be blurred and he couldn't really see anything much. He kept on swimming. After fifty strokes he decided he'd stop and tread water and look around. The idea of treading water now seemed like the greatest pleasure ever vouchsafed the human race.

He started to count the strokes. Fourteen, fifteen, sixteen . . . Lord, he thought, what if he's bald? He tried to remember what the man's head had looked like, far out, splashing away from the overturned boat. There had been a funny pale gleam. Bald, Munnie decided desperately. Nothing is going to go right.

He started counting strokes all over again. By the time he got to thirty-five he knew he would have to stop for awhile. He made himself do five more, then stopped and rolled over on his back, gasping and blowing water and looking up at the sky. He got his breath back and turned again and trod water, searching for the Frenchman.

He blinked his eyes and rubbed them with the back of his hand, sinking up to his mouth as he did so. The Frenchman wasn't there. Oh, God, he thought, he went down.

Then he heard the chugging and twisted in the water. A fishing boat was bearing away from the spot where Munnie had last seen the Frenchman, and was going toward the overturned dory. Munnie trod water, watching while the tuna boat stopped, and two fishermen reached down and pulled the woman on board. The tuna boat, Munnie realized, must have been coming up from the south, concealed by the little headland on which the fort was built, and must have coasted along the seaward side of the wall and entered the channel while he was swimming blindly out from the beach.

The men on the tuna boat threw a line onto the dory, then swung around and headed for Munnie. He waited for it, fighting his lungs. The tuna boat, painted blue, and slow and old, approached him, looking big and safe as it drew nearer. Munnie saw grinning, tanned wide faces, capped by blue berets in the bow, and he waved, with great effort, as the tuna boat slowed down and came to a stop next to him.

"*Ça va?*" a fisherman shouted, grinning down at him. A cigarette, burned almost to the end, hung plastered to his lips.

Munnie managed to smile. "*Ça va bien,*" he called. "*Très bien.*"

The man who had been rescued came to the rail, still naked to the waist, and peered curiously down at Munnie. Munnie saw that he had plenty of hair. The Frenchman didn't say anything. He was a fat young man with a hurt and dignified expression on his face. At his side appeared a woman. She had been heavily made up and the seawater had done a great deal of damage to the rouge and mascara. She stared furiously down at Munnie, then turned to the Frenchman. She grabbed him by both ears and shook him. "*Crapaud!*" she said loudly. "*Espèce de cochon.*"

The Frenchman closed his eyes and allowed his head to be shaken, keeping his face sad and dignified. The fisherman grinned more broadly.

"*Alors,*" one of the fishermen said, throwing a line out toward Munnie, "*Allons-y.*"

Munnie looked longingly at the line. Then he remembered that he was naked. He shook his head. One thing that was not going to happen to him that afternoon was to be fished out of the sea naked in front of that woman pulling her friend's ears and calling him a pig and a toad. "I'm O.K.," Munnie said, up to the brown, tough, amused faces, used to all sorts of comical, salty accidents and escapes. "*Je suis O.K.* I want to swim. I mean—*Je voudrais bien nager.*"

"O.K., O.K.," the fisherman said, laughing, as though what he had said was enormously witty. They pulled in the line and waved and the tuna boat swung around and started in toward the harbor, towing the dory. As it went, over the sound of the engine, Munnie could still hear the sound of the woman screaming.

Well, Munnie thought, watching the boat sail off, at least they understood me.

Then he turned and looked at the beach. It looked miles away and Munnie was surprised that he had swum that far. He had never swum that far before in his life. On the beach, at the water line, with the tower of the fort behind them, Bert and Martha were standing, small, sharp figures, throwing long shadows now in the declining sun.

Taking a deep breath, Munnie started to swim in.

He had to turn over and float every ten yards or so and for awhile it seemed to him that he wasn't moving at all, only going through the motions of swimming, but finally, putting his feet down, he touched bottom. It was still fairly deep, up to his chin, and he pulled his feet up and stubbornly kept on swimming. And as a gesture, which he didn't try to understand, even as he did it, he swam all the way in, making himself spurt and do a proper crawl, until the water was so shallow that his finger tips scraped the sand.

Then he stood up. He wavered a little, but he stood up and, making himself smile, walked slowly, naked, with the water streaming off him, toward where Bert and Martha stood next to the little pile of his clothes on the beach.

"Well," Bert said as Munnie came up to them, "what part of Switzerland are *you* from, Bud?"

As he bent over and picked up the towel and began to dry himself, shivering under the rough cloth, Munnie heard Martha laugh.

He rubbed himself dry. He took a long time, shivering badly, too weary and not interested enough to try to cover his nakedness. They drove back to the hotel in silence and when Munnie said that he thought he'd lie down and try to rest for awhile, they both agreed that it was probably the best thing to do.

He slept uneasily, his ears half deaf and stopped with water and the blood pounding in them like a distant, fitful sea. When Bert came in and said it was time for dinner, Munnie told him he wasn't hungry and that he wanted to rest. "We're going to the Casino after dinner," Bert said, "should we stop by and pick you up?"

"No," Munnie said. "I don't feel lucky tonight."

There was a little silence in the darkened room. Then Bert said, "Good night. Sleep well, Fat Man," and went out.

Alone, Munnie lay staring at the shadowed ceiling, thinking. *I'm not fat. Why does he call me that? He only started it in the middle of the summer.* Then he slept again and only awakened when he heard the car drive up outside the hotel and the steps going softly up the stairs, past his door, to the floor above. He heard a door open and close gently upstairs and he made himself shut his eyes and try to sleep.

When he awoke the pillow was wet, where the water had run out of his ears, and he felt better. When he sat up the blood stopped pounding inside his head, too. He turned on the lamp and looked at Bert's bed. It was empty. He looked at his watch. It was four-thirty.

He got out of bed and lit a cigarette and went to the window and opened it. The moon was just going down and the sea was milky and was making an even, grumbling sound, like an old man complaining about the life that lay behind him.

For a moment, he wondered where he would have been at this hour if the tuna boat hadn't come in around the breakwater. Then he doused his cigarette and began to pack. It didn't take long, because they had been traveling light all summer.

When he finished he made sure that the extra key for the car was on his ring. Then he wrote a short note for Bert, telling him that he'd decided to take off for Paris. He hoped to get to Paris in time to catch the boat. He hoped this wouldn't inconvenience Bert too much and he knew that Bert would understand. He didn't mention Martha.

He carried his bag out to the car through the dark hotel and threw the bag into the empty space next to the driver's seat. He put on a rain-coat and a pair of gloves and started the car and drove carefully out the driveway, without looking back to see whether the sound of the engine had awakened anyone or whether anyone had come to a window to watch him leave.

There was mist in the low places on the road, and he drove slowly, feeling it wet against his face. With the sighing regular noise of the windshield wipers and the steady, damp light of the headlights on the road ahead of him almost hypnotizing him, he drove mechanically, not thinking of anything at all.

It was only far past Bayonne, when the dawn had broken and he had cut off the lights and the road stretched gray and glistening through the dark pine aisles of Les Landes, that he allowed himself to remember the day and night that had just passed. And then all he could think was, It's my fault. I let the summer go on one day too long.

A WICKED STORY

THE CURTAIN CAME DOWN and the applause began. The theatre was warm now, after the three long acts, and Robert Harvey applauded lightly, only from the wrists, because he didn't want to sweat. He was a big, heavy man, and he had found that when he permitted himself enthusiasm in the overheated midtown auditoriums, he came away soaking wet. He had once caught a bad cold that way, going out into a rainstorm after *A Streetcar Named Desire,* and he had learned to temper his gratitude, moving his hands politely but making very little noise. The curtain went up again and the cast took their bows, smiling widely because the play had been running three months and was going to run at least a year and they were all eating. Robert regarded them coolly, thinking, Well, they certainly aren't worth four-eighty a seat. What has happened, he thought, to the plays I used to see when I was a younger man?

Virginia, in the next seat, was applauding briskly. Her eyes were shining, as they did when she was enjoying herself. Robert decided not to say anything about the four-eighty a seat when he talked to her later about the play. The actors were taking individual curtain calls now, and when the girl who played the cynical friend of the heroine came on, Robert clapped his hands quite powerfully, risking perspiration, because he had met her once at a party. Besides, she was not a bad-looking girl, with longish black hair, cut in an unusual way, and large blue eyes. She was a bit too big and eventually she was going to be fat and you had the feeling she never was going to get very far as an actress, but none of these things would be crucial for several more years.

Robert felt the beads of perspiration coming out on his forehead, and he was glad when the girl, after a bosomy curtsy, went off into the wings.

The lights came on and the Harveys moved slowly up the aisle in the newly disturbed waves of perfume and fur. Virginia said, "That was a very nice little play, wasn't it?" and Robert nodded, hoping that there were no relatives of the playwright within earshot. In the lobby, as he put on his coat, he saw a young man with a yellow muffler who was leaning against the box-office window staring at Virginia. In a more realistic society, he thought, taking Virginia's arm and moving her toward the street, you would be permitted to walk over and punch the nose of any man who looked at your wife that way.

They spurted across the street among the taxis, Virginia fleet on her high heels, and went through the alley, between the stage doors and the gay posters for musical comedies. There were three hits playing on the next street, and the people flowing from the theaters sounded good-natured and jubilant, and you knew that they would remain that way for at least another half hour, and it was pleasant to be among them in the windless, cold night air. The lights of the restaurant across the street were warm among the dark buildings, and the doorman, while not effusive, was agreeably polite as he swung the door open for them. The headwaiter was a little chillier than the doorman and seated them at the rear of the restaurant, although there were several empty tables closer to the entrance. Robert humbly accepted the table, thinking philosophically, Well, this is a theatrical restaurant; there are dozens of places where they'd put me near the front of the room and actors'd be lucky to get through the door.

Virginia settled herself on the banquette with a hundred small subsiding movements, then took out her glasses and carefully surveyed the room. After a minute, she put the glasses down on the table and turned toward Robert. "What're you smiling at?" she asked.

"Because you're so pleased," said Robert.

"Who says I'm pleased?"

"You examined the terrain and you said to yourself, 'Isn't this nice? I'm prettier than any of them,' and now you can enjoy your supper."

"Oh, you're so sharp," Virginia said. She smiled, "You're such a sharp man."

The waiter came, and they ordered spaghetti and half a bottle of Chianti, and watched the restaurant fill up with people who had been to the theatre and actors who still had traces of greasepaint around their collars and tall, astonishing-looking girls in mink coats from the musicals across the street. Robert ate hungrily and drank his wine slowly, nursing it.

"That play tonight," Virginia was saying, delicately winding spaghetti on her fork against a spoon, "was all right and I enjoyed it while I was there, but I'm getting tired of how awful all the female characters are in plays these days. All the women always are drunks or nymphomaniacs or they drive their sons crazy or they ruin the lives of two or three people an act. If I were a playwright, I'd write a nice, old-fashioned play in which the heroine is pure and beautiful and makes a man out of her husband, even though he's weak and drinks too much and occasionally robs his boss to bet on the horses."

"If you were a playwright, you'd be in Hollywood," Robert said.

"Anyway, I bet it'd be a big success," Virginia insisted. "I bet people are just dying to go to see a play that they can come out of and say, 'Yes, that's just how Mother was the time Dad had his trouble down at the bank and those two men in plainclothes came to see him from New York.'"

"If anything like that comes up," Robert said comfortably, "you go to see it some matinée. By yourself."

"And all the actresses these days. They try to act so ordinary. Just like anybody you'd meet in the street. Sometimes you wonder how they dare charge you admission to watch them. When I was a little girl, actresses used to be so affected you'd *know* you had to pay to see them, because you'd never meet anybody like that in real life in a million years."

"How did you like Duse?" Robert asked. "What did you think of Bernhardt when you were ten?"

"Don't be so witty. You know what I mean. That girl you liked so much tonight, for example . . ."

"Which girl I liked so much?" Robert asked, puzzled.

"The big one. The one that played the friend."

"Oh, that one," Robert said. "I didn't like her so much."

"You certainly sounded as though you did. I thought your hands'd be a bloody pulp by the time she got off the stage."

"I was just being neighborly," Robert said. "I met her once at a party."

"Whose party?" Virginia stopped eating.

"The Lawtons'. She went to school with Anne Lawton," Robert said. "Didn't you meet her?"

"I didn't go to that party. I had the flu that week." Virginia sipped her wine. "What's her name?"

"Carol Something. Look at the program."

"I left the program in the theater. Was she nice?"

Robert shrugged. "I only talked to her for five minutes. She told me she came from California and she hates working for television and she was divorced last year but they're still good friends. The usual kind of talk you get at the Lawtons'."

"She looks as though she came from California," Virginia said, making it sound like a criticism.

"Oakland," Robert said. "It's not exactly the same thing."

"There she is now," said Virginia. "Near the door."

Robert looked up. The girl was alone and was making her way down the center of the room. She wasn't wearing a hat, and her hair looked careless, and she had on a shapeless polo coat and flat shoes, and Robert decided, looking at her, that actresses were getting plainer every year. She stopped briefly once or twice to greet friends at other tables, then headed for a table in the corner, where a group of three men and two women were waiting for her. Robert realized that she was going to pass their table, and wondered if he ought to greet her. The party at which they'd met had been almost two months before, and he had a modest theory that people like actresses and book publishers and movie directors never remembered anyone they met who wasn't in a related profession. He doubted whether the girl would recognize him, but he arranged a slight, impersonal smile on his face, so that if she did happen to remember, he would seem to be saluting her. If she just passed by, Robert hoped that it would merely look as though he were responding with polite amusement to one of Virginia's remarks.

But the girl stopped in front of the table, smiling widely. She put out her hand and said, "Why, Mr. Harvey, isn't it nice seeing you again!"

She wasn't any prettier close up, Robert decided, but when she smiled, she seemed friendly and simple, and her voice sounded as though she really was glad to see him again after the five minutes in the noisy corner at the Lawtons' two months ago. Robert stood up and took her hand. "Hello," he said. "May I present my wife. Miss Byrne."

"How do you do, Miss Byrne," Virginia said. "We were just talking about you."

"We saw your show tonight," Robert said. "We thought you were very good indeed."

"Aren't you dear to say that," the girl said. "I love to hear it, even if you don't mean it at all."

"What about the man who wrote the play?" Virginia asked. "He must be rather strange."

"Mother trouble." Miss Byrne glanced significantly up at the ceiling. "All the young writers coming into the theater these days seem to have the same thing. You'd think it'd be the war that would be haunting them, but it isn't at all. It's only Mama."

Virginia smiled. "Not only young writers," she said. "Is this your first play, Miss Byrne?"

"Heavens, no," the girl said. "I've been in three others. *Regret, The Six-Week Vacation.* . . . I don't even remember the name of the third one. Turkeys. Here today and closed by Saturday."

Virginia turned to Robert. "Did you happen to see any of them, dear?" she asked.

"No," Robert said, surprised. He never went to the theatre without Virginia.

"Three other plays," Virginia went on pleasantly, sounding genuinely interested. "You must have been in New York quite a long time."

"Two years," Miss Byrne said. "A single blink of the eye of a drama critic."

"Two years," Virginia said, politely. She turned to Robert again. "Where did you say Miss Byrne came from? Hollywood?"

"Oakland," Robert said.

"New York must be quite exciting," Virginia said. "After Oakland."

"I love it," Miss Byrne said, sounding young and enthusiastic. "Even with the flops."

"I'm so sorry," Virginia said. "Keeping you standing there like that, talking on and on about the theatre. Wouldn't you like to sit down and join us for a drink?"

"Thanks," the girl said, "I really can't. They're waiting for me over in the corner."

"Some other time, perhaps," Virginia said.

"I'd love it," said Miss Byrne. "It's been fun meeting you, Mrs. Harvey. Mr. Harvey told me about you. I do hope we see each other again. Good night." She waved and smiled widely again and strode over toward her waiting friends.

Robert sat down slowly. There was silence at the table for a moment.

"It's a hard life," Virginia said after a while, "for actresses, isn't it?"

"Yes."

"*The Six-Week Vacation,*" Virginia said. "No wonder it failed, with a title like that. Did she play the lead in it, that girl?"

"I don't know," Robert said, waiting. "I told you I didn't see it."

"That's right," Virginia said. "You told me."

They were silent again. Virginia began to twist the stem of her wineglass with little, jerky movements. "You told me," she repeated. "It's too bad she couldn't have a drink with us. We might have learned a great deal about the theatre tonight. I find people in the theatre so fascinating. Don't you?"

"What's the matter with you?" Robert asked.

"Nothing," Virginia said flatly. "There's nothing the matter with me at all. Are you finished with your food?"

"Yes."

"Let's pay the check and get out of here."

"Virginia . . ." Robert said, drawling the name out complainingly.

"Rah-ahbert . . ." Virginia said, mimicking him.

"All right," said Robert. "What is it?"

"I said nothing."

"I know what you said. What is it?"

Virginia lifted her eyes and looked at him closely. "Miss Byrne," she said. "I thought you didn't know her name."

"Oh," Robert said. "Now it's turning into one of those evenings."

"It's not turning into any kind of evening. Get the check," Virginia said. "I want to go home."

"Waiter!" Robert called. "The check, please." He stared at Virginia. She was beginning to look martyred. "Listen," Robert said. "I didn't know her name."

"Carol Something," said Virginia.

"It came to me just as she got to the table. While I was standing up. Hasn't that ever happened to you?"

"No," said Virginia.

"Well, it's a common phenomenon."

Virginia nodded. "Very common," she said, "I'm sure."

"Don't you believe me?"

"You haven't forgotten a girl's name since you were six years old," Virginia said. "You remember the name of the girl you danced with once the night of the Yale game in 1935."

"Gladys," Robert said. "Gladys McCreary. She played field hockey for Bryn Mawr."

"No wonder you were so eager to get to the Lawtons' that night."

"I wasn't eager to get to the Lawtons' that night," Robert said, his voice beginning to rise. "And anyway I didn't even know she existed. At least be logical."

"I had a hundred and three fever," Virginia said, pitying herself all over again for the damp eyes, the hot forehead, the painful cough of two months earlier. "I was just lying there all alone, day after day . . ."

"Don't make it sound as though you were on the point of death for the whole winter," Robert said loudly. "You were in bed three days, and on Saturday you went to lunch in a snowstorm."

"Oh," Virginia said, "you can remember that it snowed one Saturday two months ago, but you can't remember the name of a girl you talked to for hours at a party, that you exchanged the most intimate confidences with."

"Virginia," Robert said, "I'm going to get up on this seat and scream at the top of my voice."

"Divorced, she said, but they're still good friends. I'll bet they are. I'll bet that girl is good friends with a lot of people. How about you and *your* ex-wife?" Virginia demanded. "Are you good friends with her, too?"

"You know as well as I do," Robert said, "that the only time I see my ex-wife is when she wants the alimony adjusted."

"If you keep talking in that tone of voice, they'll never let you in this restaurant again," Virginia whispered.

"Let's get out of here," Robert said blindly. "Waiter, where's that check?"

"She's thick." Virginia stared at Miss Byrne, who was sitting with her back to them twenty feet away, talking brightly and waving a cigarette. "Through the middle. Grotesquely thick."

"Grotesquely," Robert agreed.

"You don't fool me," Virginia said, "I know your tastes."

"Oh, God," Robert murmured.

"Always pretending to be such a connoisseur of beautiful women," Virginia said, "and secretly what you really like are old-fashioned, disgusting brood mares."

"Oh, God," Robert said again.

"Like that Elise Cross," Virginia rolled on, "two summers ago on the Cape. She always looked as though she had to be packed into her girdle under pressure. And whenever I looked around for you at a party, you both were gone, out on the dunes."

"I thought we had agreed never to discuss that subject again," Robert said with dignity.

"What subject am I permitted to discuss?" Virginia demanded. "The United Nations?"

"There never was anything between me and Elise Cross. Not anything. And you know it," Robert said firmly and convincingly. It was true that there had been something, but that had been two years ago, and he hadn't seen Elise Cross since then, or anyone else, for that matter. And anyway it had been summertime then, and he had been drunk a good deal of the time for a reason he could no longer recall, and the people around them had been of that peculiar, handsome, neurotic, wife-changing type that appears at places like that in August and infects the atmosphere. He had been ashamed of himself by Labor Day and had resolved to change his ways once and for all. Now he felt blameless and aggrieved at being called upon to defend himself after all that abstinence.

"You spent more time on the beach than the Coast Guard," Virginia said.

"If the waiter doesn't come with the check," Robert said, "I'm going to walk out of here and they can follow me in a taxi if they want their money."

"I should have known," Virginia said, and there was a remote throb in her voice. "People told me about you before we were married. I knew your reputation."

"Look, that was more than five years ago," Robert said doggedly. "I was younger then and more energetic and I was married to a woman I didn't like and who didn't like me. I was unhappy and lonely and restless—"

"And now?"

"And now," Robert said, thinking how wonderful it would be to get up and walk away from his wife for six or seven months, "and now I am married to a woman I love and I am settled and profoundly happy. I haven't had lunch or a drink with anyone for years. I barely tip my hat to women I know when I pass them in the street."

"And what about that fat actress over there?"

"Look," Robert said, feeling hoarse, as though he had been shouting into the wind for hours. "Let's get it straight. I met her at a party. I spoke to her for five minutes. I don't think she's very pretty. I don't think she's much as an actress. I was surprised when she recognized me. I forgot her name. Then I remembered her name when she came to the table."

"I suppose you expect me to believe that." Virginia smiled coldly.

"I certainly do. Because it's an exact statement of fact."

"I saw that smile," Virginia said. "Don't think I didn't."

"What smile?" Robert asked, honestly puzzled.

"Why, Mr. Harvey," Virginia said, cooing, "isn't it nice seeing you again? And then the teeth and the girlish crinkling of the nose and the long, direct stare . . ."

"Finally," Robert said to the waiter, who was leaning over the table, putting the check down. "Don't go away." Robert counted out some bills, feeling his hands shaking minutely with rage. He watched the waiter going toward the cashier's desk, near the kitchen, for change. Then he spoke, trying to keep his voice under control. "Now," he said, turning back to Virginia, "what, exactly, did you mean by that?"

"I may not be very smart," Virginia said, "but if there's one thing I have, it's intuition. Especially where you're concerned. And anyway that smile was unmistakable."

"Now, wait a minute." Robert felt his fists opening and closing spasmodically. "It's charming of you to think, even after being married to me for five years, that women just drop at my feet after speaking to me for five minutes, but I have to disillusion you. It has never happened to me. Never," he said slowly and distinctly and with some disappointment.

"If there's one thing I can't stand, it's fake modesty," Virginia said. "I've seen you looking at yourself in the mirror, approving of yourself by the hour, pretending you were shaving or looking for gray hairs. And," she added bitterly, "I've talked to your mother. I know how she brought you up. Drilling it into your head that the whole panting female sex was after you because you were a Harvey and you were so dazzling—"

"Good God," Robert said. "Now we have my mother, too."

"She has a lot to answer for," Virginia said, "your mother. Don't think she hasn't."

"All right," Robert said. "My mother is a low, terrible woman and everybody agrees on that. But what has that got to do with the fact that a woman I met at a party happened to smile at me?"

"Happened," Virginia said.

"I still don't see how it could be my fault," Robert said, trying to sound patient. "I can't control the way people smile in restaurants."

"It's always your fault," Virginia said. "Even if you don't say a word. It's just the way you come into the room and stand there and decide to look . . . male."

Robert jumped up, pushing the table back. "I can't stand it," he said. "I can't stand it any more. The hell with the change."

Virginia stood up, too, her face rigid. "I have an idea," Robert said as he helped her on with her coat. "Let's you and I not talk to each other for a week."

"Fine," said Virginia crazily. "That's perfectly fine with me." She walked swiftly toward the door, through the middle of the restaurant, without looking back.

Robert watched her striding down the narrow aisle between the tables, her black coat floating behind her. He wished that he had a worse temper. He wished that he had a temper so bad that he could stay out all night and get drunk.

The waiter came with the change, and Robert fumbled with the tip. Over the waiter's shoulder he saw Miss Byrne swing her head slowly toward him. Everybody else at her table was talking animatedly. For the first time, Robert looked at her carefully. It *is* true, he thought numbly. Most women these days *are* too damn thin.

Then Miss Byrne smiled at him. Her nose crinkled and her teeth showed and she seemed to be looking at him for a long time. He felt flattered and considerably younger and very curious. And as he dropped his eyes and left a large tip for the waiter, he knew, helplessly, that he was going to call her next day and he knew what her voice was going to sound like on the telephone.

Then he got his coat and hurried out of the restaurant after his wife.

PETER TWO

IT WAS SATURDAY night and people were killing each other by the hour on the small screen. Policemen were shot in the line of duty, gangsters were thrown off roofs, and an elderly lady was slowly poisoned for her pearls, and her murderer brought to justice by a cigarette company after a long series of discussions in the office of a private detective. Brave, unarmed actors leaped at villains holding forty-fives, and ingénues were saved from death by the knife by the quick thinking of various handsome and intrepid young men.

Peter sat in the big chair in front of the screen, his feet up over the arm, eating grapes. His mother wasn't home, so he ate the seeds and all as he stared critically at the violence before him. When his mother was around, the fear of appendicitis hung in the air and she watched carefully to see that each seed was neatly extracted and placed in an ashtray. Too, if she were home, there would be irritated little lectures on the quality of television entertainment for the young, and quicktempered fiddling with the dials to find something that was vaguely defined as educational. Alone, daringly awake at eleven o'clock, Peter ground the seeds between his teeth, enjoying the impolite noise and the solitude and freedom of the empty house. During the television commercials Peter closed his eyes and imagined himself hurling bottles at large unshaven men with pistols and walking slowly up dark stairways toward the door behind which everyone knew the Boss was waiting, the bulge of his shoulder holster unmistakable under the cloth of his pencilstriped flannel jacket.

Peter was thirteen years old. In his class there were three other boys with the same given name, and the history teacher, who thought he was a funny man, called them Peter One, Peter Two (now eating grapes, seeds and all), Peter Three, and Peter the Great. Peter the Great was, of course, the smallest boy in the class. He weighed only sixty-two pounds, and he wore glasses, and in games he was always the last one to be chosen. The class always laughed when the history teacher called out "Peter the Great," and Peter Two laughed with them, but he didn't think it was so awfully funny.

He had done something pretty good for Peter the Great two weeks ago, and now they were what you might call friends. All the Peters were what you might call friends, on account of that comedian of a history teacher. They weren't *real* friends, but they had something together, something the other boys didn't have. They didn't like it, but they had it, and it made them responsible for each other. So two weeks ago, when Charley Blaisdell, who weighed a hundred and twenty, took Peter the Great's cap at recess and started horsing around with it, and Peter the Great looked as if he was going to cry, he, Peter Two, grabbed the cap and gave it back and faced Blaisdell. Of course, there was a fight, and Peter thought it was going to be his third defeat of the term, but a wonderful thing happened. In the middle of the fight, just when Peter was hoping one of the teachers would show up (they sure showed up plenty of times when you didn't need them), Blaisdell let a hard one go. Peter ducked and Blaisdell hit him on the top of the head and broke his arm. You could tell right off he broke his arm, because he fell to the ground yelling, and his arm just hung like a piece of string. Walters, the gym teacher, finally showed up and carried Blaisdell off, yelling all the time, and Peter the Great came up and said admiringly, "Boy, one thing you have to admit, you sure have a hard head."

Blaisdell was out of class two days, and he still had his arm in the sling, and every time he was excused from writing on the blackboard because he had a broken arm, Peter got a nice warm feeling all over. Peter the Great hung around him all the time, doing things for him and buying him sodas, because Peter the Great's parents were divorced and gave him all the money he wanted, to make up to him. And that was O.K.

But the best thing was the feeling he'd had since the fight. It was like what the people on the television must feel after they'd gone into a room full of enemies and come out with the girl or with the papers or with the suspect, leaving corpses and desolation behind them. Blaisdell weighed a hundred and twenty pounds but that hadn't stopped Peter any more than the fact that the spies all had two guns apiece ever stopped the F.B.I. men on the screen. They saw what they had to do and they went in and did it, that was all. Peter couldn't phrase it for himself, but for the first time in his life he had a conscious feeling of confidence and pride in himself.

"Let them come," he muttered obscurely, munching grape seeds and watching the television set through narrowed eyes, "just let them come."

He was going to be a dangerous man, he felt, when he grew up, but one to whom the weak and the unjustly hunted could safely turn. He was sure he was going to be six feet tall, because his father was six feet tall, and all his uncles, and that would help. But he would have to develop his arms. They were just too thin. After all, you couldn't depend on people breaking their bones on your head every time. He had been doing pushups each morning and night for the past month. He could only do five and a half at a time so far, but he was going to keep at it until he had arms like steel bars. Arms like that really could mean the difference between life and death later on, when you had to dive under the gun and disarm somebody. You had to have quick reflexes, too, of course, and be able to feint to one side with your eyes before the crucial moment. And, most important of all, no matter what the odds, you had to be fearless. One moment of hesitation and it was a case for the morgue. But now, after the battle of Peter the Great's cap, he didn't worry about that part of it, the fearless part. From now on, it would just be a question of technique.

Comedians began to appear all over the dial, laughing with a lot of teeth, and Peter went into the kitchen and got another bunch of grapes and two tangerines from the refrigerator. He didn't put on the light in the kitchen and it was funny how mysterious a kitchen could be near midnight when nobody else was home, and there was only the beam of the light from the open refrigerator, casting shadows from the milk bottles onto the linoleum. Until recently he hadn't liked the dark too much and he always turned on lights wherever he went, but you had to practice being fearless, just like anything else.

He ate the two tangerines standing in the dark in the kitchen, just for practice. He ate the seeds, too, to show his mother. Then he went back into the living room, carrying the grapes.

The comedians were still on and still laughing. He fiddled with the dial, but they were wearing funny hats and laughing and telling jokes about the income tax on all the channels. If his mother hadn't made him promise to go to sleep by ten o'clock, he'd have turned off the set and gone to bed. He decided not to waste his time and got down on the floor and began to do pushups, trying to be sure to keep his knees straight. He was up to four and slowing down when he heard the scream. He stopped in the middle of a pushup and waited, just to make sure. The scream came again. It was a woman and it was real loud. He looked up at the television set. There was a man there talking about floor wax, a man with a mustache and a lot of teeth, and it was a cinch *he* wasn't doing any screaming.

The next time the scream came there was moaning and talking at the end of it, and the sound of fists beating on the front door. Peter got up and turned off the television, just to be sure the sounds he was hearing weren't somehow being broadcast.

The beating on the door began again and a woman's voice cried "Please, please, *please* . . ." and there was no doubt about it any more.

Peter looked around him at the empty room. Three lamps were lit and the room was nice and bright and the light was reflected off the grapes and off the glass of the picture of the boats on Cape Cod that his Aunt Martha painted the year she was up there. The television set stood in the corner, like a big blind eye now that the light was out. The cushions of the soft chair he had been sitting in to watch the programs were pushed in and he knew his mother would come and plump them out before she went to sleep, and the whole room looked like a place in which it was impossible to hear a woman screaming at midnight and beating on the door with her fists and yelling, "Please, please, *please* . . ."

The woman at the door yelled "Murder, murder, he's killing me!" and for the first time Peter was sorry his parents had gone out that night.

"Open the door!" the woman yelled. "Please, *please* open the door!" You could tell she wasn't saying please just to be polite by now.

Peter looked nervously around him. The room, with all its lights, seemed strange, and there were shadows behind everything. Then the woman yelled again, just noise this time. Either a person is fearless, Peter thought coldly, or he isn't fearless. He started walking slowly toward the front door. There was a long mirror in the foyer and he got a good look at himself. His arms looked very thin.

The woman began hammering once more on the front door and Peter looked at it closely. It was a big steel door, but it was shaking minutely, as though somebody with a machine was working on it. For the first time he heard another voice. It was a man's voice, only it didn't sound quite like a man's voice. It sounded like an animal in a cave, growling and deciding to do something unreasonable. In all the scenes of threat and violence on the television set, Peter had never heard anything at all like it. He moved slowly toward the door, feeling the way he had felt when he had the flu, remembering how thin his arms looked in the mirror, regretting that he had decided to be fearless.

"Oh, God!" the woman yelled, "Oh, God, don't do it!"

Then there was some more hammering and the low, animal sound of the beast in the cave that you never heard over the air, and he threw the door open.

Mrs. Chalmers was there in the vestibule, on her knees, facing him, and behind her Mr. Chalmers was standing, leaning against the wall, with the door to his own apartment open behind him. Mr. Chalmers was making that funny sound and he had a gun in his hand and he was pointing it at Mrs. Chalmers.

The vestibule was small and it had what Peter's mother called Early American wallpaper and a brass light fixture. There were only the two doors opening on the vestibule, and the Chalmers had a mat in front of theirs with "Welcome" written on it. The Chalmers were in their mid-thirties, and Peter's mother always said about them, "One thing about our neighbors, they *are* quiet." She also said that Mrs. Chalmers put a lot of money on her back.

Mrs. Chalmers was kind of fat and her hair was pretty blond and her complexion was soft and pink and she always looked as though she had been in the beauty parlor all afternoon. She always said "My, you're getting to be a big boy" to Peter when she met him in the elevator, in a soft voice, as though she was just about to laugh. She must have said that fifty times by now. She had a good, strong smell of perfume on her all the time, too.

Mr. Chalmers wore pince-nez glasses most of the time and he was getting bald and he worked late at his office a good many evenings of the week. When he met Peter in the elevator he would say, "It's getting colder," or "It's getting warmer," and that was all, so Peter had no opinion about him, except that he looked like the principal of a school.

But now Mrs. Chalmers was on her kness in the vestibule and her dress was torn and she was crying and there were black streaks on her cheeks and she didn't look as though she'd just come from the beauty parlor. And Mr. Chalmers wasn't wearing a jacket and he didn't have his glasses on and what hair he had was mussed all over his head and he was leaning against the Early American wallpaper making this animal noise, and he had a big, heavy pistol in his hand and he was pointing it right at Mrs. Chalmers.

"Let me in!" Mrs. Chalmers yelled, still on her knees. "You've got to let me in. He's going to kill me. *Please!*"

"Mrs. Chalmers . . ." Peter began. His voice sounded as though he were trying to talk under water, and it was very hard to say the "s" at the end of her name. He put out his hands uncertainly in front of him, as though he expected somebody to throw him something.

"Get inside, you," Mr. Chalmers said.

Peter looked at Mr. Chalmers. He was only five feet away and without his glasses he was squinting. Peter feinted with his eyes, or at least later in his life he thought he had feinted with his eyes. Mr. Chalmers didn't do anything. He just stood there, with the pistol pointed, somehow, it seemed to Peter, at both Mrs. Chalmers and himself at the same time. Five feet was a long distance, a long, long distance.

"Good night," Peter said, and he closed the door.

There was a single sob on the other side of the door and that was all.

Peter went in and put the uneaten grapes back in the refrigerator, flicking on the light as he went into the kitchen and leaving it on when he went out. Then he went back to the living room and got the stems from the first bunch of grapes and threw them into the fireplace, because otherwise his mother would notice and look for the seeds and not see them and give him four tablespoons of milk of magnesia the next day.

Then, leaving the lights on in the living room, although he knew what his mother would say about that when she got home, he went into his room and quickly got into bed. He waited for the sound of shots. There were two or three noises that might have been shots, but in the city it was hard to tell.

He was still awake when his parents came home. He heard his mother's voice, and he knew from the sound she was complaining about the lights in the living room and kitchen, but he pretended to be sleeping when she came into his room to look at him. He didn't want to start in with his mother about the Chalmers, because then she'd ask when it had happened and she'd want to know what he was doing up at twelve o'clock.

He kept listening for shots for a long time, and he got hot and damp under the covers and then freezing cold. He heard several sharp, ambiguous noises in the quiet night, but nothing that you could be sure about, and after a while he fell asleep.

In the morning, Peter got out of bed early, dressed quickly, and went silently out of the apartment without waking his parents. The vestibule looked just the way it always did, with the brass lamp and the flowered wallpaper and the Chalmers' doormat with "Welcome" on it. There were no bodies and no blood. Sometimes when Mrs. Chalmers had been standing there waiting for the elevator, you could smell her perfume for a long time after. But now there was no smell of perfume, just the dusty, apartment-house usual smell. Peter stared at the Chalmers' door nervously while waiting for the elevator to come up, but it didn't open and no sound came from within.

Sam, the man who ran the elevator and who didn't like him, anyway, only grunted when Peter got into the elevator, and Peter decided not to ask him any questions. He went out into the chilly, bright Sunday-morning street, half expecting to see the morgue wagon in front of the door, or at least two or three prowl cars. But there was only a sleepy woman in slacks airing a boxer and a man with his collar turned up hurrying up from the corner with the newspapers under his arm.

Peter went across the street and looked up to the sixth floor, at the windows of the Chalmers' apartment. The Venetian blinds were pulled shut in every room and all the windows were closed.

A policeman walked down the other side of the street, heavy, blue and purposeful, and for a moment Peter felt close to arrest. But the policeman continued on toward the avenue and turned the corner and disappeared and Peter said to himself, They never know anything.

He walked up and down the street, first on one side, then on the other, waiting, although it was hard to know what he was waiting for. He saw a hand come out through the blinds in his parents' room and slam the window shut, and he knew he ought to get upstairs quickly with a good excuse for being out, but he couldn't face them this morning, and he would invent an excuse later. Maybe he would even say he had gone to the museum, although he doubted that his mother would swallow that. Some excuse. Later.

Then, after he had been patrolling the street for almost two hours, and just as he was coming up to the entrance of his building, the door opened and Mr. and Mrs. Chalmers came out. He had on his pince-nez and a dark-gray hat, and Mrs. Chalmers had on her fur coat and a red hat with feathers on it. Mr. Chalmers was holding the door open politely for his wife, and she looked, as she came out the door, as though she had just come from the beauty parlor.

It was too late to turn back or avoid them, and Peter just stood still, five feet from the entrance.

"Good morning," Mr. Chalmers said as he took his wife's arm and they started walking past Peter.

"Good morning, Peter," said Mrs. Chalmers in her soft voice, smiling at him. "Isn't it a nice day today?"

"Good morning," Peter said, and he was surprised that it came out and sounded like good morning.

The Chalmers walked down the street toward Madison Avenue, two married people, arm in arm, going to church or to a big hotel for Sunday breakfast. Peter watched them, ashamed. He was ashamed of Mrs. Chalmers for looking the way she did the night before, down on her knees, and yelling like that and being so afraid. He was ashamed of Mr. Chalmers for making the noise that was not like the noise of a human being, and for threatening to shoot Mrs. Chalmers and not doing it. And he was ashamed of himself because he had been fearless when he opened the door, but had not been fearless ten seconds later, with Mr. Chalmers five feet away with the gun. He was ashamed of himself for not taking Mrs. Chalmers into the apartment, ashamed because he was not lying now with a bullet in his heart. But most of all he was ashamed because they had all said good morning to each other and the Chalmers were walking quietly together, arm in arm, in the windy sunlight, toward Madison Avenue.

It was nearly eleven o'clock when Peter got back to the apartment, but his parents had gone back to sleep. There was a pretty good program on at eleven, about counterspies in Asia, and he turned it on automatically, while eating an orange. It was pretty exciting, but then there was a part in which an Oriental held a ticking bomb in his hand in a roomful of Americans, and Peter could tell what was coming. The hero, who was fearless and who came from California, was beginning to feint with his eyes, and Peter reached over and turned the set off. It closed down with a shivering, collapsing pattern. Blinking a little, Peter watched the blind screen for a moment.

Ah, he thought in sudden, permanent disbelief, after the night in which he had faced the incomprehensible, shameless, weaponed grownup world and had failed to disarm it, ah, they can have that, that's for kids.

THE KISS AT CROTON FALLS

FREDERICK MULL WAS a huge rollicking man, with a russet mustache, but when they took the trolleys off Third Avenue and put him on a pension he sickened and died, he who had never missed a day of work in his life except for drunkenness or wounds incurred in the kind of arguments a man from time to time could not avoid on evenings out with high-spirited and honorable companions. It was bad enough when they took away his conductor and made him make his own change in the front of the trolley, with all the traffic of New York charging and howling around him, but when they put the buses on and told him he'd have to learn how to drive if he wanted to stay with the company, he knew and the company knew he was finished.

All this shows how long ago it all was, when there was snow in the city every winter and the lakes froze over and all the comfortable brown buildings hadn't been torn down for gray and glass office slabs and it didn't take all day to go from the Bridge to Yorkville by surface transportation.

He had his faults. He drank whisky when he could afford it and beer when he couldn't and they carried him home to his wife one night with a concussion that lasted two days that he got defending the hanging of Roger Casement in a bar owned by a man named Mulloy near Fortieth Street. His father had fought in the Union Army, under Mc-Clellan, and he was an unswerving patriot. He was part-everything, he said, because his father's family had come from the Midlands and his mother was one-eighth Indian. He had a slow, barrelling baritone and when he had drunk one or two he would sing "Flow Gently, Sweet

Afton" and "Good King Wenceslaus" and "Oh, Susannah." But most of all he was partial to "John Brown's Body Lies A-Mouldering in the Grave" and "Who Is Sylvia?"

According to his wife, he also had a weakness for women.

The sole basis for this belief came from something that happened in the summer of 1921, when they were at a hotel at Croton Falls, recovering from the birth of their daughter, and Mrs. Mull looked out of her window on a moonlit night and saw her husband kissing a redheaded woman whose husband was not due to arrive until Labor Day. Mr. Mull's story was that before he knew what she was up to, the redheaded woman pinned him against a pillar after dinner, while he was quietly smoking his pipe, and threw her arms around him and kissed him, missing his mouth, in her anxiety, by a good margin. But Mrs. Mull would have none of that, and from that moment until the day he died, Mr. Mull enjoyed the reputation with his wife of being a wild, philandering ladies' man.

It was her contention that the women of the great city of New York rode on the Third Avenue trolley for the sole purpose of corrupting her husband. There was a story, it is true, that on a spring day in 1919 a widow in a veil walked forward along the aisle and slipped her address on an embossed card into his hand while she was waiting for the car to stop at Seventy-ninth Street, but there were many stories in those days about motormen and locomotive engineers and people like that, not all of them worthy of belief.

To forestall any other widows or soft-eyed virgins or dissatisfied wives with similar cunning tricks, his wife took to waiting along the route at odd and unsuspected hours for his trolley to appear. Once or twice he saw her in time, standing there next to the elevated pillar holding their little dark-haired daughter, Clarice, by the hand and he merely passed her by. She would scream like a forsaken bride, shaking her fist after the yellow car rattling down the tracks toward the Bowery, with the taxi-drivers stopping their cabs to gawk at her in wonder, but naturally, she couldn't denounce him to the company. So she descended to guile and picked corners where there'd be sure to be at least eight or ten other passengers waiting that, for his job's sake, he couldn't dare sail by. Even years after she had given up the practice, he'd tighten visibly at the box when he approached Twenty-third Street, Thirty-fourth Street, or the back entrance of Bloomingdale's.

When she climbed into the car, she'd nod icily to Mr. Coombs, who was her husband's conductor the best part of the time, pay her nickel, march up the aisle toward the head of the car, daring any other woman who happened to be sitting there to look at her. She'd never say a word to her husband. She'd just sit there, boring holes in the back of his head with her eyes, until he couldn't stand it anymore and he'd draw the leather curtain they had around the motorman's position to keep the reflection of the lights within the car from confusing him on the night run.

The night shifts were of course the worst. She'd sit up for him in the dark cold kitchen with a blanket wrapped around her like a fisherman's wife during a storm waiting for the lighthouse keeper to come knocking on the door with the bad news. And when he did come home she'd pretend to be making coffee and getting out the biscuits, but all the time she was sniffing him for perfume like a hound on new tracks and her eyes would be going over him for lipstick and signs of disarray like a pirate over a bloodstained map.

He was a good-natured man and he made no complaint. He'd only been married that once and he supposed that was what the institution was like.

He was content enough. He had his whisky on and off the route and played with Clarice and taught her "Who Is Sylvia?" He endured the reproaches of his wife as he endured the weather and traffic policemen, and in the end he took it as a sign of love, which indeed it was, and he would have been lonely and lost without it. Everything considered, they lived together for nearly thirty years in what would certainly pass in these days as happiness.

He lived to see his only daughter married to a good man by the name of Smalley, who had a dependable job as an insurance adjuster, and at the wedding he said to the groom, "Ah, man, at least in your trade they'll never tear the tracks out from under you."

Mr. Smalley was of a different breed from Mr. Mull, which was only to be expected, since Mrs. Mull had spent a good part of her life warning her daughter not to marry a man like her father. Mr. Mull had heard many of these warnings in his time and while he had not actively set the seal of his approval upon them, he had been seen to nod in quiet agreement with his wife's directives. He admired her intelligence vastly and took her word for gospel in all questions of taste and affection.

The only pleasure Mr. Smalley took outside his home was prevailing upon people who had broken their legs in industrial accidents or who had lost their goods by fire to settle for less than they had originally asked from the company. He had never been seen inside a saloon and he looked at his shoetops when he passed women in the street. He was a good provider, and while he did not seem capable of presenting his wife with an heir, he insisted upon her having a maid come in three afternoons a week to help with the cleaning and ironing.

When Mr. Mull died, Mrs. Mull mourned him truly, keeping his photograph on the mantelpiece, with his mustaches brushed, and saying to visitors, over a cup of tea, "Ah, nobody knows the life that man led me."

She dreamt about him constantly through the years, conversing with him in her sleep in wifely tones and walking over the next morning to her daughter's home to tell her about it. "Your father visited me again last night," Mrs. Mull would say, "and we had a nice long talk about the time we went up the river to Newburgh and the picnic steamer almost capsized in the rain." Or, "We had a serious talk last night and he promised to drink only beer until the Sunday after Easter." And sometimes Mrs. Mull would hurry over with her eyes shining, to say, "He was in very good spirits last night, not affected by drink or anything like that, you understand, but jolly, and he sang 'Flow Gently, Sweet Afton' and four verses of 'They're Hanging Danny Deever in the Morning.'"

Clarice took the reports of these conversations calmly. She had loved her father and thought him by far the most interesting man she had ever known and it seemed to her entirely natural that his memory died hard. And her mother was a lonely old woman, living in one room with very little to occupy her after an exhilarating lifetime of nagging an obstreperous and lovable man, and Clarice felt that these matter-of-fact nocturnal visits from the grave lightened her mother's solitude and gave point to her days.

But one morning the whole atmosphere changed. Her mother appeared early, white-lipped and angry. "He came again last night," she said, almost as soon as she walked through the door of Clarice's apartment.

"Did you have a nice visit?" Clarice asked, according to her usual formula.

"We did not," Mrs. Mull said. "We had a mortifying evening."

"Oh, Mother," Clarice said, "is that nice?"

"I would like to see what you would have done," said Mrs. Mull, "in my place."

"You must be careful not to hurt him," Clarice said soothingly. "Remember, he's an old man."

"Hurt him!" Mrs. Mull snorted. "Try and hurt that man. He has the hide of an elephant."

"What happened?" Clarice asked.

"The bell rang," said Mrs. Mull, "and there he was, standing there, with that smirk on his face he always has when he knows he's doing something that will annoy me."

"Now, Mother," Clarice began, "you mustn't read into things . . ."

"Read into things!" Mrs. Mull said. "Wait until you hear the story and then say read into things. Do you know what that man had the cold, icy courage to do last night?" She paused and Clarice dutifully said, "What?"

"Finally," Mrs. Mull said, "he overstepped the bounds. I'm a tolerant woman and I've learned to take the bad with the good, but even saints have their limits. And when I saw them standing there outside the door last night, I knew. . . ."

"What?" Clarice asked, puzzled. "What do you mean, *them?*"

"What I mean, exactly," Mrs. Mull said tightly, "is *them.* Your father and that red-headed woman in a crepe-de-Chine dress so tight you'd wonder how she could breathe the air or digest her food, and the child."

"What child?" Clarice asked faintly.

"A big, lumpish boy," said Mrs. Mull, "growing out of his clothes, with the same smirk on his face. Put a mustache on him and he could go down to the carbarn any day of the week and take out a car and run the full length of Third Avenue and nobody would know the difference."

"Now, Mother," Clarice said. She had heard, of course, of the red-headed woman on the porch at Croton Falls in the summer of 1921, but this was the first intimation of issue. "I never heard of any child."

"Neither did I," Mrs. Mull said, "until last night. Oh, he was the most deceptive man who ever walked the streets of the city. But last night he tore away the veil. Standing there, as cool as you please, with that woman's hand on his arm and that unmistakable child, saying, 'Bertha, I've brought some friends. Are there any refreshments in the house?' "

"And what did you do then?" Clarice asked, humoring her mother, but curious, also.

"Oh, I was polite," Mrs. Mull said. "I never held with making scenes before strangers and your father knows that and depends upon it. I gave her a cold bow and I took the boy's cap and I ushered them in with all civility and I made them tea and set out half a loaf of crumb-cake that I had in the cupboard. I sat there, putting in a yes or no from time to time while that woman talked about Croton Falls and how she found the summer weather a little sticky and how she suspected they used margarine in the kitchen for cooking, although they swore they used butter. I'll tell the truth, I didn't go out of my way to make them comfortable, and they cut their visit mercifully short. I took the opportunity of getting your father off to one side for a moment and I told him, in no uncertain terms, that that was the last I wanted to see of that woman and their child of sin. I said, clear and definite, so there would be no misunderstanding in the future, that if he expected to see me again, he would have to make his visits alone."

"What did Father say to that?" Clarice asked.

"He didn't say anything," Mrs. Mull said. "Before he could open his mouth, she came into the hall and put her hand on his arm and said, 'Frederick, it's getting late, we're expected downtown,' and off they went together, after kindly thanking me for the tea, all unholy shameless three of them."

Clarice was a sensible girl and she said the right thing to restore order and harmony. "I don't think you have anything more to worry about now," she told her mother. "I'm sure he'll take the hint."

"He'd better," Mrs. Mull said fiercely, "or he'll find the door locked in his face."

For the next week or so, Mrs. Mull reported, all went well. Mr. Mull visited her three times, rather quiet and absent-minded, but alone. She herself had decided to be tolerant and keep her own counsel, and she had tactfully not brought up the subject of the red-headed woman and the unmistakable boy.

But then the devil came up in him again, and on a Saturday night he rang the bell and there he was with the smirk on his lips and the red-headed woman on his arm with every wrinkle of her corset showing as clear as light through her skin-tight dress, and of course, that lump of a boy, with his father's Saturday-night expression built into his face.

"He stood there in the hallway," Mrs. Mull told Clarice on the following Monday morning, "grinning and enjoying his guilt, saying, 'We were just passing by and we thought maybe you'd be in the mood for a little company.'"

Mrs. Mull had had to wait until Monday to tell Clarice, because Clarice had been in Providence for the weekend, visiting the family of Mr. Smalley. The enforced delay had enabled Mrs. Mull to arrange the details eloquently in her mind and she started her story even before she took off her hat in Clarice's living room.

"I took one look at him," Mrs. Mull said, "and I let my eyes pass significantly over that woman and her criminal son and it wasn't wasted on your father, you can be assured of that. But he brazened it out. 'Aren't you going to invite us in for a minute, Bertha?' he says, standing there between the two of them, like a prize bull at a fair. 'I warned you, Frederick,' I told him, polite but final. 'Now go away and never come up these stairs again.' 'Now, Bertha,' he began, in that wheedling, sugary tone he knows how to put on when there is a woman in question. But I cut him off quick. 'I told you to go away,' I said, 'I wash my hands of you. I have stood enough. Don't waste your time trying,' I said. 'This door is locked.' And I closed it in his face, not slamming it, because I wouldn't give that woman the pleasure of knowing I was angry, but sharp and definite. I heard regretful whispering on the other side for a minute or two and then they shuffled off and I went to bed. He came back an hour later and he rang the bell and he called through the door, 'I'm alone now, Bertha, let me in for the love of God,' but I made not a move and I said not a word. He rang the bell all the night long and whimpered outside the door, but my decision was made and I didn't let him know, even by a whisper, that I so much as heard a sound. And in the end, with the sun coming up, he gave a last, despairing ring, and he called, 'I'm going, Bertha, it's good-bye forever' and even though my heart fell down inside me like a weight, I didn't answer him, because it's about time he was taught a lesson. And that," Mrs. Mull said, "is the end of your father."

Clarice started to tell her mother that she ought to give him one more chance, but she gave up when she saw the set of Mrs. Mull's jaw and made her a cup of tea and tried to calm her as best she could and watched her put on her hat, squarely on her head, like a soldier putting on his helmet before a battle, and descend the stairs to do her day's shopping, implacable and alone.

Clarice thought all day about her mother and about how the love she bore her father could burn so fiercely for forty years that she could find the strength to turn him away from her door, even though he had been dead so long, because of a kiss on a porch in Croton Falls in 1921. And when Mr. Smalley came home that night, she looked at him coldly and knew, as he took off his shoes and sat down mildly and faithfully in an easy chair, putting on his glasses to read the evening newspaper, that he never could inspire such passion in any woman, and that ten days after he had been lowered into his grave she would not be able to remember even his most obnoxious mannerism.

"Ah," he said wearily, settling into his chair and folding his paper, "I've been busy today."

Clarice looked at him for a long, bitter moment. "Doing what?" she asked. "Cheating the poor and doing sad souls that have been destroyed by fire out of their rightful damages?"

"Clarice . . ." Mr. Smalley said, looking up from his newspaper, frightened and surprised, sensing a new, disturbing note of passion in the marriage that he knew would never be to his advantage. "What have I done?"

But Clarice did not answer. She was putting on her coat, and she was out of the apartment, without a word, on her way to a saloon on Third Avenue, not far from the Bloomingdale corner.

THE WEDDING OF A FRIEND

It is impossible to attend a wedding without a sense of foreboding or regret. Depending upon which side you are ranged, you are bound to have some unpleasant reservations about the bride or the groom, or perhaps both, and if you are cynical you are likely to remember other weddings you have witnessed and how the marriages eventually turned out. And if you are a man and the bride is beautiful, there is almost certain to be a moment during which you will feel a sharp, ignoble twinge of deprivation.

But at Ronny Biddell's wedding, although the bride was young and lovely and regarded Ronny with the most obvious bridal pleasure, I felt nothing but satisfaction and a strange kind of relief, a relief, I imagine, which must have been very close to the emotion felt by the brother of a matador who has watched a particularly dangerous fight, in which the matador has been upon the horns and has done foolhardy things all afternoon and has finally, exhausted and covered with blood, made a triumphant kill.

Ronny was not my brother and he was, of course, not covered with blood. He stood at the altar, ruddy, growing bald, sweating slightly, as he always did, a sturdy, round man in his tailcoat and striped trousers, looking, as he stood there, not quite being able to refrain from smiling a little, as though he had never been in danger in his life.

I was at the wedding by accident. I had arrived in London planning vaguely to look up Ronny, and had, in fact, made a desultory inquiry or two, but everyone in England seemed to have changed addresses several times since the war, and I had not taken the time to track him down.

The truth was, too, that I was a little afraid of what I might find if I finally did locate him, and I invented excuses not to press the search too assiduously.

Then, one day, in a restaurant on Jermyn Street, I saw him across the room, sitting with a young, dark-haired girl of superlative beauty, who kept looking at Ronny with that narrowness and intensity of focus which is, in our era, in a crowded restaurant, the public advertisement of love. Fifteen minutes later I was being invited to the wedding.

Now I was sitting in the church, among the polished, strange British faces, listening to the ceremony, staring at Ronny's reddish scalp and his solid, polite shoulders, enjoying the curious feeling of relief for Ronny, who, unexpectedly, among all the men I had known during the war who had later suffered or vanished or failed to live up to the hopes we had entertained for them, had arrived at this shining and victorious moment.

I had met Ronny in London in 1943. He was at that time a lieutenant in the British Army, hazily attached to the same project to which I was assigned, one of those inter-allied missions which had very little to do with winning the war, but which served, while the armies waited for the invasion of Europe, as an occasion of Anglo-American good-will and co-operation at almost no military cost. Ronny at first sight looked like the sort of man who had been deprived, only because of his youth, of a colonelcy in the Indian Army. He wore a mustache, he boomed, he carried himself like a soldier and drank like one—he was in fact so markedly the type of regular colonial officer, at least to American eyes, that we called him, much to his enjoyment, the Beefeater. The flaw in the picture was that under the robust martial exterior he was hideously shy, especially with women. He had been brought up by aunts with so much circumspection that his respect for women at the age of twenty-eight was carried to an extreme which was, to all practical purposes, impotence.

He was childishly candid about himself with his friends and I knew all his history within two weeks of meeting him. He was abnormally susceptible to women—the sight of a pretty face across a theater lobby could make him blush, almost as though all the confused thoughts and emotions that flooded through him at the sight of the girl were somehow guiltily plain to her, at a distance of twenty feet, and to everyone else present. And once, when a girl whom I had invited to have dinner with Ronny and me kissed him good night on the cheek, he confessed that it kept him up, half smiling and half in despair, for the entire night. He also had an uncomfortable tendency to breathe brokenly, like a sufferer from asthma, when talking to a girl, and sometimes even when talking *about* a girl. In all that time in London, which, not to put too fine a point upon it, was a period of almost unprecedented *camaraderie* between the sexes, I never saw Ronny out with a girl of his own.

That is not to say that Ronny had never been involved with a woman. For two years before the war, he had lived in Paris, on a small income, wearing a beret, according to his report, and studying what he vaguely called Art. During that time he had met Virginie, or rather, as he later admitted, had permitted himself to be picked up by her in a café on a rainy evening and allowed to pay for her drink.

"Frenchwomen, my dear fellow," he confided in me, on the basis of his knowledge of Virginie, "are more in my line. Forthright. Not always playing that damned game with a man. Direct."

It developed that Virginie had not been as direct as all that. She was young, with black hair and what Ronny called drowning gray eyes and that French thing about the mouth. But she lived, so she said, with her family, who were so savagely devout that Ronny was not even permitted to meet them. After the numberless dinners, evenings at the opera and theater to which Ronny escorted her, she would leave him, severely, at the door. He himself lived with a family and he had to go through the salon to reach his room, and there never was any hope of inviting her there. He fell very much in love with her and had reached a point at which he was taking her out three nights a week and kissing her at her doorway and mentioning marriage when the war broke out.

There was a tearful and public parting in the Luxembourg Gardens and Ronny went back to England, promising a letter a day and a quick victory for the linked arms of their two countries. Healthy, willing and with no discernible military talent, he was enlisted as a private and put at a desk in a motor-repair depot near Salisbury. Feigning patriotism and an overwhelming desire to come to grips with the enemy, he pulled what wires he could to get himself transferred to a position of greater danger, and some months later happily found himself en route to France. He never got as far as Paris, but was set down at Rennes, where he was put behind a desk once more, again in a motor-repair depot. Virginie could not come to visit him, because of parental objections, but Ronny managed two leaves in Paris, where he made up for the ignominy of his trooper's uniform with prodigal tête à tête dinners with Virginie in the elegant restaurants and with substantial gifts bought from his dwindling income, in the most expensive shops.

Marriage was, for the moment, out of the question, but Ronny's ardor, fanned by two years of devotion, could no longer be stayed, and he so far forgot the maxims of his aunts as to press Virginie, finally, for a rendezvous. After a suitable hesitation, Virginie, taking into account the perils of the time and the patriotic claims of the poor boys in uniform who might be here today and God-knows-where tomorrow, relented. But after so much waiting, so many unassuaged sighs, so many whispered nighttime conversations under lampposts and outside darkened doors, she could not relent all in one piece or in a single moment. She agreed—but for the future. On his next leave in Paris, when they had had time to prepare themselves properly, she promised that the event would take place. Ronny went back to Rennes, blistered with anticipation, and put in, as soon as he dared, for another leave. The leave was promised him some three weeks in the future and he made thorough arrangements, through the mails, with a small but excellent hotel, for a two-room suite with bath and even went so far as to order the dinner and the wine for the crucial evening. Four years later, when he told me all this, he still remembered the exact menu and wines that he had ordered—smoked Scotch salmon, roast duck, cooked with peaches, salad and wild strawberries. The wines were a Haut-Brion, 1928, and a Veuve Cliquot, 1919.

Something of a hypochondriac, despite his robust appearance, and fearful that the prolonged state of tension under which he was living would bring him disastrously to sick parade and hospital, he began taking long, brisk, health-giving walks in the drab purlieus of Rennes and he gave up all drink, even wine, for the three weeks. As the day grew near, despite the fact that he no longer was able to sleep more than four or five hours a night, he began to feel that he would be able to arrive in Paris in acceptable condition.

His uniform glittering, his duties meticulously completed, all his rather extensive banking arrangements carefully made, Ronny was ready to take off for Paris when the German Army, after eight months of stationary and non-bellicose war on the Western front, struck through the Low Countries. All leaves, including Ronny's, were cancelled, and he spent the next twenty days praying, more fervently than any general in command of the engaged armies, for a stabilization of the front. As one turning movement, one counterattack after another was crushed and swept aside by the German armor, Ronny fell deeper and deeper into apathy. When the British Army, in accordance with the modern doctrine of saving the clerks first, loaded him on a truck to a port in Southern Brittany, where, without hearing a gun fired, he was put on a comfortable excursion steamer and carried across to England, Ronny had lost all interest in the war and hardly even bothered to listen to the ship's radio reports of the disintegration of the Allied Armies to the North.

For six months after that, Ronny sat on a hill in Sussex, serving a tank which was parked permanently in a meadow, since its engine had long since been removed to a more active unit. Neither the tank's immobility nor the fact that for a long time there were only four shells at the disposal of the crew in the event that the Germans appeared on the road below them served to disturb his melancholy tranquillity. Like those philosophers who have been driven into monasteries by a secret but overpowering disappointment, Ronny was for that period far past caring about such remote temporal matters as the passage of armies, death in battle, or the collapse of governments. He sat in the meadow, beside the useless weapon, among the summer flowers, agreeable, silent, smiling distantly at his fellow-soldiers, rereading the curt letters he had received from Virginie before the fall of Paris, and going over and over again the communication to the hotel manager, with the menu of the celebration dinner, of which he had kept a copy.

When America entered the war and it began to seem as if, some time in the future, English armies would once more stand on the Continent, Ronny aroused himself and applied for O.T.C., under the sensible assumption that if he ever returned to Paris, in a military condition, he would be received more gratefully by Virginie if he were in the uniform of an officer. He worked conscientiously and won his commission, in an honorable middle place in his class, distinguishing himself among his fellow-officers only by signing his name to a petition for a Second Front which was being circulated at that time by the Communists, although he came from an unswervingly Tory family, and his personal politics would have been considered medieval even by the Duke of Wellington.

When I met him in London, in 1943, he was cheerful, lively and blindly pro-American, mostly because of the fact that with the arrival in England of each new troopship from the United States, the liberation of Paris became, in his eyes, more and more of a certainty. He admired, above all, the easy American familiarity, especially pronounced at that time, with the opposite sex, although he found it quite beyond his powers to emulate it. He was one of those unfortunate men in whom the conception of love, of sex, even, is irrevocably bound up with one woman—and the fact that he was separated from that woman by four years, the English Channel, and sixty divisions of the German Army, altered his attitude not at all, and, indeed, only served to strengthen it.

When it became plain that the Invasion was imminent, Ronny volunteered for a position of danger, garnering a promotion in the process, and managed to get himself set down on the beach on the first day. From then on he became the image of the perfect soldier, making his country's cause completely his own, cheerfully offering himself at all times for patrols, reconnaissance, liaison and attacks, although the mission of the unit to which he was attached was not primarily combat. But I think it could fairly be said that whatever one humble lieutenant in an obscure post could do to pierce the encircling lines and drive the German Army back toward the Rhine, Ronny did.

On the day that Paris fell, Ronny rode into the city amid the cheers and the snipers' fire with the first Allied troops. The driver of the small truck in which Ronny had made his entry into the capital was a forty-year-old corporal named Watkins, who, although the father of five children, was sympathetically romantic, and, under Ronny's direction, guided the truck along doubtful streets, sometimes dangerously deserted, sometimes swarming with celebrating Parisians, toward the address behind the Gare St. Lazare at which Ronny had last visited Virginie.

There is a whole tribe of men, who, at the end of a similar quest, would have found the lady waiting, perfumed and appropriately dressed, in her living room, ready to be embraced. Needless to say, Ronny was not one of those. Virginie was nowhere on the premises and there was no one there who even remembered her. In her old apartment was living a cranky couple from Caen who took the occasion, upon hearing Ronny speak French, to complain bitterly to him about certain bombings they had undergone from the R.A.F.

That evening, in the midst of the revelry which marked the first twenty-four hours of freedom for the city, Ronny moved absently, a fixed smile upon his lips, because he was too good and kindly a man to impose his sorrow upon his friends' pleasure, but facing tragically the conviction that for him love was over, once and for all, even before it had fairly begun.

Our unit, as though exhausted by the approach to Paris, remained there, under ambiguous orders, billeted in a small hotel off the Rue de Rivoli, while the lines of battle moved farther and farther off. Ronny had the room next to mine and night after night I heard his steady, military pacing up and down, like a guardsman who is making up his mind to face his colonel and tell him he has betrayed the honor of the regiment.

Then the miracle happened. While driving in the truck along the Boulevard des Italiens one afternoon, three or four days after our arrival in Paris, Ronny saw Virginie. She was on a bicycle and moving fast in the opposite direction and her hair was now blond, but Ronny, who had been scanning every female face in the city with the nervous persistence of a radar antenna, was not to be deceived. He waved at Watkins, who was at the wheel of the truck, to turn around. Watkins, by now himself imbued with some of Ronny's passion, swung recklessly through the press of bicycles, jeeps and pedestrians and finally caught up with Virginie at the corner of the Rue Lafitte. Ronny jumped out of the truck while it was still moving but managed to hold his feet, calling Virginie's name wildly and reaching out for the handlebars of her bicycle. She recognized him almost immediately and they embraced in the middle of the street, with Watkins, grinning delightedly, and a good many others, watching with interest. As Ronny admitted to me later, at that moment, standing there in the busy street, blocking traffic, with the sound of horns in his ears, holding Virginie in his arms, the war had reached its culminating point.

Virginie, it turned out, had an appointment that could not wait, but she took time for a hurried drink in a nearby café and a conversation which Ronnie could not repeat coherently when he tried to report it to me an hour later. They made a date for six o'clock at a bar near our hotel and kissed in parting, and Ronny, to whom loving was synonymous with giving, spent the rest of the afternoon collecting, from all possible sources, gifts for Virginie. He bought a pink scarf, although the rate of exchange was ruinous; he traded a pair of captured German binoculars for five yards of parachute silk; he managed to pry loose from a friend who had been hoarding them in his knapsack for two months, three cans of sardines; he ordered Watkins, who was more than willing, to impose mercilessly upon his connections with certain American mess-sergeants, and Watkins turned up with a box of ten-in-one rations and a five-pound can of orange marmalade, no mean accomplishment in a city in which everyone, soldiers and civilians alike, were on severely curtailed diets.

Ronny insisted that I meet the lady, although I tried to persuade him that on this first day, while the shock of the lost years was being absorbed, it would perhaps be better for him to be alone with her. But Ronny, whose concept of happiness was involved automatically with the idea of sharing, and who was understandably nervous about these first delicate moments with Virginie, insisted that I meet her, at least, even if I left after a few minutes.

When I got to the bar, shortly after six o'clock, Ronny was sitting tensely in a corner, sweating, alone, surrounded by his pile of gifts, looking anxiously at his watch.

"She's not here," he said, as I sat down. "I'm a fool. I should have told her I'd go and get her. She probably can't find the bar."

"She's been living in Paris all her life, hasn't she?" I said. "She'll find the bar."

"I don't know," Ronny said, keeping his eyes on the entrance. "And then there's the question of time. I said six o'clock but I don't remember whether I said French time or Army time." At that period, because of the manipulations with daylight-saving schemes that the Germans had introduced, in an effort to conserve fuel and lengthen the working day, the French were always an hour in advance of us. "Maybe she was here," Ronny said, troubledly, "and hung around and gave up and went home and like an idiot I never asked her for her address. . . ."

"Did you ask the bartender if he saw her?" I said.

"He says he hasn't seen anybody," Ronnie said. "But maybe she looked in and decided to wait outside. She's shy and sitting in here with a lot of soldiers might have . . ." He stopped and stood up, smiling tremulously. "Virginie," he said.

He shook hands formally with the girl and introduced us immediately, and carefully held her chair while she sat down.

"I'm terribly pressed, Ronneee," Virginie said. She had a full skirt and she settled herself in little ballooning movements. She was pretty enough, although the blond hair was a misfortune and she had a wary, speculative look about her, like a gambler measuring an opponent's luck before putting down his bet. She was a small, neat, clever-looking, big-city girl and it was hard to think of her saying good night so demurely and insistently at her door just four years before. "Would they have whisky?"

"Of course they have whisky," Ronny said, in the tone of a man who was prepared to distill it out of his own veins on the spot if necessary. He called to the bartender for a whisky and, clumsy and beaming in front of her, began shoveling his various gifts onto the table. "I brought you a few things. A scarf, and this silk is . . ."

"Ah," Virginie said, "the American rations." She ran her hand caressingly over the carton. "So ingenious." The look on her face changed subtly, the gambler deciding that the man opposite is not lucky. She smiled sentimentally and touched Ronny's hand. "The same old Ronneee," she said. "Always so thoughtful." She wrinkled her nose troubledly. "But how am I to get it all home?" she said. "I only have a bicycle."

"I have a lorry," Ronny said, his happiness increased by this opportunity for further service. "I'll take you home."

"There is room for the bicycle, too?"

"Of course."

"Good," the girl said. "Now I can stay an additional fifteen minutes." She smiled softly at Ronny, although I still did not see the drowning look about the eyes that Ronny had described, or anything particularly French about the mouth. "I am so anxious to hear about the kind of war you have made and . . ." she looked at me significantly, "there are one or two things I wish to explain when we are alone."

I stood up. "I have to go along to dinner," I said.

"Americans," Virginie said, smiling charmingly, "are so tactful."

Ronny beamed, proud that his friend had won Virginie's approval. I left them, Ronny breathing hoarsely and talking in intimate whispers, Virginie sitting there, her eyes gently downcast, her fingers from time to time stroking the edges of the box of ten-in-one rations.

I was in my room, reading, later that night, when Ronny knocked on the door and came in. He was nervous and he had obviously had something more to drink and he could not sit still, but walked back and forth uneasily on the worn rug next to my bed.

"What do you think of her?" he asked.

"I. . . ."

"Isn't she marvelous?"

"Marvelous," I said.

"It's that thing about Frenchwomen," he said. "I'm spoiled forever for English girls."

"Well," I said, "maybe you . . ."

"Can you lay your hands on a carton of cigarettes?" he asked.

"Well," I said, "it's pretty difficult . . ."

"I'll pay, of course," he said hastily.

"Why do you need them?" I asked. "Does Virginie smoke?"

"No," Ronny said. "It's the man she's living with."

"Oh," I said, closing my book.

"He's a chain smoker," Ronny said. "But he only likes American cigarettes."

"I see."

Ronny made two more trips up and down the carpet. "That's why she was in a hurry," he said. "He's terribly jealous. What I mean is, after four years, and during a war and all, and she never knew whether I was alive or dead."

"Of course," I said.

"What I mean is, it would be childish to be surprised, wouldn't it?"

"I suppose so."

"He's one of those dark, intense types. He rather smouldered at me in the beginning." Ronny smiled briefly, and I could see that along with the disappointment of discovering that Virginie had been claimed in his absence there was a little sense of gratification that he had finally found someone who was jealous of him. "He was in the Underground or something like that and now that that's finished he just sits around the apartment all day, chain-smoking and keeping track of Virginie. Can't blame him, can you, with a girl as attractive as Virginie?"

"Well," I began.

"She doesn't love him, though," Ronny said, breathing heavily. "She told me in the truck going there. They live all the way up on top of Montmartre and that poor girl has to pedal up and down that hill in all weathers. She took him in when he was hiding from the police. Simple patriotism. And then one thing led to another. They've been together three years, but she isn't happy. I promised the cigarettes for tomorrow. Do you think you can manage it?"

"I'll try," I said. "In the morning."

"By Jove," he said, "after four years. Seeing her there riding down the Boulevard des Italiens on a bicycle. They opened the marmalade and it was pathetic to see how they spooned it up. I'm seeing her tomorrow afternoon. It's not as though they were married or she loved him or anything like that. What I mean is, it's not a violation of principle or taking advantage. I mean, I declared myself long before he appeared on the scene, didn't I? After all, if my leave hadn't been cancelled when the Germans went through Belgium . . ." He allowed himself a half-sigh, remembering that inconvenient invasion. "And I'm just meeting her in a bar. I can't go to their place, because he just sits there all day, chain-smoking, checking on her movements. Rum luck, eh?" He smiled wanly, moving to the door. "After four years. A man who sits home all day."

He went out and long after I had turned out the light I heard him striding steadily back and forth in his room, the boards creaking sadly through the long hours of the night in trouble and love.

For the next few days Ronny was of very little use to the British Army. Whenever Virginie had fifteen minutes that she could spare from her lover, Ronny would make himself available, meeting her in bars, in front of monuments, in the lobbies of hotels, and at the approaches to whatever bridges over the Seine Virginie had to cross in her various errands around Paris. There would be hurried, murmuring, serious talks, often with Virginie holding the handlebars of her bicycle and walking briskly with it down a street as Ronny strode alongside her, both of them followed, at a ceremonial pace, by Watkins, in the truck. Ronny would return from these tantalizing meetings red-faced, breathing hoarsely, with an obsessed glitter in his eyes, very much like the light that one might imagine as having shone in the eye of Captain Ahab as he was finally certain that he was closing in on the white whale. In the intervals of the day when he was not rushing to one point or another of the city to meet Virginie, Ronny devoted his energies to the amassing of treasure from the Allied Commissaries, which he delivered dutifully, by truck, to the apartment of Virginie and her lover. They had short, amiable conversations, the three of them, Ronny said, about what it had been like in Paris under the Germans and about how clumsily the Americans were conducting the war. Virginie's lover reserved his admiration for things American only to our cigarettes. The apartment, which was a small one, must have soon taken on the appearance of a small auxiliary depot of the Supply Services of two armies, with cases of bully beef, packaged rations, cans of coffee and cocoa powder, bottles of whisky, stacked cartons of cigarettes, and occasionally even loins of pork and cuts of beef piled all over the place, the substantial evidence of Ronny's devotion. I am sure that if by any chance Ronny, who until that time had been the most timid obeyer of regulations, had been investigated by the C.I.D., he would have run a fair chance of being sent to jail for ten years.

But neither this nor any other consideration could sway him for a moment. There was a continual procession of shifty-eyed sergeants carrying loaded barracks bags in and out of our hotel and Watkins was kept permanently in a state of readiness to drive Ronny to Virginie's apartment with each new acquisition. I know that Ronny dreamed of the hour when he would arrive, unannounced (Virginie had no telephone), with his musette bag stuffed with cigarettes or bar chocolate, to find Virginie alone, finally, after the six years. But this never happened. He often found her lover, whose name was Emile, alone, and Emile would sometimes even go so far as to offer Ronny a small drink from the ration Scotch which Ronny had turned over to the couple, but Virginie never.

Like a gambler who is deep in the hole who keeps blindly doubling his bets to get even, Ronny poured his gifts into the little apartment.

He was not completely ingenuous about what he was doing. "I'll tell you something," he confided to me. "That Emile doesn't really like me. Everything else being equal, he'd tell Virginie that she couldn't see me anymore. But this way, with the cigarettes and the tinned bully beef and the whisky, he's torn. Understand," Ronny said, "I wouldn't be doing this if he treated Virginie well. But he treats her horribly and I feel no compunctions."

"But you haven't done anything to feel any compunctions about," I pointed out.

"In due time, old man," Ronny said confidently. "All in due time."

Then, the very next day, which was a Saturday, it turned out that his confidence was justified. I was washing up in my room, preparatory to going out for dinner, when Ronny knocked and came in. I knew that he had had a date with Virginie, in front of the Opera, and that she had said she could only spare a quarter of an hour. Usually, when he came from seeing Virginie, he was exceptionally red-faced and booming, speaking in exhilarated half-sentences, chuckling for no apparent reason, and moving restlessly, with a nervous excess of energy. But tonight he seemed pale and subdued and he spoke with a curious combination of languor and jumpily repressed emotion.

"Well," he said, "tomorrow is the day."

"What?" I asked, puzzled.

"I just saw her," he said. "I'm to come to the apartment tomorrow at three-fifteen. It's Sunday, and Emile is going to the prize fights. He's interested in a middleweight. It's the only moment in the week when he leaves her alone for more than an hour at a time. There are people coming in at four-thirty, though. It's rather split-second—one hour and fifteen minutes." He smiled wanly, not looking at all like the Indian colonel. "After six years. But a chap must finally make a start, don't you think?"

"Yes," I said.

"It's almost inconceivable," he said. "Isn't it?"

"Almost," I agreed.

"My aunts would be amazed," he said.

"Would they?" I said noncommittally.

"There are chaps that do things like this every day of their lives, aren't there?"

"So I hear," I said.

"Amazing." He shook his head. "What time have you got?" he asked anxiously.

I looked at my watch. "Ten minutes to seven," I said.

He looked worriedly at his watch. "I have thirteen minutes to seven. Do you think my watch is slow?"

"I'm a little fast, I think."

He listened carefully to the ticking of his watch. "I'd better get the right time tomorrow morning," he said. "I told Watkins to meet me in front of the hotel at three sharp. He's more excited than I am." He smiled jerkily at the thought of the loyalty of Watkins. "Tell me, old man," he said, flushing a little, "is there anything I ought to know?"

"What?"

"I mean anything in particular?"

I hesitated, then decided that there wasn't enough time. "No," I said.

"Amazing," he said.

We sat in silence, not looking at each other.

"Curious," he said.

"What's curious?"

"Next January," he said, "I'm going to be twenty-nine years old."

I stood up and put on my tie. "I'm going down to dinner. Do you want to eat with me?"

"Not tonight, old man," he said. "I don't think I could eat tonight."

I nodded sympathetically, pretending to be more sensitive than I was, and went down to dinner. Ronny went into his room to write his weekly letter to his aunts.

The next morning I was on duty and the man who was supposed to relieve me didn't appear until well after two o'clock. I had lunch in a transient officers' mess and then, because it was a hot, sunny day, I walked leisurely, stopping often to enjoy the bright September sunlight on the old buildings and the quiet streets, toward the hotel. I was glad that I would be too late to see Ronny before he set out on his adventure. I had the feeling that it would be almost impossible to avoid saying the wrong thing at a moment like that, and I did not wish to complicate, by a slip of the tongue or an inadvertent smile, Ronny's climactic hour.

I reached the hotel at twenty minutes past three, and I was just going in, when Ronny came charging out of the open door. He was sweating heavily in his beautifully pressed battledress, and his face was red, his eyes were rolling, and his mouth was hanging open as if he had been bellowing. He grabbed me by both arms, his hands crazily powerful, crushing my shirt.

"Where's Watkins?" he shouted, although his face was no more than six inches from mine.

"What?" I asked, stupidly.

"Have you seen Watkins?" Ronny shouted, even more loudly, shaking me. "I'll kill the bastard."

"What's happened, Ronny?"

"Have you got a jeep?" he roared. "I'll have him court-martialed."

"You know I haven't got a jeep, Ronny," I said.

He dropped my arms and leaped out into the middle of the empty street and peered in both directions, wheeling around on his heels, waving his arms. "No transport," he cried. "No bloody transport!" He looked at his watch. "Twenty-five minutes past three." The numerals came out in a sob. "I'll have him transferred to the infantry, the swine!" He jumped back onto the sidewalk and began a short, running step, back and forth in front of the hotel entrance. "I should have been there ten minutes ago."

"Did you call the garage, Ronny?" I asked, trying to be helpful.

"He was there all morning," Ronny shouted, "washing the damn truck. Then he left about an hour ago. He's probably joy-riding in the Bois with his damned black-market friends."

This was a little unfair, since Watkins' by now extensive acquaintanceship in the black market had been built up solely in Ronny's service, but I didn't feel that this was the moment to see justice done to the reputation of the absent driver.

Ronny looked at his watch once more and moaned. "He's been driving for me for a year and a half," Ronny cried, "and he hasn't been a minute late yet. And he picks this day for it! Don't you know somebody with a jeep?"

"Well," I said doubtfully, "I guess I could rustle one up if you give me an hour or so."

"An hour or so!" Ronny laughed horribly. "There're people coming in at four-thirty! An hour or so!" He gazed wildly at the blank faces of the buildings and the calm, deserted street. "What a city! No Metro, no buses, no taxi! God, do you know anybody who has a bicycle?"

"I'm afraid not, Ronny," I said. "I wish I could help . . ."

"You wish you could help," he said, snarling, turning on me. "I don't believe you. I don't believe you for a minute."

"Ronny," I said, reproachfully. In all the time we had known each other, this was the first unfriendly word I had heard from him.

"Nobody gives a damn!" he shouted. "You don't fool me!" The sweat was pouring off him now and his face was alarmingly red. "The hell with you all! All right, all right," he shouted incoherently, waving his arms, "I'll go on foot."

"It'll take you at least a half hour," I said.

"Forty-five minutes," Ronny said. "What's the difference? If that bloody driver comes, tell him to come after me and watch for me on the street. He knows the route."

"Yes, Ronny," I said. "Good luck."

He looked at me bleakly, breathing hard. Then he said something obscene and short and started running. I watched him running heavily down the sunny street, past the shuttered windows, the sturdy khaki figure growing smaller and smaller, the sound of the thick boots on the pavement going farther and farther away, diminishing, in the direction of Montmartre. He turned a corner and the street was quiet, lost in its bright, Sunday stillness.

Somehow, I felt guilty, as though there were something I might have done for Ronny that I had callously left undone, and I stayed in front of the hotel, smoking, watching for Watkins and the truck. Finally, at ten minutes to four, I saw it turn the corner and come down our street. It was thoroughly washed and polished and looked as neat as any truck could possibly be expected to look which had made the entire campaign from the beaches to Paris. Watkins, too, I saw as he drove up, had taken great pains with himself. He had shaved himself painfully close and his skin was shining pink and raw, his hair was plastered down under his hat, and he had a sly, benignant, anticipatory smile on his face as he parked the truck in front of the hotel with an unaccustomed flourish. On the seat beside him, I saw, there was a large bunch of flowers.

He sprang out and saluted me smartly, still smiling. "Well," he said, "I'm a little early, but I thought, on a day like this, the lieutenant might be waiting for me on the pavement."

"Where the hell have you been, Watkins?" I asked, exasperated for Ronny's sake with the man's idiotic pleasure in himself.

"Been?" Watkins asked, puzzled. "Been?"

"The lieutenant called the garage nearly an hour ago," I said, "and they said you'd left."

"Well," Watkins said, "I thought it might be a pleasant touch if the lieutenant carried some flowers in for the lady and I took a little tour looking for them. Carnations," he said, pointing to them. "You'd be shocked if I told you what they ask for them . . ."

"Watkins," I said, "you're an hour late."

"What?" Watkins' mouth fell open. He looked at his watch. "The lieutenant said specifically three o'clock, and I allowed a little extra time and it's not ten to three yet."

"It's ten to four, Watkins," I said.

"What?" Watkins closed his eyes, as though he could not bear to look at my face.

"It's ten to four," I said. "Weren't you told that as of last midnight, all clocks would be advanced one hour, to coincide with French time?"

"Oh," Watkins said in a whisper. "Oh, suffer me, suffer me." His face looked drained and loose, like the face of a man going under anesthesia. "I heard about it during the week, but I didn't spend the night in billets, and I was off duty this morning and nobody happened to mention it at the garage. Oh, suffer me, Mother . . . Where's the lieutenant now?"

"At this moment," I said, "he's probably just passing Sacre Coeur, on the dead run."

Watkins turned slowly, like a prizefighter who has been hit and is senselessly seeking the support of the ropes. He leaned against the door of the truck, his forehead pressed against the metal. When he lifted his head, I saw that there were tears in his eyes. There he stood, bowlegged and hunched over in his neat uniform, his scraggly, cruelly shaven, Cockney face twisted in grief as he thought of Ronny pounding hopelessly up the hills of Montmartre.

"What can I do?" he asked brokenly. "What can I ever bloody well do?"

"Well," I said, "at least go wait for him so he doesn't have to walk home."

Watkins nodded mechanically. Then he got into the cab of the truck, carelessly knocking the carnations onto the floor, and started the motor. He drove off, looking neither to the right nor left.

Ronny got back to the hotel at six o'clock. I heard the truck drive up to the door and I looked out my window and saw him descend from the truck, slowly, without saying a word to Watkins, and move exhaustedly into the hotel. He came directly to my room and entered without knocking and sank into a chair, keeping his cap on his head. There were dark sweat stains around his collar and there were hollows under his eyes, as though he hadn't slept in weeks. I poured him a whisky and put the glass in his hand. He didn't even look up at me, but sat there, a round, diminished, rumpled figure, staring blankly ahead of him at the stained wall above the bed.

"You heard," he said finally.

"Yes."

"The Army," he said flatly. "Whenever anything good is liable to happen to you, the Army does something." He sat slumped in the chair, with his cap on, thinking of the declaration of war in 1939 and the collapse in Belgium less than a year later. He shook his head and took a long drink. "French time," he muttered, obscurely.

I poured some whisky into his glass.

"I've got to get out," he said. "I've been in this war long enough."

"What happened?" I asked, thinking that perhaps talking about it would help him.

"Nothing," he said. He chuckled once, shortly. "I got there at five minutes past four. Watkins caught up with me one block from the house. Did you see the flowers?"

"Yes," I said.

"That was thoughtful of him, wasn't it?"

"Yes."

"She was making canapés for her guests. Sardines. She had oil all over her fingers."

"Was she angry?"

"Not exactly," Ronny said. "When I told her what had happened, she began to laugh. I thought she was going to strangle, she laughed so hard. I never heard a woman laugh like that in my whole life."

"Well," I said, trying to be comforting, "another time."

Ronny shook his head. "No. When she finally got through laughing, she kissed my forehead and she said, 'It's fate, Chérie, we will remain good friends.'"

There was nothing to be said to this, and I poured myself a drink. We sat in silence.

"She asked me to help her with the canapés," Ronny said. "I opened two tins of bully beef and I cut my finger." He held up his right hand and I saw a nasty, jagged cut, sticky with dried blood. "The only blood I've lost in the whole damned war," he said. "Her friends came in early. Four-fifteen. They devoured everything. I had to open three more tins of bully. They kept complaining about the American Army. Emile came in early, too. Four-thirty-five." Ronny by now was as conscious of time as a railroad engineer. "His middleweight won," Ronny said bitterly, as though this was finally too much to bear. "A knockout in the first round. He drank three glasses of whisky to celebrate and he kept clapping me on the back and calling me *mon petit Anglais* and showing me how it was done. Three lefts, *mon petit Anglais*, like lightning, to the nose, and a straight right, like a bomb, to the point of the jaw. The other man didn't wake up for ten minutes. He was feeling so good, Emile, he let Virginie say goodbye to me alone in the hallway." Ronny smiled wanly. "She got sardine oil all over my battledress. And she gave me some information. She said her conscience was bothering her; the time had come to speak frankly. She was very queer. When she talked it was as though she was having a hard time to keep from laughing. She said she had known Emile since 1937. She hasn't lived with her family since she was fifteen years old. Her family lives in Nice. They've never been to Paris. And Emile wasn't in the Underground. I got *that* from her friends. He smuggled butter from Normandy all during the war."

Ronny got up from the chair, slowly and painfully, like a man whose bones are giving him trouble. "I've got to get out," he said. "I've just got to get out." He turned and faced me, looking at me with brooding intensity. "Don't be surprised," he said mysteriously, "no matter what you hear."

He went out slowly, the bones not moving very well in the martial, chubby flesh. I heard him go into his room and the springs creak as he lay heavily down on his bed.

The very next day, I noticed a change in Ronny. Whenever he moved, he gave off a strong smell of a particularly sweet toilet water, and he began to cultivate the habit of wearing his handkerchief in his sleeve. He also began to walk in a curious, short-stepped way and his speech suddenly took on a slight lisp, very disturbing in a man who looked as though he should be leading a regiment of Sikhs. He began to avoid me, too, and there were no longer the long, candid conversations in my room at night. When I invited him to have dinner with me, he giggled nervously and said he was terribly busy these days.

Then, a week later, I was visited by a British Medical Officer, a bleak, graying captain, who, it turned out, was a specialist in psychic disorders and cases of combat fatigue.

"I wonder if you could help me, Lieutenant," the captain said, after ascertaining that I had known Ronny for almost a year. "It's about your friend, Lieutenant Biddell."

"Is anything wrong with him?" I asked, cautiously, wishing Ronny had briefed me.

"I'm not sure," the captain said. "Would you say there was something abnormal about him?"

"Well," I said, wondering how I might answer a question like that honestly without harming Ronny, "that would be hard to say. Why? What's the matter?"

"Lieutenant Biddell has been to see me three or four times this week," the captain said, "with a most unusual story. Most unusual." The captain hesitated, then decided to plunge ahead. "Well, there's no sense in being ambiguous. He seems to believe that he should be discharged for the good of the service."

"What?" I asked, surprised.

"He claims to have discovered, quite recently, that—well we're both grown men, we don't have to beat around the bush . . ." the captain said. "It's not the first time we've heard about something like this. Particularly in time of war, with men taken out of their normal life and deprived of the companionship of women for years on end. Bluntly," the captain said, "Lieutenant Biddell claims that he finds himself attracted irresistibly to—uh—men."

"Oh," I said, thinking, Poor Ronny; the toilet water and the handkerchief.

"The external evidence is all there, of course," the captain said, "the perfume, the manner of speech, et cetera. But he scarcely seems to be the type, although in my profession, of course, we are hardly surprised . . . You understand. At any rate, he says he's afraid that if he remains in the . . . uh . . . military atmosphere . . . he will be tempted into an overt act . . . which would, of course, have grave consequences. I've spoken to other of his fellow officers, and, as tactfully as possible, to his driver, and they all seem surprised. I hear that you've been very close and I wonder if you might be able to throw light on the situation."

"Well . . ." I hesitated. For a moment, I thought of telling the doctor the entire story. Then I decided against it. Maybe, I thought, it's really time for Ronny to get out. "I've noticed little indications here and there," I said. "He's had an exhausting war," I added loyally.

The captain nodded. "Who hasn't?" he said gloomily and got up and left, after shaking my hand.

The next day, without warning, our unit was ordered to move out of Paris. At the same time, Ronny was detached from us and assigned to a headquarters in Paris, where, I presumed, it would be easier for the doctor to conclude his examination. In the confusion of the move, I didn't see Ronny, and I didn't get back to Paris until the war was over and by that time he had departed. I heard that, whatever else had happened, he had not been given the discharge he had asked for. Somebody said that he thought Ronny had been sent back to England, but he wasn't sure, and it was impossible, without compromising Ronny, to make the only kind of inquiry that would enlighten me.

I was sent back to America without getting to England again, and over the years, from time to time, I wondered rather sadly about my friend and speculated, not without pity, on what paths he might have strayed into in peacetime London. I did not judge him harshly. It is not only twenty-four-hour barrages and being in the line without relief for months on end that destroys the will to continue in men, and in a war casualties are suffered in a variety of ways that have nothing to do with gunfire. But, occasionally, when I met a man who spoke with a little lilt or dressed in a certain, overfastidious way, I wondered if perhaps he would have been a different man at that moment if sometime in his past, at a moment of crisis, someone had arrived a half hour sooner or later.

Ronny kissed the bride before the altar, then they both turned and walked up the aisle, the music swelling behind them. As he came even with me, red-faced, triumphant, tender, bull-like, he winked. I winked back, thinking, Isn't this nice; not everything has turned out badly since 1944. As he went out of the church with his bride, I wondered if I could get the name and address of the psychiatrist from him for one or two of my other friends.

GOD ON FRIDAY NIGHT

SOL LET HIMSELF quietly into the house and walked softly down the long hall toward the kitchen, the only sound the fashionable creaking of his pale tan shoes. He saw his mother bending over the stove, red-faced, peering into the roaster, basting a chicken.

"Ma," he said softly.

Ma grunted, busily pushing the potatoes.

"It's me, Ma. It's Sol."

Ma closed the oven and stood up wearily, her hand pushing helpfully at the hip.

"Kiss Mama," she said.

Sol kissed her and she sat down and looked at him. "You don't look so good, Sol. You don't look the way you looked when you were a young boy."

Every time she saw him she told him the same thing.

"What do you want, Ma?" Sol sighed, voicing the hopeless argument. "I'm not a young boy any more. I'm a man thirty-three years old."

"Even so." Ma wiped her forehead and looked anxiously at him. "The life you lead."

"A man who makes his living entertaining in night clubs can't live like a prize horse," Sol said. He sat down across the table and stretched his hand out tenderly to cover hers. "How're yuh, Ma?"

Ma sighed. "What do you expect? My kidneys. Always my kidneys. A woman with a family gets old like an express train." She looked closely at her son. "Sol, darling," she said, "you wear the worst clothes I've ever seen on a man's back. You belong on a merry-go-round."

"In my profession," Sol said with sober pride, "this is the way they dress."

"They should not be allowed out in the daytime." She shook her head. "That tie. That material would be good to line closets with."

"Violet picked out this tie."

"How is Violet? Why can't she come visit her mother-in-law once in a while? Is the Bronx another world?"

"Violet's all right," Sol said flatly, looking at the glitter on his shoe tips. "Only . . ."

Ma sighed, her large, fashionably supported bosom heaving under the black net. "O.K., Baby, tell Mama."

Sol leaned over anxiously. "I must talk to you, private."

Ma looked around the kitchen. "Are we in Grand Central Station?"

"Real private, Ma. I don't want *nobody* to hear this. *Nobody*. Not even Pop."

"What've you done, Sol?" There was a note of stern alarm in Ma's voice, and she grabbed Sol's arm tightly. "Tell Mama the truth."

"I ain't done nothing. Honest. At least nothing bad. Don't worry, Ma."

"Nobody's sick?"

"Nobody's sick."

"All right." Ma sat back in her chair, holding her feet off the floor to take the weight off them. "Do you want to stay to dinner? You can always cut an extra portion out of a chicken."

"Lissen, Ma," Sol said intensely, "you got to lissen to me and you got to promise you won't tell nobody."

"I promise. All right, I promise. Will you stay to dinner?"

"Yeah," Sol said. "Well . . ." He hesitated. "This is complicated."

Lawrence came into the kitchen, throwing his books on the floor. "Hiya, Sol. Hello, Mom. Am I hungry, oh, Momma, am I hungry . . . Mom, whatta ye got to eat? Oh, am I hungry!"

"I'm talkin' to Ma, private," Sol said.

"I'm hungry," Lawrence said, looking in the icebox. "Go ahead and talk. I'll forget it anyway."

"I want to talk to Ma private," Sol said in measured tones.

"What the hell's so private?" Lawrence asked, gesturing with a bottle of milk. "What're you, a German spy? Boy, am I hungry!"

"Don't say 'hell,' Larry," Ma said. "And get out of here."

"I'm taking the bottle with me," Lawrence announced, marching toward the door. He patted his mother on the head. "Mata Hari." He went out.

"A brilliant boy," Ma said. "He leads his class."

Sol cleared his throat.

"Yes, Sol," Ma said. "I'm listening."

"I been thinking, Ma," he began in a low thoughtful voice, twisting his heavy gold ring slowly around on his finger. "I ain't a good boy."

"That's not such private news." Ma laughed at the expression on Sol's face. She pinched his arm. "You got a good heart, Sol," she said. "My baby Sol, with a heart like a house."

"I have done things, Ma," Sol said slowly, choosing his words with great care, "that were not so good."

"If we were all angels, we wouldn't need airplanes," Ma said with finality. "Let me look at the chicken."

She went over and looked at the chicken. "That butcher!" she said. "He is selling me eagles." She closed the oven door and sat down again.

"I have done things," Sol said quietly, "that God wouldn't like."

"I think God has other things on His mind, these days, Sol."

"Ma," Sol said, not looking at his mother, "Ma, would you light candles on Friday night and make the prayer?"

There was silence in the kitchen, broken only by the small crackle from the oven, where the chicken was browning.

"I haven't lighted candles for a long time, Sol," Ma said gently. "Ever since the day I married your father. He was a Socialist, your father."

"Would yuh light 'em now, Ma?" Sol pleaded. "Every Friday night?"

"What is it, Sol? Why should I light candles?"

Sol took a deep breath and stood up and walked back and forth in the kitchen. "Violet," he said, "Violet's goin' to have a baby."

"Oh!" Ma gasped, fanning herself. "Oh! Well! That blonde girl! Oh! A grandchild! Oh! Sol, Baby!" She grabbed Sol and kissed him. "My Sol!"

"Don't cry, Ma. Ma, please . . ." Sol patted her solid wide back. "It's all right."

"It's about time, Sol. I thought you'd never . . ." She kissed him on the forehead and smiled widely. "I thought Violet was beginning to look very good in the breasts. Congratulations from the bottom of my heart. We'll name him after my father."

"Yeah," Sol said. "Thanks. How about the candles now, Ma?"

"What do you need candles for? I had five children without burning a single candle."

"Violet's different," Sol said uneasily. "She's not like you."

"She is just built for children," Ma declared. "She is built like a horse. When I had you I weighed ninety-five pounds. Including you. She doesn't need candles."

"You don't know, Ma." Sol looked intently into his mother's eyes. "Today Violet slipped in the bathtub."

"Well?"

"She coulda killed herself. As it is, she fainted."

"So you want me to pray because your wife doesn't know how to take a bath. Sol!" Ma waved him away. "Every day millions of people fall down in bathtubs."

"Lissen, Ma," Sol said, holding both her hands. "Nuthin' can't happen to Violet. And nuthin' can happen to the kid. See, Ma? We been tryin' to have a kid for five years now and . . ." He stopped.

Ma shook her head in wonderment. "That big blonde horse."

"We want that kid, Ma. We gotta have that kid. Everybody should have a kid. What've I got if I haven't got a son?"

"Sssh, Baby," Ma said. "Sure, you're right. Only don't yell. You're too nervous to yell."

"All right, I won't yell." Sol wiped the sweat off his forehead with a blue silk handkerchief with a green monogram. "All right. What I want to say is, Violet's dumpin' herself in the bathtub was a omen."

"A what?"

"A omen. It's a . . ."

"I know."

"It shows us we can't take any chances, Ma."

"Loose in the head, my baby Sol," Ma said. "Too much night life."

"We got to pray to God, Ma," Sol said, "that nuthin' happens to that baby."

"If you want to pray to God, go ahead and pray. Did I make the baby?" Ma asked. "Let Violet pray."

Sol swallowed. "Violet's not fit to pray," he said gently. "She's a first-class girl and I would lay down on railroad tracks for her, but she ain't fit to pray to God."

"That's no way to talk about your own wife, Solly," Ma said. "Shame on you."

"I love her like she was my right arm," Sol said. "But she's not a very good woman, Ma. What's the sense in kiddin' ourselves? Violet has a weak character, Ma, and she has done two or three or five things . . . Give Violet four drinks, Ma, and she says 'Yes' to the man from Macy's. She's young, she'll outgrow it an' settle down, but right now . . ." Sol nervously lit a cigarette. "Right now, Ma, Violet's prayers'd carry top weight in the field."

"So, Sol," Ma said gravely, "why can't *you* pray?"

Sol sat quietly, observing his cigarette. The blush came up over his purple collar, like dye soaking in cloth. "I am not one hundred percent perfect in any respect, myself," he said. "First of all, Ma, in my business if yuh don't tell the customers dirty jokes, yuh might just as well apply to the WPA."

"You should've been a doctor, like I said."

"I know, Ma," Sol said patiently. "But I'm not. I'm a man who has to play in cheap night clubs in Philadelphia and Lowell, Massachusetts, and Boston, weeks at a time. Yuh don't know how lonely it can get at night in Lowell, Massachusetts."

"A lot, Sol?"

"A lot, Ma, a lot," Sol cast his eyes up at the kitchen ceiling.

"A boy with a face like yours." Ma shrugged. "Girls're funny."

"If I prayed, Ma, the words'd stick in my throat."

"So you want me. I don't even believe in God, Baby."

"That's all right, Ma," Sol said. "You're a good woman. Yuh never hurt anybody in all yer life."

Ma sighed hugely. "I'll have to go down to Mrs. Aaronson and get her to teach me the prayer. Sol, darling, you're a nuisance."

Sol kissed her, his eyes shining.

"I got to see what's happening to that bird," Ma said, bending over the chicken. "I'll pray that it's a boy," she said, "while I'm at it."

Every Friday night the candles were lighted and Ma steadfastly said the old words: *"Burach ee, burach shmoi, Burach ee, burach shmoi. Burach ee, burach shmoi. Burach ata adanoi eluchainu melach huoilom. Chaleck necht shil shabos."* And then she prayed for a boy.

It was on a Friday night that Sol and Violet brought the baby over to Ma's for the first time.

Sol held the smiling and pink and robust boy in his arms as if he were wood.

"See, Ma?" he said, holding the baby out.

Ma put her hand out slowly, and gently rubbed the little soft head. "Hair," she said. "He's got hair." She chuckled and took the baby's hand out and kissed it. "Take him into the bedroom, Violet," she said. "I'm busy here for a minute."

She turned and lighted the seven candles in the window, one by one.

"The last stronghold of religion," Lawrence said. "All of a sudden. This house."

"Shut up," Ma said. "City College philosopher."

And she said, *"Burach ee, burach shmoi. Burach ee . . ."* as the candles burned.

FREE CONSCIENCE,
VOID OF OFFENCE

"To Chamberlain!" one of the women at the bar was saying, her glass held high, as Margaret Clay and her father came into the small, pleasant room, lit by candles, with a big oak fire burning steadily in the fireplace and the glassware and cutlery on the tables winking softly in the firelight. "He saved my son for me," the woman said loudly. She was a woman of nearly fifty who had obviously been pretty once. "To my good friend Neville Chamberlain!"

The other two women and the three men at the bar drank soberly as Margaret and her father sat down at a table.

"That Dorothy Thompson!" said the friend of Neville Chamberlain. "She makes me so mad! Did you see what she wrote about him? If I had her here!" She waved her fist and the wrinkles in her face suddenly bit deeper. "I won't read her any more. Not once more. You know what she is? She's a Red. She's rabid!"

"This is a nice place," Margaret's father said, looking around him with a happy expression. "It has a pleasant atmosphere. Do you come here often?"

"Boys take me here," Margaret said. "It's only about ten miles from school, and they like the candlelight and the open fire, even though it costs three bucks a dinner. Boys always think candlelight and an open fire act like heavy artillery on a girl's resistance. Two hours of that, they figure, and they can just walk in and mop up."

"Margaret," Mr. Clay said, like a father, "I don't like to hear you talk like that."

Margaret laughed, and leaned over and patted her father's hand.

"What's the matter, Pop?" she asked. "Your long years at the Stork Club turn you tender?"

"You're too young to talk like that," Mr. Clay said, disliking the fact that she had called him Pop, disliking her thinking that he went often to the Stork Club. "A twenty-year-old girl should . . ."

The owner of the place, a beautifully dressed, pink-faced man of forty who looked like a boy, was standing beside their table, smiling, having come out from behind the bar, where at dinner-time he mixed the drinks scrupulously himself.

"Hello, Mr. Trent," Margaret said. "This is my father. He likes your place."

"Thank you," Trent said, bowing a little, smiling like a little boy. "I'm pleased."

"It has a very pleasant atmosphere," Mr. Clay said.

"Mr. Trent has a specialty," Margaret said. "He makes it with rum."

"Rum, lime juice, sugar, a little Cointreau in the bottom of the glass." Trent waved his hands delicately as he spoke.

"It comes out foamy," Margaret said. "It's nice on the teeth."

"I'm making it now with black Jamaica rum," Trent said. "Myers' rum, it's heavier, for the autumn. I make it on the electric mixer. It gives it a nice quality."

"Two," said Mr. Clay, wishing he had the courage to order a Martini.

The six people at the bar were singing now. "The old gray mare," they sang, loudly, consciously having a good time, consciously being gay and lively, and yet singing with a slight touch of burlesque, so that anybody could see these were no yokels. "The old gray mare," they sang, "she ain't what she used to be, Oh, she ain't what she used to be . . ."

Margaret watched them, grouped at the bar, their heads together—a cluster of men's middle-aged sparse gray hair, neatly brushed; and carefully curled and elaborately arranged coiffures on the women that in this light, at least, had a last, desperate look of youth. The woman who had toasted Chamberlain had been here once before when Margaret had come for dinner. Mrs. Taylor, Trent had called her, and she'd been in with a man other than her husband, whose hand she was holding now. Margaret had noticed her quick look around the room before she seated herself, her tiny adjustment of her corset, betraying the fact that the achievement of that trim and almost elegant figure came only as a result of engineering and torture under the smart silk print dress. A man they called Oliver, who looked slightly older than the others, somehow more confident and breezy, as though he had more money in the bank than any of his friends, led the singing with elaborate gestures of his hands, like a burlesque of Stokowski. Mr. Taylor was the least noisy of the three men. He wheezed a little and drank sparingly. Margaret was sure he had a bad stomach and was already looking sorrowfully ahead to the aspirin and Alka-Seltzer the next morning. The third man was fat, and his scalp bloomed through his hair and he had a piped vest, which made him look like a businessman in the movies, except that when he wasn't singing his face looked intelligent and very cold. The other two women were standard suburban mothers nearing fifty, forlornly carrying on their battle against age, loneliness, and death with powder, rouge, rejuvenating cream, accustomed now to neglect from their husbands and children, full of mild, half-formed regrets for their lives as they drove behind their middle-aged chauffeurs down to New York in the late mornings for lunch and shopping.

"What does that sign say?" Mr. Clay said loudly, over the noise of the singing. He was peering out the window at the large sign on the lawn with the name of the inn on it.

" 'Free conscience, void of offence, 1840,' " Margaret said.

"That's a queer thing to have on a sign advertising a restaurant," Mr. Clay said.

Trent had come to their table with the drinks. "It came with the place," he apologized. "I didn't have the heart to take it down."

"There's nothing wrong with it," Mr. Clay said quickly, hoping he hadn't hurt Trent's feelings. "It's an admirable sentiment." He tasted the drink. "Wonderful!" he said loudly, over the singing, to make Trent feel better. "Absolutely wonderful!"

Trent smiled and went back to the bar, where his six customers were calling for more drinks.

Mr. Clay settled back in his chair, savoring his drink, expecting a good dinner. "Now, tell me," he said, "why you dragged me up here."

Margaret played reflectively with her glass. "I wanted to ask your advice," she said.

Mr. Clay sat forward and stared intently at his daughter. Usually when girls that age asked advice in that sober, reflective tone, it was on only one subject. Margaret noticed him leaning forward, staring at her, his handsome gray eyes now full of worry and suspicion.

"What's the matter?" Margaret asked. "What're you looking so scared about?"

"You can tell me everything," Mr. Clay said, wishing she wouldn't.

"Oh!" Margaret said. "Please sit back. The patient isn't dying. All I brought you up here for was to tell you I wanted to quit school. Now, take that look out of your eyes." She laughed, but her laugh was nervous, and over her glass she eyed her father, who ran a great business and paid a huge income tax each year to the government.

"I didn't have any look in my eyes," Mr. Clay said, laughing, deciding instantly that that was the way to handle it—gently, with an easy laugh, pretending that it was all light and cheerful, that he was a good fellow, practically her own age, that he understood everything. "Who's the boy?"

"It isn't any boy."

"Now, Margaret," he said lightly, "your father's been around . . ."

"I know my father's been around," Margaret said. "The headwaiters' delight." Mr. Clay looked hurt, his eyes narrowing, his mouth falling into the straight line Margaret remembered, and she spoke hurriedly. "I don't mind it," she said. "In fact, I like it. It makes me feel I come from durable yet light-footed stock. Every time I see your picture with one of those girls in a mink coat, I feel proud. Honest."

"What I meant to say," Mr. Clay said coldly, "was that you could tell me the truth."

"There isn't any boy."

"To my daughter!" Mrs. Taylor said loudly, her glass held high. "This is an anniversary. A year ago I gave my pure and beautiful daughter away in marriage. Now I'm a grandmother. To my daughter!"

"To the grandmother!" said Oliver, the one who spoke the loudest and oftenest and with the most assurance. "To the poor, broken-down, pure, and beautiful old grandmother!"

All the people at the bar laughed, as though this was a wonderful joke, and Oliver slapped Mrs. Taylor heartily on the back. "Now, Oliver," she said mildly, wriggling her back.

"I just want to quit school," Margaret said, scowling a little at the people making so much noise at the bar. "It bores me."

"It's the best school for women in the country," Mr. Clay said. "And you've done very well. And you've only got two more years to go."

"It bores me."

"I've always thought," Mr. Clay said carefully, "that a good school was the best place for a young and unsettled girl to spend four very important years of her life."

"I'm in abeyance in school," Margaret said. "My whole life's in abeyance. Everything's happening outside and nothing's happening inside. A girls' school is a continual Junior League ball!"

"It seems to me there're a couple of classes to be attended," Mr. Clay said with heavy irony. "Or so I've heard."

"Remote, remote," Margaret said dreamily. "Anglo-Saxon literature.
The development of the novel. The nervous system of the worm. You
look at the front page of one newspaper, you listen to one conversation
in the subway in New York, when you go in on a week-end, you see
one play, and your mind begins to itch because you're stuck in that
organdie-and-douche-bag nunnery."

"Margaret!" Mr. Clay said, honestly shocked.

"The French novel, Elizabethan poetry, *exclusive* of the drama—remote, remote, the world's racing by. Mr. Trent," Margaret called, "we
want two more."

"A good college affords protection." Mr. Clay felt uneasy saying it,
but felt he had to say it or something like it, play the father decently
and in good form, although he had never played the father with Margaret, had always been friendly and easy with her until the past year,
when she had suddenly changed. "It affords protection to a young girl
at a time when she's unstable, easily swayed . . ."

"I don't want to be afforded protection," Margaret said. "I want to be
easily swayed." She looked out at the sign, standing, lit, on the lawn.
" 'Free conscience, void of offence, 1840.' That's the nicest thing about
this whole place."

Trent came over with the drinks. Neatly and ceremoniously, he
cleared away the old glasses, the wet paper napkins, flicked ashes, put
down the fresh glasses, smiling admiringly at Mr. Clay, because his suit,
shoes, wrist watch, the complexion of his skin were all handsome, expensive, rigorously correct.

Margaret watched the people at the bar while Trent fussed over the
table. The men all had on dark-gray or blue double-breasted suits and
starched white collars, as sharp and neat as knives, and ties, small, precise, of heavy silk, fitted into the collars so snugly that they seemed to
spring from the throat itself. Cuff links, neat but expensive, gleamed at
all their wrists, and their shoes, deeply shining and brought from England, made them look as though they were all equipped with exactly
the same feet. Their faces, Margaret thought, were familiar, the faces
of her friends' fathers, well barbered, controlled, with not too much fat
on them; the lines not deep now but soon to be deep; the eyes, the
mouths, assured, arrogant, superior, because the men had never found a
place in the last forty years of their lives where they hadn't made themselves at home, felt themselves superior. They were the faces of businessmen ready to assume responsibility, give orders, watch machines run for
them, money be counted for them. They had come from the same colleges, married the same girls, listened to the same sermons, were marked

similarly, the way bullets fired from the same gun are similarly marked, can be identified when dug out of walls, picture frames, car moldings, victims.

"I'm going to get drunk tonight," Mrs. Taylor was saying. "I'm not going to church tomorrow. I prayed all week and I don't have to go to church tomorrow. I'm going to get drunk."

"Mrs. Chamberlain prayed every morning," one of the suburban mothers, a bright blonde, said. "She went in and prayed in Westminster Abbey while her husband was flying day after day to Germany."

"That's the sort of wife to have," Mr. Taylor said.

"It was the old man's first trip," the fattest man said. "He'd never been up in an airplane before. Sixty-nine years old. That's a hell of a first trip!"

" 'Out of this nettle, danger,' " the blonde said, " 'we pluck this flower, safety,' he said when he came back. It's from Shakespeare. He's a well-educated man."

"All those Englishmen are well educated," Mr. Taylor said. "The ruling class. They know how to run a country. Not like what we have here."

"The contacts you make at college," Mr. Clay said, "are the most important . . ."

"Sh-h-h." Margaret waved impatiently at him. "I'm listening."

"I'm going to get drunk tonight," Mrs. Taylor said. "I prayed for peace so my son wouldn't have to go to war, and I got peace. What do I have to go to church for any more? Let's have another round."

" 'Peace in our time,' " the blonde said. "That's what he said when he got off the plane. That old man with the umbrella."

"Do you want my advice?" Mr. Clay asked.

Margaret looked at him, at the face she remembered as the first thing in her life, deep down at the bottom of memory, the handsome, easy, cheerful face, now troubled, puzzled, in a funny way helpless, loaded tonight with this problem of a twenty-year-old daughter. "Sure," Margaret said softly, feeling suddenly sorry for her father. "I want your advice. That's why I asked you to come. You're dependable," she said, smiling. "After all, you were the one who advised me to cut my hair the first time."

Mr. Clay smiled happily. He sipped his drink, spread his beautiful, well-kept hands lightly on the table, talked gently to his daughter. She watched the people at the bar as he talked about the friends you made at college, the people you could live with for the rest of your life, the memories you stored up, the important contacts.

A new party had come in, two men and two women, all of them with cold, red faces, as though they had been riding in an open car. One of the men was just like the other men at the bar—neat, double-breasted in blue, with English feet—and the women, though younger, lived on the same streets as the women already at the bar. The second man was a huge, fat man in a light tweed suit with a black slip-on sweater under it, and a white shirt, very white now under the heavy-hanging, deep-red jowls.

"Roar, Lion, Roar," the man in tweeds was singing. "Twenty-seven—fourteen."

"Who won?" asked Mr. Taylor.

"Columbia," the man in tweeds said. "Twenty-seven—fourteen. Hail Columbia! I'm a Columbia man."

"Who'd've thought that a team from New York City would ever beat Yale?" Mr. Taylor said.

"I don't believe it," Oliver said.

"Twenty-seven—fourteen," the man in tweeds said. "Luckman ran over them."

"We're from Yale," Mr. Taylor said. "All of us. Yale, 1912."

"Have a drink on a Columbia man," the man in tweeds said. "Everybody." He ordered the drinks and they sang "Roar, Lion, Roar," the two parties melting happily and naturally together.

Margaret heard her father going on seriously about your needing solid friends to depend on later on, and, by God, the place where you developed them, people of your own kind that you could cleave to through thick and thin. . . . She watched the huge man in tweeds as he drank, sang out "Roar, Lion, Roar," his behind quivering deeply under the expanse of heavy cloth.

"Can you sing 'Stand, Columbia'?" Mrs. Taylor asked. "That's a Columbia song. You ought to be able to sing it."

"I would," said the fat man, "only my throat's too hoarse for a song like that."

They sang "Heigh-ho, Heigh-ho, It's Off to Work We Go," their voices hearty, full of whisky and pleasure and loud good-fellowship.

"I would like to hear 'Stand, Columbia,' " Mrs. Taylor said.

"Did you hear this one?" the fat man said. And he sang, "Heigh-ho, heigh-ho, I joined the C.I.O., I pay my dues to a bunch of Jews, heigh-ho, heigh-ho!"

Oliver, who had been slapping Mrs. Taylor on the back, slapped the fat man on the back in appreciation, and all the others laughed and beat on the bar approvingly, and Trent, who was standing behind the bar, looked out nervously across the room, scanning it for a Jewish face. Seeing none, he permitted himself to smile.

"Once again," the fat man said, beaming, standing up to lead with large gestures of his arms, "before we leave for Poughkeepsie."

All the voices, middle-aged, hoarse, joined happily in the chorus, the song more spontaneous, full of more joy and celebration and real pleasure, than any before that evening. "Heigh-ho," they sang joyously, "heigh-ho, we've joined the C.I.O., We've paid our dues to a bunch of Jews, heigh-ho, heigh-ho!"

They laughed and clapped each other on the back, the room echoing and re-echoing as they banged the bar and roared.

"Oh, I love it!" Mrs. Taylor gasped.

Margaret turned her back on them and looked at her father. He was laughing, too.

Margaret looked carefully at him, as though he were a man whom she had just met. Her father's face was not fat, Margaret noticed, but almost so. His gray suit was double-breasted and his collar was sharp, starched white. The heavy silk necktie flowed like a spring from his lined though ruddy throat, and his shoes looked as though they had been brought from England for carefully custom-built feet. She looked at his face, like the faces of the fathers of her friends, the men who had been graduated from the good colleges around 1910 and had gone on to stand at the head of businesses, committees, charity organizations, lodges, lobbies, political parties, who got brick red when they thought of the income tax, who said, "That lunatic in the White House." Her father was sitting across the table with that face, laughing.

"What're you laughing at?" Margaret asked. "What the hell are you laughing at?"

Mr. Clay stopped laughing, but a look of surprise seemed to hang over as a kind of transition expression on his face. Margaret stood up as the man in tweeds and his friends left to go to Poughkeepsie.

"Where're you going?" Mr. Clay asked.

"I don't feel like eating here," Margaret said, putting on her coat.

Mr. Clay left some bills for the check, and put his coat on. "I thought you wanted me to tell you what I thought," he said. "I thought you wanted me to advise . . ."

Margaret said nothing as they started out.

"I don't believe he was a Columbia man at all," Mrs. Taylor was saying as Margaret passed her. "He couldn't sing 'Stand, Columbia.'"

"That's right," said Mr. Taylor. "Too tweedy, too much sweater."

"To Neville Chamberlain!" Mrs. Taylor said, her thin, white fingers holding her cocktail glass high. "I'm going to get drunk tonight. I don't have to go to church tomorrow."

Margaret closed the door behind her and walked with her father toward their car, past the sign on the lawn, lit and shaking in the wind, with the dry leaves blowing against it.

This was in the autumn of 1938, the year Columbia beat Yale 27–14 in the first game of the season.

MATERIAL WITNESS

LESTER BARNUM WALKED down the steps, across the street and around the corner without looking back. He was a small, worn-out, neat, married-looking man, walking slowly, as though he never got enough sleep, his head lowered politely and humbly into his gray overcoat, his gray face pursed vaguely and undramatically over some inner problem.

A year in jail, he thought. He shook his head and turned to look at the huge gray prison that had held him, but he had gone around the corner without realizing it, and the jail and the year were behind him and out of sight. He walked aimlessly on, looking without real interest at the free men about him.

He hadn't liked the men he'd met in prison. In the movies, cellblocks were invariably inhabited by warm, great-hearted, harmless persons, but in the year he had spent behind bars no convicts of that particular type had turned up. There had only been rough, large, desperate men who had put pepper in his coffee, nails in his bed, and occasionally, in moments of extreme emotion, had hit him with mophandles and slop buckets. And there was always a small, pasty-faced man turning up every month or so, whispering gratingly into his ear in the exercise yard, "Talk an' the next stop is Woodlawn. Fer yer own good . . ."

Everybody took it for granted that he owned some secret, deadly information—the police, the district attorney, the convicts. Barnum sighed as he walked listlessly along the bustling, free streets. He stopped irresolutely at a corner. No direction was more inviting than any other direction, no street offered any final destination. There was no home for him to go to. For the first time in his forty-three years there was no definite, appointed place where his clothes were hanging, his bed ready to be slept in. His wife had gone to St. Louis with an automobile mechanic and had taken his two daughters with her. "I might as well tell you," she'd said flatly in the visiting room at the jail after he'd been there three months. "This has been going on a long time, but now he's going to St. Louis and I guess it's about time you found out." And she'd pulled at one of the curly little hats she was always wearing and adjusted her corset a little angrily as though Barnum had insulted her and she'd started west. And he'd found out that the printing shop he'd worked in for seventeen years had been unionized and his job had been taken over, at a much higher salary, by a Rumanian with a beard.

Barnum whistled bleakly through his teeth, thinking vaguely of the years behind him when he had led an ordinary, simple existence, bringing home the comic papers to his children every evening, dozing after dinner while his wife complained of one thing and another, a plain, unnoticed, uncomplicated life, in which he never talked to such important, improbable persons as district attorneys and Irish detectives, never had pepper put in his coffee by exasperated swindlers and dope-peddlers.

It had all started because he'd turned down Columbus Avenue, instead of Broadway. A year ago he had been walking slowly and quietly home from work, worrying over the fact that the Boss had marched back and forth behind him in the shop all afternoon, muttering, "I can't stand it! There are limits! I can't stand it!" Barnum hadn't known what it was that the Boss couldn't stand, but, vaguely, it had worried him, as there was always the possibility that the thing that the Boss couldn't stand might be Barnum. But he had been walking wearily home, knowing there would be haddock for dinner and that he would have to mind the children that evening because his wife was going to some woman's club where, she said, instruction was to be had in knitting.

Dimly Barnum had felt the evening was not going to be pleasant—dull, aimless, like thousands of other evenings in his life.

Then it had happened. A tall, very dark man had walked swiftly past Barnum, holding his hands in his pockets. Suddenly another man, in a gray hat and topcoat, had leaped out of a doorway and tapped the tall dark man on the shoulder. "Here you are, you son of a bitch," the man in the gray hat had said loudly and the dark man had started to run and the man in the gray hat had pulled a gun from under his armpit and yelled, "Not this time, Spanish!" and shot the dark man four times. The dark man slid quietly to the pavement and the man in the gray coat said, "How do you like that?" and looked once, coldly, at Barnum, who was standing there, with his mouth open. "Aah!" the man in the gray coat said loudly, pulling up one corner of his mouth in a snarl—and then he'd disappeared.

Barnum just stood there looking at the tall dark man who was lying quietly on the sidewalk, looking not so tall now, with the blood coming from him. After a while Barnum closed his mouth. He moved dreamily over to the man lying on the sidewalk. The man's eyes looked up at Barnum, calmly dead.

"Say—say, Mister! What happened?" a man in a butcher's apron was standing next to Barnum, looking down excitedly.

"I saw it," Barnum said slowly. "This fellow walked past me and a man in a gray hat jumped out of a doorway and he said, 'Here you are, you son of a bitch!' and then he said, 'Not this time, Spanish' and he went bang! bang! bang! bang! and he said, 'How do you like that?' and he looked at me and he went 'Aaah!' and he disappeared and this gentleman was dead."

"What happened?" a fat lady ran across the street from a millinery shop, shouting as she ran.

"A man's been shot," the butcher said. "He saw it." He pointed at Barnum.

"How did it happen?" the milliner asked, respectfully. Three more men had run up by this time, and four small boys, all looking at the corpse.

"Well," Barnum said, feeling important as the babel of talk died down as he began to speak, "I was walking along and this fellow walked past me and a man in a gray hat jumped out of a doorway and he said, 'Here you are, you son of a bitch!' and this fellow started to run and the man in the gray hat pulled out a gun and he said, 'Not this time, Spanish' and he went bang! bang! bang! bang!" Barnum shouted the bangs and pointed his finger violently at the corpse on the sidewalk. "And he said, 'How do you like that?' and he looked at me and he went 'Aaah!'" Barnum curled his lip into an imitation of the murderer's snarl. "And he disappeared and this gentleman was dead."

By now there were fifty people gathered around Barnum and the corpse. "What happened?" the latest arrival asked.

"I was walking along," Barnum said in a loud voice, conscious of every eye upon him, "and this fellow walked past me. . . ."

"Lissen, Buddy," A small rough-looking man nudged his elbow. "Why don't you go home? You didn't see nuthin'."

"I saw," Barnum said excitedly. "I saw with my own eyes. A man in a gray hat jumped out of a doorway . . ." Barnum leaped to demonstrate, the crowd respectfully falling back to give him room, as Barnum landed catlike, his knees bent but tense. "And he said, 'Here you are, you son of a bitch!' And this fellow"—with a wave for the corpse—"started to run . . ." Barnum took two quick little steps to show how the dead man had started to run ". . . and the man in the gray hat pulled out a gun and said . . ."

"Why don't you go home?" the rough little man said pleadingly. "It's nuthin' to me, but you're only complicating yerself. Why don't you go home?"

Barnum looked at him coldly for a moment.

"Then what happened?" a voice demanded from the crowd.

"'Not this time, Spanish!'" Barnum cried. "And he went bang! bang! bang! bang!" Barnum moved his hand as though he was firing a heavy gun and fighting the recoil. "And he said, 'How do you like that?' and he looked at me and he went 'Aaah!'" Barnum snarled it out, with every eye upon him, "and he disappeared, and this gentleman was dead."

"As a good friend of yours," the small rough man said earnestly, "I advise you to go home. You didn't see nuthin' . . ."

"What happened?" A voice shouted across the bobbing heads. By now it seemed to Barnum nearly a thousand people must be congregated around him, all with their eyes fixed eagerly on him, who never, even in his own home, could get three people at one time, even his wife and two children, to listen to him for as long as a minute without interruption.

"I was walking along," Barnum said in a loud, ringing voice, "and this fellow . . ."

"Mistuh!" The small man shook his head despairingly. "Why're you doing this? What's it goin' to get you? Trouble!"

"This fellow," Barnum went on, disregarding the small, rough man, "walked past me and a man in a gray hat jumped out of a doorway . . ." Once more Barnum demonstrated. "'There you are, you son of a bitch!' he hollered and this fellow started to run and the man in the gray hat pulled out a gun . . ." Barnum snatched an imaginary pistol from under his armpit, pointed it at the corpse. "And he yelled, 'Not this time, Spanish!' and he went bang! bang! bang! bang! and he said, 'How do you like that?' and he looked at me and he went 'Aaah!' and he disappeared and this gentleman was dead." Barnum was sweating heavily now from his leaps and snarls and the unaccustomed strain of talking so that a thousand people could hear every word, and his eyes were rolling with excitement. "And it was all over," Barnum said dramatically, "and this gentleman was lying there looking up at me before you could blink your eyes."

"Jesus Christ!" one of the four little boys in the inner circle said in deep admiration.

"Whoever you are," the small man said to Barnum, "you're a dope. Remember I told you. Good-bye." And he pushed his way out of the crowd.

A big man with a red face tapped Barnum's arm. He smiled engagingly at Barnum. "Did you really see it?" he asked.

"Did I see it!" Barnum waved his hand. "The bullets went past my head."

"What happened?" the red-faced man asked.

"I was walking along," Barnum began while the red-faced man listened with deep interest. "And this fellow was walking in front of me . . ."

"Louder!" a voice cried deep in the crowd.

"I WAS WALKING ALONG," Barnum shouted, "AND THIS FELLOW WAS WALKING IN FRONT OF ME AND A MAN IN A GRAY HAT . . ." And Barnum went through the story, with gestures, while the red-faced man listened with respect.

"You saw the murderer close up?" the red-faced man inquired.

"Like you." Barnum stuck his face right next to the other man's.

"You'd know his face again if you saw it?"

"Like my wife's . . ."

"Good," said the red-faced man, taking Barnum by the elbow and starting out through the crowd, as the sirens of radio cars howled to a halt at the corner. "You'll come with me to the police station and when we catch the murderer you'll identify him. You're a material witness. I'm glad I found you."

Barnum, a year later, sighed in retrospect. For a whole year the murderer was not caught, and he sat in jail and lost his wife and children and a bearded Rumanian took his job and highwaymen and forgers beat him with mop handles and slop buckets. Every three days he would be taken down to look at some new collection of thugs. Each time he would have to shake his head because the man in the gray hat was not among them and then the young district attorney would say, sneeringly, "You're one hell of a fine material witness, Barnum. Get him the hell out of here!" and the detectives would wearily drag him back to his cell. "We're pertectin' yuh," the detectives would say when Barnum would ask to be freed. "Yuh wanna go out and have 'em blow yer brains out? That was Sammy Spanish that was killed. He's an important figure. You know too much. Take it easy, yuh're gettin' yer three squares a day, ain't yuh?"

"I don't know anything," Barnum would say wearily, in a low voice, as they locked him into his cell, but they never paid any attention. Luckily, the district attorney got a good job with an insurance company and gave up looking for the murderer of Sammy Spanish, otherwise Barnum was sure he'd have been kept until either he or the district attorney died.

Walking aimlessly down the street, with the year behind him, homeless, wifeless, childless, jobless, Barnum sighed. He stood on a corner, rubbing his chin sadly, trying to decide which way to turn. A car swung around the corner past him, too close to a car parked just below the corner. There was the sound of the grating of fenders and then the forlorn wail of brakes and the crumpling of metal. A man jumped out of the parked car, waving his hands.

"Where the hell do you think you're going?" he cried to the driver of the other car, looking wildly at his mashed fender. "Lemme see your license! Somebody's got to pay for that fender and it ain't going to be me, brother!" While the reckless driver was getting out of his car, the owner of the damaged car turned sadly to Barnum.

"Did you see that?" he asked.

Barnum looked hurriedly at him, at the fender, at the street around him. "Oh, no," he said. "I didn't see anything."

And he turned and walked swiftly back in the direction from which he had come.

THE HOUSE OF PAIN

"Tell her Mr. Bloomer wants to see her," Philip said, holding his hat, standing straight before the elegant, white-handed hotel clerk.

"It's a Mr. Bloomer, Miss Gerry," the hotel clerk said elegantly, looking through Philip's plain, clean face, far across the rich lobby.

Philip heard the famous voice rise and fall in the receiver. "Who the hell is Mr. Bloomer?" the famous, sweet voice said.

Philip moved his shoulders uncomfortably in his overcoat. His country-boy ears, sticking out from his rough hair, reddened.

"I heard that," he said. "Tell her my name is Philip Bloomer and I wrote a play called *The House of Pain*."

"It's a Mr. Philip Bloomer," the clerk said languidly, "and he says he wrote a play called *A House of Pain*."

"Did he come all the way up here to tell me that?" the deep rich voice boomed in the receiver. "Tell him that's dandy."

"Let me talk to her, please." Philip grabbed the receiver from the clerk's pale hand. "Hello," he said, his voice shaking in embarrassment. "This is Philip Bloomer."

"How do you do, Mr. Bloomer?" the voice said with charm.

"The thing is, Miss Gerry, this play I wrote," Philip tried to find the subject, the object, the predicate before she hung up, "*The House of Pain*."

"The clerk said *A House of Pain*, Mr. Bloomer."

"He's wrong," Philip said.

"He's a very stupid man, that clerk," the voice said. "I've told him so many times."

"I went to Mr. Wilkes' office," Philip said desperately, "and they said you still had the script."

"What script?" Miss Gerry asked.

"*The House of Pain*," Philip cried, sweating. "When I brought it into Mr. Wilkes' office I suggested that you play the leading part and they sent it to you. Now, you see, somebody at the Theatre Guild wants to see the script, and you've had it for two months already, so I thought you mightn't mind letting me have it."

There was a pause, an intake of breath at the other end of the wire. "Won't you come up, Mr. Bloomer?" Miss Gerry said, her voice chaste but inviting.

"Yes, ma'am," Philip said.

"1205, sir," the clerk said, delicately taking the phone from Philip's hands and placing it softly on its pedestal.

In the elevator Philip looked anxiously at his reflection in the mirror, arranged his tie, tried to smooth down his hair. The truth was he looked like a farm boy, a dairy-hand who had perhaps gone to agricultural school for two years. As far as possible he tried to avoid meeting theater people because he knew nobody would believe that anybody who looked like him could write plays.

He got out of the elevator and went down the softly carpeted hall to 1205. There was a sheet of paper stuck in a clip on the metal door. He braced himself and rang the bell.

Miss Adele Gerry opened the door herself. She stood there, tall, dark-haired, perfumed, womanly, in an afternoon dress that showed a square yard of bosom. Her eyes held the same dark fire that had commanded admiring attention on many stages from Brooks Atkinson, from Mantle, from John Mason Brown. She stood there, her hand lightly on the doorknob, her hair swept up simply, her head a little to one side, looking speculatively at Philip Bloomer in the hallway.

"I'm Mr. Bloomer," Philip said.

"Won't you come in?" Her voice was sweet, simple, direct, fitted exactly to the task of allaying the nervousness of farm boys and dairy-hands.

"There's a note for you on the door," Philip said, glad of one sentence, at least, with which to get inside.

"Oh, thank you," she said, taking it.

"Probably a letter from some secret admirer," Philip said, with a smile, suddenly resolved to be gallant, to fight the farm boy, destroy the dairy-hand.

Miss Gerry took the sheet of paper over to the window, scanned it, her eyes close to it near-sightedly, her whole body beautifully intent on the written word.

"It's a menu," she said, tossing it on a table. "They have lamb stew tonight."

Philip closed his eyes for a moment, hoping that when he opened them, Miss Gerry, the room, the hotel would have disappeared.

"Won't you sit down, Mr. Bloomer?" Miss Gerry said.

He opened his eyes and marched across the room and sat upright on a little gilt chair. Miss Gerry arranged herself beautifully on a sofa, her hand outstretched along the back, the fingers dangling, the legs girlishly tucked in.

"You know, Mr. Bloomer," Miss Gerry said, her voice charmingly playful, "you don't look like a playwright at all."

"I know," Philip said, gloomily.

"You look so healthy." She laughed.

"I know."

"But you *are* a playwright?" She leaned forward intimately, and Philip religiously kept his eyes away from her bosom. This, he suddenly realized, had become the great problem of the interview.

"Oh, yes," he said, looking steadfastly over her shoulder. "Yes, indeed. As I told you over the phone, I came up for my play."

"*The House of Pain.*" She shook her head musingly. "A lovely title. Such a strange title for such a healthy-looking boy."

"Yes, ma'am," Philip said, rigorously holding his head steady, his gaze up.

"It was so good of you to think of me for it," Miss Gerry said, leaning forward even farther, her eyes liquid and grateful enough to project to the third row, balcony. "I've practically been in retirement for three years. I thought nobody even remembered Adele Gerry any more."

"Oh, no," Philip said, gallantly. "I remembered you." He saw that this was bad, but was sure that anything else he might add would be worse.

"The Theatre Guild is going to do your play, Mr. Bloomer?" Miss Gerry asked fondly.

"Oh, no. I didn't say that. I said somebody I knew up there thought it might not be a bad idea to send it around, and since you'd had the play for two months . . ."

Some of the interest fled from Miss Gerry's deep eyes. "I haven't a copy of your play, Mr. Bloomer. My director, Mr. Lawrence Wilkes, has it." She smiled beautifully at him, although the wrinkles showed clearly then. "I was interested in seeing you. I like to keep an eye on the new blood of the theater."

"Thank you," Philip mumbled, feeling somehow exalted. Miss Gerry beamed at him and he felt his eyes, unable to withstand the full glory of her glance, sinking to her bosom. "Mr. Wilkes," he said loudly. "I've seen many of his plays. You were wonderful in his plays. He's a wonderful director."

"He has his points," Miss Gerry said coldly. "But he has limitations. Grave limitations. It is the tragedy of the American theater that there is no man operating in it today who does not suffer from grave limitations."

"Yes," Philip said.

"Tell me about your play, Mr. Bloomer. Tell me about the part you had in mind for me." She recrossed her legs comfortably, as though preparing for a long session on the sofa.

"Well," Philip said, "it's about a boarding house. A low, dreary, miserable boarding house with bad plumbing and poor devils who can't pay the rent. That sort of thing."

Miss Gerry said nothing.

"The presiding genius of this boarding house," Philip went on, "is a slatternly, tyrannical, scheming, harsh woman. I modeled her on my aunt, who keeps a boarding house."

"How old is she?" Miss Gerry asked, her voice small and flat.

"Who? My aunt?"

"The woman in the play."

"Forty-five." Philip got up and started to stride up and down the room as he talked of his play. "She's continually snooping around, listening at keyholes, piecing together the tragedies of her boarders from overheard snatches, fighting with her family, fighting with . . ." He stopped. "Why, Miss Gerry," he said. "Miss Gerry . . ."

She was bent over on the couch and the tears were dropping slowly and bitterly from her eyes.

"That man," she wept, "that man . . ." She jumped up and swept across to the phone, dialed a number. Unheeded, the tears streamed down through the mascara, eye-shadow, rouge, powder, in dark channels. "That man," she wept, "that man . . ."

Philip backed instinctively against a wall between a table and a chest, his hands spread coldly out behind him. Silently he stood there, like a man awaiting an attack.

"Lawrence!" she cried into the phone. "I'm glad you were home. There's a young man up here and he's offered me a part in his play."

The tears coursed bitterly down the dark channels on her cheeks. "Do you know what part it is? I'm going to tell you and then I'm going to throw the young man right the hell out of this hotel!"

Philip cowered against the wall.

"Keep quiet, Lawrence!" Miss Gerry was shouting. "I've listened to your smooth excuses long enough. A woman of forty-five," she wept, her mouth close to the phone, "a bitter, slatternly, ugly, hateful boarding-house keeper who listens at keyholes and fights with her family." Miss Gerry was half bent over in grief now, and she gripped the telephone desperately and clumsily in her two hands. Because her tears were too much for her, she listened and Philip heard a man's voice talking quickly, but soothingly, over the phone.

Finally, disregarding the urgent voice in the receiver, Miss Gerry stood straight. "Mr. Bloomer," she said, her teeth closing savagely over the name, "please tell me why you thought of me for this rich and glamorous role."

Philip braced himself weakly against the wall between the chest and the table. "You see," he said, his voice high and boyish and forlorn, "I saw you in two plays."

"Shut up, for the love of God!" Miss Gerry called into the phone. Then she looked up and with a cold smile, spoke to Philip. "What plays, Mr. Bloomer?"

"*Sun in the East*," Philip croaked, "and *Take the Hindmost*."

A new and deeper flood of tears formed in her dark eyes. "Lawrence," she sobbed into the phone. "Do you know why he's offering me this part? He saw me in two plays. Your two great successes. He saw me playing a hag of sixty in *Sun in the East* and he saw me playing the mother of a goddamned brood of Irish hoodlums in *Take the Hindmost*. You've ruined me, Lawrence, you've ruined me."

Philip slipped out of his niche against the wall and walked quickly over to the window and looked out. Twelve stories, his mind registered automatically.

"*Everybody's* seen me in those parts. Everybody! Now, whenever there's a play with a mother, a crone in it, they say, 'Call up Adele Gerry.' I'm a woman in the full flush of my powers. I should be playing Candida, Hedda, Joan, and I'm everybody's candidate for the hero's old mother! Boarding-house keepers in children's first efforts!"

Philip winced, looking down at Madison Avenue.

"Who did this to me?" Miss Gerry's tones were full, round, tragic. "Who did it? Who cajoled, pleaded, begged, drove me into those two miserable plays? Lawrence Wilkes! Lawrence Wilkes can claim the credit for ruining the magnificent career of a great actress. The famous Lawrence Wilkes, who fooled me into playing a mother at the age of thirty-three!"

Philip hunched his shoulders as the deep, famous voice crowded the room with sound.

"And now you wonder," even at the phone, her wide gesture of shoulder and arm was sharp with irony, "now you wonder why I won't marry you. Send me flowers, send me books, send me tickets to the theater, write me letters telling me you don't care if I go out wih other men. From now on I'm going out with the entire garrison of Governor's Island! I'll eat dinner next to you with a different man every night! I hate you, I hate you, Larry, I hate you . . ."

Her sobs finally conquered her. She let the phone drop heedlessly, walked slowly and with pain over to a deep chair and sank into it, damp, bedraggled, undone, like a sorrowing child.

Philip breathed deeply and turned around. "I'm sorry," he said hoarsely.

Miss Gerry waved her hand wearily. "It's not your fault. I've been getting this for three years. You're the agent of events, that's all."

"Thank you," Philip said gratefully.

"A young woman like me," Miss Gerry moaned, looking like a little girl, miserable in the deep chair. "I'll never get a decent part. Never. Never. Mothers! That man has done me in. Don't ever get mixed up with that man. He's an egotistic maniac. He would crucify his grandmother for a second-act curtain." She wiped her eyes in a general smear of cosmetics. "He wants me to marry him." She laughed horribly.

"I'm so sorry," Philip said, feeling finally, because that was all he could say, like a farm boy, a dairy-hand. "I'm so, so sorry."

"He says go up and get your script," Miss Gerry said. "He lives across the street in the Chatham. Just call up from the desk and he'll bring it down."

"Thank you, Miss Gerry," Philip said.

"Come here," she said, the tears departing. He walked slowly over to her and she pulled his head down to her bosom and kissed his forehead and held his ears with her two hands. "You're a nice, clean, stupid boy," she said. "I'm glad to see there's a new crop springing up. Go."

Philip limped to the door, turned there, meaning to say something, saw Adele Gerry sitting in her chair, looking blankly at the floor, with her face a ruin of sorrow and mascara and age. Philip softly opened the door and softly closed it behind him.

He went across the street, breathing the cold air deeply, and called Lawrence Wilkes on the phone. Philip recognized Wilkes when he got out of the elevator with a copy of *The House of Pain* under his arm. Wilkes was neatly and beautifully dressed and had a hit running and had just been to a barber, but his face was worn and tortured and weary, like the faces of the people in the newsreels who have just escaped an air-raid, but who do not hope to escape the next.

"Mr. Wilkes," Philip said softly.

Wilkes looked at Philip and smiled and put his head forgivingly and humorously to one side. "Young man," he said, "in the theater you must learn one thing. Never tell an actress what type of part you think she can play." And he gave Philip *The House of Pain* and turned and went back into the elevator. Philip watched the door close on his well-tailored, tortured back, then sprang out into the street and fled across town to the Theatre Guild.

TRIUMPH OF JUSTICE

MIKE PILATO PURPOSEFULLY threw open the door of Victor's shack. Above him the sign that said, "Lunch, Truckmen Welcome," shook a little, and the pale shadows its red bulbs threw in the twilight waved over the State Road.

"Victor," Mike said, in Italian.

Victor was leaning on the counter, reading Walter Winchell in a spread-out newspaper. He smiled amiably. "Mike," he said, "I am so glad to see you."

Mike slammed the door. "Three hundred dollars, Victor," he said, standing five feet tall, round and solid as a pumpkin against the door. "You owe me three hundred dollars, Victor, and I am here tonight to collect."

Victor shrugged slightly and closed the paper on Walter Winchell.

"As I've been telling you for the past six months," he said, "business is bad. Business is terrible. I work and I work and at the end . . ." He shrugged again. "Barely enough to feed myself."

Mike's cheeks, farmer-brown, and wrinkled deeply by wind and sun, grew dark with blood. "Victor, you are lying in my face," he said slowly, his voice desperately even. "For six months, each time it comes time to collect the rent you tell me, 'Business is bad.' What do I say? I say, 'All right, Victor, don't worry, I know how it is.'"

"Frankly, Mike," Victor said sadly, "there has been no improvement this month."

Mike's face grew darker than ever. He pulled harshly at the ends of his iron-gray mustache, his great hands tense and swollen with anger, repressed but terrible. "For six months, Victor," Mike said, "I believed you. Now I no longer believe you."

"Mike," Victor said reproachfully.

"My friends, my relatives," Mike said, "they prove it to me. Your business is wonderful, ten cars an hour stop at your door; you sell cigarettes to every farmer between here and Chicago; on your slot machine alone . . ." Mike waved a short thick arm at the machine standing invitingly against a wall, its wheels stopped at two cherries and a lemon. Mike swallowed hard, stood breathing heavily, his deep chest rising and falling sharply against his sheepskin coat. "Three hundred dollars!" he shouted. "Six months at fifty dollars! I built this shack with my own hands for you, Victor. I didn't know what kind of man you were. You were an Italian, I trusted you! Three hundred dollars or get out tomorrow! Finish! That's my last word."

Victor smoothed his newspaper down delicately on the counter, his hands making a dry brushing sound in the empty lunchroom. "You misunderstand," he said gently.

"I misunderstand nothing!" Mike yelled. "You are on my land in my shack and you owe me three hundred dollars . . ."

"I don't owe you anything," Victor said, looking coldly at Mike. "That is what you misunderstand. I have paid you every month, the first day of the month, fifty dollars."

"Victor!" Mike whispered, his hands dropping to his sides. "Victor, what are you saying . . . ?"

"I have paid the rent. Please do not bother me any more." Calmly Victor turned his back on Mike and turned two handles on the coffee urn. Steam, in a thin little plume, hissed up for a moment.

Mike looked at Victor's narrow back, with the shoulder blades jutting far out, making limp wings in the white shirt. There was finality in Victor's pose, boredom, easy certainty. Mike shook his head slowly, pulling hard at his mustache. "My wife," Mike said, to the disdainful back, "she told me not to trust you. My wife knew what she was talking about, Victor." Then, with a last flare of hope, "Victor, do you really mean it when you said you paid me?"

Victor didn't turn around. He flipped another knob on the coffee urn. "I mean it."

Mike lifted his arm, as though to say something, pronounce warning. Then he let it drop and walked out of the shack, leaving the door open. Victor came out from behind the counter, looked at Mike moving off with his little rolling limp down the road and across the cornfield.

Victor smiled and closed the door and went back and opened the paper to Walter Winchell.

Mike walked slowly among the corn stalks, his feet crunching unevenly in the October earth. Absently he pulled at his mustache. Dolores, his wife, would have a thing or two to say. "No," she had warned him, "do not build a shack for him. Do not permit him onto your land. He travels with bad men; it will turn out badly. I warn you!" Mike was sure she would not forget this conversation and would repeat it to him word for word when he got home. He limped along unhappily. Farming was better than being a landlord. You put seed into the earth and you knew what was coming out. Corn grew from corn, and the duplicity of Nature was expected and natural. Also no documents were signed in the compact with Nature, no leases and agreements necessary, a man was not at a disadvantage if he couldn't read or write. Mike opened the door to his house and sat down heavily in the parlor, without taking his hat off. Rosa came and jumped on his lap, yelling, "Poppa, Poppa, tonight I want to go to the movies, Poppa, take me to the movies!"

Mike pushed her off. "No movies," he said harshly. Rosa stood in a corner and watched him reproachfully.

The door from the kitchen opened and Mike sighed as he saw his wife coming in, wiping her hands on her apron. She stood in front of Mike, round, short, solid as a plow horse, canny, difficult to deceive.

"Why're you sitting in the parlor?" she asked.

"I feel like sitting in the parlor," Mike said.

"Every night you sit in the kitchen," Dolores said. "Suddenly you change."

"I've decided," Mike said loudly, "that it's about time I made some use of this furniture. After all, I paid for it, I might as well sit in it before I die."

"I know why you're sitting in the parlor," Dolores said.

"Good! You know!"

"You didn't get the money from Victor," Dolores wiped the last bit of batter from her hands. "It's as plain as the shoes on your feet."

"I smell something burning," Mike said.

"Nothing is burning. Am I right or wrong?" Dolores sat in the upright chair opposite Mike. She sat straight, her hands neatly in her lap, her head forward and cocked a little to one side, her eyes staring directly and accusingly into his. "Yes or no?"

"Please attend to your own department," Mike said miserably. "I do the farming and attend to the business details."

"Huh!" Dolores said disdainfully.

"Are you starving?" Mike shouted. "Answer me, are you starving?"

Rosa started to cry because her father was shouting.

"Please, for the love of Jesus," Mike screamed at her, "don't cry!"

Dolores enfolded Rosa in her arms . . . "Baby, baby," she crooned, "I will not let him harm you."

"Who offered to harm her?" Mike screamed, banging on a table with his fist like a mallet. "Don't lie to her!"

Dolores kissed the top of Rosa's head soothingly. "There, there," she crooned. "There." She looked coldly at Mike. "Well. So he didn't pay."

"He . . ." Mike started loudly. Then he stopped, spoke in a low reasonable voice. "So. To be frank with you, he didn't pay. That's the truth."

"What did I tell you?" Dolores said as Mike winced. "I repeat the words. 'Do not permit him onto your land. He travels with bad men; it will turn out badly. I warn you!' Did I tell you?"

"You told me," Mike said wearily.

"We will never see that money again," Dolores said, smoothing Rosa's hair. "I have kissed it good-bye."

"Please," said Mike. "Return to the kitchen. I am hungry for dinner. I have made plans already to recover the money."

Dolores eyed him suspiciously. "Be careful, Mike," she said. "His friends are gangsters and he plays poker every Saturday night with men who carry guns in their pockets."

"I am going to the law," Mike said. "I'm going to sue Victor for the three hundred dollars."

Dolores started to laugh. She pushed Rosa away and stood up and laughed.

"What's so funny?" Mike asked angrily. "I tell you I'm going to sue a man for money he owes me, you find it funny! Tell me the joke."

Dolores stopped laughing. "Have you got any papers? No! You trust him, he trusts you, no papers. Without papers you're lost in a court. You'll make a fool of yourself. They'll charge you for the lawyers. Please, Mike, go back to your farming."

Mike's face set sternly, his wrinkles harsh in his face with the gray stubble he never managed completely to shave. "I want my dinner, Dolores," he said coldly, and Dolores discreetly moved into the kitchen, saying, "It is not my business, my love, truly, I merely offer advice."

Mike walked back and forth in the parlor, limping, rolling a little from side to side, his eyes on the floor, his hands plunged into the pockets of his denims like holstered weapons, his mouth pursed with thought and determination. After a while he stopped and looked at Rosa, who prepared to weep once more.

"Rosa, baby," he said, sitting down and taking her gently on his lap. "Forgive me."

Rosa snuggled to him. They sat that way in the dimly lit parlor.

"Poppa," Rosa said finally.

"Yes," Mike said.

"Will you take me to the movies tonight, Poppa?"

"All right," Mike said. "I'll take you to the movies."

The next day Mike went into town, dressed in his neat black broadcloth suit and his black soft hat and his high brown shoes. He came back to the farm like a businessman in the movies, bustly, preoccupied, sober, but satisfied.

"Well?" Dolores asked him, in the kitchen.

He kissed her briskly, kissed Rosa, sat down, took his shoes off, rubbed his feet luxuriously, said paternally to his son who was reading *Esquire* near the window, "That's right, Anthony, study."

"Well?" asked Dolores.

"I saw Dominic in town," Mike said, watching his toes wriggling. "They're having another baby."

"Well," asked Dolores. "The case? The action?"

"All right," Mike said. "What is there for dinner?"

"Veal," Dolores said. "What do you mean 'all right'?"

"I've spoken to Judge Collins. He is filling out the necessary papers for me and he will write me a letter when I am to appear in court. Rosa, have you been a good girl?"

Dolores threw up her hands. "Lawyers. We'll throw away a fortune on lawyers. Good money after bad. We could put in an electric pump with the money."

"Lawyers will cost us nothing," Mike stuffed his pipe elaborately. "I have different plans. Myself. I will take care of the case myself." He lit up, puffed deliberately.

Dolores sat down across the table from him, spoke slowly, carefully. "Remember, Mike," she said. "This is in English. They conduct the court in English."

"I know," said Mike. "I am right. Justice is on my side. Why should I pay a lawyer fifty, seventy-five dollars to collect my own money? There is one time you need lawyers—when you are wrong. I am not wrong. I will be my own lawyer."

"What do you know about the law?" Dolores challenged him.

"I know Victor owes me three hundred dollars." Mike puffed three times, quickly, on his pipe. "That's all I need to know."

"You can hardly speak English, you can't even read or write, nobody will be able to understand you. They'll all laugh at you, Mike."

"Nobody will laugh at me. I can speak English fine."

"When did you learn?" Dolores asked. "Today?"

"Dolores!" Mike shouted. "I tell you my English is all right."

"Say Thursday," Dolores said.

"I don't want to say it," Mike said, banging the table. "I have no interest in saying it."

"Aha," Dolores crowed. "See? He wants to be a lawyer in an American court, he can't even say Thursday."

"I can," Mike said. "Keep quiet, Dolores."

"Say Thursday." Dolores put her head to one side, spoke coquettishly, slyly, like a girl asking her lover to say he loved her.

"Stirday," Mike said, as he always said. "There!"

Dolores laughed, waving her hand. "And he wants to conduct a law case! Holy Mother! They will laugh at you!"

"Let them laugh!" Mike shouted. "I will conduct the case! Now I want to eat dinner! Anthony!" he yelled. "Throw away that trash and come to the table."

On the day of the trial, Mike shaved closely, dressed carefully in his black suit, put his black hat squarely on his head, and with Dolores seated grimly beside him drove early into town in the 1933 family Dodge.

Dolores said nothing all the way into town. Only after the car was parked and they were entering the courthouse, Mike's shoes clattering bravely on the legal marble, did Dolores speak. "Behave yourself," she said. Then she pinched his arm. Mike smiled at her, braced his yoke-like shoulders, took off his hat. His rough gray hair sprang up like steel wool when his hat was off, and Mike ran his hand through it as he opened the door to the courtroom. There was a proud, important smile on his face as he sat down next to his wife in the first row and patiently waited for his case to be called.

When Victor came, Mike glared at him, but Victor, after a quick look, riveted his attention on the American flag behind the Judge's head.

"See," Mike whispered to Dolores. "I have him frightened. He doesn't dare look at me. Here he will have to tell the truth."

"Sssh!" hissed Dolores. "This is a court of law."

"Michael Pilato," the clerk called, "versus Victor Fraschi."

SHORT STORIES OF IRWIN SHAW

"Me!" Mike said loudly, standing up.

"Sssh," said Dolores.

Mike put his hat in Dolores' lap, moved lightly to the little gate that separated the spectators from the principals in the proceedings. Politely, with a deep ironic smile, he held the gate open for Victor and his lawyer. Victor passed through without looking up.

"Who's representing you, Mr. Pilato?" the Judge asked when they were all seated. "Where's your lawyer?"

Mike stood up and spoke in a clear voice. "I represent myself. I am my lawyer."

"You ought to have a lawyer," the Judge said.

"I do not need a lawyer," Mike said loudly. "I am not trying to cheat anybody." There were about forty people in the courtroom and they all laughed. Mike turned and looked at them, puzzled. "What did I say?"

The Judge rapped with his gavel and the case was opened. Victor took the stand, while Mike stared, coldly accusing, at him. Victor's lawyer, a young man in a blue pinstripe suit and a starched tan shirt, questioned him. Yes, Victor said, he had paid each month. No, there were no receipts, Mr. Pilato could neither read nor write and they had dispensed with all formalities of that kind. No, he did not understand on what Mr. Pilato based his claim. Mike looked incredulously at Victor, lying under solemn oath, risking Hell for three hundred dollars.

Victor's lawyer stepped down and waved to Mike gracefully. "Your witness."

Mike walked dazedly past the lawyer and up to the witness stand, round, neat, his bull neck, deep red-brown and wrinkled, over his pure white collar, his large scrubbed hands politely but awkwardly held at his sides. He stood in front of Victor, leaning over a little toward him, his face close to Victor's.

"Victor," he said, his voice ringing through the courtroom, "tell the truth, did you pay me the money?"

"Yes," said Victor.

Mike leaned closer to him. "Look in my eye, Victor," Mike said, his voice clear and patient, "and answer me. Did you pay me the money?"

Victor lifted his head and looked unflinchingly into Mike's eyes. "I paid you the money."

Mike leaned even closer. His forehead almost touched Victor's now. "Look me *straight* in the eye, Victor."

Victor looked bravely into Mike's eyes, less than a foot away now.

"Now, Victor," Mike said, his eyes narrowed, cold, the light in them small and flashing and gray, "DID YOU PAY ME THE MONEY?"

Victor breathed deeply. "Yes," he said.

Mike took half a step back, almost staggering, as though he had been hit. He stared incredulously into the perjurer's eyes, as a man might stare at a son who has just admitted he has killed his mother, beyond pity, beyond understanding, outside all the known usage of human life. Mike's face worked harshly as the tides of anger and despair and vengeance rolled up in him.

"You're a goddam liar, Victor!" Mike shouted terribly. He leapt down from the witness platform, seized a heavy oak armchair, raised it murderously above Victor's head.

"Mike, oh, Mike!" Dolores' wail floated above the noise of the courtroom.

"Tell the truth, Victor!" Mike shouted, his face brick red, his teeth white behind his curled lips, almost senseless with rage, for the first time in his life threatening a fellow-creature with violence. "Tell it fast."

He stood, the figure of Justice, armed with the chair, the veins pulsing in his huge wrists, the chair quivering high above Victor's head in his huge gnarled hands, his tremendous arms tight and bulging in their broadcloth sleeves. "Immediately, Victor!"

"Pilato," shouted the Judge. "Put that chair down!"

Victor sat stonily, his eyes lifted in dumb horror to the chair above his head.

"Pilato," the Judge shouted, "you can be sent to jail for this!" He banged sternly but helplessly on his desk. "Remember, this is a court of law!"

"Victor?" Mike asked, unmoved, unmoving. "Victor? Immediately, please."

"No," Victor screamed, cringing in his seat, his hands now held in feeble defense before his eyes. "I didn't pay! I didn't!"

"Pilato," screamed the Judge, "this is not evidence!"

"You were lying?" Mike said inexorably, the chair still held, ax-like, above him.

"Mike, oh, Mike," wailed Dolores.

"It was not my idea," Victor babbled. "As God is my judge, I didn't think it up. Alfred Lotti, he suggested it, and Johnny Nolan. I am under the influence of corrupt men. Mike, for the love of God, please don't kill me, Mike, it would never have occurred to me myself, forgive me, forgive me . . ."

"Guiness!" the Judge called to the court policeman. "Are you going to stand there and let this go on? Why don't you do something?"

"I can shoot him," Guiness said. "Do you want me to shoot the plaintiff?"

"Shut up," the Judge said.

Guiness shrugged and turned his head toward the witness stand, smiling a little.

"You were lying?" Mike asked, his voice low, patient.

"I was lying," Victor cried.

Slowly, with magnificent calm, Mike put the chair down neatly in its place. With a wide smile he turned to the Judge. "There," he said.

"Do you know any good reason," the Judge shouted, "why I shouldn't have you locked up?"

Victor was crying with relief on the witness stand, wiping the tears away with his sleeve.

"There is no possible excuse," the Judge said, "for me to admit this confession as evidence. We are a court of law in the State of Illinois, in the United States. We are not conducting the Spanish Inquisition, Mr. Pilato."

"Huh?" Mike asked, cocking his head.

"There are certain rules," the Judge went on, quickly, his voice high, "which it is customary to observe. It is not the usual thing, Mr. Pilato," he said harshly, "to arrive at evidence by bodily threatening to brain witnesses with a chair."

"He wouldn't tell the truth," Mike said simply.

"At the very least, Mr. Pilato," the Judge said, "you should get thirty days."

"Oh, Mike," wept Dolores.

"Mr. Fraschi," the Judge said, "I promise you that you will be protected. That nobody will harm you."

"I did it," sobbed Victor, his hands shaking uncontrollably in a mixture of fear, repentance, religion, joy at delivery from death. "I did it. I will not tell a lie. I'm a weak man and influenced by loafers. I owe him three hundred dollars. Forgive me, Mike, forgive me . . ."

"He will not harm you," the Judge said patiently. "I guarantee it. You can tell the truth without any danger. Do you owe Mr. Pilato three hundred dollars?"

"I owe Mr. Pilato three hundred dollars," Victor said, swallowing four times in a row.

The young lawyer put three sheets of paper into his briefcase and snapped the lock.

The Judge sighed and wiped his brow with a handkerchief as he looked at Mike. "I don't approve of the way you conducted this trial,

Mr. Pilato," he said. "It is only because you're a working man who has many duties to attend to on his land that I don't take you and put you away for a month to teach you more respect for the processes of law."

"Yes, sir," Mike said faintly.

"Hereafter," the Judge said, "kindly engage an attorney when you appear before me in this court."

"Yes, sir," Mike said.

"Mr. Pilato," the Judge said, "it is up to you to decide when and how he is to pay you."

Mike turned and walked back to Victor. Victor shrank into his chair. "Tomorrow morning, Victor," Mike said, waving his finger under Victor's nose, "at eight-thirty o'clock, I am coming into your store. The money will be there."

"Yes," said Victor.

"Is that all right?" Mike asked the Judge.

"Yes," said the Judge.

Mike strode over to the young lawyer. "And you," he said, standing with his hands on his hips in front of the young man with the pinstripe suit. "Mr. Lawyer. You knew he didn't pay me. A boy with an education. You should be ashamed of yourself." He turned to the Judge, smiled broadly, bowed. "Thank you," he said. "Good morning." Then, triumphantly, smiling broadly, rolling like a sea captain as he walked, he went through the little gate. Dolores was waiting with his hat. He took the hat, put Dolores' arm through his, marched down the aisle, nodding, beaming to the spectators. Someone applauded and by the time he and Dolores got to the door all the spectators were applauding.

He waited until he got outside, in the bright morning sunshine down the steps of the courthouse before he said anything to Dolores. He put his hat on carefully, turned to her, grinning. "Well," he said, "did you observe what I did?"

"Yes," she said. "I was never so ashamed in my whole life!"

"Dolores!" Mike was shocked. "I got the money. I won the case."

"Acting like that in a court of law!" Dolores started bitterly toward the car. "What are you, a red Indian?"

Dolores got into the car and slammed the door and Mike limped slowly around and got into the other side. He started the car without a word and shaking his head from time to time, drove slowly toward home.

SELECT CLIENTELE

"'Figaro, Figaro, Figaro!'" they sang as their bicycles rolled downhill through the shaking shadow and sunlight between the close rows of trees. "'Figaro!'"

"My native wood notes wild," Sam said. "The red-necked Mirapole, native to the Bronx, but found frequently in more northern latitudes. His song is distinguished by a long wail, followed by a short wail, and the influence of Debussy is marked in this species."

"'Figaro!'" Max sang, leaning far over on a curve. "'My bonnie lies over the ocean, My bonnie lies over the sea . . .'"

"Max, the bald Austrian lark," Esther said, leaning over for the curve, following Max. "Plumage of the male, yellow, with green pants. None genuine unless wearing one-quarter-inch gold-rimmed spectacles."

"If I were going to have a baby," Max said, slowing down, "I wouldn't go bicycle-riding all over the mountains of New York State, like you. It wouldn't be the best thing for the baby."

"It'll be wonderful for the baby," Esther said. "He'll be athletic and skinny. I don't want a fat baby. I want a baby who looks lean and sad and soulful, like his father." She looked at Sam and they laughed at each other.

"That'll be some beautiful baby," said Sam.

There were four men down at the bottom of the hill, and as the bicycles drew nearer they spread across the road with an appearance of casualness, but with something under the appearance that was purposeful and not casual. As the bicycles approached, the four men stood, moving a little, raising the dust of the road nervously. Two of the men had heavy, trimmed branches that they tapped against the road gently again and again. They looked like men who had been loafing aimlessly and unhappily in small towns for a long time. One of them snapped open a long jackknife.

"Some of the boys out to make a couple of bucks for Saturday night," Sam whispered, going as slowly as he could on his bicycle. "You got anything on you?"

"Fifteen cents," said Max. "I'll donate it."

"I got three bobbie pins," Esther said.

"I have a quarter," Sam said. "Let's go through."

But they had to stop at the bottom of the hill because the four men had spread out across the road, without words, examining Sam, Max and Esther with businessmen's eyes. The men didn't move. One of them wore an old maroon football jersey spotted with moth holes, and with the number "38" in black on it.

"What's the matter?" Sam asked. The men didn't say anything.

"Nice boys," Esther said softly. "Very nice boys. Did you ever go to Princeton, boys?" she asked loudly.

The men didn't say anything.

Max whistled between his teeth a theme from one of his own piano sonatas. He moved his bicycle around in front of him, between himself and the men.

The men took in Sam's and Max's old clothes, and the old slacks, stained with cooking and bicycle grease, that Esther was wearing, and her frayed cotton shirt.

"Nothing there," said the man in the maroon jersey. "I bet there isn't a buck between them."

"Intelligent," Max said, smiling behind his glasses, rubbing his bald head slowly. "A real intelligent character."

"Don't be smart," the man in the football jersey said.

"Jews," the man with the jackknife said. "A coupla Jews from old lady Spear's free-love colony."

"Get out of here." The man in the football jersey moved back to the side of the road, leaving room for the bicycles to pass. "Get the hell out of here."

With Esther between them, Sam and Max pedaled slowly between the men.

"Jew bastards," said the man with the knife. "Lousy Jew bastards."

He waited until the bicycles were fifteen yards down the road and threw a stone. Then all the men bent and picked up stones and threw them. Sam dropped behind Esther and covered her as they pedaled swiftly but stiff-backed, upright in their saddles, without looking behind them. A stone hit Max high up on the shoulder; his face turned very white and his hands shook on the handlebars, but he didn't lean forward and he didn't look back.

They turned a bend in the road and slowed down.

"Poor Max," Esther said. "Not even a Jew. You hang around with the wrong people."

"Thomas's barn is right up the road," Max said, keeping his eyes straight ahead. "We can pick up a couple of pitchforks and maybe Thomas, and come back to those four gentlemen."

"Sure," Sam said. "You can do a lot of damage with a pitchfork."

"Now, Sam," Esther began, "stay out of trouble," then stopped when she saw the set expression on Sam's face.

"I left Berlin, I left Vienna," said Max. "I thought I wouldn't see any more things like that. It must be a terrible thing"—Max, watching the road for ruts, was still pale—"to be a Jew."

"You manage," Sam said. "One way or another."

"Old lady Spear," Max said, "invites fifteen artists without money to her place every summer because she believes in art and because she's lonely. How many Jews are there up here now?"

"Four," Sam said.

"Artists," Max said, "so the people in the town hate them, so they call them Jews. Fifteen artists in one place, painting and composing and writing poetry and playing string quartets, so they hate them, call it old lady Spear's free-love colony. What have artists done to Americans, they should dislike them so much? What have the Jews done?"

They came to a fork in the road and stopped.

"Go home," Sam said to Esther. "Take it easy and go home."

Esther looked hard at Sam and Max. "What the hell do you think you're going to accomplish?"

"Go home," Sam said.

"O.K." Esther shrugged. "I'm hungry anyway. I eat like a horse these days." She got on her bicycle and pedaled away. Sam watched her as she went down the road between the trees with his child within her. You had to be real selfish to have a baby these days. It used to be the other way around, he thought, but we're turning everything cockeyed these days.

Sam and Max mounted their bicycles and rode toward Thomas's house.

Those four bastards with the rocks, Sam thought, riding. Pogroms are being planned in odd corners of the United States for my kid who still has five months to go before he comes out of his mother. There're people who hate my son while he still has gills in his mother's womb. Sam laughed a little.

"What's so funny?" Max asked.

"Nothing," Sam said. "I just thought of something silly."

Four hoodlums, Sam thought; don't take them too seriously. But day by day the American people were becoming like them. Men and boys selling Father Coughlin on the street corners and the mean little middle-aged ladies buying him. The undernourished, baleful faces on those newsboys and their customers. The disease was growing stronger in the veins and organs of America. All the time there were more hotels you couldn't go to, apartment houses right in New York City you couldn't live in. Sam sold stories to magazines that published advertisements for vacation places that said "Distinguished clientele" or "Exclusive clientele" or "Select clientele." A hotel advertises that its clientele is exclusive, Sam thought, if it allows in everybody but six million Jews and fifteen million Negroes. It's exclusive for a hundred and ten million people. All right, Sam thought, you had been able to overlook it, it was static, a condition of existence, there was still room to breathe, it wasn't static any more.

"Say," said Sam, "maybe there's something in what they say. Where there's so much smoke . . . Maybe I'm in on the Protocols of Zion, maybe I'm plotting world dominion and I don't know it. Maybe I'm an international Jew. I've voted Democrat for eight years. I voted for LaGuardia, maybe I'm a Communist. I got eight hundred dollars in the bank, I'm a plutocratic banker. I can't bear to watch prizefights, maybe I'm thirsting for Christian blood. What're you supposed to do?"

"Work," Max said, keeping his eyes on the road ahead of him.

"Work. What can you say today? Stop this! Please stop shooting each other. Please stop shooting my brother, my wife, my child. Please become reasonable human beings. I'm a fiction writer. I write, 'The moon shone down brilliantly. She looked into his eyes with mixed emotions.'"

Max smiled. "That's not exactly the way you write, Sam," he said.

"The world's burning up," said Sam, "and I write, 'She looked into his eyes with mixed emotions.'"

"You could write what you want to say, the truth as you see it."

"The truth as I see it." Sam laughed. "The world stinks. People are terrible and there is only despair. Should I write that? Who gets any good out of that? Why should I be the one to tell it?"

They saw Thomas's house at the crossroads and moved faster.

Thomas came out of the barn when he saw them. He was a tall, stringy man who did odd jobs around Mrs. Spear's place and listened patiently to the string quartets. He played an accordion and sang in a trio with Sam and Max on afternoons when they were too lazy to work. They sang "Casey Jones" and "Night and Day" and "Do Ye Ken John Peel?"

"There're four boys up the road, Thomas, who would've held us up," Sam said, "if they thought we had any money."

"They called us Jew bastards," Max said, "and threw rocks at us. We thought we'd get you and go back and . . ."

"There've been gangs around all summer," Thomas said, "bothering the summer people." He gave Max a pitchfork and took another himself. He had tough farmer's arms and a pitchfork suddenly looked like a deadly weapon in his hands. There was a battered baseball bat leaning against the barn wall, and Sam took that.

They started back on foot. Max was still pale and he looked queer, short and round and bald, with his indoor complexion and his soft, pianist's hands tight and mean against the fork handle as he walked, rolling a little in the ruts, between Thomas and Sam. Sam carried the old baseball bat easily over his shoulder.

"Harry Heilmann," he said. "This bat is signed by Harry Heilmann. He played for Detroit. He led the league a few years in batting. It's a nice, heavy bat." Sam swung it experimentally a few times. "I once made five hits in one game." He laughed, feeling better now that he was on his way to some concrete and violent action. "I hope I haven't lost my eye."

Max didn't laugh. He walked eagerly, his face tight and angry.

"This remind you of your duelling days in old Heidelberg?" Sam asked, trying to take the desperation out of Max's face. "Honor at the point of a pitchfork? This remind you? Hey, Max?"

"No," said Max.

They were getting near the bend in the road.

"They'll probably run as soon as they see us," Thomas said. "We can chase 'em a little and give 'em a poke or two. Be careful. You can kill a man without much trouble with a fork."

"Say, Max," Sam said, "you hear that?"

"Yes," said Max. He was walking faster now, two or three yards ahead of the two taller men, the dust flying around his feet.

The four men were still down at the bottom of the hill. They were sitting on the grass alongside the road, but they stood up when Max appeared around the bend of the road with Sam and Thomas right behind him. Max walked swiftly toward them, the pitchfork steady in front of him, color coming back into his face finally, a childish smile on his lips. He didn't look like a little, bald, fat, forty-four-year-old musician any more. "Hello," he was saying, even when he was a long distance from the men, with Sam and Thomas rushing to keep up with him. "Hello, boys. Here we are again, boys."

The men retreated a little, unconsciously casting about for shelter as Max bore down on them.

Suddenly the man with the jackknife smiled. "Hello," he said. "Hi, Tom."

Thomas stopped. He lowered his pitchfork. "Hello, Alec," he said, his voice low, uneasy.

Max stopped. He threw back his head and squinted through his glasses at a bird on a high branch. Sam held onto the baseball bat with one hand.

"There seems to've been a little trouble with my friends here, Alec," Thomas said.

"Misunderstanding," Alex mumbled. "Great misunderstanding. A coupla drinks too much, Thomas. You know how it is." He attempted to make believe he was drunk, bobbing his head from side to side and thickening his speech heavily. The other men took the cue and hung their heads and rocked on their feet and one of them inspiredly hiccoughed.

"Playful," the man in the football jersey said. "No harm meant. Apologize. We apologize if there's any hard feelings. Don't we, boys?"

The boys nodded.

"You see," Thomas said to Sam, embarrassed because he had to make believe that he thought the men were drunk, "they didn't mean anything by it. They apologize. They didn't mean no harm."

"That's right, Thomas, old boy," Alec said. "We didn't mean no harm."

"Go away," Max said. "Go away fast."

The four men turned. "So long, Thomas," Alec called back.

"So long," said Thomas.

Sam and Max and Thomas watched the four men, no longer pretending to be drunk, walk swiftly up the road.

"They're a little foolish," Thomas said, troubled. "They can't get no jobs and they just sit around all day in town, drinkin' when they can manage it, and they get foolish notions. Don't pay any attention to 'em. They're really pretty good fellers."

"I'm sorry," Max said. "I'm really sorry you knew them, Thomas, really sorry."

"I play pool with 'em once in a while," Thomas said, fingering the pitchfork prongs, "an' go to dances and drink beer with 'em a coupla times a month. It'd been a little hard for me to go at 'em with the fork. You see how it is."

"Sure," said Sam.

They walked back to the barn in silence. Max looked straight ahead of him as he walked, his forehead creased, his eyes squinting thoughtfully far down the road.

"I think he batted over four hundred one year," Sam said, as they neared the barn, trying to pull Max out of his anger. "Harry Heilmann. A righthanded batter."

But Max didn't turn his eyes. He and Sam got on their bicycles at the barn and Sam said "Thanks" to Thomas, and Thomas picked gently at his ear with his big hand and looked to one side of Sam and said, "Don't mention it." Sam had to pedal fast to catch up with Max.

On the way back they didn't talk and Max turned off to his cottage with a wave of his hand.

Sam rode on to his cottage, put his bicycle against the wall, and went inside. Esther was eating grapes in the living room, and she smiled when she saw he was unhurt. "Everything all right?" she asked.

"Everything's fine." Sam lay down on the couch and stared at the ceiling. "I'm going to call my agent."

"Catch," Esther said, tossing a grape at him. He caught it and rolled it around in his hand.

"I'm going to tell him to get me a job in Hollywood." Sam put the grape into his mouth. "I want to write about things that never happened and people that never happened. I need a vacation."

Esther looked obliquely at him. She went over to the couch and lay beside him. She kissed him under the ear.

"Tastes better than grapes," she said.

"I want my child to be born under the Western stars." Sam put his arm loosely around her. "Under the stars that look down on Darryl Zanuck and Garbo."

Esther kissed him again.

THE INDIAN IN DEPTH OF NIGHT

THE CITY LAY around Central Park in a deep hush, the four-o'clock-in-the-morning sky mild with stars and a frail softly rising mist. Now and then a car went secretly by, with a sigh of tires and wind and a sudden small flare of headlights. The birds were still, and the trolley cars and buses; the taxicabs waited silently at scattered corners; the drunks were lying by this time in the doorways; the bums bedded for the night, the lights of the tall choked buildings out, save for a window here and there lit in lust or illness. There was no wind and the smell of earth, heavy and surprising in the concrete city, rose with the mist.

O'Malley walked slowly from east to west on the rolling footpaths of the park, free now of nurses and children and policemen and scholars and old men retired heartbrokenly from business. The paths were free now of everything but the soft night and the mist and the country smell of spring earth and the endless and complex memory of all the feet that had trod and worn the paths in the green park in the palm of the city's hand.

O'Malley walked slowly, carrying his head with the exaggerated and conscious care of a man who feels he has drunk one whisky past absolute clarity. He breathed deeply of that rare and fragrant early morning air which seemed to O'Malley to have been made especially by God, in assurance of His mercy and benign tolerance, to follow whisky.

O'Malley looked around him at the city slumbering magnificently past the trees of the park and was glad to know his home was there, his work, his future. He walked slowly from east to west, breathing in the quiet air, holding his head carefully, but comfortably.

"Pardon me." A man slipped out in front of him. "Have you got a light?"

O'Malley stopped and struck a match. He held the match to the man's cigarette, noticing the touch of rouge on the cheeks, the long, carefully waved hair, the white trembling hands cupping the match, the slight smear of rouge on the man's lips.

"Thanks." The man lifted his head, looked sidewise, but challengingly, at O'Malley. O'Malley put the matches away and started to move westward, holding his head in gentle balance.

"Lovely night," said the man hurriedly. His voice was shrill and girlish and came from high in his throat, all breath, nervous, almost hysterical. "I adore walking in the park at this time on a night like this. Breathe," he said. "Just breathe the air."

O'Malley breathed the air.

"All alone?" the man asked nervously.

"Uhuh," O'Malley said.

"You're not lonesome?" The man's hands pulled at each other as he talked. "You're not afraid to walk all alone through the park at this hour?"

"No," O'Malley said, ready, with the drinks and the sweetness of the air, and the feeling of living in and, in a way, owning the great city of New York, to pass on a kind word to every living thing. "I never get lonesome and I like to walk through the park when it's empty and dark like this."

The man nodded unhappily. "Are you sure you don't want company?" he asked desperately, looking up at O'Malley with that sidewise and challenging look, like the look of a frightened but determined woman at a man she has decided to catch.

"I'm sure," O'Malley said gently. "I'm sorry." And he left the man with the carefully waved hair standing next to a tree with the little light of the cigarette gleaming in his hand and walked slowly on. He walked on, feeling sorry for the man, feeling good that he had enough of a fund of sympathy and human feeling so that he could sorrow, even slightly, over a man like that, rouged and roaming the park on a sinful and illicit errand, met for sixty seconds in the middle of the night.

"Say, Buddy," another man, small, and even in the darkness, knobby and gnarled, stepped out from behind a tree. "I want a dime."

O'Malley dug dreamily in his pocket. There was nothing there. "I haven't got a dime," he said.

"I want a dime," the man said. O'Malley saw that his face was dark and savage-looking, not a city face, grimy, hard, gleaming in the light of a distant lamppost. The clothes the man wore were too large and improvised and torn and he continually lifted his arms to slide the sleeves back from his wrist, giving him a supplicant and religious look.

"I told you I haven't got a dime," O'Malley said.

"Gimme a dime!" the little man said loudly. His voice was rough and hoarse, as though he had been shouting in noisy places for years on end.

O'Malley took out his wallet and opened it and showed it to the man. "There's nothing there," he said. "Look."

The man looked. He lifted his arms to free his wrists from his sleeves, looked uneasily over O'Malley's shoulder up at the lamppost. O'Malley put his wallet away.

"Gimme a dollar," the man said.

"I showed you my wallet," O'Malley said. "I haven't got a dollar. I haven't got anything. I'm busted."

The man walked thoughtfully around O'Malley, walking lightly, on his toes, as though he expected to take O'Malley by surprise. "I'll beat you up," he said. "No matter how big you are. I'm a prizefighter. I'm an Indian. I'm a Creek Indian. My name's Billy Elk. Gimme a dime!" He put out his hand as though he was absolutely confident now that he'd convinced O'Malley and the money would be dropped in his hand.

"I'm busted," O'Malley said. "Honest."

Billy Elk circled O'Malley slowly, his large and ragged garments flapping around him. O'Malley stood there, gently willing, in the fragrance and loneliness and peace of the night, to befriend a penniless Creek Indian prizefighter astray far from home in Central Park.

Billy Elk's face creased in thought as he tip-toed around O'Malley. "Give me the wallet," he said suddenly. "I can get a dollar for that."

"It only cost seventy-five cents," O'Malley said.

Billy Elk's face creased in thought again. Only half-consciously now, he walked lightly in a circle around O'Malley, who stood there dreamily, looking up at the towers of the city rearing dark and magnificent against the clear soft sky, with here and there the scattered lights, lust and illness, keeping the city from total sleep in the depths of the night.

Suddenly Billy Elk leaped at him, snatched from his outside breast pocket the fountain pen O'Malley carried there. Billy Elk covered it proudly and lovingly in his gnarled hands, half-bent over it, his dark and savage face lit now by wild satisfaction. "I can get a dollar for this," he said.

"It only cost twenty-five cents," O'Malley said gently. "In the five and ten."

Billy Elk considered the pen in his hands. "All right," he said. "I can get twenty-five."

"Who'll give you twenty-five?" O'Malley asked.

Billy Elk backed up three steps to think about this. He sighed, came up to O'Malley and gave him the pen. O'Malley put the pen in his pocket, smiled in a pleasant, brotherly way at the Indian.

"Give me a dollar!" Billy Elk said harshly.

O'Malley smiled again and patted him on the shoulder. "Good night," he said, and started slowly home.

"If you don't give me the dollar," Billy Elk shouted, keeping pace with him, talking up at him, "I'll report you to the police."

O'Malley stopped. "For what?" he asked, smiling dreamily, pleased that the city and the night had produced, after the one Scotch too many, this wild and tiny creature.

"For talking to a fairy," Billy Elk shouted. "I saw you!"

"What did you see?" O'Malley asked mildly.

"I saw you with that fairy," Billy Elk said. "I'll take you to a policeman. Don't try to get away. I'm a prizefighter. Keep your hands in your pockets!"

"Take me to a policeman," O'Malley said, feeling somehow that it was his duty, as one of the few citizens of the city awake and moving, to be pleasant, hospitable, at the service of visitors, beggars, lunatics, lost children and young girls fled from home.

They walked out of the park in silence. Billy Elk's face was cast in harsh, savage lines, his eyes glittered, his mouth was set. At a corner on Central Park West, a fat policeman was wearily talking to a cab driver slouched in his seat. All the weight of the night hung over them, the deaths in the hospitals, the pain endured, the crimes committed in the dark hours, the hearts broken and the torture of men betrayed by women while the city slept, distilled and poured down in the bleak lamplight over the officer of the law and the tired man at the wheel of the old cab under the lamppost.

O'Malley stopped ten yards away and Billy Elk strode up to the policeman, who was lamenting the fact that his wife had kidney trouble and that his daughter was free with the boys, although she was only in the third term of high school.

The policeman stopped talking when Billy Elk stopped in front of him, and looked at the Indian slowly, mournfully, expecting only trouble, the night's everlasting gift to him.

"Well?" he asked Billy Elk sadly.

Billy Elk looked fleetingly and wildly over his shoulder at O'Malley, then turned back to the policeman. "Is there an Indian Reservation around here?" he asked loudly.

The policeman, grateful that no murder had turned up, no entry, rape, arson, assault, double-parking, committed, thought seriously for a full minute. "No," he said. "I don't know of any Indian Reservation in these parts."

"There's a place called Indian Point," said the cab driver. "It's up the river."

Billy Elk nodded soberly, with ancient dignity, came back to O'Malley and the policeman went on to tell the cab driver that although his daughter was merely sixteen years old she was built in all respects like a full-blooded woman of thirty.

Billy Elk stood in front of O'Malley and smiled, his face suddenly broken by the flash of teeth and gleam of eye into cheerful warm childishness. "See," he said. "I'm not such a bad guy."

He waved and departed into the park, slipping silently and expertly among the trees, like Tecumseh's braves and the slippery, valiant red defenders of Kentucky's bloody ground.

O'Malley walked slowly home, breathing deeply the clear morning air, pleased to be in a city in which Indians roamed the streets and went to great lengths to prove their friendliness and goodness of heart.

IT HAPPENED IN ROCHESTER

THERE WERE FOUR GIRLS sitting on the wooden benches of the agency's front room. They had on big hats and they talked fast and kept their gloves on and made believe they were very happy and high-spirited and every time one of the office doors opened and a man ran from one room to another through the front office the girls would spring up and cry gaily, "Jules, oh, Jules, darling," or "Harry, now Harry, darling," and Jules or Harry would grunt and wave and disappear and the girls would sit down slowly, not so gay, and wouldn't sound happy or high-spirited for five minutes after that.

I sat between two of the girls, trying to look old, keeping my hat on, flipping through the script of *It Happened in Rochester* and making notes in pencil on the margins to show the girls I was not an actor hanging around for a job.

The girl at the switchboard said, "Mr. McCleary," and I stood up. "In the back office, Mr. McCleary."

The girls watched me coldly as I went through the little swinging gate and toward the back office, holding *It Happened in Rochester* negligently under my arm.

There was a little blond man in the back office. He looked like a boy for the first five minutes, clean and red-cheeked, with all his teeth, and bright eyes.

"My name is Sundstrom," he said, shaking hands with me. "And this is Mrs. Sundstrom."

I looked at Mrs. Sundstrom. She was a round, tall woman who had been Sundstrom's assistant in his juggling act, handing him the Indian

clubs and plates and clapping her hands and throwing him a handkerchief after each trick. She smiled at me, a nice, fat, middle-aged
woman with good false teeth, who kept her hand always lightly touching her husband's sleeve. When I looked back at Sundstrom I saw that
he wasn't a boy at all, but this woman's husband, slim, with a boy's
direct, simple appearance, but forty-five years old.

"Sit down, Mr. McCleary," Sundstrom said.

I sat down, finally unhappily taking my hat off.

"Isn't he young to be a director?" Mrs. Sundstrom said, taking a good
look at me with my hat off. She smiled at me, but there was doubt in
her eye.

"I'm twenty-seven," I said, lying for four years. "I got a young look.
When I die I'll have a young look."

Both of them laughed, gently.

"In the theater, dear," Sundstrom said, "age doesn't make any difference. Talent is the thing in the theater. Wouldn't you say so, Mr. Mc-
Cleary?"

"Yes," I said.

"Still," said Mrs. Sundstrom, "a play like *It Happened in Rochester*,
it's full of emotion, it takes an advanced understanding of human nature, very advanced. With all due respect, Mr. McCleary."

I couldn't say that I had an advanced understanding of human nature, so I kept quiet.

"Mr. McCleary is very well recommended, dear," Sundstrom said.
"He's the best one left." He turned to me, speaking seriously. "We tried
many other directors, Mr. McCleary. The best. All the best. Older men.
Some were busy and others didn't like the script."

"They didn't understand the play," Mrs. Sundstrom said. "They want
yelling and shooting and movie stars. A simple, honest play like *It
Happened in Rochester* is beyond them."

"It's a true story," Mr. Sundstrom said. "It happened to me and I
wrote it. I waited twenty years to write this play. It's an absolutely true
story. The girl is a young woman I knew in Rochester. That was before
I met Mrs. Sundstrom." He smiled at her and patted her hand in apology for ever having known another woman.

"That story is absolutely typical," Mrs. Sundstrom said. "It shows how
some women are. People will flock to see it."

I looked at the blue covers of *It Happened in Rochester* and fiddled
with my hat. "Where's the money coming from?" I asked.

"I'm backing it," Sundstrom said. "My own money. Mrs. Sundstrom
and I worked steadily for twenty years. From one end of the country to

another. When vaudeville was good. We made as high as three-fifty a week. We retired comfortably. We bought a house in New Jersey."

"You must visit us," Mrs. Sundstrom said. "Come on a Sunday for the whole day."

"Yes," I said. "Why don't you try a regular producer with the play? Why risk your money?" I asked, trying, then, in the first fifteen minutes, to save them.

"We've tried other producers," Sundstrom said.

"They're like the directors," Mrs. Sundstrom said. "They don't understand real-life drama."

"Maybe," I said, "maybe they know what the public wants. Maybe you oughtn't to take a chance. This'll cost about twelve thousand dollars."

"The public will flock to it," Mrs. Sundstrom said.

"I am willing to take the chance," Sundstrom said, smiling kindly at me. "I have faith in this play. It's an absolutely true story."

"What is your opinion of the play?" Mrs. Sundstrom asked, suspicion for the first time in her voice.

I thought of all the offices I waited in for jobs, and all the "No's," and all the years going past without plays to stage or actors to direct. I thought of my bank account, which read, "Thirty-seven dollars and ninety cents." I looked at the Sundstroms, happy and confident, determined to do the play with me or without me.

I nodded soberly. "It has the ring of an absolutely true story," I said.

The Sundstroms beamed at each other and shook my hand and we agreed to start rehearsals in two weeks and Mrs. Sundstrom asked, "What's your first name?"

"Robert," I said.

"Very nice." She smiled. "It's so silly to call a young boy like you Mr. McCleary."

We shook hands again and I put on my hat and went down and bought a drink.

I cast the play in the little back office. The office belonged to the Lazarus Agency for Actors and Artists, and Jules Lazarus, out of pity or gambler's hope, loaned the Sundstroms the little office and a telephone and the firm's secretary. I sat behind the desk and talked to the actors and actresses and the Sundstroms sat behind me quietly, smiling, Mrs. Sundstrom's hand on her husband's sleeve, trusting me, approving delightedly of every choice I made. From time to time members of their families would come in and silently stand in front of the window and watch and listen. Then they would go out into the hall and confer in whispers with the Sundstroms. Then they'd come back with a grave look of deliberation and take up their old places. I never found out what they said to each other out in the halls because they never questioned any decision I made.

"Young," I heard Mrs. Sundstrom saying to her mother one afternoon, "but definitely talented."

All the Sundstrom relatives who came to stand in front of the window in the Lazarus Agency's back office looked somehow as though they'd never been in New York before.

In the two weeks that I took to cast the play I carefully avoided reading *It Happened in Rochester*. By the time the cast assembled on the stage of the theater for the first rehearsal I had worked myself into a condition of hope.

The Sundstroms and their relatives, now about fifteen in number, came in and sat themselves down along the rear of the dark auditorium as I gave out the sides to the actors.

"Ladies and gentlemen," I said to the actors, "this is a simple, true play, and I would like it to be played simply and truly. Act One, Scene One . . ."

By the time the first act was over the actors were suppressing giggles. In the first act the good but simple hero met and fell in love with the pretty but bad heroine. The pretty heroine told three different men in the first act that she loved them and spent a great deal of her time buying new dresses. The hero at the first act curtain was building dreams of a cottage in the country and children and raises in salary.

I called a recess after the first act, and all the actors fled the stage without looking at me. I sat at the director's table, with my back to the Sundstroms and their families out in the theater. I counted the steampipes along the back wall.

The man who was playing the hero came back for his pipe, passed close to my table, whispered as he passed, "Lemons, Mister? Any lemons today, Mr. McCleary?"

He was a good friend of mine.

"Shut up!" I said.

He bowed soberly, got his pipe, smiled like a juvenile at the Sundstroms out in the theater. They all smiled back.

He passed me on the way out, tamping down his pipe, "Turkeys, Mister, are you interested in turkeys today, Mr. Belasco?"

I sat there, rubbing my eyes, feeling as though I was going to have a headache in five minutes. I thought hard about my rent and my chances of getting anything else for the season. I got up and jumped down from the stage and walked up the aisle toward the fifteen Sundstroms. I didn't know what I was going to say, but I was going to say something.

They were all smiling widely at me as I came toward them. Sundstrom had an automatic pencil with a little light in it and a notebook for suggestions. He hadn't opened the notebook yet.

He patted my shoulder as I stopped next to his seat. "We think it's wonderful," he said, smiling happily, thinking about his words, planned for twenty years, being spoken that afternoon on the stage. "My whole family and Mrs. Sundstrom's whole family think it's wonderful."

And all the fifteen Sundstroms leaned over so I could see them and nodded and smiled at me.

"That's good," I said. "Have you any suggestions?"

Sundstrom patted my shoulder again. "We think it's wonderful," he said.

I went back and started the cast on Act Two, Scene One.

For the next three weeks Sundstrom arrived promptly, with his notebook and automatic pencil with the light in it, for every rehearsal. Always, too, Mrs. Sundstrom sat next to him in the last row of the theater. The number of relatives varied, with the biggest collection of them coming in for the Sunday rehearsals when they were free of whatever work they did during the week.

The actors had given up by now and were just mumbling through their lines and looking for other parts during lunch hour. Sundstrom sat with the notebook. Occasionally he would draw a careful six-pointed star on the first page and then close the book with a decisive snap.

My headache had lasted for two and a half weeks now and I lived on coffee and aspirin, watching through half-closed eyes the weary rambling of the actors around the stage.

"Elspeth," the hero was saying, "I do not think that it is necessary for you to talk in that manner."

"What manner do you mean?" Elspeth asked. She always sat down on this line as though she had been out for five nights steadily before it.

"You know what manner I mean," the hero said.

"I do not understand you," said Elspeth. She was chewing gum. Suddenly I couldn't bear the fact that she was chewing gum.

"Please, for the love of God," I shouted, "throw that gum away!"

There was a hush in the theater. It was the first time a voice had been raised in all three weeks.

"Well," said the heroine, coldly, "there's no need to scream."

She got up deliberately and walked all the way across the stage, chewing slowly. With a large sweeping gesture she stuck the gum on the gilt paint of the proscenium arch. Then she marched slowly and arrogantly back to her place and fell heavily into her chair.

"Move!" I stood up and yelled. "You're supposed to be a young, passionate girl. You're supposed to dance around the stage! You're not supposed to act like a lead safe, darling! I want to see some signs of life! That goes for the whole damned company! We've been conducting a funeral around here for three weeks!"

There was silence for a moment, and then the heroine started to cry. She cried for five minutes with no signs of stopping, so I dismissed the company for the day.

"Tomorrow," I said, "we're going to put some life into this play. We're going to really try."

They all went quietly off the stage, except for the heroine, who was still crying as loudly as ever.

"Now, Robert." It was Sundstrom behind me, with Mrs. Sundstrom right next to him. "Was that absolutely necessary, Robert?"

I looked at them, standing there, puzzled, neatly dressed for Sunday, and I felt like crying, too.

"I wanted to make it move a little faster, Mr. Sundstrom," I said gently. "It's been pretty dead up there."

"We don't think so," Sundstrom said, tapping his wrist with the notebook in which he had not entered one suggestion in three weeks. "We think it's very nice."

"My family thinks it's wonderful," Mrs. Sundstrom said. "And they've been watching for three weeks now."

"It's not wonderful," I said, wanting to help them, to save them. "I think you and I ought to sit down tonight, Mr. Sundstrom, and map out a complete job of rewriting."

"Now, Robert . . ." Sundstrom began, his little-boy face wrinkling up.

"We start with the first act," I said, talking fast, to get it over with, to make the last desperate attempt as easy and as quick as possible, "and we go right through to the third act. We work mostly on the character of Elspeth. She's on the stage all the time, and we've got to make her talk like a human being . . ."

"But that's the way she talked," Sundstrom said. "I knew her for five years and that's the way she talked."

"It's very natural talk," Mrs. Sundstrom said.

"It's terrible, Mr. Sundstrom," I said, being cruel, hoping to save him. "If you leave it this way we're all completely sunk."

"That's what you honestly think, Robert?" he asked.

"That's what I honestly think." I sat down suddenly on the arm of one of the aisle chairs.

"I thought about this play for twenty years," Sundstrom said, his hands going over his eyes, forty-five years old. "It's the absolute truth."

"I think we ought to talk it over with Momma and the boys," Mrs. Sundstrom said.

"You don't mind?" Sundstrom asked me.

"No," I said. "I'll be across the street in the bar."

I walked up the aisle, past the fifteen Sundstroms, who had been listening intently. They watched me silently as I went out.

I had three whiskies before Sundstrom came into the bar. He bought me another drink and put his hand on my shoulder before he said anything.

"They like it," he said. "The family. They think it will draw the public. They don't see anything wrong in it. I agree with them."

"Sure," I said, without knowing exactly what I was saying "sure" to.

"I feel, Robert," he went on, "in the light of what you have just told me, that you are not quite in sympathy at this time with the play."

I shook the ice in my glass.

"It's clear to me now," he said, "that you don't really understand this play. That's natural, Robert. You're a little young for such a play."

"Sure," I said.

"So if you don't mind, I'll relieve you of the responsibility of directing it."

"Who'll direct it?" I asked.

"I will," he said. "After all, it happened to me. I ought to know how it happened."

"Uhuh," I said, remembering the notebook empty of all notes. "I'll give you back as much money as I have left."

"Half," Sundstrom said. "We talked it over and we decided that you should get half your pay. Is that fair?"

"Sure," I said. "Well, I hope *It Happened in Rochester* wins the Pulitzer Prize."

"Thank you, Robert. Come and visit us in New Jersey."

"I will." I waved to him and he went back to the theater to his family and his wife's family and the leading lady who sat down like a lead safe and to the play he had thought of writing for twenty years.

I stayed at the bar.

The reviews were very bad. The *Times* said: *"It Happened in Rochester* opened last night at the Jackson Theater. It was written, produced and directed by Leon Sundstrom."* That was all it said. It was the kindest review.

I didn't go to see it and I didn't see Sundstrom until two weeks later. He was walking along Broadway, very slowly, like an old man. He hadn't shaved and I noticed with surprise that his beard was gray. He had two advertising sandwich boards strapped on him.

"See *It Happened in Rochester"* the boards read. "It Is an Absolutely True Story. Now Playing at the Jackson Theater."

He saw me and I had to stop.

"Hello, Robert," he said, without smiling.

"Hello," I said.

"Do you think this'll help, Robert?" he asked.

"What?"

"These signs. Will it bring people into the theater? Will it help them understand that this is a real true story?"

"Of course," I said.

"The critics didn't understand," he said, shaking his head, the last trace of the little boy gone. "They wrote about it as though it was impossible. I've written them. They won't believe that it actually happened to me. I could introduce them to the girl. She's married now and she has three children. In Rochester. Have you got a cigarette, Robert?"

I gave him a cigarette and lit it for him.

"I kept it running two weeks," he said. "Some people saw it. They liked it very much. They saw it was real life. Critics aren't real people. It cost me eight thousand dollars to keep it running two weeks. I sold my house and my car." He sighed. "I thought word would get around that it was a real life story. I'm going to go back to juggling—if I can get a start. There's not much demand for jugglers these days and I'm not so steady any more. I would like to put enough aside so I could write another play." He never smiled, not once. "Could you lend me two or three cigarettes, Robert?"

I gave him my pack.

"Why don't you come and see the play?" he asked. "I'll get you in for nothing."

"Thanks."

"That's all right. You better come tonight. It's closing tonight. I haven't got any more money to keep it going any more, and the family chipped in as much as they had." He sighed. "I guess I don't understand the theater," he said. "Well, I like to keep moving. I like to give as many people as I can a look at this sign."

"That's a good idea," I said.

"It's not a bad sign, is it?"

"It's a very good sign."

"It's the truth," he said, and walked off, up Broadway, shifting the shoulder straps.

I haven't found another job yet.

THE DRY ROCK

"WE'RE LATE," Helen said, as the cab stopped at a light. "We're twenty minutes late." She looked at her husband accusingly.

"All right," Fitzsimmons said. "I couldn't help it. The work was on the desk and it had to . . ."

"This is the one dinner party of the year I didn't want to be late for," Helen said. "So naturally . . ."

The cab started and was halfway across the street when the Ford sedan roared into it, twisting, with a crashing and scraping of metal, a high mournful scream of brakes, the tinkling of glass. The cab shook a little, then subsided.

The cabby, a little gray man, turned and looked back, worriedly. "Everybody is all right?" he asked nervously.

"Everybody is fine," Helen said bitterly, pulling at her cape to get it straight again after the jolting.

"No damage done," said Fitzsimmons, smiling reassuringly at the cabby, who looked very frightened.

"I am happy to hear that," the cabby said. He got out of his car and stood looking sadly at his fender, now thoroughly crumpled, and his headlight, now without a lens. The door of the Ford opened and its driver sprang out. He was a large young man with a light gray hat. He glanced hurriedly at the cab.

"Why don't yuh watch where the hell yer goin'?" he asked harshly.

"The light was in my favor," said the cabby. He was a small man of fifty, in a cap and a ragged coat, and he spoke with a heavy accent. "It turned green and I started across. I would like your license, Mister."

"What for?" the man in the gray hat shouted. "Yer load's all right. Get on yer way. No harm done." He started back to his car.

The cabby gently put his hand on the young man's arm. "Excuse me, friend," he said. "It is a five-dollar job, at least. I would like to see your license."

The young man pulled his arm away, glared at the cabby. "Aaah," he said and swung. His fist made a loud, surprising noise against the cabby's nose. The old man sat down slowly on the running board of his cab, holding his head wearily in his hands. The young man in the gray hat stood over him, bent over, fists still clenched. "Didn't I tell yuh no harm was done?" he shouted. "Why didn't yuh lissen t' me? I got a good mind to . . ."

"Now, see here," Fitzsimmons said, opening the rear door and stepping out.

"What d'*you* want?" The young man turned and snarled at Fitzsimmons, his fists held higher. "Who asked for *you*?"

"I saw the whole thing," Fitzsimmons began, "and I don't think you . . ."

"Aaah," snarled the young man. "Dry up."

"Claude," Helen called. "Claude, keep out of this."

"Claude," the young man repeated balefully. "Dry up, Claude."

"Are you all right?" Fitzsimmons asked, bending over the cabby, who still sat reflectively on the running board, his head down, his old and swollen cap hiding his face, blood trickling down his clothes.

"I'm all right," the cabby said wearily. He stood up, looked wonderingly at the young man. "Now, my friend, you force me to make trouble. Police!" he called, loudly. "*Police!*"

"Say, lissen," the man in the gray hat shouted. "What the hell do yuh need to call the cops for? Hey, cut it out!"

"*Police!*" the old cabby shouted calmly, but with fervor deep in his voice. "Police!"

"I ought to give it to yuh good." The young man shook his fist under the cabby's nose. He jumped around nervously. "This is a small matter," he shouted, "nobody needs the cops!"

"Police!" called the cabby.

"Claude," Helen put her head out the window. "Let's get out of here and let the two gentlemen settle this any way they please."

"I apologize!" The young man held the cabby by his lapels with both large hands, shook him, to emphasize his apology. "Excuse me. I'm sorry. Stop yelling police, for God's sake!"

"I'm going to have you locked up," the cabby said. He stood there, slowly drying the blood off his shabby coat with his cap. His hair was gray, but long and full, like a musician's. He had a big head for his little shoulders, and a sad, lined little face and he looked older than fifty, to Fitzsimmons, and very poor, neglected, badly nourished. "You have committed a crime," the cabby said, "and there is a punishment for it."

"Will yuh talk to him?" The young man turned savagely to Fitzsimmons. "Will yuh tell him I'm sorry?"

"It's entirely up to him," Fitzsimmons said.

"We're a half hour late," Helen announced bitterly. "The perfect dinner guests."

"It is not enough to be sorry," said the cab driver. "*Police . . .*"

"Say, lissen, Bud," the young man said, his voice quick and confidential, "what's yer name?"

"Leopold Tarloff," the cabby said. "I have been driving a cab on the streets of New York for twenty years and everybody thinks just because you're a cab driver they can do whatever they want to you."

"Lissen, Leopold," the young man pushed his light gray hat far back on his head. "Let's be sensible. I hit yer cab. All right. I hit you. All right."

"What's all right about it?" Tarloff asked.

"What I mean is, I admit it, I confess I did it, that's what I mean. All right." The young man grabbed Tarloff's short ragged arms as he spoke, intensely. "Why the fuss? It happens every day. Police are unnecessary. I'll tell yuh what I'll do with yuh, Leopold. Five dollars, yuh say, for the fender. All right. And for the bloody nose, another pound. What do yuh say? Everybody is satisfied. Yuh've made yerself a fiver on the transaction; these good people go to their party without no more delay."

Tarloff shook his arms free from the huge hands of the man in the gray hat. He put his head back and ran his fingers through his thick hair and spoke coldly. "I don't want to hear another word. I have never been so insulted in my whole life."

The young man stepped back, his arms wide, palms up wonderingly. "I insult him!" He turned to Fitzsimmons. "Did you hear me insult this party?" he asked.

"Claude!" Helen called. "Are we going to sit here all night?"

"A man steps up and hits me in the nose," Tarloff said. "He thinks he makes everything all right with five dollars. He is mistaken. Not with five hundred dollars."

"How much d'yuh think a clap in the puss is worth?" the young man growled. "Who d'yuh think y'are—Joe Louis?"

"Not ten thousand dollars," Tarloff said, on the surface calm, but quivering underneath. "Not for twenty thousand dollars. My dignity."

"His dignity!" the young man whispered. "For Christ's sake!"

"What do you want to do?" Fitzsimmons asked, conscious of Helen glooming in the rear seat of the cab.

"I would like to take him to the station house and make a complaint," Tarloff said. "You would have to come with me, if you'd be so kind. What is your opinion on the matter?"

"Will yuh tell him the cops are not a necessity!" the young man said hoarsely. "Will yuh tell the bastidd?"

"Claude!" called Helen.

"It's up to you," Fitzsimmons said, looking with what he hoped was an impartial, judicious expression at Tarloff, hoping he wouldn't have to waste any more time. "You do what you think you ought to do."

Tarloff smiled, showing three yellow teeth in the front of his small and childlike mouth, curved and red and surprising in the lined and weatherbeaten old hackie's face. "Thank you very much," he said. "I am glad to see you agree with me."

Fitzsimmons sighed.

"Yer drivin' me crazy!" the young man shouted at Tarloff. "Yer makin' life impossible!"

"To you," Tarloff said with dignity, "I talk from now on only in a court of law. That's my last word."

The young man stood there, breathing heavily, his fists clenching and unclenching, his pale gray hat shining in the light of a street lamp. A policeman turned the corner, walking in a leisurely and abstracted manner, his eyes on the legs of a girl across the street.

Fitzsimmons went over to him. "Officer," he said, "there's a little job for you over here." The policeman regretfully took his eyes off the girl's legs and sighed and walked slowly over to where the two cars were still nestling against each other.

"What are yuh?" the young man was asking Tarloff, when Fitzsimmons came up with the policeman. "Yuh don't act like an American citizen. What are yuh?"

"I'm a Russian," Tarloff said. "But I'm in the country twenty-five years now, I know what the rights of an individual are."

"Yeah," said the young man hopelessly. "Yeah . . ."

The Fitzsimmonses drove silently to the police station in the cab, with Tarloff driving slowly and carefully, though with hands that shook on the wheel. The policeman drove with the young man in the young man's Ford. Fitzsimmons saw the Ford stop at a cigar store and the young man jump out and go into the store, into a telephone booth.

"For three months," Helen said, as they drove, "I've been trying to get Adele Lowrie to invite us to dinner. Now we've finally managed it. Perhaps we ought to call her and invite the whole party down to night court."

"It isn't night court," Fitzsimmons said patiently. "It's a police station. And I think you might take it a little better. After all, the poor old man has no one else to speak up for him."

"Leopold Tarloff," Helen said. "It sounds impossible. Leopold Tarloff. Leopold Tarloff."

They sat in silence until Tarloff stopped the cab in front of the police station and opened the door for them. The Ford with the police-man and the young man drove up right behind them and they all went in together.

There were some people up in front of the desk lieutenant, a dejected-looking man with long mustaches and a loud, blonde woman who kept saying that the man had threatened her with a baseball bat three times that evening. Two Negroes with bloody bandages around their heads were waiting, too.

"It will take some time," said the policeman. "There are two cases ahead of you. My name is Kraus."

"Oh, my," said Helen.

"You'd better call Adele," Fitzsimmons said. "Tell her not to hold dinner for us."

Helen held her hand out gloomily for nickels.

"I'm sorry," Tarloff said anxiously, "to interrupt your plans for the evening."

"Perfectly all right," Fitzsimmons said, trying to screen his wife's face from Tarloff by bending over to search for the nickels in his pocket.

Helen went off, disdainfully holding her long formal skirt up with her hand, as she walked down the spit- and butt-marked corridor of the police station toward a pay telephone. Fitzsimmons reflectively watched her elegant back retreat down the hallway.

"I am tired," Tarloff said. "I think I will have to sit down, if you will excuse me." He sat on the floor, looking up with a frail apologetic smile on his red face worn by wind and rain and traffic-policemen. Fitzsim-mons suddenly felt like crying, watching the old man sitting there among the spit and cigarette butts, on the floor against the wall, with his cap off and his great bush of musician's gray hair giving the lie to the tired, weathered face below it.

Four men threw open the outside doors and walked into the police station with certainty and authority. They all wore the same light-gray hats with the huge flat brims. The young man who had hit Tarloff greeted them guardedly. "I'm glad you're here, Pidgear," he said to the man who, by some subtle mixture of stance and clothing, of lift of eyebrow and droop of mouth, announced himself as leader.

They talked swiftly and quietly in a corner.

"A Russian!" Pidgear's voice rang out angrily. "There are 10,000 cab drivers in the metropolitan area, you have to pick a Russian to punch in the nose!"

"I'm excitable!" the young man yelled. "Can I help it if I'm excitable? My father was the same way; it's a family characteristic."

"Go tell that to the Russian," Pidgear said. He went over to one of the three men who had come in with him, a large man who needed a shave and whose collar was open at the throat, as though no collar could be bought large enough to go all the way around that neck. The large man nodded, went over to Tarloff, still sitting patiently against the wall.

"You speak Russian?" the man with the open collar said to Tarloff.

"Yes, sir," Tarloff said.

The large man sat down slowly beside him, gripped Tarloff's knee confidentially in his tremendous hairy hand, spoke excitedly, winningly, in Russian.

Pidgear and the young man who had hit Tarloff came over to Fitzsimmons, leaving the other two men in the gray hats, small, dark men with shining eyes, who just stood at the door and looked hotly on.

"My name is Pidgear," the man said to Fitzsimmons, who by now was impressed with the beautiful efficiency of the system that had been put into motion by the young driver of the Ford—an obviously legal mind like Pidgear, a man who spoke Russian, and two intense men with gray hats standing on call just to see justice done, and all collected in the space of fifteen minutes. "Alton Pidgear," the man said, smiling professionally at Fitzsimmons. "I represent Mr. Rusk."

"Yeah," said the young man.

"My name is Fitzsimmons."

"Frankly, Mr. Fitzsimmons," Pidgear said, "I would like to see you get Mr. Tarloff to call this whole thing off. It's an embarrassing affair for all concerned; nobody stands to gain anything by pressing it."

Helen came back and Fitzsimmons saw by the expression on her face that she wasn't happy. "They're at the soup by now," she said loudly to Fitzsimmons. "Adele said for us to take all the time we want, they're getting along fine."

"Mr. Rusk is willing to make a handsome offer," Pidgear said. "Five dollars for the car, five dollars for the nose . . ."

"Go out to dinner with your husband," Helen muttered, "and you wind up in a telephone booth in a police station. 'Excuse me for being late, darling, but I'm calling from the 8th precinct, this is our night for street-fighting.'"

"Sssh, Helen, please," Fitzsimmons said. He hadn't eaten since nine that morning and his stomach was growling with hunger.

"It was all a mistake," Pidgear said smoothly. "A natural mistake. Why should the man be stubborn? He is being reimbursed for everything, isn't he? I wish you would talk to him, Mr. Fitzsimmons; we don't want to keep you from your social engagements. Undoubtedly," Pidgear said, eyeing their evening clothes respectfully, "you and the madam were going to an important dinner party. It would be too bad to spoil an important dinner party for a little thing like this. Why, this whole affair is niggling," he said, waving his hand in front of Fitzsimmons' face. "Absolutely niggling."

Fitzsimmons looked over to where Tarloff and the other Russian were sitting on the floor. From Tarloff's face and gestures, even though he was talking in deepest Russian, Fitzsimmons could tell Tarloff was still as firm as ever. Fitzsimmons looked closely at Rusk, who was standing looking at Tarloff through narrow, baleful eyes.

"Why're you so anxious?" Fitzsimmons asked.

Rusk's eyes clouded over and his throat throbbed against his collar with rage. "I don't want to appear in court!" he yelled. "I don't want the whole goddamn business to start all over again, investigation, lawyers, fingerprints . . ."

Pidgear punched him savagely in the ribs, his fist going a short distance, but with great violence.

"Why don't you buy time on the National Broadcasting System?" Pidgear asked. "Make an address, coast to coast!"

Rusk glared murderously for a moment at Pidgear, then leaned over toward Fitzsimmons, pointing a large blunt finger at him. "Do I have to put my finger in your mouth?" he whispered hoarsely.

"What does he mean by that?" Helen asked loudly. "Put his finger in your mouth? Why should he put his finger in your mouth?"

Rusk looked at her with complete hatred, turned, too full for words, and stalked away, with Pidgear after him. The two little men in the gray hats watched the room without moving.

"Claude?" Helen began.

"Obviously," Fitzsimmons said, his voice low, "Mr. Rusk isn't anxious for anyone to look at his fingerprints. He's happier this way."

"You picked a fine night!" Helen shook her head sadly. "Why can't we just pick up and get out of here?"

Rusk, with Pidgear at his side, strode back. He stopped in front of the Fitzsimmonses. "I'm a family man," he said, trying to sound like one. "I ask yuh as a favor. Talk to the Russian."

"I had to go to Bergdorf Goodman," Helen said, too deep in her own troubles to bother with Rusk, "to get a gown to spend the evening in a police station. 'Mrs. Claude Fitzsimmons was lovely last night in blue velvet and silver fox at Officer Kraus's reception at the 8th Precinct. Other guests were the well-known Leopold Tarloff, and the Messrs. Pidgear and Rusk, in gray hats. Other guests included the Russian Ambassador and two leading Italian artillerymen, also in gray hats.'"

Pidgear laughed politely. "Your wife is a very witty woman," he said.

"Yes," said Fitzsimmons, wondering why he'd married her.

"Will yuh for Christ's sake *ask?*" Rusk demanded. "Can it hurt yuh?"

"We're willing to do our part," Pidgear said. "We even brought down a Russian to talk to him and clear up any little points in his own language. No effort is too great."

Fitzsimmons' stomach growled loudly. "Haven't eaten all day," he said, embarrassed.

"That's what happens," Pidgear said. "Naturally."

"Yeah," said Rusk.

"Perhaps I should go out and get you a malted milk," Helen suggested coldly.

Fitzsimmons went over to where Tarloff was sitting with the other Russian. The others followed him.

"Are you sure, Mr. Tarloff," Fitzsimmons said, "that you still want to prosecute?"

"Yes," Tarloff said promptly.

"Ten dollars," Rusk said. "I offer yuh ten dollars. Can a man do more?"

"Money is not the object." With his cap Tarloff patted his nose which was still bleeding slowly and had swelled enormously, making Tarloff look lopsided and monstrous.

"What's the object?" Rusk asked.

"The object, Mr. Rusk, is principle."

"*You* talk to him," Rusk said to Fitzsimmons.

"All right," Officer Kraus said, "you can go up there now."

They all filed in in front of the lieutenant sitting high at his desk.

Tarloff told his story, the accident, the wanton punch in the nose.

"It's true," Pidgear said, "that there was an accident, that there was a slight scuffle after by mistake. But the man isn't hurt. A little swelling in the region of the nose. No more." He pointed dramatically to Tarloff.

"Physically," Tarloff said, clutching his cap, talking with difficulty because his nose was clogged, "physically that's true. I am not badly hurt. But in a mental sense . . ." He shrugged. "I have suffered an injury."

"Mr. Rusk is offering the amount of ten dollars," Pidgear said. "Also, he apologizes; he's sorry."

The lieutenant looked wearily down at Rusk. "Are you sorry?" he asked.

"I'm sorry," said Rusk, raising his right hand. "On the Bible, I swear I'm sorry."

"Mr. Tarloff," the lieutenant said, "if you wish to press charges, there are certain steps you will have to take. A deposition will have to be taken. Have you got witnesses?"

"Here," Tarloff said with a shy smile at the Fitzsimmonses.

"They will have to be present," the lieutenant said sleepily.

"Oh, God," Helen said.

"A warrant will have to be sworn out, there must be a hearing, at which the witnesses must also be present . . ."

"Oh, God," Helen said.

"Then the trial," said the lieutenant.

"Oh, God!" Helen said loudly.

"The question is, Mr. Tarloff," said the lieutenant, yawning, "are you willing to go through all that trouble?"

"The fact is," Tarloff said unhappily, "he hit me in the head without provocation. He is guilty of a crime on my person. He insulted me. He did me an injustice. The law exists for such things. One individual is not to be hit by another individual in the streets of the city without legal punishment." Tarloff was using his hands to try to get everyone, the Fitzsimmonses, the lieutenant, Pidgear, to understand. "There is a principle. The dignity of the human body. Justice. For a bad act a man suffers. It's an important thing . . ."

"I'm excitable," Rusk shouted, "If yuh want, yuh can hit me in the head."

"That is not the idea," Tarloff said.

"The man is sorry," the lieutenant said, wiping his eyes, "he is offering you the sum of ten dollars; it will be a long, hard job to bring this man to trial; it will cost a lot of the taxpayers' money; you are bothering these good people here who have other things to do. What is the sense in it, Mr. Tarloff?"

Tarloff scraped his feet slowly on the dirty floor, looked sadly, hopefully, at Fitzsimmons. Fitzsimmons looked at his wife, who was glaring at Tarloff, tapping her foot sharply again and again. Fitzsimmons looked back at Tarloff, standing there, before the high desk, small, in his ragged coat and wild gray hair, his little worn face twisted and grotesque with the swollen nose, his eyes lost and appealing. Fitzsimmons shrugged sadly. Tarloff drooped inside his old coat, shook his head wearily, shrugged, deserted once and for all before the lieutenant's desk, on the dry rock of principle.

"O.K.," he said.

"Here," Rusk brought the ten-dollar bill out with magical speed.

Tarloff pushed it away. "Get out of here," he said, without looking up.

No one talked all the way to Adele Lowrie's house. Tarloff opened the door and sat, looking straight ahead, while they got out. Helen went to the door of the house and rang. Silently, Fitzsimmons offered Tarloff the fare. Tarloff shook his head. "You have been very good," he said. "Forget it."

Fitzsimmons put the money away slowly.

"Claude!" Helen called. "The door's open."

Fitzsimmons hated his wife, suddenly, without turning to look at her. He put out his hand and Tarloff shook it wearily.

"I'm awfully sorry," Fitzsimmons said. "I wish I . . ."

Tarloff shrugged. "That's all right," he said. "I understand." His face, in the shabby light of the cab, worn and old and battered by the streets of the city, was a deep well of sorrow. "There is no time. Principle." He laughed, shrugged. "Today there is no time for anything."

He shifted gears and the taxi moved slowly off, its motor grinding noisily.

"Claude!" Helen called.

"Oh, shut up!" Fitzsimmons said as he turned and walked into Adele Lowrie's house.

PRIZE FOR PROMISE

They stood in their raincoats, with the rain still dripping off them, and their shoes making sodden marks on the rug, outside the railing that divided the office in two. Behind the railing the girl at the switchboard kept saying, "Mr. Van Meter's office. Mr. Van Meter is not in. He is expected at three o'clock. Mr. Van Meter is not casting." From time to time she looked up at the four soaked prize-winners without curiosity or surprise.

"It's ten minutes past three," Miss Tittle said. She rubbed at her nose with her handkerchief and dabbed at her eyes. She kept crying and blowing her nose because she had walked all the way from Grand Central in the cold. "I do wish he'd come. I have to get back to Stamford. I go on at six o'clock."

"Are you playing in something at Stamford?" Schwartz asked politely.

"No," Miss Tittle said. "I work in the library. I go on at six o'clock."

"I see," Schwartz nodded and smiled at her and shifted his weight from one side to the other and leaned more heavily on his cane.

"That's a nice cane," Midkiff said.

"It cost ninety-five cents," said Schwartz. "I have rheumatism."

"Oh," said Midkiff. He nodded. Dowd, leaning with elaborate negligence on the railing, nodded too. Miss Tittle moved over on the little bench against the wall and Schwartz sat down. He stretched his feet out stiffly and sighed. "This is some weather for rheumatism," he said.

Nobody said anything for a while except the girl at the switchboard, who said, "This is *not* Circle seven-niun-seven-three-one."

"Maybe they changed their minds," Midkiff said. He was a big chunky man, with large, workman's hands, scarred by tools, twisted from labor. He had been a farmer and later a plasterer, and it showed in his hands. "After all," his gesture bespoke logic, "there's no reason they should give us a thousand dollars apiece."

"You're joking," Dowd said nervously.

"That's right," Midkiff said, looking down at Dowd. Midkiff was bald, although he was only thirty-three, and he seemed much older than the others. "That's right, little boy." He unbuttoned his coat and flapped it to shake some of the rain out of it. It was a light coat, even though it was midwinter, and the rain had soaked through it. The cloth was badly worn around the buttons and buttonholes and ravelled at the cuffs. "Playwrights in the movies," Midkiff said, "wear high hats." He looked around him gravely, his heavy Russian eyebrows contracted. "We're not dressed for the occasion. What're you going to do with your money?" he asked Dowd.

Dowd licked his upper lip nervously. He had a little sandy mustache that he wet again and again. "I'm going to move to the city," he said. "To Bank Street. I live in Brooklyn now. It's hard to find the proper atmosphere for work in Brooklyn."

He lived with his wife's family. His wife worked for an insurance company and her family hated Dowd because he lived off her salary in the same upstairs room his wife had had before she married him. They sent him on errands, to the store to get butter and potatoes, to pay the telephone bills, to complain about the assessments. Every time he sat down at the typewriter his mother-in-law would try to think up some errand she could send him on.

"I work very carefully," Dowd said apologetically. "It takes me a long time to finish anything." He had had two stories in *Story*. They had taken him three months apiece and he'd got twenty-five dollars for them and his brother-in-law had grimly figured this out on a weekly basis.

"I need a quiet place. Among artists. Where people understand the necessities of creative work." He smiled nervously.

Midkiff nodded.

"Mr. Van Meter is not in," the girl at the switchboard said with great finality.

Midkiff began to walk up and down in the little space between the railing and the wall. "I intend to make certain improvements on my country house," he said.

He lived in a semi-detached six-room house in Astoria with his wife and three children. "We've been burning egg crates in the furnace." He shook his head. "Unsatisfactory . . . I intend to experiment with coal for the furnace, with the thousand dollars. Also, I intend to experiment with the gas company. I will pay them and see what happens."

Twice producers had bought plays from Midkiff and nearly put them on. Plastering was behind him, definitely.

"I wish it was the summertime," Midkiff said.

"Me too," said Schwartz, rubbing his knee. He was only twenty-nine, but he moved like an old man, and he'd written one success, his first play, and three failures, and the critics kept saying he was finished. "I'm going to New Mexico, Albuquerque. The air's warm, but clear. I have to be away from cold, dampness." He rubbed his knee vigorously. "You know, it's damned nice of the Foundation to put up the dough for something like this."

"I think it's admirable," Miss Tittle said. She giggled.

"Six thousand dollars for Art," Midkiff said. "From the Steel Kings. Conscience money."

The girl behind the switchboard glanced at Midkiff. He waved his hand in a courtly greeting.

"Mr. Van Meter is not in," she said coldly into the phone.

Midkiff stood over Miss Tittle. "What're you going to do with your money?"

She blushed, blew her nose. Midkiff waited patiently. "I'm putting my money in the bank," she said soberly. "For my trousseau. When I get married."

Midkiff nodded. "Are you engaged?"

Miss Tittle drew in her breath through her soaked handkerchief. "No," she said.

Midkiff looked at Dowd, shrugged. He turned and walked to the open door and looked out down the hall.

"I'm honestly surprised," Schwartz said, "that they picked me. I thought everybody agreed I was finished." He laughed a little. "Maybe the Foundation doesn't read John Mason Brown. That's the nice thing about Albuquerque, it's a long distance from John Mason Brown." He laughed again, but nobody laughed with him. He tapped his cane slowly against the sole of his shoe. He was a little, ugly man, with heavy glasses, but when he smiled he looked pleasant and sad and eager to please.

Johnny Marble hurried through the door. "Am I late?" he asked Midkiff anxiously.

"No," Midkiff said. "Mr. Van Meter is out eating lunch, dining off rich roasts, with beautiful women, whose names are known from coast to coast."

"I had to rehearse two actors who're going in tomorrow night," Marble said, lighting a cigarette with quick, sharp movements. Marble was the stage manager for a play that was struggling along from week to week. "If we last the month out, it'll be a miracle."

Midkiff took him by the hand, led him up to Miss Tittle. "Miss Tittle, another thousand-dollar genius, Mr. Marble."

Miss Tittle said, "How do you do?" and Marble shook hands with her. He had very long black hair and he left his collar open to show that he was not really a stage manager, but a poet.

"She comes from Stamford," Midkiff said.

"That's a damned funny place for a playwright to come from," Marble said. He was constantly speaking in what he hoped were witty generalities, like Noel Coward, and he was very dashing with women.

"She's a librarian," Midkiff said.

"Wonderful place for a playwright," Marble said, smiling widely, "a library. Tried and proved materials." He laughed.

"What do you feel so happy about?" Midkiff asked.

Marble doused his cigarette against a filing cabinet. "Do you want the truth?"

"I want the truth," Midkiff said.

"I don't feel so happy," Marble said.

Gentling strode in, his deep mustache glistening with rain, his black hat like a sombrero dashingly to one side of his head.

"The sixth and most promising playwright," Marble said. "He's as tall as Robert Sherwood."

Miss Tittle giggled and Gentling looked fiercely at her, standing near the door, his long dirty coat cape-like and romantic on his shoulders. Miss Tittle stopped giggling.

"Ah," Gentling said. He came from Mississippi and his speech was very dramatic. "The beggars've come early to wait in line for the cold Presbyterian charity of the Fountain Foundation." There was nothing to say to this, and the playwrights kept silence. Gentling posed effectively against the filing cabinet.

"A thousand dollars," Marble said. "I never had a thousand dollars in one lump in my whole life. Can you believe it?"

"Playwriting," Midkiff said, "is the avocation of a rich man, like shooting grouse."

Marble laughed and repeated it under his breath so he could write it down when he got outside. Miss Tittle giggled.

"Who's she?" Gentling asked.

"Miss Tittle," Marble said. "She's a librarian."

"Pleased to meet you," Gentling said, with fierce Southern charm, lifting his black sombrero, with holes along the creases. "Remain a librarian."

Miss Tittle flushed and wiped her nose with her handkerchief and swung around on the bench so she didn't have to face Gentling.

"Frankly," Gentling said, "I'm very much surprised that they're giving me a prize. It's the first time in the modern theater anything but garbage has received any notice. They like tricks and nonsense, the concoctions of Park Avenue note-takers."

"Where do you live?" Midkiff asked.

"Twenty-third Street."

"All right," Midkiff said.

"No good writing can come out of New York City," said Gentling. Nobody asked him to explain this. He brushed his mustache up at the ends. "I'm leaving for Natchez tomorrow," he announced. He was going over to the Pennsylvania Station immediately to buy his ticket, before he got drunk again. He wasn't going to drink in Natchez. He was going to sit down and write eight hours a day and . . . He shook his head, looked around him fiercely, strode over to the switchboard. "I've waited long enough," he said. "Where the hell's Van Meter?"

"Hey," Marble ran over to him anxiously. "Go easy. I owe this thousand bucks already."

"Mr. Van Meter is out," the girl said coldly.

"Who the hell does he think he is?" Gentling said loudly to the other playwrights. "If he said three o'clock, let him keep his appointments like a gentleman."

"Sssh," Marble said soothingly.

"A fat old man throws a crumb to Art," Gentling called, "and thinks he's entitled to act like the King of England! The day of patrons has passed, young lady!" He waved his finger at the girl at the switchboard. "I'm leaving. If you want me, you know my address." He started for the door.

Van Meter came in, his face flushed with hurry. "I'm so sorry I kept you waiting," he said, out of breath. "Please come in."

He held the little gate open, smiled at Miss Tittle, followed the playwrights into his private office—tall, well-groomed, his face the best color a barber could make it, looking fifteen years under his fifty-five. His office was paneled in light pine and there were pictures of celebrities of stage and screen, all the pictures lovingly inscribed, "To Ralph" or "To dearest Ralph." There was a picture of Herbert Hoover, looking very grave and solid among the actresses.

"Be seated, ladies and gentlemen," Van Meter said, with a hospitable wave of his hand, as he sat down behind the large ash-colored desk. "It appears that I've been appointed by the Foundation to make, well—something of a speech. . . ."

The playwrights sat silently watching him.

"I don't know what to say," Van Meter went on, a little uneasy because of the dead silence he was talking into, "except that the Foundation is proud to be able to help six persons of such talent. . . ." He looked hopefully at Schwartz. Schwartz was tapping on the sole of his shoe with his cane and looking thoughtfully at Herbert Hoover.

"We think the American theater cannot die," Van Meter said, embarrassed now at this noble statement which had seemed fine to him when he put it down in his notes at lunch, "if it is in the hands of young people like you." He looked at Midkiff, who slowly rotated his hand on his bald head.

"It is unfortunate," Van Meter went on, his voice faster and higher now, "that none of the six plays was considered quite ready for production by the managers who made the choice for the Foundation." Gentling laughed harshly and Van Meter jumped a little in his seat, but went on quickly. "What we want you to understand is that the prizes have been given you for your promise—rather than . . ." He shook his head, wishing he hadn't had three Manhattans at luncheon. "A small investment in the future of the American drama is the way we look at it—in a way. . . ."

"When do we get the money?" It slipped out of Dowd's mouth almost by itself. Dowd looked around him apologetically, took out his handkerchief, wiped his lips.

Van Meter drew a deep breath. He smiled with strained warmth at Dowd. "In due time, my friend, in due time. . . ."

"Sorry," Dowd muttered.

"It is the purpose of the Foundation," Van Meter went on, a low note of desperation creeping into his voice, "to get the greatest good—that is, artistically speaking, of course, out of the money."

Gentling laughed again. Van Meter looked at him curiously. Gentling leaned back easily in his chair, negligently lifted his torn, soaked shoe to full view as he crossed his leg over on the other knee.

"We want to make sure," Van Meter said, his hands clenching, "that the money helps you people in the best way to write more and better plays."

"Do we get paid in cash or by check?" Midkiff asked.

Van Meter smiled at Midkiff, making believe Midkiff had been witty.

"In order to give you young people the longest possible time free from financial worry, the Foundation has decided to split the prizes into weekly payments."

Gentling's foot came down to the heavy rug on the floor with a soft boom. "Oh, my God," Dowd said miserably.

"Now, the Foundation has no desire to impose any particular standard of living upon you, but they have decided that—" Van Meter hesitated, spoke in louder tones, "that on twenty-five dollars a week it is possible to live fairly comfortably and do your work." The playwrights looked past his shoulders at the pictures of the movie stars on the walls. "Also—when you divide one thousand by twenty-five, you find it lasts about ten months. Frankly, ladies and gentlemen, it is impossible for a good play to be written in less than ten months. You all know the saying, 'A play is not written, it is rewritten.'"

"Do we get paid in checks or cash?" Midkiff asked. "I don't know anybody who would cash a twenty-five dollar check for me."

"I'm sure an arrangement can be made, Mr. Midkiff," Van Meter said smoothly, hating Midkiff, who kept rubbing his head every time Van Meter called them "young people."

"That's good," Midkiff said.

"You see," Van Meter smiled with obvious charm, "you see, we've dealt with artists before, and we have the highest respect for them. But we understand them. They're children. Talented, wonderful children. Especially about money . . . I'm sure in ten months you'll all be very grateful for this arrangement."

He stood up and everyone else stood up. Van Meter nodded at them, smiling. Miss Tittle nodded back. They stood in the pine-paneled office, among the pictures of the immortals, Van Meter neat and healthy, Dowd gray-faced, Miss Tittle sniffling, Gentling lordlike in his indifference, Schwartz thoughtful, Marble wondering if his creditors would wait, a dark air clearly blowing on their spirits, no one able to get gracefully out of the office.

"Yes," Van Meter said, happy now that it was all over, "yes, indeed."

"Well," said Midkiff finally, wrapping his thin, raveled, sopping coat around him with dignity, like a war flag, "I don't know what you bastards're going to do with your money, but I'm going out to buy a Packard." He made a little bow to Van Meter, put on his hat and strode magnificently out of the office, toward Astoria.

The other prize-winners followed quickly.

LEMKAU, POGRAN AND BLAUFOX

THE MACHINE OPERATORS, the cutters, the boys from the shipping room had departed for the night. One light burned in the partitioned-off showroom of Lemkau, Pogran & Blaufox, Knit Goods, Girdles, Brassières, Corsets of All Descriptions. It was quiet as only a factory can be quiet twenty minutes after the machines have stopped, the girls gone, and the lights been extinguished. Through the soft new dark, outside the windows, came the distant sounds of taxis and people hurrying home to dinner. A low wail rose from the elevator shafts as the elevators dropped toward the ground floor.

In the showroom, Lemkau and Pogran sat, not looking at each other and not talking. They heard the elevator doors and a lively, skipping step approaching along the hall. The door swung open and Maurice Blaufox bustled in, singing softly, "I didn't know what time it was." He stopped when he saw them. His hands went up in cordial surprise as he stood there, fresh from the barber, his face pink and well conditioned, his pince-nez swinging smartly on a black ribbon, his spats immaculate. "Lemkau! Pogran!" he cried. "My partners. You don't work hard enough all day, you got to work at night, too!" He laughed heartily. "You can't make money day and night, boys. You got to live from time to time." He slapped them on the back, one with each hand. He was only five feet five inches tall, but standing next to his partners, Maurice Blaufox was a large man, full of juice and confidence.

"We were not making money," Pogran said.

"In a manner of speaking," Lemkau said, "we were waiting for you, Maurice."

"Ah!" Blaufox threw up his hands. "I have overdrawn my expense account. Give me a lecture, boys," he said good-naturedly. "Sometimes the money slips through the fingers with a buyer on the hook."

"It is not the expense account," Pogran said.

Blaufox lit a cigar. "Some day I will take you boys out for the night on the expense account. Dinner in Longchamps, a musical comedy with speculator's tickets, a night club." He laughed. "All on the firm's money. Just like you were a buyer. Wouldn't that be nice?"

"That would be very nice," Pogran said.

"Thank you very much," said Lemkau.

"So, boys," Blaufox asked, waving the cigar, "so what is it?"

Lemkau ran his hand over his bald head, ruffling the few gray hairs still clinging there. "Maurice," he began in a stiff voice. "It is this way . . ." He stopped.

"Anything you want to say to me," Blaufox said kindly, "I will listen to. Anything my friends have on their mind."

"Maurice," Pogran broke in, much louder than he expected, "it is about that girl, that woman, that lady from the French Follies."

Blaufox's face settled into hard lines under the barber's finish, and he put away his cigar. "Excuse me," he said, starting toward the door. "I have an appointment."

"Maurice," Lemkau cried, following him, "please don't take that attitude! What is the use of taking an attitude like that?"

"Listen to us." Pogran held Blaufox's elbow. "Five minutes of your time. We are all friends, we can listen to each other."

Blaufox stopped, his hand on the door. He said nothing, but he didn't move.

"We have seen checks," Pogran said, "made out to her, signed by Maurice Blaufox. We saw you in the Chesterfield Restaurant with her. We found out the telephone number you leave on rainy afternoons is the Hotel Lowrie on Twenty-third Street. We saw you go in and come out with Anna Gerenson."

"My partners," Blaufox said bitterly. "The Secret Police. Dick Tracy and his friends."

"We don't hold it against you," Lemkau said. "Not one little tiny bit."

"On the contrary," Pogran said. "Quite on the contrary."

"So," Blaufox said. "Assuming, for the sake of argument, it is true. So?"

"She is a fine-looking woman," Lemkau said. He sighed.

"A first-class figure of a woman," Pogran said.

"All my life," said Lemkau, "I have dreamed of a woman like that."

The expression on Blaufox's face changed. A slight hint of satisfaction, of complacency, crept over his lips. "She is not a bad-looking girl," he said. "She is really an actress, you know, not just a showgirl. Only there are no parts for her. The theater is dying; there are six thousand actresses out of work."

"Yes," said Pogran and Lemkau.

"She has to make a living, don't she?" Blaufox asked. "The French Follies is merely temporary."

"Yes," said his partners. "Yes, yes."

"The truth is"—Blaufox sat down and crossed his neat legs—"the whole truth is I contribute to the support of her apartment. I won't hide it from you, because, after all, we have been partners for sixteen years. Why should we hide things from each other?"

"Oh," Lemkau sighed, "oh, the life a salesman leads."

"I do not keep her on the expense account," Blaufox said. "Please understand that from the beginning."

There was quiet in the showroom. The faraway noise of New York on a winter evening sifted through the windows.

"I am not doing anything wrong," Blaufox continued in a troubled voice. "I still love my wife. But she is a sick woman, Bertha. She's fat, she has upset glands. I take care of her, hand and foot. I would die for Bertha. I spend a fortune of money on her. But"—he flicked the cigar that he had put down on the showroom table off into a wastebasket— "the fact is she is away six months of the year for her health. Arizona in the winter for her asthma. New Hampshire in the summer for her hay fever. A man gets lonely. He can't spend all his time with buyers."

"We are not blaming you." Lemkau went over and patted Blaufox on the shoulder. "Believe me."

Blaufox tilted his head and examined his partners closely for the first time that evening. "What is the reason," he asked, "for bringing this subject up?"

Lemkau looked at Pogran, who in turn looked down at the carpet and shuffled his feet uneasily.

"Kindly talk up," Blaufox said. "We have gone so far, let us go further."

"You are a lucky man," Lemkau said.

Blaufox shrugged.

"In your way, Maurice," said Lemkau. "Other people are lonely, too."

"Poor Lemkau." Blaufox shook his head. "A man should not live alone in a hotel room. I have told you that three thousand times."

"Maurice . . ." Lemkau stopped and looked despairingly at Pogran.

"Maurice," Pogran said, "I will get to the hilt of the matter. You have a girl. She is a fine girl. We admire her. It would be a great pleasure to us if from time to time we could all go out together. A purely social evening. Say, every other Thursday. It would break up the month." He talked hurriedly, his hands in his pockets, his eyes fixed on the third button of Blaufox's vest. "Dinner in a nice sea-food restaurant, three friends, and a handsome woman."

"Oh," said Blaufox.

"It would be pleasant," Lemkau said, "to make the acquaintance of a person we would not normally make the acquaintance of. A lady of the theatrical profession, for example, who—oh, my God!" he said, and dropped, shaking, into a chair.

They sat in silence, looking out of the window.

"Never mind," Lemkau said after a time. "I did not really expect— I am a little, funny-looking man, and she wouldn't want to be seen with me."

"You are not so funny-looking, Lemkau," Blaufox said loyally.

"Don't tell me lies. I am little and I look like a rabbit. Where is my hat?" Lemkau reached absently toward the hatrack. "It was a wild idea from the beginning," he said to Pogran. "Blaufox is tall, he is merry, he knows what to say to women, he makes jokes and drinks cocktails. Me?" He shrugged, and put on his hat.

"I wish I had your talent," Blaufox said. "There is not another knit-goods designer in the whole country like Adolph Lemkau. An artist!"

Lemkau laughed. "An artist. The artist goes home by himself. Pogran, you coming down with me?"

Pogran took his hat off the rack.

"Wait a minute," Blaufox said. "I tell you what. We will go and talk to the lady. We will let her decide whether or not she wants to have dinner with us."

"That is fair," Pogran said. "That is altogether equitable."

They marched out together, forgetting to lock the showroom door.

"Rest assured," Pogran said solemnly in the elevator, "that all expenses will be divided three ways."

"The firm," Lemkau suggested. "Why can't we put it on the books of the firm?"

They all nodded in agreement and took a taxi to the Lowrie Hotel.

Pogran and Lemkau waited downstairs in the lobby after Blaufox had left them to go up to Anna Gerenson's room. They sat, flanked by palms, making believe they were calm, blushing when the clerk looked at them.

"It is no go," Lemkau said after a while. "I have that feeling in my bones. Frankly . . ."

Blaufox came out of the elevator and walked toward them with dignity. "Kindly follow me," he said, and they got into the elevator. "She wants to look at you," he said.

Lemkau's mouth drooped. "What is the use?" he asked as they got out on the eighth floor.

Anna shook hands with them gravely and said, "Please be seated, gentlemen."

They sat, looking at the floor.

"Mr. Blaufox has told me about you gentlemen," Anna said. She looked at Lemkau. "Mr. Blaufox told me you was afraid you was so awful-looking I wouldn't want to be seen with you. I don't think you're awful-looking at all."

Lemkau beamed at her. "Thank you, Miss Gerenson," he said. "Very kind of you, indeed."

She turned to Pogran. "Mr. Blaufox tells me you're a family man, Mr. Pogran."

Pogran sighed. "True," he said. "Absolutely true. A wife and three daughters."

"He lives in a house on Albemarle Road in Brooklyn," Blaufox said. "A first-class property."

"If the truth must be told, Miss Gerenson," Pogran said, "I am as alone as a cat in an alley. For the last sixteen years, Miss Gerenson, I have worked morning, noon, and night . . ."

"He is the brains of the business," Blaufox said. "No exaggeration. A human dynamo."

"In those sixteen years my wife has drifted apart from me." Pogran looked at the ceiling and spoke with his head tilted back. "She attends lectures, she is on committees, she reads new books. Frankly, she is ashamed of me, Miss Gerenson. Also, my daughters. They go to New York University."

"That's a very nice school," Anna said politely.

"When I stay in town at night to work," Pogran said, "my wife and my daughters feel much better."

Anna shook her head, reflecting. "You are very nice guys," she said at last. "Gentlemen." She smiled at them, showing her fine white teeth. "What do you say, boys," she said, "we all have dinner together?"

They nodded briskly at each other, and Blaufox patted Anna's cheek, standing on his toes to do so. "A celebration is in order!" He picked up the telephone and got the bar and said, "Champagne. A nice medium-priced bottle of champagne with four glasses in Room 804." He turned to his partners as he put the phone down. "On the expense account," he said, laughing.

They laughed with him, their voices ringing out loud and cheerful in the room.

"Would you gentlemen object," Anna asked, "if I invited in two girl friends after dinner? Two very nice ladies."

Lemkau and Pogran looked at each other. "No," said Pogran, "we wouldn't object."

They watched Anna as she picked up the phone and asked for a Chelsea number.

"Isn't this nice?" Lemkau asked Blaufox. "Isn't this wonderful?"

DINNER IN A GOOD RESTAURANT

They sat in the good restaurant, with the wineglasses between them, and the waiter coming over every five minutes and regarding the table critically, with one eye squinted a little, and from time to time putting a dab of butter on their plates.

"One thing," the woman said. "One thing I'm no longer going to stand for. Just one thing."

The man smiled and drank slowly from his wineglass. He put the wineglass down and looked across at her and one eyebrow went up to add to the smile something that was more than the smile. The woman was plain, with a long face, and she looked forty-five, even though she had on a little tilted white straw hat, like a funny little basket, and a blue veil over her eyes, and a smart suit over soft white lace and excellent corsets.

"You always smile," the woman said. "Every time I tell you there's one thing I won't stand, you smile."

"That's right, dear," the man said, the eyebrow up again.

"This time, darling," the woman said, putting down her knife and fork carefully for a moment, "this time I mean it."

"Sure," the man said. He cut neatly at the steak on his plate. "Sure, dear."

The woman picked up her knife and fork and went on eating. She moved her bony hands with sharp, accurate energy. She had on long sleeves, but her arms showed thin and middle-aged anyway, and when she swallowed, the wrinkles on her throat moved and made you notice how thin she was there, too.

"You haven't worked one day in fifteen years and I haven't said a thing, darling, but . . ."

The waiter leaned over. "The bottle is killed, Mr. Hood," he said. "Another?"

"Darling," the man said, "do you want any more wine?"

"Yes." The woman finished her glass.

The waiter walked swiftly down the room to get another bottle of Burgundy.

"I've been watching," the woman said. "Every time Laura Chapin comes into a room, your face lights up. And sometime before the end of the evening you're not in the room and she's not in the room. At the same time." The man went on eating, calmly, enjoying himself, his healthy red cheeks moving regularly, his teeth doing justice to the meal. "And her dresses've gotten to show more and more of her week by week. And there's plenty to show."

The man laughed. "There sure is," he said. He smiled as he talked, but he knew he was hurting the lank woman across the table from him, and was glad he was doing it. "She certainly is a solid woman."

"We don't have to go there to play bridge," the woman said slowly. "That house has been boring me for a long time. It might not be a bad idea to stop going there altogether."

"Anything you say, dear." The man didn't stop smiling. "My one ambition, dear, as everyone knows, is to make you happy."

"Don't talk like that," the woman said. "Don't make fun."

"The wine, sir," the waiter said. The two people watched him as he poured. "Will Mrs. Hood have some more steak?" the waiter asked, leaning over, with waiter's imploring hands.

"Yes, please."

They watched while the waiter served them with more steak, thick and rare, and poured a little sauce over it, and delicately portioned out potatoes and green peas with a spoon and fork in one hand.

The woman watched the man as he cut at the food on his table. "You eat," the woman said. "You certainly do eat."

The man nodded, smiling. He had a soft full little mouth that was always curled close to a smile on his red full face. He had blond, little-boy eyebrows, and clear blue eyes that helped the smile.

"You never have indigestion. You eat like a horse, darling, and you're never sick, and you don't even get real fat. You're just round and firm, darling. At forty-three." The woman smiled back at him. "A better man than you would be living on soda crackers and bromo-seltzer by this time if he'd eaten and drunk like you."

The man nodded in sober mockery. "I lived a careful youth. I was a poor honest boy and I lived a poor honest life." He chuckled. "Until I learned better, dear. At the age of fifteen, dear."

The waiter came over and poured some more wine.

"Good?" the waiter asked. "You like it, Mr. Hood?"

"Fine," said the man. "It's a very nice bottle."

The waiter nodded solemnly and backed off.

"What would you do, darling?" the woman leaned forward over the table and looked sharply at her husband. He noticed again that she had short sparse lashes, and her eyes had a dry look to them. "What would you do," she was saying, "if I said, 'no more money; you go out and earn your money.' Where would you eat then?"

"The same restaurants, dear," the man said.

"You wouldn't go out and work, would you, darling?"

The man grinned at his wife. "Oh, no. There'd be people who'd buy me dinners. I have good friends."

"You're no good." The woman wiped her mouth with her napkin, her fingers holding it tightly. "You're no good at all."

"Yes, dear," the man said. He drank half his glass of wine.

"You've lived off women all your life, darling. Your Aunt Margaret supported you for seventeen years, with you wearing clothes from Brooks Brothers and eating in good restaurants and never lifting a finger to help yourself; not doing anything more than visit her on Thursday afternoons and remember her birthday."

"April," the man said. "April ninth. My dear Aunt Margaret."

"And your cousin," the woman said. "She and her famous husband."

The man went on eating, slowly, with care and love for the food.

"There were fine things going on in your family while your cousin was alive," the woman said. "And you did more for it than just remembering her birthday, darling."

"Don't speak badly of the dead, dear," the man said, the same smile on his face. "When you're dead, you wouldn't want people to sit around a nice restaurant full of nice polite people and speak badly of you."

"When I'm dead," the woman said, "people will sit in restaurants and say, 'What a fool!' and they'll be partly right and partly wrong because they don't know the whole story."

The man patted her hand playfully. "Don't be vulgar, dear," he said. "Not in a good restaurant."

"It's a lucky thing for you," the woman said, "there are women in this world, women with incomes."

"You bet," said the man.

"Every time you got a job you found one excuse or another to get out of it. You're a man who's managed to avoid all responsibilities. You're forty-three now, and you've eaten better than anyone else in New York, darling, and done less work than anybody else in the country."

"I've led a successful life." He picked up the wine bottle and made a little laughing gesture with it before pouring another glassful for himself.

The waiter came and took away the dirty plates and put down their dessert and poured coffee for them and went away.

"You're a pimp, darling," the woman said, looking directly at her husband. He stirred his coffee with a regular slow motion. "You've been a pimp for good meals and French wines for twenty-five years." She stirred her own coffee. Her voice was low and even and did not rise above the level of diners' talk in the room. "Six years ago you were in love with Edith Bleeker, the only time you were in love in your whole life, and you let her go, because you'd have to work to support yourself with her and the work you have to do to support yourself with me you don't mind doing—too much."

"It's a privilege," he said, the smile set on his face.

"I lost my last shred of respect for you," the woman said. "For six years, darling, I've been living with you, disgusted with you."

"So you've told me," the man said. "Dinner conversation in the Hood family."

"Where were you this afternoon?" For the first time the woman's voice was raised. "With whom? Tell the truth."

The man smiled. "The Metropolitan Museum of Art. With six sailors."

The woman finished her coffee and took out her powder puff and mirror and powdered her nose. She went back to the earnest conversational dinner tone. "At least if you felt ashamed once in a while. But you don't. You took money from your Aunt Margaret and your cousin and God knows how many other women and now me, and you've never been ashamed for a minute. You ought to get up and hit me in the face for calling you the names I call you, darling. But you won't. You just sit there, eating good dinners, taking it all. You have no pride, darling. You're a man in one respect, only."

The man grinned and leaned over, took her hand in his and kissed it calmly. He dropped her hand and took out a twenty-dollar bill and laid it on the waiter's silver tray, over the check, without looking at the check.

"But there's one thing I won't stand for," the woman said. "I mean it. You'll be out in the cold."

"I don't know what you're talking about." The man spoke with deliberate amusement.

"I just won't stand for it," the woman said desperately, knowing she would stand for it and knowing that he knew it. "I'm warning you here and now."

"Sure," the man said. He took three dollars change from the twenty-dollar bill. The waiter bowed to him.

They got up and started out of the restaurant.

"What do you want to do now?" the man asked.

"I want to go home."

"So early?"

"So early," the woman said, grimly, holding his arm tightly. He bowed ironically to her and held the restaurant door open for her.

"In my will," the woman said flatly, "I'm cutting you off without a cent. You won't have a penny. When I'm dead and I'll have no need for you any more. Let's walk fast."

Arm in arm, they walked toward home.

THE LAMENT OF MADAM RECHEVSKY

THE TELEPHONE RANG and rang through the silken room, tumbled with sleep, lit here and there by the morning sunlight that broke through the hangings in little bright patches. Helen sighed and wriggled in the bed, and, still with her eyes closed, reached out and picked up the phone. The ringing stopped and Helen sighed in relief and wearily put the phone to her ear.

The sound of weeping, deep and bitter, welled along the wires.

"Hello, Momma," Helen said, still with her eyes closed.

"Helen," Madam Rechevsky said. "How are you, Helen?"

"Fine, Momma." Helen stretched desperately under the covers. "What time is it?"

"Nine o'clock." Helen winced, closed her eyes more tightly. "Momma, darling," she said gently, "why must you call so early?"

"When I was your age," Madam Rechevsky said, weeping, "I was up at six in the morning. Working my fingers to the bone. A woman thirty-eight shouldn't spend her whole life sleeping."

"Why do you always say thirty-eight?" Helen protested. "Thirty-six. Why can't you remember—thirty-six!"

"On this subject, Helen, darling," Madam Rechevsky said coldly, through her tears, "I am absolutely definite."

Helen finally opened her eyes, slowly, with effort, looked wearily up at the sun-streaked ceiling. "Why're you crying, Momma?"

There was a pause over the wires, then the weeping started afresh, on a new high pitch, deep, despairing, full of sorrow.

"Tell me, Momma," Helen said.

"I must go to Poppa's grave. You must come right downtown and take me to Poppa's grave."

Helen sighed. "Momma, I have three different places I have to be today."

"My own child!" Madam Rechevsky whispered. "My own daughter! Refuses to take her mother to the grave of her own father."

"Tomorrow," Helen pleaded. "Can't you make it tomorrow?"

"Today!" Madam Rechevsky's voice reached across Manhattan high and tragic, as in the old days, when she strode on the stage and discovered that her stepmother was wearing her dead mother's jewels. "I woke up this morning and a voice spoke to me. 'Go to Abraham's grave! Immediately! Go to the grave of your husband!'"

"Momma," Helen said gently. "Poppa's been dead fifteen years. How much difference can one day make to him?"

"Never mind," Madam Rechevsky said, with magnificent, resounding resignation. "Forgive me if I have troubled you on this trifling matter. Go. Go to your appointments. Go to the beauty parlor. Go to the cocktail parties. I will take the subway to your dead father's grave."

Helen closed her eyes. "I'll pick you up in an hour, Momma."

"Yes," said Madam Rechevsky decisively. "And please don't wear that red hat. For your father's sake."

"I won't wear the red hat." Helen lay back and wearily put the phone back on its pedestal.

"This is a fine car to be going to a cemetery in," Madam Rechevsky was saying as they drove out through Brooklyn. She sat up straight as a little girl in school, savagely denying her seventy-three years with every line of her smart seal coat, every expert touch of rouge, every move of her silken legs. She looked around her contemptuously at the red-leather and chromium of Helen's roadster. "A sport model. A great man lies buried, his relatives come to visit him in a cream-colored convertible automobile."

"It's the only car I have, Momma." Helen delicately twisted the wheel in her eloquent, finely gloved hands. "And I'm lucky they haven't taken it away from me by now."

"I told you that was the wrong man for you, in the first place, didn't I?" Madam Rechevsky peered coldly at her daughter, her deep gray eyes flashing and brilliant, rimmed beautifully in mascara, with a touch of purple. "Many years ago I warned you against him, didn't I?"

"Yes, Momma."

"And now—now you are lucky when you collect alimony six months out of twelve." Madam Rechevsky laughed bitterly. "Nobody ever listened to me, not my own children. Now they suffer."

"Yes, Momma."

"And the theater." Madam Rechevsky waved her hands fiercely. "Why aren't you on the stage this season?"

Helen shrugged. "The right part hasn't come along this season."

"The right part!" Madam Rechevsky laughed coldly. "In my day we did seven plays a year, right part or no right part."

"Momma, darling . . ." Helen shook her head. "It's different now. This isn't the Yiddish Theater and this isn't 1900."

"That was a better theater," Madam Rechevsky said loudly. "And that was a better time."

"Yes, Momma."

"Work!" Madam Rechevsky hit her thighs emphatically with her two hands. "We worked! The actor acted, the writer wrote, the audience came! Now—movies! Pah!"

"Yes, Momma."

"Even so, you're lazy." Madam Rechevsky looked at herself in her handbag mirror to make sure that the violence of her opinions had not disarranged her face. "You sit back and wait for alimony and even so it doesn't come. Also . . ." She examined her daughter critically. "The way you dress is very extreme." She squinted to sharpen the image. "But you make a striking impression. I won't deny that. Every one of my daughters makes a striking impression." Madam Rechevsky shook her head. "But nothing like me, when I was a little younger . . ." She sat back and rode in silence. "Nothing like me . . ." she murmured. "Nothing like me, at all . . ."

Helen walked briskly beside her mother through the marble-crowded cemetery, their feet making a busy scuffle along the well-kept gravel walks. Madam Rechevsky clutched a dozen yellow chrysanthemums in her hands and on her face was a look of anticipation, almost pleasure, as they approached the grave.

"Perhaps . . ." A bearded old man in holy black, all very clean and pink-faced came up to them and touched Madam Rechevsky's arm. "Perhaps you would like me to make a prayer for the dead, lady?"

"Go away!" Madam Rechevsky pulled her arm away impatiently. "Abraham Rechevsky does not need professional prayers!"

The old man bowed gently, spoke softly. "For Abraham Rechevsky I will pray for nothing."

Madam Rechevsky stopped, looked at the man for a moment. Her cold gray eyes smiled a little. "Give the old man a dollar, Helen," she said and touched the man's arm with royal condescension.

Helen dug in her bag and produced a dollar and the old man bowed gravely again.

Helen hurried after her mother.

"See," Madam Rechevsky was muttering as she charged along. "See. Dead fifteen years and still he is famous, all over the world. I bet that old man hasn't offered to pray for anyone free for twenty-five years." She turned on Helen. "And yet you didn't want to come!" She strode on, muttering, "All over the world."

"Don't walk so fast, Momma," Helen protested. "Your heart . . ."

"Don't worry about my heart." Madam Rechevsky stopped, put her arm out sharply to stop her daughter. "We are in sight. You stay here. I want to go to the grave alone." She spoke without looking at Helen, her eyes on the massive gray granite tombstone thirty yards away, with her husband's name on it and underneath his, space for her own. She spoke very softly. "Turn around, Helen, darling. I want this to be private. I'll call you when I'm ready for you."

She walked slowly toward the tombstone, holding the chrysanthemums before her like a gigantic bride's bouquet. Helen sat on a marble bench near the grave of a man named Axelrod, and turned her head.

Madam Rechevsky approached her husband's grave. Her face was composed, the lips set, the chin high, out of the smart seal collar. She knelt gracefully, placed the chrysanthemums in a compact spray of yellow on the cold earth against the granite. She patted the flowers lightly with one hand to make a pattern more pleasing to the eye, and she stood up. She stood without speaking, looking at the even, dead, winter-brown grass that spread across the grave.

Slowly, still looking at the faded grass, she took off first one glove, then the other and absently stuffed them into a pocket, leaving her white and brilliantly manicured hands bare.

Then she spoke.

"Abraham!" she cried, her voice ringing and imperious and fiercely intimate. "Abraham!" the proud, useful voice echoed and re-echoed among the marble on the small rolling hills of the cemetery. "Abraham, listen to me!"

She took a deep breath, and disregarding the formal stone, spoke directly to the earth beneath her. "You've got to help me, Abraham. Trouble, trouble . . . I'm old and I'm poor and you've left me alone for fifteen years." The resonance and volume had gone from her voice, and she spoke quietly, with the little touch of impatience that comes to women's voices when they are complaining to their husbands. "Money. All your life you never made less than fifteen hundred dollars a week and now they bother me for rent." Her lips curled contemptuously as she thought of the miserable men who came to her door on the first of each month. "You rode in carriages, Abraham. You always owned at least four horses. Wherever you went everybody always said, 'There goes Abraham Rechevsky!' When you sat down to eat, fifty people always sat down with you. You drank wine with breakfast, dinner and supper, and fifty people always drank it with you. You had five daughters by me and God knows how many by other women and every one of them was dressed from Paris from the day she could walk. You had six sons and each one of them had a private tutor from Harvard College. You ate in the best restaurants in New York, London, Paris, Budapest, Vienna, Berlin, Warsaw, Rio de Janeiro. You ate more good food than any other man that ever lived. You had two overcoats at one time lined with mink. You gave diamonds and rubies and strings of pearls to enough women to make up three ballet companies! Sometimes you were paying railroad fare for five women at one time crossing the country after you, on tour. You ate and you drank and you always had a baby daughter in your lap till the day you died, and you lived like a king of the earth, in all respects." Madam Rechevsky shook her head at the grave. "And I? Your wife? Where is the rent?"

Madam Rechevsky paced deliberately to the foot of the grave and addressed herself even more directly to her husband. "A king, to the day you died, with a specialist from Vienna and three trained nurses and four consulting doctors for an old man, seventy-seven, who had exhausted himself completely with eating and drinking and making love. Buried . . . Buried like a king. Three blocks long. The line behind your coffin was three blocks long on Second Avenue at the funeral, thousands of grown men and women crying into their handkerchiefs in broad daylight. And I? Your wife? Forgotten! Money spent, theater gone, husband dead, no insurance . . . Only one thing left—children."

Madam Rechevsky smiled coldly at her husband. "And the children —like their father. Selfish. Thinking of themselves. Silly. Doing crazy things. Getting mixed up with ridiculous people. Disastrous. The whole world is disastrous, and your children have led disastrous lives. Alimony, movies, trouble with girls, never any money, never . . . Relatives are dying in Germany. Five hundred dollars would have saved them. No five hundred dollars. And I am getting older day by day and the ones that can help won't, and the ones that want to help, can't.

Three times a week the dressmaker calls me with old bills. Disastrous! Why should it happen to me?"

Once more, for a moment, Madam Rechevsky's voice went high and clear and echoed among the small graveyard hills. "Why should it happen to me? I worked for you like a slave. I got up at five o'clock in the morning. I sewed the costumes. I rented the theaters. I fought with the authors about the plays. I picked the parts for you. I taught you how to act, Abraham. The Great Actor, they said, the Hamlet of the Yiddish Theater, people knew your name from South Africa to San Francisco, the women tore off their gowns in your dressing room. You were an amateur before I taught you; on every line you tried to blow down the back of the theater. I worked on you like a sculptor on a statue. I made you an artist. And in between . . ." Madam Rechevsky shrugged ironically. "In between I took care of the books, I hired the ushers, I played opposite you better than any leading lady you ever had, I gave you a child every two years and fed all the others other women gave you the rest of the time. With my own hands I polished the apples they sold during intermission!"

Madam Rechevsky slumped a little inside her fashionable seal coat, her voice sank to a whisper. "I loved you better than you deserved and you left me alone for fifteen years and I'm getting older and now they bother me for rent. . . ." She sat down on the cold earth, on the dead winter grass covering the grave. "Abraham," she whispered, "you've got to help me. Please help me. One thing . . . One thing I can say for you —whenever I was in trouble, I could turn to you. Always. Help me, Abraham."

She was silent a moment, her bare hands outspread on the grass. Then she shrugged, stood up, her face more relaxed, confident, at peace, than it had been in months. She turned away from the grave and called.

"Helen, darling," she called. "You can come here now."

Helen left the marble bench on the plot of the man named Axelrod and walked slowly toward her father's grave.

PATTERN OF LOVE

"I'll go into a nunnery," Katherine said, holding her books rigidly at her side, as they walked down the street toward Harold's house. "I'll retire from the world."

Harold peered uneasily at her through his glasses. "You can't do that," he said. "They won't let you do that."

"Oh, yes, they will." Katherine walked stiffly, looking squarely in front of her, wishing that Harold's house was ten blocks farther on. "I'm a Catholic and I can go into a nunnery."

"There's no need to do that," said Harold.

"Do you think I'm pretty?" Katherine asked. "I'm not looking for compliments. I want to know for a private reason."

"I think you're pretty," Harold said. "I think you're about the prettiest girl in school."

"Everybody says so," Katherine said, worrying over the "about," but not showing it in her face. "Of course I don't really think so, but that's what everybody says. You don't seem to think so, either."

"Oh, yes," said Harold. "Oh, yes."

"From the way you act," Katherine said.

"It's hard to tell things sometimes," Harold said, "by the way people act."

"I love you," Katherine said coldly.

Harold took off his glasses and rubbed them nervously with his handkerchief. "What about Charley Lynch?" he asked, working on his glasses, not looking at Katherine. "Everybody knows you and Charley Lynch . . ."

"Don't you even like me?" Katherine asked stonily.

"Sure. I like you very much. But Charley Lynch . . ."

"I'm through with him." Katherine's teeth snapped as she said it. "I've had enough of him."

"He's a very nice fellow," Harold said, putting his glasses on. "He's the captain of the baseball team and he's the president of the eighth grade and . . ."

"He doesn't interest me," Katherine said, "any more."

They walked silently. Harold subtly increased his speed as they neared his house.

"I have two tickets to Loew's for tonight," Katherine said.

"Thanks," said Harold. "I've got to study."

"Eleanor Greenberg is giving a party on Saturday night." Katherine subtly slowed down as she saw Harold's house getting nearer. "I can bring anyone I want. Would you be interested?"

"My grandmother's," Harold said. "We're going to my grandmother's on Saturday. She lives in Doylestown, Pennsylvania. She has seven cows. I go there in the summertime. I know how to milk the cows and they . . ."

"Thursday night," Katherine said, speaking quickly. "My mother and father go out on Thursday night to play bridge and they don't come home till one o'clock in the morning. I'm all alone, me and the baby, and the baby sleeps in her own room. I'm all alone," she said in harsh invitation. "Would you like to come up and keep me company?"

Harold swallowed unhappily. He felt the blush come up over his collar, surge under his glasses. He coughed loudly, so that if Katherine noticed the blush, she'd think it came from the violence of his coughing.

"Should I slap you on the back?" Katherine asked eagerly.

"No, thank you," Harold said clearly, his coughing gone.

"Do you want to come up Thursday night?"

"I would like to very much," Harold said, "but my mother doesn't let me out at night yet. She says when I'm fifteen . . ."

Katherine's face set in grim lines. "I saw you in the library at eight o'clock at night, Wednesday."

"The library's different," Harold said weakly. "My mother makes an exception."

"You could tell her you were going to the library," Katherine said. "What's to stop you?"

Harold took a deep, miserable breath. "Every time I lie my mother knows it," he said. "Anyway, you shouldn't lie to your mother."

Katherine's lip curled with cold amusement. "You make me laugh," she said.

They came to the entrance to the apartment house in which Harold lived, and halted.

"In the afternoons," Katherine said, "a lot of times nobody's home in the afternoons but me. On your way home from school you could whistle when you pass my window, my room's in front, and I could open the window and whistle back."

"I'm awful busy," Harold said, noticing uneasily that Johnson, the doorman, was watching him. "I've got baseball practice with the Montauk A.C. every afternoon and I got to practice the violin a hour a day and I'm behind in history, there's a lot of chapters I got to read before next month and . . ."

"I'll walk home every afternoon with you," Katherine said. "From school. You have to walk home from school, don't you?"

Harold sighed. "We practice in the school orchestra almost every afternoon." He stared unhappily at Johnson, who was watching him with the knowing, cynical expression of doormen who see everyone leave and everyone enter and have their own opinions of all entrances and exits. We're working on 'Poet and Peasant' and it's very hard on the first violins and I never know what time we'll finish and . . ."

"I'll wait for you," Katherine said, looking straight into his eyes, bitterly, not hiding anything. "I'll sit at the girls' entrance and I'll wait for you."

"Sometimes," said Harold, "we don't get through till five o'clock."

"I'll wait for you."

Harold looked longingly at the doorway to the apartment house, heavy gilt iron and cold glass. "I'll admit something," he said. "I don't like girls very much. I got a lot of other things on my mind."

"You walk home from school with Elaine," Katherine said. "I've seen you."

"O.K.," Harold shouted, wishing he could punch the rosy, soft face, the large, coldly accusing blue eyes, the red, quivering lips. "O.K.!" he shouted, "I walk home with Elaine! What's it to you? I like to walk home with Elaine! Leave me alone! You've got Charley Lynch. He's a big hero, he pitches for the baseball team. I couldn't even play right field. Leave me alone!"

"I don't want him!" Katherine shouted. "I'm not interested in Charley Lynch! I hate you!" she cried, "I hate you! I'm going to retire to a nunnery!"

"Good!" Harold said. "Very good!" He opened the door of the apartment house. Johnson watched him coldly, unmoving, knowing everything.

"Harold," Katherine said softly, touching his arm sorrowfully, "Harold—if you happen to pass my house, whistle 'Begin the Beguine.' Then I'll know it's you. 'Begin the Beguine,' Harold . . ."

He shook her hand off, went inside. She watched him walk without looking back at her, open the elevator door, go in, press a button. The door closed finally and irrevocably behind him. The tears nearly came, but she fought them down. She looked miserably up at the fourth-story window behind which he slept.

She turned and dragged slowly down the block toward her own house. As she reached the corner, her eyes on the pavement before her, a boy spurted out and bumped her.

"Oh, excuse me," said the boy. She looked up.

"What do you want, Charley?" she asked coldly.

Charley Lynch smiled at her, forcing it. "Isn't it funny, my bumping into you? Actually bumping into you. I wasn't watching where I was going, I was thinking of something else and . . ."

"Yeah," said Katherine, starting briskly toward home. "Yeah."

"You want to know what I was thinking about?" Charley asked softly, falling in beside her.

"Excuse me," Katherine said, throwing her head back, all tears gone, looking at a point thirty feet up in the evening sky. "I'm in a hurry."

"I was thinking of that night two months ago," Charley said quickly. "That party Norah O'Brien gave. That night I took you home and I kissed your neck. Remember that?"

"No," she said. She walked at top speed across the street corner, down the row of two-story houses, all alike, with the children playing potsy and skating and leaping out from behind stoops and going, "A-a-a-a-a-a-h," pointing pistols and machine guns at each other. "Pardon me, I've got to get home and mind the baby; my mother has to go out."

"You weren't in a hurry with Harold," Charley said, his eyes hot and dry, as he matched her step for step. "You walked slow enough with him."

Katherine looked briefly and witheringly at Charley Lynch. "I don't know why you think that's your business," she said. "It's my own affair."

"Last month," Charley said, "you used to walk home with me."

"That was last month," Katherine said loudly.

"What've I done?" Pain sat clearly on Charley Lynch's face, plain over the freckles and the child's nose with the bump on it where a baseball bat had once hit it. "Please tell me what I've done, Katie."

"Nothing," said Katherine, her voice bored and businesslike. "Absolutely nothing."

Charley Lynch avoided three small children who were dueling seriously with wooden swords that clanged on the garbage-pail cover shields with which they protected themselves. "I must have done something," he said sorrowfully.

"Nothing!" Katherine's tones were clipped and final.

"Put 'em up, Stranger!" a seven-year-old boy said right in front of Charley. He had a pistol and was pointing it at a boy who had another pistol. "This town ain't big enough for you and me, Stranger," said the first little boy as Charley went around him, keeping his eyes on Katherine. "I'll give you twenty-four hours and then come out shooting."

"Oh, yeah?" said the second little boy with the pistol.

"Do you want to go to the movies tonight?" Charley asked eagerly, rejoining Katherine, safely past the Westerners. "Cary Grant. Everbody says it's a very funny picture."

"I would love to go," said Katherine, "but I've got to catch up on my reading tonight."

Charley walked silently among the dueling, wrestling, gun-fighting children. Katherine walked slightly ahead of him, head up, pink and round and rosy-kneed, and Charley looked at the spot on her neck where he had kissed her for the first time and felt his soul drop out of his body.

He laughed suddenly, falsely. Katherine didn't even look at him. "I was thinking about that feller," Charley said. "That Harold. What a name—Harold! He went out for the baseball team and the coach threw him out the first day. The coach hit three balls at him and they went right through his legs. Then he hit another one at him and it bounced and smacked him right in the nose. You should've seen the look on that Harold's face." Charley chuckled shrilly. "We all nearly died laughing. Right square in the nose. You know what all the boys call him? 'Four-eyed Oscar.' He can't see first base from home plate. 'Four-eyed Oscar.' Isn't that funny?" Charley asked miserably.

"He's very nice about you," Katherine turned into the vestibule of her own house. "He tells me he admires you very much; he thinks you're a nice boy."

The last trace of the manufactured smile left Charley's face. "None of the other girls can stand him," Charley said flatly. "They laugh at him."

Katherine smiled secretly, remembering the little girls' conversations in the wardrobes and at recess.

"You think I'm lying!" Charley shouted. "Just ask."

Katherine shrugged coolly, her hand on the inner door leading to her house. Charley moved close to her in the vestibule gloom.

"Come to the movies with me," he whispered. "Please, Katie, please . . ."

"As I told you," she said, "I'm busy."

He put his hand out gropingly, touched hers. "Katie," he begged.

She pulled her hand away sharply, opened the door. "I haven't the time," she said loudly.

"Please, please . . ." he whispered.

Katherine shook her head.

Charley spread his arms slowly, lunged for Katherine, hugged her, tried to kiss her. She pulled her head savagely to the side, kicked him sharply in the shins. "Please . . ." Charley wept.

"Get out of here!" Katherine slapped his chest with her hands.

Charley backed up. "You used to let me kiss you," he said. "Why not now?"

"I can't be bothered," Katherine pulled down her dress with sharp, decisive, warning movements.

"I'll tell your mother," Charley shouted desperately. "You're going around with a Methodist! With a Protestant!"

Katherine's eyes grew large with fury, her cheeks flooded with blood, her mouth tightened. "Now get out of here!" she said. "I'm through with you! I don't want to talk to you. I don't want you to follow me around!"

"I'll walk wherever I goddamn please!" Charley yelled.

"I heard what you said," Katherine said. "I heard the word you used."

"I'll follow whoever I goddamn please!" Charley yelled even louder. "This is a free country."

"I'll never talk to you as long as I live," Katherine stamped for emphasis, and her voice rang off the mailboxes and doorknobs of the vestibule. "You bore me! I'm not interested in you. You're stupid! I don't like you. You're a big idiot! Go home!"

"I'll break his neck for him!" Charley shouted, his eyes clouded, his hands waving wildly in front of Katherine's face. "I'll show him! A violin player! When I get through with him you won't be so anxious to be seen with him. Do you kiss him?"

"Yes!" Katherine's voice clanged triumphantly. "I kiss him all the time. And he really knows how to kiss! He doesn't slobber all over a girl, like you!"

"Please," Charley whimpered, "please . . ." Hands out gropingly, he went toward Katherine. She drew back her arm coldly, and with all her round, solid, well-nourished eighty-five pounds, caught him across the face, turned, and fled up the stairs.

"I'll kill him!" Charley roared up the stairwell. "I'll kill that violinist with my bare hands!"

The door slammed in answer.

"Please tell Mr. Harold Pursell," Charley said soberly to Johnson, the doorman, "that a certain friend of his is waiting downstairs; he would like to see him, if it's convenient."

Johnson went up in the elevator and Charley looked with grim satisfaction around the circle of faces of his eight friends, who had come with him to see that everything was carried out in proper order.

Harold stepped out of the elevator, walked toward the boys grouped at the doorway. He peered curiously and short-sightedly at them, as he approached, neat, clean, white-fingered, with his glasses.

"Hello," Charley stepped out and faced Harold. "I would like to talk to you in private."

Harold looked around at the silent ring of faces, drained of pity, brimming with punishment. He sighed, realizing what he was in for.

"All right," he said, and opened the door, holding it while all the boys filed out.

The walk to the vacant lot in the next block was performed in silence, broken only by the purposeful tramp of Charley Lynch's seconds.

"Take off your glasses," Charley said when they reached the exact center of the lot.

Harold took off his glasses, looked hesitantly for a place to put them. "I'll hold them," Sam Rosenberg, Charley's lieutenant, said politely.

"Thanks," Harold said, giving him the glasses. He turned and faced Charley, blinking slowly. He put up his hands. "O.K.," he said.

Charley stood there, breathing deeply, his enemy, blinking, thin-armed, pale, twenty pounds lighter than Charley, before him. A deep wave of exultation rolled through Charley's blood. He put up his hands carefully, stepped in and hit Harold square on the eye with his right hand.

The fight did not take long, although it took longer than Charley had expected. Harold kept punching, advancing into the deadly fire of Charley's fists, the most potent and sharp and brutal in the whole school. Harold's face smeared immediately with blood, and his eye closed, and his shirt tore and the blood soaked in down his clothes. Charley walked in flat-footed, not seeking to dodge or block Harold's weak punches. Charley felt his knuckles smashing against skin and bone and eye, and running with blood, half-delirious with pleasure, as Harold reeled and fell into the cruel, unpitying fists. Even the knuckles on his hands, and the tendons in Charley's fists, carrying the shock of the battle up to his shoulders, seemed to enjoy the pitiless administration of punishment.

From time to time Harold grunted, when Charley took time off from hitting him in the head to hit him, hooking upward from his ankles, in the belly. Except for that, the battle was conducted in complete quiet. The eight friends of Charley watched soberly, professionally, making no comment, finally watching Harold sink to the ground, not unconscious, but too exhausted to move a finger, and lie, spread out, his bloody face pressed harshly, but gratefully, into the dust and rubble of the vacant lot.

Charley stood over the fallen enemy, breathing heavily, his fists tingling joyfully, happy to see the weak, hated, frail figure face down and helpless on the ground, sorry that the pleasure of beating that figure was over. He watched in silence for a minute until Harold moved.

"All right," Harold said, his face still in the dirt. "That's enough." He lifted his head, slowly sat up, then, with a trembling hand, pulled himself to his feet. He wavered, his arms out from his sides and shaking uncontrollably, but he held his feet. "May I have my glasses?" he asked.

Silently, Sam Rosenberg, Charley's lieutenant, gave Harold his glasses. Harold fumblingly, with shaking hands, put them on. Charley watched him, the incongruously undamaged glasses on the damaged face. Suddenly Charley realized that he was crying. He, Charley Lynch, victor in fifty more desperate battles, who had shed no tear since the time he was spanked at the age of four, was weeping uncontrollably, his body shaken with sobs, his eyes hot and smarting. As he wept, he realized that he had been sobbing all through the fight, from the first right-hand to the eye until the final sinking, face-first, of the enemy into the dirt. Charley looked at Harold, eye closed, nose swollen and to one side, hair sweated and muddy, mouth all gore and mud, but the face, the spirit behind it, calm, unmoved. Harold wasn't crying then, Charley knew, as he sobbed bitterly, and he wouldn't cry later, and nothing he, Charley Lynch, could ever do would make him cry.

Harold took a deep breath and slowly walked off, without a word.

Charley watched him, the narrow, unheroic, torn and bedraggled back, dragging off. The tears swelled up in a blind flood and Harold disappeared from view behind them.

PREACH ON THE DUSTY ROADS

NELSON WEAVER SAT at his desk and wrote, "Labor . . . Bridgeport plant . . . $1,435,639.77." Then he put his sharply pointed hard pencil down among the nine other sharply pointed hard pencils arrayed in severe line on the right side of the shining desk, below the silver-framed photograph of his dead wife.

He looked at the leather clock on the back edge of his desk. 10:35. Robert wouldn't be along for ten minutes yet.

Nelson Weaver picked up his pencil and looked at the long sheets of paper, closely covered with typewritten figures, to his right. "Depreciation . . . $3,100,456.25," he wrote.

The tax sheets for Marshall and Co., Valves and Turbines, were nearly done. He had sat at this desk for thirty-five days, working slowly and carefully, from time to time deliberately putting down a number on the page, like Cézanne with his six strokes a day on a water color, until the huge elaborate structure of Marshall and Co.'s finances, which reached from bank to bank and country to country, from Wilmington, Delaware, where it was incorporated, to Chungking, China, where it sold electrical equipment to Chiang Kai-shek; until all this sprawling, complex history of money paid and money gained and credit offered and rejected and profit and loss, palpable and impalpable, was laid bare and comprehensible on five short pages of his clean accountant's figures.

Nelson looked at the leather clock. 10:40. The train was leaving at 11:15. Robert had better hurry.

Nelson looked at the $3,100,456.25 he had written. For the thousandth time he admired the delicate, tilted, bookkeeper's 2 he had early in his career learned to make. Somehow that 2 was to him a badge of his profession, a sign of his talents, an advertisement of the difficult rare world of figures in which he moved skilfully and at ease, turning sweat and clamor, heat and smoke, bonanza and disaster, into clear, rigid, immutable tables.

10:43. Where was Robert? Nelson got up and went to the window and looked out. He looked down the steel and granite fifty stories to the street. He laughed a little to himself when he realized he was trying to pick his son out of the hurry and confusion of 49th Street five hundred feet below.

He went back to his desk and sat down and picked up the sheet of paper on which he had been working. Tax sheets represented a formal and intricate game in which the players solemnly and conventionally juggled abstractions, like Spinoza proving God, to bring about very real and tangible results, like the great man who, in 1932, proved that J. P. Morgan had no taxable income. Once, in 1936, Nelson, in a rare burst of capriciousness, had made up two tax sheets. One, that Marshall and Co. had actually submitted to the government. And the other, with a change here and there to conform more to the actual realities of iron and sweat rather than the formal accountant's symbolism of numbers and deductible percentages. There had been a difference of $700,962.12. Nelson had carried the second sheet around with him for his private amusement for a week and then burned it, wisely.

This year, with the blossoming expansion of Marshall and Co. for war orders and the jump in the surplus profits tax, the difference between the real and the formal would be immense, over a million dollars, Nelson figured. Marshall and Co. paid him $40,000 a year. He was quite a bargain, he told himself grimly.

10:47. No Robert yet. Nelson put down the paper because the figures were beginning to jump before his eyes. More and more frequently he found that happening to him. Well, along with the waistline that grew an inch a year and the tendency to wake at five in the morning and his lack of shock at overhearing people calling him a middle-aged gentleman, that had to be expected of a man who had led a quiet, rather unhealthy life at a desk and was now over fifty. . . .

The door opened and Robert came in in his new lieutenant's uniform, with the rawhide suitcase Nelson had given him in his hand.

"On our way, Pop," Robert said. "The U.S. Army is waiting on tiptoe."

They smiled at each other and Nelson took his beautiful gray Homburg out of the closet and put it carefully on before the mirror.

"I was afraid you wouldn't make it," he said, delicately fingering the brim of the hat.

Robert was over at the window, staring out at New York, shining all around in the early summer sun, with the Hudson a flat blue highway against the cliffs of New Jersey and the buildings piled against each other like stiff confectionery in the light morning air. "Lord, Lord . . ." Robert murmured. "What a place to work! You ought to be sitting here writing the Ninth Symphony, Pop."

Nelson smiled at him and took his arm. "I'm not writing the Ninth Symphony." He would have liked to carry Robert's bag for him to the elevator and even made a move for it, but Robert detected it and switched the bag without a word to the other hand.

There was a pretty, dark-haired woman in a fine, severe black dress that looked on her as black dresses are supposed to look on smart women who work in fashionable businesses, and rarely do. She had her hair swept up for the summer morning and she looked pert and sharp and pretty and grownup all at once, and she looked coolly and approvingly, Nelson noticed, at his tall son, standing beside him, very slender and straight and self-consciously handsome in his new dark-green lieutenant's blouse with the proud gold bar shining on each shoulder.

Robert smiled a little to himself, conscious of the cool approving stare, helplessly and a little ashamedly pleased with himself for provoking it.

"Sometimes," he said, as he and Nelson got out of the elevator and walked toward Fifth Avenue, with the woman lost behind them, "sometimes, Pop, they ought to be allowed to arrest a man for the thoughts that pass through his head."

They grinned at each other and Robert took a deep full breath, looking around him, the smile still on his lips, before he got into the taxicab and said, "Grand Central, please."

They sat quietly as the cab dodged through the streets. Nelson looked steadfastly at the shining rawhide bag. You saw bags like that, he thought, on Friday afternoons in the summertime, on station platforms where people in summer clothes gaily waited for trains going to New England, to the Adirondacks, to Cape Cod . . . Somehow, he felt, to make the picture complete, there should be a tennis racket lying beside it, in its bright rubber case, and a girl's voice, light and excited, dominating the scene, saying swiftly, laughing, "Olive oil and vinegar in equal parts and a few drops of glycerin and just smear yourself, darling, every hour. There was this lifeguard at Hobe Sound and he was out in the sun twelve hours a day and that was all he used and he was as brown as the outside of an old piece of roast beef . . ."

But instead it was Robert's voice saying, "Five medium tanks . . ."

"What was that?" Nelson looked at his son, apologetically. "I'm sorry. I didn't quite . . ."

"When I get back," Robert said, "I'm put in command of five medium tanks. Twelve tons apiece, with a crew of four men. They represent an investment of about three hundred thousand bucks. And I've got to tell them, start, stop, go here, go there, kindly demolish that hot dog stand to the left, would you be so good as to put six shells into that corset and lingerie shop five blocks down the street." He grinned widely. "Me. I never even ran a set of electric trains before in my life. The faith that the U.S. Government has in me! I'm going to develop a beautiful case of stage fright when the time comes for me to look those five medium tanks in the eye."

"You'll do all right," Nelson said soberly.

Robert stared at him seriously for a moment, the smile gone. "I suppose so," he said.

The cab wheeled into Grand Central and they got out.

"We have fifteen minutes," Robert said, looking up at the clock. "How about one quick one, to oil the wheels?"

"Is anyone else seeing you off?" Nelson asked, as they walked through the dim, shuffling, echoing vault, toward the bar of the Commodore Hotel. "No girls?"

"Nope," said Robert, smiling. "Can't start that. If you invite one you've got to invite them all. It'd look like a reunion of Vassar graduates, classes of 38 to 41, inclusive." He laughed aloud. "I wouldn't like to make such a showy exit."

Nelson smiled at the joke, but was aware that the joke covered the fact that Robert had saved his final private good-bye before he went to war for his father. He wished there was some way to tell Robert he understood and was grateful, but whatever words he could think of would be clumsy and tragic, so he said nothing. They went into the Commodore and stood at the long bar, quiet now and cool and dim in the eleven o'clock pause before the day's drinking began.

"Two martinis," Robert said to the bartender.

"I haven't had a drink in the morning," Nelson said, "since Arthur Parker's wedding. 1936."

"What the hell," Robert said. "There's a war on."

There was the pleasant sound of the ice clinking in the mixer and the faint strange smell of the gin rising in the empty bar and the pungent tiny smell of the lemon peel that the bartender twisted delicately over the full cold glasses.

They lifted their drinks and Nelson looked past his son's lean, well-loved head, capped and young and martial, with the gold and leather of the United States Army shining on it. Nelson looked along the bar into the dim recesses of the low-ceilinged, long room, as neat and orderly and expectant with its empty and regular tables and chairs as only a bar or restaurant prepared for the day's eating and drinking can be. How many farewells had been said in this room, this drinking place next to the trains that spread out across the whole huge continent. How many final good-byes. How many last kisses between husband and wife. How many gulped and tasteless drinks, how much shock of alcohol to take the first terrible edge off the pain of loss and distance. How many farewelling ghosts sat at those regular tables, their endless irrevocable good-byes echoing among the frivolous glasses. How full the company of grieving leavetakers, each of them tasting death in this snatched last moment over whisky, before the train rolled out. . . .

Nelson looked squarely, steadily at his one child's military head. He raised his glass a little higher, touching his son's glass. "To a quick end of the business," he said.

They drank. The drink tasted powerful and rich and burning and immediately effective against his morning palate. Robert drank with zest, tasting the full savor of the drink happily, rolling it over his tongue. "You'd be surprised," he said, "how hard it is to get a good martini in the Tank Corps."

Nelson watched him drink and remembered a day in the country, three years ago, when Robert was twenty. It was summertime and they were both on vacation and had a house in Vermont and Robert had been out swimming all afternoon and had come in, wet-haired, tan, barefoot, wrapped in a huge white bathrobe, with a faded blue towel swung around his shoulders, summertime printed on his freckled nose and the tan backs of his lake-washed hands . . . He had swung through the screen door, singing loudly, "Stormy weather, since my gal and I ain't together. . . ." He had padded along barefoot, leaving high-arched stains of lakewater on the grass rugs directly to the kitchen. When Nelson had gone into the kitchen, he saw Robert sitting at the porcelain table, still humming "Stormy Weather," with an open bottle of cold beer in one hand, the moisture condensing coolly on the glass, and in the other hand a huge, ludicrous sandwich he had made for himself with two great jagged slices of rye bread and a quarter pound of Swiss cheese and two mountainous slices of cold baked ham and a tremendous cold beefsteak tomato cut in three fat, meaty slices. Robert was sitting there, tilted back in the flimsy kitchen chair, the late afternoon sun shining obliquely on him through the high old-fashioned window, slowly dripping lakewater, the giant of a sandwich and the bottle of beer happily in his hands, his mouth full of cheese and tomato and ham and bread and cold beer, the song somehow working out of his throat in a bumbling joyous monotone. He waved the sandwich airily at Nelson when Nelson appeared at the door.

"Starving," he mumbled. "Swam four miles. Got to keep my energy up."

"You've got to eat dinner in an hour," Nelson said.

Robert grinned through the food. "I'll eat dinner. Let nobody worry." And he took another fabulous bite from the monstrous sandwich.

Nelson watched him eat, smiling a little to himself.

"Want me to make you a sandwich?" Robert asked.

"No, thanks."

"Great maker of sandwiches . . ."

Nelson shook his head, smiling. "I'll wait for dinner." He watched his son eat. The full white teeth shining in the sunburned face, biting strongly and evenly into the food, the lean muscles of the strong throat, rising out of the white bathrobe, moving calmly as he tilted the bottle back and gulped the beer. . . .

"When I was your age," Nelson said, "I ate just like that. . . ."

And suddenly Robert had looked at him very soberly as though seeing his father twenty years old—and loving him—and seeing the long years that came after with pride and pity . . .

"Well . . ." Robert ate the olive at the bottom of his glass and put the glass down with a little flat tinkle that ran lightly through the quiet bar. "Well, the train's waiting. . . ."

Nelson looked around and shook his head and the Vermont kitchen and the sunburned boy and the bottle of beer beaded with icebox-cold all disappeared. He finished his drink and paid and together he and Robert hurried across the station to the gate where Robert's train was waiting. There was an air of bustle and impatience about the gate, and a soldier and his mother and two female relatives were weeping together in a sodden mass and somehow he and Robert shook hands and there was a last wave and no words because they each knew that any word through the tortured throat would bring with it sobs—and Robert went down the long incline to the dark station below. His rawhide bag gleamed among the descending passengers and he was gone. . . .

Nelson turned and walked slowly toward the street. As he walked he thought of the capped head and the rawhide bag going down the long incline to the waiting train, to the medium tanks, to the waiting guns, the waiting agony, going lightly and zealously and unquestioningly off to war. He remembered, although a little mistily, with the martini and the shuffling steps on the marble floor, and the weeping at the gates of the soldier's women, all serving to blur and confuse and make remote, he remembered watching Robert playing tennis last summer. Robert played very smoothly and well, lanky and easy over the court, like those tall kids in California who play 365 days a year in a kind of lazy, expert boredom. Robert had a habit of talking jovially and half-irritably to himself when he missed a shot, looking up to heaven and muttering under his breath, "Weaver! *Weaver!* Why don't you just give up? Why don't you just go home?" He had seen his father looking down at him, smiling, and knew that his father understood the mumbled tirade he was delivering to himself. He had grinned and waved his racket and slammed the next three services so hard no returns were possible. . . .

Nelson walked up Madison Avenue toward the office of Marshall and Co., toward the formal and intricate sheets of figures waiting on his desk, toward the neat, professional, bookkeeper's 2 he was proud of. . . .

As he walked he wondered where his son would be sent to meet the enemy. Africa? Australia? India? England? Russia? Desert, plain, mountain, jungle, seacoast—and a twenty-three-year-old boy, ex-swimmer, ex-tennis-player, ex-eater of great sandwiches and drinker of cold beer, ex-lover of his father, hungry and full of jokes and ready for any climate, while his father, full of his slack fifty years, walked daily to his office . . .

Nelson walked along Madison Avenue before the windows of the fine shops. Two women passed him and a high woman's voice said, "Taffeta. Baby-blue taffeta, shirred, with the back bare down to the hips. It has a startling effect."

It never occurred to me it could happen, Nelson thought, walking slowly and blindly away from the station where his son had set off to battle. There was one war and that was all. It's my fault. I had a son, but I didn't take my responsibility seriously enough. I worked and I dressed him and fed him and sent him to a good college and bought him books and gave him money to take out girls and took him with me on vacations to Vermont, but I didn't take my responsibility seriously enough. I worked, and it wasn't easy, and I was poor for a long time and only the poor know how hard it is to stop being poor. I worked, but for the wrong things. I've added millions of rows of figures, detailed the maneuverings of many corporations, year by year, and sometimes it was eighteen hours a day and no time for meals. . . . Nonsense! I'm guilty. I should've been out stopping this. . . . I am nearly the same age as Hitler. He could do something to kill my son. I should've been doing something to save him. I'm guilty. I should be ashamed to stand in the same room with my son in his lieutenant's green blouse. Money . . . I thought about the grocer, the insurance man, the electric light company . . . Nonsense, nonsense . . . I've wasted my life. I'm an old man and alone and my son has gone to war and all I did was pay rent and taxes. I was playing with toys. I was smoking opium. Me and millions like me. The war was being fought for twenty years and I didn't know it. I waited for my son to grow up and fight it for me. I should've been out screaming on street corners, I should've grabbed people by their lapels in trains, in libraries and restaurants and yelled at them. "Love, understand, put down your guns, forget your profit, remember God . . ." I should have walked on foot through Germany and France and England and America. I should've preached on the dusty roads and used a rifle when necessary. I stayed in the one city and paid the grocer. Versailles, Manchuria, Ethiopia, Warsaw, Madrid— battlefields, battlefields—and I thought there was one war and it was over.

He stopped and looked up. He was sweating now and the salt was in his eyes and he had to rub them to see that he was standing in front of the great monument of a building, serene and immutable, in which, in war and peace, Marshall and Co. conducted its business. His charts and figures were waiting for him, all the clever, legal, evasive, money-saving numbers that a global dealer in valves and turbines could as-semble in this bloody and profitable year to turn over in its solemn annual report to the government of the republic. Depreciation . . . $3,100,456.25.

He looked up at the soaring shining building sharp against the soft summer sky.

He stood there, before the graven entrance, and people jostled him and came and went, but he didn't go in.

FAITH AT SEA

LIEUTENANT PETER GIFFORD LAWRENCE stood on the foredeck of the SS *Rascoe*, holding on lightly to the canvas-sheathed three-inch gun as the bow dipped and trembled in the harsh chop of the North Atlantic. Twelve men of the gun crew stood at ease before him, shifting easily with the soaring lift and fall of the SS *Rascoe* as she chewed busily into the slate waves that had been hacking at her for six days, getting stronger and stronger as the 6,000-ton tramp steamer ploughed at nine knots toward England.

"The duties of the gun captain," Constantini was chanting, like a child in school. "A, on manning gun, reports through sight-setter to group control officer when gun is ready. B, operates plug as necessary. C, calls 'Ready,' to pointer when breech is closed . . ."

Lawrence only half listened as Constantini's voice droned on, in the regular Thursday afternoon gunnery class that Lawrence conducted to keep the Navy gun crew alert and interested on the long, monotonous trips. He looked at the twelve men outlined in mufflers and coats, against the low-hanging cold sun. These, plus the four men on duty now at the rear gun, had been given him by the Navy to guard the gray and shabby and valuable life of the SS *Rascoe*, and as always, when he saw them assembled he felt with a mixture of amusement and pity how old he was.

He was only thirty-five, but except for Farrell, the Chief Petty Officer, who was older than he, and Benson, the gunner's mate, who was twenty-five, all the men were twenty-one or under, their faces bronzed and unlined and boyish, always solemn and youthfully important when they were assembled like this for any official function, and especially solemn today because they had lost the convoy the night before in a storm and were now plodding over the gray wastes toward port, vulnerable and alone.

"He is responsible for the conduct, efficiency and spirit of the crew," Constantini was saying, "and must be made to realize that he is the representative of his battery officer."

"Very good," Lawrence said. "Harris."

"Yes, sir." Harris stood stiffly at attention.

"The duties of the sight setter."

"To set the sights," Harris rattled off glibly, "and to transmit all communications between gun and group control officer."

Lawrence looked up over Harris's head to the bridge. Captain Linsey, his beard patchy and crooked in the wind, was peering angrily down at what he called the Navy kindergarten.

"To call 'Set,'" Harris was saying, "to pointer when sights have been set . . ."

Suddenly Harris stopped. Lawrence turned from looking at Linsey on the bridge. The man next to Harris, William Doneger, was on his knees by Harris's side, gripping Harris's arm with a tortured, clutching hand. Harris stood there stupidly, frightened, looking blankly at the sweating tense face.

"Doneger . . ." Lawrence started toward him. Doneger let loose his grip and dropped, bent over and rocking, to the deck.

Constantini sank swiftly to his knees and took Doneger's head in his hands, tenderly.

"What is it?" Lawrence kneeled beside the two of them, with the other men crowded silent and helpless around them.

Doneger looked up at him wildly, the sweat breaking from his forehead, even in this bitter winter evening.

"He's been sick all day, sir," Constantini said, his hands almost unconsciously going slowly and soothingly over his friend's forehead. "Terrible bellyache, sir."

Lawrence looked down at the suffering boy. His lips were bleeding from biting them and his face had grown terribly, greenly pale, morbid and alarming in the cold Atlantic dusk. His legs pulled spasmodically and unreasonably as he lay on the wet deck.

"Let's get him below," Lawrence said. "To my quarters." There was no doctor on board and Lawrence's quarters had the medical chest and served as clinic for the Navy men.

Constantini got Doneger under the armpits and one of the other men got him around the knees and they started down with him. Constantini was a broad, powerful boy and held his friend firmly and lightly and maneuvered him delicately up the steps, his face tense and wary as he attempted to beat the cruel roll of the ship which at any moment threatened to smash the sick boy against a bulkhead.

Lawrence looked out across the ocean for a last survey. The water hissed by the SS *Rascoe* and the gray waves piled endlessly and monotonously on top of each other and the clouds came down, and that was all. He swallowed a little drily, thinking of Doneger lying racked and contorted in his room, then braced his shoulders consciously and walked slowly toward his quarters.

When he opened the door, Doneger was lying on the extra berth and Constantini was whispering to him, a steady, soft stream of comforting words. Constantini had a deep melodious voice, like a singer, and it sounded like a lullaby as he whispered to his friend.

"Nothing at all, William, nothing at all." He was the only one on the ship who called Doneger William. All the other men called him Bill and Billy, but Constantini gave him his full and proper name, like a doting mother, at all times. "Something you ate. I've had bellyaches in my time. . . ." Constantini was seventeen years old. "I thought I was going to split down the middle and two hours later I'd be out eating two plates of spaghetti and a quart of dago red. . . ."

When he saw Lawrence come into the room, he stopped his whispering and stood up at attention, trying to make his face impassive and military. But he had a child's face with deep soft-brown Italian eyes, with heavy curled black eyelashes, and a full, almost girlish mouth, and the military mask at the moment was not deceptive.

Lawrence looked down at the suffering boy. Doneger looked up at him wanly. "Sorry, sir," he whispered.

"Sssh," Lawrence said.

"He's been puking, sir," Constantini said. "All day, sir . . ."

Lawrence sighed and sat down on the berth next to Doneger. That's what it's going to turn out to be, he thought, as he put his hand on the boy's side. The worst possible thing . . .

The right side was swollen and tight and Doneger jumped even with the slightest pressure.

"He has a very sensitive belly, sir," Constantini was speaking quickly and anxiously, as though somehow his words and explanations could make the disease less. "I took him to my cousin's wedding and he got drunk faster than anyone else, even faster than the sixteen-year-old girls . . . We had a stew yesterday that was a little greasy and maybe . . ."

"He has appendicitis, Salvatore," Lawrence said slowly.

Constantini looked at his friend's face in silence. Doneger closed his eyes. Lying down here, in the warm stateroom, on a dry bed, he seemed more comfortable, better able to meet the pain.

"Everything will be all right, William," Constantini murmured to Doneger. "The Lieutenant has already diagnosed the disease."

The door opened and Captain Linsey came in. He stood above Doneger, staring down at him, without a word, his mouth curled, as always when he had anything to do with the Navy men on board his ship, into a sour and ancient snarl.

"Sick," Linsey said. "This son-of-a-bitch is very sick."

"Yes," Lawrence said. Captain Linsey would make amusing conversation after the war at dinner parties in Boston. Crusty old merchant seadog. Ignored the Navy. Ignored the war, even in the middle of a pack of submarines.

"This son-of-a-bitch'll die." Captain Linsey leaned over and peered harshly into the pale suffering face.

Very amusing after the war at dinner parties, Lawrence thought. Right now I'd like to kill him.

"We'll take care of him," Lawrence said.

Suddenly Captain Linsey poked Doneger in the side with a huge, wrinkled finger. Doneger cried and jumped. "Sorry, Sonny," Captain Linsey said. He turned to Lawrence. "Ready to bust. Boy out with me on the way to Wilhelmshaven in 1931 died in three days. Same thing."

Out of the corner of his eye, Lawrence saw Constantini look quickly down at Doneger, then look up and take a long, deep breath.

"Please," Lawrence said. "I'll come up to the bridge later and you can tell me whatever you . . ."

"This son-of-a-bitch needs an operation."

"There's no doctor on board."

Captain Linsey sucked at the wet ends of his mustache, looked with crazy slyness at Lawrence. "We won't make port for seven days. At least. He ain't going to last no week."

I'd like to kill him, Lawrence thought, looking up at Captain Linsey's old, harsh seaman's face. I'd like to kill him, but he's right, he's right.

"I thought we could freeze it," Lawrence said. "After all, we have ice. Maybe it'll subside . . ."

"Too late." Captain Linsey wagged his head finally. "Surgery. Surgery or nothing."

"There're no surgeons here," Lawrence said loudly. "If you insist on arguing, let's get out of this room."

"You ever see an operation?" Captain Linsey asked.

"Yes." Lawrence's brother-in-law was a fashionable surgeon and over a period of ten years Lawrence had seen seven or eight operations. "That isn't the same thing."

"There was a Dutchman we took to Capetown in 1927," Captain Linsey said. "A doctor. Studied in America. He left a book on board. All kinds of operations. Every once in a while I read in it. Very interesting reading. I bet it's got appendicitis in it."

"That's ridiculous," Lawrence stood up and went over to the door. "Thank you for your interest, Captain . . ."

Captain Linsey touched Doneger's head. "Fever. I bet it's over 104. An operation really isn't so much. A little common sense and a little nerve. What the hell, what has this boy got to lose?" He leaned close to Doneger and spoke with surprising softness. "Sonny, you got any objections to being operated on?"

Doneger stared at Constantini. Constantini turned away, giving no answer one way or another with his eyes.

"I have no objections," Doneger said faintly.

Captain Linsey strode briskly toward the door. "I'll send the book down," he said cheerfully. "We'll save the son-of-a-bitch yet." He clapped Lawrence on the back. "I'd do it myself only I'm old and jumpy and I've drunk too much whisky in my day. I'll be on the bridge. I'll keep this tub as steady as possible."

He went out quickly.

Lawrence closed his eyes so that he wouldn't have to look at Doneger or Crowley or Constantini, all standing stiffly watching him.

A moment later a seaman came in with a worn and broken-backed book. He put it on the table and went out. Crowley and Doneger and Constantini and Lawrence all looked at the fat, dog-eared book, lying alone on the table. Lawrence stood up and went over and opened to the index. Under A Pg. 941—Appendectomy.

The first time he read through it, the words were a weird and incomprehensible blur. He looked up once or twice only to see the staring, serious eyes of the three other men scanning his face, as though they somehow could tell from that distance whether or not the words he was reading were of any value to him or not.

Lawrence took off his coat and started slowly to read it from the beginning, once more.

Before operating, try to locate the situation of the appendix. The incision should be over the seat of the disease. In the rare left-sided cases and in median cases, the incision is median . . .

The words began to group themselves in his mind into English sentences, capable of being understood by a man who could read and write.

In an acute case in a man I separate the muscular fibres. Battle's incision at the outer edge of the rectus muscle is preferred by many surgeons . . .

In a biology course in college he had dissected the earthworm, the frog, the white rat—but all dead, beyond the reach of pain, unmoved by clumsiness or error.

If there be infection, surround the region involved with packs of plain gauze, each strip being two and a half inches wide, fifteen inches long, and four layers in thickness. Pass a ligature through the meso appendix as shown in Fig. 691, A, tie the ligature and . . .

Fig. 691, A, was very simple and if flesh and muscle and organ were anything like the diagram, it was conceivable that a deft, though unpracticed man might be able to manage . . .

"William," Lawrence said. "Are you sure?"

Doneger sighed. "I'm sure."

"Crowley," Lawrence said. "Go to the galley and get a pot of boiling water."

"Yes, sir," Crowley said, and went out softly, already making a hospital out of the room.

Lawrence went back to the close print of the book. He read and reread, studied the diagrams until he felt he could draw them with his eyes closed.

He stood up and unlocked the medical chest. He threw open the doors and stared at the rows of bottles, the serried bandages, the fateful gleaming instruments. Behind him he heard the soft child's voice of Constantini, rough with the accent of the streets of New York, soft with compassion and fear.

"It ain't hardly nothing, William. A cousin of mine had this and he was operated on and three days later he slept with the nurse." Constantini had a cousin for all eventualities of discussion, naval and civilian. "Everybody ought to have his appendix out. They don't do you no good. None at all. If I had the time I'd have 'em out myself. . . ."

Lawrence stared at the bottles, the bandages, the steel instruments. He made his eyes go slowly and calmly from one thing to another in the chest, taking a deliberate inventory. The thing is, he thought, not to hurry. After all, men have done more difficult things than this. The instruments are there, the one can of ether, the bandage, the scalpel, the needles, the catgut, the clamps, the sponges, the alcohol, sulfanila-mide. And the Navy had given him a course in First Aid. How to stop bleeding. How to avoid gangrene. How to set a broken leg.

"You hardly feel it," Constantini was saying in his deep melodious boy's voice. "You take a little nap. You wake up. Appendix absent. You feel a little stiff for a day or two, you get a good rest, the other guys stand your watches, you read the magazines and drink hot soup. You get to England, you get three weeks sick leave, you'll have the time of your life. The English girls're crazy about American sailors. I got a cousin in the merchant marine and he says that an American in London is like a king, far as the girls're concerned. They can't do enough for them . . ."

Why, Lawrence thought with a remote and bitter detachment, did this have to happen the first time we lost a convoy? In a convoy the boy could be transferred to one of the cruisers accompanying them and there a first-rate naval surgeon in a shining, brilliantly equipped operating room would do the job as a matter of simple routine in ten minutes.

Crowley came in with the pot of hot water and Lawrence put the scalpel, the needles and the clamps into it.

"Anything I can do," Constantini said, as Lawrence watched the steel gleaming dully as it sank among the bubbles of the boiling water. "Anything at all."

Lawrence nodded. "There'll be plenty for you to do. Clear that table and get a sheet out of the locker and spread it over it." Constantini listened eagerly and nodded. "Wash your hands first."

While Crowley and Constantini scrubbed their hands and the strong smell of the soap pricked his nostrils, Lawrence re-read, slowly, the entire description of the operation.

Even after he had finished and after the gentle watery sound of scrubbing behind him had long ceased, he sat with his head in his hands, staring at the page before him.

He stood up. Well, that was that . . .

He turned briskly and without words he and Constantini and Crow-ley lifted Doneger onto the white-covered table. He washed and scrubbed his hands with alcohol. Gently, he shaved the slight downy fuzz from the boy's belly. Then he washed it with alcohol.

Crowley behaved wonderfully. He was a little, impassive Irishman, to whom all things seemed to come as a matter of course, promotions, overwork, murders, drownings, wars. Lawrence was glad it was Crow-ley who had silently volunteered for this job.

Constantini, too, handled Doneger with soft hands, lifting him gently and securely, making no unnecessary move. Together they bound Doneger to the table with linen bandage, so that the roll of the ship would not throw him off the table.

Lawrence noticed that the ship had swung around and was heading directly into the wind and was much steadier now. He would remember to thank Captain Linsey later.

He took the ether cone and stood at Doneger's shoulder. Doneger and Constantini and seven or eight of the other boys had had their heads shaven when they were last in the States. They had done it as a kind of joke, after Lawrence had complained at inspection that they were letting their hair grow too long. All seven of them had marched solemnly back onto the SS Rascoe from their shore leaves and had with one gesture swept their hats off their heads as they reported in. Lawrence had stared at the seven shining pates, scarred with the incredibly numerous battles of childhood, and had lowered his eyes to keep from laughing and had said, "Very good."

They had saluted and swept out and he had heard them roaring with laughter on the deck . . .

Doneger's head, now with a slight baby fuzz standing up all over it, lay flatly, in the shadows, on the table in the small cabin as the old plates on the SS Rascoe creaked and wailed under the attack of the sea. . . .

"All right, William," Lawrence said softly. "Are you ready now?"

"I'm ready, sir." Doneger spoke in a whisper and smiled up at him.

Lawrence put the cone gently over the boy's face and said, "Breathe deeply." He poured the ether in and the smell, sweet and deadly leaked into the cabin, making it strange and deathly suddenly. "Count," Lawrence said. "Keep counting."

"One, two, three," Doneger said clearly. "Four, five, six, seven, eight . . ." The young voice began to blur and thicken. "Nine, ten, eleven, twelve, thir—thir . . ." The voice mumbled heavily and wearily through the cone. The long chubby body on the table relaxed for the first time and Crowley gently straightened the legs out. The voice died away completely and the noise of the creaking plates of the old ship was the only sound to be heard.

Lawrence lifted the ether cone. Doneger's face was calm and showed no trace of pain. He gave the cone to Constantini. "If I tell you to," he said, "put this over his face. In case he moves . . ."

"Yes, sir," Constantini said, and moved quickly to Doneger's head.

Lawrence went to the pot of boiling water, and with a forceps took out the instruments he had put in there to sterilize. Crowley had arranged a clean towel on the bunk and Lawrence put the instruments there in a neat and shining row, remembering how dentists who had filled his teeth had done the same thing.

He picked up the scalpel and arranged the lamp so that its full glare fell on the bare stomach of the sleeping boy.

The skin was very pink, and there was a firm small layer of fat under it. Doneger was very young and his belly still had a round little baby-swell. He was breathing softly and the muscles trembled rhythmically and gently in the harsh light of the single lamp.

How smooth, how subtle, how complex, Lawrence thought, how close to death. How vulnerable to knife and powder. How irrevocably naked to damage. He closed his eyes for a moment, unable to look any more at the smooth childish skin. With his eyes closed and the moaning and creaking of the tumbling ship in his ears, it all seemed dreamlike and impossible. He, Peter Gifford Lawrence, gently reared, nursed and fed and tended all his years by mother and aunt and teacher and doctor, every boyhood scratch mercurochromed and overbandaged, soft-blanketed sleeper in neat, well-ventilated rooms, student at Harvard where he had taken notes on Plato and Geoffrey Chaucer, on the architecture of the Renaissance and the metrics of John Milton, Peter Gifford Lawrence, gentleman, formal guest at pleasant dinners, polite talker to old ladies at Lenox garden parties, dealer in books and fine prints, now standing scalpel in hand in the cramped, peeling First-Officer's quarters of a wheezing freighter groaning and heaving in a Middle Atlantic gale, with four miles of black sea water and countless drowned sailors under the keel, the prey of deadly vessels that struck unseen and mortal in the turn of a man's head . . .

Battle's incision at the outer edge of the rectus muscle is preferred by many surgeons . . . After opening the peritoneum examine very gently to detect the situation of the . . . This divides the mucous membrane, submucous tissue and muscular coat . . .

He opened his eyes and looked up. Constantini was staring at him. In the soft girlish eyes, beside the worry for his friend's agony, there was deep trust, deep confidence that this kindly, efficient, understanding, courageous man, this officer who had been designated by great authority to guide his wartime fate, would, this time and all times, do well what had to be done. There was no doubt in the soft steady eyes of Salvatore Constantini.

Lawrence bent his head and firmly made the necessary incision . . .

When the operation was over and Doneger had been gently lifted into the extra bunk and Constantini had silently taken the watch at his side, Lawrence opened the door and stepped out onto the deck. The black wind flung bitter spray into his face and he had to half-shut his eyes against it. But he stood there, holding onto the rail, peering sightlessly into the roaring darkness, hardly thinking, hardly feeling, rolling crazily and aimlessly with the roll of the ship.

He stood there drunkenly for a long time, then suddenly turned and went into his room. Doneger was lying there, steady and still, the ether still in control. Constantini sat quietly at his side, never taking his eyes off the pale, exhausted face.

Lawrence lay down in all his clothes and slept immediately.

When he awoke, he opened his eyes slowly and came up deeply from the well of sleep, as though he had slept for weeks on end. Slowly he became aware of Constantini sitting across the room from him, still looking steadfastly at Doneger, as though he hadn't moved all night.

Lawrence opened his eyes wide.

"Good morning, Lieutenant." Constantini smiled shyly at him. His eyes were sunken and he rubbed them like a sleepy infant.

"Morning, Salvatore." Lawrence sat up suddenly and looked at Doneger, remembering in a rush that across from him lay a man whom he had operated upon the night before. Doneger was awake, and drowsily smiled, his face creased by a kind of remote pain.

"Hello, Lieutenant," Doneger whispered.

Lawrence jumped out of his bunk. "How are you?"

"Fine," Doneger whispered. "First class. Thanks."

Lawrence peered at him closely. There were wrinkles of pain in the boy's smooth face, but there was a little color in the cheeks and something in the eyes that seemed to announce that death had once and for all passed by.

Lawrence looked at Constantini. "You get any sleep last night?"

"Not much, sir. I'm pleased to watch William."

"Get below and get some sleep. Someone else'll watch William."

"Yes, sir." Constantini looked shyly at him and then turned to Doneger. "My God," he whispered, as Lawrence poured some water to wash, "will you have a picnic with those English girls . . ."

And he touched his friend's forehead lightly and chuckled as he went out and deep, deep, from the depths of his eighteen years and recovery from death, Doneger chuckled softly in return.

Later in the day, Lawrence started forward toward the bow gun, where the men were assembled for the interrupted examination in gunnery. The sun was shining and the ocean was a sharp, wintry blue, with the whitecaps in the distance looking like the bobbing sails of a regatta with a million entries. He had left Doneger smiling and sipping tea and the bright wind felt festive and alive against his freshly shaven face. He saw the cluster of blue uniforms and the ruddy faces of the gun crew around the gun and heard Constantini's voice, melodious and terribly earnest, chanting in final review before his arrival. Lawrence smiled to himself and was proud of the Navy and the red-faced earnest boys, and the gun and the SS *Rascoe* and himself, abroad, dependable and unafraid, on the wide ocean.

"'Tention!" Benson called as he approached, and the boys stiffened rigidly, their faces stern and set, their hands tight at their sides. Lawrence looked sternly at them, carrying out his share of the military drama.

He looked at them and felt once more with the old amusement and pity how old he was at the age of thirty-five, confronted by and responsible for these large, determined, valuable, fearless children.

"At ease," he said.

The tight little knot relaxed and the men shuffled about, making themselves comfortable. They kept their eyes on Lawrence, seriously. Constantini's lips mumbled inaudibly as he ran over the list of questions he might be asked to answer.

"We'll go right into it," Lawrence said. "Harris . . ." he started with the boy nearest him. "What're the duties of the first loader?"

"To receive the shell from the second loader," Harris said. "And to load the gun."

"Levine." Lawrence spoke to the next man. "Duties of the second loader?"

"To pass shells to the first loader," Levine said carefully. "To arrange shells on deck in rear of gun in probable arc of train."

"Constantini . . ." Lawrence went down the line. He saw Constantini's face tense almost painfully with anticipation. "What are the duties of the third loader?"

Constantini's lips started to move. Then he licked them uneasily. He took in a deep breath, looked suddenly, blankly and despairingly at Lawrence. Lawrence glanced at him and saw that all knowledge had fled from his head, like an actor on opening night, with four weeks of rehearsals behind him, who is stricken dumb by the overpowering desire to do well.

A deep red flush surged up over Constantini's collar and stained his cheeks, his ears. He licked his lips in misery, looked straight ahead, hopelessly . . .

Lawrence looked away, called the next man, Moran, went on with the questioning.

Moran answered the question briskly.

One by one, Lawrence went down the line of men. Each man snapped out his answer, their voices ringing clear and triumphant in the bright wind. Once more it was Constantini's turn.

Lawrence looked surreptitiously at him. He was next in line and he was standing as stiff as though all the admirals of all the fleets of the world were passing him in review. His jaws were clenched and the muscles stood out in them like rope. His eyes stared ahead of him like a man watching the execution of his father, wild, hopeless, full of guilt.

Lawrence knew in his heart that no matter what question he put to Constantini, no answer would come from that mourning brain, no word pass those locked, despairing lips. For a moment Lawrence thought of passing him up and going on to the next man. But then, to the shame of Constantini's ignorance and defection would be added the ignominy of official pity.

"Constantini," Lawrence said as crisply as he could, hoping to shock him out of his trancelike trauma. He carefully sought out the simplest, most transparent, easily answered question in the whole book. "Constantini," he said, slowly and clearly and loudly, "what is the purpose of shrapnel?"

Constantini did not move. The tongue froze between the lips, the eyes stared without hope across the Atlantic Ocean, while no answer came to show this good man, this Boston Lieutenant who had done a brave and noble thing to save his friend's life that he, Salvatore Constantini, loved and admired him and would be grateful to him for the rest of his life. The blush settled like a permanent blight on his cheeks, but no answer came from the rockbound brain. The deep, ordinary thanks that a man could give by the crisp performance of his duty could not be given. William lived and Salvatore failed the man who had saved him.

Suddenly the tears started from his eyes and rolled down his rigid cheeks.

Lawrence looked at the weeping boy, staring blindly out to sea, among the men who kindly stared out to sea with him. Lawrence saw the bitter tears and almost put out his hand to comfort the boy, but held back just in time, since comfort now, before his ten friends, would be agony later.

Lawrence glanced once more at him and tried to call the next man's name and ask him the purpose of shrapnel, but the name stuck in his throat and he turned his back on the men and wept and felt the tears cold on his cheeks without surprise.

RETREAT

THE COLUMN OF TRUCKS wound into the little square beside the Madeleine and stopped there, under the trees. They were furry with dust, the black cross almost indistinguishable even in the bright Paris sunlight under the harsh dry coat they had accumulated in the retreat from Normandy.

The engines stopped and suddenly the square was very quiet, the drivers and the soldiers relaxing on the trucks, the people at the little tables in the cafés staring without expression at the line of vehicles, bullet-scarred and fresh from war against the trees and Greek columns of the Madeleine.

A major at the head of the column slowly raised himself and got out of his car. He stood looking up at the Madeleine, a dusty, middle-aged figure, the uniform no longer smart, the lines of the body sagging and unmilitary. The major turned around and walked slowly toward the Café Bernard across the square, his face grimy and worn and expressionless, with the dust in heavy, theatrical lines in the creases of his face and where his goggles had been. He walked heavily, thoughtfully, past his trucks and his men, who watched him dispassionately and incuriously, as though they had known him for many years and there was nothing more to be learned from him. Some of the men got out of their trucks and lay down in the sunshine on the pavement and went to sleep, like corpses in a town where there has been a little fighting, just enough to produce several dead without doing much damage to the buildings.

The major walked over to the little sidewalk tables of the Café Bernard, looking at the drinkers there with the same long, cold, thoughtful stare with which he had surveyed the Madeleine. The drinkers stared back with the guarded, undramatic faces with which they had looked at the Germans for four years.

The major stopped in front of the table where Segal sat alone, the half-finished glass of beer in his hand. A little twist of a smile pulled momentarily at the German's mouth as he stood there, looking at Segal, small and pinned together with desperate neatness in his five-year-old suit, his shirt stitched and cross-stitched to hold it together, his bald head shining old and clean in the bright sun.

"Do you mind . . . ?" the major indicated the empty chair beside Segal with a slow, heavy movement of his hand.

Segal shrugged. "I don't mind," he said.

The major sat down, spread his legs out deliberately in front of him. "*Garçon*," he said, "two beers."

They sat in silence and the major watched his men sleeping like corpses on the Paris pavement.

"For this drink," the major said, in French, "I wanted to sit with a civilian."

The waiter brought the beers and set them down on the table and put the saucers in the middle, between them. The major absently pulled the saucers in front of him.

"To your health," he said. He raised his glass. Segal lifted his and they drank.

The major drank thirstily, closing his eyes, almost finishing his glass before he put it down. He opened his eyes and licked the tiny scallop of froth from the beer off his upper lip, as he slowly turned his head, regarding the buildings around him. "A pretty city," he said. "A very pretty city. I had to have one last drink."

"You've been at the front?" Segal asked.

"Yes," said the major. "I have been at the front."

"And you are going back?"

"I am going back," the major said, "and the front is going back." He grinned a little, sourly. "It is hard to say which precedes which. . . ." He finished his beer, then turned and stared at Segal. "Soon," he said, "the Americans will be here. How do you feel about that?"

Segal touched his face uncomfortably. "You don't really want a Parisian to answer a question like that," he said, "do you?"

"No," the major smiled. "I suppose not. Though, it's too bad the Americans had to meddle. However, it's too late to worry about that now." Under the warlike dust his face now was tired and quiet and intellectual, not good-looking, but studious and reasonable, the face of a man who read after business hours and occasionally went to concerts without being pushed into it by his wife. He waved to the waiter. "*Garçon,* two more beers." He turned to Segal. "You have no objections to drinking another beer with me?"

Segal looked across at the armored vehicles, the two hundred sprawling men, the heavy machine guns mounted and pointing toward the sky. He shrugged, his meaning cynical and clear.

"No," said the major. "I would not dream of using the German army to force Frenchmen to drink beer with me."

"Since the Germans occupied Paris," Segel said, "I haven't drunk with one or conducted a conversation with one. Four years. As an experience, perhaps, I should not miss it. And now is the time to try it. In a little while it will no longer be possible, will it?"

The major disregarded the jibe. He stared across at his command stretched wearily and incongruously in front of the Greek temple Paris had faithfully erected in her midst. He never seemed to be able to take his eyes off the armor and the men, as though there was a connection there, bitter and unsatisfactory and inescapable, that could never really be broken, even for a moment, in a café, over a glass of beer. "You're a Jew," he said quietly to Segal, "aren't you?"

The waiter came and put the two beers and the saucers on the table.

Segal put his hands into his lap, to hide the trembling and the terror in the joints of the elbows and knees and the despair in all the veins of the body that the word had given rise to in him, each time, every day, since the bright summer days of 1940. He sat in silence, licking his lips, automatically and hopelessly looking for exits and doorways, alleys and subway entrances.

The major lifted his glass. "To your health," he said. "Come on. Drink."

Segal wet his lips with the beer.

"Come on," the major said. "You can tell me the truth. If you don't talk, you know, it would be the easiest thing in the world to call over a sergeant and have him look at your papers. . . ."

"Yes," said Segal. "I'm a Jew."

"I knew it," said the major. "That's why I sat down." He stared at his men with the same look of bondage, devoid of affection, devoid of warmth or loyalty or hope. "There are several questions in my mind you can answer better than anyone."

"What are they?" Segal asked uneasily.

"No rush," said the major. "They'll wait for a minute." He peered curiously at Segal. "You know, it's forbidden for Jews to enter a café in France . . . ?"

"I know," said Segal.

"Also," said the major, "all Jews are instructed to wear the yellow star on their coats. . . ."

"Yes."

"You don't wear yours and I find you in a café in broad daylight."

"Yes."

"You're very brave." There was a little note of irony in the major's voice. "Is it worth it for a drink—to risk being deported?"

Segal shrugged. "It isn't for the drink," he said. "Maybe you won't understand, but I was born in Paris, I've lived all my life in the cafés, on the boulevards."

"What is your profession, Mr. . . . ? Mr. . . . ?"

"Segal."

"What do you do for a living?"

"I was a musician."

"Ah," there was an involuntary little tone of respect in the German's voice. "What instrument?"

"The saxophone," said Segal, "in a jazz orchestra."

The major grinned. "An amusing profession."

"I haven't played in four years," said Segal. "Anyway, I was getting too old for the saxophone and the Germans permitted me to make a graceful exit. But imagine, for a jazz musician, the cafés are his life, his studio, his club, his places to make love, his library and place of business. If I am not free to sit down on a *terrasse* and have a *vin blanc* in Paris, I might just as well go to a concentration camp. . . ."

"Every man," said the major, "to his own particular patriotism."

"I think," said Segal, starting to rise, "that perhaps I'd better go now. . . ."

"No. Sit down. I have a little time." The German stared once more at his men. "We will arrive in Germany a half hour later, if at all. It doesn't matter. Tell me something. Tell me about the French. We have not behaved badly in France. Yet, I feel they hate us. They hate us, most of them, almost as much as the Russians hate us. . . ."

"Yes," said Segal.

"Fantastic," said the major. "We have been most correct, within the bounds of military necessity."

"You believe that. It's wonderful, but you really believe it." Segal was beginning to forget where he was, whom he was talking to, the argument rising hot within him.

"Of course I believe it."

"And the Frenchmen who have been shot . . . ?"

"The army had nothing to do with it. The SS, the Gestapo . . ."
Segal shook his head. "How many times I have heard that!" he said.
"And all the dead Jews, too."

"The army knew nothing about it," the major said stubbornly. "I,
myself, have never lifted my hand, or done one bad thing against any
Jew in Germany or Poland or here in France. At this point, it is necessary to judge accurately who did what . . ."

"Why is it necessary?" Segal asked.

"Let us face the facts." The major looked around him suddenly, lowered his voice. "It is very probable now that we are beaten . . ."

"It is probable," Segal smiled. "It is also probable that the sun will rise
sometime about six o'clock tomorrow morning."

"A certain amount of revenge—what you call justice, will be demanded. The army has behaved in a civilized manner and that must
not be forgotten."

Segal shrugged. "I do not recall seeing the Gestapo in Paris until
after the German army came in. . . ."

"Ah, well," said the major, "you are not representative. You are a
Jew, and naturally a little more bitter, although you seem to have done
very well, I must say."

"I've done very well," said Segal. "I am still alive. It is true that my
two brothers are no longer alive, and my sister is working in Poland,
and my people have been wiped out of Europe, but I have done very
well. I have been very clever." He took out his wallet and showed it to
the major. The Star of David was tucked in so that it could be snapped
out in a moment, and there was a needle already threaded, wound
round a piece of yellow cardboard right next to it. "In a tight spot,"
said Segal, "I could always take out the star and put it on. It took six
stitches, exactly." His hand trembled as he closed the wallet and put
it away. "Four years, major, imagine four years praying each moment
you will have thirty seconds somewhere to sew in six stitches before
they ask to look at your papers. I've done very well. I've always found
the thirty seconds. And do you know where I slept at night, because I
was clever? In the woman's jail. So, when the Gestapo came to my
house looking for me, I was comfortably locked in a cell among the
whores and shoplifters. I could arrange that because my wife is Catholic
and a nurse at the jail. Again, I've done very well. My wife decided
finally she had had enough of me. I don't blame her, it's difficult for a
woman. It's all right for a year, two years, but then the gesture wears

out, you yearn not to have the millstone around your neck. So she decided to divorce me. A very simple procedure for a Christian. You merely go to court and say, 'My husband is a Jew,' and that's the end of it. We have three children, and I have not seen them for a year. Well enough. And the propaganda agencies, who also have no connection to the correct German army, also have done well. The French hate the Germans, but they have been fed the lies for four years and I think maybe they will never quite get over the lies about the Jews. The Germans have various accomplishments to their credit, and this is another one . . ."

"I think perhaps you're being too pessimistic," the major said. "People change. The world goes back to normal, people get tired of hatred and bloodshed."

"You're getting tired of hatred and bloodshed," said Segal. "I can understand that, after all this time."

"Myself," said the major, "I never wanted it. Look at me. Fundamentally, I'm not a soldier. Come to Germany after the war and I'll sell you a Citroen. I'm an automobile salesman, with a wife and three children, dressed in uniform."

"Maybe," said Segal. "Maybe . . . Now we will hear that from many people. Fundamentally, I am not a soldier, I am an automobile salesman, a musician, a pet-fancier, a stamp-collector, a Lutheran preacher, a schoolteacher, anything. . . . But in 1940 we did not hear that as you marched down the boulevards. There were no automobile salesmen then—only captains and sergeants, pilots, artillerists . . . Somehow, the uniform was not such an accident in 1940."

They sat silent. A passing automobile backfired twice, and one of the sleeping soldiers screamed in his sleep, the noise echoing strangely in the sunny square. One of the other soldiers woke the sleeping man and explained to him what had happened and the sleeper sat up against a truck wheel, wiped his face nervously with his hand, went to sleep again, sitting up.

"Segal," said the major, "after this war is over, it will be necessary to salvage Europe. We will all have to live together on the same continent. At the basis of that, there must be forgiveness. I know it is impossible to forgive everyone, but there are the millions who never did anything. . . ."

"Like you?"

"Like me," said the German. "I was never a member of the Party. I lived a quiet middle-class existence with my wife and three children."

"I am getting very tired," Segal said, "of your wife and three children."

The major flushed under the dust. He put his hand heavily on Segal's wrist. "Remember," he said, "the Americans are not yet in Paris."

"Forgive me," said Segal. "I believed you when you told me I could talk freely."

The major took his hand off Segal's wrist. "I mean it," he said. "Go ahead. I have been thinking about these things for a long time, I might as well listen to you."

"I'm sorry," said Segal. "I have to go home and it's a long walk, to the other bank."

"If you have no objection," said the major, "I'll drive you there."

"Thank you," said Segal.

The major paid and they walked together across the square, in front of the men, who stared at them both with the same incurious, hostile expressions. They got into the major's car and started off. Segal couldn't help enjoying his first ride in an automobile in four years and smiled a little as they crossed the Seine, with the river blue and pleasant below them.

The major barely looked at where they were going. He sat back wearily, an aging man who had been pushed beyond the limits of his strength, his face worn and gentle now with exhaustion as they passed in front of the great statues that guard the Chambre des Députés. He took off his cap and the fresh wind blew his sparse hair in thin curls.

"I am ready to face the fact," he said, his voice soft and almost pleading, "that there is a price to be paid for what could be called our guilt. We have lost and so we are guilty."

Segal chuckled drily. By this time he was feeling exhilarated by the beer he had drunk, and the ride, and the sense of danger and victory that came with talking to the major in a town full of German troops.

"Perhaps," said the major, "even if we hadn't lost we would be guilty. Honestly, Mr. Segal, for the last two years I have thought that. In the beginning, a man is swept up. You have no idea of the pressure that is applied when a country like Germany goes to war, to make a man join in with a whole heart, to try to succeed in the profession of soldiering. But even so, it wasn't the older ones like me . . . It was the young ones, the fanatics, they were like a flood, and the rest of us were carried along. You've seen for yourself. . . ."

"I've seen the young ones myself," said Segal. "But also the older ones, sitting at the best restaurants, eating butter and steaks and white bread for four years, filling the theatres, wearing the pretty uniforms, signing orders to kill ten Frenchmen a day, twenty . . ."

"Weakness," said the major. "Self-indulgence. The human race is not composed of saints. Somewhere, forgiveness has to begin."

Segal leaned over and touched the driver on the shoulder. "Stop here, please," he said in German. "I have to get off."

"Do you live here?" the major asked.

"No. Five streets from here," said Segal. "But with all due respect, major, I prefer not showing a German, any German, where I live."

The major shrugged. "Stop here," he told the driver.

The car pulled over to the curb and stopped. Segal opened the door and got out.

The major held his hand. "Don't you think we've paid?" he asked harshly. "Have you seen Berlin, have you seen Hamburg, were you at Stalingrad, have you any idea what the battlefield looked like at Saint Lô, at Mortain, at Falaise? Have you any notion of what it's like to be on the road with the American air force over you all the time and Germans trying to get away in wagons, on foot, on bicycles, living in holes like animals, like cattle in slaughter pens in an abattoir? Isn't that paying, too?" His face worked convulsively under the dust and it seemed to Segal as though he might break into tears in a moment. "Yes," he said, "yes, we're guilty. Granted, we're guilty. Some of us are more guilty than the rest. What are we to do now? What can I do to wash my hands?"

Segal pulled his arm away. For a moment, helplessly, he felt like comforting this aging, wornout, decent-looking man, this automobile salesman, father of three children, this weary, frightened, retreating soldier, this wavering, hopeless target on the straight, long roads of France. Then he looked at the rigid face of the driver, sitting at attention in the front of the car, with his machine pistol, small, and clever, well-oiled and ready for death in the sling under the windshield.

"What can I do?" the major cried again, "to wash my hands?"

Segal sighed wearily, spoke without exultation or joy or bitterness, speaking not for himself, but for the first Jew brained on a Munich street long ago and the last American brought to earth that afternoon by a sniper's bullet outside Chartres, and for all the years and all the dead and all the agony in between. "You can cut your throat," he said, "and see if the blood will take the stain out."

The major sat up stiffly and his eyes were dangerous, cold with anger and defeat, and for a moment Segal felt he had gone too far, that after the four years' successful survival, he was going to die now, a week before the liberation of the city, and for the same moment, looking at the set, angry, beaten face, he did not care. He turned his back and walked deliberately toward his home, the space between his shoulder blades electric and attendant, waiting tightly for the bullet. He had walked ten steps, slowly, when he heard the major say something in German. He walked even more slowly, staring, stiff and dry-eyed, down the broad reaches of the Boulevard Raspail. He heard the motor of the car start up, and the slight wail of the tires as it wheeled around sharply, and he did not look back as the car started back toward the Seine and the Madeleine and the waiting troops sleeping like so many dead by their armored cars before the Madeleine, back along the open, unforgiven road to Germany.

PART IN A PLAY

ALEXIS CONSTANTIN was a pleasant man, and there were many people who thought he had talent, even before the war, when the theatre in Paris was crowded with good actors of his type, heavy, pleasant-appearing men nearing middle age with an aptitude for shrewd comedy who could also be counted upon to be sympathetic and emotional when playing the aging rich husbands of flighty and unfaithful young women. He had been to Hollywood for a year or two and did an imitation of Boyer that was always amusing at parties. He had been married and amicably divorced when considerably younger and before the war had shared an apartment with Philippe Tournebroche, another actor, in the Saint Germain district. They had been friends ever since they had carried spears as young men together at the Odéon, and their friendship continued even though Tournebroche had become known as one of the most brilliant and successful actors in France before the Nazis came in and Constantin had merely plodded along, dependably, making a living, but always playing secondary parts, drawing a mildly approving paragraph from the reviewers here and there, but no more.

The actors' apartment was an agreeable place. Tournebroche made a great deal of money and was thoughtlessly open-handed with it. The two men got along together much better than either of them had got along with their wives, and there were a great many parties always going on there, with people from Broadway and Hollywood wandering through, and many bottles of champagne, and representatives of all the arts and always the new crop of pretty girls whom the two friends

scrupulously shared, and a generous sprinkling of rich ladies and gentlemen with country places in Normandy and villas in Cannes who could
be counted upon when Paris turned dull. All in all, it was the sweet,
rich, glorious life it was possible for an artist to live in the 1930's and
which we are repeatedly warned will never return to the face of the
earth.

Occasionally, when he was offered a part in a new play, Constantin
would have his bad moments. "The same thing," he said one morning
to Philippe, morosely leafing through a new script. "Always the same
thing."

"Let me guess," said Philippe. It was at breakfast, and Philippe was
sitting across from him, meditatively tapping an egg. "An industrialist.
You manufacture perfumes."

"Automobiles."

"Automobiles. A play of superior quality. Your wife deceives you
with an Italian."

"A Hungarian. I have been cuckolded enough," Constantin said bitterly, "to have grounds for divorce against a nunnery full of English
schoolgirls."

Philippe grinned. "Alexis Constantin," he chanted oratorically, "the
eternal pillar of the French theatre. What would we do without the
cuckold? The head reels at the thought. Pass the salt."

"Some day," Alexis said darkly, "they are going to be surprised.
They're going to offer me this part and I'm not going to take it. This
isn't a career—it's a disease. . . ."

"Some day," Philippe said gently, "you're going to play Cyrano. I'm
sure of it." Philippe was sensitive and decent and he was very fond of
Alexis, and as much as he could do to assuage the pain of disappointed
ambition, he did.

But these were only the occasional moments, the flashes of dark
clarity when Alexis saw his career slipping hurriedly past in a confused,
unremembered succession of drab roles. He was not jealous of Philippe,
or as little jealous as an actor can be, and there was always the human
dream that next year would be different, a last-minute change in casting,
a friend dying in a difficult and rewarding role and he called upon to
fill in between matinee and evening performance; a peculiarly discerning producer suddenly appearing on the Parisian scene and calling him,
and saying, "Constantin, I've been watching you. You've been wasting
yourself in those parts. I have here a new play in which the leading
man runs from the age of nineteen to the age of eighty-five. He is irre-

sistible to women and he is on the stage for two hours and twelve minutes. . . ."

But his friends never died, or died in bad roles; no discerning producers arrived in Paris; the pattern of his career was as even and predictable as wallpaper until the Germans entered Paris.

The Germans, who loved Paris much better than they loved Berlin, and who thought of themselves as connoisseurs and patrons of European art, interfered very little with the capital's theatre. Of course they closed down the plays written by Jews and handed Jewish-owned theatres over to more acceptable Frenchmen, for a price, and, naturally, they forbade the production of plays in which the English, Americans, or Russians were presented in a good light, but by and large they did no more harm to the theatre than a large motion-picture concern would do if given the same power.

The play Philippe was appearing in was a fiery story of the Franco-Prussian War, in which Frenchmen died eloquently on Uhlan lances in the third and fourth acts, so there was no question of its reopening. But Alexis was in one of his standard confections, acceptable to all parties except lovers of the theatre, and its producer was invited by the German commissar of culture, a romantic Bavarian colonel, to put the play back on the boards.

"It's a problem," Alexis was saying. He and Philippe had been talking around the subject all night. It was late now, and quiet outside, and there had been considerable brandy drunk over the problem.

"After all, I have only one profession. I am an actor."

"Yes," said Philippe. He was lying outstretched on the couch, staring into the brandy glass he held on his chest.

"A baker continues to bake. A doctor continues to practice medicine, Germans or no Germans. . . ."

"Yes," said Philippe.

"After all," Alexis said, "the play is one that was a success under the Third Republic."

"Yes," said Philippe. "That play was a success under Caligula."

"It does no one any harm."

"Yes," said Philippe. "Pass the brandy."

"There is nothing in it to give comfort to the Nazis."

"Yes," said Philippe.

There was a pause. From the street came the sound of marching, three or four men only, but the hobnails hit the pavement like an army.

"The Germans," said Philippe. "They march to weddings, assignations, toilets. . . ."

"Are you going to play this season?" Alexis asked.

Philippe rolled the liquor around in his glass. "I am not going to play this season," he said.

"What are you going to do?" Alexis asked.

"I'm going to drink brandy," said Philippe, "and read the collected works of Molière."

Alexis listened to the marching dying away in the direction of Montparnasse.

"Are you going to play next season?" he asked.

"No," said Philippe. "I am going to play the season the only Germans in Paris are dead Germans."

"You don't think it's right, even in a play like mine . . . ?"

Philippe waved his glass slowly past his nose. "Each man has to decide for himself. I am not going to influence anyone on a question like this."

"You don't think it's right?" Alexis persisted.

"I . . ." Philippe spoke slowly and softly into the large, delicate glass. "I think it's treason. I am not in the market as an entertainer for the brave, blond German troops."

The two friends remained in silence. From the street came a hoarse voice, bellowing a Schubert *lied,* and a woman's high giggle.

"Well," said Alexis finally, "I'll call Lamarque in the morning and tell him he has to find someone else for the part."

Philippe slowly put down his glass. He got up and came over to where Alexis was sitting. For the first time since the Germans had entered the city, Alexis saw emotion breaking through the bored, remote, cold mask of Philippe's famous face. With surprise, Alexis saw that Philippe was crying. Philippe held out his hand.

"I was afraid," he said. "I was afraid you wouldn't. . . . Forgive me, Alex, forgive me. . . ."

They shook hands, and Alexis was surprised again to see that he, too, had tears in his eyes as he clasped the hand of this man he had known for twenty years.

For a while it was not so bad. The Germans were correct, especially to well-known people in the theatre, and Alexis and Philippe remained aloof, pretending to be taking their time finding suitable parts, politely rejecting all manuscripts offered them. Philippe had a good deal of money, which he shared unstintingly with Alexis. They had a kind of prolonged vacation, reading, lying abed late, even spending seasons in the country after arming themselves with passes which were given graciously and without question by the Germans. There were long, quiet parties now at the apartment, at which painters showed new work which they refused to exhibit publicly, and playwrights read new plays that were meant for the boards sometime in the hazy future when the Germans were finally cleared out of Paris. That time, as the occupation wore on, seemed more and more dreamlike and impossible of achievement, and occasionally men and women of their circle would drop out and take once more their accustomed places on the stage, making their separate peace with the fact that the stalls were packed with German troops, in Paris on leave as a reward for their work on the various fronts.

The holiday began to pall on both Alexis and Philippe, especially as new faces appeared on the Parisian stage, new favorites claimed the attention of the public. Also, Philippe's money gave signs of running out and the Germans confiscated their apartment and they were forced to live, both of them together, in a small room on the fifth floor of a building without an elevator on a bad street in the Saint Denis section.

Finally, there was the day Lamarque sent a note to Alexis. He wanted to see Alexis alone and he wished Alexis to keep quiet about it for the time being.

Alexis dressed carefully for the interview, his best remaining suit, and a sober, expensive necktie he hadn't worn in two years. He had his hair cut on his way to Lamarque's office, and just before he went up the stairs bought a flower for his buttonhole. He mounted the stairs slowly, a solid, fleshy, handsome citizen, his face somber and reserved, hiding the sharp, nervous pangs of excitement and premonitory guilt as he opened the door of the producer's office.

"Germans or no Germans," Lamarque was saying, "this play"—he waved the manuscript excitedly above his desk—"this play is theatrical literature. It's a contribution to the culture of France. And the leading part . . . My God!" Lamarque looked religiously up to heaven. "An old man, but powerful, in the full flush of his maturity, on the stage half the first act, the whole second act, and a death scene in the third act Racine couldn't've done better." Lamarque was a little fat man from Marseilles with small, shrewd, dark, promoter's eyes. He had done well under the Third Republic, he had done well under the Germans, and he would do well under the Ninth Dictatorship of the Proletariat.

"Alexis," he gripped the actor's arm fiercely, "Alexis, when I read this I could only think of one man. You. I know the trash you've been playing. The same old thing, year after year. Same tricks, same notices. Death for an actor. This would be a new Constantin. Raimu, Bauer, they'll seem like schoolboys next to you. I've always felt that when the right part came along you could astonish the world."

"It's true," Alexis said tentatively, knowing that it was only because so many of the old standbys were no longer playing that Lamarque was talking to him, "I have somehow not had the opportunity to . . ."

"This is it, Alex," Lamarque said solemnly. "Believe me I've been in the theatre all my life and I know when a part and an actor get together like electricity."

"However," Alexis said, in a troubled voice, "it's very kind of you, but in a way, I thought I'd wait for awhile. . . ."

"He's a miser," Lamarque said reverently. "A huge, powerful miser. He's the hard-fisted, ruthless, scheming king of an industrial empire, with a pathologic love for money. He was disappointed in love in his youth and he has turned from women. All his passion is given to his money. His money is his wife, his mistress, his children, his life, and he ruins men with a laugh for a thousand francs. There's a scene when his best friend comes to him and pleads . . . but you have to read it for yourself, Alex, the power, the power, I don't want to spoil it for you. And there's a pure young girl he meets . . . And his change. The blossoming in December, the laughter. And then the discovery. The girl's a slut. Off with a captain in the Algerian cavalry at the moment he is buying a large pure diamond in a simple setting for her in the Place Vendôme. And a mad scene, Alex, a mad scene that makes *Hamlet* look like a game of dominoes on a Sunday afternoon. And the murder and the speech before he takes the poison! And the bloody, raging prayer to his God, with the glass in his hand! Alex," he said solemnly, "as God is my judge, this is the time for you to take your place in the history of the French theatre. . . . Here!" He thrust the manuscript into Alexis' hand. "Don't say another word. Take it with you and read it, and come back to me at five o'clock this afternoon and take my hand and say, "Lamarque, I want to thank you from the bottom of my heart. I am ready for rehearsals tomorrow morning!"

A little dazedly, Alexis left the office. He walked slowly toward the Seine and sat down on one of the benches overlooking the river, and in the pale spring sunlight read the play. The play was written with bite and energy, and was not as lurid as Lamarque had described it, although it was studded with big, showy scenes for the principal character. As he stared unseeingly across the river, Alexis could imagine himself striding a richly lit stage, cruel, monstrous, pitiful, torn, charming, stricken, corrupt, murderous, suicidal, evil, calling down the powers of hell upon the world he was leaving behind him.

It was a role the vision of which had haunted his dreams ever since he had first set foot on a stage, and Alexis knew, as he walked slowly toward his apartment, that whatever Philippe would say, he was going to take it. . . .

It was a great success. Overnight his name became a tradition in the French theatre. The comic, aging cuckold was forgotten, and in his place was a tragic actor of historic stature. Every new script of any importance was submitted to him and he did two films in the suburbs that made his face famous throughout Europe. It was true that several of his more hotheaded friends cut him on the street and there were one or two savage articles about him in some of the flimsy resistance sheets that were unkindly sent to him and, of course, Philippe had broken with him, on that first afternoon. . . .

"Yes, yes," Philippe had said wearily, "I know all the arguments. Argument one: we must eat. Argument two: the baker bakes, the doctor medicines, etc. Argument three: the Germans have won and will continue to win. Are we to make no arrangements for the rest of our lives? Argument four: we all know French misers, must we only present Frenchmen as angels, etc? Argument five: I'm through with you."

And Philippe had packed and that was the last Alexis had seen of him. Later, he heard vaguely that Philippe was serving with the maquis in the Haute Savoie, and on one or two occasions had even been glimpsed in Paris, looking considerably older and shabbier than he had before. Alexis suffered a twinge of uneasiness each time he heard Philippe had been seen in Paris, but he was busy and successful and honored on all sides and consolation came easy.

It was in July, 1944, when Alexis next saw Philippe. The Americans were at Saint Lô, and Paris had become an uneasy city, tremors of guilt and joyful anticipation running through its secret life. Shots were heard in the streets at night, the Germans strode through the city searching the eyes of the inhabitants, calculating and puzzled; other Germans were found obscurely murdered along the river or floating face down toward the sea. Everyone knew that resistance battalions had been formed and the seventeen-year-old child who cleared the dishes from your table in a restaurant might be a Communist captain with an arsenal under his mattress and your name quite possibly on his list for retribution. Among the men who had done well under the Germans, or who had done nothing against them, there was a quiet, nervous, unhappy adding up of interior accounts. Alexis was no exception. He was not playing at the time and he took to long slow, speculative walks and sitting up late and alone at night, staring out the dark windows of his apartment at the waiting, trembling city around him. He followed the war maps closely, and examined his reactions as honestly as he could, and was pleased to see, that despite the danger to himself, he felt a thin, undeniable thrill of joy when the Americans broke through in Normandy and clearly took the road to Paris.

Philippe, when he saw him near the Etoile, was almost unrecognizable. He had grown much older, with gray hair and deep furrows in a face that had become very thin and weatherbeaten. This, added to his clumsy clothes and heavy boots, made him seem like a farmer, and a poor one at that, committed to a bleak ten acres of unprofitable land, in town for a day. Alexis walked behind him, watching, and noticed painfully the harsh, wounded limp with which Philippe moved past the little tables of the cafés.

For a moment Alexis almost stopped, feeling that he must avoid this scarred, bitter-seeming veteran. But looking at the awkward, weathered, familiar back, thinking of the twenty years of friendship, twisted in the uncertain guilty currents of that bloody August, he walked more quickly, overtook Philippe, put his hand on his arm.

Philippe stopped, looked around. There was a quick, momentary tightening around his eyes, but that was all. "Yes, monsieur?" he asked politely.

"Please, Philippe," Alexis begged. "Don't say monsieur."

Philippe started to pull his arm away.

"Please talk to me. . . ." But Philippe began to walk away, deliberately, but not slowly, before the café tables.

Alexis followed him. "I'm sorry," he said. "I was a fool. I was weak. Anything you say. I should have gone with you. I've heard of what you've been doing. I'm proud you were once my friend."

Philippe limped slowly along, looking straight ahead, as though he heard not a word.

"Anything," Alexis said, pleadingly. "I'm ashamed of myself. I have a lot of money. I know you people need it. Take it. All of it."

For the first time a look of interest came into Philippe's face. He glanced sidelong at his friend, speculatively.

"Money buys guns," Alexis said hurriedly. "Everybody knows the Germans sell guns, but expensive . . . You haven't got the right to turn me away. No matter what you think of me. I want to do something to help. Maybe it's late, but I want to help. Myself, too. There'll be fighting. I'm willing to fight. Forget the last three years. At least now, for the time being, forget . . ."

Philippe stopped. He stared coldly, without friendship at Alexis. "Don't talk so loud," he said.

"Forgive me," said Alexis humbly.

"And get out of here and go back to your home. And wait there."

"Will you come there?" Alexis asked happily.

"Maybe." Philippe shrugged, smiled sourly. "Maybe we will."

"My address is . . ."

"We know what your address is. Good-bye, monsieur." Without a smile, without a handshake, Philippe walked off. Alexis looked after the harsh, limping figure losing itself among the bright dresses, and the bicycles and the green uniforms in the sunlight, feeling sick for the lost twenty years, but also feeling a quickening and a hope he had not felt for months. He turned and went back to his apartment and sat there and waited.

"This gentleman," Philippe was saying, his voice touched with a light, scornful amusement, the first sign Alexis had seen of the long years this civilian soldier had spent on the stage, "this gentleman is known to me."

There were three of them who had come up to Alexis' apartment with Philippe just after dark. They were small, quiet men, very young, shabby and deadly-looking, and Alexis felt himself being weighed candidly and swiftly in their steady glances, as they sat across from him in his bright, comfortable living room.

"Early in the Occupation," Philippe went on, "he turned himself over to the service of the Germans, as so many did. . . ."

Alexis opened his mouth to protest, to say that continuing at his profession, keeping a theatre lit, in French, even though Germans did attend, was not so irrevocably sinful, especially when measured against the full-hearted co-operation so common in other and more important fields—but looking at the four, cool, quiet faces, he decided merely to sit there and remain silent.

"Now"—there was a slight stagey, amused mockery in Philippe's voice—"now the Americans are in Rennes and this gentleman has suffered a new growth of patriotism. . . ."

"Philippe," Alexis protested regretfully, "may I talk for myself?"

One of the other men nodded.

"I was wrong," Alexis said. "I wish to make up for it. Money. As much as I have. Myself, if I can be of assistance. It's as simple as that."

The three men looked at each other. Philippe turned his back, stared at a Derain drawing on the wall.

One of the men stood up, came over and shook Alexis' hand. The others smiled at him a little, with a touch of warmth, but Philippe didn't look at him, even when he took out the huge pile of franc notes and turned them over. Philippe did not say good night when he left.

When the fighting started in the city, at barricades and windows and on the roofs, they called for Alexis and he went with them, in old flannels, that he had used to lounge on the beach at Cannes, with the new armband that marked him as a member of the French Forces of the Interior. In the crowded room near the Hotel de Ville, waiting to receive what arms were available, with the preliminary crackling of automatic fire coming in through the windows, he looked again and again at the badge of acceptance on his arm. He felt too old for this and fear was a stone lump at the back of his throat and he was ashamed that his shirt was stained with nervous sweat, but when he looked down at the mark on his arm, there was a sense of religion and peace that almost compensated for the cold trembling nerves and the pumping blood.

They gave him four potato-masher grenades, which he stuck in his belt, after surreptitiously watching what the other men did with theirs, like a country cousin at a banquet watching the host pick up knives and forks.

Philippe came in and the room fell silent. Philippe stood before them and spoke in a low, even voice. "We do not intend to fight pitched battles at this point," he said. "We will harass them, pick them off when we can, try to make them stay and take cover and hole up until the Americans get here. We will try to make it expensive for them to move anywhere in Paris. We will be frugal with ammunition and weapons. I am sorry we are not better armed. Anyone who feels that he is not well enough equipped to go into this engagement is at liberty to leave. . . ." He looked thoughtfully at Alexis as he spoke. Alexis stroked the handle of one of the grenades.

Philippe came over and stood before him. "Monsieur," he said, "do you know how to use your weapon?"

"I—uh . . . Not exactly."

Philippe pulled one of the grenades out of Alexis' belt and showed him how to hold it, how to withdraw the pin, how to throw it. Alexis thanked him and Philippe gave him back the grenade and spoke sharply to all of them. "All right. We are ready. . . ."

They slid out into the night.

The next two days were a confused series of clanging dreams for Alexis; the first, biting smell of powder, the sharp, malicious chips of

stone flying off window sills past your head and the mean, continuing
searching noise of German machine guns, and a man falling beside
you with a bullet through his lung and your taking his 1918 rifle and
firing into the dust a hundred yards away and perhaps hitting the
running gray figure there; and the heavy-footed trotting from one
barricade of stones and tree trunks to another, with the inexorable noise
of the Tiger tank turning the corner behind you and churning through
the debris, and the hopeless, dissolving sound of shells hitting around
you and the bloody disintegration before your eyes when the overturned
car in front of you was hit by a shell and the two men and a woman
pinned under it vanished . . . The boys around him were pleased with
him and called him "Poppa" and loyally swore one of his grenades had
fallen inside a tank turret when he dropped it from a third-floor window
near the Opera and from time to time, in little flashes in the heat and
fear and exhaustion, he was pleased with himself and surprised that
there was so much of the soldier hidden under the boulevardier and
artist. Philippe alone spoke to him coldly and professionally, not dis-
criminating against him, but showing him no favor. Alexis did not mind.
In the ambush and counter ambush, in the sudden burst from the
roof, and the dry-mouthed stalking down the moonlit streets, there
was no time to think of anything except the next German, the nearest
cover, a hurried sip of wine to dissolve for an instant the stone of thirst
and terror in the throat, a place to lie down and sleep for an hour to
keep from dying of fatigue on your feet. . . .

He was alone with Philippe, hiding behind a wooden door that was
just open a slit, so they could cover the street. Seven men of the group
had just left them, going down the street to investigate the report that
there were four or five Germans hiding in a wine merchant's cellar
half a block away.

He could hear Philippe breathing hard beside him, because they
had run a hundred yards down the broad street to get here, with two
shots fired at them from snipers on the roofs. There were strange,
wonderful colored gyrations of the atmosphere before his eyes and he
heard his breath coming like the noise of some ancient machine, creaking and in need of oil. He sank to one knee, leaning against the door,
feeling the door get wet from the sweat that was thick on his forehead.
For a moment, looking up at the gaunt, red-eyed, scarred, be-stubbled
face above him, wavering in the gyrating lights of his own exhaustion,
he thought of Philippe and himself sitting across from each other,
many years before at breakfast, the coffee steaming between them, the
newspapers fresh and black before them, themselves newly washed

in crisp silk robes. . . . "Your wife," Philippe had said jokingly at breakfast a long time ago, "deceives you with an Italian. . . ."

"They're going too slow. Too slow," Philippe was looking out the door. He had opened it wider and was watching his patrol cautiously make its way, hugging the sides of the buildings toward the wine merchant's cellar. "Stay here," he said to Alexis. "I've got to get them to move faster. . . ." He looked down at Alexis curiously. "Are you all right?" he asked.

With an effort, Alexis got to his feet, essayed a smile. "Sure," he said. "I'm a little old for this sort of thing. That's all."

"Yes," said Philippe and slipped out after the patrol.

He had only been gone five seconds when Alexis saw the truck. It ground around the corner and stopped for an instant at the end of the street. It was a big open German army truck, with a machine gun mounted on it above the driver's cab in front, and it seemed to be full of men, with rifles bristling on all sides.

Alexis threw open the door. "Philippe!" he screamed.

Philippe turned and he and the men of the patrol saw the truck just at the moment that the truck driver and the man at the machine gun saw them. The Frenchmen started to run and the driver threw his vehicle into gear and picked up speed, pursuing them. The machine gunner fired several bursts, but the jolting of the truck made him wild and the bullets ricocheted around Philippe and the others as they ran toward the corner, where they would get a moment's respite. Alexis took one last look at Philippe, the limping, exhausted figure running grotesquely, rifle in hand, with stone chips and machine-gun bullets flickering around him. . . .

Alexis left the protection of the doorway and began to run across the street at an angle that would bring the truck even with him as it passed him. For a moment, no one in the truck saw him and he had time to pull the pin from a grenade as he ran heavily, diagonally, almost in the same direction as the careening truck, like a man running to swing on a trolley car. Then the machine gunner saw him and swung his weapon around at him. The first burst missed him and Alexis lumbered on, his breath singing weirdly in his ears, the grenade clutched tight in his sweating hand. The riflemen in the body of the truck saw him too, and the weapons appeared over the wooden sides, converging on him. Alexis never heard the shots, but he heard the sick whistle of the missiles past his head. One hit him high on the left shoulder and he stumbled, then picked himself up and, scrambling and stumbling, continued toward the approaching truck. The machine gunner swung his weapon around and there was the hysterical triphammer noise and Alexis felt something hit him in the head and there was the strange taste of blood in his mouth, although his tongue for some reason could not move to swallow it. He kept on, his shoes making a deliberate, shuffling, weary clatter on the pavement, amid all the other sounds, the grinding of the truck, the shots, the yelling German. His arms out to keep his balance, his legs moving with the insane deliberation of the mechanism of an automatic phonograph, staggering and sliding in his ruined fashionable flannels that had looked so well on the bright Mediterranean beach, blood streaming from his shoulder and head, leaving a plain dark wavering trail behind him on the pavement, his cheekbone exposed, broken and white in the bloody face, and the eye drooped close, its muscles torn and useless, and the other eye frantic and singed and dusty, he caught up with the rolling truck, put one hand on the cab, was dragged along for an instant while the man inside beat at the hand with the butt of his gun. With the homely, everyday grunt of a fat man swinging upon the platform of a suburban train, just reached in the morning, he pulled himself for a moment onto the running board and heaved the grenade up and over the wooden side into the mass of rifles and uniforms and ammunition and screaming men. . . .

He fell back and dropped peacefully to the pavement. Far off, it seemed to him, there was an explosion. Somehow he sat himself up in the middle of the street and regarded his handiwork with the one crazy eye. The truck had overturned and was burning brightly. Here and there a gray uniform dragged itself painfully for a yard or two, but most of the gray uniforms lay still and some were still burning.

The ghost and spectre of a grin crossed what was left of his face.

Philippe walked slowly up to him. Alexis brokenly raised one arm to wipe the blood and stone dust out of his one eye so that he could see his friend more clearly. For a single mangled moment Alexis thought of the things that lay between them, the thousand drinks and the pretty girls and the vacations and the idle debonair hours after the theatre and the afternoon he had been no more than an actor and had decided to play the big, ludicrous, sinful part . . . The bloody mouth and the broken teeth mumbled something, lost in blood, and the single wild eye stared up, dying, begging forgiveness.

But Philippe said, gently, but coldly, "Lie down, monsieur. We will look for the aid men."

Alexis shook his smashed, tangled head, grieving, knowing in this last instant that he was unforgiven, and lay down on the stained and fractured pavement.

THE PRIEST

THE PRIEST WALKED leisurely across the Besancon Bridge. The Doubs flowed swiftly past, springlike and ruffled and green, carrying with it a bright mountain breeze through the sunny valley. The priest was round and small and his dark, tanned face was rosy and cheerful in the pleasant morning as he walked with little steps next to the stone balustrade, keeping off to the side as a tank marked with the black cross rumbled past a wagonload of cabbages into town. Two young blond paratroopers, with their caps off, were leaning on the balustrade, staring quietly into the rushing water, their hair blowing in the wind, and the priest stopped next to them and stood by their side looking east to the mountains.

"Very pretty morning," the priest said, smiling.

"Excuse us, Father," one of the paratroopers said, haltingly, "we do not speak French. We speak only German."

The priest shrugged, smiled, patted one of the boys in a fatherly gesture, on the shoulder. *"Guten tag,"* he said, moving off.

"Auf Wiedersehen, Father," the boy said, standing up straight. He was almost a foot taller than the priest and he seemed very young, seventeen, eighteen perhaps, standing there with his hair blowing over his unlined, rather pale face.

The priest moved on, his small scuffed dusty shoes making a little mincing pattern under the swinging, worn folds of his cassock. He walked slowly along the busy street, pleased with the morning traffic, nodding agreeably at the housewives with their net shopping bags stuffed with vegetables. He stopped in front of one of the shops which was used as an art gallery, and looked at a local painter's water color of the Besancon cathedral, his dark round face grave with judgment.

In the same window, by the same artist, there were three plump, long-legged nudes lying in abandoned positions on rugs and sofas, and the priest glanced rather hastily at the pink and fleshy confections. A little grin played around the corners of his mouth as he turned away from the window and continued up the street.

He crossed the cobbled square at the end of the street, and, holding the skirts of his cassock, skipped nimbly and good-naturedly to dodge a large German army truck that was rumbling through. A little out of breath, and smiling, he walked to a table on the open terrace of the large café that stood under the new foliage of the trees along one side of the square. The man sitting at the table stood up as he approached.

"Good morning, Father," he said, holding a chair for the priest, and smiling with pleasure.

"Good morning, my son." The priest sat down, smiling at him, but sighing, too, as a fat man does at sudden changes of position.

The man seated himself beside the priest, so that they both could look out over the square and enjoy the fresh bustle of the spring morning. He was a large, slender man, with weary dark eyes and a sharp mouth and he was dressed in faded workman's clothes, with old, washed oil and grease stains evident here and there in the worn cloth.

"I hope," said the priest, "I didn't keep you waiting long."

"I just arrived," the man said.

The waiter trotted to their table. "Messieurs," he said.

"White wine for me," said the priest.

"Two," said the other man.

The waiter trotted off.

The man in workman's clothes surveyed the priest fondly, but with amusement. "Solomon," he said, "you're getting fatter every week."

The priest sighed. "Flesh is the curse of man. I live on cabbage and skimmed milk and I walk a hundred kilometers a week up and down mountain roads and I grow more and more like a pincushion. Still, Maurice, in a way, it has its points. Everyone expects a priest to be fat."

"That's true," said Maurice.

The waiter came back with the two glasses of white wine and the saucers. "Messieurs," he said, serving them. He trotted off.

The priest looked after him absently, noticing that there was no one at the near-by tables. "All right, Maurice," he said.

Maurice sipped his wine. "In Marcel Artois' barn, in the hay-loft . . ."

"Yes," said the priest.

"On the road to Epinal."

"I know the house." The priest sipped his drink, nodding absently, his eyes squinted a little, looking out over the square.

"Two Sten guns with a thousand rounds of ammunition . . ."

"Well," said the priest.

"Three Enfield rifles with two hundred and fifty rounds of ammunition. A Luger and six grenades. How many men does Philip have with him?"

"Ten."

"Does that include you?"

"That includes me." The priest nodded.

"The difficulty with the child," Maurice said loudly, as two German lieutenants passed, "is that he refuses to recognize the authority of his mother."

"I will come by Wednesday afternoon," the priest said clearly, "and attempt to reason with him."

"There will be a gasoline convoy passing the crossroad two miles north of Epinal around eleven o'clock tomorrow night," said Maurice. "Ordinarily, the convoys are lightly guarded in this area, and there is brush right down to the roadside, and they stop at the crossroads for a minute or two to wait for stragglers. Tell Philip I suggest that that is the most profitable place. . . ."

"I'll tell him," said the priest.

"However, he understands," Maurice said, "that it is his business and I am merely offering suggestions."

"I'll tell him," said the priest.

"Messieurs?" The waiter was standing over them, questioning.

"Nothing more for me, thank you," said the priest.

Maurice put down the money for the drinks and the waiter cleared away the glasses and the saucers.

"Gasoline trucks," said Maurice, "make a very satisfactory target. They have a tendency to blow up."

"Philip will be pleased." The priest nodded again, with a trace of amusement in his dark eyes.

"Tell Philip I pray that God smiles upon your enterprise," said Maurice, very seriously.

The priest smiled a little. "I will pass on yours and God's good wishes. . . ."

Maurice turned and stared soberly at the priest for the first time. "Solomon," he said softly, "I think you are taking too much of a risk."

The priest grinned. "Again," he said, "the old song . . ."

"But to pretend to be a priest!" Maurice shook his head. "You're always on the verge of being discovered. Any curé with his eyes half-open . . . Any sudden or unexpected situation . . ."

The priest looked around him, his eyes crinkled. "I know this will offend your deep religious sensibilities, Maurice," he said, "but it is amazing how little people expect of the servants of the Church. And priests're always rambling around, poking their noses into other people's business. They make perfect messengers for the Underground. If we could really get the holy men of France into the movement, we would have a system of intelligence better than any telephone network. . . ."

"The Church has its own spiritual problems," Maurice said bleakly.

"Forgive me." The priest stretched out his hand and touched Maurice's arm. "I mean no offense."

"It still strikes me as dangerous," Maurice said.

The priest shook his head. "Look at me," he said.

Maurice stared at him. "Well?"

"In every magazine," the priest said, "on every wall, there are pictures of criminals against Germany who look just like me—Jews, swarthy, with thick lips, and hooked noses. . . . Why, Maurice," the priest said, grinning, "I could make a fortune as a photographer's model in Berlin."

Maurice chuckled. "I must admit . . ."

"But dressed like this . . ." The priest shrugged. "A priest is expected to look like anything at all in the world. Anyway, I've got away with it for three years now. I couldn't conduct Mass, but I tell my beads in public, and I carry a breviary and read a little Latin and I got a smattering of the sacraments from Father Morand before they killed him, and my papers look more authentic than a monastery full of Benedictine brothers, and the cassock is very handy when it comes to hiding my pistol."

Maurice stood up, smiling. "You always win this argument. Still, it gives me a chill every time I see you pass a church."

"I promise to defrock myself," the priest said, "ten minutes after the Germans're out of France."

"Well," said Maurice, "I must get back to work." They shook hands. "Good-bye, Father."

"I promise," Solomon said gravely, "to do nothing to disgrace the cloth. God be with you, my son."

Solomon sat at the table in the playful, sunny wind, watching Maurice cross the square. Maurice had a square, upright way of walking, and, knowing him, Solomon felt that by his walk Maurice betrayed himself to all the world—honest, righteous, devoid of subservience or fear. Each time, after their meetings, when they said good-bye, Solomon was moved by worriment and sorrow for his friend, and a bitter sense that they would not meet again. The trick was, in their business, to feel nothing, no affection, no sympathy, no regrets for the dead and dying. But fighting beside men in this obscure war, with your lives on the tips of each other's tongues a hundred times a day, with your life dependent every moment on their rectitude and sacrifice, you found yourself loving the good ones better than a wife or a son, and then the trick, of course, did not work. . . .

Maurice disappeared around a corner and Solomon sighed and stood up heavily, pulling his cassock down.

He stared back across the terrace, but at that moment a canvas-covered army truck drove up and the soldiers jumped out and the young lieutenant said loudly, "Nobody will move, if you please. All the patrons of this establishment will come with me, if you please. . . ."

Solomon looked at the corner to make sure that Maurice had disappeared and then sat down, sighing like a fat man, waiting for the Germans to reach him.

The interior of the truck was dark and crowded with some twenty patrons of the café. An odor of fear hung over the twenty heads and people attempted to remain frigid and remote from neighbors pressing on all sides.

"This is a formidable nuisance," one gentleman said in a loud voice, looking angrily at the impassive guard at the rear of the truck. "I have a very important business engagement at one o'clock. And I have a pass signed personally by General Meister, himself, who is a personal acquaintance of mine."

"I have a personal request," a voice cut into the semi-gloom under the canvas from near the front of the truck. "Please keep personally quiet."

"I will remember that voice," said the personal acquaintance of General Meister threateningly.

The priest wriggled a little on his bench and his two neighbors looked at him sourly.

"Excuse me," he said apologetically. "A fat man finds it difficult to be comfortable in his clothes. . . ." He put his hands under his cassock, through the side slits and pulled at his belt.

"What's the matter?" a man across the aisle muttered. "The priest wearing a corset?"

Two or three of the men tittered a little sourly.

"Excuse me, again," the priest said, lifting himself a little from the narrow wooden bench, under which there were some tow chains loosely stowed.

"Only the priests," said his neighbor loudly, "still remain uncomfortably fat in France."

Solomon sat back once more, sighing, a tiny smile on his lips in the darkness. Below him, hidden by the chains, lay the small pistol he had contrived to loosen from his belt and drop there.

"What did you have for dinner last night, Father?" his neighbor asked unpleasantly. "A whole stuffed duck?"

"God be with you, my son," Solomon said serenely, as the truck rattled into the courtyard of Gestapo headquarters.

Solomon was sleeping when they came to his cell and opened the door. It was near dawn and dark and cold and he woke shivering when the two SS men drew back the bolt and shone the beam of the electric lantern in his face, where he lay on the wooden bench that served the cell as a bed.

"You," one of the jailers said. "Get up."

Solomon sat up, rubbing the ruffled thin hair on the top of his head, still half-caught in the sharp darkness in the vague, delicious dream he'd been having in which he had been eating a large dinner in a warm, sunny café in Marseilles. A warm, peppery soup and lobster with a tomato sauce . . .

"Well," he said, blinking, struggling with the old, familiar cold knot of fear at the sight of the black uniforms, "well, gentlemen . . ."

"Get up."

Solomon stood up.

"Are you dressed?" The man with the lantern played it up and down the ragged cassock.

"Yes." Solomon swallowed and he felt himself shiver, thin waves of cold trembling from his groin upwards, finally tightening the skin on his forehead and around his ears in little spasms.

"This way," said the man with the flashlight.

Between the two SS men, Solomon walked out of the cell and down the stone corridor, his knees hurting as though the act of walking was a shocking and unnatural activity. Too bad, too bad, Solomon thought, licking the corner of his lips drily, as he followed the dark figure along the dim stone. He had thought that he was going to get away with it. His papers had been in perfect order, excellently forged, and they had searched him only perfunctorily and questioned him hardly at all, and had even been slightly apologetic, or as apologetic as you could ever expect a German to be. When he had dropped off to his cold sleep he had really thought they would release him in the morning. Well, he thought wryly, there are several different kinds of release.

The SS men stopped in front of a door.

"There's a man in there," the German with the lantern said, "who's going to be shot in a few minutes. He wants the last rites of the Church. Ordinarily, we are not so agreeable, but"—with a small grin in the weak light—"since we had the Church so handy this evening, we saw no harm in letting him make his soul comfortable. I, myself, am a Catholic, and I understand that a man, before he . . . At any rate, you have fifteen minutes."

He swung the door open and put his lantern down on the floor inside the cell. Solomon walked slowly in and stood still as the door closed behind him.

The lantern diffused a thin pale light along the floor, leaving the corners and walls of the cell in heavy darkness. A man was standing with his back to the door, his head lost in the shadows in the bare room. He turned when the sound of the Germans at the door had ceased.

"Father," he said softly, but mechanically, as though he had rehearsed the speech, "I am very glad you came. I have lived by the Church all my life and I believe in the life everlasting and I wish to make my peace with God in accordance with the sacraments before facing judgment . . ." The voice was bruised and muffled in the shadowy room, as though it came from a throat and lips that had been sorely torn and battered, but Solomon recognized it.

"We have fifteen minutes, my son," he said, trying to control the sorrow in his own throat. He stepped forward so that Maurice could see his face.

Maurice slowly lifted his eyes to look at Solomon. His lips were puffed and cut and three teeth were missing, with the blood still coming from the sockets. He held his hands stiffly in front of him. They were torn and swollen and covered with blood from the places at the fingertips where his nails had been torn out.

"The Germans told me," Maurice said evenly, "that I was lucky to be killed on just this night, being a good Catholic. They happened to have a priest here and they were releasing him in the morning. Shall we begin, Father?"

"Are you sure . . ." Solomon could not keep his voice from trembling.

"Yes, Father," said Maurice, staring at the door of the cell, behind which the Germans might or might not be listening.

Solomon sat on the small three-legged stool in the center of the room and, stiffly, with the pale light making his ruined face look clotted and grotesque, Maurice knelt before him.

The jail was absolutely quiet and Solomon could hear the breath whistling brokenly through Maurice's smashed nose. Solomon closed his eyes, trying to remember some scraps of what Father Morand had taught him before the Germans killed him.

"Son, I will hear your confession now," he said, surprised at the clarity and steadiness of his own voice.

Maurice bowed his head at Solomon's knee. "Forgive me, Father," he said evenly, "for my sins. . . ." Then, in the quiet night, he confessed. He confessed to the sin of doubt, the sins of anger and murder, the sins of envy and desire, the sin of despair. Kneeling rigidly, his wounded hands resting for support on Solomon's knees, staining the old cloth with the slow dark blood, he spoke soberly and clearly, his voice swelling occasionally in the stone room, loud enough to be heard through the open grating of the oak door, if anyone were listening there. . . .

As the voice went on, Solomon remembered another man he had talked with, played another game with, before death. It was when he was a boy of fourteen and a neighbor was dying and too weak to leave the house and Solomon had gone every afternoon and played chess with the dying man in the sickroom. The man had once been fat and red of face, but now his skin was yellow and old and hung in loose folds from his bones. He was an avid player and loved to win, and occasionally cheated, moving pieces surreptitiously and taking back moves, falling back to his pillows in exhausted triumph after the game was over. Solomon had played with him on the day of his death, and at the funeral had watched with dry eyes as the coffin was lowered, the mourners and the cold earth, and stone crosses of the cemetery somehow mixed in his mind with bishops taking pawns and black wooden knights held in a yellow hand advancing over red squares. Ever since then, death and chess had lain in troubled confusion in his mind, funerals and ivory, flowers and squares, tears and pawns tumbled in a box mingling in obscure painful symbols in his brain. As he regarded his friend, kneeling before him, he felt as though he were betraying him in this double game of priest and chessman, and he wrenched at his will to focus all his pity and affection on the dying man. He put his hand out humbly and touched the bloody fingers of his friend. The Jews did it differently, he thought. They went into death hot and guilty, as to a roaring battle in a dark, bloody doubtful abyss, with intercession to their wrathy, fitful God not to be hoped for. He thought of the times he had seen Maurice coldly skirt death, and the times he had seen him wash his child's face, and of the times he had seen Maurice kill, with a rather abstracted, calm, regretful air, and of the times he had seen him walk side by side with his wife, dressed for Sunday, on the road to church.

As the voice went on in the cold stone room, Solomon thought of the times he had looked at Maurice's slender strained face, and known deep in his heart that he was going to die before their business came to an end. You felt that about yourself from time to time, and often about others, and you took a drink, or you got into an argument, and tried to forget it, but he had been sure of Maurice. Solomon was not a religious man, and he doubted that God would condemn Maurice because he had been shriven by a Jew, but he looked closely at Maurice to see if the orthodox Catholic soul, so obedient to the ordered sacraments and hierarchy, was suffering at the deception. But Maurice's face and voice were calm and clear, as though he were being granted absolution for all his earthly deeds by the Bishop of Rome, himself.

Finally, the droning broken voice stopped in the cold cell. Somewhere down the corridor there was the chilly clank of steel and a young German voice singing the mournful words of "Lili Marlene," the sorrowing, sentimental melody hanging cloyingly on the stale, condemned, frozen air. Solomon stared at the austere, destroyed face of his friend. If there were only some way of giving him one word to carry with him to the final wall, one word to tell him, you are loved, you will not be forgotten, we do not believe the shallow coffin and the quick lime pit are the end, we will mention your name later in the century . . . His hands groped in a small, lost gesture before him, but there was the sound of steps outside the door, and the fiddling with the lock.

He blindly ruffled the pages of his brieviary and read a scrap of Latin for the absolution, and as the door swung open, made vague, wandering motions with his hands, from some dim memory of another deathbed.

Maurice stood up as the Germans came in. "I am very happy, Father," he said courteously as the Germans bound his hands, "that you were here tonight. I hope it has not interfered too much with your business in these parts."

Solomon stared at the Germans, knowing that Maurice was telling him he had not broken, that he had told the Germans nothing, that no plans were invalidated by his death.

"It has not interfered, son," he said. He stood up and followed them out to the corridor and watched Maurice walk away between the Germans, the familiar walk unchanged by the prison, or the cords on his wrists, or the knowledge that the wall was waiting. Maurice walked away, as he had walked away from the terrace of the café, the lean shoulders set square and upright, betraying himself to all the world.

A third guard came up to Solomon, touched his elbow. "This way, Father," he said, and led him back to his cell. He was sitting there, waiting for his deliverance, when he heard the small muffled sound, like a door closing sharply far away, from the other side of the prison.

NIGHT IN ALGIERS

It was late at night in Algiers and in the army newspaper office the clatter of typewriters had long since died down. Most of the men had gone to sleep upstairs and the halls were empty. The wisecracks and decisions and sudden laughter were over for the day, and in another building the presses were comfortably turning out the next day's paper.

On the walls, the pictures of all the pretty girls with big bosoms looked a littly weary in the dim light. Down on the street outside the Red Cross building, late-traveling soldiers whistled for hitches in the dark and a soldier who had had some wine was singing the "Marseillaise" in English, the brave words and the brave tune floating up a little uncertainly through the darkness until a truck stopped and picked the singer up. In the office the radio was on and Tchaikovsky's piano concerto was coming in, moody and sorrowful, from London.

An assistant editor with sergeant's stripes on his sleeves came in and sat down wearily in front of the radio. He stared at it, remembering many things that had nothing to do with his job, remembering home and what his college campus looked like in June and how it had felt to sail out of New York harbor in the rain.

"Have some wine," said the reporter who was sitting there listening to the music. The reporter had no stripes on his sleeves at all. The assistant editor took the wine and forgot to drink, just sitting there holding the bottle.

"There's a bar in New York," the assistant editor said. "Ralph's. On Forty-fifth Street. Ugly little joint. I like to drink there. Ever been there?"

"Uhuh," the reporter said.

"Scotch whisky," the assistant editor said. "Cold beer."

The concerto ended in wild, mournful thunder and a polite English voice said it had been Toscanini conducting and Horowitz at the piano, the names sounding strange on the nighttime African coast. The polite voice said good night and the reporter got Berlin. There were waltzes on from Berlin, very prettily played, lilting through the small, paper-littered room. A polite German voice described the waltzes and once more the violins and trumpets swept out of the radio.

"The Germans," the assistant editor said. "They should be deprived of music for fifty years. Should be part of the peace treaty."

A rewrite man, a corporal, on his way up to bed, stuck his head in. "Anybody want a gumdrop?" He brought out the box. "Just got my rations today."

The assistant editor and the reporter reached out. They chewed consideringly on the gumdrops, listening to the waltz.

"Nice music," the rewrite man said.

"Fifty years," said the assistant editor.

The rewrite man yawned and stretched. "Going to bed," he said, and started out. "Maybe when I wake up tomorrow the war'll be over. Good night." He went out and the assistant editor washed down the rationed gumdrop with a little wine.

"Did you ever eat a gumdrop in civilian life?" he asked.

"No," said the reporter.

"Neither did I." He rolled the wine around reflectively in the bottle. "God, it's dull around here. I wish I could have gone to Italy." The radio turned to Hungarian dances and the assistant editor stared gloomily at it. He drank a little wine. "That's the trouble, though. Now that the invasion has come at last, other guys are covering it. Other guys'll write great stories. I'll be sitting here on my can in Africa. The editor. The assistant editor . . . When I got out of college I wrote better than I do now. Eight years ago." He rubbed his bald spot thoughtfully. "Somehow I got to be an editor. Eight years." He finished the wine. "Maybe I should've got married."

"Probably wouldn't make any difference," said the reporter, who was married.

"Probably not." The assistant editor shrugged. "There was a girl back in college in my sophomore year. She was a year older than me. You had to date her up in October for the spring prom. There was a fellow with a car who used to drive her to breakfast, lunch and dinner and send her flowers every day, but she used to take walks with me and lunch sometimes. She did the most marvelous thing that anyone ever

did for me. I was a kid then and maybe it oughtn't to seem like so much
to me now, but it still does. She broke a date with this other guy and
went to the spring prom with me, I gave her orchids and we went to a
couple of speakeasies and it was the best night I ever had in my whole
life." He sat back, remembering the orchids and the speakeasies. "I introduced her to a friend of mine that summer. He had a lot of dough
and called her long distance three times a week and six months later
they got married. You can't blame a girl. Want to see her picture?"

"Yes," the reporter said.

The assistant editor took out the picture, yellowed and ravelled at the
edges. It was of a pretty, graceful girl, in a white dress, sitting erect, a
hint of strength in her face, mixed with ancient coquetry. "I don't
know why I keep it," the assistant editor said, looking at the picture.
"Maybe for luck." He put it back carefully into his wallet. He leaned
back and his thick glasses and square, angular, plain, decent face shone
in the dim light, clearly and painfully the face of a man who all his
life might expect to find his best friends taking his girl.

"There was another girl. A Danish girl," the assistant editor went
on. "I met her at a party in the Village. She'd come down from Boston
with a friend, to be an actress. She worked at the Filmarte as an usher.
I must have seen the last part of 'Grand Illusion' twelve times."

He smiled.

"I'd go around for the last reel or two of the pictures," he said, "and
take her out to Sunnyside. She lived there with her friend. She liked
me, but she wouldn't have anything much to do with me, even though
I used to sleep out on the living-room couch five times a week. We had a
fight and she decided she didn't want to be an actress and she went
home to Boston. I guess I would've married her then if I hadn't fought
with her so much." He took off his glasses and stared wearily at them.
"About six months later she came down to New York on a visit and it
was different. She moved right in and we had a wonderful time. We'd
go out on weekends in the country. Just drive around in the summertime
and stop in for drinks here and there and go swimming and laugh. She
met me in Provincetown and we stayed with a Danish family. There
was a great party. Provincetown, on Cape Cod. I don't think I've ever
had a better time and I keep remembering it. . . . Maybe I should've
married her. I don't know."

The assistant editor leaned over and put the bottle down. On the
street below, three Frenchmen passed, singing loudly.

"I'm thirty years old and I write worse than I ever did. I don't know
what I'll do after the war. Once, when I was in the Engineers, I sent

her a letter. She was married, she wrote me, and she was having a kid on May seventeenth. She was going to call it David, after her husband's uncle, she said. She asked me to pray for it. I haven't written back. Well, what's the difference?" He put his glasses on again. "The Filmarte Theatre." He laughed and stood up. "I wish I had two hack writers I could throw stories to and know they'd come out right," he said. "I wouldn't get so tired. Well, it's pretty late. Got to go to bed. Tomorrow's another war."

The radio was sending out American jazz now, the deep, familiar horns of America pounding like all the music in all the dance halls and all the night clubs and at all the spring proms any American ever went to, any girl in a white dress ever danced at.

The assistant editor listened, his eyes blinking behind the thick lenses of his glasses. When it was over, he got up and walked into his own room slowly, his shirt dumpy and wrinkled, to take one last look at his desk and make sure everything was all right before going to bed.

THE VETERANS REFLECT

THE BELLS were ringing everywhere and the engineer blew the locomotive whistle over and over as they roared up the springtime valley. The hills rolled back from the blue river, and the frail green of the young leaves made them look as though pale green velvet cloth, thready and worn, had been thrown as drapery over their winter sides.

Peter Wylie sat at the window staring dreamily out at the Hudson Valley rolling sweetly and familiarly past him. He smiled when a little girl in front of a farmhouse gravely waved an American flag at the speeding train, and the engineer gravely saluted her in return with a deep roar of the whistle.

Peter Wylie sat at the window of the speeding train and avoided listening to the booming voice of the gentleman talking to the pretty woman across the aisle. He stretched his legs comfortably and half-closed his eyes as he watched the green, quiet country over which, faintly, between towns, came the pealing of bells, because that morning the war had ended.

". . . Dead two years," the gentleman was saying. "His ship went down off Alaska and that was the last we heard of him. Twenty-one years old. Here's his picture, in uniform."

"He looks so young," the woman said.

"He had a blond beard. Hardly had to shave. The ship went down in eighteen minutes . . ."

The bells were ringing, Peter thought, and the graves were full of young men who had hardly had to shave, in uniform. His two cousins on his mother's side, killed in Africa, and Martin, who had been his roommate for three years, killed in India, and all the boys from the squadron . . . The graves on the plains and the mountains, the shallow graves on the hard coral islands, and the long well-kept cemetery of the military dead outside the hospital which you looked at through the tall window of your ward as nurses whispered outside in the corridor, and the doctors hurried fatefully by on their crepe soles. "Convenient," you said with a slow, remote wave of your hand and with what you hoped was a smile, to the nurse, who seemed always to have come from behind a screen where she wept continuously when not actually needed at a bedside. "Modern design."

"What?" the red-eyed nurse had asked blankly.

You had been too tired to explain and merely closed your eyes with the beautiful rudeness of the dying. But you hadn't died. There was a strange platter-like excavation in your abdomen and you would never really enjoy your food any more, and you would always have to climb stairs slowly even though you were only twenty-nine now on this day when the bells were ringing, but the cemetery and the military dead were still there, and here you were on a train up the Hudson Valley on your way home to see your wife and child, and the guns were quiet and the airplanes idled in the hangars, and the pilots sat around and played cards and tried to remember the telephone numbers of the girls in their home towns.

You were on your way home to see your wife and child. For three years, alone at night, sleepless in strange rooms on other continents; on leave, at a bar, sleepless, drinking and laughing, and the brassy old juke boxes playing songs that cried *far away and long ago, far away and long ago,* and all the women being earnest about the war and patri- otically anxious to jump into bed with all the pilots, navigators, bombardiers, flight-sergeants, wing-commanders, meteorologists, radio- operators of the air forces of all the United Nations, including the Russian; for three years on the long droning flights across the hundred- mile ripples of the Pacific; for three years, even sometimes at the mo- ment when the bombardier said, "OK, I'll take it from here," as the plane ducked in over the target and the anti-aircraft fire bloomed roughly about you, the faces of your wife and daughter slid through your mind, the woman's firm-boned jaw, the moody blue eyes, the wide, full mouth, familiar, loving, changing, merry, tragic, tenderly and laughingly mocking in the secret, wifely, female understanding of the beloved weaknesses of the man of the family—and the child's face, small, unformed, known only from photographs sent across the oceans, looking out at him through the night with sober, infant gravity. Three years, he thought, and tomorrow morning the train will pull into the dirty old station at Chicago and there they'll be, standing in the soot and clangor, hand in hand, the quick, delightful woman and the fat child, picking his uniform out among the other uniforms, with three years' waiting and loving and hoping showing in the faces as he strode down the platform. . . .

"Bong-bong!" shouted a little bald man, who was leading two women drunkenly down the aisle toward the diner. "Bong-bong. We did it!"

"Ding-a-ling! Ring out the wild bells!" The blonde woman right behind the bald man cried out. "Welcome to America!"

"We applied the crusher," the bald man told the crowded car. "The old steel spring technique. Coil back, coil back, coil back, then . . ."

They disappeared around the bend of the car over which the small sign said modestly, "Women."

Across the ocean, in the mountains of another country, a man strode out of a darkened house to the long, armored automobile waiting on the night-deserted road. Two men, bundled in army greatcoats, hurried behind him, their boots sighing softly in the damp earth of the courtyard. The chauffeur had the door open, but the man stopped and turned around before he got in and looked at the dark shapes of the mountains rising behind him against the starry sky. He put his hand uncertainly to his collar and pulled at it and took a deep breath. The two men in the greatcoats waited, without looking up, shadowed by the slowly fluttering young foliage of the oaks that bordered the path. The man turned and slowly got into the car, carefully, like an old man who has fallen recently and remembers that his bones are brittle and mend slowly. The other two men sprang into the front seat, and the chauffeur slammed the rear door and ran around to the front and leaped in and started the motor. The automobile sped quietly down the dark road, the noise of its going making a private and faraway *whoosh* that died on the huge and growing darkness of the mountain-circled spring night.

In the back of the car, the man sat bolt upright, his eyes narrow and unseeing, staring straight ahead of him. Off in the hills a church bell pealed and pealed again and again, musical and lonely in the echoing darkness. The lips of the man in the back seat curled slightly, bitterly, as the sound of the pealing village bell wavered on the wind. Germans! he thought. Five million German dead all over the world and the Russians on the road to Berlin and everything worse than 1918 and their leader skulking through the night on back-roads toward the Swiss border with a chauffeur and two frightened first-lieutenants and they ring bells as though this was the day after the Fall of France! Germans! Idiots! Imitation suits, imitation rubber, imitation eggs, finally imitation men . . . What was a man expected to do with material like that? And he'd come so close—so close . . . The gates of Moscow. But he sat. The statue sat. Everyone else ran, the diplomats, the newspapermen, the government, and Stalin sat there and the people sat . . . Peasant. Sitting there in his burning house with his gun and his plow—and somehow the house didn't burn. Storm-troopers, assault-guards, blitzkrieg veterans at the gates of Moscow and they died. A little cold and they dropped like hot-house violets. So close—so close . . .

The bell rang more strongly and in other villages other bells answered.

They'd hang him if they caught him. He'd cried at the last Armistice, he'd hang at this. . . . The British use a silk rope when they hang nobility. They wouldn't use silk on him. . . . And the bells ringing all around him . . .

He leaned forward and jabbed the chauffeur fiercely in the back.

"Faster!"

The car spurted forward.

"Production," the booming gentleman across the aisle was saying to the pretty woman, who was leaning closer to him, prettily attentive. "It was inevitable. American production won this war."

Peter thought of the graves, of the English and Chinese and Australians and Russians and Serbs and Greeks and Americans who filled them, who had fought bitterly with rifle and cannon and plane across the torn fields and stripped forests where they now quietly lay, under the illusion that if the war was to be won, it was to be won by them, standing there, hot gun in hand, with the shells dropping around them and the scream of the planes overhead and the tanks roaring at them at fifty miles an hour. . . .

"I know," the gentleman was saying. "I was in Washington from 1941 right to the finish and I saw. I'm in machine tools and I had my hand on the pulse of production and I know what I'm talking about. We performed miracles."

"I'm sure," the pretty woman murmured. "I'm absolutely sure." She was not as young as she had looked at first, Peter noticed, and her clothes were much shabbier than he had thought, and she looked pretty and impressed and tired and ready to be invited to dinner.

". . . Plants in seven states," the man was saying. "We expanded four hundred per cent. The war's over now, I can talk freely. . . ."

The war's over, Peter thought deliciously, settling deeper into his chair, and letting his head rumble pleasantly with the click of the wheels as he leaned back against the cushion, the war's over and machine-tool manufacturers who expanded four hundred per cent can talk freely to women in Pullman cars and tomorrow I see my wife and child and I never have to climb into an airplane again. From now on I walk down to the station and buy a ticket when I want to go some place and I sit down with a magazine and a whisky and soda and the train clicks along on steel and solid gravel and the only enemy activity will be an occasional small boy throwing a rock hopefully at the bright windows of the diner flashing by. Tomorrow afternoon he would be walking slowly along the lake front in the spring wind, hand in hand with his wife and child. "And that, darling, is Lake Michigan. Do you know the water you took a bath in this morning? It comes right from here, especially for you. When your father was a boy he used to stand here and watch the red Indians sail by in their war canoes at forty miles an hour, reciting Henry Wadsworth Longfellow at the top of their voices. I can see by the look in your mother's eye that she doesn't believe me and wants an ice-cream soda. I can also see by the look in her eye that she doesn't think you should have an ice-cream soda so soon after lunch, but I've been thinking about buying you this ice-cream soda for three years and the war's over, and I don't think she's going to make too much of a fuss. . . ."

And tomorrow night, they would lie, soft on their backs in the soft bed, staring idly up at the dark ceiling, his arm under her head, their voices murmuring and mingling with the distant quiet night sounds of the sleeping city, the clack and rumble from the lakefront railroad yards and the soft whisper of automobiles on the highway. . . . "I slept in the same bed in Cairo, Egypt, with a boy from Texas who weighed two hundred and thirty pounds. He wanted to get in the Navy, but he was six feet six inches tall and they said he wouldn't fit on any ship afloat or building. Also he was in love with a girl he met in New York who sold gloves in Saks and he talked about her all night long. She has a thirty-six inch bust and she lives with four girls from Vassar in Greenwich Village and she has a scar on her right buttock six inches long that she got when she fell down iceskating and a man with racing skates ran over her. This is an improvement over sleeping with a two-hundred-and-thirty-pound Texan in the same bed in Cairo, Egypt. Yes, I'll kiss you if you want . . ."

And her voice, close to his ear, in the gentle, tumbled darkness, alive with the fresh night wind off the lake and the familiar smell of her perfume and the frail dry smell of her hair, remembered all the years deep in his nostrils. ". . . And she went to the nursery school in Tucson all day while I was on duty in the hospital and they all liked her very much but she had a habit of hitting the other little boys and girls with her shovel and I had to leave her with my sister. I knew you'd laugh. Stop laughing or I'll stuff a pillow in your mouth, Mr. Veteran. You can afford to laugh, out flying around ten thousand miles away with nothing to worry about but Japs and Germans. Wait till you're a mother and seven young mothers descend upon you to tell you your child has swiped at their children with a wooden shovel every day of the school term . . ." And the kiss to stop the laughter and her head under his chin after that and the slow, diminishing chuckles together for the child sleeping in the next room dreaming of other children and more wooden shovels.

And again, her hand thrown softly and possessively on his chest. "There's a lot more hair here than I remember."

"War. I always put on a lot of hair on my chest in a war. Any objections?"

"No. I'm well-known as a woman who's partial to hairy men. Or is talk like that too vulgar for young soldiers? Am I too fat? I put on eight pounds since 1942. . . . Have you noticed?"

"I'm noticing now."

"Too fat?"

"Ummmmmnnn . . ."

"Tell the truth."

"Ummnnn."

"I'm going to diet. . . ."

"You just wait here and I'll go down and get you a plate of mashed potatoes. . . ."

"Oh, shut up! Oh, darling, darling, I'm glad you're home . . ."

Or perhaps they wouldn't talk at all in the beginning. Perhaps they would just touch each other's hand and weep cheek to cheek for the three years behind them and the years ahead and cling to each other desperately through the long cool night and go to his parents' farm in Wisconsin and walk hand in hand in morning sunlight slowly over the greening fields, their feet sinking into the soft loam, content in the first hours with love and silence, until finally they could sit under the wide peaceful sky, off to themselves, with the rich smell of the newly plowed fields and the watermelon-cucumber smell of the river in their nostrils, and then, finally, the words would come . . . The things he had thought on the long flights, the decisions and doubts of the thousand wartime nights, the deep, deep hallelujah of his spirit as the train covered the sweet final miles between the war and home. He would tell her the things he had had to bury deep within him through the noisy, bleeding years . . . The times he had been afraid . . . The first time he had seen an enemy squadron small against the horizon, harmless-looking dots, growing nearer and larger with insane speed, and the ridiculous way it made him see, over and over again, for some reason, *Acrobatics,* as it was printed in the March Field Bulletin. And at the time he had been shot, six hours away from base, on a rough day, lying bleeding on his parachute while Dennis pushed the bomber toward home, and he had managed to keep quiet for the first four hours, but had wept for the last two hours, almost mechanically, although he had felt very calm. And because he was certain he was going to die, he had for the first time permitted himself to think about whether the whole thing was worth it or not, as the plane bucked in the cold air. He could tell her how he had thought, in those long six hours, of all the boys who had lightly roared off at four hundred miles an hour and lightly and thoughtlessly, or at least silently died. . . . He would be able to tell her that he had soberly decided, bullet in his belly and sure of death in the roaring plane, that it was worth it, that if he had it to do again he would leave home, wife, child, father, mother, country, and search the German bullet out of the cloud once more, part of the enormous anguish and enormous courage of all the men on sea and beach and mountain locked with him in final struggle against the general enemy. And, then, weeping, on the edge of death, as he thought, he could let himself go . . . and for the first time, in the mist of pain, break down the barrier of reserve that had kept him, even in his most secret thoughts, from admitting even to himself how much he loved all those men behind guns—his friends, boys from the same schools, coldly diving, cannons and machine guns tearing out of their wings, at enemy bombers; the pleasant Englishmen foolishly and desperately confident of their ships, sailing formally and arrogantly into hopeless battle like Englishmen in books; the quilted Chinese rifleman standing forlornly on the brown China earth against tanks and artillery; and huge, muffled Russians, fighting by day and night and snow and rain, implacably and ingeniously and tirelessly killing, oblivious to agony or doubt, intent only on burning and crippling and starving and murdering the enemy. . . . He could tell her how deep inside him he had loved all those bloody, weary, cruel, reliable men, how he had felt borne up on that huge tide of men careless of death, and had felt himself to be a part of that tide, agonized, stricken, familiar with defeat, often falsely and frivolously led, but better than the leaders, dangerous, brawling, indivisible—and how he had felt linked with those men for all their lives and his, closer to them even though he could not speak their language nor they his, than to his own mother and father, responsible forever for their comfort and glory as they were for his. And he could tell her of the sober exhilaration of these reflections, this deep dredging to his thoughts, this ultimate examination in the light of pain and exhaustion and terror of himself, who never before this had thought deeply or reflected much beyond the everyday cares of average life in a small town, seated at a desk from nine to five, sleeping comfortable in a quiet room in a warm house, going to the pictures twice a week, playing tennis on Sunday, worrying about whether the car was good for another year or not . . .

The long automobile sped down the winding road among the hills on its way through the night to the Swiss border. The man still sat bolt upright on the back seat, his eyes narrow and unseeing, straight ahead of him.

Victories, he thought, how many victories can a man be expected to win? Paris, Rotterdam, Singapore, Athens, Kiev, Warsaw—and still they kept coming. . . . There was a certain limit to the number of victories that were humanly possible. Napoloen discovered, too . . . Napoleon . . . Napoleon . . . He was tired of that name. In the last days he had ordered that it was not to be spoken in his presence. And now they were all hunting for him, like a world full of bloodhounds—Germans, English, Russians, Americans, French, Austrians, Poles, Dutch, Bulgarians, Serbs, Italians . . . Well, they had reason. Fools. For a long time it hadn't been hard. The cities fell like rotten apples. But then America and Russia . . . The timing was not quite exact. In politics everything happened before schedule. In war everything happened behind schedule . . . So close, so close . . . The Russians . . . Everything else being equal, the bells would be ringing for another reason tonight if not for the Russians . . . Just that winter had to be the coldest in fifty years. There has to be a certain element of luck. Well, all things considered, he had had a successful career. He had started out as a nobody, with his father always yelling at him that he'd never amount to anything and he never could hold a job . . . Today his name was known in every home on the face of the earth, in every jungle . . . Thirty million people had died earlier than they expected because of him and hundreds of cities were leveled to the ground because of him and the entire wealth of all nations of the earth had been strained by him, mines and factories and farms . . . All things considered, he had had a successful career. Even his father would have to admit that. Though, to be fair, if he hadn't grabbed first, someone else would have grabbed. The thing would have happened without him. He had to admit that. But he had grabbed first and the name known in every home on the face of the earth was Hitler, not any other name. So close, so close . . . A little cold and they died . . . Idiots! And now they wanted to hang him. If he could only get across the border, lie low . . . Until the rest of them got tired of killing the Germans. After all, Napoleon came back off Elba. A hundred days. With a little luck he could have stuck . . . Napoloen . . . The name was not to be mentioned. They were going to start worrying about the Russians very soon. The Russians, the Russians . . . The armies had been cut up, they had died by the millions . . . And yet, today they were on the road to Berlin. They were going to need someone to stop the Russians and if he could only lie low for a few months, his name would be mentioned . . . And once he got back, there'd be no more mistakes. With a little luck . . .

The man on the rear seat relaxed against the cushions and a little smile played around the raw mouth.

"I was interviewed by the Washington *Post*," the booming gentleman was saying, his voice cutting into Peter's reverie. "Right before I left. And I told them straight up and down—production must not stop." Peter looked absently at the booming gentleman. He was a tall fat man with a bald head, but somehow he reminded Peter of all the teacher's pets who had ever been in his classes in grammar school—pink, fat face, small, round, pink, satisfied mouth, always impressing everyone with how much he knew and how much in favor he was. Peter closed his eyes and imagined the tall, fat man in an Eton collar with a bow tie and grinned. "Stop a machine for a day," the man was saying, "and industrial obsolescence comes a month nearer. Whether we like it or not we are geared to wartime production."

"You're so right," the pretty woman murmured. Peter looked at her closely for the first time. Her clothes were shabby and she had the same wornout, rundown look that the whole country seemed to have, as though the war had rubbed people and things down to the grain, as though the war had kept the whole continent up too many nights, working too hard . . . Teacher's pet was bright and shining, as though he had stepped out of 1941 into a world many years older . . .

"Nobody ever had too many guns. I told them right to their faces."

"You're so right," the pretty woman murmured.

"My son was sunk off Alaska . . ." Peter tightened as he recognized the note of boasting in the voice, as though the man were saying he had been elected to an exclusive club. "My son was sunk off Alaska, and I produced machine tools twenty-four hours a day, seven days a week and I have a right to talk. We got it on our hands, I told them, and we have to face the problem fair and square, what are we going to do with them . . ."

"Yes," murmured the pretty woman, hoping for dinner, over the rumble of the wheels.

He would walk slowly, Peter thought, in the evening, after dinner in the big farm kitchen, with the smell of cooking rich and fragrant in the warm kitchen air and his mother red-faced and aproned and his father tall and scrubbed and quiet, smoking his nickel cigar . . . He would walk slowly along the rutted wagon road with Laura beside him in the bright twilight, full of the warm knowledge that he was in no hurry to get any place, that he could leisurely regard the small hills, accepting the night, and leisurely listen to the last evening concert of the birds, leisurely scuff his shoes in the light country dust of the road over which armored tread had never passed, which had never known blood. He could tell Laura finally that of all the good things that had happened to him in this savage, ecstatic century, the best had happened in the moment when he had walked toward her on a train platform in Chicago the day after the war was over. He could tell her finally how tired he was, how tired he had been when bone and blood and nerve had collapsed, when no effort had ever seemed possible again, when his body had given up all knowledge of victory or defeat. And when somehow planes had to be flown and guns manned and swift, deadly action taken by that sodden bone and blood and nerve . . . And somehow the action taken because of the feeling deep within him that on other fields and in other skies, wearier and more desperate men were still manning guns for him and flying more dangerous skies . . . And the promise he made to himself that when it was over and he was home, surrounded by care and love, he was never going to hurry again, never knowingly perform a violent act, never even raise his voice except in laughter and song, never argue with anyone about anything . . . He wasn't going back to his job. Nine to five in a bank at a desk was no way to crown a career of bloodshed thirty thousand feet over three continents. Perhaps Laura would be able to suggest something for him to do, something quiet and unhurried and thoughtless . . . But first he was going to do nothing. Just wander around the farm and teach the baby how to spell and listen to his father explain his particular reasons for rotating his crops in his own particular way. Maybe two, three, five months, a year of that, as long as it took to drain off the blood and weariness, as long as it took for his crippled spirit to open the door of its wartime hospital and step out firmly—as long as it took . . .

"The job's just begun," the booming gentleman was saying. "Let them ring the bells. It amuses them. But tomorrow morning . . ."

"Yes," said the pretty woman, eager to agree with everything.

"We've got to face the facts. A businessman faces the facts. What are the facts? The Russians are near Berlin. Right?"

"Yes," said the woman, "of course."

"Berlin. Fine. Unavoidable. The Russians are sitting on Europe . . ."

Peter tried to close his eyes, close his ears, go back to the dear dream of the twilight country road and his wife's hand in his and the dust that had never known blood. But the man's voice tore through and he couldn't help but listen.

"As a businessman I tell you it's an impossible situation." The man's voice grew louder. "Intolerable. And the sooner we realize it, the better. The truth is, maybe it's a good thing this war was fought. Dramatizes the real problem. Makes the American people see what the real danger is. And what's the answer? Production! Guns and more guns! I don't care what those Communists in Washington say, I say the war has just begun."

Peter stood up wearily and went over to the booming gentleman. "Get out of here," he said as quietly as he could. "Get out of here and keep quiet or I'll kill you."

The booming gentleman looked up at him, his face still with surprise. His little red mouth opened twice and closed silently. His pale eyes stared harshly and searchingly at Peter's worn, bitter face. Then he shrugged, stood up, put out his arm for the lady.

"Come," he said, "we might as well eat."

The pretty woman stood up and started hesitantly, frightenedly, toward the door.

"If it weren't for your uniform," the booming man said loudly, "I'd have you arrested. Armistice or no Armistice."

"Get out of here," Peter said.

The booming gentleman turned and walked swiftly after the woman and they disappeared toward the diner. Peter sat down, conscious of every eye in the car on him, regretting that he had found his next years' work placed so soon before him and crying so urgently to be done.

Well, he comforted himself, at least I don't have to travel for this one.

The engineer blew his whistle on a ten-mile stretch of clear track because the war was over and as the hoarse, triumphant sound floated back, Peter closed his eyes and tried to think of his wife and child waiting in the noisy station in Chicago. . . .

THE PASSION OF
LANCE CORPORAL HAWKINS

Lance Corporal Alfred Hawkins stood on the Haifa dock, his fingers wet on the long nightstick in his hands, the unaccustomed helmet heavy on his head, watching a naval launch slowly bring in the two-masted schooner *Hope*, its decks and tattered rigging swarming with people, who looked like clustered dark bees, so far away, and not like people at all. Please, Lord, Hawkins prayed to himself, standing at ease with his platoon, warm in the yellow Mediterranean sun, please, Lord, keep me from hitting any of them.

"Don't take any nonsense from the buggers," Lieutenant Madox said, standing in front of the platoon. "Whack 'em a couple of times and they'll behave like bloody gentlemen." He turned and peered at the shabby schooner slowly approaching the dock, and Hawkins was sure that the look on the Lieutenant's thick red face was one of pleasurable anticipation. Hawkins looked at the other men of the platoon. Except for Hogan, you couldn't tell anything from their faces. In London once, during the war, Hawkins had overheard an American Air Force major saying, "The British would watch Hitler hanging or their daughters marrying into the Royal Family or their own legs being chopped off at the knee and not change expression by one twitch of the eyebrow. You can't beat an army like that." The American had been drunk, of course, but, looking around him now, and remembering other times, too—like the day outside Caen and the day on the Rhine and the day his company went into the concentration camp at Belsen—Hawkins could understand what the American had been talking about. In ten or fifteen minutes, the men around him might be in the middle of a very mean fight on board the schooner, against clubs and knives, perhaps, and maybe even home-made bombs, and except for Hogan, again, all of them looked as though they were merely lined up for a routine roll call outside their barracks in the morning. And Hogan, of course, was an Irishman, and not the same thing at all. He was a small, thin boy, with a tough, broken-nosed, handsome face, and now he was fidgeting uneasily, his jaw rigid with excitement, pushing his helmet back and forth on his head, shifting his nightstick, breathing loudly enough to be heard over all the small noises of the harbor and the platoon around him.

They were singing now on the schooner. The rising and falling, chanting, foreign melody came thinly and defiantly across the oily green water. Hawkins could understand several words of Hebrew, but he could not make out what the song was about. It sounded wild and somehow menacing, as though it should not be sung in sunshine and in the morning or by women's voices but late at night, in the desert, by lawless and desperate men. Esther had translated two or three Hebrew songs for Hawkins in the last few weeks, and he had noticed that the words "freedom" and "justice" figured in them prominently, but those words did not seem to fit with the flat, dangerous, hoarse music hammering across the harbor from the slowly moving old boat.

Hawkins wished they wouldn't sing. It made it harder if they sang and you knew they were singing about freedom or justice. After all, they were singing to him, and to the other men around him, and what did they expect him to do?

Hawkins closed his eyes, as though by shutting out the sight of the dark-clustered boat inexorably being pushed to the dock, and the clubs, and the transport waiting to take them to the stockade on Cyprus, he could somehow also shut out the sound of the rough, challenging voices of the Jews.

He closed his eyes, his youthful, almost childish face, sweating under the hot helmet, painfully composed, painfully disclosing nothing to the Lieutenant or the men around him or to the eyes of the fugitives he was expected to punish. He closed his eyes. He was uncomfortable in his wool battle dress and the tight canvas belting, and was sorry he was in Palestine, sorry he was in the Army, sorry he was an Englishman, sorry he was alive. This was not what he had expected when he had reënlisted, six months after the war was over. He didn't know exactly what he had expected. He had just known he did not want to live in Southampton, in the foggy weather, among the ruined docks and the torn buildings; in the same house with his father, who had had his arm torn off during a raid in 1941; in the same house with his sister, whose husband had been killed at Bari in 1943; in the same house in which he had lived for such a short while with Nancy, who had later divorced him and married an American sergeant in the port battalion—and that was a soft job for a soldier, wasn't it, during a war. He had just known that after four years in the Army, ever since he was seventeen, he did not want to start looking for a job as a longshoreman on the wrecked wharves, he did not want to stand in a queue collecting the unemployment dole, he did not want the bitter weather of unheated winter England after glimpses of Africa and summer France. And the only thing he had known was soldiering. They had made it a little more attractive —they had raised the pay and promised many rather vague benefits— and, if the truth must be told, the only time anyone had ever really taken care of him was in the Army. It was certain no one was really going to take care of you as a civilian, Socialist government or no Socialist government. Though he had voted for them, of course. He had read all the pamphlets and he knew what he was doing, a common soldier in the Army of the King, the son of a workingman, the grandson of a workingman, the great-grandson of a workingman. That was another thing about the Army. It had given him the chance to read for the first time in his life. Especially the two periods he'd been in the hospital, first with the bullet in his hip and then with the piece of shrapnel he'd picked up twelve days before the end of the war. The hospital library had had a complete set of H. G. Wells, and he had slowly and studiously gone through it all, soberly agreeing with the energetic arguments of the old man. By the time he'd got out of the hospital, he had become a confirmed Socialist, believing that education could change the world, and that violence was a hangover from primitive times, and that year by year the human race was certain to improve. He opened his eyes for a moment and looked at the schooner. It was much closer now, and he could smell it, too. There were perhaps three hundred people jammed onto it, men and women, and they had obviously not had the most complete sanitation facilities. He wished H. G. Wells were on the dock in the uniform of an infantry lance corporal today; it would be interesting to see what he would do.

It had been so much simpler during the war. There were the Germans across the fields, or up on a hill two miles away, and you shot them and they shot you. They had bombed your home and torn the arm off your father's shoulder and killed your brother-in-law, and there were no further decisions to be made about them. And all the men around you felt exactly as you did, no matter who they were. But now . . . There was Lieutenant Madox, who hated all Jews and was delighted with this duty on the dock this morning. Of course, Lieutenant

Madox hated everybody, except Englishmen, and if he had been in India or Malaya or France, he would have looked forward to cracking Indian or Malayan or French skulls with equal pleasure. But he happened to be in Palestine, and he happened to be looking forward to hitting Jews. Then there was Private Fleming, a quiet, capable man of thirty-five. Private Fleming was a Communist. Communists, Hawkins knew, did not think much of Zionism, but certainly they didn't believe in braining Jews, and yet there was Private Fleming, an excellent soldier, standing quietly at ease, ready to do his duty, gripping his nightstick like all the others. And there was Hogan, who was one of Hawkins' best friends, with whom he drank beer in Jerusalem and Tel Aviv, and who was a Catholic, like Hawkins, and went to Mass on Sunday morning with him, and whose father had been killed by the British in the trouble in Dublin in 1916. Hogan often went out with him and Esther, too. Esther would bring a friend and they would swim on the beach at Tel Aviv and go to the movies at night when they played musical pictures. Hogan hated the Jews, though, because his second cousin, who was in the Sixth Airborne, had got his foot blown off by a Jewish mine on the Rehovoth Road two months before. What would H. G. Wells have made of the Dublin orphan on the sunny dock this morning, tense with pent-up fury as he glared at the naval launch slowly pushing the tattered, dark, chanting refugees toward him?

And, supposing H. G. Wells had been a Jew, and were standing on the deck of the *Hope* this morning, after the years of murder in Germany, after the displaced persons' camps, after the illegal journey across Europe and the crooked voyage down the Mediterranean, what clever, hopeful statement would he make then, waiting there like an old bull in the knacker's yard, waiting for the clubs and the Cyprian wire?

An Arab laborer walked by, rolling a wheelbarrow. He put the wheelbarrow down in front of the platoon, his long, skinny arms dark mahogany, dangling out of his tattered shirt. He had a little black scraggly beard, and he didn't smell so good, either. He grinned at the soldiers. His teeth were not all there, but when he smiled, he looked childlike and ingratiating, and some of the men smiled back at him. The Arab looked over his shoulder at the approaching boat, grinned more widely, and moved his finger across his Adam's apple in the gesture of throat slitting.

"Get out of here, you filthy old rascal," Lieutenant Madox said, smiling broadly. "Go ahead. Out of the way. We'll have no international incidents on this dock."

The Arab bobbed his head, the grin fixed on his face, and made the throat-cutting gesture again, like a child who repeats a trick that he sees has pleased his elders. Then he bent and picked up the handles of the wheelbarrow again and trundled it off, giggling to himself.

Hawkins didn't remember what H. G. Wells had had to say about the Arabs. He was sure there must have been something on the subject, because there was something on every subject in the old man's books, but he couldn't remember. The Arabs, Hawkins had to admit, were much more pleasant to have around than the Jews. For one thing, they did what you told them. For another thing, they weren't likely to get you off in a corner and engage you in a loud political argument. Esther lived in the same house with a family by the name of Freedman, who were German refugees and whose two sons had been in the Jewish Brigade during the war. The two boys lay in wait for Hawkins when he came to call for Esther and battered him with questions like "Why doesn't Britain live up to the Balfour Declaration?" and "Why does Britain allow the Grand Mufti of Jerusalem, who worked with the Nazis during the war, to come back to lead the Arabs from Cairo?" It was very queer, sitting in the small white living room of the apartment house, with your rifle leaning against the wall (from time to time, Division Headquarters ordered that all troops be armed when they left the barracks), drinking tea and eating little sweet cookies that Mrs. Freedman kept pressing on you, debating politely with the two fierce young veterans, who were probably members of the Jewish underground and had probably blown up a sergeant major in the morning.

"It's not fair," he had said to Esther after one such session, when he had finally managed to get her away from the house. "They talk as though I was personally responsible."

Esther had glanced at him obliquely, then looked away. "Maybe," she said softly, "maybe that's what they think about every British soldier."

"Is that what you think?"

Esther had shaken her head and gripped his arm more firmly. "No," she had said gravely, her low, soft voice solemn and warm. "No, I do not think of you as a British soldier." They had been walking along the quiet, white street, in the clear, foreign evening air—his boots making a hob-nailed clatter on the pavement and his rifle sling pulling at his shoulder and the girl beside him in a thin white dress with a blue sweater over it, her hair blowing gently, soft and pale brown, in the stirring wind.

"Listen to them sing," Hogan said, his voice nervous and angry.

"The murderin' heathen! They'll sing a different tune an hour from now, they will!"

Hawkins opened his eyes. The ship was much closer now, and the songs clamored across the water from the packed ship, with the soprano of the women shrill and glittering over the menacing bass of the men's voices. Hogan, Hawkins remembered, also sang songs in another language—in Gaelic—and the words "freedom" and "justice" figured prominently in them, too. They were songs Hogan's grandfather had taught him in memory of his dead father, shot through the throat on a Dublin pavement by men in the same uniform that Hogan was wearing now so far away, seventy-five miles north of Jerusalem.

Hawkins closed his eyes again. It would do no good to watch the boat come nearer, foot by foot. There would be time enough to look, later. He thought of Esther. He had arranged to meet her that night in Tel Aviv and take her to a movie if he got off duty early. He had not known what the duty would be, though, and he doubted if he would tell her later on. Matters were complicated enough with Esther as it was. She looked so cheerful and agreeable, so pretty and young, like the very nicest kind of girl you might meet by a lucky accident at home, but there had been the terrible times when she had suddenly broken down, for no apparent reason, and wept in his arms, wildly and inconsolably, clutching him as though to make certain again and again that he was there and alive. She was a German girl, whose mother and father had been killed in Munich, and whose husband had been caught by the British near Haifa unloading illegal immigrants in 1939. He had been put into a camp, where he had caught typhus and died. The authorities had permitted Esther to visit her husband the day he died, and once Esther had told Hawkins about it, although most of the time they avoided talking about things like that. The husband, who was twenty-four years old and had been a robust, laughing young man (Hawkins had seen his picture), had been wasted by the disease to ninety pounds and was screaming in his delirium when Esther finally saw him. He did not recognize his wife at all when she came into the room, and that, somehow, was Esther's bitterest memory—the screaming, skeleton-like boy turning his head senselessly to the wall in the bare, barred room. Then, after that, all through the war, Esther had been kept under house arrest and had not been permitted to go out into the streets from sunset to dawn. When Hawkins had first known her, she had been quiet, almost fearful, and perhaps it was because she had matched his own shyness and fearfulness so well that he had begun to love her.

For the past several months, whenever Hawkins was waiting somewhere, and closed his eyes, as he was doing now, he had had a recurrent daydream. It was winter in the dream, a cold, windy night, and he and Esther were sitting before a warm fire in their own house. He could never decide whether the house was in England, in a quiet village, or on a farm in Palestine, cupped in the small, old hills, among the orange orchards. They were reading, and occasionally they looked up from their books and smiled at each other, not having to talk, in the firelight. After a time, there was a knock on the door and guests began to come in; not many of them, just good friends. Hogan, with his wild hair plastered down politely. Fleming, with the schoolteacher wife from Leeds he talked about so often. Robinson, who had been in Hawkins' platoon in Africa—it was always hard to remember, especially in a daydream, that Robinson was dead, buried in the small, windy cemetery near Constantine. They talked quietly in the warm room, and Hawkins opened up the tall bottles of heavy beer, and after a while Hogan sang, in his hoarse, accurate boy's voice, the sad, thrilling songs his grandfather had taught him in his father's honor, songs whose words no one understood but whose melodies made you somehow melancholy and proud.

Hawkins blinked and refused himself the pleasure of taking the daydream through to its quiet ending. It was ridiculous to allow himself to moon like that, and it only made it worse when he finally opened his eyes and looked around him. There he was, on the dock, in the hot, bare sun, with the nightstick, waiting for Lieutenant Madox to order him to fight. And in the hills behind him, among the orange groves, people were hiding rifles and knives and machine guns to murder each other in the long winter nights. And in England, from all the letters he got from his family, they were preparing to starve and freeze to celebrate their victory in the war. He was sorry he was not older. Perhaps if he were thirty or forty or fifty, he could understand it better. During the war they had been warm, during the war they had been fed, during the war the Russians had loved them, the Americans had admired them, the French had kissed them when they came into a town; wherever they had gone, they had been heroes and saviors. He remembered the day that the election returns came out. He was still in Germany, in Hamburg, and an American sergeant had come over to him and said, very solemnly, "Soldier, my name is McCarthy. I'm a paid-up C.I.O. member from Indianapolis. I decided I wanted to tell some Englishman how wonderful I think they are, and you're the first one I've come across since I made the decision. You've shown the whole world how civilized human beings should behave." The American had been drunk, of course (was it possible that Americans appreciated other people only when they had ten drinks under their belts?), but he had shaken Hawkins' hand sternly and clapped him on the back, and Hawkins had walked away grinning and feeling proud because he had voted for Attlee and the others who were going to prove that a country could be run for the benefit of the workingman without violence or disaster. He was glad the American wasn't around to see him standing on the dock today with helmet and nightstick, in this land of widows and orphans, in this land where there were no whole families, only survivors, in this land where everyone—every girl on the street, every child in a schoolroom, every farmer plowing a furrow—had a story like Esther's, memories like Esther's, nightmares like Esther's, where the memory of the furnace flickered across every face, the knocking of the midnight arrest broke into every dream, where agony was so commonplace that no one even remarked it. What a puzzling, sad thing it was to be an Englishman today, Hawkins thought, staring at the boat, which was so close now. If he was in England, he was caught between cold and hunger, in Palestine between Jew and Arab, in India between Hindu and Moslem, in the East Indies between Dutchman and Javanese, and no friends anywhere, no approval anywhere, just the helmet and the nightstick, the barbed wire and the Lieutenant, the songs in the strange languages hurled at your head like hand grenades. You could read all the pamphlets, vote all the elections, pray all the Sundays, and each day it became worse, each day made you more of a villain, each day your uniform was cursed on the streets of more cities, in more languages. He closed his eyes.

"Hawkins!"

Hawkins jumped and straightened up. Lieutenant Madox was standing in front of him. "Damn you, Hawkins!" Madox was saying. "Will you keep your bloody eyes open! Get over here!"

"Yes, sir," said Hawkins. He gripped his club and moved to where two sailors were swinging a gangplank up to the railing of the boat. The boat was tied to the dock now, and a terrible stillness had settled over the people on it.

"Spread out, spread out," Madox was shouting to the platoon. "Don't let anyone jump onto the dock. Make 'em all come down the gangplank."

The smell was awful now, and in the silence the Jews stared down at the Lieutenant and the men of the platoon with cold, devouring hatred. Over a loudspeaker came a cool, pleasant voice.

"Ladies and gentlemen," the voice said, and it sounded like at least a colonel in the Guards, "we wish to do this in as orderly a fashion as possible. You will please come down the gangplank in twos and march to your right and go aboard the vessel moored directly behind your boat. You are going to be transferred to Cyprus, where you will be taken care of in British Army camps. Your sick will be treated and you will be given every consideration possible. Now, if you please, start leaving your vessel."

The voice halted in a mechanical crackle. No one moved.

"All right," Madox said. "Let's get on board."

Slowly and deliberately, the men of the platoon started up the gangplank. Hawkins was right behind the Lieutenant, with Hogan at his side. For a moment, at the top of the gangplank, he stopped. He looked down at the deck of the schooner. There was a blur of eyes, dark, staring, wild; a confusion of gaunt, ravaged faces; a wavering mass of tattered clothing such as might have been recovered from the corpses of a dug-up graveyard. Hawkins tottered momentarily, feeling dizzily, this has happened to me before. Then he remembered. Belsen, he thought—wherever you turn, it is Belsen. In Belsen, he remembered, there had been the smell, too, and the same eyes, the same clothes, and there had been the old man (although later Hawkins had found out the man was only thirty) who had opened a door of one of the huts and come slowly out, holding his hands in front of him, his hands like claws, his face twisted skull-like and horrible in what Hawkins had later realized the man had meant as a glorious smile of greeting but which at the moment had seemed weird and threatening. Then, just as he had reached Hawkins, he had dropped to the ground, and when Hawkins had bent over him, he had died. But no one here approached Hawkins; there was no expression here that might later be deciphered into a smile. On the other side of the deck, there were the women, and standing, facing the gangplank, were the young men, and then Hawkins knew there was going to be a fight. Crazily, he thought: I'll bet there are some of these people here who will recognize me from Belsen. What will they think of me?

"Come on!" Madox was shouting furiously. "Come on, Hawkins, get in there!"

Slowly, with dreamy obedience, Hawkins moved toward the first line of men. I am not going to hit them, he thought as he walked through the stinking, unreal silence. No matter what, I am not going to hit them. Then he saw Hogan swing and there was the flat, awful noise of the stick hitting a shoulder. Then the screams began, and the shouting, which closed around you in a savage, wild, echoing vault of sound, and the bodies slamming into you, and the spurt of someone's blood, hot and slippery, in your face, and the confused flailing of arms and the black gleam of wood flashing against the yellow sky and a form dropping with a scream out of the rigging. Hawkins tried to keep his arms over his head, so that he wouldn't be pinned in helplessly, but hands grabbed at his club, and stabbed into his face, and he had to move his arms furiously to keep the club from being torn away. Then, suddenly, there was a pair of hands at his throat and he was staring into a dark, grimacing face, the eyes, just six inches from his, pitiless, mad, as the powerful fingers pressed and pressed. Hawkins tried to pull away, but there was no escaping the hands. Oh, God, Hawkins thought, feeling the blood pounding in his head, oh, God, he is going to kill me. No, he wanted to say, you don't understand. I am not doing anything. I was at Belsen. I was one of the people at Belsen. But the hands gripped firmer and firmer, the eyes stared coldly and triumphantly close to his own, as though the man who was choking him were finally taking vengeance for the ghetto in Poland, the death of his children, the locked cars, the whips, the furnaces, the graves of Europe. Hawkins felt his eyes clouding, his throat being torn, his knees slowly crumpling, as he pressed back and back, with the screams and the wet smashing of blows all around him. With his waning strength, he wrenched away. Then he hit the man. The man did not let go. Hawkins hit him again, across the face, and the man's face disappeared in a fuzz of blood, but still the fingers gripped, as strong as ever. Then, again and again, with all the desperate strength in his arms and body, Hawkins lashed out at the man who was trying to strangle him. The man's face seemed to crumble in a red, dissolving tissue, his jaw hanging queer and sidewise in a broken leer, only his eyes, steadfast and full of hatred, still glaring into Hawkins' own. There was a last, convulsive spasm of the fingers at Hawkins' throat; then the man slowly and silently slid down and away. Hawkins stared at him, then fell on top of him, and something crashed across his head, and when he opened his eyes again, he was lying on the dock and everything was very quiet, except for the weeping of women, soft and far away.

Hawkins sat up. The fight was over. Now they were taking the women down the gangplank, and that was where the weeping was coming from—from the raddled bundles of living rags being carried by troopers onto the soil of Palestine and back onto the other ship, thirty-five feet away. Hawkins felt his throat. It was terribly sore, and blood was still oozing from a cut under his ear. He felt sick and lightheaded. He turned his head away from the women. He did not want to look at them. Lying next to him on the dock, very quiet, face downward, was a man. He had on an American Army shirt and a pair of Royal Air Force pants. He was barefooted and his feet were terribly cut and swollen, black with blood. Slowly, Hawkins took the man's shoulder and rolled him over. The eyes were still open. The face was smashed, the jaw leering and dislocated, the teeth broken and red at the roots. But the eyes were open and they were the eyes of the man who had tried to kill Hawkins on board the schooner *Hope*.

Hawkins stood up. It was hard to walk, but he moved slowly over to the gate in the barbed wire at the other end of the dock. Madox was there, sweating but looking pleased.

"Very well done, Hawkins," Madox said. "I watched you. Are you hurt?"

"A little, sir," Hawkins said, surprised at the croaking, strange noise that came from his throat. "Not too bad."

"Good," said Madox. "It's just about finished here. We'll be going back to camp in a minute." He looked solicitously at Hawkins' torn throat. "You're in rather bad shape. You'd better not go with the others in the lorry. I'll take you with me in my jeep."

"Yes, sir," said Hawkins flatly. He walked slowly over to where the jeep was parked and laboriously climbed into the back. He leaned against the canvas. He closed his eyes, thinking of nothing.

Ten minutes later, Madox and his driver got into the jeep, and the jeep rolled slowly through the gate. Hawkins did not look back purposely, but he could not help seeing the dock, the two boats, the old, silent, broken, deserted schooner, and the full transport, beginning to work up steam for the voyage to Cyprus. They were singing again on board the transport, but softer now, and wearily, and Hawkins thought, I must get Esther to translate that song for me. And on the dock, with the Arab laborer, still holding his wheelbarrow, standing curiously over him, lay the dead man, flat and alone. Hawkins closed his eyes as the jeep spurted away from the waterfront.

I wonder, he was thinking, slowly and painfully, because his head did not seem familiar or normal to him any more, I wonder if I can get off tonight to go into Tel Aviv to take Esther to the movies. Then there was the explosion, and even as he felt himself slamming through the air, Hawkins thought, They must have got hold of some Army mines. Then he hit. He moved with crawling, broken slowness, feeling everything slippery and sliding all around him, thinking with dull persistence, I must tell them, they mustn't do this to me, they don't understand, I was at Belsen. Then he lay still.

WIDOWS' MEETING

THE NOISE of the plane came fitfully from the dark, foggy sky. Emily Clemens stood on the edge of the field, lightly holding her daughter Peggy's arm, listening to the muffled, searching, ebbing and flowing roar in the night mist that swirled in from the wintry Pacific. Occasionally, a door was opened in the operations room of the terminal and a figure came silently out, gliding through the fog in a weak glow of neon light, like a nurse coming out of an operating room, quiet, sad, and abstracted.

Emily was seventy years old and she felt tired. In the plane that had come out of New York and was now circling blindly through the dangerous soft gray stuff between the mountains and the sea was her other daughter, whom she had not seen in eleven years.

It had been a very bad day for Emily. There had been the bitter argument with Peggy at breakfast in the sunny dining room of the peeling stucco house which they had shared for the past three years. Then the slow hours of nervous anticipation. Now, this was almost too much to bear. The engines whined and coughed hesitantly in the wet darkness. Emily could feel the mist condensing in fine, sharp drops on her skin. She wanted to sit down some place, but it did not seem like the proper thing to do, to sit comfortably while your daughter wandered overhead in danger of her life. Unreasonably, Emily felt that if she stood, and accepted the ache in her legs and back and the piercing dizziness at the base of her skull, it would somehow make her daughter's safety more certain.

She looked sidelong at Peggy. Peggy's face was reserved and distant, outlined softly by the neon edge of the wet light. Peggy had on a scarf and had her hands plunged into the pockets of her loose, schoolgirlish coat, and looked younger by far than her fifty years.

"Do you think," Emily asked hesitantly, "do you think they'll be all right?"

"I don't know, Mother," Peggy said. Her voice was calm and terribly cool. "You heard what the man said. They expect a break in the fog within the next thirty minutes."

"Yes," Emily said. She sighed. At least, she reflected, at least Peggy should sound worried. No matter what she'd thought about her sister for the last ten years. Peggy had acted so well about everything during the war; she had been so reasonable and sane when Lawrence, her husband, had died; she had been so stolidly brave when she'd heard that Bud had been killed in Germany, and Bud, after all, had been her only child. Peggy had acted so well that it had come as a shock when she had showed such violence about Irene. It was almost as though she didn't care whether Irene lived or died, arrived or didn't arrive, crashed or not. It was one thing to have a family quarrel, but to carry it to such lengths, for so many years, with so many deaths along the way, leaving them three lone women out of the whole gay, hopeful family. . . . It was the new type of woman, Emily thought resentfully, the modern woman, who had shaken off so many claims of convention and order and had lost some of the capacity to forgive and to love that her mother had had.

The plane creaked painfully through the sky very close by. You could almost sense the effort of the engines, the straining eyes of the pilot, the rain-stained, sweating windshield a dim glow of light in the unrelenting obscurity. And back in the passenger compartment, strapped into her seat in case of a crash, Irene, after all the years.

Emily closed her eyes and remembered her two daughters in better days.

There was only one year between them, and they had been almost like twins—always together, always playing side by side, wearing each other's clothes, scolding each other's dolls in the sunny back yard in the sunny time before the other war, when they all had lived in the big house in Los Angeles and Mr. Clemens had been alive. The girls had been so pretty—both of them blonde and slender, with large, grave, dark eyes; each of them given to looking at the other and going off into spasms of secretive, little-girl laughter, private, dear, unapproachable by the outside, adult world.

"I am going to sit back," Mr. Clemens would tell them, tilted on the porch in the fragrant California night, peering down at the two small girls at his feet. "I am going to sit back and take it easy and preserve myself until you ripen. Then you are both going to marry Eastern millionaires with railroad stock, because you are going to be so beautiful that no one will be able to resist you, and I'll throw up my job with the oil company and live off the fat of the land. I'll live for six months of the year with Irene and her husband on his yacht off the summer colony of Newport, Rhode Island, eating lobster and clam chowder out of silver bowls. Then I'll go and live with Peggy and her husband on his hunting preserve in Georgia, chasing the fox and the pheasant all the day and drinking fine wines all the night."

Her eyes closed, the sound of the airplane engines dwindling in the misted distance, Emily could almost hear her husband's low voice in the homely garden so many years ago, could almost hear the high, shrill laughter of the girls and their "Daddy, Daddy, you *are* a fool!"

There was a five-story factory building, now, where the garden had been. And Mr. Clemens had died in 1914, and the girls' marriages had not been exactly as he had prophesied. They had been pretty enough and there had been a flood of young men, of astonishing variety in looks, fortune, and talents, passing through the apartment in New York to which Emily and the girls had moved after Mr. Clemens died. Peggy and Irene had handled the young men with charming mercilessness, trading them off to each other, giggling icily, late at night in the bedroom they shared, over the lame and pathetic pretensions of first one suitor, then another. They had almost invariably gone out together in those days, sternly insisting on a kind of double courtship from their stricken lovers, and it had seemed to Emily then that her two daughters far preferred each other's company to that of any of the young men they fleetingly favored.

Coldly, and with cynical girlish precision, they had worked out contrasting and complementary personalities for themselves, so that if a young man escaped one, he would be taken by the other; if he slipped the flame, he would succumb to the ice. Irene, who had been the taller and more handsome of the two, had played the role of the independent, dashing young woman, outspoken, sardonic, intellectual. Peggy, smaller and softer, had been all sliding smiles and oblique glances, and Emily had overheard them roaring, in the privacy of their room, over their campaigns, like pirates adding up the season's haul and recalling the season's saltiest stratagems.

Emily, who had been a simple girl, rather afraid of men, would shake her head and, half in earnest, half mockingly, say, over breakfast the next morning, in the confusion of newspapers and toast and coffee and lace and satin, "There's a reckoning coming, my dears, there's a reckoning coming. There's a man waiting for each of you, and he'll make you pay up, and double and triple, for all your clever tricks."

There had been a man, of course, and Emily had been right, but what she hadn't foreseen was that it would be the same one for both her daughters.

Emily blinked and looked around her strangely and tried to remember what she had come here for, what she was doing standing in the cold mist near midnight, with the ebbing noise of a plane overhead. Then she remembered, but it took an effort. Old age, she thought—everything gets jumbled. The images and memories slide in one on top of another, like a doubly exposed film, and something that happened thirty years ago is much brighter and more intense than something that happened yesterday, and dead men speak in more lively tones than the substantial people all around you, and your daughter at the age of twenty seems more real and more familiar than the cold-faced woman standing beside you holding your arm.

She was sitting in the living room in the apartment in New York City. 1915, was it? 1916? She was sewing a blouse for Irene. It was a wet night and the rain was snapping at the windows and the curtains were shaking a little. She looked at the curtains and said to Irene, "Next week they have to be washed." Irene didn't answer. She was lying stretched out on the couch, staring up at the ceiling.

The door opened and Peggy came in with a man. They were both glistening with rain, and Peggy was laughing as she shook her head to get the water out of her hair. "This is Reinhold Weigen, Mother," Peggy said. "He's a German. He's a journalist and he likes the opera. He'll sing Wagner for you if you're not careful. Reinhold, my sister Irene."

He was a very polite man. He was rather small and a little chubby. He did not look like the dark agent of disaster. He bowed and he kissed Emily's hand, and bowed and kissed Irene's hand. By this time Irene was sitting up and looking curiously at him.

"Ah," the German said. "What a delightful family." He wore old-fashioned clothes, and there was something old-fashioned about the way he spoke. He had practically no accent.

"Tea," Peggy said. "We're dying for a cup of tea. Sit here, Reinhold," she said, "and charm my mother and sister and I'll be right back with a gallon."

Peggy went into the kitchen, and Irene stood up and went over to the brocade chair under the lamp and sat there, her skirt flaring out, catching the light. "I don't suppose," Irene said, her voice low and suddenly melodious, "our opera sounds like much to somebody like you, Mr. Weigen—somebody who's heard it in Europe."

"Oh," said Reinhold gallantly, "quite the opposite. I find it excellent. Excellent. Do you go often?"

"Occasionally." Irene smiled. "It's difficult to get American men to take you there."

"Do you like the opera?"

"I adore it," Irene said, and Emily looked at her in surprise, because Irene hadn't gone more than two or three times since she'd come to New York. "I can't get enough of it."

"Ah," said Reinhold, beaming gravely. "Perhaps you would do me the honor of attending with me?"

"I'd adore it," Irene said.

Weigen took a deep breath. "They are singing 'Siegfried' Friday night," he said. "Is that agreeable?"

"Wonderful," said Irene. "I can hardly wait till Friday night."

They looked at each other, and Emily, sitting in the easy chair near the window with her sewing, thought: Poor Peggy, she needn't come out with that tea at all; it won't do her any good, any good in the world.

Emily blinked again. She was with the girls in their bedroom, with the pink satin ruffling on the dressing table. Peggy was sitting white-lipped and silent on the bed, and Irene was talking, loudly and harshly. "I'm going to marry him. If they let me, I'd go down to Georgia now and and marry him right there in the prison cell. I don't care what people say. I don't care if he's a German agent or an Egyptian agent or any kind of an agent. They have no right to put a man like that in jail, war or no war. I don't care about the war. We ought to lose it! We're barbarians, we don't know how to treat civilized human beings, it would be the best thing for us if we *did* lose."

The door of the operations room opened and a man came out, bare-headed. He stood there, holding the door open with one hand, looking sadly and reflectively up at the swirling sky, from which came the even, heavy sound of the engines. He shook his head and went back inside. The door closed, muffled and dull in the fog.

Weddings, Emily thought. An old woman had so many weddings to remember, so many brides, so many flowers, so many guests. . . . Irene in white satin in the church on Twenty-fourth Street that had been torn down later on. The triumphant, challenging look she gave the guests, not at all like a polite, joyous bride. Reinhold, thin and pale from the jail but composed and happy. Peggy very pretty in yellow tulle as bridesmaid, but with slight dark smudges under her eyes, as though she hadn't been sleeping for the past few nights.

Then Peggy's wedding, six months later. Lawrence, very handsome, so tall, with an angular, long, honest face. Irene hadn't been there, because she was in Germany by then. But she had sent a long cable, and at the wedding party Peggy had opened it first among the messages, because she knew whom it was from, and handed it to Lawrence. "From my sister," Peggy had said. "She sends us her blessings. She's going to have a baby and she urges us to do likewise. She also wants me to send a picture of you. She says my descriptions are useless. No man could look like that." Lawrence had grinned and stuffed the cable in his pocket, and it had lain around the house in one of those card-board files, with all the other telegrams and letters, for years, until a new maid had thrown them out.

The plane passed overhead again in its slow, blind circle of the field, and Emily sighed as she listened to the fateful engines. If Peggy had been a little more knowing or crafty about the German all those years ago, if Irene had not been so certain and shrewd, would it have been Peggy circling in the mist tonight and Irene standing waiting, tight-lipped and frozen, beside her? Or if Peggy just hadn't brought the man home . . . Or if Irene had been out that night . . . You tried so hard to be sensible about your daughters, to protect them, guide them, mold the stubborn clay of circumstance, and at the age of seventy there you were, standing, exhausted, on a closed-in field, like a bankrupt gambler, afflicted by accident, pushing the last, pathetic bet out to the croupier's rake on the checkered board.

Among the faces that you remembered, and the rooms where you had been happy or where terrible things had happened to you, among the confused images that tumbled in an old woman's brain, there were the letters. You remembered how they looked—the foreign postmark; Irene's racing, large handwriting; the heavy, gray envelopes; even the slight smell of Irene's perfume that somehow managed to survive the long crossing of the ocean. "This is Hans." (How curious it was to have a grandson called Hans in a family whose men had always been called John and Peter and Luke and Thomas.) "It is true that he looks a little like Bismarck, but we expect that by the time he is three, he will give up the resemblance." And "Reinhold is not doing so well, but nobody is doing very well in this poor country and we do not mind at all. Hans now has seven teeth and we are going to stop counting when he reaches ten." And "Dietrich weighed ten pounds when he was born and it was a minor scandal, in this hungry country, like being caught hoarding food or taking bribes. I insisted upon calling him Dietrich Jonathan, after Papa, and all of Reinhold's very Prussian relatives raised their eyebrows, but I didn't budge an inch, and I suppose they went home and said to each other, 'That is what you must expect if you insist upon marrying an American.'" And "Please send me some new pictures of Bud. He must be off that bear rug by now. If we don't get some new pictures here, his German cousins will be terribly surprised when they finally see him and find out that he is not always naked and lying on his belly."

But the cousins never met. When Irene wrote, in 1936, that she and Reinhold were coming over for three months on a wonderful assignment that Reinhold had got from his paper, she had added that she couldn't take the boys out of school. Peggy had redecorated the guest room in her house (the wallpaper with the large, full-blown red roses, and the new blue rug). And she had taught Bud to say, in German, "Good morning, Aunt Irene and Uncle Reinhold," and "How is the health of my cousins? I hope it is good." Bud, who was very proud of his accomplishment in the field of languages, and who was twelve then, had gone on independently to learn "*Auf Wiedersehen*" and "My father is very fond of the beer of Munich." Emily smiled, even now, in the midnight mist, remembering Bud standing in a worn sweatshirt and an old pair of long white ducks in the middle of the living room, grinning, slowly and proudly announcing that his father was very fond of the beer of Munich.

It was hard to remember the day they arrived. Nineteen thirty-six was so far away and so many things had happened. The handsome big German boat—was it the *Europa*?—with its soaring prow that seemed to jut over the street from its berth on the North River. The band playing. (What was it playing in 1936? A German song, but she didn't remember it, although later, in newsreels, she heard it during pictures of German Army parades.) The cold biting in off the ice-filled river. Bud, delighted with the ship, shuffling around in a new blue coat that already seemed too short in the sleeves. Lawrence holding Peggy's arm, smiling, but pale, because even then his health was beginning to fail. Peggy grave, but with her eyes shining, searching the gangplank and the railings for the first glimpse of her sister. Then a tall, beautiful woman coming down the gangplank in a fur coat, a woman with a flashing, barely familiar face. Emily remembered thinking: That woman must be very wealthy. And then, the sudden realization that it was her daughter and the fumbling through her handbag to find her glasses to make sure. And the man beside Irene looking rather small and dumpy, and comfortably fat, and when he took his hat off, Emily realized that it was Reinhold and that he had grown bald.

The gaps that opened up in your memory as you reached seventy . . . You remembered that there had been a great deal of excitement and everybody was kissing everybody else and everybody was talking and laughing at once, but what, exactly, it was like—what it was, exactly, that Peggy said to Reinhold, and how she looked when she said it, and if there was any indication there of any old pain or regret—you couldn't remember at all. And then the next thing you remembered was the party.

It was a big dinner party, or at least big for Peggy and Lawrence, in their basement dining room, which led out into a small back garden. You remembered that somehow you'd found out that Reinhold had been doing very well recently in Germany, and that he was very highly thought of and had moved to Berlin, and he and Irene had a large house in the country, where their sons were staying now, as well as an apartment in Berlin, and you were quite proud of him, fat and bald as he was, as he sat beaming, pleasant, deferential, his clothes still somehow old-fashioned, at the dark table, among all Lawrence's and Peggy's friends.

Then Irene's voice had cut across the mild confusion of the general conversation, saying, "Hitler? Of course I believe in Hitler." And the whole room had fallen silent, and Emily had watched Mr. Rosen, Lawrence's partner, slowly and carefully put his fork down on his plate, as though it weighed a great deal and were terribly fragile. "I think it's impudent," Irene's voice had gone on, "for your Mr. Roosevelt to make speeches complaining about what's happening in Germany. How would you like it if Herr Hitler made speeches complaining about the internal affairs of America?"

"Darling," Reinhold had said smoothly, "I think we ought not talk about politics at dinner. It is bad for the digestion."

"Nonsense," Irene had said. "This gentleman on my right"—she gestured toward Henry Connolly, who was one of Lawrence's oldest friends—"has been making a political speech for a half hour, and I think we ought to straighten him out. He's been saying we need a revolution in Germany, that if we don't get the Nazis out, the world will have to destroy us, that we are barbarians—the whole silly bill of fare." Irene had looked challengingly around the table, and Emily had thought anxiously: Perhaps she has had too much to drink; women really should not drink when they go out. "I've been reading the papers ever since I got here," Irene had said loudly, "and I've been listening to people talk, and I must confess it makes me sick. You don't know what's happening. You swallow all that Communist propaganda about us without trying to find out the truth at all. I've been living there and you haven't, and I tell you that if Hitler hadn't come along—"

"Darling," Reinhold had said, "please talk on another subject."

"I will not," Irene had said. "You were sent here to convince the Americans. This is just as good a place to begin as any." She spoke once more to all the guests. "I tell you that if Hitler hadn't come along, we'd have all been destroyed by the Jews and the Communists."

"Lawrence"—Mr. Rosen had stood up quietly—"I'm afraid Carol and I will have to go now." Then Carol Rosen had got up, too, and Emily remembered the pale wash of fright on her face. Lawrence had taken a deep breath and got up slowly and wearily from his chair and followed the Rosens out into the hall. There had been a mumble of voices from the hall, but Emily had been unable to hear what they were saying there, because Irene had continued loudly, "I suppose Mr. Rosen is a Jew. I'm sorry if I've hurt his feelings, but if he's so tender, he oughtn't to go out in company where he can hear a few of the facts of life."

Then Lawrence had come back. He had stopped behind Irene's chair, looking exhausted and drained, and had said quietly, "I'm afraid there's no use pretending this is a party any more. I imagine you're all as anxious to go home as I am for you to go. Peggy, darling"—he had turned to his wife—"may I speak to you alone for a moment?"

"Of course," Peggy had said. She had stood up and gone out with Lawrence, and Emily had heard their slow footsteps mounting the stairs.

"Irene," Emily had said sorrowfully, "why can't you keep quiet about things like this? It's not for women to make speeches, one way or another."

"Oh, Mother," Irene had said. "Don't be any sillier than you have to be. Go read your grandchild a bedtime story and leave the grownups alone." She had stared coldly around at the other guests. "I'm sorry if I've made an ugly scene, but I couldn't help it. I've been in America three days and I am thoroughly disgusted with it and hope I never have to see it again. I suppose you all think more or less the way your friend Lawrence does. It's no wonder Europeans laugh at you. You don't know any more about what's really happening in the world than a Sioux Indian in the middle of the Dakota prairie. In Berlin I spend most of my time defending you people, telling my friends it's just that you're a little slow, that you're really intelligent, progressive people. I'm going to go back to Berlin and apologize."

The other guests stood up and said good night politely to Emily and left. Reinhold was sitting slumped in his chair, reflectively moving his coffee cup around in its saucer.

Emily had stared, puzzled, at her daughter. It was hard to understand what had provoked her to such violence. Emily hadn't even voted since 1924, and politics to her was something you left to the Irish.

"I certainly am glad my sons aren't growing up in this idiotic country," Irene said.

The door opened and Peggy came in. She looked nervous but in control of herself, and Emily knew that it was going to be bad.

"Irene," Peggy said, "I'd like to talk to you."

"Now, girls," Emily said anxiously. "Don't say anything you're going to regret later."

"I know what she's going to say," Irene said. "Her woolly-headed husband has been lecturing her and she's going to tell us that she wants us to leave."

"Exactly," Peggy said. "Tonight, if possible."

"Peggy!" Emily cried. "Irene!"

"Delighted," said Irene. "Reinhold . . ."

Reinhold stood up, trying to hold his belly in. "It is necessary for civilized human beings," he began loudly, "to consider a question like this impersonally, in abstract terms, if you understand, in its historical perspec—"

"Get out of here," Peggy said evenly.

"Peggy," said Emily faintly. "Irene."

Irene had swept out of the room and Reinhold had stopped at the door to bow stiffly before he followed his wife.

And now Peggy was standing coldly beside Emily, with the noise of the doubtful plane in their ears, far away from New York. And Lawrence was dead, and Reinhold was dead, killed by the Eighth Air Force in Berlin, his body unrecovered even now from the ruins of the apartment house. And not so far from where his uncle lay, Bud was dead, at the Saar River, which he had tried to cross but had not managed; and Irene's two sons were dead in Russia, and what rivers had they failed to cross? And the letters from Irene finally had been so sad, so broken—widowed, sonless, bereft in a shattered country. ("I said good-bye to Reinhold at eleven in the morning and the bombers came over at one and I never saw him again." And "Dietrich was only seventeen years old, but they took him anyway. They told me they would only put him in the anti-aircraft, but they put him in the infantry just the same, and what chance did he have? His comrades said he died very bravely, and they are all dead now themselves." And "Of course, our lovely home in Berlin is no more, but luckily there is still the country place. And, thanks to God, it is in the American zone, and I cannot tell you the thrill and the way the tears came to my eyes when I saw those blessed American faces and heard the first American say, 'Ma'am, I come from Milwaukee, Wisconsin.' The Americans have been very kind to me and even went so far as to put a guard of three men in my house when they heard that I was an American citizen. A guard is absolutely essential, because there are wild bands of released prisoners from the concentration camps, who roam the country and kill and rob and burn and have no more mercy in their hearts than so many tigers. Most of my money is in the Russian zone and I have been to Berlin three times to try to negotiate with them to get some of it back from the banks, but they are very cunning and they do not wish to coöperate at all. So your money order, sent through the very charming Lieutenant Wilson, who has been extraordinarily good to me, was most welcome. I can't tell you how anxious I am to see my native land again and settle down with you, as in the old days, and forget the horrible things that have happened.")

That was what the fight with Peggy at breakfast had been about. "I will not have that woman living in the same house with me," she had repeated stubbornly over and over again when Emily had pleaded with her.

"What is Irene going to do?" Emily had asked. "She's over fifty. We're the only flesh and blood she has in the whole world, the only ones she can turn to."

Peggy had suddenly begun to weep. "Every time I look at her," she'd said, "I'll think of Bud, drowning in that river. Why should I have to put up with anything like that? Flesh and blood? What sort of flesh and blood is that?"

"Peggy, darling," Emily had said. "She's changed, she's changed. You can see from her letters. That's all behind her. You've got to forgive her, you have to. . . ." Then she'd begun to weep, too, thinking of all the wrong, tragic, hopeless things that lay behind her, thinking of the graves and the hatred and the ended hopes. The sight of her mother crying, the old, worn, faded face gripped in rigid grief, had softened Peggy.

She had put her arms about Emily, comforting her. "There. There," she had said. "All right. Don't cry. All right. She can come here. If she's changed, she can come here."

And after breakfast, pretending that she had to go to town to do some shopping, Emily had gone to church and had sat stiffly in the empty building, with the mild, religious sunlight sifting in through the colored windows, and had prayed that Irene had changed. Emily knew she was not going to go on much longer, and for that little time she wanted to live in the small, secure atmosphere of love, in the same house with her two aging daughters, who had started out so brightly, with such promise of full, gay lives, and had ended, somehow, so badly, so lonely, bereaved, poor, plagued by the dead.

The lights of the field went on, watery and weak in the fog. The noise of the plane suddenly became much stronger, and then Emily saw its lights tentatively sliding down out of the veiled sky. The plane side-slipped, almost stalled, roared unnervingly, then hit the ground hard. It jarred up into the air, then crashed down again. It skidded; one wing touched the strip; then it righted itself and went in a crazy half circle before it ground to a halt in front of them.

The engines stopped and the propellers turned more and more slowly, throwing moisture off their surfaces in pale, lighted arcs. Emily sighed.

"All right, Mother," Peggy said. "She's safe."

"I think I must sit down now," Emily said. Peggy led her along the fence to a bench near the gate through which the passengers would come, and Emily sat down heavily, feeling her knees trembling under her thick wool dress.

The attendants wheeled the steps over to the plane. The door was opened and the passengers slowly started to come out.

"Disgraceful!" one of the women getting off the plane was saying. "Absolutely disgraceful. It's a wonder we weren't all killed."

A stream of eight or nine people moved slowly toward the gate. There were three women and five or six men. Emily stared anxiously at them, searching for Irene. One of the women was very young and was carrying a child in her arms. That could not be Irene. The two other women were much older. They were both about Irene's size, and as they came into the light, Emily stood up and moved swiftly over to the gate, with Peggy holding her arm, to scan them more closely. Neither of the faces was known to her. She turned to Peggy. "Do you see her?" she asked.

Peggy shook her head slowly. One of the women, quite well dressed, came toward them, smiling, and Emily half started to smile, thinking: Oh, dear Lord, this is Irene and I don't recognize her, my own daughter! But the woman went right past her and was swept into the arms of a large young man who was standing behind them and who said, "My God, Mother, don't do that to me again!"

The other woman who had come off the plane was standing in the full glare of the light at the gate. She was obviously at least sixty, dowdy, poorly dressed, in a frayed coat with a beaver collar. She had a fat, wrinkled, commanding face, very red from the cold.

"Peggy," Emily said nervously, "don't you think you ought to go ask the stewardess if . . ."

"Wait a minute," Peggy said. "I think perhaps that woman . . ."

"Disgusting," the dowdy woman was saying to the man who was standing next to her. "A sickening performance. Risking all our lives like that. What a country! I can tell you, it would never have happened in Germany! America! We had fog-dispellers on every field as long ago as 1937. Disgusting!"

Emily felt Peggy's hand tightening on her arm. The dowdy woman looked around her disdainfully once more, her eyes passing over Peggy's face without stopping. "They must be waiting for me over there," she said to the man, pointing toward the dim headlights of the cars on the parking lot. She started to walk away, toward the parking lot, a heavy, aged, slow-moving figure gradually being lost in the dark mist. Emily wanted Peggy to call out before the woman wandered out of sight.

"Peggy," she said, speaking with difficulty, her tongue almost uncontrollable between her teeth. "I think that's your sister Irene."

"I know," Peggy said. "I know it is."

Then Emily knew that Peggy would never call out. "Irene," Emily said weakly. Then, more strongly, "Irene! We're over here." The dim figure in the fog stopped and turned, then started slowly toward them, growing more real and more familiar with each step. "Over here, Irene," Emily said, weeping. "Welcome home."

THE MAN WITH ONE ARM

"I WOULD LIKE complete reports on these three people," Captain Mikhailov was saying. He pushed a slip of paper across the desk to Garbrecht, and Garbrecht glanced at the names. "They are interpreters at the American civil affairs headquarters. The Americans have a charming habit of hiring ex-Nazis almost exclusively for those jobs, and we have found it rewarding to inquire into the pasts of such gentlemen." Mikhailov smiled. He was a short, stocky man with a round, shielded face, and pale, unsmiling eyes, and when he smiled it was like a flower painted unconvincingly on stone.

Garbrecht recognized two of the three names. Mikhailov was right. They were Nazis. It would take some thinking out, later, though, to decide whether to expose them to Mikhailov, or exactly how far to expose them. Garbrecht watched Mikhailov unlock a drawer in his desk and take out some American marks. Methodically, Mikhailov counted the notes out in his square, machine-like hands. He locked the drawer and pushed the money across the desk to Garbrecht.

"There," Mikhailov said, "that will keep you until we see each other next week."

"Yes, Captain," Garbrecht said. He reached out and pulled the money toward him, leaving it on the top of the desk. He took out his wallet, and, slowly, one by one, put the notes into the wallet. He was still slow and clumsy with things like that, because he had not yet learned how to handle things deftly with his left hand, and his right hand and arm were buried behind the field hospital in the brewery fourteen hundred miles away. Mikhailov watched him impassively, without offering aid.

Garbrecht put his wallet away and stood up. His overcoat was thrown over a chair and he picked it up and struggled to get it over his shoulders.

"Till next week," he said.

"Next week," Mikhailov said.

Garbrecht did not salute. He opened the door and went out. At least, he thought, with a nervous sensation of triumph, as he went down the grimy steps past the two plain-clothes men loitering in the dark hall, at least I didn't salute the bastard. That's the third week in a row I didn't salute him.

The plain-clothes men stared at him with a common, blank, threatening look. By now he knew them too well to be frightened by them. They looked that way at everything. When they looked at a horse or a child or a bunch of flowers, they threatened it. It was merely their comfortable professional adjustment to the world around them, like Mikhailov's smile. The Russians, Garbrecht thought as he went down the street, what a people to have in Berlin!

Garbrecht walked without looking about him. The landscape of the cities of Germany had become monotonous—rubble, broken statues, neatly swept lanes between piled cracked brick, looming blank single walls, shells of buildings, half-demolished houses in which dozens of families somehow lived. He moved briskly and energetically, like everyone else, swinging his one arm a little awkwardly to maintain his balance, but very little of what he saw around him made any impression on him. A solid numbness had taken possession of him when they cut off his arm. It was like the anesthesia which they injected into your spine. You were conscious and you could see and hear and speak and you could understand what was being done to you, but all feeling was absent. Finally, Garbrecht knew, the anesthesia would wear off, but for the present it was a most valuable defense.

"Lieutenant." It was a woman's voice somewhere behind him, and Garbrecht did not look around. "Oh, Lieutenant Garbrecht."

He stopped and turned slowly. Nobody had called him lieutenant for more than a year now. A short, blonde woman in a gray cloth coat was hurrying toward him. He looked at her, puzzled. He had never seen her before, and he wondered if it were she who had called his name.

"Did you call me?" he asked as she stopped in front of him.

"Yes," she said. She was thin, with a pale, rather pretty face. She did not smile. "I followed you from Mikhailov's office."

"I'm sure," Garbrecht said, turning and starting away, "that you have made some mistake."

The woman fell in beside him, walking swiftly. She wore no stockings and her legs showed a little purple from the cold. "Please," she said, "do not behave like an idiot."

Then, in a flat, undemanding voice, she said several things to him that he had thought nobody alive remembered about him, and finally she called him by his correct name, and he knew that there was no escaping it now. He stopped in the middle of the ruined street and sighed, and said, after a long time, "Very well. I will go with you."

There was a smell of cooking in the room. Good cooking. A roast, probably, and a heavy, strong soup. It was the kind of smell that had seemed to vanish from Germany sometime around 1942, and even with all the other things happening to him, Garbrecht could feel the saliva welling helplessly and tantalizingly up from the ducts under his tongue. It was a spacious room with a high ceiling that must have been at one time quite elegant. There was a bricked-up fireplace with a large, broken mirror over it. By some trick of fracture the mirror reflected separate images in each of its broken parts, and it made Garbrecht feel that something shining and abnormal was hidden there.

The girl had ushered him without formality into the room and had told him to sit down and had disappeared. Garbrecht could feel his muscles slowly curling as he sat rigidly in the half-broken wooden chair, staring coldly at the battered desk, the surprising leather chair behind the desk, the strange mirror, the ten-inch high portrait of Lenin which was the only adornment on the wall. Lenin looked down at him from the wall, across the years, through the clumsy heroics of the lithographer, with a remote, ambiguous challenge glaring from the dark, wild eyes.

The door through which he had himself come was opened and a man entered. The man slammed the door behind him and walked swiftly across the room to the desk. Then he wheeled and faced Garbrecht.

"Well, well," the man said, smiling, his voice hearty and welcoming, "here you are. Here you are. Sorry to keep you waiting. Terribly sorry." He beamed across the room, leaning forward hospitably from his position in front of the desk. He was a short, stocky man with a light, pink face, and pale, silky hair that he wore long, possibly in an attempt to hide what might be an increasing tendency to baldness. He looked like an amiable butcher's boy, growing a little old for his job, or the

strong man in a tumbling act in a small-time circus, the one on the
bottom that the others climbed on. Garbrecht stood up and peered at
him, trying to remember if he had ever seen the man before.

"No, no," the man said, waving his pudgy hands, "no, we have never
met. Do not trouble your brain. Sit down, sit down. Comfort first.
Everything else after." He leapt lightly across the room and almost
pushed Garbrecht into his chair. "It is a lesson I have learned from our
friends, the Americans. How to slouch. Look what they've accomplished
merely by spending most of their time on the base of their spines." He
laughed uproariously, as though the joke were too merry not to be enjoyed, and swept quickly across the room, with his almost leaping, light
gait, and hurled himself into the large leather chair behind the desk.
He continued beaming at Garbrecht.

"I want to say," said Garbrecht, "that I have no notion of why I was
asked to come here. I merely came," he said carefully, "because the
young lady made me curious, and I had an hour to spare, anyway,
and . . ."

"Enough, enough." The man rocked solidly back and forth in the
squeaking chair. "You came. Sufficient. Delighted. Very pleased. Have
a cigarette. . . ." With a sudden movement, he thrust out the brass
cigarette box that lay on the desk.

"Not at the moment, thank you," Garbrecht said, although his throat
was quivering for one.

"Ah," the fat man said, grinning. "A rarity. Only German known to
refuse a cigarette since the surrender. Still, no matter. . . ." He took
a cigarette himself and lighted it deftly. "First, introductions, Lieutenant. My name. Anton Seedorf. Captain, Hermann Goering Division.
I keep the title." He grinned. "A man saves what he can from a war."

"I imagine," Garbrecht said, "you know my name."

"Yes." Seedorf seemed to bubble with some inward humor. "Oh, yes,
I certainly do. Yes, indeed. I've heard a great deal about you. Been most
anxious to meet you. The arm," he said, with sudden solemnity. "Where
was that?"

"Stalingrad."

"Ah, Stalingrad," Seedorf said heartily, as though he were speaking
the name of a winter resort at which he had spent a marvelous holiday.
"A lot of good souls left there, weren't there, many good souls. A mis-
calculation. One of many. Vanity. The most terrible thing in the world,
the vanity of a victorious army. A most interesting subject for historians
—the role of vanity in military disasters. Don't you agree?" He peered
eagerly at Garbrecht.

"Captain," Garbrecht said coldly, "I cannot remain here all afternoon."

"Of course," Seedorf said. "Naturally. You're curious about why I invited you here. I understand." He puffed swiftly on his cigarette, wreathing his pale head in smoke before the cracked mirror. He jumped up and perched himself on the desk, facing Garbrecht, boyishly. "Well," he said, heartily, "it is past time for hiding anything. I know you. I know your very good record in the Party . . ."

Garbrecht felt the cold rising in his throat. It's going to be worse, he thought, worse than I expected.

". . . promising career in the army until the unfortunate accident at Stalingrad," Seedorf was saying brightly, "loyal, dependable, et cetera; there is really no need to go into it at this moment, is there?"

"No," said Garbrecht, "none at all." He stood up. "If it is all the same to you, I prefer not to be reminded of any of it. That is all past and, I hope, it will soon all be forgotten."

Seedorf giggled. "Now, now," he said. "There is no need to be so cautious with me. To a person like you or me," he said, with a wide, genial gesture, "it is never forgotten. To a person who has said the things we have said, who did the things we have done, for so many years, a paid Party official, a good soldier, a good German . . ."

"I am not interested any more," Garbrecht said loudly but hopelessly, "in being what you call a good German."

"It is not a question," Seedorf said, smiling widely and dousing his cigarette, "of what you are interested in, Lieutenant. I beg your pardon. It is a question of what must be done. Simply that."

"I am not going to do anything," said Garbrecht.

"I beg your pardon once more." Seedorf rocked happily back and forth on the edge of the desk. "There are several little things that you can be very useful doing. I beg your pardon, you will do them. You work for the Russians, collecting information in the American zone. A useful fellow. You also work for the Americans, collecting information in the Russian zone." Seedorf beamed at him. "A prize!"

Garbrecht started to deny it, then shrugged wearily. There might be a way out, but denial certainly was not it.

"We, too, several of us, maybe more than several, could use a little information." Seedorf's voice had grown harder, and there was only an echo of jollity left in it, like the sound of laughter dying down a distant alley on a cold night. "We are not as large an organization at the moment as the Russians; we are not as well equipped for the time being, as the Americans . . . but we are even more . . . more . . ." He chuckled as he thought of the word . . . "curious. And more ambitious."

There was silence in the room. Garbrecht stared heavily at the pale, fat head outlined against the broken mirror with its insane, multiplied reflections. If he were alone, Garbrecht knew he would bend his head and weep, as he did so often, without apparent reason, these days.

"Why don't you stop?" he asked heavily. "What's the sense? How many times do you have to be beaten?"

Seedorf grinned. "One more time, at least," he said. "Is that a good answer?"

"I won't do it," Garbrecht said. "I'll give the whole thing up. I don't want to get involved any more."

"I beg your pardon," said Seedorf happily, "you will give up nothing. It is terrible for me to talk to a man who gave his arm for the Fatherland this way," he said with a kind of glittering facsimile of pity, "but I am afraid the Russians would be told your correct name and Party position from 1934 on, and they would be told of your affiliations with the Americans, and they would be told of your job as adjutant to the commanding officer of Maidanek concentration camp in the winter of 1944, when several thousand people died by orders with your name on them. . . ."

Seedorf drummed his heels softly and cheerfully against the desk. "They have just really begun on their war trials . . . and these new ones will not run ten months, Lieutenant. I beg your pardon for talking this way, and I promise you from now on, we will not mention any of these matters again." He jumped up and came across the room in his swift, round walk. "I know how you feel," he said softly. "Often, I feel the same way. Quit. Quit now, once and for all. But it is not possible to quit. In a little while you will see that and you will be very grateful."

"What is it?" Garbrecht said. "What is it that you want me to do?"

"Just a little thing," Seedorf said. "Nothing at all, really. Merely report here every week and tell me what you have told the Russians and the Americans and what they have told you. Fifteen minutes a week. That's all there is to it."

"Fifteen minutes a week." Garbrecht was surprised that he had actually laughed. "That's all."

"Exactly." Seedorf laughed. "It won't be so bad. There's always a meal to be had here, and cigarettes. It is almost like old times. There!" He stepped back, smiling widely. "I am so happy it is settled." He took Garbrecht's hand and shook it warmly with both his. "Till next week," he said.

Garbrecht looked heavily at him. Then he sighed. "Till next week," he said.

Seedorf held the door open for him when he went out. There was no one else in the corridor and no guards at the door, and he walked slowly down the creaking hall, through the rich smell of cooking, and on into the street and the gathering cold evening air.

He walked blankly through the broken brick wastes toward the American control post, staring straight ahead of him. Next week, he thought, I must ask him what the picture of Lenin is doing on the wall.

The office of Captain Peterson was very different from the bleak room in which Captain Mikhailov conducted his affairs. There was a clerk in the corner and an American flag on the wall, and the busy sound of American typewriters from the next room. There was a water cooler and a warm radiator, and there was a picture of a pretty girl with a small blond child on Peterson's disordered desk. Garbrecht took his coat off and sat down in one of the comfortable looted plush chairs and waited for Peterson. The interviews with Peterson were much less of a strain than the ones with Mikhailov. Peterson was a large young man who spoke good German and, amazingly, fair Russian. He was good-natured and naïve, and Garbrecht was sure he believed Garbrecht's excellently forged papers and innocuous, false record, and Garbrecht's quiet, repeated insistence that he had been anti-Nazi from the beginning. Peterson was an enthusiast. He had been an enthusiast about the war, in which he had performed quite creditably, he was an enthusiast about Germany, its scenery, its art, its future, its people, whom he regarded as the first victims of Hitler. Mikhailov was different. He bleakly made no comment on the official soft tones issuing from Moscow on the subject of the German people, but Garbrecht knew that he regarded the Germans not as the first victims, but as the first accomplices.

Of late, Garbrecht had to admit, Peterson had not seemed quite so enthusiastic. He had seemed rather baffled and sometimes hurt and weary. In the beginning, his naïveté had spread to cover the Russians in a rosy blanket, too. The assignments he gave to Garbrecht to execute in the Russian zone were so routine and so comparatively innocent, that if Garbrecht had had a conscience he would have hesitated at taking payment for their fulfillment.

Peterson was smiling broadly when he came in, looking like a schoolboy who has just been promoted to the first team on a football squad. He was a tall, heavy young man with an excited, swift manner of talking. "Glad to see you, Garbrecht," he said. "I was afraid I was going to miss you. I've been busy as a bartender on Saturday night, hand-carrying orders all over the place, packing, saying good-bye . . ."

"Good-bye?" Garbrecht said, shaken by a small tremor of fear. "Where are you going?"

"Home." Peterson pulled out three drawers from his desk and started emptying them in a swift jumble. "The United States of America."

"But I thought," Garbrecht said, "that you had decided to stay. You said your wife and child were coming over and . . ."

"I know . . ." Peterson threw a whole batch of mimeographed papers lightheartedly into the trash basket. "I changed my mind." He stopped working on the drawers and looked soberly at Garbrecht. "They're not coming here. I decided I didn't want my child to grow up in Europe." He sat down heavily, staring over Garbrecht's head at the molding around the ceiling. "In fact," he said, "I don't think I want to hang around Europe any more myself. In the beginning I thought I could do a lot of good here. Now . . ." He shrugged. "They'd better try someone else. I'd better go back to America and clear my head for a while. It's simpler in a war. You know whom you're fighting and you have a general idea about where he is. Now . . ." Once more the shrug.

"Maybe I'm too stupid for a job like this," he continued. "Or maybe I expected too much. I've been here a year, and everything seems to be getting worse and worse. I feel as though I'm sliding downhill all the time. Slowly, not very perceptibly . . . but downhill. Maybe Germany has always struck everybody the same way. Maybe that's why so many people have always committed suicide here. I'm going to get out of here before I wake up one morning and say to myself, 'By God, they have the right idea.' "

Suddenly he stood up, swinging his big feet in their heavy army shoes down to the floor with a commanding crash. "Come on," he said. "I'll take you in to see Major Dobelmeir. He's going to replace me." Peterson opened the door for Garbrecht, and they went out into the anteroom with the four desks and the girls in uniform typing. Peterson led the way. "I think the United States Army is going to begin to get its money's worth out of you now, Garbrecht," Peterson said, without looking back. "Dobelmeir is quite a different kettle of fish from that nice, simple young Captain Peterson."

Garbrecht stared at the back of Peterson's head. So, he thought coldly, he wasn't so completely fooled by me, after all. Maybe it's good he's going.

But then Peterson opened the door to one of the rooms along the hall and they went in, and Garbrecht took one look at the major's leaf and the heavy, brooding, suspicious face, and he knew that he was wrong; it would have been much better if Peterson had stayed.

Peterson introduced them and the Major said, "Sit down," in flat, heavy-voiced German, and Peterson said, "Good luck, I have to go now," and left. The Major looked down at the papers on his desk and read them stolidly, for what seemed to Garbrecht like a very long time. Garbrecht felt the tension beginning again in his muscles, as it had in Seedorf's room. Everything, he thought, gets worse and worse, more and more complicated.

"Garbrecht," the Major said, without looking up, "I have been reading your reports." He did not say anything else, merely continued to read slowly and effortfully, his eyes covered, his heavy chin creasing in solid fat as he bent his head over the desk.

"Yes?" Garbrecht said finally, because he could no longer stand the silence.

For a moment, Dobelmeir did not answer. Then he said, "They aren't worth ten marks, all of them together, to anybody. The United States Government ought to sue you for obtaining money on false pretenses."

"I am very sorry," Garbrecht said hurriedly, "I thought that that is what was wanted, and I . . ."

"Don't lie." The Major finally lifted his head and stared fishily at him.

"My dear Major . . ."

"Keep quiet," the Major said evenly. "We now institute a new regime. You can do all right if you produce. If you don't, you can go find another job. Now we know where we stand."

"Yes, sir," said Garbrecht.

"I should not have to teach you your business at this late date," the Major said. "There is only one way in which an operation like this can pay for itself; only one rule to follow. All our agents must act as though the nation on which they are spying is an active enemy of the United States, as though the war has, in fact, begun. Otherwise the information you gather has no point, no focus, no measurable value. When you bring me information it must be information of an enemy who is probing our line for weak spots, who is building up various depots of supplies and troops and forces in specific places, who is choosing certain specific fields on which to fight the crucial battles. I am not interested in random, confusing gossip. I am only interested in indications of the disposition of the enemy's strength and indications of his aggressive intentions toward us. Is that clear?"

"Yes, sir," said Garbrecht.

The Major picked up three sheets of clipped-together papers. "This is your last report," he said. He ripped the papers methodically in half and then once more in half and threw them on the floor. "That is what I think of it."

"Yes, sir," said Garbrecht. He knew the sweat was streaming down into his collar and he knew that the Major must have noticed it and was probably sourly amused at it, but there was nothing he could do to stop it.

"This office has sent out its last chambermaid-gossip report," the Major said. "From now on, we will send out only useful military information, or nothing at all. I'm not paying you for the last two weeks' work. You haven't earned it. Get out of here. And don't come back until you have something to tell me."

He bent down once more over the papers on his desk. Garbrecht stood up and slowly went out the door. He knew that the Major did not look up as he closed the door behind him.

Greta wasn't home, and he had to stand outside her door in the cold all evening because the janitress refused to recognize him and let him in. Greta did not get back till after midnight, and then she came up with an American officer in a closed car, and Garbrecht had to hide in the shadows across the street while the American kissed Greta clumsily again and again before going off. Garbrecht hurried across the broken pavement of the street to reach Greta before she retreated into the house.

Greta could speak English and worked for the Americans as a typist and filing clerk, and perhaps something else, not quite so official, in the evenings. Garbrecht did not inquire too closely. Greta was agreeable enough and permitted him to use her room when he was in the American zone, and she always seemed to have a store of canned food in her cupboard, gift of her various uniformed employers, and she was quite generous and warm-hearted about the entire arrangement. Greta had been an energetic patriot before the defeat, and Garbrecht had met her when she visited the hospital where he was lying with his arm freshly severed after the somber journey back from Russia. Whether it was patriotism, pity, or perversity that had moved her, Garbrecht did not know, nor did he inquire too deeply; at any rate, Greta had remained a snug anchorage in the wild years that had passed, and he was fond of her.

"Hello," he said, as he came up behind her. She was struggling with the lock, and turned abruptly as though frightened.

"Oh," she said. "I didn't think you'd be here tonight."

"I'm sorry," he said. "I couldn't get in touch with you."

She opened the door, and he went in with her. She unlocked the door of her own room, which was on the ground floor, and slammed it irritably behind her. Ah, he thought unhappily, things are bad here, too, tonight.

He sighed. "What is it?" he said.

"Nothing," she said. She started to undress, methodically, and without any of the usual graceful secrecy she ordinarily managed even in the small drab room.

"Can I be of any help?" Garbrecht asked.

Greta stopped pulling off her stockings and looked thoughtfully at Garbrecht. Then she shook her head and yanked at the heel of the right stocking. "You could," she said, contemptuously. "But you won't."

Garbrecht squinted painfully at her. "How do you know?" he asked.

"Because you're all the same," Greta said coldly. "Weak. Quiet. Disgusting."

"What is it?" he asked. "What would you want me to do?" He would have preferred it if Greta had refused to tell him, but he knew he had to ask.

Greta worked methodically on the other stocking. "You ought to get four or five of your friends, the ex-heroes of the German Army," she said disdainfully, "and march over to Freda Raush's house and tear her clothes off her back and shave her head and make her walk down the street that way."

"What?" Garbrecht sat up incredulously. "What are you talking about?"

"You were always yelling about honor," Greta said loudly. "Your honor, the Army's honor, Germany's honor."

"What's that got to do with Freda Raush?"

"Honor is something Germans have only when they're winning, is that it?" Greta pulled her dress savagely over her shoulders. "Disgusting."

Garbrecht shook his head. "I don't know what you're talking about," he said. "I thought Freda was a good friend of yours."

"Even the French," Greta said, disregarding him, "were braver. They shaved their women's heads when they caught them. . . ."

"All right, all right," Garbrecht said wearily. "What did Freda do?"

Greta looked wildly at him, her hair disarranged and tumbled around her full shoulders, her large, rather fat body shivering in cold and anger in her sleazy slip. "Tonight," she said, "she invited the Lieutenant I was with and myself to her house. . . ."

"Yes," said Garbrecht, trying to concentrate very hard.

"She is living with an American captain."

"Yes?" said Garbrecht, doubtfully. Half the girls Greta knew seemed to be living with American captains, and the other half were trying to. That certainly could not have infuriated Greta to this wild point of vengeance.

"Do you know what his name is?" Greta asked rhetorically. "Rosenthal! A Jew. Freda!"

Garbrecht sighed, his breath making a hollow, sorrowful sound in the cold midnight room. He looked up at Greta, who was standing over him, her face set in quivering, tense lines. She was usually such a placid, rather stupid, and easygoing girl that moments like this came as a shocking surprise.

"You will have to find someone else," Garbrecht said wearily, "if you want to have Freda's head shaved. I am not in the running."

"Of course," Greta said icily. "I knew you wouldn't be."

"Frankly," Garbrecht said, trying to be reasonable with her, "I am a little tired of the whole question of the Jews. I think we ought to drop it, once and for all. It was all right for a while, but I think we've probably just about used it all up by now."

"Ah," Greta said, "keep quiet. I should have known better than to expect anything from a cripple."

They both were silent then. Greta continued undressing with contemptuous asexual familiarity, and Garbrecht slowly took his clothes off and got into bed, while Greta, in a black rayon nightgown that her American Lieutenant had got for her, put her hair up in curlers before the small, wavy mirror. Garbrecht looked at her reflection in the mirror and remembered the nervous, multiple reflections in the cracked mirror in Seedorf's office.

He closed his stinging eyes, feeling the lids trembling jumpily. He touched the folded, raw scar on his right shoulder. As long as he lived, he probably would never get over being shocked at the strange, brutal scar on his own body. And he would never get over being shocked when anybody called him a cripple. He would have to be more diplomatic with Greta. She was the only girl he was familiar with, and occasionally there was true warmth and blessed hours of forgetfulness in her bed. It would be ridiculous to lose that over a silly political discussion in which he had no real interest at all. Girls were hard to get these days. During the war it was better. You got a lot of girls out of pity. But pity went out at Rheims. And any German, even a whole, robust one, had a hard time competing with the cigarettes and chocolates and prestige of the victors. And for a man with one arm . . . It had been a miserable day, and this was a fitting, miserable climax to it.

Greta put out the light and got aggressively into bed, without touching him. Tentatively he put his hand out to her. She didn't move. "I'm tired," she said. "I've had a long day. Good night."

In a few moments she was asleep.

Garbrecht lay awake a long time, listening to Greta snore; a wavering, troubling reflection from a street light outside played on his lids from the small mirror across the room.

As he approached the house in which Seedorf kept his headquarters, Garbrecht realized that he had begun to hurry his pace a little, that he was actually looking forward to the meeting. This was the fourth week that he had reported to the fat ex-Captain, and he smiled a little to himself as he reminded himself of how affectionately he had begun to regard Seedorf. Seedorf had not been at all demanding. He had listened with eager interest to each report of Garbrecht's meetings with Mikhailov and Dobelmeir, had chuckled delightedly here and there, slapped his leg in appreciation of one point or another, and had shrewdly and humorously invented plausible little stories, scraps of humor, to give first to the Russian, then to the American. Seedorf, who had never met either of them, seemed to understand them both far better than Garbrecht did, and Garbrecht had risen steadily in the favor of both Captain Mikhailov and Major Dobelmeir since he had given himself to Seedorf's coaching.

As Garbrecht opened the door of Seedorf's headquarters, he remembered with a little smile the sense of danger and apprehension with which he had first come there.

He did not have to wait long at all. Miss Renner, the blonde who had first talked to him on the street, opened the door to the ex-Captain's room almost immediately.

Seedorf was obviously in high spirits. He was beaming and moving up and down in front of his desk with little, mincing, almost dancing steps. "Hello, hello," he said warmly, as Garbrecht came into the room. "Good of you to come."

Garbrecht never could make out whether this was sly humor on Seedorf's part, or perfectly automatic good manners, this pretense that Garbrecht had any choice in the matter.

"Wonderful day," Seedorf said. "Absolutely wonderful day. Did you hear the news?"

"What news?" Garbrecht asked cautiously.

"The first bomb!" Seedorf clasped his hands delightedly. "This afternoon at two-thirty the first bomb went off in Germany. Stuttgart! A solemn day. A day of remembrance! After 1918 it took twelve years before the Germans started any real opposition to the Allies. And now . . . less than a year and a half after the surrender . . . the first bomb! Delightful!" He beamed at Garbrecht. "Aren't you pleased?" he asked.

"Very," said Garbrecht diplomatically. He was not fond of bombs. Maybe for a man with two arms, bombs might have an attraction, but for him . . .

"Now we can really go to work." Seedorf hurled himself forcefully into his leather chair behind the desk and stared piercingly out at Garbrecht. "Until now, it hasn't meant very much. Really only developing an organization. Trying out the parts. Seeing who could work and who couldn't. Instituting necessary discipline. Practice, more than anything else. Now the maneuvers are over. Now we move onto the battlefield!"

Professional soldiers, Garbrecht thought bitterly, his new-found peace of mind already shaken, they couldn't get the jargon of their calling out of their thinking. Maneuvers, battlefields . . . The only accomplishment they seemed to be able to recognize was the product of explosion, the only political means they really understood and relished, death.

"Lieutenant," Seedorf said, "we have been testing you, too. I am glad to say," he said oratorically, "we have decided that you are dependable. Now you really begin your mission. Next Tuesday at noon Miss Renner will meet you. She will take you to the home of a friend of ours. He will give you a package. You will carry it to an address that Miss Renner will give you at the time. I will not hide from you that you will be in a certain danger. The package you will carry will include a timing mechanism that will go into the first bomb to be exploded in the new war against the Allies in Berlin. . . ."

Seedorf seemed to be far away and his voice distant and strange. It had been too good to be true, Garbrecht thought dazedly, the easygoing, undangerous, messenger-boy life that he had thought he was leading. Merely a sly, deadly game that Seedorf had been playing, testing him.

"Captain," he whispered, "Captain . . . I can't . . . I can't . . ."

"The beginning," Seedorf said, ecstatically, as though he had not heard Garbrecht's interruption. "Finally, there will be explosions day and night, all over the city, all over the country. . . . The Americans will blame the Russians, the Russians will blame the Americans, they will become more and more frightened, more and more distrustful of each other. They will come to us secretly, bargain with us, bid for us against each other. . . ."

It will never happen, Garbrecht said dazedly to himself, never. It is the same old thing. All during the war they told us that. The Americans would break with the British, the British with the Russians. And here they all were in what was left of Berlin: Cockneys, Tartars from Siberia, Negroes from Mississippi. Men like Seedorf were victims of their own propaganda, men who listened and finally believed their own hopes, their own lies. And, he, Garbrecht, next week, would be walking among the lounging American MP's, with the delicate, deadly machinery ticking under his arm, because of Seedorf's hallucination. Any other nation, Garbrecht thought, would be convinced. They'd look around at the ruin of their cities, at the ever-stretching cemeteries, at the marching enemy troops in the heart of their capital, and they'd say, "No, it did not work." But not the Germans. Goering was just dead in the Nuremberg jail, and here was this fat murderer with the jolly smile who even looked a bit like Goering, rubbing his hands and shouting, "A day of remembrance! The first bomb has exploded!"

Garbrecht felt lost and exhausted and hopeless, sitting in the wooden chair, watching the fat man move nervously and jubilantly behind the desk, hearing the rough, good-natured voice saying, "It took fourteen years last time, it won't take four years this time! Garbrecht, you'll be a full colonel in 1950, one arm and all."

Garbrecht wanted to protest, say something, some word that would stop this careening, jovial, bloodthirsty, deluded lunatic, but he could get no sound out between his lips. Later on, perhaps, when he was alone, he might be able to figure some way out of this whirling trap. Not here, not in this tall, dark room, with the fat, shouting captain, the broken mirror, the somber, incongruous, brooding picture of Lenin, Seedorf's obscure, mocking joke, that hung on the cracked wall.

"In the meantime," Seedorf was saying, "you continue your regular work. By God!" he laughed, "you will be the richest man in Berlin when they all get through paying you!" His voice changed. It became low and probing. "Do you know two men called Kleiber and Machewski who work out of Mikhailov's office?" He peered shrewdly at Garbrecht.

"No," said Garbrecht after a moment. He knew them. They were both on Mikhailov's payroll and they worked in the American zone, but there was no sense in telling that, yet, to Seedorf.

"No matter," Seedorf laughed, after an almost imperceptible pause. "You will give their names and this address to your American Major." He took a piece of paper out from his pocket and put it down on the desk before him. "You will tell the Major that they are Russian spies and that they can be found at this place." He tapped the paper. "It will be quite a haul for the Major," Seedorf said ironically, "and he will be sure to reward you handsomely. And he will have a very strong tendency after that to trust you with quite important matters."

"Yes," said Garbrecht.

"You're sure," Seedorf said inquiringly, smiling a little at Garbrecht, "you're sure you don't know these men?"

Then Garbrecht knew that Seedorf knew he was lying, but it was too late to do anything about it.

"I don't know them," he said.

"I could have sworn . . ." Seedorf shrugged. "No matter." He got up from the desk, carrying the slip of paper, and came over to the chair where Garbrecht was sitting. "Some day, my friend," he said, putting his hand lightly on Garbrecht's shoulder, "some day you will learn that you will have to trust me, too. As a matter of . . ." He laughed. "A matter of discipline."

He handed Garbrecht the slip of paper and Garbrecht put it in his pocket and stood up. "I trust you, sir," he said flatly. "I have to."

Seedorf laughed uproariously. "I like a good answer," he shouted. "I do like a good answer." He put his arm around Garbrecht in a brotherly hug. "Remember," he said, "my first and only lesson—the one principle in being a hired informer is to tell the man who is paying you exactly what he wishes to hear. Any information must fit into theories which he already holds. Then he will trust you, pay you well, regard you as a more and more valuable employee. However . . ." and he laughed again, "do not try to work this on me. I am different. I don't pay you . . . and therefore, I expect the truth. You will remember that?" He turned Garbrecht around quite roughly and peered into his eyes. He was not smiling now.

"Yes, sir," said Garbrecht. "I will remember it."

"Good." Seedorf pushed him toward the door. "Now go downstairs and talk to Miss Renner. She will make all arrangements."

He pushed Garbrecht gently through the door and closed it sharply behind him. Garbrecht stared at the closed door for a moment, then walked slowly downstairs to Miss Renner.

Later, on the street, on his way to Mikhailov's office, he tried not to think of Seedorf's conversation, or the ingenious, deadly device that even now was waiting for him on the other side of the city.

He felt like stopping and leaning his head against the cold, cracked brick wall of a gutted house he was passing, to weep and weep in the twisting, cutting wind. After so much, after all the fighting, all the death, after the operating room in the brewery at Stalingrad, a man should be entitled to something, some peace, some security. And, instead, this onrushing dilemma, this flirtation with next week's death, this life of being scraped against every rock of the jagged year by every tide that crashed through Germany. Even numbness was no longer possible.

He shuffled on dazedly, not seeing where he was going. He stumbled over a piece of pavement that jutted crazily up from the sidewalk. He put out his hand to try to steady himself, but it was too late, and he fell heavily into the gutter. His head smashed against the concrete, and he felt the hot laceration of broken stone on the palm of his hand.

He sat up and looked at his hand in the dim light. There was blood coming from the dirty, ripped wounds, and his head was pounding. He sat on the curb, his head down, waiting for it to clear before he stood up. No escape, he thought, heavily, there never would be any escape. It was silly to hope for it. He stood up slowly, and continued on his way to Mikhailov's office.

Mikhailov was crouched over his desk, the light of a single lamp making him look froglike and ugly as he sat there, without looking up at Garbrecht. ". . . Tell the man who is paying you exactly what he wishes to hear. . . ." Garbrecht could almost hear Seedorf's mocking, hearty voice. Maybe Seedorf knew what he was talking about. Maybe the Russian was that foolish, maybe the American was that suspicious. . . . Suddenly, Garbrecht knew what he was going to tell Mikhailov.

"Well?" Mikhailov said finally, still peering down at his desk. "Anything important? Have you found out anything about that new man the Americans are using?"

Mikhailov had asked him to find out what he could about Dobelmeir last week, but Garbrecht had silently resolved to keep his mouth shut about the American. If he said too much, if he slipped once, Mikhailov would become suspicious, start prying, set someone on Garbrecht's trail. But now he spoke in a loud, even voice. "Yes," he said. "He is a second generation German-American. He is a lawyer in Milwaukee in civilian life. He was under investigation early in the war because he was said to have contributed to the German-American Bund in 1939 and 1940." Garbrecht saw Mikhailov slowly raise his head and look at him, his eyes beginning to glisten with undisguised interest. It's working, Garbrecht thought, it actually is working. "The case was never pressed," he went on calmly with his invention, "and he was given a direct commission late in the war and sent to Germany on special orders. Several members of his family are still alive in the British zone, Hamburg, and a cousin of his was a U-boat commander in the German Navy and was sunk off the Azores in 1943."

"Of course," said Mikhailov, his voice triumphant and satisfied. "Of course. Typical." He did not say what it was typical of, but he looked at Garbrecht with an expression that almost approached fondness.

"There are two things you might work on for the next few weeks," Mikhailov said. "We've asked everyone working out of this office to pick up what he can on this matter. We are quite sure that the Americans have shipped over a number of atomic bombs to Great Britain. We have reason to believe that they are being stored in Scotland, within easy distance of the airfield at Prestwick. There are flights in from Prestwick every day, and the crews are careless. I would like to find out if there are any preparations, even of the most preliminary kind, for basing a group of B-29's somewhere in that area. Skeleton repair shops, new fuel storage tanks, new radar warning stations, et cetera. Will you see if you can pick up anything?"

"Yes, sir," said Garbrecht, knowing that for Mikhailov's purpose he would make certain to pick up a great deal.

"Very good," said Mikhailov. He unlocked the drawer in his desk and took out the money. "You will find a little bonus here," he said with his mechanical smile.

"Thank you, sir," said Garbrecht, picking up the money.

"Till next week," Mikhailov said.

"Till next week," said Garbrecht. He saluted and Mikhailov returned the salute as Garbrecht went out the door.

Although it was dark and cold outside, and his head was still throbbing from his fall, Garbrecht walked lightly, grinning to himself, as he moved toward the American zone.

He didn't see Dobelmeir till the next morning. "You might be interested in these men," he said, placing before the Major the slip of paper with the names of the men Seedorf had instructed him to denounce. "They are paid agents for the Russians, and the address is written down there, too."

Dobelmeir looked at the names, and a slow, delighted grin broke over his heavy face. "Very, very interesting," he said. "Excellent." His large hand went slowly over the crumpled paper, smoothing it out in a kind of dull caress. "I've had some more inquiries for information about that Professor I asked you to check. Kittlinger. What did you find out?"

Garbrecht had found out, more by accident than anything else, that the Professor, an aging, obscure physics teacher in the Berlin Medical School, had been killed in a concentration camp in 1944, but he was sure that there was no record anywhere of his death. "Professor Kittlinger," Garbrecht said glibly, "was working on nuclear fission from 1934 to the end of the war. Ten days after the Russians entered Berlin, he was arrested and sent to Moscow. No word has been heard since."

"Of course," Dobelmeir said flatly. "Of course."

The atom, Garbrecht thought, with a slight touch of exhilaration, is a marvelous thing. It hands over everything like a magic charm. Mention the atom, and they will solemnly believe any bit of nonsense you feed them. Perhaps, he thought, grinning inwardly, I will become a specialist. Garbrecht, Atomic Secrets Limited. An easy, rich, overflowing, simple field.

Dobelmeir was industriously scratching down the doubtful history of Professor Kittlinger, Atomic Experimenter. For the first time since he had begun working for the Americans, Garbrecht realized that he was actually enjoying himself.

"You might be interested," he said calmly, "in something I picked up last night."

Dobelmeir looked up assiduously from his desk. "Of course," he said gently.

"It probably doesn't amount to anything, just drunken, irresponsible raving . . ."

"What is it?" Dobelmeir leaned forward keenly.

"Three days ago a General Bryansky, who is on the Russian General Staff . . ."

"I know, I know," said Dobelmeir impatiently. "I know who he is. He's been in Berlin for a week now."

"Well," said Garbrecht, deliberately playing with Dobelmeir's impatience, "he made a speech before a small group of officers at the Officers' Club, and later on he got quite drunk, and there are rumors about certain things that he said. . . . I really don't know whether I ought to report anything as vague as this, as I said, just a rumor. . . ."

"Go ahead," Dobelmeir said hungrily. "Let me hear it."

"He is reported to have said that there will be war in sixty days. The atomic bomb is meaningless, he said. The Russian army can march to the Channel from the Elbe in twenty-five days. Then let the Americans use the atomic bomb on them. They will be in Paris, in Brussels, in Amsterdam, and the Americans won't dare touch them. . . . Of course, I cannot vouch for this, but . . ."

"Of course he said it," Dobelmeir said. "Or if he didn't, some other of those murderers did." He leaned back wearily. "I'll put it in the report. Maybe it'll make somebody wake up in Washington. And don't worry about reporting rumors. Very often there's more to be learned from a rumor than from the most heavily documented evidence."

"Yes, sir," said Garbrecht.

"I don't know," said Dobelmeir, "whether you heard about the bombing in Stuttgart yesterday."

"Yes, sir. I did."

"I have my own theory about it. There are going to be more, too, take my word for it. I think if you got to the bottom of it, you'd find our friends, the Russians, there. I want you to work on that, see what you can pick up this week. . . ."

"Yes, sir," Garbrecht said. What a wonderful man Seedorf is, Garbrecht thought. How astute, how correct in his intuition. How worthy of faith. He stood up. "Is that all, sir?"

"That's all." Dobelmeir handed him an envelope. "Here's your money. You'll find two weeks' pay I held back in the beginning are added to this week's money."

"Thank you very much, sir," Garbrecht said.

"Don't thank me," said the Major. "You've earned it. See you next week."

"Next week, sir." Garbrecht saluted and went out.

There were two MP's standing at the door, in the clear winter sunshine, their equipment glittering, their faces bored. Garbrecht smiled and nodded at them, amused now, long in advance, as he thought of himself scornfully carrying the delicate parts of the first bomb past them, right under their noses.

He walked briskly down the street, breathing deeply the invigorating air, patting the small bulge under his coat where the money lay. He could feel the numbness that had held him for so long deserting him, but it was not pain that was taking its place, not pain at all.

ABOUT THE AUTHOR

IRWIN SHAW was born in New York in 1913 and grew up in Brooklyn. He received his secondary education in city schools and was admitted to Brooklyn College, where trouble with calculus caused him to leave at the end of his freshman year. At intervals during the following year he held jobs in a cosmetics factory, an installment furniture house and a department store. Returning to school the next fall semester, he played varsity football and wrote a column for the college paper. He was graduated with a bachelor's degree in 1934.

While still in his early twenties, Shaw began writing serial scripts for radio—"The Gumps" and "Dick Tracy." He presently attracted critical attention for his more serious writing, including an expressionist anti-war play, "Bury the Dead," and a more conventional drama, "The Gentle People," which in 1939 enjoyed a good run on Broadway. At the same time, he began selling a stream of short stories to *The New Yorker* and other magazines of literary distinction.

Enlisting in the army early in World War II, he saw service with the Signal Corps and as a correspondent for *Yank* and *Stars and Stripes* in Africa and Europe. Out of this war experience came his major best-selling novel, "The Young Lions." Several novels followed, "The Troubled Air," "Lucy Crown," "Two Weeks in Another Town," and "Voices of a Summer Day." But he never lost his interest in the short story form. "Walking Wounded" won the O. Henry Memorial Prize in 1944, and later stories have since appeared in The O'Brien and other collections. Two, "A Year to Learn the Language," and "In the French

Style," were made into a movie, also titled "In the French Style," for which Shaw wrote the script.

In retrospect, Shaw has said of his stories: ". . . they all seem to be anchored in some remembered, isolated moment of my own time, and they reflect, I believe, the moods which I experienced in common with many of the men and women of my generation, and the ideas that moved us in the time which these stories span. In that time, in the places I have passed through, there have been hope, despair, defiance, courage, resignation, brutality, laughter, and love, as in all other times, but all in the special and peculiar light of our epoch." *

Married since 1939, Irwin Shaw spends most of the year with his wife in their home in Klosters, Switzerland, with frequent returns to the U.S. He has one son, at present in school in Connecticut. He prefers the U.S. in the fall, when the football season is on and the new plays are opening on Broadway.

The present collection includes all his short stories from 1938 to 1962.

* Selected Short Stories, Random House, © Irwin Shaw